THIS BOOK
BELONGS TO

_____

_____

CW00868576

Louisa May Alcott

LITTLE WOMEN

VINTAGE BOOKS
London

Published by Vintage 2012

Chapter illustrations © Georgie McAusland 2012

Little Women was first published in 1868

Vintage
Random House, 20 Vauxhall Bridge Road,
London SW1V 2SA

www.vintage-classics.info

Addresses for companies within The Random House Group Limited can
be found at: www.randomhouse.co.uk/offices.htm

The Random House Group Limited Reg. No. 954009

A CIP catalogue record for this book
is available from the British Library

The Random House Group Limited supports The Forest Stewardship
Council (FSC®), the leading international forest certification organisation.
Our books carrying the FSC label are printed on FSC® certified paper.
FSC is the only forest certification scheme endorsed by the leading
environmental organisations, including Greenpeace. Our paper
procurement policy can be found at
www.randomhouse.co.uk/environment

Printed and bound in Great Britain by
CPI Group (UK) Ltd, Croydon CR0 4YY

Contents

Little Women
or, Meg, Jo, Beth and Amy

Preface

'Go then, my little Book, and show to all
That entertain and bid thee welcome shall,
What thou dost keep close shut up in thy breast;
And wish what thou dost show them may be blest
To them for good, may make them choose to be
Pilgrims better by far, than thee or me.
Tell them of Mercy; she is one
Who early hath her pilgrimage begun.
Yea, let young damsels learn of her to prize
The world which is to come, and so be wise;
For little tripping maids may follow God
Along the ways which saintly feet have trod.'

Adapted from JOHN BUNYAN

1

Playing Pilgrims

'CHRISTMAS won't be Christmas without any presents,' grumbled Jo, lying on the rug.

'It's so dreadful to be poor!' sighed Meg, looking down at her old dress.

'I don't think it's fair for some girls to have lots of pretty things, and other girls nothing at all,' added little Amy, with an injured sniff.

'We've got father and mother, and each other, anyhow,' said Beth, contentedly, from her corner.

The four young faces on which the firelight shone brightened at the cheerful words, but darkened again as Jo said sadly,—

'We haven't got father, and shall not have him for a long time.' She didn't say 'perhaps never,' but each silently added it, thinking of father far away, where the fighting was.

Nobody spoke for a minute; then Meg said in an altered tone,—

'You know the reason mother proposed not having any presents this Christmas, was because it's going to be a hard winter for every one; and she thinks we ought not to spend money for pleasure, when our men are suffering so in the army. We can't do much, but we can make our little sacrifices, and ought to do it gladly. But I am afraid I don't;' and Meg shook her head, as she thought regretfully of all the pretty things she wanted.

'But I don't think the little we should spend would do any good. We've each got a dollar, and the army wouldn't be much helped by our giving that. I agree not to expect anything from mother or you, but I do want to buy Undine and Sintram for myself; I've wanted it *so* long,' said Jo, who was a bookworm.

'I planned to spend mine in new music,' said Beth, with a little sigh, which no one heard but the hearth-brush and kettle-holder.

'I shall get a nice box of Faber's drawing pencils; I really need them,' said Amy, decidedly.

'Mother didn't say anything about our money, and she won't wish us to give up everything. Let's each buy what we want, and have a little fun; I'm sure we grub hard enough to earn it,' cried Jo, examining the heels of her boots in a gentlemanly manner.

'I know *I* do,—teaching those dreadful children nearly all day, when I'm longing to enjoy myself at home,' began Meg, in the complaining tone again.

'You don't have half such a hard time as I do,' said Jo. 'How would you like to be shut up for hours with a nervous, fussy old lady, who keeps you trotting, is never satisfied, and worries you till you're ready to fly out of the window or box her ears?'

'It's naughty to fret,—but I do think washing dishes and keeping things tidy is the worst work in the world. It makes me cross; and my hands get so stiff, I can't practise good a bit.' And Beth looked at her rough hands with a sigh that any one could hear that time.

'I don't believe any of you suffer as I do,' cried Amy; 'for you don't have to go to school with impertinent girls, who plague you if you don't know your lessons, and laugh at your dresses, and label your father if he isn't rich, and insult you when your nose isn't nice.'

'If you mean *libel* I'd say so, and not talk about *labels*, as if pa was a pickle-bottle,' advised Jo, laughing.

'I know what I mean, and you needn't be "statirical" about it. It's proper to use good words, and improve your *vocabilary*,' returned Amy, with dignity.

'Don't peck at one another, children. Don't you wish we had the money papa lost when we were little, Jo? Dear me, how happy and good we'd be, if we had no worries,' said Meg, who could remember better times.

'You said the other day you thought we were a deal happier than the King children, for they were fighting and fretting all the time, in spite of their money.'

'So I did, Beth. Well, I guess we are; for though we do have to work, we make fun for ourselves, and are a pretty jolly set, as Jo would say.'

'Jo does use such slang words,' observed Amy, with a reproving look at the long figure stretched on the rug. Jo immediately sat up, put her hands in her apron pockets, and began to whistle.

'Don't, Jo; it's so boyish.'

'That's why I do it.'

'I detest rude, unlady-like girls.'

'I hate affected, niminy piminy chits.'

'Birds in their little nests agree,' sang Beth, the peacemaker, with such a funny face that both sharp voices softened to a laugh, and the 'pecking' ended for that time.

'Really, girls, you are both to be blamed,' said Meg, beginning to lecture in her elder sisterly fashion. 'You are old enough to leave off boyish tricks, and behave better, Josephine. It didn't matter so much when you were a little girl; but now you are so tall, and turn up your hair, you should remember that you are a young lady.'

'I ain't! and if turning up my hair makes me one, I'll wear it in two tails till I'm twenty,' cried Jo, pulling off her net, and shaking down a chestnut mane. 'I hate to think I've got to grow up and be Miss March, and wear long gowns, and look as prim as a China-aster. It's bad enough to be a girl, anyway, when I like boys' games, and work, and manners. I can't get over my disappointment in not being a boy, and it's worse than ever now, for I'm dying to go and fight with papa, and I can only stay at home and knit like a poky old woman;' and Jo shook the blue army-sock till the needles rattled like castanets, and her ball bounded across the room.

'Poor Jo; it's too bad! But it can't be helped, so you must try to be contented with making your name boyish, and playing brother to us girls,' said Beth, stroking the rough head at her knee with a hand that all the dishwashing and dusting in the world could not make ungentle in its touch.

'As for you, Amy,' continued Meg, 'you are altogether too particular and prim. Your airs are funny now, but you'll grow up an affected little goose if you don't take care. I like your nice manners, and refined ways of speaking, when you don't try to be elegant; but your absurd words are as bad as Jo's slang.'

'If Jo is a tom-boy, and Amy a goose, what am I, please?' asked Beth, ready to share the lecture.

'You're a dear, and nothing else,' answered Meg, warmly; and no one contradicted her, for the 'Mouse' was the pet of the family.

As young readers like to know 'how people look,' we will take this moment to give them a little sketch of the four sisters, who sat knitting away in the twilight, while the December snow fell quietly without, and the fire crackled cheerfully within. It was a comfortable old room, though the carpet was faded and the furniture very plain, for a good picture or two hung on the walls, books filled the recesses, chrysanthemums and Christmas roses bloomed in the windows, and a pleasant atmosphere of home-peace pervaded it.

Margaret, the eldest of the four, was sixteen, and very pretty, being plump and fair, with large eyes, plenty of soft brown hair, a sweet mouth, and white hands, of which she was rather vain. Fifteen-year old Jo was very tall, thin and brown, and reminded one of a colt; for she never seemed to know what to do with her long limbs, which were very much in her way. She had a decided mouth, a comical nose, and sharp gray eyes, which appeared to see everything, and were by turns fierce, funny, or thoughtful. Her long, thick hair was her one beauty; but it was usually bundled into a net, to be out of her way. Round shoulders had Jo, big hands and feet, a fly-away look to her clothes, and the uncomfortable appearance of a girl who was rapidly shooting up into a woman, and didn't like it. Elizabeth,—or Beth, as every one called her,—was a rosy, smooth-haired, bright-eyed girl of thirteen, with a shy manner, a timid voice, and a peaceful expression, which was seldom disturbed. Her father called her 'Little Tranquillity,' and the name suited her excellently; for she seemed to live in a happy world of her own, only venturing out to meet the few whom she trusted and loved. Amy, though the youngest, was a most important person, in her own opinion at least. A regular snow maiden, with blue eyes, and yellow hair curling on her shoulders; pale and slender, and always carrying herself like a young lady mindful of her manners. What the characters of the four sisters were, we will leave to be found out.

The clock struck six; and, having swept up the hearth, Beth put a pair of slippers down to warm. Somehow the sight of the old shoes had a good effect upon the girls, for mother was coming, and every one brightened to welcome her. Meg stopped lecturing, and lit the lamp, Army got out of the easy-chair without being asked, and Jo forgot how tired she was as she sat up to hold the slippers nearer to the blaze.

'They are quite worn out; Marmee must have a new pair.'

'I thought I'd get her some with my dollar,' said Beth.

'No, I shall!' cried Amy.

'I'm the oldest,' began Meg, but Jo cut in with a decided—

'I'm the man of the family now papa is away, and I shall provide the slippers, for he told me to take special care of mother while he was gone.'

'I'll tell you what we'll do,' said Beth; 'let's each get her something for Christmas, and not get anything for ourselves.'

'That's like you, dear! What will we get?' exclaimed Jo.

Every one thought soberly for a minute; then Meg announced, as if the idea was suggested by the sight of her own pretty hands, 'I shall give her a nice pair of gloves.'

'Army shoes, best to be had,' cried Jo.

'Some handkerchiefs, all hemmed,' said Beth.

'I'll get a little bottle of Cologne; she likes it, and it won't cost much, so I'll have some left to buy something for me,' added Amy.

'How will we give the things?' asked Meg.

'Put 'em on the table, and bring her in and see her open the bundles. Don't you remember how we used to do on our birthdays?' answered Jo.

'I used to be so frightened when it was my turn to sit in the big chair with a crown on, and see you all come marching round to give the presents, with a kiss. I liked the things and the kisses, but it was dreadful to have you sit looking at me while I opened the bundles,' said Beth, who was toasting her face and the bread for tea, at the same time.

'Let Marmee think we are getting things for ourselves, and then surprise her. We must go shopping tomorrow afternoon, Meg; there is lots to do about the play for Christmas night,' said Jo, marching up and down with her hands behind her back, and her nose in the air.

'I don't mean to act any more after this time; I'm getting too old for such things,' observed Meg, who was as much a child as ever about 'dressing up' frolics.

'You won't stop, I know, as long as you can trail round in a white gown with your hair down, and wear gold-paper jewelry. You are the best actress we've got, and there'll be an end of everything if you quit the boards,' said Jo. 'We ought to rehearse tonight; come here, Amy, and do the fainting scene, for you are as stiff as a poker in that.'

'I can't help it; I never saw any one faint, and I don't choose to make myself all black and blue, tumbling flat as you do. If I can go down easily, I'll drop; if I can't, I shall fall into a chair and be graceful; I don't care if Hugo does come at me with a pistol,' returned Amy, who was not gifted with dramatic power, but was chosen because she was small enough to be borne out shrieking by the hero of the piece.

'Do it this way; clasp your hands so, and stagger across the room, crying frantically, "Roderigo! save me! save me!"' and away went Jo, with a melodramatic scream which was truly thrilling.

Amy followed, but she poked her hands out stiffly before her, and jerked herself along as if she went by machinery; and her 'Ow!' was more suggestive of pins being run into her than of fear and anguish. Jo gave a despairing groan, and Meg laughed outright, while Beth let her bread burn as she watched the fun, with interest.

'It's no use! do the best you can when the time comes, and if the audience shout, don't blame me. Come on, Meg.'

Then things went smoothly, for Don Pedro defied the world in a speech of two pages without a single break; Hagar, the witch, chanted an awful incantation over her kettleful of simmering toads, with weird effect; Roderigo rent his chains asunder manfully, and Hugo died in agonies of remorse and arsenic, with a wild 'Ha! ha!'

'It's the best we've had yet,' said Meg, as the dead villain sat up and rubbed his elbows.

'I don't see how you can write and act such splendid things, Jo. You're a regular Shakespeare!' exclaimed Beth, who firmly believed that her sisters were gifted with wonderful genius in all things.

'Not quite,' replied Jo, modestly. 'I do think "The Witch's Curse, an Operatic Tragedy," is rather a nice thing; but I'd like to try Macbeth, if we only had a trapdoor for Banquo. I always wanted to do the killing part. "Is that a dagger that I see before me?"' muttered Jo, rolling her eyes and clutching at the air, as she had seen a famous tragedian do.

'No, it's the toasting fork, with ma's shoe on it instead of the bread. Beth's stage struck!' cried Meg, and the rehearsal ended in a general burst of laughter.

'Glad to find you so merry, my girls,' said a cheery voice at the door, and actors and audience turned to welcome a stout, motherly lady, with a 'can-I-help-you' look about her which was truly delightful. She wasn't a particularly handsome person, but mothers are always lovely to their children, and the girls thought the gray cloak and unfashionable bonnet covered the most splendid woman in the world.

'Well, dearies, how have you got on today? There was so much to do, getting the boxes ready to go tomorrow, that I didn't come home to dinner. Has any one called, Beth? How is your cold, Meg? Jo, you look tired to death. Come and kiss me, baby.'

While making these maternal inquiries Mrs March got her wet things off, her hot slippers on, and sitting down in the easy-chair, drew Amy to her lap, preparing to enjoy the happiest hour of her busy day. The girls flew about, trying to make things comfortable, each in her own way. Meg arranged the tea-table; Jo brought wood and set chairs, dropping, overturning, and clattering everything she touched; Beth trotted to and fro between parlor and kitchen, quiet and busy; while Amy gave directions to every one, as she sat with her hands folded.

As they gathered about the table, Mrs March said, with a particularly happy face, 'I've got a treat for you after supper.'

A quick, bright smile went round like a streak of sunshine. Beth clapped her hands, regardless of the hot biscuit she held, and Jo tossed up her napkin, crying, 'A letter! a letter! Three cheers for father!'

'Yes, a nice long letter. He is well, and thinks he shall get through the cold season better than we feared. He sends all sorts of loving wishes for Christmas, and an especial message to you girls,' said Mrs March, patting her pocket as if she had got a treasure there.

'Hurry up, and get done. Don't stop to quirk your little finger, and prink over your plate, Amy,' cried Jo, choking in her tea, and dropping her bread, butter side down, on the carpet, in her haste to get at the treat.

Beth ate no more, but crept away, to sit in her shadowy corner and brood over the delight to come, till the others were ready.

'I think it was so splendid in father to go as a chaplain when he was too old to be draughted, and not strong enough for a soldier,' said Meg, warmly.

'Don't I wish I could go as a drummer, a *vivan*—what's its name? or a nurse, so I could be near him and help him,' exclaimed Jo, with a groan.

'It must be very disagreeable to sleep in a tent, and eat all sorts of bad-tasting things, and drink out of a tin mug,' sighed Amy.

'When will he come home, Marmee?' asked Beth, with a little quiver in her voice.

'Not for many months, dear, unless he is sick. He will stay and do his work faithfully as long as he can, and we won't ask for him back a minute sooner than he can be spared. Now come and hear the letter.'

They all drew to the fire, mother in the big chair

with Beth at her feet, Meg and Amy perched on either arm of the chair, and Jo leaning on the back, where no one would see any sign of emotion if the letter should happen to be touching.

Very few letters were written in those hard times that were not touching, especially those which fathers sent home. In this one little was said of the hardships endured, the dangers faced, or the homesickness conquered; it was a cheerful, hopeful letter, full of lively descriptions of camp life, marches, and military news; and only at the end did the writer's heart overflow with fatherly love and longing for the little girls at home.

'Give them all my dear love and a kiss. Tell them I think of them by day, pray for them by night, and find my best comfort in their affection at all times. A year seems very long to wait before I see them, but remind them that while we wait we may all work, so that these hard days need not be wasted. I know they will remember all I said to them, that they will be loving children to you, will do their duty faithfully, fight their bosom enemies bravely, and conquer themselves so beautifully, that when I come back to them I may be fonder and prouder than ever of my little women.'

Everybody sniffed when they came to that part; Jo wasn't ashamed of the great tear that dropped off the end of her nose, and Amy never minded the rumpling of her curls as she hid her face on her mother's shoulder and sobbed out, 'I *am* a selfish pig! but I'll truly try to be better, so he mayn't be disappointed in me by and by.'

'We all will!' cried Meg. 'I think too much of my looks, and hate to work, but won't any more, if I can help it.'

'I'll try and be what he loves to call me, "a little woman," and not be rough and wild; but do my duty here instead of wanting to be somewhere else,' said Jo, thinking that keeping her temper at home was a much harder task than facing a rebel or two down South.

Beth said nothing, but wiped away her tears with the blue army-sock, and began to knit with all her might, losing no time in doing that duty that lay nearest her, while she resolved in her quiet little soul to be all that father hoped to find her when the year brought round the happy coming home.

Mrs March broke the silence that followed Jo's words, by saying in her cheery voice, 'Do you remember how you used to play Pilgrim's Progress when you were little things? Nothing delighted you more than to have me tie my piece-bags on your backs for burdens, give you hats and sticks, and rolls of paper, and let you travel through the house from the cellar, which was the City of Destruction, up, up, to the house-top, where you had all the lovely things you could collect to make a Celestial City.'

'What fun it was, especially going by the lions, fighting Apollyon, and passing through the Valley where the hobgoblins were,' said Jo.

'I liked the place where the bundles fell off and tumbled down stairs,' said Meg.

'My favorite part was when we came out on the flat roof where our flowers and arbors, and pretty things were, and all stood and sung for joy up there in the sunshine,' said Beth, smiling, as if that pleasant moment had come back to her.

'I don't remember much about it, except that I was afraid of the cellar and the dark entry, and always liked the cake and milk we had up at the top. If I wasn't too old for such things, I'd rather like to play it over again,' said Amy, who began to talk of renouncing childish things at the mature age of twelve.

'We never are too old for this, my dear, because it is a play we are playing all the time in one way or another. Our burdens are here, our road is before us, and the longing for goodness and happiness is the guide that leads us through many troubles and mistakes to the peace which is a true Celestial City. Now, my little pilgrims, suppose you begin again, not in play, but in earnest, and see how far on you can get before father comes home.'

'Really, mother? where are our bundles?' asked Amy, who was a very literal young lady.

'Each of you told what your burden was just now, except Beth; I rather think she hasn't got any,' said her mother.

'Yes, I have; mine is dishes and dusters, and envying girls with nice pianos, and being afraid of people.'

Beth's bundle was such a funny one that everybody wanted to laugh; but nobody did, for it would have hurt her feelings very much.

'Let us do it,' said Meg, thoughtfully. 'It is only another name for trying to be good, and the story may help us; for though we do want to be good, it's hard work, and we forget, and don't do our best.'

'We were in the Slough of Despond tonight, and mother came and pulled us out as Help did in the book. We ought to have our roll of directions, like Christian. What shall we do about that?' asked Jo, delighted with the fancy which lent a little romance to the very dull task of doing her duty.

'Look under your pillows, Christmas morning, and you will find your guide-book,' replied Mrs March.

They talked over the new plan while old Hannah cleared the table; then out came the four little workbaskets, and the needles flew as the girls made sheets for Aunt March. It was uninteresting sewing, but tonight no one grumbled. They adopted Jo's plan of dividing the long seams into four parts, and calling the quarters Europe, Asia, Africa and America, and in that way got on capitally, especially when they talked about the different countries as they stitched their way through them.

At nine they stopped work, and sang, as usual, before they went to bed. No one but Beth could get much music out of the old piano; but she had a way of softly touching the yellow keys, and making a pleasant accompaniment to the simple songs they sung. Meg had a voice like a flute, and she and her mother led the little choir. Amy chirped like a cricket, and Jo wandered through the airs at her own sweet will, always coming out at the wrong place with a crook or a quaver that spoilt the most pensive tune. They had always done this from the time they could lisp

'Crinkle, crinkle, 'ittle 'tar,'

and it had become a household custom, for the mother was a born singer. The first sound in the morning was her voice, as she went about the house singing like a lark; and the last sound at night was the same cheery sound, for the girls never grew too old for that familiar lullaby.

2

A Merry Christmas

JO WAS the first to wake in the gray dawn of Christmas morning. No stockings hung at the fireplace, and for a moment she felt as much disappointed as she did long ago, when her little sock fell down because it was so crammed with goodies. Then she remembered her mother's promise, and slipping her hand under her pillow, drew out a little crimson-covered book. She knew it very well, for it was that beautiful old story of the best life ever lived, and Jo felt that it was a true guide-book for any pilgrim going the long journey. She woke Meg with a 'Merry Christmas,' and bade her see what was under her pillow. A green-covered book appeared, with the same picture inside, and a few words written by their mother, which made their one present very precious in their eyes. Presently Beth and Amy woke, to rummage and find their little books also,—one dove-colored, the other blue; and all sat looking at and talking about them, while the East grew rosy with the coming day.

In spite of her small vanities, Margaret had a sweet and pious nature, which unconsciously influenced her sisters, especially Jo, who loved her very tenderly, and obeyed her because her advice was so gently given.

'Girls,' said Meg, seriously, looking from the tumbled head beside her to the two little night-capped ones in the room beyond, 'mother wants us to read and love and mind these books, and we must begin at once. We used to be faithful about it; but since father went away, and all this war trouble unsettled us, we have neglected many things. You can do as you please; but *I* shall keep my book on the table here, and read a little every morning as soon as I wake, for I know it will do me good, and help me through the day.'

Then she opened her new book and began to read. Jo put her arm round her, and, leaning cheek to cheek, read also, with the quiet expression so seldom seen on her restless face.

'How good Meg is! Come, Amy, let's do as they do. I'll help you with the hard words, and they'll explain things if we don't understand,' whispered Beth, very much impressed by the pretty books and her sisters' example.

'I'm glad mine is blue,' said Amy; and then the rooms were very still while the pages were softly turned, and the winter sunshine crept in to touch the bright heads and serious faces with a Christmas greeting.

'Where is mother?' asked Meg, as she and Jo ran down to thank her for their gifts, half an hour later.

'Goodness only knows. Some poor creeter come a-beggin', and your ma went straight off to see what was needed. There never *was* such a woman for givin' away vittles and drink, clothes and firin',' replied Hannah, who had lived with the family since Meg was born, and was considered by them all more as a friend than a servant.

'She will be back soon, I guess; so do your cakes, and have everything ready,' said Meg, looking over the presents which were collected in a basket and kept under the sofa, ready to be produced at the proper time. 'Why, where is Amy's bottle of Cologne?' she added, as the little flask did not appear.

'She took it out a minute ago, and went off with it to put a ribbon on it, or some such notion,' replied Jo, dancing about the room to take the first stiffness off the new army-slippers.

'How nice my handkerchiefs look, don't they?

Hannah washed and ironed them for me, and I marked them all myself,' said Beth, looking proudly at the somewhat uneven letters which had cost her such labor.

'Bless the child, she's gone and put "Mother" on them instead of "M. March;" how funny!' cried Jo, taking up one.

'Isn't it right? I thought it was better to do it so, because Meg's initials are "M. M.," and I don't want any one to use these but Marmee,' said Beth, looking troubled.

'It's all right, dear, and a very pretty idea; quite sensible, too, for no one can ever mistake now. It will please her very much, I know,' said Meg, with a frown for Jo, and a smile for Beth.

'There's mother; hide the basket, quick!' cried Jo, as a door slammed, and steps sounded in the hall.

Amy came in hastily, and looked rather abashed when she saw her sisters all waiting for her.

'Where have you been, and what are you hiding behind you?' asked Meg, surprised to see, by her hood and cloak, that lazy Amy had been out so early.

'Don't laugh at me, Jo, I didn't mean any one should know till the time came. I only meant to change the little bottle for a big one, and I gave *all* my money to get it, and I'm truly trying not to be selfish any more.'

As she spoke, Amy showed the handsome flask which replaced the cheap one; and looked so earnest and humble in her little effort to forget herself, that Meg hugged her on the spot, and Jo pronounced her 'a trump,' while Beth ran to the window, and picked her finest rose to ornament the stately bottle.

'You see I felt ashamed of my present, after reading and talking about being good this morning, so I ran round the corner and changed it the minute I was up; and I'm *so* glad, for mine is the handsomest now.'

Another bang of the street-door sent the basket under the sofa, and the girls to the table eager for breakfast.

'Merry Christmas, Marmee! Lots of them! Thank you for our books; we read some, and mean to every day,' they cried, in chorus.

'Merry Christmas, little daughters! I'm glad you began at once, and hope you will keep on. But I want to say one word before we sit down. Not far away from here lies a poor woman with a little newborn baby. Six children are huddled into one bed to keep from freezing, for they have no fire. There is nothing to eat over there; and the oldest boy came to tell me they were suffering hunger and cold. My girls, will you give them your breakfast as a Christmas present?'

They were all unusually hungry, having waited nearly an hour, and for a minute no one spoke; only a minute, for Jo exclaimed impetuously,—

'I'm so glad you came before we began!'

'May I go and help carry the things to the poor little children?' asked Beth, eagerly.

'*I* shall take the cream and the muffins,' added Amy, heroically giving up the articles she most liked.

Meg was already covering the buckwheats, and piling the bread into one big plate.

'I thought you'd do it,' said Mrs March, smiling as if satisfied. 'You shall all go and help me, and when we come back we will have bread and milk for breakfast, and make it up at dinner-time.'

They were soon ready, and the procession set out. Fortunately it was early, and they went through back streets, so few people saw them, and no one laughed at the funny party.

A poor, bare, miserable room it was, with broken windows, no fire, ragged bed-clothes, a sick mother, wailing baby, and a group of pale, hungry children cuddled under one old quilt, trying to keep warm. How the big eyes stared, and the blue lips smiled, as the girls went in!

'Ach, mein Gott! it is good angels come to us!' cried the poor woman, crying for joy.

'Funny angels in hoods and mittens,' said Jo, and set them laughing.

In a few minutes it really did seem as if kind spirits had been at work there. Hannah, who had carried wood, made a fire, and stopped up the broken panes with old hats, and her own shawl. Mrs March gave the mother tea and gruel, and comforted her with promises of help, while she dressed the little baby as tenderly as if it had been her own. The girls, meantime, spread the table, set the children round the fire, and fed them like so many hungry birds; laughing, talking, and trying to understand the funny broken English.

'Das ist gute!' 'Der angel-kinder!' cried the poor things, as they ate, and warmed their purple hands at the comfortable blaze. The girls had never been called angel children before, and thought it very agreeable, especially Jo, who had been considered 'a Sancho' ever since she was born. That was a very happy breakfast, though they didn't get any of it; and when they went away, leaving comfort behind, I think there were not in all the city four merrier people than the hungry little girls who gave away their breakfasts, and contented themselves with bread and milk on Christmas morning.

'That's loving our neighbor better than ourselves, and I like it,' said Meg, as they set out their presents, while their mother was upstairs collecting clothes for the poor Hummels.

Not a very splendid show, but there was a great deal of

love done up in the few little bundles; and the tall vase of red roses, white chrysanthemums, and trailing vines, which stood in the middle, gave quite an elegant air to the table.

'She's coming! strike up, Beth, open the door, Amy. Three cheers for Marmee!' cried Jo, prancing about, while Meg went to conduct mother to the seat of honor.

Beth played her gayest march, Amy threw open the door, and Meg enacted escort with great dignity. Mrs March was both surprised and touched; and smiled with her eyes full as she examined her presents, and read the little notes which accompanied them. The slippers went on at once, a new handkerchief was slipped into her pocket, well scented with Amy's Cologne, the rose was fastened in her bosom, and the nice gloves were pronounced 'a perfect fit.'

There was a good deal of laughing, and kissing, and explaining, in the simple, loving fashion which makes these home-festivals so pleasant at the time, so sweet to remember long afterward, and then all fell to work.

The morning charities and ceremonies took so much time, that the rest of the day was devoted to preparations for the evening festivities. Being still too young to go often to the theatre, and not rich enough to afford any great outlay for private performances, the girls put their wits to work, and, necessity being the mother of invention, made whatever they needed. Very clever were some of their productions; pasteboard guitars, antique lamps made of old-fashioned butter-boats, covered with silver paper, gorgeous robes of old cotton, glittering with tin spangles from a pickle factory, and armor covered with the same useful diamond-shaped bits, left in sheets when the lids of tin preserve-pots were cut out. The furniture was used to being turned topsy-turvy, and the big chamber was the scene of many innocent revels.

No gentlemen were admitted; so Jo played male parts to her heart's content, and took immense satisfaction in a pair of russet-leather boots given her by a friend, who knew a lady who knew an actor. These boots, an old foil, and a slashed doublet once used by an artist for some picture, were Jo's chief treasures, and appeared on all occasions. The smallness of the company made it necessary for the two principal actors to take several parts apiece; and they certainly deserved some credit for the hard work they did in learning three or four different parts, whisking in and out of various costumes, and managing the stage besides. It was excellent drill for their memories, a harmless amusement, and employed many hours which otherwise would have been idle, lonely, or spent in less profitable society.

On Christmas night, a dozen girls piled on to the bed, which was the dress circle, and sat before the blue and yellow chintz curtains, in a most flattering state of expectancy. There was a good deal of rustling and whispering behind the curtain, a trifle of lamp-smoke, and an occasional giggle from Amy, who was apt to get hysterical in the excitement of the moment. Presently a bell sounded, the curtains flew apart, and the Operatic Tragedy began.

'A gloomy wood,' according to the one play-bill, was represented by a few shrubs in pots, a green baize on the floor, and a cave in the distance. This cave was made with a clothes-horse for a roof, bureaus for walls; and in it was a small furnace in full blast, with a black pot on it, and an old witch bending over it. The stage was dark, and the glow of the furnace had a fine effect, especially as real steam issued from the kettle when the witch took off the cover. A moment was allowed for the first thrill to subside; then Hugo, the villain, stalked in with a clanking sword at his side, a slouched hat, black beard, mysterious cloak, and the boots. After pacing to and fro in much agitation, he struck his forehead, and burst out in a wild strain, singing of his hatred for Roderigo, his love for Zara, and his pleasing resolution to kill the one and win the other. The gruff tones of Hugo's voice, with an occasional shout when his feelings overcame him, were very impressive, and the audience applauded the moment he paused for breath. Bowing with the air of one accustomed to public praise, he stole to the cavern and ordered Hagar to come forth with a commanding 'What ho! minion! I need thee!'

Out came Meg, with gray horse-hair hanging about her face, a red and black robe, a staff, and cabalistic signs upon her cloak. Hugo demanded a potion to make Zara adore him, and one to destroy Roderigo. Hagar, in a fine dramatic melody, promised both, and proceeded to call up the spirit who would bring the love philter:—

> 'Hither, hither, from thy home,
> Airy sprite, I bid thee come!
> Born of roses, fed on dew,
> Charms and potions canst thou brew?
> Bring me here, with elfin speed,
> The fragrant philter which I need;
> Make it sweet, and swift and strong;
> Spirit, answer now my song!'

A soft strain of music sounded, and then at the back of the cave appeared a little figure in cloudy white, with glittering wings, golden hair, and a garland of roses on its head. Waving a wand, it sang:—

> *'Hither I come,*
> *From my airy home,*
> *Afar in the silver moon;*
> *Take the magic spell,*
> *Oh, use it well!*
> *Or its power will vanish soon!'*

and dropping a small gilded bottle at the witch's feet, the spirit vanished. Another chant from Hagar produced another apparition,—not a lovely one, for, with a bang, an ugly, black imp appeared, and having croaked a reply, tossed a dark bottle at Hugo, and disappeared with a mocking laugh. Having warbled his thanks, and put the potions in his boots, Hugo departed; and Hagar informed the audience that, as he had killed a few of her friends in times past, she has cursed him, and intends to thwart his plans, and be revenged on him. Then the curtain fell, and the audience reposed and ate candy while discussing the merits of the play.

A good deal of hammering went on before the curtain rose again; but when it became evident what a masterpiece of stage carpentering had been got up, no one murmured at the delay. It was truly superb! A tower rose to the ceiling; half-way up appeared a window with a lamp burning at it, and behind the white curtain appeared Zara in a lovely blue and silver dress, waiting for Roderigo. He came, in gorgeous array, with plumed cap, red cloak, chestnut love-locks, a guitar, and the boots, of course. Kneeling at the foot of the tower, he sang a serenade in melting tones. Zara replied, and after a musical dialogue, consented to fly. Then came the grand effect of the play. Roderigo produced a rope-ladder with five steps to it, threw up one end, and invited Zara to descend. Timidly she crept from her lattice, put her hand on Roderigo's shoulder, and was about to leap gracefully down, when, 'alas, alas for Zara!' she forgot her train,—it caught in the window; the tower tottered, leaned forward, fell with a crash, and buried the unhappy lovers in the ruins!

A universal shriek arose as the russet boots waved wildly from the wreck, and a golden head emerged, exclaiming, 'I told you so! I told you so!' With wonderful presence of mind Don Pedro, the cruel sire, rushed in, dragged out his daughter with a hasty aside,—

'Don't laugh, act as if it was all right!' and ordering Roderigo up, banished him from the kingdom with wrath and scorn. Though decidedly shaken by the fall of the tower upon him, Roderigo defied the old gentleman, and refused to stir. This dauntless example fired Zara; she also defied her sire, and he ordered them both to the deepest dungeons of the castle. A stout little retainer came in with chains, and led them away, looking very much frightened, and evidently forgetting the speech he ought to have made.

Act third was the castle hall; and here Hagar appeared, having come to free the lovers and finish Hugo. She hears him coming, and hides; sees him put the potions into two cups of wine, and bid the timid little servant 'Bear them to the captives in their cells, and tell them I shall come anon.' The servant takes Hugo aside to tell him something, and Hagar changes the cups for two others which are harmless. Ferdinando, the 'minion,' carries them away, and Hagar puts back the cup which holds the poison meant for Roderigo. Hugo, getting thirsty after a long warble, drinks it, loses his wits, and after a good deal of clutching and stamping, falls flat and dies; while Hagar informs him what she has done in a song of exquisite power and melody.

This was a truly thrilling scene; though some persons might have thought that the sudden tumbling down of a quantity of long hair rather marred the effect of the villain's death. He was called before the curtain, and with great propriety appeared leading Hagar, whose singing was considered more wonderful than all the rest of the performance put together.

Act fourth displayed the despairing Roderigo on the point of stabbing himself, because he has been told that Zara has deserted him. Just as the dagger is at his heart, a lovely song is sung under his window, informing him that Zara is true, but in danger, and he can save her if he will. A key is thrown in, which unlocks the door, and in a spasm of rapture he tears off his chains, and rushes away to find and rescue his lady-love.

Act fifth opened with a stormy scene between Zara and Don Pedro. He wishes her to go into a convent, but she won't hear of it; and, after a touching appeal, is about to faint, when Roderigo dashes in and demands her hand. Don Pedro refuses, because he is not rich. They shout and gesticulate tremendously, but cannot agree, and Roderigo is about to bear away the exhausted Zara, when the timid servant enters with a letter and a bag from Hagar, who has mysteriously disappeared. The latter informs the party that she bequeaths untold wealth to the young pair, and an awful doom to Don Pedro if he doesn't make them happy. The bag is opened, and several quarts of tin money shower down upon the stage, till it is quite glorified with the glitter. This entirely softens the 'stern sire;' he consents without a murmur, all join in a joyful chorus, and the curtain falls upon the lovers kneeling to receive Don Pedro's blessing, in attitudes of the most romantic grace.

Tumultuous applause followed, but received an unexpected check; for the cot-bed on which the 'dress circle' was built, suddenly shut up, and extinguished the enthusiastic audience. Roderigo and Don Pedro flew to the rescue, and all were taken out unhurt, though many were speechless with laughter. The excitement had hardly subsided when Hannah appeared, with 'Mrs March's compliments, and would the ladies walk down to supper.'

This was a surprise, even to the actors; and when they saw the table they looked at one another in rapturous amazement. It was like 'Marmee' to get up a little treat for them, but anything so fine as this was unheard of since the departed days of plenty. There was ice cream, actually two dishes of it,—pink and white,—and cake, and fruit, and distracting French bonbons, and in the middle of the table four great bouquets of hot-house flowers!

It quite took their breath away; and they stared first at the table and then at their mother, who looked as if she enjoyed it immensely.

'Is it fairies?' asked Amy.

'It's Santa Claus,' said Beth.

'Mother did it;' and Meg smiled her sweetest, in spite of her gray beard and white eyebrows.

'Aunt March had a good fit, and sent the supper,' cried Jo, with a sudden inspiration.

'All wrong; old Mr Laurence sent it,' replied Mrs March.

'The Laurence boy's grandfather! What in the world put such a thing into his head? We don't know him,' exclaimed Meg.

'Hannah told one of his servants about your breakfast party; he is an odd old gentleman, but that pleased him. He knew my father, years ago, and he sent me a polite note this afternoon, saying he hoped I would allow him to express his friendly feeling toward my children by sending them a few trifles in honor of the day. I could not refuse, and so you have a little feast at night to make up for the bread and milk breakfast.'

'That boy put it into his head, I know he did! He's a capital fellow, and I wish we could get acquainted. He looks as if he'd like to know us; but he's bashful, and Meg is so prim she won't let me speak to him when we pass,' said Jo, as the plates went round, and the ice began to melt out of sight, with ohs! and ahs! of satisfaction.

'You mean the people who live in the big house next door, don't you?' asked one of the girls. 'My mother knows old Mr Laurence, but says he's very proud, and don't like to mix with his neighbors. He keeps his grandson shut up when he isn't riding or walking with his tutor, and makes him study dreadful hard. We invited him to our party, but he didn't come. Mother says he's very nice, though he never speaks to us girls.'

'Our cat ran away once, and he brought her back, and we talked over the fence, and were getting on capitally, all about cricket, and so on, when he saw Meg coming, and walked off. I mean to know him some day, for he needs fun, I'm sure he does,' said Jo, decidedly.

'I like his manners, and he looks like a little gentleman, so I've no objection to your knowing him if a proper opportunity comes. He brought the flowers himself, and I should have asked him in if I had been sure what was going on upstairs. He looked so wistful as he went away, hearing the frolic, and evidently having none of his own.'

'It's a mercy you didn't, mother,' laughed Jo, looking at her boots. 'But we'll have another play some time, that he *can* see. Maybe he'll help act; wouldn't that be jolly?'

'I never had a bouquet before; how pretty it is,' and Meg examined her flowers with great interest.

'They *are* lovely, but Beth's roses are sweeter to me,' said Mrs March, sniffing at the half dead posy in her belt.

Beth nestled up to her, and whispered, softly, 'I wish I could send my bunch to father. I'm afraid he isn't having such a merry Christmas as we are.'

3

The Laurence Boy

'JO! JO! where are you?' cried Meg, at the foot of the garret stairs.

'Here,' answered a husky voice from above; and running up, Meg found her sister eating apples and crying over the 'Heir of Redcliffe,' wrapped up in a comforter on an old three-legged sofa by the sunny window. This was Jo's favorite refuge; and here she loved to retire with half a dozen russets and a nice book, to enjoy the quiet and the society of a pet rat who lived near by, and didn't mind her a particle. As Meg appeared, Scrabble whisked into his hole. Jo shook the tears off her cheeks, and waited to hear the news.

'Such fun! only see! a regular note of invitation from Mrs Gardiner for tomorrow night!' cried Meg, waving the precious paper, and then proceeding to read it, with girlish delight.

'"Mrs Gardiner would be happy to see Miss March and Miss Josephine at a little dance on New-Year's-Eve." Marmee is willing we should go; now what *shall* we wear?'

'What's the use of asking that, when you know we shall wear our poplins, because we haven't got anything else,' answered Jo, with her mouth full.

'If I only had a silk!' sighed Meg; 'mother says I may when I'm eighteen, perhaps; but two years is an everlasting time to wait.'

'I'm sure our pops look like silk, and they are nice enough for us. Yours is as good as new, but I forgot the burn and the tear in mine; whatever shall I do? the burn shows horridly, and I can't take any out.'

'You must sit still all you can, and keep your back out of sight; the front is all right. I shall have a new ribbon for my hair, and Marmee will lend me her little pearl pin, and my new slippers are lovely, and my gloves will do, though they aren't as nice as I'd like.'

'Mine are spoilt with lemonade, and I can't get any new ones, so I shall have to go without,' said Jo, who never troubled herself much about dress.

'You *must* have gloves, or I won't go,' cried Meg, decidedly. 'Gloves are more important than anything else; you can't dance without them, and if you don't I should be *so* mortified.'

'Then I'll stay still; I don't care much for company dancing; it's no fun to go sailing round, I like to fly about and cut capers.'

'You can't ask mother for new ones, they are so expensive, and you are so careless. She said, when you spoilt the others, that she shouldn't get you any more this winter. Can't you fix them any way?' asked Meg, anxiously.

'I can hold them crunched up in my hand, so no one will know how stained they are; that's all I can do. No! I'll tell you how we can manage—each wear one good one and carry a bad one; don't you see?'

'Your hands are bigger than mine, and you will stretch my glove dreadfully,' began Meg, whose gloves were a tender point with her.

'Then I'll go without. 1 don't care what people say,' cried Jo, taking up her book.

'You may have it, you may! only don't stain it, and do behave nicely; don't put your hands behind you, or stare, or say "Christopher Columbus!" will you?'

'Don't worry about me; I'll be as prim as a dish, and not get into any scrapes, if I can help it. Now go and answer your note, and let me finish this splendid story.'

So Meg went away to 'accept with thanks,' look over her dress, and sing blithely as she did up her one real lace frill; while Jo finished her story, her four apples, and had a game of romps with Scrabble.

On New-Year's-Eve the parlor was deserted, for the two younger girls played dressing maids, and the two elder were absorbed in the all-important business of 'getting ready for the party.' Simple as the toilets were, there was a great deal of running up and down, laughing and talking, and at one time a strong smell of burnt hair pervaded the house. Meg wanted a few curls about her face, and Jo undertook to pinch the papered locks with a pair of hot tongs.

'Ought they to smoke like that?' asked Beth, from her perch on the bed.

'It's the dampness drying,' replied Jo.

'What a queer smell! it's like burnt feathers,' observed Amy, smoothing her own pretty curls with a superior air.

'There, now I'll take off the papers and you'll see a cloud of little ringlets,' said Jo, putting down the tongs.

She did take off the papers, but no cloud of ringlets appeared, for the hair came with the papers, and the horrified hair-dresser laid a row of little scorched bundles on the bureau before her victim.

'Oh, oh, oh! what *have* you done? I'm spoilt! I can't go! my hair, oh my hair!' wailed Meg, looking with despair at the uneven frizzle on her forehead.

'Just my luck! you shouldn't have asked me to do it; I always spoil everything. I'm no end sorry, but the tongs were too hot, and so I've made a mess,' groaned poor Jo, regarding the black pancakes with tears of regret.

'It isn't spoilt; just frizzle it, and tie your ribbon so the ends come on your forehead a bit, and it will look like the last fashion. I've seen lots of girls do it so,' said Amy, consolingly.

'Serves me right for trying to be fine. I wish I'd let my hair alone,' cried Meg, petulantly.

'So do I, it was so smooth and pretty. But it will soon grow out again,' said Beth, coming to kiss and comfort the shorn sheep.

After various lesser mishaps, Meg was finished at last, and by the united exertions of the family Jo's hair was got up, and her dress on. They looked very well in their simple suits, Meg in silvery drab, with a blue velvet snood, lace frills, and the pearl pin; Jo in maroon, with a stiff, gentlemanly linen collar, and a white chrysanthemum or two for her only ornament. Each put on one nice light glove, and carried one soiled one, and all pronounced the effect 'quite easy and nice.'

Meg's high-heeled slippers were dreadfully tight, and hurt her, though she would not own it, and Jo's nineteen hair-pins all seemed stuck straight into her head, which was not exactly comfortable; but, dear me, let us be elegant or die.

'Have a good time, dearies,' said Mrs March, as the sisters went daintily down the walk. 'Don't eat much supper, and come away at eleven, when I send Hannah for you.' As the gate clashed behind them, a voice cried from a window,—

'Girls, girls! *have* you both got nice pocket-handkerchiefs?'

'Yes, yes, spandy nice, and Meg has Cologne on hers,' cried Jo, adding, with a laugh, as they went on, 'I do believe Marmee would ask that if we were all running away from an earthquake.'

'It is one of her aristocratic tastes, and quite proper, for a real lady is always known by neat boots, gloves, and handkerchief,' replied Meg, who had a good many little 'aristocratic tastes' of her own.

'Now don't forget to keep the bad breadth out of sight, Jo. Is my sash right; and does my hair look *very* bad?' said Meg, as she turned from the glass in Mrs Gardiner's dressing-room, after a prolonged prink.

'I know I shall forget. If you see me doing anything wrong, you just remind me by a wink, will you?'

returned Jo, giving her collar a twitch and her head a hasty brush.

'No, winking isn't lady-like; I'll lift my eyebrows if anything is wrong, and nod if you are all right. Now hold your shoulders straight, and take short steps, and don't shake hands if you are introduced to any one, it isn't the thing.'

'How *do* you learn all the proper quirks? I never can. Isn't that music gay?'

Down they went, feeling a trifle timid, for they seldom went to parties, and, informal as this little gathering was, it was an event to them. Mrs Gardiner, a stately old lady, greeted them kindly, and handed them over to the eldest of her six daughters. Meg knew Sallie, and was at her ease very soon; but Jo, who didn't care much for girls or girlish gossip, stood about with her back carefully against the wall, and felt as much out of place as a colt in a flower-garden. Half a dozen jovial lads were talking about skates in another part of the room, and she longed to go and join them, for skating was one of the joys of her life. She telegraphed her wish to Meg, but the eyebrows went up so alarmingly that she dared not stir. No one came to talk to her, and one by one the group near her dwindled away, till she was left alone. She could not roam about and amuse herself, for the burnt breadth would show, so she stared at people rather forlornly till the dancing began. Meg was asked at once, and the tight slippers tripped about so briskly that none would have guessed the pain their wearer suffered smilingly. Jo saw a big red-headed youth approaching her corner, and fearing he meant to engage her, she slipped into a curtained recess, intending to peep and enjoy herself in peace. Unfortunately, another bashful person had chosen the same refuge; for, as the curtain fell behind her, she found herself face to face with the 'Laurence boy.'

'Dear me, I didn't know any one was here!' stammered Jo, preparing to back out as speedily as she had bounced in.

But the boy laughed, and said, pleasantly, though he looked a little startled,—

'Don't mind me; stay, if you like.'

'Shan't I disturb you?'

'Not a bit; I only came here because I don't know many people, and felt rather strange at first, you know.'

'So did I. Don't go away, please, unless you'd rather.'

The boy sat down again and looked at his boots, till Jo said, trying to be polite and easy,—

'I think I've had the pleasure of seeing you before; you live near us, don't you?'

'Next door;' and he looked up and laughed outright, for Jo's prim manner was rather funny when he remembered how they had chatted about cricket when he brought the cat home.

That put Jo at her ease; and she laughed too, as she said, in her heartiest way,—

'We did have such a good time over your nice Christmas present.'

'Grandpa sent it.'

'But you put it into his head, didn't you, now?'

'How is your cat, Miss March?' asked the boy, trying to look sober, while his black eyes shone with fun.

'Nicely, thank you, Mr Laurence; but I ain't Miss March. I'm only Jo,' returned the young lady.

'I'm not Mr Laurence, I'm only Laurie.'

'Laurie Laurence; what an odd name.'

'My first name is Theodore, but I don't like it, for the fellows called me Dora, so I made them say Laurie instead.'

'I hate my name, too—so sentimental! I wish every one would say Jo, instead of Josephine. How did you make the boys stop calling you Dora?'

'I thrashed 'em.'

'I can't thrash Aunt March, so I suppose I shall have to bear it;' and Jo resigned herself with a sigh.

'Don't you like to dance, Miss Jo?' asked Laurie, looking as if he thought the name suited her.

'I like it well enough if there is plenty of room, and

every one is lively. In a place like this I'm sure to upset something, tread on people's toes, or do something dreadful, so I keep out of mischief, and let Meg do the pretty. Don't you dance?'

'Sometimes; you see I've been abroad a good many years, and haven't been about enough to know how you do things here.'

'Abroad!' cried Jo, 'oh, tell me about it! I love dearly to hear people describe their travels.'

Laurie didn't seem to know where to begin; but Jo's eager questions soon set him going, and he told her how he had been at school in Vevey, where the boys never wore hats, and had a fleet of boats on the lake, and for holiday fun went on walking trips about Switzerland with their teachers.

'Don't I wish I'd been there!' cried Jo. 'Did you go to Paris?'

'We spent last winter there.'

'Can you talk French?'

'We were not allowed to speak anything else at Vevey.'

'Do say some. I can read it, but can't pronounce.'

'Quel nom a cette jeune demoiselle en les pantoufles jolis?' said Laurie, good-naturedly.

'How nicely you do it! Let me see—you said, "Who is the young lady in the pretty slippers," didn't you?'

'Oui, mademoiselle.'

'It's my sister Margaret, and you knew it was! Do you think she is pretty?'

'Yes; she makes me think of the German girls, she looks so fresh and quiet, and dances like a lady.'

Jo quite glowed with pleasure at this boyish praise of her sister, and stored it up to repeat to Meg. Both peeped, and criticized, and chatted, till they felt like old acquaintances. Laurie's bashfulness soon wore off, for Jo's gentlemanly demeanor amused and set him at his ease, and Jo was her merry self again, because her dress was forgotten, and nobody lifted their eyebrows at her. She liked the 'Laurence boy' better than ever, and took several good looks at him, so that she might describe him to the girls; for they had no brothers, very few male cousins, and boys were almost unknown creatures to them.

Curly black hair, brown skin, big black eyes, long nose, nice teeth, little hands and feet, tall as I am; very polite for a boy, and altogether jolly. Wonder how old he is?

It was on the tip of Jo's tongue to ask; but she checked herself in time, and, with unusual tact, tried to find out in a roundabout way.

'I suppose you are going to college soon? I see you pegging away at your books—no, I mean studying hard;' and Jo blushed at the dreadful 'pegging' which had escaped her.

Laurie smiled, but didn't seem shocked, and answered, with a shrug,—

'Not for two or three years yet; I won't go before seventeen, anyway.'

'Aren't you but fifteen?' asked Jo, looking at the tall lad, whom she had imagined seventeen already.

'Sixteen, next month.'

'How I wish I was going to college; you don't look as if you liked it.'

'I hate it! nothing but grinding or sky-larking; and I don't like the way fellows do either, in this country.'

'What do you like?'

'To live in Italy, and to enjoy myself in my own way.'

Jo wanted very much to ask what his own way was; but his black brows looked rather threatening as he knit them, so she changed the subject by saying, as her foot kept time, 'That's a splendid polka; why don't you go and try it?'

'If you will come too,' he answered, with a queer little French bow.

'I can't; for I told Meg I wouldn't, because—' there Jo stopped, and looked undecided whether to tell or to laugh.

'Because what?' asked Laurie, curiously.

'You won't tell?'

'Never!'

'Well, I have a bad trick of standing before the fire, and so I burn my frocks, and I scorched this one; and, though it's nicely mended, it shows, and Meg told me to keep still, so no one would see it. You may laugh if you want to; it is funny, I know.'

But Laurie didn't laugh; he only looked down a minute, and the expression of his face puzzled Jo, when he said very gently,—

'Never mind that; I'll tell you how we can manage: there's a long hall out there, and we can dance grandly, and no one will see us. Please come.'

Jo thanked him, and gladly went, wishing she had two neat gloves, when she saw the nice pearl-colored ones her partner put on. The hall was empty, and they had a grand polka, for Laurie danced well, and taught her the German step, which delighted Jo, being full of swing and spring. When the music stopped they sat down on the stairs to get their breath, and Laurie was in the midst of an account of a students' festival at Heidelberg, when Meg appeared in search of her sister. She beckoned, and Jo reluctantly followed her into a side-room, where she found her on a sofa holding her foot, and looking pale.

'I've sprained my ankle. That stupid high heel turned,

and gave me a horrid wrench. It aches so, I can hardly stand, and I don't know how I'm ever going to get home,' she said, rocking to and fro in pain.

'I knew you'd hurt your foot with those silly things. I'm sorry; but I don't see what you can do, except get a carriage, or stay here all night,' answered Jo, softly rubbing the poor ankle, as she spoke.

'I can't have a carriage without its costing ever so much; I dare say I can't get one at all, for most people come in their own, and it's a long way to the stable, and no one to send.'

'I'll go.'

'No, indeed; it's past ten, and dark as Egypt. I can't stop here, for the house is full; Sallie has some girls staying with her. I'll rest till Hannah comes, and then do the best I can.'

'I'll ask Laurie; he will go,' said Jo, looking relieved as the idea occurred to her.

'Mercy, no! don't ask or tell any one. Get me my rubbers, and put these slippers with our things. I can't dance any more; but as soon as supper is over, watch for Hannah, and tell me the minute she comes.'

'They are going out to supper now. I'll stay with you; I'd rather.'

'No, dear; run along, and bring me some coffee. I'm so tired, I can't stir.'

So Meg reclined, with the rubbers well hidden, and Jo went blundering away to the dining-room, which she found after going into a china-closet and opening the door of a room where old Mr Gardiner was taking a little private refreshment. Making a dive at the table, she secured the coffee, which she immediately spilt, thereby making the front of her dress as bad as the back.

'Oh dear! what a blunderbuss I am!' exclaimed Jo, finishing Meg's glove by scrubbing her gown with it.

'Can I help you?' said a friendly voice; and there was Laurie, with a full cup in one hand and a plate of ice in the other.

'I was trying to get something for Meg, who is very tired, and some one shook me, and here I am, in a nice state,' answered Jo, glancing, dismally, from the stained skirt to the coffee-colored glove.

'Too bad! I was looking for some one to give this to; may I take it to your sister?'

'Oh, thank you; I'll show you where she is. I don't offer to take it myself, for I should only get into another scrape if I did.'

Jo led the way; and, as if used to waiting on ladies, Laurie drew up a little table, brought a second instalment of coffee and ice for Jo, and was so obliging that even particular Meg pronounced him a 'nice boy.' They had a merry time over the bonbons and mottos, and were in the midst of a quiet game of 'buzz' with two or three other young people who had strayed in, when Hannah appeared. Meg forgot her foot, and rose so quickly that she was forced to catch hold of Jo, with an exclamation of pain.

'Hush! don't say anything,' she whispered; adding aloud, 'It's nothing; I turned my foot a little,—that's all,' and limped up stairs to put her things on.

Hannah scolded, Meg cried, and Jo was at her wits' end, till she decided to take things into her own hands. Slipping out, she ran down, and finding a servant, asked if he could get her a carriage. It happened to be a hired waiter, who knew nothing about the neighborhood; and Jo was looking round for help, when Laurie, who had heard what she did, came up and offered his grandfather's carriage, which had just come for him, he said.

'It's so early,—you can't mean to go yet,' began Jo, looking relieved, but hesitating to accept the offer.

'I always go early,—I do, truly. Please let me take you home; it's all on my way, you know, and it rains, they say.'

That settled it; and telling him of Meg's mishap, Jo gratefully accepted, and rushed up to bring down the rest of the party. Hannah hated rain as much as a cat does; so she made no trouble, and they rolled away in the luxurious close carriage, feeling very festive and elegant. Laurie went on the box, so Meg could keep her foot up, and the girls talked over their party in freedom.

'I had a capital time; did you?' asked Jo, rumpling up her hair, and making herself comfortable.

'Yes, till I hurt myself. Sallie's friend, Annie Moffat, took a fancy to me, and asked me to come and spend a week with her when Sallie does. She is going in the spring, when the opera comes, and it will be perfectly splendid if mother only lets me go,' answered Meg, cheering up at the thought.

'I saw you dancing with the red-headed man I ran away from; was he nice?'

'Oh, very! his hair is auburn, not red; and he was very polite, and I had a delicious *redowa* with him!'

'He looked like a grasshopper in a fit, when he did the new step. Laurie and I couldn't help laughing; did you hear us?'

'No, but it was very rude. What were you about all that time, hidden away there?'

Jo told her adventures, and by the time she had finished they were at home. With many thanks, they said 'Good-night,' and crept in, hoping to disturb no one; but the instant their door creaked, two little night-caps bobbed up, and two sleepy but eager voices cried out,—

'Tell about the party! tell about the party!'

With what Meg called 'a great want of manners,' Jo had saved some bonbons for the little girls, and they soon subsided, after hearing the most thrilling events of the evening.

'I declare, it really seems like being a fine young lady, to come home from my party in my carriage, and sit in my dressing-gown with a maid to wait on me,' said Meg, as Jo bound up her foot with arnica, and brushed her hair.

'I don't believe fine young ladies enjoy themselves a bit more than we do, in spite of our burnt hair, old gowns, one glove apiece, and tight slippers, that sprain our ankles when we are silly enough to wear them.' And I think Jo was quite right.

4

Burdens

'OH DEAR, how hard it does seem to take up our packs and go on,' sighed Meg, the morning after the party; for now the holidays were over, the week of merry-making did not fit her for going on easily with the task she never liked.

'I wish it was Christmas or New-Year all the time; wouldn't it be fun?' answered Jo, yawning dismally.

'We shouldn't enjoy ourselves half so much as we do now. But it does seem so nice to have little suppers and bouquets, and go to parties, and drive home in a carriage, and read and rest, and not grub. It's like other people, you know, and I always envy girls who do such things; I'm so fond of luxury,' said Meg, trying to decide which of two shabby gowns was the least shabby.

'Well, we can't have it, so don't let's grumble, but shoulder our bundles and trudge along as cheerfully as Marmee does. I'm sure Aunt March is a regular Old Man of the Sea to me, but I suppose when I've learned to carry her without complaining, she will tumble off, or get so light that I shan't mind her.'

This idea tickled Jo's fancy, and put her in good spirits; but Meg didn't brighten, for her burden, consisting of four spoilt children, seemed heavier than ever. She hadn't heart enough to make herself pretty, as usual, by putting on a blue neck-ribbon, and dressing her hair in the most becoming way.

'Where's the use of looking nice, when no one sees me but those cross midgets, and no one cares whether I'm pretty or not,' she muttered, shutting her drawer with a jerk. 'I shall have to toil and moil all my days, with only little bits of fun now and then, and get old and ugly and sour, because I'm poor, and can't enjoy my life as other girls do. It's a shame!'

So Meg went down, wearing an injured look, and wasn't at all agreeable at breakfast-time. Every one seemed rather out of sorts, and inclined to croak. Beth had a headache, and lay on the sofa trying to comfort herself with the cat and three kittens; Amy was fretting because her lessons were not learned, and she couldn't find her rubbers; Jo *would* whistle, and make a great racket getting ready; Mrs March was very busy trying to finish a letter, which must go at once; and Hannah had the grumps, for being up late didn't suit her.

'There never *was* such a cross family!' cried Jo, losing her temper when she had upset an inkstand, broken both boot-lacings, and sat down upon her hat.

'You're the crossest person in it!' returned Amy, washing out the sum, that was all wrong, with the tears that had fallen on her slate.

'Beth, if you don't keep these horrid cats down cellar I'll have them drowned,' exclaimed Meg, angrily, as she tried to get rid of the kitten, who had swarmed up her back, and stuck like a burr just out of reach.

Jo laughed, Meg scolded, Beth implored, and Amy wailed, because she couldn't remember how much nine times twelve was.

'Girls! girls! do be quiet one minute. I *must* get this off by the early mail, and you drive me distracted with your worry,' cried Mrs March, crossing out the third spoilt sentence in her letter.

There was a momentary lull, broken by Hannah, who bounced in, laid two hot turn-overs on the table, and bounced out again. These turn-overs were an institution; and the girls called them 'muffs,' for they had no others, and found the hot pies very comforting to their hands on cold mornings. Hannah never forgot to make them, no matter how busy or grumpy she might be, for the walk was long and bleak; the poor things got no other lunch, and were seldom home before three.

'Cuddle your cats, and get over your headache, Bethy. Good-by, Marmee; we are a set of rascals this morning, but we'll come home regular angels. Now then, Meg,' and Jo tramped away, feeling that the pilgrims were not setting out as they ought to do.

They always looked back before turning the corner, for their mother was always at the window, to nod, and smile, and wave her hand to them. Somehow it seemed as if they couldn't have got through the day without that, for whatever their mood might be, the last glimpse of that motherly face was sure to affect them like sunshine.

'If Marmee shook her fist instead of kissing her hand to us, it would serve us right, for more ungrateful minxes than we are were never seen,' cried Jo, taking a remorseful satisfaction in the slushy road and bitter wind.

'Don't use such dreadful expressions,' said Meg, from the depths of the veil in which she had shrouded herself like a nun sick of the world.

'I like good, strong words, that mean something,' replied Jo, catching her hat as it took a leap off her head, preparatory to flying away altogether.

'Call yourself any names you like; but *I* am neither a rascal nor a minx, and I don't choose to be called so.'

'You're a blighted being, and decidedly cross today, because you can't sit in the lap of luxury all the time. Poor dear! just wait till I make my fortune, and you shall revel in carriages, and ice-cream, and high-heeled slippers, and posies, and red-headed boys to dance with.'

'How ridiculous you are, Jo!' but Meg laughed at the nonsense, and felt better in spite of herself.

'Lucky for you I am; for if I put on crushed airs, and tried to be dismal, as you do, we should be in a nice state. Thank goodness, I can always find something funny to keep me up. Don't croak any more, but come home jolly, there's a dear.'

Jo gave her sister an encouraging pat on the shoulder as they parted for the day, each going a different way, each hugging her little warm turn-over, and each trying to be cheerful in spite of wintry weather, hard work, and the unsatisfied desires of pleasure-loving youth.

When Mr March lost his property in trying to help an unfortunate friend, the two oldest girls begged to be allowed to do something toward their own support, at least. Believing that they could not begin too early to cultivate energy, industry, and independence, their parents consented, and both fell to work with the hearty goodwill which, in spite of all obstacles, is sure to succeed at last. Margaret found a place as nursery governess, and felt rich with her small salary. As she said, she *was* 'fond of luxury,' and her chief trouble was poverty. She found it harder to bear than the others, because she could remember a time when home was beautiful, life full of ease and pleasure, and want of any kind unknown. She tried not to be envious or discontented, but it was very natural that the young girl should long for pretty things, gay friends, accomplishments, and a happy life. At the Kings she daily saw all she wanted, for the children's older sisters were just out, and Meg caught frequent glimpses of dainty ball-dresses and bouquets, heard lively gossip about theatres, concerts, sleighing parties and merry-makings of all kinds, and saw money lavished on trifles which would have been so precious to her. Poor Meg seldom complained, but a sense of injustice made her feel bitter toward every one sometimes, for she had not yet learned to know how rich she was in the blessings which alone can make life happy.

Jo happened to suit Aunt March, who was lame, and needed an active person to wait upon her. The childless old lady had offered to adopt one of the girls when the troubles came, and was much offended because her offer was declined. Other friends told the Marches that they had lost all chance of being remembered in the rich old lady's will; but the unworldly Marches only said,—

'We can't give up our girls for a dozen fortunes. Rich or poor, we will keep together and be happy in one another.'

The old lady wouldn't speak to them for a time, but, happening to meet Jo at a friend's, something in her comical face and blunt manners struck the old lady's fancy, and she proposed to take her for a companion. This did not suit Jo at all; but she accepted the place, since nothing better appeared, and, to every one's surprise, got on remarkably well with her irascible relative. There was an occasional tempest, and once Jo had marched home, declaring she couldn't bear it any longer; but Aunt March always cleared up quickly, and sent for her back again with such urgency that she could not refuse, for in her heart she rather liked the peppery old lady.

I suspect that the real attraction was a large library of fine books, which was left to dust and spiders since Uncle March died. Jo remembered the kind old gentleman who used to let her build railroads and bridges with his big dictionaries, tell her stories about the queer pictures in his Latin books, and buy her cards of gingerbread whenever he met her in the street. The dim, dusty room, with the busts staring down from the tall book-cases, the cosy chairs, the globes, and, best of all, the wilderness of books, in which she could wander where she liked, made the library a region of bliss to her. The moment Aunt March took her nap, or was busy with company, Jo hurried to this quiet place, and, curling herself up in the big chair, devoured poetry, romance, history, travels, and pictures, like a regular book-worm. But, like all happiness, it did not last long; for as sure as she had just reached the heart of the story, the sweetest verse of the song, or the most perilous adventure of her traveller, a shrill voice called, 'Josy-phine! Josy-phine!' and she had to leave her paradise to wind yarn, wash the poodle, or read Belsham's Essays, by the hour together.

Jo's ambition was to do something very splendid; what it was she had no idea; but left it for time to tell her; and, meanwhile, found her greatest affliction in the fact that she couldn't read, run, and ride as much as she liked. A quick temper, sharp tongue, and restless spirit were always getting her into scrapes, and her life was a series of ups and downs, which were both comic and pathetic. But the training she received at Aunt March's was just what she needed; and the thought that she was doing something to support herself made her happy, in spite of the perpetual 'Josy-phine!'

Beth was too bashful to go to school; it had been tried, but she suffered so much that it was given up, and she did her lessons at home, with her father. Even when he went away, and her mother was called to devote her skill and energy to Soldiers' Aid Societies, Beth went faithfully on by herself, and did the best she could. She was a housewifely little creature, and helped Hannah keep home neat and comfortable for the workers, never thinking of any reward but to be loved. Long, quiet days she spent, not lonely nor idle, for her little world was peopled with imaginary friends, and she was by nature a busy bee. There were six dolls to be taken up and dressed every morning, for Beth was a child still, and loved her pets as well as ever; not one whole or handsome one among them; all were outcasts till Beth took them in; for, when her sisters outgrew these idols, they passed to her, because Amy would have nothing old or ugly. Beth cherished them all the more tenderly for that very reason, and set up a hospital for infirm dolls. No pins were ever stuck into their cotton vitals; no harsh words or blows were ever given them; no neglect ever saddened the heart of the most repulsive, but all were fed and clothed, nursed and caressed, with an affection which never failed. One forlorn fragment of *dollanity* had belonged to Jo; and, having led a tempestuous life, was left a wreck in the rag-bag, from which dreary poorhouse it was rescued by Beth, and taken to her refuge. Having no top to its head, she tied on a neat little cap, and, as both arms and legs were gone, she hid these deficiencies by folding it in a blanket, and devoting her best bed to this chronic invalid. If any one had known the care lavished on that dolly, I think it would have touched their hearts, even while they laughed. She brought it bits of bouquets; she read to it, took it out to breathe the air, hidden under her coat; she sung it lullabys, and never went to bed without kissing its dirty face, and whispering tenderly, 'I hope you'll have a good night, my poor dear.'

Beth had her troubles as well as the others; and not being an angel, but a very human little girl, she often 'wept a little weep,' as Jo said, because she couldn't take music lessons and have a fine piano. She loved music so dearly, tried so hard to learn, and practised away so patiently at the jingling old instrument, that it did seem as if some one (not to hint Aunt March) ought to help her. Nobody did, however, and nobody saw Beth wipe the tears off the yellow keys, that wouldn't keep in tune when she was all alone. She sung like a little lark about her work, never was too tired to play for Marmee and the girls, and day after day said hopefully to herself, 'I know I'll get my music some time, if I'm good.'

There are many Beths in the world, shy and quiet, sitting in corners till needed, and living for others so cheerfully, that no one sees the sacrifices till the little cricket on the hearth stops chirping, and the sweet, sunshiny presence vanishes, leaving silence and shadow behind.

If anybody had asked Amy what the greatest trial of her life was, she would have answered at once, 'My nose.' When she was a baby, Jo had accidentally dropped her into the coal-hod, and Amy insisted that the fall had ruined her nose forever. It was not big, nor red, like poor "Petrea's;' it was only rather flat, and all the pinching in the world could not give it an aristocratic point. No one minded it but herself, and it was doing its best to grow, but Amy felt deeply the want of a Grecian nose, and drew whole sheets of handsome ones to console herself.

'Little Raphael,' as her sisters called her, had a decided talent for drawing, and was never so happy as when copying flowers, designing fairies, or illustrating stories with queer specimens of art. Her teachers complained that instead of doing her sums, she covered her slate with animals; the blank pages of her atlas were used to copy maps on, and caricatures of the most ludicrous description came fluttering out of all her books at unlucky moments. She got through her lessons as well as she could, and managed to escape reprimands by being a model of deportment. She was a great favorite with her mates, being good-tempered, and possessing the happy art of pleasing without effort. Her little airs and graces were much admired, so were her accomplishments; for beside her drawing, she could play twelve tunes, crochet, and read French without mispronouncing more than two-thirds of the words. She had a plaintive way of saying, 'When papa was rich we did so-and-so,' which was very touching; and her long words were considered 'perfectly elegant' by the girls.

Amy was in a fair way to be spoilt; for every one petted her, and her small vanities and selfishnesses were growing nicely. One thing, however, rather quenched the vanities; she had to wear her cousin's clothes. Now Florence's mamma hadn't a particle of taste, and Amy suffered deeply at having to wear a red instead of a blue bonnet, unbecoming gowns, and fussy aprons that did not fit. Everything was good, well made, and little worn; but Amy's artistic eyes were much afflicted, especially this winter, when her school dress was a dull purple, with yellow dots, and no trimming.

'My only comfort,' she said to Meg, with tears in her eyes, 'is, that mother don't take tucks in my dresses whenever I'm naughty, as Maria Parks' mother does. My dear, it's really dreadful; for sometimes she is so bad, her frock is up to her knees, and she can't come to school. When I think of this *deggerredation*, I feel that I can bear even my flat nose and purple gown, with yellow sky-rockets on it.'

Meg was Amy's confidant and monitor, and, by some strange attraction of opposites, Jo was gentle Beth's. To Jo alone did the shy child tell her thoughts; and over her big, harum-scarum sister, Beth unconsciously exercised more influence than any one in the family. The two older girls were a great deal to each other, but both took one of the younger into their keeping, and watched over them in their own way; 'playing mother' they called it, and put their sisters in the places of discarded dolls, with the maternal instinct of little women.

'Has anybody got anything to tell? It's been such a dismal day I'm really dying for some amusement,' said Meg, as they sat sewing together that evening.

'I had a queer time with aunt today, and, as I got the best of it, I'll tell you about it,' began Jo, who dearly loved to tell stories. 'I was reading that everlasting Belsham, and droning away as I always do, for aunt soon drops off, and then I take out some nice book, and read like fury, till she wakes up. I actually made myself sleepy; and, before she began to nod, I gave such a gape that she asked me what I meant by opening my mouth wide enough to take the whole book in at once.

'"I wish I could, and be done with it," said I, trying not to be saucy.

'Then she gave me a long lecture on my sins, and told me to sit and think them over while she just "lost" herself for a moment. She never finds herself very soon; so the minute her cap began to bob, like a top-heavy dahlia, I whipped the "Vicar of Wakefield" out of my pocket, and read away, with one eye on him, and one on aunt. I'd just got to where they all tumbled into the water, when I forgot, and laughed out loud. Aunt woke up; and, being more good-natured after her nap, told me to read a bit, and show what frivolous work I preferred to the worthy and instructive Belsham. I did my very best, and she liked it, though she only said,—

'"I don't understand what it's all about; go back and begin it, child."

'Back I went, and made the Primroses as interesting as ever I could. Once I was wicked enough to stop in a thrilling place, and say meekly, "I'm afraid it tires you, ma'am; shan't I stop now?"

'She caught up her knitting which had dropped out of her hands, gave me a sharp look through her specs, and said, in her short way,—

'"Finish the chapter, and don't be impertinent, miss."'

'Did she own she liked it?' asked Meg.

'Oh, bless you, no! but she let old Belsham rest; and, when I ran back after my gloves this afternoon, there she was, so hard at the Vicar, that she didn't hear me laugh as I danced a jig in the hall, because of the good time coming. What a pleasant life she might have, if she only chose. I don't envy her much, in spite of her money, for after all rich people have about as many worries as poor ones, I guess,' added Jo.

'That reminds me,' said Meg, 'that I've got something to tell. It isn't funny, like Jo's story, but I thought about it a good deal as I came home. At the Kings today I found everybody in a flurry, and one of the children said that her oldest brother had done something dreadful, and papa had sent him away. I heard Mrs King crying, and Mr King talking very loud, and Grace and Ellen turned away their faces when they passed me, so I shouldn't see how red their eyes were. I didn't ask any questions, of course; but I felt so sorry for them, and was rather glad I hadn't any wild brothers to do wicked things, and disgrace the family.'

'I think being disgraced in school is a great deal tryinger than anything bad boys can do,' said Amy, shaking her head, as if her experience of life had been a deep one. 'Susie Perkins came to school today with a lovely red carnelian ring; I wanted it dreadfully, and wished I was her with all my might. Well, she drew a picture of Mr Davis, with a monstrous nose and a hump, and the words, "Young ladies, my eye is upon you!"

coming out of his mouth in a balloon thing. We were laughing over it, when all of a sudden his eye *was* on us, and he ordered Susie to bring up her slate. She was *parry*lized with fright, but she went, and oh, what *do* you think he did? He took her by the ear, the ear! just fancy how horrid! and led her to the recitation platform, and made her stand there half an hour, holding that slate so every one could see.'

'Didn't the girls shout at the picture?' asked Jo, who relished the scrape.

'Laugh! not a one; they sat as still as mice, and Susie cried quarts, I know she did. I didn't envy her then, for I felt that millions of carnelian rings wouldn't have made me happy after that. I never, never should have got over such a agonizing mortification;' and Amy went on with her work, in the proud consciousness of virtue, and the successful utterance of two long words in a breath.

'I saw something that I liked this morning, and I meant to tell it at dinner, but I forgot,' said Beth, putting Jo's topsy-turvy basket in order as she talked. 'When I went to get some oysters for Hannah, Mr Laurence was in the fish shop, but he didn't see me, for I kept behind a barrel, and he was busy with Mr Cutter, the fish-man. A poor woman came in with a pail and a mop, and asked Mr Cutter if he would let her do some scrubbing for a bit of fish, because she hadn't any dinner for her children, and had been disappointed of a day's work. Mr Cutter was in a hurry, and said "No," rather crossly; so she was going away, looking hungry and sorry, when Mr Laurence hooked up a big fish with the crooked end of his cane, and held it out to her. She was so glad and surprised she took it right in her arms, and thanked him over and over. He told her to "go along and cook it," and she hurried off, so happy! wasn't it nice of him? Oh, she did look so funny, hugging the big, slippery fish, and hoping Mr Laurence's bed in heaven would be "aisy."'

When they had laughed at Beth's story, they asked their mother for one; and, after a moment's thought, she said soberly,—

'As I sat cutting out blue flannel jackets today, at the rooms, I felt very anxious about father, and thought how lonely and helpless we should be if anything happened to him. It was not a wise thing to do, but I kept on worrying, till an old man came in with an order for some things. He sat down near me, and I began to talk to him, for he looked poor, and tired, and anxious.

'"Have you sons in the army?" I asked, for the note he brought was not to me.

'"Yes, ma'am; I had four, but two were killed; one is a prisoner, and I'm going to the other, who is very sick in a Washington hospital," he answered, quietly.

' "You have done a great deal for your country, sir," I said, feeling respect now, instead of pity.

' "Not a mite more than I ought ma'am. I'd go myself, if I was any use; as I ain't, I give my boys, and give 'em free."

'He spoke so cheerfully, looked so sincere, and seemed so glad to give his all, that I was ashamed of myself. I'd given one man, and thought it too much, while he gave four, without grudging them; I had all my girls to comfort me at home, and his last son was waiting, miles away, to say "good-by" to him, perhaps. I felt so rich, so happy, thinking of my blessings, that I made him a nice bundle, gave him some money, and thanked him heartily for the lesson he had taught me.'

'Tell another story, mother; one with a moral to it, like this. I like to think about them afterwards, if they are real, and not too preachy,' said Jo, after a minute's silence.

Mrs March smiled, and began at once; for she had told stories to this little audience for many years, and knew how to please them.

'Once upon a time there were four girls, who had enough to eat, and drink, and wear; a good many comforts and pleasures, kind friends and parents, who loved them dearly, and yet they were not contented.' (Here the listeners stole sly looks at one another, and began to sew diligently.) 'These girls were anxious to be good, and made many excellent resolutions, but somehow they did not keep them very well, and were constantly saying, "If we only had this," or "if we could only do that," quite forgetting how much they already had, and how many pleasant things they actually could do; so they asked an old woman what spell they could use to make them happy, and she said, "When you feel discontented, think over your blessings, and be grateful."' (Here Jo looked up quickly, as if about to speak, but changed her mind, seeing that the story was not done yet.)

'Being sensible girls, they decided to try her advice, and soon were surprised to see how well off they were. One discovered that money couldn't keep shame and sorrow out of rich people's houses; another that though she was poor, she was a great deal happier with her youth, health, and good spirits, than a certain fretful, feeble old lady, who couldn't enjoy her comforts; a third, that, disagreeable as it was to help get dinner, it was harder still to have to go begging for it; and the fourth, that even carnelian rings were not so valuable as good behavior. So they agreed to stop complaining, to enjoy the blessings already possessed, and try to deserve them, lest they should be taken away entirely, instead of increased; and I believe they were never disappointed, or sorry that they took the old woman's advice.'

'Now, Marmee, that is very cunning of you to turn our own stories against us, and give us a sermon instead of a "spin,"' cried Meg.

'I like that kind of sermon; it's the sort father used to tell us,' said Beth, thoughtfully, putting the needles straight on Jo's cushion.

'I don't complain near as much as the others do, and I shall be more careful than ever now, for I've had warning from Susie's downfall,' said Amy, morally.

'We needed that lesson, and we won't forget it. If we do, you just say to us as Old Chloe did in Uncle Tom,— "Tink ob yer marcies, chillen, tink ob yer marcies,"' added Jo, who could not for the life of her help getting a morsel of fun out of the little sermon, though she took it to heart as much as any of them.

5

Being Neighborly

'WHAT in the world are you going to do now, Jo?' asked Meg, one snowy afternoon, as her sister came clumping through the hall, in rubber boots, old sack and hood, with a broom in one hand and a shovel in the other.

'Going out for exercise,' answered Jo, with a mischievous twinkle in her eyes.

'I should think two long walks, this morning, would have been enough. It's cold and dull out, and I advise you to stay, warm and dry, by the fire, as I do,' said Meg, with a shiver.

'Never take advice; can't keep still all day, and not being a pussycat, I don't like to doze by the fire. I like adventures, and I'm going to find some.'

Meg went back to toast her feet, and read 'Ivanhoe,' and Jo began to dig paths with great energy. The snow was light; and with her broom she soon swept a path all round the garden, for Beth to walk in when the sun came out; and the invalid dolls needed air. Now the garden separated the Marches' house from that of Mr Laurence; both stood in a suburb of the city, which was still country like, with groves and lawns, large gardens, and quiet streets. A low hedge parted the two estates. On one side was an old brown house, looking rather bare and shabby, robbed of the vines that in summer covered its walls, and the flowers which then surrounded it. On the other side was a stately stone mansion, plainly betokening every sort of comfort and luxury, from the big coach-house and well-kept grounds to the conservatory, and the glimpses of lovely things one caught between the rich curtains. Yet it seemed a lonely, lifeless sort of house; for no children frolicked on the lawn, no motherly face ever smiled at the windows, and few people went in and out, except the old gentleman and his grandson.

To Jo's lively fancy this fine house seemed a kind of enchanted palace, full of splendors and delights, which no one enjoyed. She had long wanted to behold these hidden glories, and to know the 'Laurence boy,' who looked as if he would like to be known, if he only knew how to begin. Since the party she had been more eager than ever, and had planned many ways of making friends with him; but he had not been lately seen, and Jo began to think he had gone away, when she one day spied a brown face at an upper window, looking wistfully down into their garden, where Beth and Amy were snow-balling one another.

'That boy is suffering for society and fun,' she said to herself. 'His grandpa don't know what's good for him, and keeps him shut up all alone. He needs a lot of jolly boys to play with, or somebody young and lively. I've a great mind to go over and tell the old gentleman so.'

The idea amused Jo, who liked to do daring things, and was always scandalizing Meg by her queer performances. The plan of 'going over' was not forgotten; and, when the snowy afternoon came, Jo resolved to try what could be done. She saw Mr Laurence drive off, and then sallied out to dig her way down to the hedge, where she paused, and took a survey. All quiet; curtains down at the lower windows; servants out of sight, and nothing human visible but a curly black head leaning on a thin hand, at the upper window.

'There he is,' thought Jo; 'poor boy! all alone, and sick, this dismal day! It's a shame! I'll toss up a snow-ball, and make him look out, and then say a kind word to him.'

Up went a handful of snow, and the head turned at once, showing a face which lost its listless look in a minute, as the big eyes brightened, and the mouth began to smile. Jo nodded, and laughed, and flourished her broom as she called out,—

'How do you do? Are you sick?'

Laurie opened the window and croaked out as hoarsely as a raven,—

'Better, thank you. I've had a horrid cold, and been shut up a week.'

'I'm sorry. What do you amuse yourself with?'

'Nothing; it's as dull as tombs up here.'

'Don't you read?'

'Not much; they won't let me.'

'Can't somebody read to you?'

'Grandpa does, sometimes; but my books don't interest him, and I hate to ask Brooke all the time.'

'Have some one come and see you, then.'

'There isn't any one I'd like to see. Boys make such a row, and my head is weak.'

'Isn't there some nice girl who'd read and amuse you? Girls are quiet, and like to play nurse.'

'Don't know any.'

'You know me,' began Jo, then laughed, and stopped.

'So I do! Will you come, please?' cried Laurie.

'I'm not quiet and nice; but I'll come, if mother will let me. I'll go ask her. Shut that window, like a good boy, and wait till I come.'

With that, Jo shouldered her broom and marched into the house, wondering what they would all say to her. Laurie was in a little flutter of excitement at the idea of having company, and flew about to get ready; for, as Mrs March said, he was 'a little gentleman,' and did honor to the coming guest by brushing his curly pate, putting on a fresh collar, and trying to tidy up the room, which in spite of half a dozen servants, was anything but neat. Presently, there came a loud ring, then a decided voice, asking for 'Mr Laurie,' and a surprised looking servant came running up to announce a young lady.

'All right, show her up, it's Miss Jo,' said Laurie, going to the door of his little parlor to meet Jo, who appeared, looking rosy and kind, and quite at ease, with a covered dish in one hand, and Beth's three kittens in the other.

'Here I am, bag and baggage,' she said, briskly. 'Mother sent her love, and was glad if I could do anything for you. Meg wanted me to bring some of her blanc-mange; she makes it very nice, and Beth thought her cats would be comforting. I knew you'd shout at them, but I couldn't refuse, she was so anxious to do something.'

It so happened that Beth's funny loan was just the thing; for, in laughing over the kits, Laurie forgot his bashfulness, and grew sociable at once.

'That looks too pretty to eat,' he said, smiling with pleasure, as Jo uncovered the dish, and showed the blanc-mange, surrounded by a garland of green leaves, and the scarlet flowers of Amy's pet geranium.

'It isn't anything, only they all felt kindly, and wanted to show it. Tell the girl to put it away for your tea; it's so simple, you can eat it; and, being soft, it will slip down without hurting your sore throat. What a cosy room this is.'

'It might be, if it was kept nice; but the maids are lazy, and I don't know how to make them mind. It worries me, though.'

'I'll right it up in two minutes; for it only needs to have the hearth brushed, so,—and the things stood straight on the mantelpiece, so,—and the books put here, and the bottles there, and your sofa turned from the light, and the pillows plumped up a bit. Now, then, you're fixed.'

And so he was; for, as she laughed and talked, Jo had whisked things into place, and given quite a different air to the room. Laurie watched her in respectful silence; and, when she beckoned him to his sofa, he sat down with a sigh of satisfaction, saying, gratefully,—

'How kind you are! Yes, that's what it wanted. Now please take the big chair, and let me do something to amuse my company.'

'No; I came to amuse you. Shall I read aloud?' and Jo looked affectionately towards some inviting books near by.

'Thank you; I've read all those, and if you don't mind, I'd rather talk,' answered Laurie.

'Not a bit; I'll talk all day if you'll only set me going. Beth says I never know when to stop.'

'Is Beth the rosy one, who stays at home a good deal, and sometimes goes out with a little basket?' asked Laurie, with interest.

'Yes, that's Beth; she's my girl, and a regular good one she is, too.'

'The pretty one is Meg, and the curly-haired one is Amy, I believe?'

'How did you find that out?'

Laurie colored up, but answered frankly, 'Why, you see, I often hear you calling to one another, and when I'm alone up here, I can't help looking over at your house, you always seem to be having such good times. I beg your pardon for being so rude, but sometimes you forget to put down the curtain at the window where the flowers are; and, when the lamps are lighted, it's like looking at a picture to see the fire, and you all round the table with your mother; her face is right opposite, and it looks so sweet behind the flowers, I can't help watching it. I haven't got any mother, you know;' and Laurie poked the fire to hide a little twitching of the lips that he could not control.

The solitary, hungry look in his eyes went straight to Jo's warm heart. She had been so simply taught that there was no nonsense in her head, and at fifteen she was as innocent and frank as any child. Laurie was sick and lonely; and, feeling how rich she was in home-love and happiness, she gladly tried to share it with him. Her brown face was very friendly, and her sharp voice unusually gentle, as she said,—

'We'll never draw that curtain any more, and I give you leave to look as much as you like. I just wish, though, instead of peeping, you'd come over and see us. Mother is so splendid, she'd do you heaps of good, and Beth would sing to you if *I* begged her to, and Amy would dance; Meg and I would make you laugh over our funny stage properties, and we'd have jolly times. Wouldn't your grandpa let you?'

'I think he would, if your mother asked him. He's very kind, though he don't look it; and he lets me do what I like, pretty much, only he's afraid I might be a bother to strangers,' began Laurie, brightening more and more.

'We ain't strangers, we are neighbors, and you needn't think you'd be a bother. We *want* to know you, and I've been trying to do it this ever so long. We haven't been here a great while, you know, but we have got acquainted with all our neighbors but you.'

'You see grandpa lives among his books, and don't mind much what happens outside. Mr Brooke, my tutor, don't stay here, you know, and I have no one to go round with me, so I just stop at home and get on as I can.'

'That's bad; you ought to make a dive, and go visiting everywhere you are asked; then you'll have lots of friends, and pleasant places to go. Never mind being bashful, it won't last long if you keep going.'

Laurie turned red again, but wasn't offended at being accused of bashfulness; for there was so much good-will in Jo, it was impossible not to take her blunt speeches as kindly as they were meant.

'Do you like your school?' asked the boy, changing the subject, after a little pause, during which he stared at the fire, and Jo looked about her well pleased.

'Don't go to school; I'm a business man—girl, I mean. I go to wait on my aunt, and a dear, cross old soul she is, too,' answered Jo.

Laurie opened his mouth to ask another question; but remembering just in time that it wasn't manners to make too many inquiries into people's affairs, he shut it again, and looked uncomfortable. Jo liked his good breeding, and didn't mind having a laugh at Aunt March, so she gave him a lively description of the fidgety old lady, her fat poodle, the parrot that talked Spanish, and the library where she revelled. Laurie enjoyed that immensely; and when she told about the prim old gentleman who came once to woo Aunt March, and, in the middle of a fine speech, how Poll had tweaked his wig off to his great dismay, the boy lay back and laughed till the tears ran down his cheeks, and a maid popped her head in to see what was the matter.

'Oh! that does me lots of good; tell on, please,' he said, taking his face out of the sofa-cushion, red and shining with merriment.

Much elated with her success, Jo did 'tell on,' all about their plays and plans, their hopes and fears for father, and the most interesting events of the little world in which the sisters lived. Then they got to talking about books; and to Jo's delight she found that Laurie loved them as well as she did, and had read even more than herself.

'If you like them so much, come down and see ours. Grandpa is out, so you needn't be afraid,' said Laurie, getting up.

'I'm not afraid of anything,' returned Jo, with a toss of the head.

'I don't believe you are!' exclaimed the boy, looking at her with much admiration, though he privately thought she would have good reason to be a trifle afraid of the old gentleman, if she met him in some of his moods.

The atmosphere of the whole house being summer-like, Laurie led the way from room to room, letting Jo stop to examine whatever struck her fancy; and so at last they came to the library, where she clapped her hands, and pranced, as she always did when especially delighted. It was lined with books, and there were pictures and statues, and distracting little cabinets full of coins and curiosities, and Sleepy-Hollow chairs, and queer tables, and bronzes; and, best of all, a great, open fireplace, with quaint tiles all round it.

'What richness!' sighed Jo, sinking into the depths of a velvet chair, and gazing about her with an air of intense satisfaction. 'Theodore Laurence, you ought to be the happiest boy in the world,' she added, impressively.

'A fellow can't live on books,' said Laurie, shaking his head, as he perched on a table opposite.

Before he could say more, a bell rang, and Jo flew up, exclaiming with alarm, 'Mercy me! it's your grandpa!'

'Well, what if it is? You are not afraid of anything, you know,' returned the boy, looking wicked.

'I think I am a little bit afraid of him, but I don't know why I should be. Marmee said I might come, and I don't think you're any the worse for it,' said Jo, composing herself, though she kept her eyes on the door.

'I'm a great deal better for it, and ever so much obliged. I'm only afraid you are very tired talking to me; it was *so* pleasant, I couldn't bear to stop,' said Laurie, gratefully.

'The doctor to see you, sir,' and the maid beckoned as she spoke.

'Would you mind if I left you for a minute? I suppose I must see him,' said Laurie.

'Don't mind me. I'm as happy as a cricket here,' answered Jo.

Laurie went away, and his guest amused herself in her own way. She was standing before a fine portrait of the old gentleman, when the door opened again, and, without turning, she said decidedly, 'I'm sure now that I shouldn't be afraid of him, for he's got kind eyes, though his mouth is grim, and he looks as if he had a tremendous will of his own. He isn't as handsome as *my* grandfather, but I like him.'

'Thank you, ma'am,' said a gruff voice behind her; and there, to her great dismay, stood old Mr Laurence.

Poor Jo blushed till she couldn't blush any redder, and her heart began to beat uncomfortably fast as she thought what she had said. For a minute a wild desire to run away possessed her; but that was cowardly, and the girls would laugh at her; so she resolved to stay, and get out of the scrape as she could. A second look showed her that the living eyes, under the bushy gray eyebrows, were kinder even than the painted ones; and there was a sly twinkle in them, which lessened her fear a good deal. The gruff voice was gruffer than ever, as the old gentleman said abruptly, after that dreadful pause, 'So, you're not afraid of me, hey?'

'Not much, sir.'

'And you don't think me as handsome as your grandfather?'

'Not quite, sir.'

'And I've got a tremendous will, have I?'

'I only said I thought so.'

'But you like me, in spite of it?'

'Yes, I do, sir.'

That answer pleased the old gentleman; he gave a short laugh, shook hands with her, and putting his finger under her chin, turned up her face, examined it gravely, and let it go, saying, with a nod, 'you've got your grandfather's spirit, if you haven't his face. He *was* a fine man, my dear; but, what is better, he was a brave and an honest one, and I was proud to be his friend.'

'Thank you, sir;' and Jo was quite comfortable after that, for it suited her exactly.

'What have you been doing to this boy of mine, hey?' was the next question, sharply put.

'Only trying to be neighborly, sir;' and Jo told how her visit came about.

'You think he needs cheering up a bit, do you?'

'Yes, sir; he seems a little lonely, and young folks would do him good, perhaps. We are only girls, but we should be glad to help if we could, for we don't forget the splendid Christmas present you sent us,' said Jo, eagerly.

'Tut, tut, tut; that was the boy's affair. How is the poor woman?'

'Doing nicely, sir;' and off went Jo, talking very fast, as she told all about the Hummels, in whom her mother had interested richer friends than they were.

'Just her father's way of doing good. I shall come and see your mother some fine day. Tell her so. There's the tea-bell; we have it early, on the boy's account. Come down, and go on being neighborly.'

'If you'd like to have me, sir.'

'Shouldn't ask you, if I didn't;' and Mr Laurence offered her his arm with old-fashioned courtesy.

'What *would* Meg say to this?' thought Jo, as she was marched away, while her eyes danced with fun as she imagined herself telling the story at home.

'Hey! why what the dickens has come to the fellow?' said the old gentleman, as Laurie came running down stairs, and brought up with a start of surprise at the astonishing sight of Jo arm in arm with his redoubtable grandfather.

'I didn't know you'd come, sir,' he began, as Jo gave him a triumphant little glance.

'That's evident, by the way you racket down stairs. Come to your tea, sir, and behave like a gentleman;' and having pulled the boy's hair by way of a caress, Mr Laurence walked on, while Laurie went through a series of comic evolutions behind their backs, which nearly produced an explosion of laughter from Jo.

The old gentleman did not say much as he drank his four cups of tea, but he watched the young people, who soon chatted away like old friends, and the change in his grandson did not escape him. There was color, light and life in the boy's face now, vivacity in his manner, and genuine merriment in his laugh.

'She's right; the lad *is* lonely. I'll see what these little girls can do for him,' thought Mr Laurence, as he looked and listened. He liked Jo, for her odd, blunt ways suited him; and she seemed to understand the boy almost as well as if she had been one herself.

If the Laurences had been what Jo called 'prim and poky,' she would not have got on at all, for such people always made her shy and awkward; but finding them free and easy, she was so herself, and made a good impression. When they rose she proposed to go, but Laurie said he had something more to show her, and took her away to the conservatory, which had been lighted for her benefit. It seemed quite fairy-like to Jo, as she went up and down the walks, enjoying the blooming walls on either side,—the soft light, the damp, sweet air, and the wonderful vines and trees that hung above her,—while her new friend cut the finest flowers till his hands were full; then he tied them up, saying, with the happy look Jo liked to see, 'Please give these to your mother, and tell her I like the medicine she sent me very much.'

They found Mr Laurence standing before the fire in the great drawing-room, but Jo's attention was entirely absorbed by a grand piano which stood open.

'Do you play?' she asked, turning to Laurie with a respectful expression.

'Sometimes,' he answered, modestly.

'Please do now; I want to hear it, so I can tell Beth.'

'Won't you first?'

'Don't know how; too stupid to learn, but I love music dearly.'

So Laurie played, and Jo listened, with her nose luxuriously buried in heliotrope and tea roses. Her respect and regard for the 'Laurence boy' increased very much, for he played remarkably well, and didn't put on any airs. She wished Beth could hear him, but she did not say so; only praised him till he was quite abashed, and his grandfather came to the rescue. 'That will do, that will do, young lady; too many sugar-plums are not good for him. His music isn't bad, but I hope he will do as well in more important things. Going? Well, I'm much obliged to you, and I hope you'll come again. My respects to your mother; good-night, Doctor Jo.'

He shook hands kindly, but looked as if something did not please him. When they got into the hall, Jo asked Laurie if she had said anything amiss; he shook his head.

'No, it was me; he don't like to hear me play.'

'Why not?'

'I'll tell you some day. John is going home with you, as I can't.'

'No need of that; I ain't a young lady, and it's only a step. Take care of yourself, won't you?'

'Yes, but you will come again, I hope?'

'If you promise to come and see us after you are well.'

'I will.'

'Good-night, Laurie.'

'Good-night, Jo, good-night.'

When all the afternoon's adventures had been told, the family felt inclined to go visiting in a body, for each found something very attractive in the big house on the other side of the hedge. Mrs March wanted to talk of her father with the old man who had not forgotten him; Meg longed to walk in the conservatory; Beth sighed for the grand piano, and Amy was eager to see the fine pictures and statues.

'Mother, why didn't Mr Laurence like to have Laurie play?' asked Jo, who was of an inquiring disposition.

'I am not sure, but I think it was because his son, Laurie's father, married an Italian lady, a musician, which displeased the old man, who is very proud. The lady was good and lovely and accomplished, but he did not like her, and never saw his son after he married. They both died when Laurie was a little child, and then his grandfather took him home. I fancy the boy, who was born in Italy, is not very strong, and the old man is afraid of losing him, which makes him so careful. Laurie comes naturally by his love of music, for he is like his mother, and I dare say his grandfather fears that he may want to be a musician; at any rate, his skill reminds him of the woman he did not like, and so he "glowered," as Jo said.'

'Dear me, how romantic!' exclaimed Meg.

'How silly,' said Jo; 'let him be a musician, if he wants

to, and not plague his life out sending him to college, when he hates to go.'

'That's why he has such handsome black eyes and pretty manners, I suppose; Italians are always nice,' said Meg, who was a little sentimental.

'What do you know about his eyes and manners? you never spoke to him, hardly;' cried Jo, who was *not* sentimental.

'I saw him at the party, and what you tell shows that he knows how to behave. That was a nice little speech about the medicine mother sent him.'

'He meant the blanc-mange, I suppose.'

'How stupid you are, child; he meant you, of course.'

'Did he?' and Jo opened her eyes as if it had never occurred to her before.

'I never saw such a girl! You don't know a compliment when you get it,' said Meg, with the air of a young lady who knew all about the matter.

'I think they are great nonsense, and I'll thank you not to be silly, and spoil my fun. Laurie's a nice boy, and I like him, and I won't have any sentimental stuff about compliments and such rubbish. We'll all be good to him, because he hasn't got any mother, and he *may* come over and see us, mayn't he, Marmee?'

'Yes, Jo, your little friend is very welcome, and I hope

Meg will remember that children should be children as long as they can.'

'I don't call myself a child, and I'm not in my teens yet,' observed Amy. 'What do you say, Beth?'

'I was thinking about our "Pilgrim's Progress,"' answered Beth, who had not heard a word. 'How we got out of the Slough and through the Wicket Gate by resolving to be good, and up the steep hill, by trying; and that maybe the house over there, full of splendid things, is going to be our Palace Beautiful.'

'We have got to get by the lions, first,' said Jo, as if she rather liked the prospect.

6

Beth Finds The Palace Beautiful

THE big house did prove a Palace Beautiful, though it took some time for all to get in, and Beth found it very hard to pass the lions. Old Mr Laurence was the biggest one; but, after he had called, said something funny or kind to each one of the girls, and talked over old times with their mother, nobody felt much afraid of him, except timid Beth. The other lion was the fact that they were poor and Laurie rich; for this made them shy of accepting favors which they could not return. But after a while they found that he considered them the benefactors, and could not do enough to show how grateful he was for Mrs March's motherly welcome, their cheerful society, and the comfort he took in that humble home of theirs; so they soon forgot their pride, and interchanged kindnesses without stopping to think which was the greater.

All sorts of pleasant things happened about that time, for the new friendship flourished like grass in spring. Every one liked Laurie, and he privately informed his tutor that 'the Marches were regularly splendid girls.' With the delightful enthusiasm of youth, they took the solitary boy into their midst, and made much of him, and he found something very charming in the innocent companionship of these simple-hearted girls. Never having known mother or sisters, he was quick to feel the influences they brought about him; and their busy, lively ways made him ashamed of the indolent life he led. He was tired of books, and found people so interesting now, that Mr Brooke was obliged to make very unsatisfactory reports; for Laurie was always playing truant, and running over to the Marches.

'Never mind, let him take a holiday, and make it up afterward,' said the old gentleman. 'The good lady next door says he is studying too hard, and needs young society, amusement, and exercise. I suspect she is right, and that I've been coddling the fellow as if I'd been his grandmother. Let him do what he likes, as long as he is happy; he can't get into mischief in that little nunnery over there, and Mrs March is doing more for him than we can.'

What good times they had, to be sure! Such plays and tableaux; such sleigh-rides and skating frolics; such pleasant evenings in the old parlor, and now and then such gay little parties at the great house. Meg could walk in the conservatory whenever she liked, and revel in bouquets; Jo browsed over the new library voraciously and convulsed the old gentleman with her criticisms; Amy copied pictures and enjoyed beauty to her heart's content, and Laurie played lord of the manor in the most delightful style.

But Beth, though yearning for the grand piano, could not pluck up courage to go to the 'mansion of bliss,' as Meg called it. She went once with Jo, but the old gentleman, not being aware of her infirmity, stared at her so hard from under his heavy eyebrows, and said 'hey!' so loud, that he frightened her so much her 'feet chattered on the floor,' she told her mother; and she ran away, declaring she would never go there any more, not even for the dear piano. No persuasions or enticements could overcome her fear, till the fact coming to Mr Laurence's ear in some mysterious way, he set about mending matters. During one of the brief calls he made, he artfully led the conversation to music, and talked away about great singers whom he had seen, fine organs he had heard, and told such charming anecdotes, that Beth found it impossible to stay in her distant corner, but crept nearer and nearer, as if fascinated. At the back of his chair she stopped, and stood listening with her great eyes wide open, and her cheeks red with the excitement of this unusual performance. Taking no more notice of her than if she had been a fly, Mr Laurence talked on about Laurie's lessons and teachers; and presently, as if the idea had just occurred to him, he said to Mrs March,—

'The boy neglects his music now, and I'm glad of it, for he was getting too fond of it. But the piano suffers for want of use; wouldn't some of your girls like to run over, and practise on it now and then, just to keep it in tune, you know, ma'am?'

Beth took a step forward, and pressed her hands tightly together, to keep from clapping them, for this was an irresistible temptation; and the thought of practising on that splendid instrument quite took her breath away. Before Mrs March could reply, Mr Laurence went on with an odd little nod and smile,—

'They needn't see or speak to any one, but run in at any time, for I'm shut up in my study at the other end of the house. Laurie is out a great deal, and the servants are never near the drawing-room after nine o'clock.' Here he rose, as if going, and Beth made up her mind to speak, for that last arrangement left nothing to be desired. 'Please tell the young ladies what I say, and if they don't care to come, why, never mind;' here a little hand slipped into his, and Beth looked up at him with a face full of gratitude, as she said, in her earnest, yet timid way,—

'Oh, sir! they do care, very, very much!'

'Are you the musical girl?' he asked, without any startling 'hey!' as he looked down at her very kindly.

'I'm Beth; I love it dearly, and I'll come if you are quite sure nobody will hear me—and be disturbed,' she added, fearing to be rude, and trembling at her own boldness as she spoke.

'Not a soul, my dear; the house is empty half the day, so come and drum away as much as you like, and I shall be obliged to you.'

'How kind you are, sir.'

Beth blushed like a rose under the friendly look he wore, but she was not frightened now, and gave the big hand a grateful squeeze, because she had no words to thank him for the precious gift he had given her. The old gentleman softly stroked the hair off her forehead, and, stooping down, he kissed her, saying, in a tone few people ever heard,—

'I had a little girl once with eyes like these; God bless you, my dear; good-day, madam,' and away he went, in a great hurry.

Beth had a rapture with her mother, and then rushed

up to impart the glorious news to her family of invalids, as the girls were not at home. How blithely she sang that evening, and how they all laughed at her, because she woke Amy in the night, by playing the piano on her face in her sleep. Next day, having seen both the old and young gentleman out of the house, Beth, after two or three retreats, fairly got in at the side-door. and made her way as noiselessly as any mouse to the drawing-room, where her idol stood. Quite by accident, of course, some pretty, easy music lay on the piano; and, with trembling fingers, and frequent stops to listen and look about, Beth at last touched the great instrument, and straightway forgot her fear, herself, and everything else but the unspeakable delight which the music gave her, for it was like the voice of a beloved friend.

She stayed till Hannah came to take her home to dinner; but she had no appetite, and could only sit and smile upon every one in a general state of beatitude.

After that, the little brown hood slipped through the hedge nearly every day, and the great drawing-room was haunted by a tuneful spirit that came and went unseen. She never knew that Mr Laurence often opened his study door to hear the old-fashioned airs he liked; she never saw Laurie mount guard in the hall, to warn the servants away; she never suspected that the exercise-books and new songs which she found in the rack were put there for her especial benefit; and when he talked to her about music at home, she only thought how kind he was to tell things that helped her so much. So she enjoyed herself heartily, and found, what isn't always the case, that her granted wish was all she had hoped. Perhaps it was because she was so grateful for this blessing that a greater was given her; at any rate, she deserved both.

'Mother, I'm, going to work Mr Laurence a pair of slippers. He is so kind to me I must thank him, and I don't know any other way. Can I do it?' asked Beth, a few weeks after that eventful call of his.

'Yes, dear; it will please him very much, and be a nice way of thanking him. The girls will help you about them, and I will pay for the making up,' replied Mrs March, who took peculiar pleasure in granting Beth's requests, because she so seldom asked anything for herself.

After many serious discussions with Meg and Jo, the pattern was chosen, the materials bought, and the slippers begun. A cluster of grave yet cheerful pansies, on a deeper purple ground, was pronounced very appropriate and pretty, and Beth worked away early and late, with occasional lifts over hard parts. She was a nimble little needle-woman, and they were finished before any one got tired of them. Then she wrote a very short, simple note, and, with Laurie's help, got them smuggled on to the study-table one morning before the old gentleman was up.

When this excitement was over, Beth waited to see what would happen. All that day passed, and a part of the next, before any acknowledgement arrived, and she was beginning to fear she had offended her crotchety friend. On the afternoon of the second day she went out to do an errand, and give poor Joanna, the invalid doll, her daily exercise. As she came up the street on her return she saw three—yes, four heads popping in and out of the parlor windows; and the moment they saw her several hands were waved, and several joyful voices screamed,—

'Here's a letter from the old gentleman; come quick, and read it!'

'Oh, Beth! he's sent you—' began Amy, gesticulating with unseemly energy; but she got no further, for Jo quenched her by slamming down the window.

Beth hurried on in a twitter of suspense; at the door her sisters seized and bore her to the parlor in a triumphal procession, all pointing, and all saying at once, 'Look there! look there!' Beth did look, and turned pale with delight and surprise; for there stood a little cabinet piano, with a letter lying on the glossy lid, directed like a sign-board, to 'Miss Elizabeth March.'

'For me?' gasped Beth, holding on to Jo, and feeling as if she should tumble down, it was such an overwhelming thing altogether.

'Yes; all for you, my precious! Isn't it splendid of him? Don't you think he's the dearest old man in the world? Here's the key in the letter; we didn't open it, but we are dying to know what he says,' cried Jo, hugging her sister, and offering the note.

'You read it; I can't, I feel so queer. Oh, it is too lovely!' and Beth hid her face in Jo's apron, quite upset by her present.

Jo opened the paper, and began to laugh, for the first words she saw were:—

'Miss March:
'*Dear Madam*—'

'How nice it sounds! I wish some one would write to me so!' said Amy, who thought the old-fashioned address very elegant.

'"I have had many pairs of slippers in my life, but I never had any that suited me so well as yours,"'

continued Jo.

'"Heart's-ease is my favorite flower, and these will always remind me of the gentle giver. I like to pay my debts, so I know you will allow 'the old gentleman' to send you something which once belonged to the little granddaughter he lost. With hearty thanks, and best wishes, I remain,

'"Your grateful friend and humble servant,
                              '"James Laurence."'

'There, Beth, that's an honor to be proud of, I'm sure! Laurie told me how fond Mr Laurence used to be of the child who died, and how he kept all her little things carefully. Just think; he's given you her piano! That comes of having big blue eyes and loving music,' said Jo, trying to soothe Beth, who trembled, and looked more excited than she had ever been before.

'See the cunning brackets to hold candles, and the nice green silk, puckered up with a gold rose in the middle, and the pretty rack and stool, all complete,' added Meg, opening the instrument, and displaying its beauties.

'"Your humble servant, James Laurence;" only think of his writing that to you. I'll tell the girls; they'll think it's killing,' said Amy, much impressed by the note.

'Try it, honey; let's hear the sound of the baby pianny,'

said Hannah, who always took a share in the family joys and sorrows.

So Beth tried it, and every one pronounced it the most remarkable piano ever heard. It had evidently been newly tuned, and put in apple-pie order; but, perfect as it was, I think the real charm of it lay in the happiest of all happy faces which leaned over it, as Beth lovingly touched the beautiful black and white keys, and pressed the shiny pedals.

'You'll have to go and thank him,' said Jo, by way of a joke; for the idea of the child's really going, never entered her head.

'Yes, I mean to; I guess I'll go now, before I get frightened thinking about it;' and, to the utter amazement of the assembled family, Beth walked deliberately down the garden, through the hedge, and in at the Laurences' door.

'Well, I wish I may die, if it ain't the queerest thing I ever see! The pianny has turned her head; she'd never have gone, in her right mind,' cried Hannah, staring after her, while the girls were rendered quite speechless by the miracle.

They would have been still more amazed, if they had seen what Beth did afterward. If you will believe me, she went and knocked at the study door, before she gave herself time to think; and when a gruff voice called out, 'Come in!' she did go in, right up to Mr Laurence, who looked quite taken aback, and held out her hand, saying, with only a small quaver in her voice, 'I came to thank you, sir, for—' but she didn't finish, for he looked so friendly that she forgot her speech; and, only remembering that he had lost the little girl he loved, she put both arms round his neck, and kissed him.

If the roof of the house had suddenly flown off, the old gentleman wouldn't have been more astonished; but he liked it—oh dear, yes! he liked it amazingly; and was so touched and pleased by that confiding little kiss, that all his crustiness vanished; and he just set her on his knee, and laid his wrinkled cheek against her rosy one, feeling as if he had got his own little granddaughter back again. Beth ceased to fear him from that moment, and sat there talking to him as cosily as if she had known him all her life; for love casts out fear, and gratitude can conquer pride. When she went home, he walked with her to her own gate, shook hands cordially, and touched his hat as he marched back again, looking very stately and erect, like a handsome, soldierly old gentleman, as he was.

When the girls saw that performance, Jo began to dance a jig, by way of expressing her satisfaction; Amy nearly fell out of the window in her surprise, and Meg exclaimed, with uplifted hands, 'Well, I do believe the world is coming to an end!'

7

Amy's Valley of Humiliation

'THAT boy is a perfect Cyclops, isn't he?' said Amy, one day, as Laurie clattered by on horseback, with a flourish of his whip as he passed.

'How dare you say so, when he's got both his eyes? and very handsome ones they are, too;' cried Jo, who resented any slighting remarks about her friend.

'I didn't say anything about his eyes, and I don't see why you need fire up when I admire his riding.'

'Oh, my goodness! that little goose means a centaur, and she called him a Cyclops,' exclaimed Jo, with a burst of laughter.

'You needn't be so rude, it's only a "lapse of lingy," as Mr Davis says," retorted Amy, finishing Jo with her Latin. 'I just wish I had a little of the money Laurie spends on that horse,' she added, as if to herself, yet hoping her sisters would hear.

'Why?' asked Meg, kindly, for Jo had gone off in another laugh at Amy's second blunder.

'I need it so much; I'm dreadfully in debt, and it won't be my turn to have the rag-money for a month.'

'In debt, Amy; what do you mean?' and Meg looked sober.

'Why, I owe at least a dozen pickled limes, and I can't pay them, you know, till I have money, for Marmee forbid my having anything charged at the shop.'

'Tell me all about it. Are limes the fashion now? It used to be pricking bits of rubber to make balls;' and Meg tried to keep her countenance, Amy looked so grave and important.

'Why, you see, the girls are always buying them, and unless you want to be thought mean, you must do it, too. It's nothing but limes now, for every one is sucking them in their desks in school-time, and trading them off for pencils, bead-rings, paper dolls, or something else, at recess. If one girl likes another, she gives her a lime; if she'd mad with her, she eats one before her face, and don't offer even a suck. They treat by turns; and I've had ever so many, but haven't returned them, and I ought, for they are debts of honor, you know.'

'How much will pay them off, and restore your credit?' asked Meg, taking out her purse.

'A quarter would more than do it, and leave a few cents over for a treat for you. Don't you like limes?'

'Not much; you may have my share. Here's the money,—make it last as long as you can, for it isn't very plenty, you know.'

'Oh, thank you! it must be so nice to have pocket-money. I'll have a grand feast, for I haven't tasted a lime this week. I felt delicate about taking any, as I couldn't return them, and I'm actually suffering for one.'

Next day Amy was rather late at school; but could not resist the temptation of displaying, with pardonable pride, a moist brown paper parcel, before she consigned it to the inmost recesses of her desk. During the next few minutes the rumor that Amy March had got twenty-four delicious limes (she ate one on the way), and was going to treat, circulated through her 'set,' and the attentions of her friends became quite overwhelming. Katy Brown invited her to her next party on the spot; Mary Kingsley insisted on lending her her watch till recess, and Jenny Snow, a satirical young lady who had basely twitted Amy upon her limeless state, promptly buried the hatchet, and offered to furnish answers to certain appalling sums. But Amy had not forgotten Miss Snow's cutting remarks about 'some persons whose noses were not too flat to smell other people's limes, and stuck-up people, who were not too proud to ask for them;' and she instantly crushed 'that Snow girl's' hopes by the withering telegram, 'You needn't be so polite all of a sudden, for you won't get any.'

A distinguished personage happened to visit the school that morning, and Amy's beautifully drawn maps received praise, which honor to her foe rankled in the soul of Miss Snow, and caused Miss March to assume the airs of a studious young peacock. But, alas, alas! pride goes before a fall, and the revengeful Snow turned the tables with disastrous success. No sooner had the guest paid the usual stale compliments, and bowed himself out, than Jenny, under pretence of asking an important question, informed Mr Davis, the teacher, that Amy March had pickled limes in her desk.

Now Mr Davis had declared limes a contraband article, and solemnly vowed to publicly ferule the first person who was found breaking the law. This much-enduring man had succeeded in banishing gum after a long and stormy war, had made a bonfire of the confiscated novels and newspapers, had suppressed a private post-office, had forbidden distortions of the face, nicknames, and caricatures, and done all that one man could do to keep half a hundred rebellious girls in order. Boys are trying enough to human patience, goodness knows! but girls are infinitely more so, especially to nervous gentlemen with tyrannical tempers and no more talent for teaching than 'Dr Blimber.' Mr Davis knew any quantity of Greek, Latin, Algebra, and ologies of all sorts, so he was called a fine teacher; and manners, morals, feelings, and examples were not considered of any particular importance. It was a most unfortunate moment for denouncing Amy, and Jenny knew it. Mr Davis had evidently taken his coffee too strong that morning; there was an east wind, which always affected his neuralgia, and his pupils had not done him the credit which he felt he deserved; therefore, to use the expressive, if not elegant, language of a school-girl, 'he was as nervous as a witch and as cross as a bear.' The word 'limes' was like fire to powder; his yellow face flushed, and he rapped on his desk with an energy which made Jenny skip to her seat with unusual rapidity.

'Young ladies, attention, if you please!'

At the stern order the buzz ceased, and fifty pairs of blue, black, gray, and brown eyes were obediently fixed upon his awful countenance.

'Miss March, come to the desk.'

Amy rose to comply, with outward composure, but a secret fear oppressed her, for the limes weighed upon her conscience.

'Bring with you the limes you have in your desk,' was

the unexpected command which arrested her before she got out of her seat.

'Don't take all,' whispered her neighbor, a young lady of great presence of mind.

Amy hastily shook out half a dozen, and laid the rest down before Mr Davis, feeling that any man possessing a human heart would relent when that delicious perfume met his nose. Unfortunately, Mr Davis particularly detested the odor of the fashionable pickle, and disgust added to his wrath.

'Is that all?'

'Not quite,' stammered Amy.

'Bring the rest, immediately.'

With a despairing glance at her set she obeyed.

'You are sure there are no more?'

'I never lie, sir.'

'So I see. Now take these disgusting things, two by two, and throw them out of the window.'

There was a simultaneous sigh, which created quite a little gust as the last hope fled, and the treat was ravished from their longing lips. Scarlet with shame and anger, Amy went to and fro twelve mortal times; and as each doomed couple, looking, oh, so plump and juicy! fell from her reluctant hands, a shout from the street completed the anguish of the girls, for it told them that their feast was being exulted over by the little Irish children, who were their sworn foes. This—this was too much; all flashed indignant or appealing glances at the inexorable Davis, and one passionate lime-lover burst into tears.

As Amy returned from her last trip, Mr Davis gave a portentous 'hem,' and said, in his most impressive manner,—

'Young ladies, you remember what I said to you a week ago. I am sorry this has happened; but I never allow my rules to be infringed, and I *never* break my word. Miss March, hold out your hand.'

Amy started, and put both hands behind her, turning on him an imploring look, which pleaded for her better than the words she could not utter. She was rather a favorite with 'old Davis,' as, of course he was called, and it's my private belief that he *would* have broken his word if the indignation of one irrepressible young lady had not found vent in a hiss. That hiss, faint as it was, irritated the irascible gentleman, and sealed the culprit's fate.

'Your hand, Miss March!' was the only answer her mute appeal received; and, too proud to cry or beseech, Amy set her teeth, threw back her head defiantly, and bore without flinching several tingling blows on her little palm. They were neither many nor heavy, but that made no difference to her. For the first time in her life she had been struck; and the disgrace, in her eyes, was as deep as if he had knocked her down.

'You will now stand on the platform till recess,' said Mr Davis, resolved to do the thing thoroughly, since he had begun.

That was dreadful; it would have been bad enough to go to her seat and see the pitying faces of her friends, or the satisfied ones of her few enemies; but to face the whole school, with that shame fresh upon her, seemed impossible, and for a second she felt as if she could only drop down where she stood, and break her heart with crying. A bitter sense of wrong, and the thought of Jenny Snow, helped her to bear it; and, taking the ignominious place, she fixed her eyes on the stove-funnel above what now seemed a sea of faces, and stood there so motionless and white, that the girls found it very hard to study, with the pathetic little figure before them.

During the fifteen minutes that followed, the proud and sensitive little girl suffered a shame and pain which she never forgot. To others it might seem a ludicrous or trivial affair, but to her it was a hard experience; for during the twelve years of her life she had been governed by love alone, and a blow of that sort had never touched her before. The smart of her hand, and the ache of her heart, were forgotten in the sting of the thought,—

'I shall have to tell at home, and they will be so disappointed in me!'

The fifteen minutes seemed an hour; but they came to an end at last, and the word 'recess!' had never seemed so welcome to her before.

'You can go, Miss March,' said Mr Davis, looking, as he felt, uncomfortable.

He did not soon forget the reproachful look Amy gave him, as she went, without a word to any one, straight into the anteroom, snatched her things, and left the place 'forever,' as she passionately declared to herself. She was in a sad state when she got home; and when the older girls arrived, some time later, an indignation meeting was held at once. Mrs March did not say much, but looked disturbed, and comforted her afflicted little daughter in her tenderest manner. Meg bathed the insulted hand with glycerine and tears; Beth felt that even her beloved kittens would fail as a balm for griefs like this, and Jo wrathfully proposed that Mr Davis be arrested without delay, while Hannah shook her fist at the 'villain,' and pounded potatoes for dinner as if she had him under her pestle.

No notice was taken of Amy's flight, except by her mates; but the sharp-eyed demoiselles discovered that Mr Davis was quite benignant in the afternoon, also unusually nervous. Just before school closed, Jo appeared, wearing a grim expression, as she stalked up to the desk, and delivered a letter from her mother; then collected Amy's property, and departed, carefully scraping the mud from her boots on the door-mat, as if she shook the dust of the place off her feet.

'Yes, you can have a vacation from school, but I want you to study a little every day, with Beth,' said Mrs March, that evening. 'I don't approve of corporal punishment, especially for girls. I dislike Mr Davis' manner of teaching, and don't think the girls you associate with are doing you any good, so I shall ask your father's advice before I send you anywhere else.'

'That's good! I wish all the girls would leave, and spoil his old school. It's perfectly maddening to think of those lovely limes,' sighed Amy, with the air of a martyr.

'I am not sorry you lost them, for you broke the rules, and deserved some punishment for disobedience,' was the severe reply, which rather disappointed the young lady, who expected nothing but sympathy.

'Do you mean you are glad I was disgraced before the whole school?' cried Amy.

'I should not have chosen that way of mending a fault,' replied her mother; 'but I'm not sure that it won't do you more good than a milder method. You are getting to be altogether too conceited and important, my dear, and it is quite time you set about correcting it. You have a good many little gifts and virtues, but there is no need of parading them, for conceit spoils the finest genius. There is not much danger that real talent or goodness will be overlooked long; even if it is, the consciousness of possessing and using it well should satisfy one, and the great charm of all power is modesty.'

'So it is,' cried Laurie, who was playing chess in a corner with Jo. 'I knew a girl, once, who had a really remarkable talent for music, and she didn't know it; never guessed what sweet little things she composed when she was alone, and wouldn't have believed it if any one had told her.'

'I wish I'd known that nice girl, maybe she would have helped me, I'm so stupid,' said Beth, who stood beside him, listening eagerly.

'You do know her, and she helps you better than any one else could,' answered Laurie, looking at her with such mischievous meaning in his merry black eyes, that Beth suddenly turned very red, and hid her face in the sofa-cushion, quite overcome by such an unexpected discovery.

Jo let Laurie win the game, to pay for that praise of her Beth, who could not be prevailed upon to play for them after her compliment. So Laurie did his best, and sung delightfully, being in a particularly lively humor, for to the Marches he seldom showed the moody side of his character. When he was gone, Amy, who had been pensive all the evening said, suddenly, as if busy over some new idea,—

'Is Laurie an accomplished boy?'

'Yes; he has had an excellent education, and has much talent; he will make a fine man, if not spoilt by petting,' replied her mother.

'And he isn't conceited, is he?' asked Amy.

'Not in the least; that is why he is so charming, and we all like him so much.'

'I see; it's nice to have accomplishments, and be elegant; but not to show off, or get perked up,' said Amy, thoughtfully.

'These things are always seen and felt in a person's manner and conversation, if modestly used; but it is not necessary to display them,' said Mrs March.

'Any more than it's proper to wear all your bonnets, and gowns, and ribbons, at once, that folks may know you've got 'em,' added Jo; and the lecture ended in a laugh.

8

Jo Meets Apollyon

'GIRLS, where are you going?' asked Amy, coming into their room one Saturday afternoon, and finding them getting ready to go out, with an air of secrecy which excited her curiosity.

'Never mind; little girls shouldn't ask questions,' returned Jo, sharply.

Now if there is anything mortifying to our feelings, when we are young, it is to be told that; and to be bidden to 'run away, dear,' is still more trying to us. Amy bridled up at this insult, and determined to find out the secret, if she teased for an hour. Turning to Meg, who never refused her anything very long, she said, coaxingly, 'Do tell me! I should think you might let me go, too; for Beth is fussing over her dolls, and I haven't got anything to do, and am *so* lonely.'

'I can't, dear, because you aren't invited,' began Meg; but Jo broke in impatiently, 'Now, Meg, be quiet, or you will spoil it all. You can't go, Amy; so don't be a baby, and whine about it.'

'You are going somewhere with Laurie, I know you are; you were whispering and laughing together, on the sofa, last night, and you stopped when I came in. Aren't you going with him?'

'Yes, we are; now do be still, and stop bothering.'

Amy held her tongue, but used her eyes, and saw Meg slip a fan into her pocket.

'I know! I know! you're going to the theatre to see the "Seven Castles!"' she cried; adding, resolutely, 'and I *shall* go, for mother said I might see it; and I've got my rag-money, and it was mean not to tell me in time.'

'Just listen to me a minute, and be a good child,' said Meg, soothingly. 'Mother doesn't wish you to go this week, because your eyes are not well enough yet to bear the light of this fairy piece. Next week you can go with Beth and Hannah, and have a nice time.'

'I don't like that half as well as going with you and Laurie. Please let me; I've been sick with this cold so long, and shut up, I'm dying for some fun. Do, Meg! I'll be ever so good,' pleaded Amy, looking as pathetic as she could.

'Suppose we take her. I don't believe mother would mind, if we bundle her up well,' began Meg.

'If *she* goes *I* shan't; and if I don't, Laurie won't like it; and it will be very rude, after he invited only us, to go and drag in Amy. I should think she'd hate to poke herself where she isn't wanted,' said Jo, crossly, for she disliked the trouble of overseeing a fidgety child, when she wanted to enjoy herself.

Her tone and manner angered Amy, who began to put her boots on, saying, in her most aggravating way, 'I *shall* go; Meg says I may; and if I pay for myself, Laurie hasn't anything to do with it.'

'You can't sit with us, for our seats are reserved, and you mustn't sit alone; so Laurie will give you his place, and that will spoil our pleasure; or he'll get another seat for you, and that isn't proper, when you weren't asked. You shan't stir a step; so you may just stay where you are,' scolded Jo, crosser than ever, having just pricked her finger in a hurry.

Sitting on the floor, with one boot on, Amy began to cry, and Meg to reason with her, when Laurie called from below, and the two girls hurried down, leaving their sister wailing; for now and then she forgot her grown-up ways, and acted like a spoilt child. Just as the party was setting out, Amy called over the banisters, in a threatening tone, 'You'll be sorry for this, Jo March! see if you ain't.'

'Fiddlesticks!' returned Jo, slamming the door.

They had a charming time, for 'The Seven Castles of Diamond Lake' were as brilliant and wonderful as a heart could wish. But, in spite of the comical red imps, sparkling elves, and gorgeous princes and princesses, Jo's pleasure had a drop of bitterness in it; the fairy queen's yellow curls reminded her of Amy; and between the acts she amused herself with wondering what her sister would do to make her 'sorry for it.' She and Amy had had many lively skirmishes in the course of their lives, for both had quick tempers, and were apt to be violent when fairly roused. Amy teased Jo, and Jo irritated Amy, and semi-occasional explosions occurred, of which both were much ashamed afterward. Although the oldest, Jo had the least self-control, and had hard times trying to curb the fiery spirit which was continually getting her into trouble; her anger never lasted long, and, having humbly confessed her fault, she sincerely repented, and tried to do better. Her sisters used to say, that they rather liked to get Jo into a fury, because she was such an angel afterward. Poor Jo tried desperately to be good, but her bosom enemy was always ready to flame up and defeat her; and it took years of patient effort to subdue it.

When they got home, they found Amy reading in the parlor. She assumed an injured air as they came in; never lifted her eyes from her book, or asked a single question. Perhaps curiosity might have conquered resentment, if Beth had not been there to inquire, and receive a glowing description of the play. On going up to put away her best hat, Jo's first look was toward the bureau; for, in their last quarrel, Amy had soothed her feelings by turning Jo's top drawer upside down, on the floor. Everything was in its place, however; and after a hasty glance into her various closets, bags and boxes, Jo decided that Amy had forgiven and forgotten her wrongs.

There Jo was mistaken; for next day she made a discovery which produced a tempest. Meg, Beth and Amy were sitting together, late in the afternoon, when Jo burst into the room, looking excited, and demanding, breathlessly, 'Has any one taken my story?'

Meg and Beth said 'No,' at once, and looked surprised; Amy poked the fire, and said nothing. Jo saw her color rise, and was down upon her in a minute.

'Amy, you've got it!'

'No, I haven't.'

'You know where it is, then!'

'No, I don't.'

'That's a fib!' cried Jo, taking her by the shoulders, and

looking fierce enough to frighten a much braver child than Amy.

'It isn't. I haven't got it, don't know where it is now, and don't care.'

'You know something about it, and you'd better tell at once, or I'll make you,' and Jo gave her a slight shake.

'Scold as much as you like, you'll never get your silly old story again,' cried Amy, getting excited in her turn.

'Why not?'

'I burnt it up.'

'What! my little book I was so fond of, and worked over, and meant to finish before father got home? Have you really burnt it?' said Jo, turning very pale, while her eyes kindled and her hands clutched Amy nervously.

'Yes, I did! I told you I'd make you pay for being so cross yesterday, and I have, so—'

Amy got no farther, for Jo's hot temper mastered her, and she shook Amy till her teeth chattered in her head; crying, in a passion of grief and anger,—

'You wicked, wicked girl! I never can write it again, and I'll never forgive you as long as I live.'

Meg flew to rescue Amy, and Beth to pacify Jo, but Jo was quite beside herself; and, with a parting box on her sister's ear, she rushed out of the room up to the old sofa in the garret, and finished her fight alone.

The storm cleared up below, for Mrs March came

home, and, having heard the story, soon brought Amy to a sense of the wrong she had done her sister. Jo's book was the pride of her heart, and was regarded by her family as a literary sprout of great promise. It was only half a dozen little fairy tales, but Jo had worked over them patiently, putting her whole heart into her work, hoping to make something good enough to print. She had just copied them with great care, and had destroyed the old manuscript, so that Amy's bonfire had consumed the loving work of several years. It seemed a small loss to others, but to Jo it was a dreadful calamity, and she felt that it never could be made up to her. Beth mourned as for a departed kitten, and Meg refused to defend her pet; Mrs March looked grave and grieved, and Amy felt that no one would love her till she had asked pardon for the act which she now regretted more than any of them.

When the tea-bell rang, Jo appeared, looking so grim and unapproachable, that it took all Amy's courage to say, meekly,—

'Please forgive me, Jo; I'm very, very sorry.'

'I never shall forgive you,' was Jo's stern answer; and, from that moment, she ignored Amy entirely.

No one spoke of the great trouble,—not even Mrs March,—for all had learned by experience that when Jo was in that mood words were wasted; and the wisest course was to wait till some little accident, or her own generous nature, softened Jo's resentment, and healed the breach. It was not a happy evening; for, though they sewed as usual, while their mother read aloud from Bremer, Scott, or Edgeworth, something was wanting, and the sweet home-peace was disturbed. They felt this most when singing-time came; for Beth could only play, Jo stood dumb as a stone, and Amy broke down, so Meg and mother sung alone. But, in spite of their efforts to be as cheery as larks, the flute-like voices did not seem to chord as well as usual, and all felt out of tune.

As Jo received her good-night kiss, Mrs March whispered, gently,—

'My dear, don't let the sun go down upon your anger; forgive each other, help each other, and begin again tomorrow.'

Jo wanted to lay her head down on that motherly bosom, and cry her grief and anger all away; but tears were an unmanly weakness, and she felt so deeply injured that she really *couldn't* quite forgive yet. So she winked hard, shook her head, and said, gruffly, because Amy was listening,—

'It was an abominable thing, and she don't deserve to be forgiven.'

With that she marched off to bed, and there was no merry or confidential gossip that night.

Amy was much offended that her overtures of peace

had been repulsed, and began to wish she had not humbled herself, to feel more injured than ever, and to plume herself on her superior virtue in a way which was particularly exasperating. Jo still looked like a thunder-cloud, and nothing went well all day. It was bitter cold in the morning; she dropped her precious turn-over in the gutter, Aunt March had an attack of fidgets, Meg was pensive, Beth *would* look grieved and wistful when she got home, and Amy kept making remarks about people who were always talking about being good, and yet wouldn't try, when other people set them a virtuous example.

'Everybody is so hateful, I'll ask Laurie to go skating. He is always kind and jolly, and will put me to rights, I know,' said Jo to herself, and off she went.

Amy heard the clash of skates, and looked out with an impatient exclamation,—

'There! she promised I should go next time, for this is the last ice we shall have. But it's no use to ask such a cross patch to take me.'

'Don't say that; you *were* very naughty, and it is hard to forgive the loss of her precious little book; but I think she might do it now, and I guess she will, if you try her at the right minute,' said Meg. 'Go after them; don't say anything till Jo has got good-natured with Laurie, then take a quiet minute, and just kiss her, or do some kind thing, and I'm sure she'll be friends again, with all her heart.'

'I'll try,' said Amy, for the advice suited her; and, after a flurry to get ready, she ran after the friends, who were just disappearing over the hill.

It was not far to the river, but both were ready before Amy reached them. Jo saw her coming, and turned her back; Laurie did not see, for he was carefully skating along the shore, sounding the ice, for a warm spell had preceded the cold snap.

'I'll go on to the first bend, and see if it's all right, before we begin to race,' Amy heard him say, as he shot away, looking like a young Russian, in his fur-trimmed coat and cap.

Jo heard Amy panting after her run, stamping her feet, and blowing her fingers, as she tried to put her skates on; but Jo never turned, and went slowly zigzagging down the river, taking a bitter, unhappy sort of satisfaction in her sister's troubles. She had cherished her anger till it grew strong, and took possession of her, as evil thoughts and feelings always do, unless cast out at once. As Laurie turned the bend, he shouted back,—

'Keep near the shore; it isn't safe in the middle.'

Jo heard, but Amy was just struggling to her feet, and did not catch a word. Jo glanced over her shoulder, and the little demon she was harboring said in her ear,—

'No matter whether she heard or not, let her take care of herself.'

Laurie had vanished round the bend; Jo was just at the turn, and Amy, far behind, striking out toward the smoother ice in the middle of the river. For a minute Jo stood still, with a strange feeling at her heart; then she resolved to go on, but something held and turned her round, just in time to see Amy throw up her hands and go down, with the sudden crash of rotten ice, the splash of water, and a cry that made Jo's heart stand still with fear. She tried to call Laurie, but her voice was gone; she tried to rush forward, but her feet seemed to have no strength in them; and, for a second, she could only stand motionless, staring, with a terror-stricken face, at the little blue hood above the black water. Something rushed swiftly by her, and Laurie's voice cried out,—

'Bring a rail; quick, quick!'

How she did it, she never knew; but for the next few minutes she worked as if possessed, blindly obeying Laurie, who was quite self-possessed; and, lying flat, held Amy up by his arm and hockeystick, till Jo dragged a rail from the fence, and together they got the child out, more frightened than hurt.

'Now then, we must walk her home as fast as we can; pile our things on her, while I get off these confounded skates,' cried Laurie, wrapping his coat round Amy, and tugging away at the straps, which never seemed so intricate before.

Shivering, dripping, and crying, they got Amy home; and, after an exciting time of it, she fell asleep, rolled in blankets, before a hot fire. During the bustle Jo had scarcely spoken; but flown about, looking pale and wild, with her things half off, her dress torn, and her hands cut and bruised by ice and rails, and refractory buckles. When Amy was comfortably asleep, the house quiet, and Mrs March sitting by the bed, she called Jo to her, and began to bind up the hurt hands.

'Are you sure she is safe?' whispered Jo, looking remorsefully at the golden head, which might have been swept away from her sight forever, under the treacherous ice.

'Quite safe, dear; she is not hurt, and won't even take cold, I think, you were so sensible in covering and getting her home quickly,' replied her mother, cheerfully.

'Laurie did it all; I only let her go. Mother, if she *should* die, it would be my fault;' and Jo dropped down beside the bed, in a passion of penitent tears, telling all that had happened, bitterly condemning her hardness of heart, and sobbing out her gratitude for being spared the heavy punishment which might have come upon her.

'It's my dreadful temper! I try to cure it; I think I have, and then it breaks out worse than ever. Oh, mother! what shall I do! what shall I do?' cried poor Jo, in despair.

'Watch and pray, dear; never get tired of trying; and never think it is impossible to conquer your fault,' said Mrs March, drawing the blowzy head to her shoulder, and kissing the wet cheek so tenderly, that Jo cried harder than ever.

'You don't know; you can't guess how bad it is! It seems as if I could do anything when I'm in a passion; I get so savage, I could hurt any one, and enjoy it. I'm afraid I *shall* do something dreadful some day, and spoil my life, and make everybody hate me. Oh, mother! help me, do help me!'

'I will, my child; I will. Don't cry so bitterly, but remember this day, and resolve, with all your soul, that you will never know another like it. Jo, dear, we all have our temptations, some far greater than yours, and it often takes us all our lives to conquer them. You think your temper is the worst in the world; but mine used to be just like it.'

'Yours, mother? Why, you are never angry!' and, for the moment, Jo forgot remorse in surprise.

'I've been trying to cure it for forty years, and have only succeeded in controlling it. I am angry nearly every day of my life, Jo; but I have learned not to show it; and I still hope to learn not to feel it, though it may take me another forty years to do so.'

The patience and the humility of the face she loved so well, was a better lesson to Jo than the wisest lecture, the sharpest reproof. She felt comforted at once by the sympathy and confidence given her; the knowledge that her mother had a fault like hers, and tried to mend it, made her own easier to bear, and strengthened her resolution to cure it; though forty years seemed rather a long time to watch and pray, to a girl of fifteen.

'Mother, are you angry when you fold your lips tight together, and go out of the room sometimes, when Aunt March scolds, or people worry you?' asked Jo, feeling nearer and dearer to her mother than ever before.

'Yes, I've learned to check the hasty words that rise to my lips; and when I feel that they mean to break out against my will, I just go away a minute, and give myself a little shake, for being so weak and wicked,' answered Mrs March, with a sigh and a smile, as she smoothed and fastened up Jo's dishevelled hair.

'How did you learn to keep still? That is what troubles me—for the sharp words fly out before I know what I'm about; and the more I say the worse I get, till it's a pleasure to hurt people's feelings, and say dreadful things. Tell me how you do it, Marmee dear.'

'My good mother used to help me—'

'As you do us—' interrupted Jo, with a grateful kiss.

'But I lost her when I was a little older than you are, and for years had to struggle on alone, for I was too proud to confess my weakness to any one else. I had a hard time, Jo, and shed a good many bitter tears over my failures; for, in spite of my efforts, I never seemed to get on. Then your father came, and I was so happy that I found it easy to be good. But by and by, when I had four little daughters round me, and we were poor, then the old trouble began again; for I am not patient by nature, and it tried me very much to see my children wanting anything.'

'Poor mother! what helped you then?'

'Your father, Jo. He never loses patience,—never doubts or complains,—but always hopes, and works and waits so cheerfully, that one is ashamed to do otherwise before him. He helped and comforted me, and showed me that I must try to practise all the virtues I would have my little girls possess, for I was their example. It was easier to try for your sakes than for my own; a startled or surprised look from one of you, when I spoke sharply, rebuked me more than any words could have done; and the love, respect, and confidence of my children was the sweetest reward I could receive for my efforts to be the woman I would have them copy.'

'Oh, mother! if I'm ever half as good as you, I shall be satisfied,' cried Jo, much touched.

'I hope you will be a great deal better, dear; but you must keep watch over your "bosom enemy," as father calls it, or it may sadden, if not spoil your life. You have had a warning; remember it, and try with heart and soul to master this quick temper, before it brings you greater sorrow and regret than you have known today.'

'I will try, mother; I truly will. But you must help me, remind me, and keep me from flying out. I used to see father sometimes put his finger on his lips, and look at you with a very kind, but sober face; and you always folded your lips tight, or went away; was he reminding you then?' asked Jo, softly.

'Yes; I asked him to help me so, and he never forgot it, but saved me from many a sharp word by that little gesture and kind look.'

Jo saw that her mother's eyes filled, and her lips trembled, as she spoke; and, fearing that she had said too much, she whispered anxiously, 'Was it wrong to watch you, and to speak of it? I didn't mean to be rude, but it's so comfortable to say all I think to you, and feel so safe and happy here.'

'My Jo, you may say anything to your mother, for it is my greatest happiness and pride to feel that my girls confide in me, and know how much I love them.'

'I thought I'd grieved you.'

'No, dear; but speaking of father reminded me how much I miss him, how much I owe him, and how faithfully I should watch and work to keep his little daughters safe and good for him.'

'Yet you told him to go, mother, and didn't cry when he went, and never complain now, or seem as if you needed any help,' said Jo, wondering.

'I gave my best to the country I love, and kept my tears till he was gone. Why should I complain, when we both have merely done our duty, and will surely be the happier for it in the end? If I don't seem to need help, it is because I have a better friend, even than father, to comfort and sustain me. My child, the troubles and temptations of your life are beginning, and may be many; but you can overcome and outlive them all, if you learn to feel the strength and tenderness of your Heavenly Father as you do that of your earthly one. The more you love and trust Him, the nearer you will feel to Him, and the less you will depend on human power and wisdom. His love and care never tire or change, can never be taken from you, but may become the source of lifelong peace, happiness, and strength. Believe this heartily, and go to God with all your little cares, and hopes, and sins, and sorrows, as freely and confidingly as you come to your mother.'

Jo's only answer was to hold her mother close, and, in the silence which followed, the sincerest prayer she had ever prayed left her heart, without words; for in that sad, yet happy hour, she had learned not only the bitterness of remorse and despair, but the sweetness of self-denial and self-control; and, led by her mother's hand, she had drawn nearer to the Friend who welcomes every child with a love stronger than that of any father, tenderer than that of any mother.

Amy stirred, and sighed in her sleep; and, as if eager to begin at once to mend her fault, Jo looked up with an expression on her face which it had never worn before.

'I let the sun go down on my anger; I wouldn't forgive her, and today, if it hadn't been for Laurie, it might have been too late! How could I be so wicked?' said Jo, half aloud, as she leaned over her sister, softly stroking the wet hair scattered on the pillow.

As if she heard, Amy opened her eyes, and held out her arms, with a smile that went straight to Jo's heart. Neither said a word, but they hugged one another close, in spite of the blankets, and everything was forgiven and forgotten in one hearty kiss.

9

Meg Goes to Vanity Fair

'I DO think it was the most fortunate thing in the world, that those children should have the measles just now,' said Meg, one April day, as she stood packing the 'go abroady' trunk in her room, surrounded by her sisters.

'And so nice of Annie Moffat, not to forget her promise. A whole fortnight of fun will be regularly splendid,' replied Jo, looking like a windmill, as she folded skirts with her long arms.

'And such lovely weather; I'm so glad of that,' added Beth, tidily sorting neck and hair ribbons in her best box lent for the great occasion.

'I wish I was going to have a fine time, and wear all these nice things,' said Amy, with her mouth full of pins, as she artistically replenished her sister's cushion.

'I wish you were all going; but, as you can't, I shall keep my adventures to tell you when I come back. I'm sure it's the least I can do, when you have been so kind, lending me things, and helping me get ready,' said Meg, glancing round the room at the very simple outfit, which seemed nearly perfect in their eyes.

'What did mother give you out of the treasure-box?' asked Amy, who had not been present at the opening of a certain cedar chest, in which Mrs March kept a few relics of past splendor, as gifts for her girls when the proper time came.

'A pair of silk stockings, that pretty carved fan, and a lovely blue sash. I wanted the violet silk; but there isn't time to make it over, so I must be contented with my old tarlatan.'

'It will look nicely over my new muslin skirt, and the sash will set it off beautifully. I wish I hadn't smashed my coral bracelet, for you might have had it,' said Jo, who loved to give and lend, but whose possessions were usually too dilapidated to be of much use.

'There is a lovely old-fashioned pearl set in the treasure-box; but mother said real flowers were the prettiest ornament for a young girl, and Laurie promised to send me all I want,' replied Meg. 'Now, let me see;

there's my new gray walking-suit,—just curl up the feather in my hat, Beth,—then my poplin, for Sunday, and the small party,—it looks heavy for spring, don't it? the violet silk would be so nice; oh, dear!'

'Never mind; you've got the tarlatan for the big party, and you always look like an angel in white,' said Amy, brooding over the little store of finery in which her soul delighted.

'It isn't low-necked, and it don't sweep enough, but it will have to do. My blue house-dress looks so well, turned and freshly trimmed, that I feel as if I'd got a new one. My silk sacque isn't a bit the fashion, and my bonnet don't look like Sallie's; I didn't like to say anything, but I was dreadfully disappointed in my umbrella. I told mother black, with a white handle, but she forgot, and bought a green one, with an ugly yellowish handle. It's strong and neat, so I ought not to complain, but I know I shall feel ashamed of it beside Annie's silk one, with a gold top,' sighed Meg, surveying the little umbrella with great disfavor.

'Change it,' advised Jo.

'I won't be so silly, or hurt Marmee's feelings, when she took so much pains to get my things. It's a nonsensical notion of mine, and I'm not going to give up to it. My silk stockings and two pairs of spandy gloves are my comfort. You are a dear, to lend me yours, Jo; I feel so rich, and sort of elegant, with two new pairs, and the old ones cleaned up for common;' and Meg took a refreshing peep at her glove-box.

'Annie Moffat has blue and pink bows on her night-caps; would you put some on mine?' she asked, as Beth brought up a pile of snowy muslins, fresh from Hannah's hands.

'No, I wouldn't; for the smart caps won't match the plain gowns, without any trimming on them. Poor folks shouldn't rig,' said Jo, decidedly.

'I wonder if I shall *ever* be happy enough to have real lace on my clothes, and bows on my caps?' said Meg, impatiently.

'You said the other day that you'd be perfectly happy if you could only go to Annie Moffat's,' observed Beth, in her quiet way.

'So I did! Well, I *am* happy, and I *won't* fret; but it does seem as if the more one gets the more one wants, don't it? There, now, the trays are ready, and everything in but my ball-dress, which I shall leave for mother,' said Meg, cheering up, as she glanced from the half-filled trunk to the many-times pressed and mended white tarlatan, which she called her 'ball-dress,' with an important air.

The next day was fine, and Meg departed, in style, for a fortnight of novelty and pleasure. Mrs March had consented to the visit rather reluctantly, fearing that Margaret would come back more discontented than she went. But she had begged so hard, and Sallie had promised to take good care of her, and a little pleasure seemed so delightful after a winter of hard work, that the mother yielded, and the daughter went to take her first taste of fashionable life.

The Moffats *were* very fashionable, and simple Meg was rather daunted, at first, by the splendor of the house, and the elegance of its occupants. But they were kindly people, in spite of the frivolous life they led, and soon put their guest at her ease. Perhaps Meg felt, without understanding why, that they were not particularly cultivated or intelligent people, and that all their gilding could not quite conceal the ordinary material of which they were made. It certainly was agreeable to fare sumptuously, drive in a fine carriage, wear her best frock every day, and do nothing but enjoy herself. It suited her exactly; and soon she began to imitate the manners and conversation of those about her; to put on little airs and graces, use French phrases, crimp her hair, take in her dresses, and talk about the fashions, as well as she could. The more she saw of Annie Moffat's pretty things, the more she envied her, and sighed to be rich. Home now looked bare and dismal as she thought of it, work grew harder than ever, and she felt that she was a very destitute and much injured girl, in spite of the new gloves and silk stockings.

She had not much time for repining, however, for the three young girls were busily employed in 'having a good time.' They shopped, walked, rode, and called all day; went to theatres and operas, or frolicked at home in the evening; for Annie had many friends, and knew how to entertain them. Her older sisters were very fine young ladies, and one was engaged, which was extremely interesting and romantic, Meg thought. Mr Moffat was a fat, jolly old gentleman, who knew her father; and Mrs Moffat, a fat, jolly old lady, who took as great a fancy to Meg as her daughter had done. Every one petted her; and 'Daisy,' as they called her, was in a fair way to have her head turned.

When the evening for the 'small party' came, she found that the poplin wouldn't do at all, for the other girls were putting on thin dresses, and making themselves very fine indeed; so out came the tarlatan, looking older, limper, and shabbier than ever, beside Sallie's crisp new one. Meg saw the girls glance at it, and then at one another, and her cheeks began to burn; for, with all her gentleness, she was very proud. No one said a word about it, but Sallie offered to do her hair, and Annie to tie her sash, and Belle, the engaged sister, praised her white arms; but, in their kindness, Meg saw only pity for her poverty, and her heart felt very heavy as she stood by herself, while the others laughed and chattered, prinked, and flew about like gauzy butterflies. The hard, bitter feeling was getting pretty bad, when the maid brought in a box of flowers. Before she could speak, Annie had the cover off, and all were exclaiming at the lovely roses, heath, and ferns within.

'It's for Belle, of course; George always sends her some, but these are altogether ravishing,' cried Annie, with a great sniff.

'They are for Miss March,' the man said. 'And here's a note,' put in the maid, holding it to Meg.

'What fun? Who are they from? Didn't know you had a lover,' cried the girls, fluttering about Meg in a high state of curiosity and surprise.

'The note is from mother, and the flowers from Laurie,' said Meg, simply, yet much gratified that he had not forgotten her.

'Oh, indeed!' said Annie, with a funny look, as Meg slipped the note into her pocket, as a sort of talisman against envy, vanity, and false pride; for the few loving words had done her good, and the flowers cheered her up by their beauty.

Feeling almost happy again, she laid by a few ferns and roses for herself, and quickly made up the rest in dainty bouquets for the breasts, hair, or skirts of her friends, offering them so prettily, that Clara, the elder sister, told her she was 'the sweetest little thing she ever saw;' and they looked quite charmed with her small attention. Somehow the kind act finished her despondency; and, when all the rest went to show themselves to Mrs Moffat, she saw a happy, bright-eyed face in the mirror, as she laid her ferns against her rippling hair, and fastened the roses in the dress that didn't strike her as so *very* shabby now.

She enjoyed herself very much that evening, for she danced to her heart's content; every one was very kind, and she had three compliments. Annie made her sing, and some one said she had a remarkably fine voice; Major Lincoln asked who 'the fresh little girl, with the beautiful eyes, was;' and Mr Moffat insisted on dancing with her, because she 'didn't dawdle, but had some spring in her,' as he gracefully expressed it. So, altogether, she had a very nice time, till she overheard a bit of conversation, which disturbed her extremely. She was sitting just inside the conservatory, waiting for her partner to bring her an ice, when she heard a voice ask, on the other side of the flowery wall,—

'How old is he?'

'Sixteen or seventeen, I should say,' replied another voice.

'It would be a grand thing for one of those girls,

wouldn't it? Sallie says they are very intimate now, and the old man quite dotes on them.'

'Mrs M. has laid her plans, I dare say, and will play her cards well, early as it is. The girl evidently doesn't think of it yet,' said Mrs Moffat.

'She told that fib about her mamma, as if she did know, and colored up when the flowers came, quite prettily. Poor thing! she'd be so nice if she was only got up in style. Do you think she'd be offended if we offered to lend her a dress for Thursday?' asked another voice.

'She's proud, but I don't believe she'd mind, for that dowdy tarlatan is all she has got. She may tear it tonight, and that will be a good excuse for offering a decent one.'

'We'll see; I shall ask that Laurence, as a compliment to her, and we'll have fun about it afterward.'

Here Meg's partner appeared, to find her looking much flushed, and rather agitated. She was proud, and her pride was useful just then, for it helped her hide her mortification, anger, and disgust, at what she had just heard; for, innocent and unsuspicious as she was, she could not help understanding the gossip of her friends. She tried to forget it, but could not, and kept repeating to herself, 'Mrs M. has her plans,' 'that fib about her mamma,' and 'dowdy tarlatan,' till she was ready to cry, and rush home to tell her troubles, and ask for advice. As that was impossible, she did her best to seem gay; and, being rather excited, she succeeded so well, that no one dreamed what an effort she was making. She was very glad when it was all over, and she was quiet in her bed, where she could think and wonder and fume till her head ached, and her hot cheeks were cooled by a few natural tears. Those foolish, yet well-meant words, had opened a new world to Meg, and much disturbed the peace of the old one, in which, till now, she had lived as happily as a child. Her innocent friendship with Laurie was spoilt by the silly speeches she had overheard; her faith in her mother was a little shaken by the worldly plans attributed to her by Mrs Moffat, who judged others by herself; and the sensible resolution to be contented with the simple wardrobe which suited a poor man's daughter, was weakened by the unnecessary pity of girls, who thought a shabby dress one of the greatest calamities under heaven.

Poor Meg had a restless night, and got up heavy-eyed, unhappy, half resentful toward her friends, and half ashamed of herself for not speaking out frankly, and setting everything right. Everybody dawdled that morning, and it was noon before the girls found energy enough even to take up their worsted work. Something in the manner of her friends struck Meg at once; they treated her with more respect, she thought; took quite a tender interest in what she said, and looked at her with eyes that plainly betrayed curiosity. All this surprised and flattered her, though she did not understand it till Miss Belle looked up from her writing, and said, with a sentimental air,—

'Daisy, dear, I've sent an invitation to your friend, Mr Laurence, for Thursday. We should like to know him, and it's only a proper compliment to you.'

Meg colored, but a mischievous fancy to tease the girls made her reply demurely,—

'You are very kind, but I'm afraid he won't come.'

'Why not, chérie?' asked Miss Belle.

'He's too old.'

'My child, what do you mean? What is his age, I beg to know!' cried Miss Clara.

'Nearly seventy, I believe,' answered Meg, counting stitches, to hide the merriment in her eyes.

'You sly creature! of course, we meant the young man,' exclaimed Miss Belle, laughing.

'There isn't any; Laurie is only a little boy,' and Meg laughed also at the queer look which the sisters exchanged, as she thus described her supposed lover.

'About your age,' Nan said.

'Nearer my sister Jo's; *I* am seventeen in August,' returned Meg, tossing her head.

'It's very nice of him to send you flowers, isn't it?' said Annie, looking wise about nothing.

'Yes, he often does, to all of us; for their house is full, and we are so fond of them. My mother and old Mr Laurence are friends, you know, so it is quite natural that we children should play together;' and Meg hoped they would say no more.

'It's evident Daisy isn't out yet,' said Miss Clara to Belle, with a nod.

'Quite a pastoral state of innocence all round,' returned Miss Belle, with a shrug.

'I'm going out to get some little matters for my girls; can I do anything for you, young ladies?' asked Mrs Moffat, lumbering in, like an elephant, in silk and lace.

'No, thank you, ma'am,' replied Sallie; 'I've got my new pink silk for Thursday, and I don't want a thing.'

'Nor I—' began Meg, but stopped, because it occurred to her that she *did* want several things, and could not have them.

'What shall you wear?' asked Sallie.

'My old white one again, if I can mend it fit to be seen; it got sadly torn last night,' said Meg, trying to speak quite easily, but feeling very uncomfortable.

'Why don't you send home for another?' said Sallie, who was not an observing young lady.

'I haven't got any other.' It cost Meg an effort to say that, but Sallie did not see it, and exclaimed, in amiable surprise,—

'Only that? how funny—.' She did not finish her speech, for Belle shook her head at her, and broke in, saying, kindly,—

'Not at all; where is the use of having a lot of dresses when she isn't out? There's no need of sending home, Daisy, even if you had a dozen, for I've got a sweet blue silk laid away, which I've outgrown, and you shall wear it, to please me; won't you, dear?'

'You are very kind, but I don't mind my old dress, if you don't; it does well enough for a little girl like me,' said Meg.

'Now do let me please myself by dressing you up in style. I admire to do it, and you'd be a regular little beauty, with a touch here and there. I shan't let any one see you till you are done, and then we'll burst upon them like Cinderella and her godmother, going to the ball,' said Belle, in her persuasive tone.

Meg couldn't refuse the offer so kindly made, for a desire to see if she would be 'a little beauty' after touching up caused her to accept, and forget all her former uncomfortable feelings towards the Moffats.

On the Thursday evening, Belle shut herself up with her maid; and, between them, they turned Meg into a fine lady. They crimped and curled her hair, they polished her neck and arms with some fragrant powder, touched her lips with coralline salve, to make them redder, and Hortense would have added 'a *soupçon* of rouge,' if Meg had not rebelled. They laced her into a sky-blue dress, which was so tight she could hardly breathe, and so low in the neck that modest Meg blushed at herself in the mirror. A set of silver filagree was added, bracelets, necklace, brooch, and even ear-rings, for Hortense tied them on, with a bit of pink silk, which did not show. A cluster of tea rose-buds at the bosom, and a *ruche*, reconciled Meg to the display of her pretty white shoulders, and a pair of high-heeled blue silk boots satisfied the last wish of her heart. A laced handkerchief, a plumy fan, and a bouquet in a silver holder, finished her off; and Miss Belle surveyed her with the satisfaction of a little girl with a newly dressed doll.

'Mademoiselle is charmante, très jolie, is she not?' cried Hortense, clasping her hands in an affected rapture.

'Come and show yourself,' said Miss Belle, leading the way to the room where the others were waiting.

As Meg went rustling after, with her long skirts trailing, her ear-rings tinkling, her curls waving, and her heart beating, she felt as if her 'fun' had really begun at last, for the mirror had plainly told her that she *was* 'a little beauty.' Her friends repeated the pleasing phrase enthusiastically; and, for several minutes, she stood, like the jackdaw in the fable, enjoying her borrowed plumes, while the rest chattered like a party of magpies.

'While I dress, do you drill her, Nan, in the management of her skirt, and those French heels, or she will trip herself up. Put your silver butterfly in the middle of that white barbe, and catch up that long curl on the left side of her head, Clara, and don't any of you disturb the charming work of my hands,' said Belle, as she hurried away, looking well pleased with her success.

'I'm afraid to go down, I feel so queer and stiff, and half-dressed,' said Meg to Sallie, as the bell rang, and Mrs Moffat sent to ask the young ladies to appear at once.

'You don't look a bit like yourself, but you are very nice. I'm nowhere beside you, for Belle has heaps of taste, and you're quite French, I assure you. Let your flowers hang; don't be so careful of them, and be sure you don't trip,' returned Sallie, trying not to care that Meg was prettier than herself.

Keeping that warning carefully in mind, Margaret got safely down stairs, and sailed into the drawing-rooms, where the Moffats and a few early guests were assembled. She very soon discovered that there is a charm about fine clothes which attracts a certain class of people, and secures their respect. Several young ladies, who had taken no notice of her before, were very affectionate all of a sudden; several young gentlemen, who had only stared at her at the other party, now not only stared, but asked to be introduced, and said all manner of foolish, but agreeable things to her; and several old ladies, who sat on sofas, and criticized the rest of the party, inquired who she was, with an air of interest. She heard Mrs Moffat reply to one of them,—

'Daisy March—father a colonel in the army—one of our first families, but reverses of fortune, you know; intimate friends of the Laurences; sweet creature, I assure you; my Ned is quite wild about her.'

'Dear me!' said the old lady, putting up her glass for another observation of Meg, who tried to look as if she had not heard, and been rather shocked at Mrs Moffat's fibs.

The 'queer feeling' did not pass away, but she imagined herself acting the new part of fine lady, and so got on pretty well, though the tight dress gave her a side-ache, the train kept getting under her feet, and she was in constant fear lest her ear-rings should fly off, and get lost or broken. She was flirting her fan, and laughing at the feeble jokes of a young gentleman who tried to be witty, when she suddenly stopped laughing, and looked confused; for, just opposite, she saw Laurie. He was staring at her with undisguised surprise, and disapproval also, she thought; for, though he bowed and smiled, yet something in his honest eyes made her blush, and wish she had her old dress on. To complete her confusion, she saw Belle nudge Annie, and both glance from her to Laurie, who, she was happy to see, looked unusually boyish and shy.

'Silly creatures, to put such thoughts into my head! I won't care for it, or let it change me a bit,' thought Meg, and rustled across the room to shake hands with her friend.

'I'm glad you came, for I was afraid you wouldn't,' she said, with her most grown-up air.

'Jo wanted me to come, and tell her how you looked, so I did;' answered Laurie, without turning his eyes upon her, though he half smiled at her maternal tone.

'What shall you tell her?' asked Meg, full of curiosity to know his opinion of her, yet feeling ill at ease with him, for the first time.

'I shall say I didn't know you; for you look so grown-up, and unlike yourself, I'm quite afraid of you,' he said, fumbling at his glove-button.

'How absurd of you! the girls dressed me up for fun, and I rather like it. Wouldn't Jo stare if she saw me?' said Meg, bent on making him say whether he thought her improved or not.

'Yes, I think she would,' returned Laurie, gravely.

'Don't you like me so?' asked Meg.

'No, I don't,' was the blunt reply.

'Why not?' in an anxious tone.

He glanced at her frizzled head, bare shoulders, and fantastically trimmed dress, with an expression that abashed her more than his answer, which had not a particle of his usual politeness about it.

'I don't like fuss and feathers.'

That was altogether too much from a lad younger than herself; and Meg walked away, saying, petulantly,—

'You are the rudest boy I ever saw.'

Feeling very much ruffled, she went and stood at a quiet window, to cool her cheeks, for the tight dress gave her an uncomfortably brilliant color. As she stood there, Major Lincoln passed by; and, a minute after, she heard him saying to his mother,—

'They are making a fool of that little girl; I wanted you to see her, but they have spoilt her entirely; she's nothing but a doll, tonight.'

'Oh, dear!' sighed Meg; 'I wish I'd been sensible, and worn my own things; then I should not have disgusted other people, or felt so uncomfortable and ashamed myself.'

She leaned her forehead on the cool pane, and stood half hidden by the curtains, never minding that her favorite waltz had begun, till some one touched her; and, turning, she saw Laurie looking penitent, as he said, with his very best bow, and his hand out,—

'Please forgive my rudeness, and come and dance with me.'

'I'm afraid it will be too disagreeable to you,' said Meg, trying to look offended, and failing entirely.

'Not a bit of it; I'm dying to do it. Come, I'll be good; I don't like your gown, but I do think you are—just splendid;' and he waved his hands, as if words failed to express his admiration.

Meg smiled, and relented, and whispered, as they stood waiting to catch the time.

'Take care my skirt don't trip you up; it's the plague of my life, and I was a goose to wear it.'

'Pin it round your neck, and then it will be useful,' said Laurie, looking down at the little blue boots, which he evidently approved of.

Away they went, fleetly and gracefully; for, having practised at home, they were well matched, and the blithe young couple were a pleasant sight to see, as they twirled merrily round and round, feeling more friendly than ever after their small tiff.

'Laurie, I want you to do me a favor; will you?' said Meg, as he stood fanning her, when her breath gave out, which it did, very soon, though she would not own why.

'Won't I!' said Laurie, with alacrity.

'Please don't tell them at home about my dress tonight. They won't understand the joke, and it will worry mother.'

'Then why did you do it?' said Laurie's eyes, so plainly, that Meg hastily added,—

'I shall tell them, myself, all about it, and "'fess" to mother how silly I've been. But I'd rather do it myself; so you'll not tell, will you?'

'I give you my word I won't; only what shall I say when they ask me?'

'Just say I looked nice, and was having a good time.'

'I'll say the first, with all my heart; but how about the other? You don't look as if you were having a good time; are you?' and Laurie looked at her with an expression which made her answer, in a whisper,—

'No; not just now. Don't think I'm horrid; I only wanted a little fun, but this sort don't pay, I find, and I'm getting tired of it.'

'Here comes Ned Moffat; what does he want?' said Laurie, knitting his black brows, as if he did not regard his young host in the light of a pleasant addition to the party.

'He put his name down for three dances, and I suppose he's coming for them; what a bore!' said Meg, assuming a languid air, which amused Laurie immensely.

He did not speak to her again till supper-time, when he saw her drinking champagne with Ned, and his friend Fisher, who were behaving 'like a pair of fools,' as Laurie said to himself, for he felt a brotherly sort of right to watch over the Marches, and fight their battles, whenever a defender was needed.

'You'll have a splitting headache tomorrow, if you drink much of that. I wouldn't, Meg; your mother don't like it, you know,' he whispered, leaning over her chair, as Ned turned to refill her glass, and Fisher stooped to pick up her fan.

'I'm not Meg, tonight; I'm "a doll," who does all sorts of crazy things. Tomorrow I shall put away my "fuss and feathers," and be desperately good again,' she answered, with an affected little laugh.

'Wish tomorrow was here, then,' muttered Laurie, walking off, ill-pleased at the change he saw in her.

Meg danced and flirted, chattered and giggled, as the other girls did; after supper she undertook the German, and blundered through it nearly upsetting her partner with her long skirt, and romping in a way that scandalized Laurie, who looked on and meditated a lecture. But he got no chance to deliver it, for Meg kept away from him till he came to say good-night.

'Remember!' she said, trying to smile, for the splitting headache had already begun.

'Silence à la mort,' replied Laurie, with a melodramatic flourish, as he went away.

This little bit of by-play excited Annie's curiosity; but Meg was too tired for gossip, and went to bed, feeling as if she had been to a masquerade, and hadn't enjoyed herself as much as she expected. She was sick all the next day, and on Saturday went home, quite used up with her fortnight's fun, and feeling that she had sat in the lap of luxury long enough.

'It does seem pleasant to be quiet, and not have company manners on all the time. Home *is* a nice place, though it isn't splendid,' said Meg, looking about her with a restful expression, as she sat with her mother and Jo on the Sunday evening.

'I'm glad to hear you say so, dear, for I was afraid home would seem dull and poor to you, after your fine quarters,' replied her mother, who had given her many anxious looks that day; for motherly eyes are quick to see any change in children's faces.

Meg had told her adventures gaily, and said over and over what a charming time she had had; but something still seemed to weigh upon her spirits, and, when the younger girls were gone to bed, she sat thoughtfully staring at the fire, saying little, and looking worried. As the clock struck nine, and Jo proposed bed, Meg suddenly left her chair, and, taking Beth's stool, leaned her elbows on her mother's knee, saying, bravely,—

'Marmee, I want to "'fess."'

'I thought so; what is it, dear?'

'Shall I go away?' asked Jo, discreetly.

'Of course not; don't I always tell you everything? I was ashamed to speak of it before the children, but I want you to know all the dreadful things I did at the Moffats.'

'We are prepared,' said Mrs March, smiling, but looking a little anxious.

'I told you they rigged me up, but I didn't tell you that they powdered, and squeezed, and frizzled, and made me look like a fashion-plate. Laurie thought I wasn't proper; I know he did, though he didn't say so, and one man called me "a doll." I knew it was silly, but they flattered me, and said I was a beauty, and quantities of nonsense, so I let them make a fool of me.'

'Is that all?' asked Jo, as Mrs March looked silently at the downcast face of her pretty daughter, and could not find it in her heart to blame her little follies.

'No; I drank champagne, and romped, and tried to flirt, and was, altogether, abominable,' said Meg, self-reproachfully.

'There is something more, I think;' and Mrs March smoothed the soft cheek, which suddenly grew rosy, as Meg answered, slowly,—

'Yes; it's very silly, but I want to tell it, because I hate to have people say and think such things about us and Laurie.'

Then she told the various bits of gossip she had heard at the Moffats; and, as she spoke, Jo saw her mother fold her lips tightly, as if ill pleased that such ideas should be put into Meg's innocent mind.

'Well, if that isn't the greatest rubbish I ever heard,' cried Jo, indignantly. 'Why didn't you pop out and tell them so, on the spot?'

'I couldn't, it was so embarrassing for me. I couldn't help hearing, at first, and then I was so angry and ashamed, I didn't remember that I ought to go away.'

'Just wait till *I* see Annie Moffat, and I'll show you how to settle such ridiculous stuff. The idea of having "plans," and being kind to Laurie, because he's rich, and may marry us by and by! Won't he shout, when I tell him what those silly things say about us poor children?' and Jo laughed, as if, on second thoughts, the thing struck her as a good joke.

'If you tell Laurie, I'll never forgive you! She mustn't, must she, mother?' said Meg, looking distressed.

'No; never repeat that foolish gossip, and forget it as soon as you can,' said Mrs March, gravely. 'I was very unwise to let you go among people of whom I know so little; kind, I dare say, but worldly, ill-bred, and full of these vulgar ideas about young people. I am more sorry than I can express, for the mischief this visit may have done you, Meg.'

'Don't be sorry, I won't let it hurt me; I'll forget all the bad, and remember only the good; for I did enjoy a great deal, and thank you very much for letting me go. I'll not be sentimental or dissatisfied, mother; I know I'm a silly little girl, and I'll stay with you till I'm fit to take care of myself. But it *is* nice to be praised and admired, and I can't help saying I like it,' said Meg, looking half ashamed of the confession.

'That is perfectly natural, and quite harmless, if the liking does not become a passion, and lead one to do foolish or unmaidenly things. Learn to know and value the praise which is worth having, and to excite the admiration of excellent people, by being modest as well as pretty, Meg.'

Margaret sat thinking a moment, while Jo stood with her hands behind her, looking both interested and a little perplexed; for it was a new thing to see Meg blushing and talking about admiration, lovers, and things of that sort, and Jo felt as if during that fortnight her sister had grown up amazingly, and was drifting away from her into a world where she could not follow.

'Mother, do you have "plans," as Mrs Moffat said?' asked Meg, bashfully.

'Yes, my dear, I have a great many; all mothers do, but mine differ somewhat from Mrs Moffat's, I suspect. I will tell you some of them, for the time has come when a word may set this romantic little head and heart of yours right, on a very serious subject. You are young, Meg; but not too young to understand me, and mothers' lips are the fittest to speak of such things to girls like you. Jo, your turn will come in time, perhaps, so listen to my "plans," and help me carry them out, if they are good.'

Jo went and sat on one arm of the chair, looking as if she thought they were about to join in some very solemn affair. Holding a hand of each, and watching the two young faces wistfully, Mrs March said, in her serious yet cheery way,—

'I want my daughters to be beautiful, accomplished, and good; to be admired, loved, and respected, to have a happy youth, to be well and wisely married, and to lead useful, pleasant lives, with as little care and sorrow to try them as God sees fit to send. To be loved and chosen by a good man is the best and sweetest thing which can happen to a woman; and I sincerely hope my girls may know this beautiful experience. It is natural to think of it, Meg; right to hope and wait for it, and wise to prepare for it; so that, when the happy time comes, you may feel ready for the duties, and worthy of the joy. My dear girls, I *am* ambitious for you, but not to have you make a dash in the world,—marry rich men merely because they are rich, or have splendid houses, which are not homes, because love is wanting. Money is a needful and precious thing,—and, when well used, a noble thing,—but I never want you to think it is the first or only prize to strive for. I'd rather see you poor men's wives, if you were happy, beloved, contented, than queens on thrones, without self-respect and peace.'

'Poor girls don't stand any chance, Belle says, unless they put themselves forward,' sighed Meg.

'Then we'll be old maids,' said Jo, stoutly.

'Right, Jo; better be happy old maids than unhappy wives, or unmaidenly girls, running about to find husbands,' said Mrs March, decidedly. 'Don't be troubled, Meg; poverty seldom daunts a sincere lover. Some of the best and most honored women I know were poor girls, but so love-worthy that they were not allowed to be old maids. Leave these things to time; make this home happy, so that you may be fit for homes of your own, if they are offered you, and contented here if they are not. One thing remember, my girls, mother is always ready to be your confidant, father to be your friend; and both of us trust and hope that our daughters, whether married or single, will be the pride and comfort of our lives.'

'We will, Marmee, we will!' cried both, with all their hearts, as she bade them good-night.

10

The P. C. and P. O.

AS SPRING came on, a new set of amusements became the fashion, and the lengthening days gave long afternoons for work and play of all sorts. The garden had to be put in order, and each sister had a quarter of the little plot to do what she liked with. Hannah used to say, 'I'd know which each of them gardings belonged to, ef I see 'em in Chiny;' and so she might, for the girls' tastes differed as much as their characters. Meg's had roses and heliotrope, myrtle, and a little orange-tree in it. Jo's bed was never alike two seasons, for she was always trying experiments; this year it was to be a plantation of sunflowers, the seeds of which cheerful and aspiring plant were to feed 'Aunt Cockle-top' and her family of chicks. Beth had old-fashioned, fragrant flowers in her garden; sweet peas and mignonette, larkspur, pinks, pansies, and southernwood, with chickweed for the bird and catnip for the pussies. Amy had a bower in hers,—rather small and earwiggy, but very pretty to look at,—with honeysuckles and morning-glories hanging their colored horns and bells in graceful wreaths all over it; tall white lilies, delicate ferns, and as many brilliant, picturesque plants as would consent to blossom there.

Gardening, walks, rows on the river, and flower-hunts employed the fine days; and for rainy ones, they had house diversions,—some old, some new,—all more or less original. One of these was the 'P. C.'; for, as secret societies were the fashion, it was thought proper to have one; and, as all of the girls admired Dickens, they called themselves the Pickwick Club. With a few interruptions, they had kept this up for a year, and met every Saturday evening in the big garret, on which occasions the ceremonies were as follows: Three chairs were arranged in a row before a table, on which was a lamp, also four white badges, with a big 'P. C.' in different colors on each, and the weekly newspaper, called 'The Pickwick Portfolio,' to which all contributed something; while Jo, who revelled in pens and ink, was the editor. At seven o'clock, the four members ascended to the clubroom, tied their badges round their heads, and took their seats with great solemnity. Meg, as the eldest, was

Samuel Pickwick; Jo, being of a literary turn, Augustus Snodgrass; Beth, because she was round and rosy, Tracy Tupman; and Amy, who was always trying to do what she couldn't, was Nathaniel Winkle. Pickwick, the President, read the paper, which was filled with original tales, poetry, local news, funny advertisements, and hints, in which they good-naturedly reminded each other of their faults and shortcomings. On one occasion, Mr Pickwick put on a pair of spectacles without any glasses, rapped upon the table, hemmed, and, having stared hard at Mr Snodgrass, who was tilting back in his chair, till he arranged himself properly, began to read,—

THE PICKWICK PORTFOLIO.

MAY 20, 18—.

Poet's Corner.

ANNIVERSARY ODE.

Again we meet to celebrate
  With badge and solemn rite,
Our fifty-second anniversary,
  In Pickwick Hall, tonight.

We all are here in perfect health,
  None gone from our small band;
Again we see each well-known face,
  And press each friendly hand.

Our Pickwick, always at his post,
    With reverence we greet,
As, spectacles on nose, he reads
    Our well-filled weekly sheet.

Although he suffers from a cold,
    We joy to hear him speak,
For words of wisdom from him fall,
    In spite of croak or squeak.

Old six-foot Snodgrass looms on high,
    With elephantine grace,
And beams upon the company,
    With brown and jovial face.

Poetic fire lights up his eye,
    He struggles 'gainst his lot;
Behold ambition on his brow,
    And on his nose a blot!

Next our peaceful Tupman comes,
    So rosy, plump and sweet.
Who chokes with laughter at the puns,
    And tumbles off his seat.

Prim little Winkle too is here,
    With every hair in place,
A model of propriety,
    Though he hates to wash his face.

The year is gone, we still unite
    To joke and laugh and read,
And tread the path of literature
    That doth to glory lead.

Long may our paper prosper well.
　　Our club unbroken be,
And coming years their blessings pour
　　On the useful, gay 'P. C.'

A. SNODGRASS

THE MASKED MARRIAGE.
A TALE OF VENICE.

Gondola after gondola swept up to the marble steps, and left its lovely load to swell the brilliant throng that filled the stately halls of Count de Adelon. Knights and ladies, elves and pages, monks and flower-girls, all mingled gaily in the dance. Sweet voices and rich melody filled the air; and so with mirth and music the masquerade went on.

'Has your Highness seen the Lady Viola tonight?' asked a gallant troubadour of the fairy queen who floated down the hall upon his arm.

'Yes; is she not lovely, though so sad! Her dress is well chosen, too, for in a week she weds Count Antonio, whom she passionately hates.'

'By my faith I envy him. Yonder he comes, arrayed like a bridegroom, except the black mask. When that is off we shall see how he regards the fair maid whose heart he cannot win, though her stern father bestows her hand,' returned the troubadour.

''Tis whispered that she loves the young English artist who haunts her steps, and is spurned by the old count,' said the lady, as they joined the dance.

The revel was at its height when a priest appeared, and, withdrawing the young pair to an alcove hung with purple velvet, he motioned them to kneel. Instant silence fell upon the gay throng; and not a sound, but the dash of fountains or the rustle of orange groves sleeping in the moonlight, broke the hush, as Count de Adelon spoke thus:—

'My lords and ladies; pardon the ruse by which I have gathered you here to witness the marriage of my daughter. Father, we wait your services.'

All eyes turned toward the bridal party, and a low murmur of amazement went through the throng, for neither bride nor groom removed their masks. Curiosity and wonder possessed all hearts, but respect restrained all tongues till the holy rite was over. Then the eager spectators gathered round the count, demanding an explanation.

'Gladly would I give it if I could; but I only know that it was the whim of my timid Viola, and I yielded to it. Now, my children, let the play end. Unmask, and receive my blessing.'

But neither bent the knee; for the young bridegroom replied, in a tone that startled all listeners, as the mask fell, disclosing the noble face of Ferdinand Devereux, the artist lover, and, leaning on the breast where now flashed the star of an English earl, was the lovely Viola, radiant with joy and beauty.

'My lord, you scornfully bade me claim your daughter when I could boast as high a name and vast a fortune as the Count Antonio. I can do more; for even your ambitious soul cannot refuse the Earl of Devereux and De Vere, when he gives his ancient name and boundless wealth in return for the beloved hand of this fair lady, now my wife.'

The count stood like one changed to stone; and, turning to the bewildered crowd, Ferdinand added, with a gay smile of triumph, 'To you, my gallant friends, I can only wish that your wooing may prosper as mine has done; and that you may all win as fair a bride as I have, by this masked marriage.'

S. PICKWICK.

————

Why is the P. C. like the Tower of Babel? It is full of unruly members.

———

THE HISTORY OF A SQUASH.

Once upon a time a farmer planted a little seed in his garden, and after a while it sprouted and became a vine, and bore many squashes. One day in October, when they were ripe, he picked one and took it to market. A grocer man bought and put it in his shop. That same morning, a little girl, in a brown hat and blue dress, with a round face and snubby nose, went and bought it for her mother. She lugged it home, cut it up, and boiled it in the big pot; mashed some of it, with salt and butter, for dinner; and to the rest she added a pint of milk, two eggs, four spoons of sugar, nutmeg, and some crackers; put it in a deep dish, and baked it till it was brown and nice; and next day it was eaten by a family named March.

T. TUPMAN.

———

MR PICKWICK, *Sir:*

I address you upon the subject of sin the sinner I mean is a man named Winkle who makes trouble in his club by laughing and sometimes won't write his piece in this fine paper I hope you will pardon his badness and let him send a French fable because he can't write out of his head as he has so many lessons to do and no brains in future I will try to take time by the fetlock and prepare some work which will be all *commy la fo* that means all right I am in haste as it is nearly school time.

Yours respectably N. WINKLE.

[The above is a manly and handsome acknowledgment of past misdemeanors. If our young friend studied punctuation, it would be well.]

A SAD ACCIDENT.

On Friday last, we were startled by a violent shock in our basement, followed by cries of distress. On rushing, in a body, to the cellar, we discovered our beloved President prostrate upon the floor, having tripped and fallen while getting wood for domestic purposes. A perfect scene of ruin met our eyes; for in his fall Mr Pickwick had plunged his head and shoulders into a tub of water, upset a keg of soft soap upon his manly form, and torn his garments badly. On being removed from this perilous situation, it was discovered that he had suffered no injury but several bruises; and, we are happy to add, is now doing well.

ED.

THE PUBLIC BEREAVEMENT.

It is our painful duty to record the sudden and mysterious disappearance of our cherished friend, Mrs Snowball Pat Paw. This lovely and beloved cat was the pet of a large circle of warm and admiring friends; for her beauty attracted all eyes, her graces and virtues endeared her to all hearts, and her loss is deeply felt by the whole community.

When last seen, she was sitting at the gate, watching the butcher's cart; and it is feared that some villain, tempted by her charms, basely stole her. Weeks have passed, but no trace of her has been discovered; and we relinquish all hope, tie a black ribbon to her basket, set aside her dish, and weep for her as one lost to us forever.

A sympathizing friend sends the following gem:—

A LAMENT
for S. B. Pat Paw.

We mourn the loss of our little pet,
    And sigh o'er her hapless fate,
For never more by the fire she'll sit,
    Nor play by the old green gate.

The little grave where her infant sleeps,
    Is 'neath the chestnut tree;
But o'er *her* grave we may not weep,
    We know not where it may be.

Her empty bed, her idle ball,
    Will never see her more;
No gentle tap, no loving purr
    Is heard at the parlor door.

Another cat comes after her mice,
    A cat with a dirty face;
But she does not hunt as our darling did,
    Nor play with her airy grace.

Her stealthy paws tread the very hall
    Where Snowball used to play,
But she only spits at the dogs our pet
    So gallantly drove away.

She is useful and mild, and does her best,
    But she is not fair to see;

And we cannot give her your place, dear,
Nor worship her as we worship thee.

A. S.

ADVERTISEMENTS.

MISS ORANTHY BLUGGAGE, the accomplished Strong-Minded Lecturer, will deliver her famous Lecture on 'WOMAN AND HER POSITION,' at Pickwick Hall, next Saturday Evening, after the usual performances.

A WEEKLY MEETING will be held at Kitchen Place, to teach young ladies how to cook. Hannah Brown will preside; and all are invited to attend.

THE DUSTPAN SOCIETY will meet on Wednesday next, and parade in the upper story of the Club House. All members to appear in uniform and shoulder their brooms at nine precisely.

Mrs BETH BOUNCER will open her new assortment of Doll's Millinery next week. The latest Paris Fashions have arrived, and orders are respectfully solicited.

A NEW PLAY will appear at the Barnville Theatre, in the course of a few weeks, which will surpass anything ever seen on the American stage. 'THE GREEK SLAVE, or Constantine the Avenger,' is the name of this thrilling drama!!!

HINTS.

If S. P. didn't use so much soap on his hands, he wouldn't always be late at breakfast. A. S. is requested not to whistle in the street. T. T. please don't forget Amy's napkin. N. W. must not fret because his dress has not nine tucks.

WEEKLY REPORT.

Meg—Good.
Jo—Bad.
Beth—Very good.
Amy—Middling.

As the President finished reading the paper (which I beg leave to assure my readers is a *bona fide* copy of one written by *bona fide* girls once upon a time), a round of applause followed, and then Mr Snodgrass rose to make a proposition.

'Mr President and gentlemen,' he began, assuming a parliamentary attitude and tone, 'I wish to propose the admission of a new member; one who highly deserves the honor, would be deeply grateful for it, and would add immensely to the spirit of the club, the literary value of the paper, and be no end jolly and nice. I propose Mr Theodore Laurence as an honorary member of the P. C. Come now, do have him.'

Jo's sudden change of tone made the girls laugh; but all looked rather anxious, and no one said a word, as Snodgrass took his seat.

'We'll put it to vote,' said the President. 'All in favor of this motion please to manifest it by saying "Aye."'

A loud response from Snodgrass, followed, to everybody's surprise, by a timid one from Beth.

'Contrary minded say "no." '

Meg and Amy were contrary minded; and Mr Winkle rose to say, with great elegance, 'We don't wish any boys; they only joke and bounce about. This is a ladies' club, and we wish to be private and proper.'

'I'm afraid he'll laugh at our paper, and make fun of us afterward,' observed Pickwick, pulling the little curl on her forehead, as she always did when doubtful.

Up bounced Snodgrass, very much in earnest. 'Sir! I give you my word as a gentleman, Laurie won't do anything of the sort. He likes to write, and he'll give a tone to our contributions, and keep us from being sentimental, don't you see? We can do so little for him, and he does so much for us, I think the least we can do is to offer him a place here, and make him welcome, if he comes.'

This artful allusion to benefits conferred, brought Tupman to his feet, looking as if he had quite made up his mind.

'Yes; we ought to do it, even if we *are* afraid. I say he may come, and his grandpa too, if he likes.'

This spirited burst from Beth electrified the club, and Jo left her seat to shake hands approvingly. 'Now then, vote again. Everybody remember it's our Laurie, and say "Aye!"' cried Snodgrass, excitedly.

'Aye! aye! aye!' replied three voices at once.

'Good! bless you! now, as there's nothing like "taking time by the *fetlock*," as Winkle characteristically observes, allow me to present the new member;' and, to the dismay of the rest of the club, Jo threw open the door of the closet, and displayed Laurie sitting on a rag-bag, flushed and twinkling with suppressed laughter.

'You rogue! you traitor! Jo, how could you?' cried the three girls, as Snodgrass led her friend triumphantly forth; and, producing both a chair and a badge, installed him in a jiffy.

'The coolness of you two rascals is amazing,' began Mr Pickwick, trying to get up an awful frown, and only succeeding in producing an amiable smile. But the new member was equal to the occasion; and, rising with a grateful salutation to the Chair, said, in the most engaging manner,—'Mr President and ladies,—I beg pardon, gentlemen,—allow me to introduce myself as Sam Weller, the very humble servant of the club.'

'Good, good!' cried Jo, pounding with the handle of the old warming-pan on which she leaned.

'My faithful friend and noble patron,' continued Laurie, with a wave of the hand, 'who has so flatteringly presented me, is not to be blamed for the base stratagem of tonight. I planned it, and she only gave in after lots of teasing.'

'Come now, don't lay it all on yourself; you know I proposed the cupboard,' broke in Snodgrass, who was enjoying the joke amazingly.

'Never you mind what she says. I'm the wretch that did it, sir,' said the new member, with a Welleresque nod to Mr Pickwick. 'But on my honor, I never will do so again, and henceforth *dewote* myself to the interest of this immortal club.'

'Hear! hear!' cried Jo, clashing the lid of the warming-pan like a cymbal.

'Go on, go on!' added Winkle and Tupman, while the President bowed benignly.

'I merely wish to say, that as a slight token of my gratitude for the honor done me, and as a means of promoting friendly relations between adjoining nations, I have set up a post-office in the hedge in the lower corner of the garden; a fine, spacious building, with padlocks on the doors, and every convenience for the mails,—also the females, if I may be allowed the expression. It's the old martin-house; but I've stopped up the door, and made the roof open, so it will hold all sorts of things, and save our valuable time. Letters, manuscripts, books and bundles can be passed in there; and, as each nation has a key, it will be uncommonly nice, I fancy. Allow me to present the club key; and, with many thanks for your favor, take my seat.'

Great applause as Mr Weller deposited a little key on the table, and subsided; the warming-pan clashed and waved wildly, and it was some time before order could be restored. A long discussion followed, and every one came out surprising, for every one did her best; so it was an unusually lively meeting, and did not adjourn till a late hour, when it broke up with three shrill cheers for the new member.

No one ever regretted the admittance of Sam Weller, for a more devoted, well-behaved, and jovial member no club could have. He certainly did add 'spirit' to the meetings, and 'a tone' to the paper; for his orations convulsed his hearers, and his contributions were excellent, being patriotic, classical, comical, or dramatic, but never sentimental. Jo regarded them as worthy of Bacon, Milton, or Shakespeare; and remodelled her own works with good effect, she thought.

The P. O. was a capital little institution, and flourished wonderfully, for nearly as many queer things passed through it as through the real office. Tragedies and cravats, poetry and pickles, garden seeds and long letters, music and gingerbread, rubbers, invitations, scoldings and puppies. The old gentleman liked the fun, and amused himself by sending odd bundles, mysterious messages, and funny telegrams; and his gardener, who was smitten with Hannah's charms, actually sent a love-letter to Jo's care. How they laughed when the secret came out, never dreaming how many love-letters that little post-office would hold in the years to come!

11

Experiments

'THE first of June; the Kings are off to the seashore tomorrow, and I'm free! Three months' vacation! how I shall enjoy it!' exclaimed Meg, coming home one warm day to find Jo laid upon the sofa in an unusual state of exhaustion, while Beth took off her dusty boots, and Amy made lemonade for the refreshment of the whole party.

'Aunt March went today, for which, oh be joyful!' said Jo. 'I was mortally afraid she'd ask me to go with her; if she had, I should have felt as if I ought to do it; but Plumfield is about as festive as a churchyard, you know, and I'd rather be excused. We had a flurry getting the old lady off, and I had a scare every time she spoke to me, for I was in such a hurry to be through that I was uncommonly helpful and sweet, and feared she'd find it impossible to part from me. I quaked till she was fairly in the carriage, and had a final fright, for, as it drove off, she popped out her head, saying, "Josy-phine, won't you—?" I didn't hear any more, for I basely turned and fled; I did actually run, and whisked round the corner, where I felt safe.'

'Poor old Jo! she came in looking as if bears were after her,' said Beth, as she cuddled her sister's feet with a motherly air.

'Aunt March is a regular samphire, is she not?' observed Amy, tasting her mixture critically.

'She means *vampire*, not sea-weed; but it don't matter; it's too warm to be particular about one's parts of speech,' murmured Jo.

'What shall you do all your vacation?' asked Amy, changing the subject, with tact.

'I shall lie abed late, and do nothing,' replied Meg, from the depths of the rocking-chair. 'I've been routed up early all winter, and had to spend my days working for other people; so now I'm going to rest and revel to my heart's content.'

'Hum!' said Jo; 'that dozy way wouldn't suit me. I've laid in a heap of books, and I'm going to improve my shining hours reading on my perch in the old apple-tree, when I'm not having l—'

'Don't say "larks!"' implored Amy, as a return snub for the 'samphire' correction.

'I'll say "nightingales," then, with Laurie; that's proper and appropriate, since he's a warbler.'

'Don't let us do any lessons, Beth, for a while, but play all the time, and rest, as the girls mean to,' proposed Amy.

'Well, I will, if mother don't mind. I want to learn some new songs, and my children need fixing up for the summer; they are dreadfully out of order, and really suffering for clothes.'

'May we, mother?' asked Meg, turning to Mrs March, who sat sewing, in what they called 'Marmee's corner.'

'You may try your experiment for a week, and see how you like it. I think by Saturday night you will find that all play, and no work, is as bad as all work, and no play.'

'Oh, dear, no! it will be delicious, I'm sure,' said Meg, complacently.

'I now propose a toast, as my "friend and pardner, Sairey Gamp," says. Fun forever, and no grubbage,' cried Jo, rising, glass in hand, as the lemonade went round.

They all drank it merrily, and began the experiment by lounging for the rest of the day. Next morning, Meg did not appear till ten o'clock; her solitary breakfast did not taste good, and the room seemed lonely and untidy, for Jo had not filled the vases, Beth had not dusted, and

Amy's books lay scattered about. Nothing was neat and pleasant but 'Marmee's corner,' which looked as usual; and there she sat, to 'rest and read,' which meant yawn, and imagine what pretty summer dresses she would get with her salary. Jo spent the morning on the river, with Laurie, and the afternoon reading and crying over 'The Wide, Wide World,' up in the apple-tree. Beth began by rummaging everything out of the big closet, where her family resided; but, getting tired before half done, she left her establishment topsy-turvy, and went to her music, rejoicing that she had no dishes to wash. Amy arranged her bower, put on her best white frock, smoothed her curls, and sat down to draw, under the honeysuckles, hoping some one would see and inquire who the young artist was. As no one appeared but an inquisitive daddy-longlegs, who examined her work with interest, she went to walk, got caught in a shower, and came home dripping.

At tea-time they compared notes, and all agreed that it had been a delightful, though unusually long day. Meg, who went shopping in the afternoon, and got a 'sweet blue muslin,' had discovered, after she had cut the breadths off, that it wouldn't wash, which mishap made her slightly cross. Jo had burnt the skin off her nose boating, and got a raging headache by reading too long. Beth was worried by the confusion of her closet, and the difficulty of learning three or four songs at once; and Amy deeply regretted the damage done her frock, for Katy Brown's party was to be the next day; and now, like Flora McFlimsey, she had 'nothing to wear.' But these were mere trifles; and they assured their mother that the experiment was working finely. She smiled, said nothing, and, with Hannah's help, did their neglected work, keeping home pleasant, and the domestic machinery running smoothly. It was astonishing what a peculiar and uncomfortable state of things was produced by the 'resting and revelling' process. The days kept getting longer and longer; the weather was unusually variable, and so were tempers; an unsettled feeling possessed every one, and Satan found plenty of mischief for the idle hands to do. As the height of luxury, Meg put out some of her sewing, and then found time hang so heavily, that she fell to snipping and spoiling her clothes, in her attempts to furbish them up, à la Moffat. Jo read till her eyes gave out, and she was sick of books; got so fidgety that even good-natured Laurie had a quarrel with her, and so reduced in spirits that she desperately wished she had gone with Aunt March. Beth got on pretty well, for she was constantly forgetting that it was to be *all play, and no work*, and fell back into her old ways, now and then; but something in the air affected her, and, more than once, her tranquillity was much disturbed; so much so, that, on one occasion, she actually shook poor dear Joanna, and told her she was 'a fright.' Amy fared worst of all, for her resources were small; and, when her sisters left her to amuse and care for herself, she soon found that accomplished and important little self a great burden. She didn't like dolls; fairy tales were childish, and one couldn't draw all the time. Tea-parties didn't amount to much, neither did picnics, unless very well conducted. 'If one could have a fine house, full of nice girls, or go travelling, the summer would be delightful; but to stay at home with three selfish sisters, and a grown-up boy, was enough to try the patience of a Boaz,' complained Miss Malaprop, after several days devoted to pleasure, fretting, and *ennui*.

No one would own that they were tired of the experiment; but, by Friday night, each acknowledged to herself that they were glad the week was nearly done. Hoping to impress the lesson more deeply, Mrs March, who had a good deal of humor, resolved to finish off the trial in an appropriate manner; so she gave Hannah a holiday, and let the girls enjoy the full effect of the play system.

When they got up on Saturday morning, there was no fire in the kitchen, no breakfast in the dining-room, and no mother anywhere to be seen.

'Mercy on us! what *has* happened?' cried Jo, staring about her in dismay.

Meg ran upstairs, and soon came back again, looking relieved, but rather bewildered, and a little ashamed.

'Mother isn't sick, only very tired, and she says she is going to stay quietly in her room all day, and let us do the best we can. It's a very queer thing for her to do, she don't act a bit like herself; but she says it *has* been a hard week for her, so we mustn't grumble, but take care of ourselves.'

'That's easy enough, and I like the idea; I'm aching for something to do—that is, some new amusement, you know,' added Jo, quickly.

In fact it *was* an immense relief to them all to have a little work, and they took hold with a will, but soon realized the truth of Hannah's saying, 'Housekeeping ain't no joke.' There was plenty of food in the larder, and, while Beth and Amy set the table, Meg and Jo got breakfast; wondering, as they did so, why servants ever talked about hard work.

'I shall take some up to mother, though she said we were not to think of her, for she'd take care of herself,' said Meg, who presided, and felt quite matronly behind the teapot.

So a tray was fitted out before any one began, and taken up, with the cook's compliments. The boiled tea was very bitter, the omelette scorched, and the biscuits speckled with saleratus; but Mrs March received her repast with thanks, and laughed heartily over it after Jo was gone.

'Poor little souls, they will have a hard time, I'm afraid; but they won't suffer, and it will do them good,' she said, producing the more palatable viands with which she had provided herself, and disposing of the bad breakfast, so that their feelings might not be hurt;—a motherly little deception, for which they were grateful.

Many were the complaints below, and great the chagrin of the head cook, at her failures. 'Never mind, I'll get the dinner, and be servant; you be missis, keep your hands nice, see company, and give orders,' said Jo, who knew still less than Meg about culinary affairs.

This obliging offer was gladly accepted; and Margaret retired to the parlor, which she hastily put in order by whisking the litter under the sofa, and shutting the blinds, to save the trouble of dusting. Jo, with perfect faith in her own powers, and a friendly desire to make up the quarrel, immediately put a note in the office, inviting Laurie to dinner.

'You'd better see what you have got before you think of having company,' said Meg, when informed of the hospitable, but rash act.

'Oh, there's corned beef, and plenty of potatoes; and I shall get some asparagus, and a lobster, "for a relish," as Hannah says. We'll have lettuce, and make a salad; I don't know how, but the book tells. I'll have blanc-mange and strawberries for dessert; and coffee, too, if you want to be elegant.'

'Don't try too many messes, Jo, for you can't make anything but gingerbread and molasses candy, fit to eat. I wash my hands of the dinner-party; and, since you have asked Laurie on your own responsibility, you may just take care of him.'

'I don't want you to do anything but be clever to him, and help to the pudding. You'll give me your advice if I get stuck, won't you?' asked Jo, rather hurt.

'Yes; but I don't know much, except about bread, and a few trifles. You had better ask mother's leave, before you order anything,' returned Meg, prudently.

'Of course I shall; I ain't a fool,' and Jo went off in a huff at the doubts expressed of her powers.

'Get what you like, and don't disturb me; I'm going out to dinner, and can't worry about things at home,' said Mrs March, when Jo spoke to her. 'I never enjoyed housekeeping, and I'm going to take a vacation today, and read, write, go visiting and amuse myself.'

The unusual spectacle of her busy mother rocking comfortably, and reading early in the morning, made Jo feel as if some natural phenomenon had occurred; for an eclipse, an earthquake, or a volcanic eruption would hardly have seemed stranger.

'Everything is out of sorts, somehow,' she said to herself, going down stairs. 'There's Beth crying; that's a sure sign that something is wrong with this family. If Amy is bothering, I'll shake her.'

Feeling very much out of sorts herself, Jo hurried into the parlor to find Beth sobbing over Pip, the canary, who lay dead in the cage, with his little claws pathetically extended, as if imploring the food, for want of which he had died.

'It's all my fault—I forgot him—there isn't a seed or drop left—oh, Pip! oh Pip! how could I be so cruel to you?' cried Beth, taking the poor thing in her hands, and trying to restore him.

Jo peeped into his half-open eye, felt his little heart, and finding him stiff and cold, shook her head, and offered her domino-box for a coffin.

'Put him in the oven, and maybe he will get warm, and revive,' said Amy, hopefully.

'He's been starved, and he shan't be baked, now he's dead. I'll make him a shroud, and he shall be buried in the grave; and I'll never have another bird, never, my Pip! for I am too bad to own one,' murmured Beth, sitting on the floor with her pet folded in her hands.

'The funeral shall be this afternoon, and we will all go. Now, don't cry, Bethy; it's a pity, but nothing goes right this week, and Pip has had the worst of the experiment. Make the shroud, and lay him in my box; and, after the dinner-party, we'll have a nice little funeral,' said Jo, beginning to feel as if she had undertaken a good deal.

Leaving the others to console Beth, she departed to the kitchen, which was in a most discouraging state of confusion. Putting on a big apron, she fell to work, and got the dishes piled up ready for washing, when she discovered that the fire was out.

'Here's a sweet prospect!' muttered Jo, slamming the stove door open, and poking vigorously among the cinders.

Having rekindled it, she thought she would go to market while the water heated. The walk revived her spirits; and, flattering herself that she had made good bargains, she trudged home again, after buying a very young lobster, some very old asparagus, and two boxes of acid strawberries. By the time she got cleared up, the dinner arrived, and the stove was red-hot. Hannah had left a pan of bread to rise, Meg had worked it up early, set it on the hearth for a second rising, and forgotten it. Meg was entertaining Sallie Gardiner, in the parlor, when the door flew open, and a floury, crocky, flushed and dishevelled figure appeared, demanding, tartly,—

'I say, isn't bread "riz" enough when it runs over the pans?'

Sallie began to laugh; but Meg nodded, and lifted her eyebrows as high as they would go, which caused the apparition to vanish, and put the sour bread into the oven without further delay. Mrs March went out, after peeping here and there to see how matters went, also saying a word of comfort to Beth, who sat making a winding-sheet, while the dear departed lay in state in the domino-box. A strange sense of helplessness fell upon the girls as the gray bonnet vanished round the corner; and despair seized them, when, a few minutes later, Miss Crocker appeared, and said she'd come to dinner. Now this lady was a thin, yellow spinster, with a sharp nose, and inquisitive eyes, who saw everything, and gossiped about all she saw. They disliked her, but had been taught to be kind to her, simply because she was old and poor, and had few friends. So Meg gave her the easy-chair, and tried to entertain her, while she asked questions, criticized everything, and told stories of the people whom she knew.

Language cannot describe the anxieties, experiences, and exertions which Jo underwent that morning; and the dinner she served up became a standing joke. Fearing to ask any more advice, she did her best alone, and discovered that something more than energy and good-will is necessary to make a cook. She boiled the asparagus hard for an hour, and was grieved to find the heads cooked off, and the stalks harder than ever. The bread burnt black; for the salad dressing so aggravated her, that she let everything else go, till she had convinced herself that she could not make it fit to eat. The lobster was a scarlet mystery to her, but she hammered and poked, till it was unshelled, and its meagre proportions concealed in a grove of lettuce-leaves. The potatoes had to be hurried, not to keep the asparagus waiting, and were not done at last. The blanc-mange was lumpy, and the strawberries not as ripe as they looked, having been skillfully 'deaconed.'

'Well, they can eat beef, and bread and butter, if they are hungry; only it's mortifying to have to spend your whole morning for nothing,' thought Jo, as she rang the bell half an hour later than usual, and stood hot, tired, and dispirited, surveying the feast spread for Laurie, accustomed to all sorts of elegance, and Miss Crocker, whose curious eyes would mark all failures, and whose tattling tongue would report them far and wide.

Poor Jo would gladly have gone under the table, as one thing after another was tasted and left; while Amy giggled, Meg looked distressed, Miss Crocker pursed up her lips, and Laurie talked and laughed with all his might, to give a cheerful tone to the festive scene. Jo's one strong point was the fruit, for she had sugared it well, and had a pitcher of rich cream to eat with it. Her hot cheeks cooled a trifle, and she drew a long breath, as the pretty glass plates went round, and every one looked graciously at the little rosy islands floating in a sea of cream. Miss Crocker tasted first, made a wry face, and drank some water hastily. Jo, who had refused, thinking there might not be enough, for they dwindled sadly after the picking over, glanced at Laurie, but he was eating away manfully, though there was a slight pucker about his mouth, and he kept his eye fixed on his plate. Amy, who was fond of delicate fare, took a heaping spoonful, hid her face in her napkin, and left the table precipitately.

'Oh, what is it?' exclaimed Jo, trembling.

'Salt instead of sugar, and the cream is sour,' replied Meg, with a tragic gesture.

Jo uttered a groan, and fell back in her chair; remembering that she had given a last hasty powdering to the berries out of one of the two boxes on the kitchen table, and had neglected to put the milk in the refrigerator. She turned scarlet, and was on the verge of crying, when she met Laurie's eyes, which *would* look merry in spite of his heroic efforts; the comical side of the affair suddenly struck her, and she laughed till the tears ran down her cheeks. So did every one else, even 'Croaker,' as the girls called the old lady; and the unfortunate dinner ended gaily, with bread and butter, olives and fun.

'I haven't strength of mind enough to clear up now, so we will sober ourselves with a funeral,' said Jo, as they rose; and Miss Crocker made ready to go, being eager to tell the new story at another friend's dinner-table.

They did sober themselves, for Beth's sake; Laurie dug a grave under the ferns in the grove, little Pip was laid in, with many tears, by his tender-hearted mistress, and covered with moss, while a wreath of violets and chickweed was hung on the stone which bore his epitaph, composed by Jo, while she struggled with the dinner:—

> 'Here lies Pip March,
>   Who died the 7th of June;
> Loved and lamented sore,
>   And not forgotten soon.'

At the conclusion of the ceremonies, Beth retired to her room, overcome with emotion and lobster; but there was no place of repose, for the beds were not made, and she found her grief much assuaged by beating up pillows and putting things in order. Meg helped Jo clear away the remains of the feast, which took half the afternoon, and left them so tired that they agreed to be contented with tea and toast for supper. Laurie took Amy to drive, which was a deed of charity, for the sour cream seemed to have had a bad effect upon her temper. Mrs March came home to find the three older girls hard at work in the middle of the afternoon; and a glance at the closet gave her an idea of the success of one part of the experiment.

Before the housewives could rest, several people called, and there was a scramble to get ready to see them; then tea must be got, errands done; and one or two bits of sewing were necessary, but neglected till the last minute. As twilight fell, dewy and still, one by one they gathered in the porch where the June roses were budding beautifully, and each groaned or sighed as she sat down, as if tired or troubled.

'What a dreadful day this has been!' began Jo, usually the first to speak.

'It has seemed shorter than usual, but so uncomfortable,' said Meg.

'Not a bit like home,' added Amy.

'It can't seem so without Marmee and little Pip,' sighed Beth, glancing, with full eyes, at the empty cage above her head.

'Here's mother, dear, and you shall have another bird tomorrow, if you want it.'

As she spoke, Mrs March came and took her place among them, looking as if her holiday had not been much pleasanter than theirs.

'Are you satisfied with your experiment, girls, or do you want another week of it?' she asked, as Beth nestled up to her, and the rest turned toward her with brightening faces, as flowers turn toward the sun.

'I don't!' cried Jo, decidedly.

'Nor I,' echoed the others.

'You think, then, that it is better to have a few duties, and live a little for others, do you?'

'Lounging and larking don't pay,' observed Jo, shaking her head. 'I'm tired of it, and mean to go to work at something right off.'

'Suppose you learn plain cooking; that's a useful accomplishment, which no woman should be without,' said Mrs March, laughing audibly at the recollection of Jo's dinner-party; for she had met Miss Crocker, and heard her account of it.

'Mother! did you go away and let everything be, just to see how we'd get on?' cried Meg, who had had suspicions all day.

'Yes; I wanted you to see how the comfort of all depends on each doing their share faithfully. While Hannah and I did your work, you got on pretty well, though I don't think you were very happy or amiable;

so I thought, as a little lesson, I would show you what happens when every one thinks only of herself. Don't you feel that it is pleasanter to help one another, to have daily duties which make leisure sweet when it comes, and to bear or forbear, that home may be comfortable and lovely to us all?'

'We do, mother, we do!' cried the girls.

'Then let me advise you to take up your little burdens again; for though they seem heavy sometimes, they are good for us, and lighten as we learn to carry them. Work is wholesome, and there is plenty for every one; it keeps us from *ennui* and mischief; is good for health and spirits, and gives us a sense of power and independence better than money or fashion.'

'We'll work like bees, and love it too; see if we don't!' said Jo. 'I'll learn plain cooking for my holiday task; and the next dinner-party I have shall be a success.'

'I'll make the set of shirts for father, instead of letting you do it, Marmee. I can and I will, though I'm not fond of sewing; that will be better than fussing over my own things, which are plenty nice enough as they are,' said Meg.

'I'll do my lessons every day, and not spend so much time with my music and dolls. I am a stupid thing, and ought to be studying, not playing,' was Beth's resolution; while Amy followed their example, by heroically declaring, 'I shall learn to make buttonholes, and attend to my parts of speech.'

'Very good! then I am quite satisfied with the experiment, and fancy that we shall not have to repeat it; only don't go to the other extreme, and delve like slaves. Have regular hours for work and play; make each day both useful and pleasant, and prove that you understand the worth of time by employing it well. Then youth will be delightful, old age will bring few regrets, and life become a beautiful success, in spite of poverty.'

'We'll remember, mother!' and they did.

12
Camp Laurence

BETH was post-mistress, for, being most at home, she could attend to it regularly, and dearly liked the daily task of unlocking the little door and distributing the mail. One July day she came in with her hands full, and went about the house leaving letters and parcels, like the penny post.

'Here's your posy, mother! Laurie never forgets that,' she said, putting the fresh nosegay in the vase that stood in 'Marmee's corner,' and was kept supplied by the affectionate boy.

'Miss Meg March, one letter, and a glove,' continued Beth, delivering the articles to her sister, who sat near her mother, stitching wristbands.

'Why, I left a pair over there, and here is only one,' said Meg, looking at the gray cotton glove.

'Didn't you drop the other in the garden?'

'No, I'm sure I didn't; for there was only one in the office.'

'I hate to have odd gloves! Never mind, the other may be found. My letter is only a translation of the German song I wanted; I guess Mr Brooke did it, for this isn't Laurie's writing.'

Mrs March glanced at Meg, who was looking very pretty in her gingham morning-gown, with the little curls blowing about her forehead, and very womanly, as she sat sewing at her little work-table, full of tidy white rolls; so, unconscious of the thought in her mother's mind, she sewed and sung while her fingers flew, and her mind was busied with girlish fancies as innocent and fresh as the pansies in her belt, that Mrs March smiled, and was satisfied.

'Two letters for Doctor Jo, a book, and a funny old hat, which covered the whole post-office, stuck outside,' said Beth, laughing, as she went into the study, where Jo sat writing.

'What a sly fellow Laurie is! I said I wished bigger hats were the fashion, because I burn my face every hot day. He said, "Why mind the fashion? wear a big hat, and be comfortable!" I said I would, if I had one, and he has sent me this, to try me; I'll wear it, for fun, and show him I *don't* care for the fashion;' and, hanging the antique broad-brim on a bust of Plato, Jo read her letters.

One from her mother made her cheeks glow, and her eyes fill, for it said to her,—

'My dear:

'I write a little word to tell you with how much satisfaction I watch your efforts to control your temper. You say nothing about your trials, failures, or successes, and think, perhaps, that no one sees them but the Friend whose help you daily ask, if I may trust the well-worn cover of your guide-book. *I*, too, have seen them all, and heartily believe in the sincerity of your resolution, since it begins to bear fruit. Go on, dear, patiently and bravely, and always believe that no one sympathizes more tenderly with you than your loving

Mother.'

'That does me good! that's worth millions of money, and pecks of praise. Oh, Marmee, I do try! I will keep on trying, and not get tired, since I have you to help me.'

Laying her head on her arms, Jo wet her little romance with a few happy tears, for she *had* thought that no one saw and appreciated her efforts to be good, and this assurance was doubly precious, doubly encouraging, because unexpected, and from the person whose commendation she most valued. Feeling stronger than ever to meet and subdue her Apollyon, she pinned the note inside her frock, as a shield and a reminder, lest she be taken unaware, and proceeded to open her other letter, quite ready for either good or bad news. In a big, dashing hand, Laurie wrote,—

'Dear Jo,
What ho!

Some English girls and boys are coming to see me tomorrow, and I want to have a jolly time. If it's fine, I'm going to pitch my tent in Longmeadow, and row up the whole crew to lunch and croquet;—have a fire, make messes, gipsey fashion, and all sorts of larks. They are nice people, and like such things. Brooke will go, to keep us boys steady, and Kate Vaughn will play propriety for the girls. I want you all to come; can't let Beth off, at any price, and nobody shall worry her. Don't bother about rations,—I'll see to that, and everything else,—only do come, there's a good fellow!

'In a tearing hurry,
Yours ever, Laurie.'

'Here's richness!' cried Jo, flying in to tell the news to Meg. 'Of course we can go, mother! it will be such a help to Laurie, for I can row, and Meg see to the lunch, and the children be useful some way.'

'I hope the Vaughns are not fine, grown-up people. Do you know anything about them, Jo?' asked Meg.

'Only that there are four of them. Kate is older than you, Fred and Frank (twins) about my age, and a little girl (Grace), who is nine or ten. Laurie knew them abroad, and liked the boys; I fancied, from the way he primmed up his mouth in speaking of her, that he didn't admire Kate much.'

'I'm so glad my French print is clean, it's just the thing, and so becoming!' observed Meg, complacently. 'Have you anything decent, Jo?'

'Scarlet and gray boating suit, good enough for me; I shall row and tramp about, so I don't want any starch to think of. You'll come, Betty?'

'If you won't let any of the boys talk to me.'

'Not a boy!'

'I like to please Laurie; and I'm not afraid of Mr Brooke, he is so kind; but I don't want to play, or sing, or say anything. I'll work hard, and not trouble any one; and you'll take care of me, Jo, so I'll go.'

'That's my good girl; you do try to fight off your shyness, and I love you for it; fighting faults isn't easy, as I know; and a cheery word kind of gives a lift. Thank you, mother,' and Jo gave the thin cheek a grateful kiss, more precious to Mrs March than if it had given her back the rosy roundness of her youth.

'I had a box of chocolate drops, and the picture I wanted to copy,' said Amy, showing her mail.

'And I got a note from Mr Laurence, asking me to come over and play to him tonight, before the lamps are lighted, and I shall go,' added Beth, whose friendship with the old gentleman prospered finely.

'Now let's fly round, and do double duty today, so that we can play tomorrow with free minds,' said Jo, preparing to replace her pen with a broom.

When the sun peeped into the girls' room early next morning, to promise them a fine day, he saw a comical sight. Each had made such preparation for the fête as seemed necessary and proper. Meg had an extra row of little curl papers across her forehead, Jo had copiously anointed her afflicted face with cold cream, Beth had taken Joanna to bed with her to atone for the approaching separation, and Amy had capped the climax by putting a clothes-pin on her nose, to uplift the offending feature. It was one of the kind artists use to hold the paper on their drawing-boards; therefore, quite appropriate and effective for the purpose to which it was now put. This funny spectacle appeared to amuse the sun, for he burst out with such radiance that Jo woke up, and roused all her sisters by a hearty laugh at Amy's ornament.

Sunshine and laughter were good omens for a pleasure party, and soon a lively bustle began in both houses. Beth, who was ready first, kept reporting what went on next door, and enlivened her sisters' toilets by frequent telegrams from the window.

'There goes the man with the tent! I see Mrs Baker doing up the lunch, in a hamper, and a great basket. Now Mr Laurence is looking up at the sky, and the weathercock; I wish he would go, too! There's Laurie looking like a sailor,—nice boy! Oh, mercy me! here's a carriage full of people—a tall lady, a little girl, and two dreadful boys. One is lame; poor thing, he's got a crutch! Laurie didn't tell us that. Be quick, girls! it's getting late. Why, there is Ned Moffat, I do declare. Look, Meg! isn't that the man who bowed to you one day, when we were shopping?'

'So it is; how queer that he should come! I thought he was at the Mountains. There is Sallie; I'm glad she got back in time. Am I all right, Jo?' cried Meg, in a flutter.

'A regular daisy; hold up your dress, and put your hat straight; it looks sentimental tipped that way, and will fly off at the first puff. Now, then, come on!'

'Oh, oh, Jo! you ain't going to wear that awful hat? It's too absurd! You shall *not* make a guy of yourself,' remonstrated Meg, as Jo tied down, with a red ribbon, the broad-brimmed, old-fashioned Leghorn Laurie had sent for a joke.

'I just will, though! it's capital; so shady, light, and big. It will make fun; and I don't mind being a guy, if I'm comfortable.' With that Jo marched straight away, and the rest followed; a bright little band of sisters, all looking their best, in summer suits, with happy faces, under the jaunty hat-brims.

Laurie ran to meet, and present them to his friends, in the most cordial manner. The lawn was the reception room, and for several minutes a lively scene was enacted there. Meg was grateful to see that Miss Kate, though twenty, was dressed with a simplicity which American girls would do well to imitate; and she was much flattered by Mr Ned's assurances that he came especially to see her. Jo understood why Laurie 'primmed up his mouth' when speaking of Kate, for that young lady had a stand-off-don't-touch-me air, which contrasted strongly with the free and easy demeanor of the other girls. Beth took an observation of the new boys, and decided that the lame one was not 'dreadful,' but gentle and feeble, and she would be kind to him, on that account. Amy found Grace a well-mannered, merry little person; and, after staring dumbly at one another for a few minutes, they suddenly became very good friends.

Tents, lunch, and croquet utensils having been sent on beforehand, the party was soon embarked, and the two boats pushed off together, leaving Mr Laurence waving his hat on the shore. Laurie and Jo rowed one boat; Mr Brooke and Ned the other; while Fred Vaughn, the riotous twin, did his best to upset both, by paddling about in a wherry, like a disturbed waterbug. Jo's funny hat deserved a vote of thanks, for it was of general utility; it broke the ice in the beginning, by producing a laugh; it created quite a refreshing breeze, flapping to and fro, as she rowed, and would make an excellent umbrella for the whole party, if a shower came up, she said. Kate looked rather amazed at Jo's proceedings, especially as she exclaimed 'Christopher Columbus!' when she lost her oar; and Laurie said, 'My dear fellow, did I hurt you?' when he tripped over her feet in taking his place. But after putting up her glass to examine the queer girl several times, Miss Kate decided that she was 'odd, but rather clever,' and smiled upon her from afar.

Meg, in the other boat, was delightfully situated, face to face with the rowers, who both admired the prospect, and feathered their oars with uncommon 'skill and dexterity.' Mr Brooke was a grave, silent young man, with handsome brown eyes, and a pleasant voice. Meg liked his quiet manners, and considered him a walking encyclopaedia of useful knowledge. He never talked to her much; but he looked at her a good deal, and she felt sure that he did not regard her with aversion. Ned being in college, of course put on all the airs which Freshmen think it their bounden duty to assume; he was not very wise, but very good-natured and merry, and, altogether, an excellent person to carry on a picnic. Sallie Gardiner was absorbed in keeping her white piqué dress clean, and chattering with the ubiquitous Fred, who kept Beth in constant terror by his pranks.

It was not far to Longmeadow; but the tent was pitched, and the wickets down, by the time they arrived. A pleasant green field, with three wide-spreading oaks in the middle, and a smooth strip of turf for croquet.

'Welcome to Camp Laurence!' said the young host, as they landed, with exclamations of delight. 'Brooke is commander-in chief; I am commissary-general; the other fellows are staff-officers; and you, ladies, are company. The tent is for your especial benefit, and that oak is your drawing-room; this is the mess-room, and the third is the camp kitchen. Now let's have a game before it gets hot, and then we'll see about dinner.'

Frank, Beth, Amy, and Grace, sat down to watch the game played by the other eight. Mr Brooke chose Meg, Kate, and Fred; Laurie took Sallie, Jo, and Ned. The

Englishers played well; but the Americans played better, and contested every inch of the ground as strongly as if the spirit of '76 inspired them. Jo and Fred had several skirmishes, and once narrowly escaped high words. Jo was through the last wicket, and had missed the stroke, which failure ruffled her a good deal. Fred was close behind her, and his turn came before hers; he gave a stroke, his ball hit the wicket, and stopped an inch on the wrong side. No one was very near; and, running up to examine, he gave it a sly nudge with his toe, which put it just an inch on the right side.

'I'm through! now, Miss Jo, I'll settle you, and get in first,' cried the young gentleman, swinging his mallet for another blow.

'You pushed it; I saw you; it's my turn now,' said Jo, sharply.

'Upon my word I didn't move it! it rolled a bit, perhaps, but that is allowed; so stand off, please, and let me have a go at the stake.'

'We don't cheat in America; but *you* can, if you choose,' said Jo, angrily.

'Yankees are a deal the most tricky, everybody knows. There you go,' returned Fred, croqueting her ball far away.

Jo opened her lips to say something rude; but checked herself in time, colored up to her forehead, and stood a minute, hammering down a wicket with all her might, while Fred hit the stake, and declared himself out, with much exultation. She went off to get her ball, and was a long time finding it, among the bushes; but she came back, looking cool and quiet, and waited her turn patiently. It took several strokes to regain the place she had lost; and, when she got there, the other side had nearly won, for Kate's ball was the last but one, and lay near the stake.

'By George, it's all up with us! Good-by, Kate; Miss Jo owes me one, so you are finished,' cried Fred, excitedly, as they all drew near to see the finish.

'Yankees have a trick of being generous to their enemies,' said Jo, with a look that made the lad redden, 'especially when they beat them,' she added, as, leaving Kate's ball untouched, she won the game by a clever stroke.

Laurie threw up his hat; then remembered that it wouldn't do to exult over the defeat of his guests, and stopped in the middle of a cheer to whisper to his friend,—

'Good for you, Jo! he did cheat, I saw him; we can't tell him so, but he won't do it again, take my word for it.'

Meg drew her aside, under pretence of pinning up a loose braid, and said, approvingly,—

'It was dreadfully provoking; but you kept your temper, and I'm so glad, Jo.'

'Don't praise me, Meg, for I could box his ears this minute. I should certainly have boiled over, if I hadn't stayed among the nettles till I got my rage under enough to hold my tongue. It's simmering now, so I hope he'll keep out of my way,' returned Jo, biting her lips, as she glowered at Fred from under her big hat.

'Time for lunch,' said Mr Brooke, looking at his watch. 'Commissary-general, will you make the fire, and get water, while Miss March, Miss Sallie, and I spread the table. Who can make good coffee?'

'Jo can,' said Meg, glad to recommend her sister. So Jo, feeling that her late lessons in cookery were to do her honor, went to preside over the coffee-pot, while the children collected dry sticks, and the boys made a fire, and got water from a spring near by. Miss Kate sketched, and Frank talked to Beth, who was making little mats of braided rushes, to serve as plates.

The commander-in-chief and his aides soon spread the tablecloth with an inviting array of eatables and drinkables, prettily decorated with green leaves. Jo announced that the coffee was ready, and every one settled themselves to a hearty meal; for youth is seldom dyspeptic, and exercise develops wholesome appetites. A very merry lunch it was; for everything seemed fresh and funny, and frequent peals of laughter startled a venerable horse, who fed near by. There was a pleasing inequality in the table, which produced many mishaps to cups and plates; acorns dropped into the milk, little black ants partook of the refreshments without being invited, and fuzzy caterpillars swung down from the tree, to see what was going on. Three white-headed children peeped over the fence, and an objectionable dog barked at them from the other side of the river, with all his might and main.

'There's salt, here, if you prefer it,' said Laurie, as he handed Jo a saucer of berries.

'Thank you; I prefer spiders,' she replied, fishing up two unwary little ones, who had gone to a creamy death. 'How dare you remind me of that horrid dinner-party, when yours is so nice in every way?' added Jo, as they both laughed, and ate out of one plate, the china having run short.

'I had an uncommonly good time that day, and haven't got over it yet. This is no credit to me, you know; I don't do anything; it's you, and Meg, and Brooke, who make it go, and I'm no end obliged to you. What shall we do when we can't eat any more?' asked Laurie, feeling that his trump card had been played when lunch was over.

'Have games, till it's cooler. I brought "Authors," and I dare say Miss Kate knows something new and nice. Go and ask her; she's company, and you ought to stay with her more.'

'Aren't you company, too? I thought she'd suit Brooke; but he keeps talking to Meg, and Kate just stares at them through that ridiculous glass of hers. I'm going, so you needn't try to preach propriety, for you can't do it, Jo.'

Miss Kate did know several new games; and as the girls would not, and the boys could not, eat any more, they all adjourned to the drawing-room, to play 'Rigmarole.'

'One person begins a story, any nonsense you like, and tells as long as they please, only taking care to stop short at some exciting point, when the next takes it up, and does the same. It's very funny, when well done, and makes a perfect jumble of tragical comical stuff to laugh over. Please start it, Mr Brooke,' said Kate, with a commanding gesture, which surprised Meg, who treated the tutor with as much respect as any other gentleman.

Lying on the grass, at the feet of the two young ladies, Mr Brooke obediently began the story, with the handsome brown eyes steadily fixed upon the sun-shiny river.

'Once upon a time, a knight went out into the world to seek his fortune, for he had nothing but his sword and his shield. He travelled a long while, nearly eight-and-twenty years, and had a hard time of it, till he came to the palace of a good old king, who had offered a reward to any one who would tame and train a fine, but unbroken colt, of which he was very fond. The knight agreed to try, and got on slowly, but surely; for the colt was a gallant fellow, and soon learned to love his new master, though he was freakish and wild. Every day, when he gave his lessons to this pet of the king's, the knight rode him through the city; and, as he rode, he looked everywhere for a certain beautiful face, which he had seen many times in his dreams, but never found. One day, as he went prancing down a quiet street, he saw at the window of a ruinous castle the lovely face. He was delighted, inquired who lived in this old castle, and was told that several captive princesses were kept there by a spell, and spun all day to lay up money to buy their liberty. The knight wished intensely that he could free them; but he was poor, and could only go by each day, watching for the sweet face, and longing to see it out in the sunshine. At last, he resolved to get into the castle, and ask how he could help them. He went and knocked; the great door flew open, and he beheld—'

'A ravishingly lovely lady, who exclaimed, with a cry of rapture, "At last! at last!"' continued Kate, who had read French novels, and admired the style. '"'Tis she!" cried Count Gustave, and fell at her feet in an ecstasy of joy. "Oh, rise!" she said, extending a hand of marble fairness. "Never! till you tell me how I may rescue you," swore the knight, still kneeling, "Alas, my cruel fate condemns me to remain here till my tyrant is destroyed," "Where is the villain?" "In the mauve salon; go, brave heart, and save me from despair." "I obey, and return victorious or dead!" With these thrilling words he rushed away, and, flinging open the door of the mauve salon, was about to enter, when he received—'

'A stunning blow from the big Greek lexicon, which an old fellow in a black gown fired at him,' said Ned. 'Instantly Sir What's-his name recovered himself, pitched the tyrant out of the window, and turned to join the lady, victorious, but with a bump on his brow; found the door locked, tore up the curtains, made a rope ladder, got half-way down when the ladder broke, and he went head first into the moat, sixty feet below. Could swim like a duck, paddled round the castle till he came to a little door guarded by two stout fellows; knocked their heads together till they cracked like a couple of nuts, then, by a trifling exertion of his prodigious strength, he smashed in the door, went up a pair of stone steps covered with dust a foot thick, toads as big as your fist, and spiders that would frighten you into hysterics, Miss March. At the top of these steps he came plump upon a sight that took his breath away and chilled his blood—'

'A tall figure, all in white, with a veil over its face, and a lamp in its wasted hand,' went on Meg. 'It beckoned, gliding noiselessly before him down a corridor as dark and cold as any tomb. Shadowy effigies in armor stood on either side, a dead silence reigned, the lamp burned blue, and the ghostly figure ever and anon turned its face toward him, showing the glitter of awful eyes through its white veil. They reached a curtained door, behind which sounded lovely music; he sprang forward to enter, but the spectre plucked him back, and waved, threateningly, before him a—'

'Snuff-box,' said Jo, in a sepulchral tone, which convulsed the audience. '"Thankee," said the knight, politely, as he took a pinch, and sneezed seven times so violently that his head fell off. "Ha! ha!" laughed the ghost; and, having peeped through the keyhole at the princesses spinning away for dear life, the evil spirit picked up her victim and put him in a large tin box, where there were eleven other knights packed together without their heads, like sardines, who all rose and began to—'

'Dance a hornpipe,' cut in Fred, as Jo paused for breath; 'and, as they danced, the rubbishy old castle turned to a man-of-war in full sail. "Up with the jib, reef the tops'l halliards, helm hard a lee, and man the guns," roared the captain, as a Portuguese pirate hove in sight, with a flag black as ink flying from her foremast. "Go in and win my hearties," says the captain; and a tremendous fight began. Of course the British beat—they always do; and, having taken the pirate captain prisoner, sailed slap over the schooner, whose decks were piled with dead, and whose lee-scuppers ran blood, for the order had been "Cutlasses, and die hard." "Bosun's mate, take a bight of the flying jib sheet, and start this villain if he don't confess his sins double quick," said the British captain. The Portuguese held his tongue like a brick, and walked the plank, while the jolly tars cheered like mad. But the sly dog dived, came up under the man-of war, scuttled her, and down she went, with all sail set, "To the bottom of the sea, sea, sea," where—'

'Oh, gracious! what *shall* I say?' cried Sallie, as Fred ended his rigmarole, in which he had jumbled together, pell-mell, nautical phrases and facts, out of one of his favorite books. 'Well, they went to the bottom, and a nice mermaid welcomed them, but was much grieved on finding the box of headless knights, and kindly pickled them in brine, hoping to discover the mystery about them; for, being a woman, she was curious. By and by a diver came down, and the mermaid said, "I'll give you this box of pearls if you can take it up;" for she wanted to restore the poor things to life, and couldn't raise the heavy load herself. So the diver hoisted it up, and was much disappointed, on opening it, to find no pearls.

He left it in a great lonely field, where it was found by a—'

'Little goose-girl, who kept a hundred fat geese in the field,' said Amy, when Sallie's invention gave out. 'The little girl was sorry for them, and asked an old woman what she should do to help them. "Your geese will tell you, they know everything," said the old woman. So she asked what she should use for new heads, since the old ones were lost, and all the geese opened their hundred mouths, and screamed—'

'"Cabbages!" continued Laurie, promptly. "Just the thing," said the girl, and ran to get twelve fine ones from her garden. She put them on, the knights revived at once, thanked her, and went on their way rejoicing, never knowing the difference, for there were so many other heads like them in the world, that no one thought anything of it. The knight in whom I'm interested went back to find the pretty face, and learned that the princesses had spun themselves free, and all gone to be married, but one. He was in a great state of mind at that; and, mounting the colt, who stood by him through thick and thin, rushed to the castle to see which was left. Peeping over the hedge, he saw the queen of his affections picking flowers in her garden. "Will you give me a rose?" said he. "You must come and get it; I can't come to you; it isn't proper," said she, as sweet as honey.

He tried to climb over the hedge, but it seemed to grow higher and higher; then he tried to push through, but it grew thicker and thicker, and he was in despair. So he patiently broke twig after twig, till he had made a little hole, through which he peeped, saying, imploringly, "Let me in! let me in!" But the pretty princess did not seem to understand, for she picked her roses quietly, and left him to fight his way in. Whether he did or not, Frank will tell you.'

'I can't; I'm not playing, I never do,' said Frank, dismayed at the sentimental predicament out of which he was to rescue the absurd couple. Beth had disappeared behind Jo, and Grace was asleep.

'So the poor knight is to be left sticking in the hedge, is he?' asked Mr Brooke, still watching the river, and playing with the wild rose in his button-hole.

'I guess the princess gave him a posy, and opened the gate, after awhile,' said Laurie, smiling to himself, as he threw acorns at his tutor.

'What a piece of nonsense we have made! With practice we might do something quite clever. Do you know "Truth?"' asked Sallie, after they had laughed over their story.

'I hope so,' said Meg, soberly.

'The game, I mean?'

'What is it?' said Fred.

'Why, you pile up your hands, choose a number, and draw out in turn, and the person who draws out the number has to answer truly any questions put by the rest. It's great fun.'

'Let's try it,' said Jo, who liked new experiments.

Miss Kate and Mr Brooke, Meg and Ned, declined; but Fred, Sallie, Jo and Laurie piled and drew; and the lot fell to Laurie.

'Who are your heroes?' asked Jo.

'Grandfather and Napoleon.'

'What lady do you think prettiest?' said Sallie.

'Margaret.'

'Which do you like best?' from Fred.

'Jo, of course.'

'What silly questions you ask!' and Jo gave a disdainful shrug as the rest laughed at Laurie's matter-of-fact tone.

'Try again; Truth isn't a bad game,' said Fred.

'It's a very good one for you,' retorted Jo, in a low voice.

Her turn came next.

'What is your greatest fault?' asked Fred, by way of testing in her the virtue he lacked himself.

'A quick temper.'

'What do you most wish for?' said Laurie.

'A pair of boot-lacings,' returned Jo, guessing and defeating his purpose.

'Not a true answer; you must say what you really do want most.'

'Genius; don't you wish you could give it to me, Laurie?' and she slyly smiled in his disappointed face.

'What virtues do you most admire in a man?' asked Sallie.

'Courage and honesty.'

'Now my turn,' said Fred, as his hand came last.

'Let's give it to him,' whispered Laurie to Jo, who nodded, and asked at once,—

'Didn't you cheat at croquet?'

'Well, yes, a little bit.'

'Good! Didn't you take your story out of "The Sea Lion?"' said Laurie.

'Rather.'

'Don't you think the English nation perfect in every respect?' asked Sallie.

'I should be ashamed of myself if I didn't.'

'He's a true John Bull. Now, Miss Sallie, you shall have a chance without waiting to draw. I'll harrow up your feelings first by asking if you don't think you are something of a flirt,' said Laurie, as Jo nodded to Fred, as a sign that peace was declared.

'You impertinent boy! of course I'm not,' exclaimed Sallie, with an air that proved the contrary.

'What do you hate most?' asked Fred.

'Spiders and rice pudding.'

'What do you like best?' asked Jo.

'Dancing and French gloves.'

'Well, *I* think Truth is a very silly play; let's have a sensible game of Authors, to refresh our minds,' proposed Jo.

Ned, Frank, and the little girls joined in this, and, while it went on, the three elders sat apart, talking. Miss Kate took out her sketch again, and Margaret watched her, while Mr Brooke lay on the grass, with a book, which he did not read.

'How beautifully you do it; I wish I could draw,' said Meg, with mingled admiration and regret in her voice. 'Why don't you learn? I should think you had taste and talent for it,' replied Miss Kate, graciously.

'I haven't time.'

'Your mamma prefers other accomplishments, I fancy. So did mine; but I proved to her that I had talent, by taking a few lessons privately, and then she was quite willing I should go on. Can't you do the same with your governess?'

'I have none.'

'I forgot; young ladies in America go to school more than with us. Very fine schools they are, too, papa says. You go to a private one, I suppose?'

'I don't go at all; I am a governess myself.'

'Oh, indeed!' said Miss Kate; but she might as well have said, 'Dear me, how dreadful!' for her tone implied it, and something in her face made Meg color, and wish she had not been so frank.

Mr Brooke looked up, and said, quickly, 'Young ladies in America love independence as much as their ancestors did, and are admired and respected for supporting themselves.'

'Oh, yes; of course! it's very nice and proper in them to do so. We have many most respectable and worthy young women, who do the same; and are employed by the nobility, because, being the daughters of gentlemen, they are both well-bred and accomplished, you know,' said Miss Kate, in a patronizing tone, that hurt Meg's pride, and made her work seem not only more distasteful, but degrading.

'Did the German song suit, Miss March?' inquired Mr Brooke, breaking an awkward pause.

'Oh, yes! it was very sweet, and I'm much obliged to whoever translated it for me;' and Meg's downcast face brightened as she spoke.

'Don't you read German?' asked Miss Kate, with a look of surprise.

'Not very well. My father, who taught me, is away, and I don't get on very fast alone, for I've no one to correct my pronunciation.'

'Try a little now; here is Schiller's "Mary Stuart," and a tutor who loves to teach,' and Mr Brooke laid his book on her lap, with an inviting smile.

'It's so hard, I'm afraid to try,' said Meg, grateful, but bashful in the presence of the accomplished young lady beside her.

'I'll read a bit, to encourage you;' and Miss Kate read one of the most beautiful passages, in a perfectly correct, but perfectly expressionless, manner.

Mr Brooke made no comment, as she returned the book to Meg, who said, innocently,—

'I thought it was poetry.'

'Some of it is; try this passage.'

There was a queer smile about Mr Brooke's mouth, as he opened at poor Mary's lament.

Meg, obediently following the long grass-blade which her new tutor used to point with, read, slowly and timidly, unconsciously making poetry of the hard words, by the soft intonation of her musical voice. Down the page went the green guide, and presently, forgetting her listener in the beauty of the sad scene, Meg read as if alone, giving a little touch of tragedy to the words of the unhappy queen. If she had seen the brown eyes then, she would have stopped short; but she never looked up, and the lesson was not spoilt for her.

'Very well, indeed!' said Mr Brooke, as she paused, quite ignoring her many mistakes, and looking as if he did, indeed, 'love to teach.'

Miss Kate put up her glass, and, having taken a survey of the little tableau before her, shut her sketchbook, saying, with condescension,—

'You've a nice accent, and, in time, will be a clever reader. I advise you to learn, for German is a valuable accomplishment to teachers. I must look after Grace, she is romping;' and Miss Kate strolled away, adding to herself, with a shrug, 'I didn't come to chaperone a governess, though she *is* young and pretty. What odd people these Yankees are! I'm afraid Laurie will be quite spoilt among them.'

'I forgot that English people rather turn up their noses at governesses, and don't treat them as we do,' said Meg, looking after the retreating figure with an annoyed expression.

'Tutors, also, have rather a hard time of it there, as I know to my sorrow. There's no place like America for us workers, Miss Margaret,' and Mr Brooke looked so contented and cheerful, that Meg was ashamed to lament her hard lot.

'I'm glad I live in it, then. I don't like my work, but I get a good deal of satisfaction out of it, after all, so I won't complain; I only wish I liked teaching as you do.'

'I think you would, if you had Laurie for a pupil. I shall be very sorry to lose him next year,' said Mr Brooke, busily punching holes in the turf.

'Going to college, I suppose?' Meg's lips asked that question, but her eyes added, 'And what becomes of you?'

'Yes; it's high time he went, for he is nearly ready, and as soon as he is off I shall turn soldier.'

'I'm glad of that!' exclaimed Meg; 'I should think every young man would want to go; though it is hard for the mothers and sisters, who stay at home,' she added, sorrowfully.

'I have neither, and very few friends, to care whether I live or die,' said Mr Brooke, rather bitterly, as he absently put the dead rose in the hole he had made, and covered it up, like a little grave.

'Laurie and his grandfather would care a great deal, and we should all be very sorry to have any harm happen to you,' said Meg, heartily.

'Thank you; that sounds pleasant,' began Mr Brooke, looking cheerful again; but, before he could finish his speech, Ned, mounted on the old horse, came lumbering up, to display his equestrian skill before the young ladies, and there was no more quiet that day.

'Don't you love to ride?' asked Grace of Amy, as they

stood resting, after a race round the field with the others, led by Ned.

'I dote upon it; my sister Meg used to ride, when papa was rich, but we don't keep any horses now,—except Ellen Tree,' added Amy, laughing.

'Tell me about Ellen Tree; is it a donkey?' asked Grace, curiously.

'Why, you see, Jo is crazy about horses, and so am I, but we've only got an old side-saddle, and no horse. Out in our garden is an apple-tree, that has a nice low branch; so I put the saddle on it, fixed some reins on the part that turns up, and we bounce away on Ellen Tree whenever we like.'

'How funny!' laughed Grace. 'I have a pony at home, and ride nearly every day in the park, with Fred and Kate; it's very nice, for my friends go too, and the Row is full of ladies and gentlemen.'

'Dear, how charming! I hope I shall go abroad, some day; but I'd rather go to Rome than the Row,' said Amy, who had not the remotest idea what the Row was, and wouldn't have asked for the world.

Frank, sitting just behind the little girls, heard what they were saying, and pushed his crutch away from him with an impatient gesture, as he watched the active lads going through all sorts of comical gymnastics. Beth, who was collecting the scattered

Author-cards, looked up and said, in her shy yet friendly way,—

'I'm afraid you are tired; can I do anything for you?'

'Talk to me, please; it's dull, sitting by myself,' answered Frank, who had evidently been used to being made much of at home.

If he had asked her to deliver a Latin oration, it would not have seemed a more impossible task to bashful Beth; but there was no place to run to, no Jo to hide behind now, and the poor boy looked so wistfully at her, that she bravely resolved to try.

'What do you like to talk about?' she asked, fumbling over the cards, and dropping half as she tried to tie them up.

'Well, I like to hear about cricket, and boating, and hunting,' said Frank, who had not yet learned to suit his amusements to his strength.

'My heart! whatever shall I do! I don't know anything about them,' thought Beth; and, forgetting the boy's misfortune in her flurry, she said, hoping to make him talk, 'I never saw any hunting, but I suppose you know all about it.'

'I did once; but I'll never hunt again, for I got hurt leaping a confounded five-barred gate; so there's no more horses and hounds for me,' said Frank, with a sigh that made Beth hate herself for her innocent blunder.

'Your deer are much prettier than our ugly buffaloes,' she said, turning to the prairies for help, and feeling glad that she had read one of the boys' books in which Jo delighted.

Buffaloes proved soothing and satisfactory; and, in her eagerness to amuse another, Beth forgot herself, and was quite unconscious of her sister's surprise and delight at the unusual spectacle of Beth talking away to one of the dreadful boys, against whom she had begged protection.

'Bless her heart! She pities him, so she is good to him,' said Jo, beaming at her from the croquet-ground.

'I always said she was a little saint,' added Meg, as if there could be no further doubt of it.

'I haven't heard Frank laugh so much for ever so long,' said Grace to Amy, as they sat discussing dolls, and making tea-sets out of the acorn-cups.

'My sister Beth is a very fastidious girl, when she likes to be,' said Amy, well pleased at Beth's success. She meant 'fascinating,' but, as Grace didn't know the exact meaning of either word, 'fastidious' sounded well, and made a good impression.

An impromptu circus, fox and geese, and an amicable game of croquet, finished the afternoon. At sunset the tent was struck, hampers packed, wickets pulled up, boats loaded, and the whole party floated down the river, singing at the tops of their voices. Ned, getting sentimental, warbled a serenade with the pensive refrain,—

'*Alone, alone, ah! woe, alone,*'

and at the lines—

'*We each are young, we each have a heart,*
Oh, why should we stand thus coldly apart?'

he looked at Meg with such a lackadaisical expression, that she laughed outright, and spoilt his song.

'How can you be so cruel to me?' he whispered, under cover of a lively chorus; 'you've kept close to that starched-up English woman all day, and now you snub me.'

'I didn't mean to; but you looked so funny I really couldn't help it,' replied Meg, passing over the first part of his reproach; for it was quite true that she *had* shunned him, remembering the Moffat party and the talk after it.

Ned was offended, and turned to Sallie for consolation, saying to her, rather pettishly, 'There isn't a bit of flirt in that girl, is there?'

'Not a particle; but she's a dear,' returned Sallie,

defending her friend even while confessing her shortcomings.

'She's not a stricken deer, anyway,' said Ned, trying to be witty, and succeeding as well as very young gentlemen usually do.

On the lawn where it had gathered, the little party separated with cordial good-nights and good-byes, for the Vaughns were going to Canada. As the four sisters went home through the garden, Miss Kate looked after them, saying, without the patronizing tone in her voice, 'In spite of their demonstrative manners, American girls are very nice when one knows them.'

'I quite agree with you,' said Mr Brooke.

13

Castles In The Air

LAURIE lay luxuriously swinging to and fro in his hammock, one warm September afternoon, wondering what his neighbors were about, but too lazy to go and find out. He was in one of his moods; for the day had been both unprofitable and unsatisfactory, and he was wishing he could live it over again. The hot weather made him indolent; and he had shirked his studies, tried Mr Brooke's patience to the utmost, displeased his grandfather by practising half the afternoon, frightened the maid-servants half out of their wits, by mischievously hinting that one of his dogs was going mad, and, after high words with the stableman about some fancied neglect of his horse, he had flung himself into his hammock, to fume over

237

the stupidity of the world in general, till the peace of the lovely day quieted him in spite of himself. Staring up into the green gloom of the horse-chestnut trees above him, he dreamed dreams of all sorts, and was just imagining himself tossing on the ocean, in a voyage round the world, when the sound of voices brought him ashore in a flash. Peeping through the meshes of the hammock, he saw the Marches coming out, as if bound on some expedition.

'What in the world are those girls about now?' thought Laurie, opening his sleepy eyes to take a good look, for there was something rather peculiar in the appearance of his neighbors. Each wore a large, flapping hat, a brown linen pouch slung over one shoulder, and carried a long staff; Meg had a cushion, Jo a book, Beth a dipper, and Amy a portfolio. All walked quietly through the garden, out at the little back gate, and began to climb the hill that lay between the house and river.

'Well, that's cool!' said Laurie to himself, 'to have a picnic and never ask me. They can't be going in the boat, for they haven't got the key. Perhaps they forgot it; I'll take it to them, and see what's going on.'

Though possessed of half a dozen hats, it took him some time to find one; then there was a hunt for the key, which was at last discovered in his pocket, so that the girls were quite out of sight when he leaped the fence and ran after them. Taking the shortest way to the boat-house, he waited for them to appear; but no one came, and he went up the hill to take an observation. A grove of pines covered one part of it, and from the heart of this green spot came a clearer sound than the soft sigh of the pines, or the drowsy chirp of the crickets.

'Here's a landscape!' thought Laurie, peeping through the bushes, and looking wide awake and good-natured already.

It *was* rather a pretty little picture; for the sisters sat together in the shady nook, with sun and shadow flickering over them,—the aromatic wind lifting their hair and cooling their cheeks,—and all the little wood-people going on with their affairs as if these were no strangers, but old friends. Meg sat upon her cushion, sewing daintily with her white hands, and looking as fresh and sweet as a rose, in her pink dress, among the green. Beth was sorting the cones that lay thick under the hemlock near by, for she made pretty things of them. Amy was sketching a group of ferns, and Jo was knitting as she read aloud. A shadow passed over the boy's face as he watched them, feeling that he ought to go, because uninvited; yet lingering, because home seemed very lonely, and this quiet party in the woods most attractive to his restless spirit. He stood so still, that a squirrel, busy with its harvesting, ran down a pine close beside him, saw him suddenly, and skipped back, scolding so shrilly that Beth looked up, espied the wistful face behind the birches, and beckoned with a reassuring smile.

'May I come in, please? or shall I be a bother?' he asked, advancing slowly.

Meg lifted her eyebrows, but Jo scowled at her defiantly, and said, at once, 'Of course you may. We should have asked you before, only we thought you wouldn't care for such a girl's game as this.'

'I always like your games; but if Meg don't want me, I'll go away.'

'I've no objection, if you do something; it's against the rule to be idle here,' replied Meg, gravely, but graciously.

'Much obliged; I'll do anything if you'll let me stop a bit, for it's as dull as the desert of Sahara down there. Shall I sew, read, cone, draw, or do all at once? Bring on your bears; I'm ready,' and Laurie sat down with a submissive expression delightful to behold.

'Finish this story while I set my heel,' said Jo, handing him the book.

'Yes'm,' was the meek answer, as he began, doing his best to prove his gratitude for the favor of an admission into the 'Busy Bee Society.'

The story was not a long one, and, when it was

finished, he ventured to ask a few questions as a reward of merit.

'Please, ma'am, could I inquire if this highly instructive and charming institution is a new one?'

'Would you tell him?' asked Meg of her sisters.

'He'll laugh,' said Amy, warningly.

'Who cares?' said Jo.

'I guess he'll like it,' added Beth.

'Of course I shall! I give you my word I won't laugh. Tell away, Jo, and don't be afraid.'

'The idea of being afraid of you! Well, you see we used to play "Pilgrim's Progress," and we have been going on with it in earnest, all winter and summer.'

'Yes, I know,' said Laurie, nodding wisely.

'Who told you?' demanded Jo.

'Spirits.'

'No, it was me; I wanted to amuse him one night when you were all away, and he was rather dismal. He did like it, so don't scold, Jo,' said Beth, meekly.

'You can't keep a secret. Never mind; it saves trouble now.'

'Go on, please,' said Laurie, as Jo became absorbed in her work, looking a trifle displeased.

'Oh, didn't she tell you about this new plan of ours? Well, we have tried not to waste our holiday, but each has had a task, and worked at it with a will. The vacation is nearly over, the stints are all done, and we are ever so glad that we didn't dawdle.'

'Yes, I should think so;' and Laurie thought regretfully of his own idle days.

'Mother likes to have us out of doors as much as possible; so we bring our work here, and have nice times. For the fun of it we bring our things in these bags, wear the old hats, use poles to climb the hill, and play pilgrims, as we used to do years ago. We call this hill the "Delectable Mountain," for we can look far away and see the country where we hope to live some time.'

Jo pointed, and Laurie sat up to examine; for through an opening in the wood one could look across the wide, blue river,—the meadows on the other side,—far over the outskirts of the great city, to the green hills that rose to meet the sky. The sun was low, and the heavens glowed with the splendor of an autumn sunset. Gold and purple clouds lay on the hill-tops; and rising high into the ruddy light were silvery white peaks, that shone like the airy spires of some Celestial City.

'How beautiful that is!' said Laurie softly, for he was quick to see and feel beauty of any kind.

'It's often so; and we like to watch it, for it is never the same, but always splendid,' replied Amy, wishing she could paint it.

'Jo talks about the country where we hope to live

some time; the real country, she means, with pigs and chickens, and haymaking. It would be nice, but I wish the beautiful country up there was real, and we could ever go to it,' said Beth, musingly.

'There is a lovelier country even than that, where we *shall* go, by and by, when we are good enough,' answered Meg, with her sweet voice.

'It seems so long to wait, so hard to do; I want to fly away at once, as those swallows fly, and go in at that splendid gate.'

'You'll get there, Beth, sooner or later; no fear of that,' said Jo; 'I'm the one that will have to fight and work, and climb and wait, and maybe never get in after all.'

'You'll have me for company, if that's any comfort. I shall have to do a deal of travelling before I come in sight of your Celestial City. If I arrive late, you'll say a good word for me, won't you, Beth?'

Something in the boy's face troubled his little friend; but she said cheerfully, with her quiet eyes on the changing clouds, 'If people really want to go, and really try all their lives, I think they will get in; for I don't believe there are any locks on that door, or any guards at the gate. I always imagine it is as it is in the picture, where the shining ones stretch out their hands to welcome poor Christian as he comes up from the river.'

'Wouldn't it be fun if all the castles in the air which we make could come true, and we could live in them?' said Jo, after a little pause.

'I've made such quantities it would be hard to choose which I'd have,' said Laurie, lying flat, and throwing cones at the squirrel who had betrayed him.

'You'd have to take your favorite one. What is it?' asked Meg.

'If I tell mine, will you tell yours?'

'Yes, if the girls will too.'

'We will. Now, Laurie!'

'After I'd seen as much of the world as I want to, I'd like to settle in Germany, and have just as much music as I choose. I'm to be a famous musician myself, and all creation is to rush to hear me; and I'm never to be bothered about money or business, but just enjoy myself, and live for what I like. That's my favorite castle. What's yours, Meg?'

Margaret seemed to find it a little hard to tell hers, and moved a brake before her face, as if to disperse imaginary gnats, while she said, slowly, 'I should like a lovely house, full of all sorts of luxurious things; nice food, pretty clothes, handsome furniture, pleasant people, and heaps of money. I am to be mistress of it, and manage it as I like, with plenty of servants, so I never need work a bit. How I should enjoy it! for I wouldn't be idle, but do good, and make every one love me dearly.'

'Wouldn't you have a master for your castle in the air?' asked Laurie, slyly.

'I said "pleasant people," you know;' and Meg carefully tied up her shoe as she spoke, so that no one saw her face.

'Why don't you say you'd have a splendid, wise, good husband, and some angelic little children? you know your castle wouldn't be perfect without,' said blunt Jo, who had no tender fancies yet, and rather scorned romance, except in books.

'You'd have nothing but horses, inkstands, and novels in yours,' answered Meg, petulantly.

'Wouldn't I, though! I'd have a stable full of Arabian steeds, rooms piled with books, and I'd write out of a magic inkstand, so that my works should be as famous as Laurie's music. I want to do something splendid before I go into my castle,—something heroic, or wonderful,— that won't be forgotten after I'm dead. I don't know what, but I'm on the watch for it, and mean to astonish you all, some day. I think I shall write books, and get rich and famous; that would suit me, so that is *my* favorite dream.'

'Mine is to stay at home safe with father and mother, and help take care of the family,' said Beth, contentedly.

'Don't you wish for anything else?' asked Laurie.

'Since I had my little piano I am perfectly satisfied. I only wish we may all keep well, and be together; nothing else.'

'I have lots of wishes; but the pet one is to be an artist, and go to Rome, and do fine pictures, and be the best artist in the whole world,' was Amy's modest desire.

'We're an ambitious set, aren't we? Every one of us, but Beth, wants to be rich and famous, and gorgeous in every respect. I do wonder if any of us will ever get our wishes,' said Laurie, chewing grass, like a meditative calf.

'I've got the key to my castle in the air; but whether I can unlock the door, remains to be seen,' observed Jo, mysteriously.

'I've got the key to mine, but I'm not allowed to try it. Hang college!' muttered Laurie, with an impatient sigh.

'Here's mine!' and Amy waved her pencil.

'I haven't got any,' said Meg, forlornly.

'Yes you have,' said Laurie, at once.

'Where?'

'In your face.'

'Nonsense; that's of no use.'

'Wait and see if it doesn't bring you something worth having,' replied the boy, laughing at the thought of a charming little secret which he fancied he knew.

Meg colored behind the brake, but asked no questions, and looked across the river with the same expectant expression which Mr Brooke had worn when he told the story of the knight.

'If we are all alive ten years hence, let's meet, and see how many of us have got our wishes, or how much nearer we are them than now,' said Jo, always ready with a plan.

'Bless me! how old I shall be,—twenty-seven!' exclaimed Meg, who felt grown up already, having just reached seventeen.

'You and I shall be twenty-six, Teddy; Beth twenty-four, and Amy twenty-two; what a venerable party!' said Jo.

'I hope I shall have done something to be proud of by that time; but I'm such a lazy dog, I'm afraid I shall "dawdle," Jo.'

'You need a motive, mother says; and when you get it, she is sure you'll work splendidly.'

'Is she? By Jupiter I will, if I only get the chance!' cried Laurie, sitting up with sudden energy. 'I ought to be satisfied to please grandfather, and I do try, but it's working against the grain, you see, and comes hard. He wants me to be an India merchant, as he was, and I'd rather be shot; I hate tea, and silk, and spices, and every sort of rubbish his old ships bring, and I don't care how soon they go to the bottom when I own them. Going to college ought to satisfy him, for if I give him four years he ought to let me off from the business; but he's set, and I've got to do just as he did, unless I break away and please myself, as my father did. If there was any one left to stay with the old gentleman, I'd do it tomorrow.'

Laurie spoke excitedly, and looked ready to carry his threat into execution on the slightest provocation; for he was growing up very fast, and, in spite of his indolent ways, had a young man's hatred of subjection,—a young man's restless longing to try the world for himself.

'I advise you to sail away in one of your ships, and never come home again till you have tried your own way,' said Jo, whose imagination was fired by the thought of such a daring exploit, and whose sympathy was excited by what she called 'Teddy's wrongs.'

'That's not right, Jo; you mustn't talk in that way, and Laurie mustn't take your bad advice. You should do just what your grandfather wishes, my dear boy,' said Meg, in her most maternal tone. 'Do your best at college, and, when he sees that you try to please him, I'm sure he won't be hard or unjust to you. As you say, there is no one else to stay with and love him, and you'd never forgive yourself if you left him without his permission. Don't be dismal, or fret, but do your duty; and you'll get your reward, as good Mr Brooke has, by being respected and loved.'

'What do you know about him?' asked Laurie, grateful for the good advice, but objecting to the lecture, and glad to turn the conversation from himself, after his unusual outbreak.

'Only what your grandpa told mother about him; how he took good care of his own mother till she died, and wouldn't go abroad as tutor to some nice person, because he wouldn't leave her; and how he provides now for an old woman who nursed his mother; and never tells any one, but is just as generous, and patient, and good as he can be.'

'So he is, dear old fellow!' said Laurie, heartily, as Meg paused, looking flushed and earnest, with her story. 'It's like grandpa to find out all about him, without letting him know, and to tell all his goodness to others, so that they might like him. Brooke couldn't understand why your mother was so kind to him, asking him over with me, and treating him in her beautiful, friendly way. He thought she was just perfect, and talked about it for days and days, and went on about you all, in flaming style. If ever I do get my wish, you see what I'll do for Brooke.'

'Begin to do something now, by not plaguing his life out,' said Meg, sharply.

'How do you know I do, miss?'

'I can always tell by his face, when he goes away. If you have been good, he looks satisfied, and walks briskly; if you have plagued him, he's sober, and walks slowly, as if he wanted to go back and do his work better.'

'Well, I like that! So you keep an account of my good and bad marks in Brooke's face, do you? I see him bow and smile as he passes your window, but I didn't know you'd got up a telegraph.'

'We haven't; don't be angry, and oh, don't tell him I said anything! It was only to show that I cared how you get on, and what is said here is said in confidence, you know,' cried Meg, much alarmed at the thought of what might follow from her careless speech.

'*I* don't tell tales,' replied Laurie, with his 'high and mighty' air, as Jo called a certain expression which he occasionally wore. 'Only if Brooke is going to be a thermometer, I must mind and have fair weather for him to report.'

'Please don't be offended; I didn't mean to preach or tell tales, or be silly; I only thought Jo was encouraging you in a feeling which you'd be sorry for, by and by. You are so kind to us, we feel as if you were our brother, and say just what we think; forgive me, I meant it kindly!' and Meg offered her hand with a gesture both affectionate and timid.

Ashamed of his momentary pique, Laurie squeezed

the kind little hand, and said, frankly, 'I'm the one to be forgiven; I'm cross, and have been out of sorts all day. I like to have you tell me my faults, and be sisterly; so don't mind if I am grumpy sometimes; I thank you all the same.'

Bent on showing that he was not offended, he made himself as agreeable as possible; wound cotton for Meg, recited poetry to please Jo, shook down cones for Beth, and helped Amy with her ferns,—proving himself a fit person to belong to the 'Busy Bee Society.' In the midst of an animated discussion on the domestic habits of turtles (one of which amiable creatures having strolled up from the river), the faint sound of a bell warned them that Hannah had put the tea 'to draw,' and they would just have time to get home to supper.

'May I come again?' asked Laurie.

'Yes, if you are good, and love your book, as the boys in the primer are told to do,' said Meg, smiling.

'I'll try.'

'Then you may come, and I'll teach you to knit as the Scotchmen do; there's a demand for socks just now,' added Jo, waving hers, like a big blue worsted banner, as they parted at the gate.

That night, when Beth played to Mr Laurence in the twilight, Laurie, standing in the shadow of the curtain, listened to the little David, whose simple music always quieted his moody spirit, and watched the old man, who sat with his gray head on his hand, thinking tender thoughts of the dead child he had loved so much. Remembering the conversation of the afternoon, the boy said to himself, with the resolve to make the sacrifice cheerfully, 'I'll let my castle go, and stay with the dear old gentleman while he needs me, for I am all he has.'

14

Secrets

JO WAS very busy up in the garret, for the October days began to grow chilly, and the afternoons were short. For two or three hours the sun lay warmly in at the high window, showing Jo seated on the old sofa writing busily, with her papers spread out upon a trunk before her, while Scrabble, the pet rat, promenaded the beams overhead, accompanied by his oldest son, a fine young fellow, who was evidently very proud of his whiskers. Quite absorbed in her work, Jo scribbled away till the last page was filled, when she signed her name with a flourish, and threw down her pen, exclaiming,—

'There, I've done my best! If this don't suit I shall have to wait till I can do better.'

Lying back on the sofa, she read the manuscript

carefully through, making dashes here and there, and putting in many exclamation points, which looked like little balloons; then she tied it up with a smart red ribbon, and sat a minute looking at it with a sober, wistful expression, which plainly showed how earnest her work had been. Jo's desk up here was an old tin kitchen, which hung against the wall. In it she kept her papers, and a few books, safely shut away from Scrabble, who, being likewise of a literary turn, was fond of making a circulating library of such books as were left in his way, by eating the leaves. From this tin receptacle Jo produced another manuscript; and, putting both in her pocket, crept quietly down stairs, leaving her friends to nibble her pens and taste her ink.

She put on her hat and jacket as noiselessly as possible, and, going to the back entry window, got out upon the roof of a low porch, swung herself down to the grassy bank, and took a roundabout way to the road. Once there she composed herself, hailed a passing omnibus, and rolled away to town, looking very merry and mysterious.

If any one had been watching her, he would have thought her movements decidedly peculiar; for, on alighting, she went off at a great pace till she reached a certain number in a certain busy street; having found the place with some difficulty, she went into the doorway, looked up the dirty stairs, and, after standing stock still a minute, suddenly dived into the street, and walked away as rapidly as she came. This manoeuvre she repeated several times, to the great amusement of a black-eyed young gentleman lounging in the window of a building opposite. On returning for the third time, Jo gave herself a shake, pulled her hat over her eyes, and walked up the stairs, looking as if she was going to have all her teeth out.

There was a dentist's sign, among others, which adorned the entrance, and, after staring a moment at the pair of artificial jaws which slowly opened and shut to draw attention to a fine set of teeth, the young gentleman put on his coat, took his hat, and went down to post himself in the opposite door-way, saying, with a smile and a shiver,—

'It's like her to come alone, but if she has a bad time she'll need some one to help her home.'

In ten minutes Jo came running down stairs with a very red face, and the general appearance of a person who had just passed through a trying ordeal of some sort. When she saw the young gentleman she looked anything but pleased, and passed him with a nod; but he followed, asking with an air of sympathy,—

'Did you have a bad time?'

'Not very.'

'You got through quick.'

'Yes, thank goodness!'

'Why did you go alone?'

'Didn't want any one to know.'

'You're the oddest fellow I ever saw. How many did you have out?'

Jo looked at her friend as if she did not understand him; then began to laugh, as if mightily amused at something.

'There are two which I want to have come out, but I must wait a week.'

'What are you laughing at? You are up to some mischief, Jo,' said Laurie, looking mystified.

'So are you. What were you doing, sir, up in that billiard saloon?'

'Begging your pardon, ma'am, it wasn't a billiard saloon, but a gymnasium, and I was taking a lesson in fencing.'

'I'm glad of that!'

'Why?'

'You can teach me; and then, when we play Hamlet, you can be Laertes, and we'll make a fine thing of the fencing scene.'

Laurie burst out with a hearty boy's laugh, which made several passers-by smile in spite of themselves.

'I'll teach you, whether we play Hamlet or not; it's

grand fun, and will straighten you up capitally. But I don't believe that was your only reason for saying "I'm glad," in that decided way; was it, now?'

'No, I was glad you were not in the saloon, because I hope you never go to such places. Do you?'

'Not often.'

'I wish you wouldn't.'

'It's no harm, Jo, I have billiards at home, but it's no fun unless you have good players; so, as I'm fond of it, I come sometimes and have a game with Ned Moffat or some of the other fellows.'

'Oh dear, I'm so sorry, for you'll get to liking it better and better, and will waste time and money, and grow like those dreadful boys. I did hope you'd stay respectable, and be a satisfaction to your friends,' said Jo, shaking her head.

'Can't a fellow take a little innocent amusement now and then without losing his respectability?' asked Laurie, looking nettled.

'That depends upon how and where he takes it. I don't like Ned and his set, and wish you'd keep out of it. Mother won't let us have him at our house, though he wants to come, and if you grow like him she won't be willing to have us frolic together as we do now.'

'Won't she?' asked Laurie, anxiously.

'No, she can't bear fashionable young men, and she'd

shut us all up in bandboxes rather than have us associate with them.'

'Well, she needn't get out her bandboxes yet; I'm not a fashionable party, and don't mean to be; but I do like harmless larks now and then, don't you?"

'Yes, nobody minds them, so lark away, but don't get wild, will you? or there will be an end of all our good times.'

'I'll be a double distilled saint.'

'I can't bear saints; just be a simple, honest, respectable boy, and we'll never desert you. I don't know what I *should* do if you acted like Mr King's son; he had plenty of money, but didn't know how to spend it, and got tipsey, and gambled, and ran away, and forged his father's name, I believe, and was altogether horrid.'

'You think I'm likely to do the same? Much obliged.'

'No I don't—Oh, *dear*, no!—but I hear people talking about money being such a temptation, and I sometimes wish you were poor; I shouldn't worry then.'

'Do you worry about me, Jo?'

'A little, when you look moody or discontented, as you sometimes do, for you've got such a strong will if you once get started wrong, I'm afraid it would be hard to stop you.'

Laurie walked in silence a few minutes, and Jo watched him, wishing she had held her tongue, for his eyes looked angry, though his lips still smiled as if at her warnings.

'Are you going to deliver lectures all the way home?' he asked, presently.

'Of course not; why?'

'Because if you are, I'll take a 'bus; if you are not, I'd like to walk with you, and tell you something very interesting.'

'I won't preach any more, and I'd like to hear the news immensely.'

'Very well, then; come on. It's a secret, and if I tell you, you must tell me yours.'

'I haven't got any,' began Jo, but stopped suddenly, remembering that she had.

'You know you have; you can't hide anything, so up and 'fess, or I won't tell,' cried Laurie.

'Is your secret a nice one?'

'Oh, isn't it! all about people you know, and such fun! You ought to hear it, and I've been aching to tell this long time. Come! you begin.'

'You'll not say anything about it at home, will you?'

'Not a word.'

'And you won't tease me in private?'

'I never tease.'

'Yes, you do; you get everything you want out of people. I don't know how you do it, but you are a born wheedler.'

'Thank you; fire away!'

'Well, I've left two stories with a newspaper man, and he's to give his answer next week,' whispered Jo, in her confidant's ear.

'Hurrah for Miss March, the celebrated American authoress!' cried Laurie, throwing up his hat and catching it again, to the great delight of two ducks, four cats, five hens, and half a dozen Irish children; for they were out of the city now.

'Hush! it won't come to anything, I dare say; but I couldn't rest till I had tried, and I said nothing about it, because I don't want any one else to be disappointed.'

'It won't fail! Why, Jo, your stories are works of Shakespeare compared to half the rubbish that's published every day. Won't it be fun to see them in print; and shan't we feel proud of our authoress?'

Jo's eyes sparkled, for it's always pleasant to be believed in; and a friend's praise is always sweeter than a dozen newspaper puffs.

'Where's *your* secret? Play fair, Teddy, or I'll never believe you again,' she said, trying to extinguish the brilliant hopes that blazed up at a word of encouragement.

'I may get into a scrape for telling; but I didn't promise

not to, so I will, for I never feel easy in my mind till I've told you any plummy bit of news I get. I know where Meg's glove is.'

'Is that all?' said Jo, looking disappointed, as Laurie nodded and twinkled, with a face full of mysterious intelligence.

'It's quite enough for the present, as you'll agree when I tell you where it is.'

'Tell, then.'

Laurie bent and whispered three words in Jo's ear, which produced a comical change. She stood and stared at him for a minute, looking both surprised and displeased, then walked on, saying sharply, 'How do you know?'

'Saw it.'

'Where?'

'Pocket.'

'All this time?'

'Yes; isn't that romantic?'

'No, it's horrid.'

'Don't you like it?'

'Of course I don't; it's ridiculous; it won't be allowed. My patience! what would Meg say?'

'You are not to tell any one; mind that.'

'I didn't promise.'

'That was understood, and I trusted you.'

'Well, I won't for the present, anyway; but I'm disgusted, and wish you hadn't told me.'

'I thought you'd be pleased.'

'At the idea of anybody coming to take Meg away? No, thank you.'

'You'll feel better about it when somebody comes to take you away.'

'I'd like to see any one try it,' cried Jo, fiercely.

'So should I!' and Laurie chuckled at the idea.

'I don't think secrets agree with me; I feel rumpled up in my mind since you told me that,' said Jo, rather ungratefully.

'Race down this hill with me, and you'll be all right,' suggested Laurie.

No one was in sight; the smooth road sloped invitingly before her, and, finding the temptation irresistible, Jo darted away, soon leaving hat and comb behind her, and scattering hair-pins as she ran. Laurie reached the goal first, and was quite satisfied with the success of his treatment; for his Atalanta came panting up with flying hair, bright eyes, ruddy cheeks, and no signs of dissatisfaction in her face.

'I wish I was a horse; then I could run for miles in this splendid air, and not lose my breath. It was capital; but see what a guy it's made me. Go, pick up my things, like a cherub as you are,' said Jo, dropping down under a maple tree, which was carpeting the bank with crimson leaves.

Laurie leisurely departed to recover the lost property, and Jo bundled up her braids, hoping no one would pass by till she was tidy again. But some one did pass, and who should it be but Meg, looking particularly lady-like in her state and festival suit, for she had been making calls.

'What in the world are you doing here?' she asked, regarding her dishevelled sister with well-bred surprise.

'Getting leaves,' meekly answered Jo, sorting the rosy handful she had just swept up.

'And hair-pins,' added Laurie, throwing half a dozen into Jo's lap. 'They grow on this road, Meg; so do combs and brown straw hats.'

'You have been running, Jo; how could you? When *will* you stop such romping ways?' said Meg, reprovingly, as she settled her cuffs and smoothed her hair, with which the wind had taken liberties.

'Never till I'm stiff and old, and have to use a crutch. Don't try to make me grow up before my time, Meg; it's hard enough to have you change all of a sudden; let me be a little girl as long as I can.'

As she spoke, Jo bent over her work to hide the trembling of her lips; for lately she had felt that Margaret was fast getting to be a woman, and Laurie's secret made her dread the separation which must surely come some time, and now seemed very near. He saw the trouble in her face, and drew Meg's attention from it by asking, quickly, 'Where have you been calling, all so fine?'

'At the Gardiners; and Sallie has been telling me all about Belle Moffat's wedding. It was very splendid, and they have gone to spend the winter in Paris; just think how delightful that must be!'

'Do you envy her, Meg?' said Laurie.

'I'm afraid I do.'

'I'm glad of it!' muttered Jo, tying on her hat with a jerk.

'Why?' asked Meg, looking surprised.

'Because, if you care much about riches, you will never go and marry a poor man,' said Jo, frowning at Laurie, who was mutely warning her to mind what she said.

'I shall never "*go* and marry" any one,' observed Meg, walking on with great dignity, while the others followed, laughing, whispering, skipping stones, and 'behaving like children,' as Meg said to herself, though she might have been tempted to join them if she had not had her best dress on.

For a week or two Jo behaved so queerly, that her sisters got quite bewildered. She rushed to the door when the postman rang; was rude to Mr Brooke whenever they met; would sit looking at Meg with a woe-begone face, occasionally jumping up to shake, and then to kiss her, in a very mysterious manner; Laurie and she were always making signs to one another, and talking about 'Spread Eagles,' till the girls declared they had both lost their wits. On the second Saturday after Jo got out of the window, Meg, as she sat sewing at her window, was scandalized by the sight of Laurie chasing Jo all over the garden, and finally capturing her in Amy's bower. What went on there, Meg could not see, but shrieks of laughter were heard, followed by the murmur of voices, and a great flapping of newspapers.

'What shall we do with that girl? She never *will* behave like a young lady,' sighed Meg, as she watched the race with a disapproving face.

'I hope she won't; she is so funny and dear as she is,' said Beth, who had never betrayed that she was a little hurt at Jo's having secrets with any one but her.

'It's very trying, but we never can make her *comme la fo*,' added Amy, who sat making some new frills for herself, with her curls tied up in a very becoming way,— two agreeable things, which made her feel unusually elegant and lady-like.

In a few minutes Jo bounced in, laid herself on the sofa, and affected to read.

'Have you anything interesting there?' asked Meg, with condescension.

'Nothing but a story; don't amount to much, I guess,' returned Jo, carefully keeping the name of the paper out of sight.

'You'd better read it loud; that will amuse us, and keep you out of mischief,' said Amy, in her most grown-up tone.

'What's the name?' asked Beth, wondering why Jo kept her face behind the sheet.

'The Rival Painters.'

'That sounds well; read it,' said Meg.

With a loud 'hem!' and a long breath, Jo began to read very fast. The girls listened with interest, for the tale was romantic, and somewhat pathetic, as most of the characters died in the end.

'I like that about the splendid picture,' was Amy's approving remark, as Jo paused.

'I prefer the lovering part. Viola and Angelo are two of our favorite names; isn't that queer?' said Meg, wiping her eyes, for the 'lovering part' was tragical.

'Who wrote it?' asked Beth, who had caught a glimpse of Jo's face.

The reader suddenly sat up, cast away the paper, displayed a flushed countenance, and, with a funny mixture of solemnity and excitement, replied in a loud voice, 'Your sister!'

'You?' cried Meg, dropping her work.

'It's very good,' said Amy, critically.

'I knew it! I knew it! oh, my Jo, I *am* so proud!' and Beth ran to hug her sister and exult over this splendid success.

Dear me, how delighted they all were, to be sure; how Meg wouldn't believe it till she saw the words, 'Miss Josephine March,' actually printed in the paper; how graciously Amy criticized the artistic parts of the story, and offered hints for a sequel, which unfortunately couldn't be carried out, as the hero and heroine were dead; how Beth got excited, and skipped and sang with joy; how Hannah came in to exclaim, 'Sakes alive, well I never!' in great astonishment at 'that Jo's doin's;' how proud Mrs March was when she knew it; how Jo laughed, with tears in her eyes, as she declared she might as well be a peacock and done with it; and how the 'Spread Eagle' might be said to flap his wings triumphantly over the house of March, as the paper passed from hand to hand.

'Tell us about it.' 'When did it come?' 'How much did you get for it?' 'What *will* father say?' 'Won't Laurie laugh?' cried the family, all in one breath, as they clustered about Jo; for these foolish, affectionate people made a jubilee of every little household joy.

'Stop jabbering, girls, and I'll tell you everything,' said Jo, wondering if Miss Burney felt any grander over her 'Evelina' than she did over her 'Rival Painters.' Having told how she disposed of her tales, Jo added,—'And when I went to get my answer the man said he liked them both, but didn't pay beginners, only let them print in his paper, and noticed the stories. It was good practice, he said; and, when the beginners improved, any one would pay. So I let him have the two stories, and today this was sent to me, and Laurie caught me with it, and insisted on seeing it, so I let him; and he said it was good, and I shall write more, and he's going to get the next paid for, and oh—I *am* so happy, for in time I may be able to support myself and help the girls.'

Jo's breath gave out here; and, wrapping her head in the paper, she bedewed her little story with a few natural tears; for to be independent, and earn the praise of those she loved, were the dearest wishes of her heart, and this seemed to be the first step toward that happy end.

15

A Telegram

'NOVEMBER is the most disagreeable month in the whole year,' said Margaret, standing at the window one dull afternoon, looking out at the frost-bitten garden.

'That's the reason I was born in it,' observed Jo, pensively, quite unconscious of the blot on her nose.

'If something very pleasant should happen now, we should think it a delightful month,' said Beth, who took a hopeful view of everything, even November.

'I dare say; but nothing pleasant ever *does* happen in this family,' said Meg, who was out of sorts. 'We go grubbing along day after day, without a bit of change, and very little fun. We might as well be in a tread-mill.'

'My patience, how blue we are!' cried Jo. 'I don't

much wonder, poor dear, for you see other girls having splendid times, while you grind, grind, year in and year out. Oh, don't I wish I could fix things for you as I do for my heroines! you're pretty enough and good enough already, so I'd have some rich relation leave you a fortune unexpectedly; then you'd dash out as an heiress, scorn every one who has slighted you, go abroad, and come home my Lady Something, in a blaze of splendor and elegance.'

'People don't have fortunes left them in that style now-a-days; men have to work, and women to marry for money. It's a dreadfully unjust world,' said Meg, bitterly.

'Jo and I are going to make fortunes for you all; just wait ten years, and see if we don't,' said Amy, who sat in a corner making 'mud pies,' as Hannah called her little clay models of birds, fruit and faces.

'Can't wait, and I'm afraid I haven't much faith in ink and dirt, though I'm grateful for your good intentions.'

Meg sighed, and turned to the frost-bitten garden again; Jo groaned, and leaned both elbows on the table in a despondent attitude, but Amy spatted away energetically; and Beth, who sat at the other window, said smiling, 'Two pleasant things are going to happen right away; Marmee is coming down the street, and

Laurie is tramping through the garden as if he had something nice to tell.'

In they both came, Mrs March with her usual question, 'Any letter from father, girls?' and Laurie to say, in his persuasive way, 'Won't some of you come for a drive? I've been pegging away at mathematics till my head is in a muddle, and I'm going to freshen my wits by a brisk turn. It's a dull day, but the air isn't bad, and I'm going to take Brooke home, so it will be gay inside, if it isn't out. Come, Jo, you and Beth will go, won't you?'

'Of course we will.'

'Much obliged, but I'm busy;' and Meg whisked out her workbasket, for she had agreed with her mother that it was best, for her at least, not to drive often with the young gentleman.

'Can I do anything for you, Madam Mother?' asked Laurie, leaning over Mrs March's chair, with the affectionate look and tone he always gave her.

'No, thank you, except call at the office, if you'll be so kind, dear. It's our day for a letter, and the penny postman hasn't been. Father is as regular as the sun, but there's some delay on the way, perhaps.'

A sharp ring interrupted her, and a minute after Hannah came in with a letter.

'It's one of them horrid telegraph things, mum,' she

271

said, handling it as if she was afraid it would explode, and do some damage.

At the word 'telegraph,' Mrs March snatched it, read the two lines it contained, and dropped back into her chair as white as if the little paper had sent a bullet to her heart. Laurie dashed down stairs for water, while Meg and Hannah supported her, and Jo read aloud, in a frightened voice,—

'Mrs March:

'Your husband is very ill. Come at once.

'S. Hale,

'Blank Hospital, Washington'

How still the room was as they listened breathlessly! how strangely the day darkened outside! and how suddenly the whole world seemed to change, as the girls gathered about their mother, feeling as if all the happiness and support of their lives was about to be taken from them. Mrs March was herself again directly; read the message over, and stretched out her arms to her daughters, saying, in a tone they never forgot, 'I shall go at once, but it may be too late; oh, children, children! help me to bear it!'

For several minutes there was nothing but the sound of sobbing in the room, mingled with broken words of comfort, tender assurances of help, and hopeful whispers, that died away in tears. Poor Hannah was the first to recover, and with unconscious wisdom she set all the rest a good example; for, with her, work was the panacea for most afflictions.

'The Lord keep the dear man! I won't waste no time a cryin', but git your things ready right away, mum,' she said, heartily, as she wiped her face on her apron, gave her mistress a warm shake of the hand with her own hard one, and went away to work, like three women in one.

'She's right; there's no time for tears now. Be calm, girls, and let me think.'

They tried to be calm, poor things, as their mother sat up, looking pale, but steady, and put away her grief to think and plan for them.

'Where's Laurie?' she asked presently, when she had collected her thoughts, and decided on the first duties to be done.

'Here, ma'am; oh, let me do something!' cried the boy, hurrying from the next room, whither he had withdrawn, feeling that their first sorrow was too sacred for even his friendly eyes to see.

'Send a telegram saying I will come at once. The next train goes early in the morning; I'll take that.'

'What else? The horses are ready; I can go anywhere,—

do anything,' he said, looking ready to fly to the ends of the earth.

'Leave a note at Aunt March's. Jo, give me that pen and paper.'

Tearing off the blank side of one of her newly-copied pages, Jo drew the table before her mother, well knowing that money for the long, sad journey, must be borrowed, and feeling as if she could do anything to add a little to the sum for her father.

'Now go, dear; but don't kill yourself driving at a desperate pace; there is no need of that.'

Mrs March's warning was evidently thrown away; for five minutes later Laurie tore by the window, on his own fleet horse, riding as if for his life.

'Jo, run to the rooms, and tell Mrs King that I can't come. On the way get these things. I'll put them down; they'll be needed, and I must go prepared for nursing. Hospital stores are not always good. Beth, go and ask Mr Laurence for a couple of bottles of old wine; I'm not too proud to beg for father; he shall have the best of everything. Amy, tell Hannah to get down the black trunk; and Meg, come and help me find my things, for I'm half bewildered.'

Writing, thinking, and directing all at once, might well bewilder the poor lady, and Meg begged her to sit quietly in her room for a little while, and let them work. Every one scattered, like leaves before a gust of wind; and the quiet, happy household was broken up as suddenly as if the paper had been an evil spell.

Mr Laurence came hurrying back with Beth, bringing every comfort the kind old gentleman could think of for the invalid, and friendliest promises of protection for the girls, during their mother's absence, which comforted her very much. There was nothing he didn't offer, from his own dressing-gown to himself as escort. But that last was impossible. Mrs March would not hear of the old gentleman's undertaking the long journey; yet an expression of relief was visible when he spoke of it, for anxiety ill fits one for travelling. He saw the look, knit his heavy eyebrows, rubbed his hands, and marched abruptly away, saying he'd be back directly. No one had time to think of him again till, as Meg ran through the entry, with a pair of rubbers in one hand and a cup of tea in the other, she came suddenly upon Mr Brooke.

'I'm very sorry to hear of this, Miss March,' he said, in the kind, quiet tone which sounded very pleasantly to her perturbed spirit. 'I came to offer myself as escort to your mother. Mr Laurence has commissions for me in Washington, and it will give me real satisfaction to be of service to her there.'

Down dropped the rubbers, and the tea was very near following, as Meg put out her hand, with a face so full of gratitude, that Mr Brooke would have felt repaid for a much greater sacrifice than the trifling one of time and comfort, which he was about to make.

'How kind you all are! Mother will accept, I'm sure; and it will be such a relief to know that she has some one to take care of her. Thank you very, very much!'

Meg spoke earnestly, and forgot herself entirely till something in the brown eyes looking down at her made her remember the cooling tea, and lead the way into the parlor, saying she would call her mother.

Everything was arranged by the time Laurie returned with a note from Aunt March, enclosing the desired sum, and a few lines repeating what she had often said before, that she had always told them it was absurd for March to go into the army, always predicted that no good would come of it, and she hoped they would take her advice next time. Mrs March put the note in the fire, the money in her purse, and went on with her preparations, with her lips folded tightly, in a way which Jo would have understood if she had been there.

The short afternoon wore away; all the other errands were done, and Meg and her mother busy at some necessary needle-work, while Beth and Amy got tea, and Hannah finished her ironing with what she called a 'slap and a bang,' but still Jo did not come. They began to get anxious; and Laurie went off to find her, for no one ever knew what freak Jo might take into her head. He missed her, however, and she came walking in with a very queer expression of countenance for there was a mixture of fun and fear, satisfaction and regret in it, which puzzled the family as much as did the roll of bills she laid before her mother, saying, with a little choke in her voice, 'That's my contribution towards making father comfortable, and bringing him home!'

'My dear, where did you get it! Twenty-five dollars! Jo, I hope you haven't done anything rash?'

'No, it's mine honestly; I didn't beg, borrow, nor steal it. I earned it; and I don't think you'll blame me, for I only sold what was my own.'

As she spoke, Jo took off her bonnet, and a general outcry arose, for all her abundant hair was cut short.

'Your hair! Your beautiful hair!' 'Oh, Jo, how could you? Your one beauty,' 'My dear girl, there was no need of this.' 'She don't look like my Jo any more, but I love her dearly for it!'

As every one exclaimed, and Beth hugged the cropped head tenderly, Jo assumed an indifferent air, which did not deceive any one particle, and said, rumpling up the brown bush, and trying to look as if she liked it, 'It doesn't affect the fate of the nation, so don't wail, Beth. It will be good for my vanity; I was getting too proud of my wig. It will do my brains good to have that mop taken off; my head feels deliciously light and cool, and the barber said I could soon have a curly crop, which will be boyish, becoming, and easy to keep in order. I'm satisfied; so please take the money, and let's have supper.'

'Tell me all about it, Jo; *I* am not quite satisfied, but I can't blame you, for I know how willingly you sacrificed your vanity, as you call it, to your love. But, my dear, it was not necessary, and I'm afraid you will regret it, one of these days,' said Mrs March.

'No I won't!' returned Jo, stoutly, feeling much relieved that her prank was not entirely condemned.

'What made you do it?' asked Amy, who would as soon have thought of cutting off her head as her pretty hair.

'Well, I was wild to do something for father,' replied Jo, as they gathered about the table, for healthy young people can eat even in the midst of trouble. 'I hate to borrow as much as mother does, and I knew Aunt March would croak; she always does, if you ask for a ninepence. Meg gave all her quarterly salary toward the rent, and I only got some clothes with mine, so I felt wicked, and was bound to have some money, if I sold the nose off my face to get it.'

'You needn't feel wicked, my child, you had no winter things, and got the simplest, with your own hard earnings,' said Mrs March, with a look that warmed Jo's heart.

'I hadn't the least idea of selling my hair at first, but as I went along I kept thinking *what* I could do, and feeling as if I'd like to dive into some of the rich stores and help myself. In a barber's window I saw tails of hair with the prices marked; and one black tail, longer, but not so thick as mine, was forty dollars. It came over me all of a sudden that I had one thing to make money out of, and, without stopping to think, I walked in, asked if they bought hair, and what they would give for mine.'

'I don't see how you dared to do it,' said Beth, in a tone of awe.

'Oh, he was a little man who looked as if he merely lived to oil his hair. He rather stared, at first, as if he wasn't used to having girls bounce into his shop and ask him to buy their hair. He said he didn't care about mine, it wasn't the fashionable color, and he never paid much for it in the first place; the work put into it made it dear, and so on. It was getting late, and I was afraid, if it wasn't done right away, that I shouldn't have it done at all, and you know, when I start to do a thing, I hate to give it up; so I begged him to take it, and told him why I was in such a hurry. It was silly, I dare say, but it changed his mind, for I got rather excited, and told the story in my topsy-turvy way, and his wife heard, and said so kindly,—

'"Take it, Thomas, and oblige the young lady; I'd do as much for our Jimmy any day if I had a spire of hair worth selling."'

'Who was Jimmy?' asked Amy, who liked to have things explained as they went along.

'Her son, she said, who is in the army. How friendly such things make strangers feel, don't they? She talked away all the time the man clipped, and diverted my mind nicely.'

'Didn't you feel dreadfully when the first cut came?' asked Meg, with a shiver.

'I took a last look at my hair while the man got his things, and that was the end of it. I never snivel over trifles like that; I will confess, though, I felt queer when I saw the dear old hair laid out on the table, and felt only the short, rough ends on my head. It almost seemed as if I'd an arm or a leg off. The woman saw me look at it, and picked out a long lock for me to keep. I'll give it to you, Marmee, just to remember past glories by; for a crop is so comfortable I don't think I shall ever have a mane again.'

Mrs March folded the wavy, chestnut lock, and laid it away with a short gray one in her desk. She only said 'Thank you, deary,' but something in her face made the girls change the subject, and talk as cheerfully as they could about Mr Brooke's kindness, the prospect of a fine day tomorrow, and the happy times they would have when father came home to be nursed.

No one wanted to go to bed, when, at ten o'clock, Mrs March put by the last finished job, and said, 'Come, girls.' Beth went to the piano and played the father's favorite hymn; all began bravely, but broke down one by one till Beth was left alone, singing with all her heart, for to her music was always a sweet consoler.

'Go to bed, and don't talk, for we must be up early, and shall need all the sleep we can get. Good-night, my darlings,' said Mrs March, as the hymn ended, for no one cared to try another.

They kissed her quietly, and went to bed as silently as if the dear invalid lay in the next room. Beth and Amy soon fell asleep in spite of the great trouble, but Meg lay awake thinking the most serious thoughts she had ever known in her short life. Jo lay motionless, and her sister fancied that she was asleep, till a stifled sob made her exclaim, as she touched a wet cheek,—

'Jo, dear, what is it? Are you crying about father?'

'No, not now.'

'What then?'

'My—my hair,' burst out poor Jo, trying vainly to smother her emotion in the pillow.

It did not sound at all comical to Meg, who kissed and caressed the afflicted heroine in the tenderest manner.

'I'm not sorry,' protested Jo, with a choke. 'I'd do it again tomorrow, if I could. It's only the vain, selfish part of me that goes and cries in this silly way. Don't tell any one, it's all over now. I thought you were asleep, so I just made a little private moan for my one beauty. How came you to be awake?'

'I can't sleep, I'm so anxious,' said Meg.

'Think about something pleasant and you'll soon drop off.'

'I tried it, but felt wider awake than ever.'

'What did you think of?'

'Handsome faces; eyes particularly,' answered Meg smilingly, to herself, in the dark.

'What color do you like best?'

'Brown—that is sometimes—blue are lovely.'

Jo laughed, and Meg sharply ordered her not to talk, then amiably promised to make her hair curl, and fell asleep to dream of living in her castle in the air.

The clocks were striking midnight, and the rooms were very still, as a figure glided quietly from bed to bed, smoothing a coverlet here, setting a pillow there, and pausing to look long and tenderly at each unconscious face, to kiss each with lips that mutely blessed, and to

282

pray the fervent prayers which only mothers utter. As she lifted the curtain to look out into the dreary night, the moon broke suddenly from behind the clouds, and shone upon her like a bright benignant face, which seemed to whisper in the silence, 'Be comforted, dear heart! there is always light behind the clouds.'

16

Letters

IN THE cold gray dawn the sisters lit their lamp, and read their chapter with an earnestness never felt before, for now the shadow of a real trouble had come, showing them how rich in sunshine their lives had been. The little books were full of help and comfort; and, as they dressed, they agreed to say good-by cheerfully, hopefully, and send their mother on her anxious journey unsaddened by tears or complaints from them. Everything seemed very strange when they went down; so dim and still outside, so full of light and bustle within. Breakfast at that early hour seemed odd, and even Hannah's familiar face looked unnatural as she flew about her kitchen with her night cap on. The big trunk stood ready in the hall, mother's cloak and bonnet lay on the sofa, and mother herself sat trying to eat, but looking so pale and worn with sleeplessness and anxiety, that the girls found it very hard to keep their resolution. Meg's eyes kept filling in spite of herself; Jo was obliged to hide her face in the kitchen roller more than once, and the little girls' young faces wore a grave, troubled expression, as if sorrow was a new experience to them.

Nobody talked much, but, as the time drew very near, and they sat waiting for the carriage, Mrs March said to the girls, who were all busied about her, one folding her shawl, another smoothing out the strings of her bonnet, a third putting on her over-shoes, and a fourth fastening up her travelling bag,—

'Children, I leave you to Hannah's care, and Mr Laurence's protection; Hannah is faithfulness itself, and our good neighbor will guard you as if you were his own. I have no fears for you, yet I am anxious that you should take this trouble rightly. Don't grieve and fret when I am gone, or think that you can comfort yourselves by being idle, and trying to forget. So on with your work as usual, for work is a blessed solace. Hope, and keep busy; and, whatever happens, remember that you never can be fatherless.'

'Yes, mother.'

'Meg dear, be prudent, watch over your sisters, consult

Hannah, and, in any perplexity, go to Mr Laurence. Be patient, Jo, don't get despondent, or do rash things; write to me often, and be my brave girl, ready to help and cheer us all. Beth, comfort yourself with your music, and be faithful to the little home duties; and you, Amy, help all you can, be obedient, and keep happy safe at home.'

'We will, mother! we will!'

The rattle of an approaching carriage made them all start and listen. That was the hard minute, but the girls stood it well; no one cried, no one ran away, or uttered a lamentation, though their hearts were very heavy as they sent loving messages to father, remembering, as they spoke, that it might be too late to deliver them. They kissed their mother quietly, clung about her tenderly, and tried to wave their hands cheerfully, when she drove away.

Laurie and his grandfather came over to see her off, and Mr Brooke looked so strong, and sensible, and kind, that the girls christened him 'Mr Greatheart,' on the spot.

'Good-by, my darlings! God bless and keep us all,' whispered Mrs March, as she kissed one dear little face after the other, and hurried into the carriage.

As she rolled away, the sun came out, and, looking back, she saw it shining on the group at the gate, like a good omen. They saw it also, and smiled and waved their hands; and the last thing she beheld, as she turned the corner, was the four bright faces, and behind them, like a body-guard, old Mr Laurence, faithful Hannah, and devoted Laurie.

'How kind every one is to us,' she said, turning to find fresh proof of it in the respectful sympathy of the young man's face.

'I don't see how they can help it,' returned Mr Brooke, laughing so infectiously that Mrs March could not help smiling; and so the long journey began with the good omens of sunshine, smiles, and cheerful words.

'I feel as if there had been an earthquake,' said Jo, as their neighbors went home to breakfast, leaving them to rest and refresh themselves.

'It seems as if half the house was gone,' added Meg, forlornly.

Beth opened her lips to say something, but could only point to the pile of nicely-mended hose which lay on mother's table, showing that even in her last hurried moments she had thought and worked for them. It was a little thing, but it went straight to their hearts; and, in spite of their brave resolutions, they all broke down, and cried bitterly.

Hannah wisely allowed them to relieve their feelings;

and, when the shower showed signs of clearing up, she came to the rescue, armed with a coffee-pot.

'Now, my dear young ladies, remember what your ma said, and don't fret; come and have a cup of coffee all round, and then let's fall to work, and be a credit to the family.'

Coffee was a treat, and Hannah showed great tact in making it that morning. No one could resist her persuasive nods, or the fragrant invitation issuing from the nose of the coffee-pot. They drew up to the table, exchanged their handkerchiefs for napkins, and, in ten minutes, were all right again.

'"Hope and keep busy;" that's the motto for us, so let's see who will remember it best. I shall go to Aunt March, as usual; oh, won't she lecture, though!' said Jo, as she sipped, with returning spirit.

'I shall go to my Kings, though I'd much rather stay at home and attend to things here,' said Meg, wishing she hadn't made her eyes so red.

'No need of that; Beth and I can keep house perfectly well,' put in Amy, with an important air.

'Hannah will tell us what to do; and we'll have everything nice when you come home,' added Beth, getting out her mop and dishtub without delay.

'I think anxiety is very interesting,' observed Amy, eating sugar, pensively.

The girls couldn't help laughing, and felt better for it, though Meg shook her head at the young lady who could find consolation in a sugar-bowl.

The sight of the turn-overs made Jo sober again; and, when the two went out to their daily tasks, they looked sorrowfully back at the window where they were accustomed to see their mother's face. It was gone; but Beth had remembered the little household ceremony, and there she was, nodding away at them like a rosy-faced mandarin.

'That's so like my Beth!' said Jo, waving her hat, with a grateful face. 'Good-by, Meggy; I hope the Kings won't train today. Don't fret about father, dear,' she added, as they parted.

'And I hope Aunt March won't croak. Your hair is becoming, and it looks very boyish and nice,' returned Meg, trying not to smile at the curly head, which looked comically small on her tall sister's shoulders.

'That's my only comfort;' and, touching her hat à la Laurie, away went Jo, feeling like a shorn sheep on a wintry day.

News from their father comforted the girls very much; for, though dangerously ill, the presence of the best and tenderest of nurses had already done him good. Mr Brooke sent a bulletin every day, and, as the head of the family, Meg insisted on reading the despatches, which grew more and more cheering as the week passed. At first, every one was eager to write, and plump envelopes were carefully poked into the letter-box, by one or other of the sisters, who felt rather important with their Washington correspondence. As one of these packets contained characteristic notes from the party, we will rob an imaginary mail, and read them:—

'My Dearest Mother,—

'It is impossible to tell you how happy your last letter made us, for the news was so good we couldn't help laughing and crying over it. How very kind Mr Brooke is, and how fortunate that Mr Laurence's business detains him near you so long, since he is so useful to you and father. The girls are all as good as gold. Jo helps me with the sewing, and insists on doing all sorts of hard jobs. I should be afraid she might overdo, if I didn't know that her 'moral fit' wouldn't last long. Beth is as regular about her tasks as a clock, and never forgets what you told her. She grieves about father, and looks sober, except when she is at her little piano. Amy minds me nicely, and I take great care of her. She does her own hair, and I am teaching her to make button-holes, and mend her stockings. She tries very hard, and I know you will be pleased with her improvement when you come. Mr Laurence watches over us like a motherly old hen, as Jo says; and Laurie is very kind and neighborly. He and Jo keep us merry, for we get pretty blue sometimes, and feel like orphans, with you so far away. Hannah is a perfect saint; she does not scold at all, and always calls me 'Miss Margaret,' which is quite proper, you know, and treats me with respect. We are all well and busy; but we long, day and night, to have you back. Give my dearest love to father, and believe me, ever your own

Meg.'

This note, prettily written on scented paper, was a great contrast to the next, which was scribbled on a big sheet of thin, foreign paper, ornamented with blots, and all manner of flourishes and curly-tailed letters:—

'My Precious Marmee,—

'Three cheers for dear old father! Brooke was a trump to telegraph right off, and let us know the minute he was better. I rushed up garret when the letter came, and tried to thank God for being so good to us; but I could only cry, and say, "I'm glad! I'm glad!" Didn't that do as well as a regular prayer? for I felt a great many in my heart. We have such funny times; and now I can enjoy 'em, for every one is so desperately good, it's like living in a nest of turtle-doves. You'd laugh to see Meg head the table, and try to be motherish. She gets prettier every day, and I'm in love with her sometimes. The children are regular archangels, and I—well, I'm Jo, and never shall be anything else. Oh, I must tell you that I came near having a quarrel with Laurie. I freed my mind about a silly little thing, and he was offended. I was right, but didn't speak as I ought, and he marched home, saying he wouldn't come again till I begged pardon. I declared I wouldn't, and got mad. It lasted all day; I felt bad, and wanted you very much. Laurie and I are both so proud, it's hard to beg pardon; but I thought he'd come to it, for I *was* in the right. He didn't come; and just at night I remembered what you said when Amy fell into the river. I read my little book, felt better, resolved not to let the sun set on *my* anger, and ran over to tell Laurie I was sorry. I met him at the gate, coming for the same thing. We both laughed, begged each other's pardon, and felt all good and comfortable again.

'I made a "pome" yesterday, when I was helping Hannah wash; and, as father likes my silly little things, I put it in to amuse him. Give him the lovingest hug that ever was, and kiss yourself a dozen times, for your

'Topsy-Turvy Jo.

'A SONG FROM THE SUDS.

'Queen of my tub, I merrily sing,
   While the white foam rises high;
And sturdily wash, and rinse, and wring,
   And fasten the clothes to dry;
Then out in the free fresh air they swing,
   Under the sunny sky.

'I wish we could wash from our hearts and souls
   The stains of the week away,
And let water and air by their magic make
   Ourselves as pure as they;
Then on the earth there would be indeed
   A glorious washing-day!

Along the path of a useful life,
   Will heart's-ease ever bloom;
The busy mind has no time to think
   Of sorrow, or care, or gloom;
And anxious thoughts may be swept away,
   As we busily wield a broom.

'I am glad a task to me is given,
   To labor at day by day;
For it brings me health, and strength, and hope,
   And I cheerfully learn to say,—
"Head you may think, Heart you may feel,
   But Hand you shall work alway!"'

'Dear Mother:

'There is only room for me to send my love, and some pressed pansies from the root I have been keeping safe in the house, for father to see. I read every morning, try to be good all day, and sing myself to sleep with father's tune. I can't sing "Land of the Leal" now; it makes me cry. Every one is very kind, and we are as happy as we can be without you. Amy wants the rest of the page, so I must stop. I didn't forget to cover the holders, and I wind the clock and air the rooms every day.

'Kiss dear father on the cheek he calls mine. Oh, do come soon to your loving

'Little Beth.'

'Ma Chere Mamma:

'We are all well I do my lessons always and never corroberate the girls—Meg says I mean contradick so I put in both words and you can take the properest. Meg is a great comfort to me and lets me have jelly every night at tea its so good for me Jo says because it keeps me sweet tempered. Laurie is not as respeckful as he ought to be now I am almost in my teens, he calls me Chick and hurts my feelings by talking French to me very fast when I say Merci or Bon jour as Hattie King does. The sleeves of my blue dress were all worn out and Meg put in new ones but the full front came wrong and they are more blue than the dress. I felt bad but did not fret I bear my troubles well but I do wish Hannah would put more starch in my aprons and have buck wheats every day. Can't she? Didn't I make that interrigation point nice. Meg says my punchtuation and spelling are disgraceful and I am mortyfied but dear me I have so many things to do I can't stop. Adieu, I send heaps of love to Papa.

'Your affection daughter,
  'Amy Curtis March.'

'Dear Mis March:

'I jes drop a line to say we git on fust rate. The girls is clever and fly round right smart. Miss Meg is goin to make a proper good housekeeper; she hes the liking for it, and gits the hang of things surprisin quick. Jo doos beat all for goin ahead, but she don't stop to cal'k'late fust, and you never know where she's like to bring up. She done out a tub of clothes on Monday, but she starched em afore they was wrenched, and blued a pink calico dress till I thought I should a died a laughin. Beth is the best of little creeters, and a sight of help to me, bein so forehanded and dependable. She tries to learn everything, and really goes to market beyond her years; likewise keeps accounts, with my help, quite wonderful. We have got on very economical so fur; I don't let the girls hev coffee only once a week, accordin to your wish, and keep em on plain wholesome vittles. Amy does well about frettin, wearin her best clothes and eatin sweet stuff. Mr Laurie is as full of didoes as usual, and turns the house upside down frequent; but he heartens up the girls, and so I let em hev full swing. The old man sends heaps of things, and is rather wearin, but means wal, and it aint my place to say nothin. My bread is riz, so no more at this time. I send my duty to Mr March, and hope he's seen the last of his Pewmonia.

'Yours respectful,

'Hannah Mullet'

'Head Nurse of Ward II:

'All serene on the Rappahannock, troops in fine condition, commissary department well conducted, the Home Guard under Colonel Teddy always on duty, Commander-in-chief General Laurence reviews the army daily, Quartermaster Mullet keeps order in camp, and Major Lion does picket duty at night. A salute of twenty-four guns was fired on receipt of good news from Washington, and a dress parade took place at headquarters. Commander-in-chief sends best wishes, in which he is heartily joined by

'Colonel Teddy.'

'Dear Madam:

'The little girls are all well; Beth and my boy report daily; Hannah is a model servant, guards pretty Meg like a dragon. Glad the fine weather holds; pray make Brooke useful, and draw on me for funds if expenses exceed your estimate. Don't let your husband want anything. Thank God he is mending.

'Your sincere friend and servant,

'James Laurence.'

17
Little Faithful

FOR a week the amount of virtue in the old house would have supplied the neighborhood. It was really amazing, for every one seemed in a heavenly frame of mind, and self-denial was all the fashion. Relieved of their first anxiety about their father, the girls insensibly relaxed their praiseworthy efforts a little, and began to fall back into the old ways. They did not forget their motto, but hoping and keeping busy seemed to grow easier; and, after such tremendous exertions, they felt that Endeavor deserved a holiday, and gave it a good many.

Jo caught a bad cold through neglecting to cover the shorn head enough, and was ordered to stay at home till she was better, for Aunt March didn't like to hear people read with colds in their heads. Jo liked this, and after an energetic rummage from garret to cellar, subsided on to the sofa to nurse her cold with arsenicum and books. Amy found that house-work and art did not go well together, and returned to her mud pies. Meg went daily to her kingdom, and sewed, or thought she did, at home, but much time was spent in writing long letters to her mother, or reading the Washington despatches over and over. Beth kept on with only slight relapses into idleness or grieving. All the little duties were faithfully done each day, and many of her sisters' also, for they were forgetful, and the house seemed like a clock, whose pendulum was gone a-visiting. When her heart got heavy with longings for mother, or fears for father, she went away into a certain closet, hid her face in the folds of a certain dear old gown, and made her little moan, and prayed her little prayer quietly by herself. Nobody knew what cheered her up after a sober fit, but every one felt how sweet and helpful Beth was, and fell into a way of going to her for comfort or advice in their small affairs.

All were unconscious that this experience was a test of character; and, when the first excitement was over, felt that they had done well, and deserved praise. So they did; but their mistake was in ceasing to do well, and they learned this lesson through much anxiety and regret.

'Meg, I wish you'd go and see the Hummels; you know mother told us not to forget them,' said Beth, ten days after Mrs March's departure.

'I'm too tired to go this afternoon,' replied Meg, rocking comfortably, as she sewed.

'Can't you, Jo?' asked Beth.

'Too stormy for me, with my cold.'

'I thought it was most well.'

'It's well enough for me to go out with Laurie, but not well enough to go to the Hummels,' said Jo, laughing, but looking a little ashamed of her inconsistency.

'Why don't you go yourself?' asked Meg.

'I *have* been every day, but the baby is sick, and I don't know what to do for it. Mrs Hummel goes away to work, and Lottchen takes care of it; but it gets sicker and sicker, and I think you or Hannah ought to go.'

Beth spoke earnestly, and Meg promised she would go tomorrow.

'Ask Hannah for some nice little mess, and take it round, Beth, the air will do you good;' said Jo, adding apologetically, 'I'd go, but I want to finish my story.'

'My head aches, and I'm tired, so I thought maybe some of you would go,' said Beth.

'Amy will be in presently, and she will run down for us,' suggested Meg.

'Well, I'll rest a little, and wait for her.'

So Beth lay down on the sofa, the others returned to their work, and the Hummels were forgotten. An hour passed, Amy did not come; Meg went to her room to try on a new dress; Jo was absorbed in her story, and Hannah was sound asleep before the kitchen fire, when Beth quietly put on her hood, filled her basket with odds and ends for the poor children, and went out into the chilly air with a heavy head, and a grieved look in her patient eyes. It was late when she came back, and no one saw her creep upstairs and shut herself into her mother's room. Half an hour after, Jo went to 'mother's closet' for something, and there found Beth sitting on the medicine chest, looking very grave, with red eyes, and a camphor bottle in her hand.

'Christopher Columbus! what's the matter?' cried Jo, as Beth put out her hand as if to warn her off, and asked quickly,—

'You've had scarlet fever, haven't you?'

'Years ago, when Meg did. Why?'

'Then I'll tell you—oh, Jo, the baby's dead!'

'What baby?'

'Mrs Hummel's; it died in my lap before she got home,' cried Beth, with a sob.

'My poor dear, how dreadful for you! I ought to have gone,' said Jo, taking her sister in her lap as she sat down in her mother's big chair, with a remorseful face.

'It wasn't dreadful, Jo, only so sad! I saw in a minute that it was sicker, but Lottchen said her mother had gone for a doctor, so I took baby and let Lotty rest. It seemed asleep, but all of a sudden it gave a little cry, and trembled, and then lay very still. I tried to warm its feet, and Lotty gave it some milk, but it didn't stir, and I knew it was dead.'

'Don't cry, dear! what did you do?'

'I just sat and held it softly till Mrs Hummel came with the doctor. He said it was dead, and looked at Heinrich and Minna, who have got sore throats. "Scarlet fever, ma'am; ought to have called me before," he said, crossly. Mrs Hummel told him she was poor, and had tried to cure baby herself, but now it was too late, and she could only ask him to help the others, and trust to charity for his pay. He smiled then, and was kinder, but it was very sad, and I cried with them till he turned round all of a sudden, and told me to go home and take belladonna right away, or I'd have the fever.'

'No you won't!' cried Jo, hugging her close, with a frightened look. 'Oh, Beth, if you should be sick I never could forgive myself! What *shall* we do?'

'Don't be frightened, I guess I shan't have it badly; I looked in mother's book, and saw that it begins with headache, sore throat, and queer feelings like mine, so I did take some belladonna, and I feel better,' said Beth, laying her cold hands on her hot forehead, and trying to look well.

'If mother was only at home!' exclaimed Jo, seizing the book, and feeling that Washington was an immense way off. She read a page, looked at Beth, felt her head, peeped into her throat, and then said, gravely, 'You've been over the baby every day for more than a week, and among the others who are going to have it, so I'm afraid you're going to have it, Beth. I'll call Hannah; she knows all about sickness.'

'Don't let Amy come; she never had it, and I should hate to give it to her. Can't you and Meg have it over again?' asked Beth, anxiously.

'I guess not; don't care if I do; serve me right, selfish pig, to let you go, and stay writing rubbish myself!' muttered Jo, as she went to consult Hannah.

The good soul was wide awake in a minute, and took the lead at once, assuring Jo that there was no need to worry; every one had scarlet fever, and, if rightly treated, nobody died; all of which Jo believed, and felt much relieved as they went up to call Meg.

'Now I'll tell you what we'll do,' said Hannah, when she had examined and questioned Beth; 'we will have Dr Bangs, just to take a look at you, dear, and see that we start right; then we'll send Amy off to Aunt March's, for a spell, to keep her out of harm's way, and one of you girls can stay at home and amuse Beth for a day or two.'

'I shall stay, of course, I'm oldest;' began Meg, looking anxious and self-reproachful.

'*I* shall, because it's my fault she is sick; I told mother I'd do the errands, and I haven't,' said Jo, decidedly.

'Which will you have, Beth? there ain't no need of but one,' said Hannah.

'Jo, please;' and Beth leaned her head against her sister, with a contented look, which effectually settled that point.

'I'll go and tell Amy,' said Meg, feeling a little hurt, yet rather relieved, on the whole, for she did not like nursing, and Jo did.

Amy rebelled outright, and passionately declared that she had rather have the fever than go to Aunt March. Meg reasoned, pleaded, and commanded, all in vain. Amy protested that she would *not* go; and Meg left her in despair, to ask Hannah what should be done. Before she came back, Laurie walked into the parlor to find Amy sobbing, with her head in the sofa cushions. She told her story, expecting to be consoled; but Laurie only put his hands in his pockets and walked about the room, whistling softly, as he knit his brows in deep thought. Presently he sat down beside her, and said, in his most wheedlesome tone, 'Now be a sensible little woman, and do as they say. No, don't cry, but hear what a jolly plan I've got. You go to Aunt March's, and I'll come and take you out every day, driving or walking, and we'll have capital times. Won't that be better than moping here?'

'I don't wish to be sent off as if I was in the way,' began Amy, in an injured voice.

'Bless your heart, child! it's to keep you well. You don't want to be sick, do you?'

'No, I'm sure I don't; but I dare say I shall be, for I've been with Beth all this time.'

'That's the very reason you ought to go away at once, so that you may escape it. Change of air and care will keep you well, I dare say; or, if it don't entirely, you will have the fever more lightly. I advise you to be off as soon as you can, for scarlet fever is no joke, miss.'

'But it's dull at Aunt March's, and she is so cross,' said Amy, looking rather frightened.

'It won't be dull with me popping in every day to tell you how Beth is, and take you out gallivanting. The old lady likes me, and I'll be as clever as possible to her, so she won't peck at us, whatever we do.'

'Will you take me out in the trotting wagon with Puck?'

'On my honor as a gentleman.'

'And come every single day?'

'See if I don't.'

'And bring me back the minute Beth is well?'

'The identical minute.'

'And go to the theatre, truly?'

'A dozen theatres, if we may.'

'Well—I guess—I will,' said Amy, slowly.

'Good girl! Sing out for Meg, and tell her you'll give in,' said Laurie, with an approving pat, which annoyed Amy more than the 'giving in.'

Meg and Jo came running down to behold the miracle which had been wrought; and Amy, feeling very precious and self-sacrificing, promised to go, if the doctor said Beth was going to be ill.

'How is the little dear?' asked Laurie; for Beth was his especial pet, and he felt more anxious about her than he liked to show.

'She is lying down on mother's bed, and feels better. The baby's death troubled her, but I dare say she has only got cold. Hannah *says* she thinks so; but she *looks* worried, and that makes me fidgety,' answered Meg.

'What a trying world it is!' said Jo, rumpling up her hair in a fretful sort of way. 'No sooner do we get out of one trouble than down comes another. There don't seem to be anything to hold on to when mother's gone; so I'm all at sea.'

'Well, don't make a porcupine of yourself, it isn't becoming. Settle your wig, Jo, and tell me if I shall telegraph to your mother, or do anything?' asked Laurie, who never had been reconciled to the loss of his friend's one beauty.

'That is what troubles me,' said Meg. 'I think we ought to tell her if Beth is really ill, but Hannah says we mustn't, for mother can't leave father, and it will only make them anxious. Beth won't be sick long, and Hannah knows just what to do, and mother said we were to mind her, so I suppose we must, but it don't seem quite right to me.'

'Hum, well, I can't say; suppose you ask grandfather, after the doctor has been.'

'We will; Jo, go and get Dr Bangs at once,' commanded Meg; 'we can't decide anything till he has been.'

'Stay where you are, Jo; I'm errand boy to this establishment,' said Laurie, taking up his cap.

'I'm afraid you are busy,' began Meg.

'No, I've done my lessons for the day.'

'Do you study in vacation time?' asked Jo.

'I follow the good example my neighbors set me,' was Laurie's answer, as he swung himself out of the room.

'I have great hopes of my boy,' observed Jo, watching him fly over the fence with an approving smile.

'He does very well—for a boy,' was Meg's somewhat ungracious answer, for the subject did not interest her.

Dr Bangs came, said Beth had symptoms of the

fever, but thought she would have it lightly, though he looked sober over the Hummel story. Amy was ordered off at once, and provided with something to ward off danger; she departed in great state, with Jo and Laurie as escort.

Aunt March received them with her usual hospitality.

'What do you want now?' she asked, looking sharply over her spectacles, while the parrot, sitting on the back of her chair, called out,—

'Go away; no boys allowed here.'

Laurie retired to the window, and Jo told her story.

'No more than I expected, if you are allowed to go poking about among poor folks. Amy can stay and make herself useful if she isn't sick, which I've no doubt she will be,—looks like it now. Don't cry, child, it worries me to hear people sniff.'

Amy *was* on the point of crying, but Laurie slyly pulled the parrot's tail, which caused Polly to utter an astonished croak, and call out,—

'Bless my boots!' in such a funny way, that she laughed instead.

'What do you hear from your mother?' asked the old lady, gruffly.

'Father is much better,' replied Jo, trying to keep sober.

'Oh, is he? Well, that won't last long, I fancy; March never had any stamina,' was the cheerful reply.

'Ha, ha! never say die, take a pinch of snuff, good-by, good-by!' squalled Polly, dancing on her perch, and clawing at the old lady's cap as Laurie tweaked him in the rear.

'Hold your tongue, you disrespectful old bird! and, Jo, you'd better go at once; it isn't proper to be gadding about so late with a rattle-pated boy like—'

'Hold your tongue, you disrespectful old bird!' cried Polly, tumbling off the chair with a bounce, and running to peck the 'rattle-pated' boy, who was shaking with laughter at the last speech.

'I don't think I *can* bear it, but I'll try,' thought Amy, as she was left alone with Aunt March.

'Get along, you're a fright!' screamed Polly, and at that rude speech Amy could not restrain a sniff.

18

Dark Days

BETH did have the fever, and was much sicker than any one but Hannah and the doctor suspected. The girls knew nothing about illness, and Mr Laurence was not allowed to see her, so Hannah had everything all her own way, and busy Dr Bangs did his best, but left a good deal to the excellent nurse. Meg stayed at home, lest she should infect the Kings, and kept house, feeling very anxious, and a little guilty, when she wrote letters in which no mention was made of Beth's illness. She could not think it right to deceive her mother, but she had been bidden to mind Hannah, and Hannah wouldn't hear of 'Mrs March bein' told, and worried just for sech a trifle.' Jo devoted herself to Beth day and night; not a hard task, for Beth was very patient, and bore her pain uncomplainingly as long as she could control herself. But there came a time when during the fever fits she began to talk in a hoarse, broken voice, to play on the coverlet, as if on her beloved little piano, and try to sing with a throat so swollen, that there was no music left; a time when she did not know the familiar faces round her, but addressed them by wrong names, and called imploringly for her mother. Then Jo grew frightened, Meg begged to be allowed to write the truth, and even Hannah said she 'would think of it, though there was no danger *yet.*' A letter from Washington added to their trouble, for Mr March had had a relapse, and could not think of coming home for a long while.

How dark the days seemed now, how sad and lonely the house, and how heavy were the hearts of the sisters as they worked and waited, while the shadow of death hovered over the once happy home! Then it was that Margaret, sitting alone with tears dropping often on her work, felt how rich she had been in things more precious than any luxuries money could buy; in love, protection, peace and health, the real blessings of life. Then it was that Jo, living in the darkened room with that suffering little sister always before her eyes, and that pathetic voice sounding in her ears, learned to see the beauty and the sweetness of Beth's nature, to feel how deep and tender a place she filled in all hearts, and to acknowledge the worth of Beth's unselfish ambition, to live for others, and make home happy by the exercise of those simple virtues which all may possess, and which all should love and value more than talent, wealth or beauty. And Amy, in her exile, longed eagerly to be at home, that she might work for Beth, feeling now that no service would be hard or irksome, and remembering, with regretful grief, how many neglected tasks those willing hands had done for her. Laurie haunted the house like a restless ghost, and Mr Laurence locked the grand piano, because he could not bear to be reminded of the young neighbor who used to make the twilight pleasant for him. Every one missed Beth. The milk-man, baker, grocer and butcher inquired how she did; poor Mrs Hummel came to beg pardon for her thoughtlessness, and to get a shroud for Minna; the neighbors sent all sorts of comforts and good wishes, and even those who knew her best, were surprised to find how many friends shy little Beth had made.

Meanwhile she lay on her bed with old Joanna at her side, for even in her wanderings she did not forget her forlorn *protégé*. She longed for her cats, but would not have them brought, lest they should get sick; and, in her quiet hours, she was full of anxiety about Jo. She sent loving messages to Amy, bade them tell her mother that she would write soon; and often begged for pencil and paper to try to say a word, that father might not think she had neglected him. But soon even these intervals of consciousness ended, and she lay hour after hour tossing to and fro with incoherent words on her lips, or sank into a heavy sleep which brought her no refreshment. Dr Bangs came twice a day, Hannah sat up at night, Meg kept a telegram in her desk all ready to send off at any minute, and Jo never stirred from Beth's side.

The first of December was a wintry day indeed to them, for a bitter wind blew, snow fell fast, and the year seemed getting ready for its death. When Dr Bangs came that morning, he looked long at Beth, held the hot hand in both his own a minute, and laid it gently down, saying, in a low tone, to Hannah,—

'If Mrs March *can* leave her husband, she'd better be sent for.'

Hannah nodded without speaking, for her lips twitched nervously; Meg dropped down into a chair as the strength seemed to go out of her limbs at the sound of those words, and Jo, after standing with a pale face for a minute, ran to the parlor, snatched up the telegram, and, throwing on her things, rushed out into the storm. She was soon back, and, while noiselessly taking off her cloak, Laurie came in with a letter, saying that Mr March was mending again. Jo read it thankfully, but the heavy weight did not seem lifted off her heart, and her face was so full of misery that Laurie asked, quickly,—

'What is it? is Beth worse?'

'I've sent for mother,' said Jo, tugging at her rubber boots with a tragical expression.

'Good for you, Jo! Did you do it on your own responsibility?' asked Laurie, as he seated her in the hall chair and took off the rebellious boots, seeing how her hands shook.

'No, the doctor told us to.'

'Oh, Jo, it's not so bad as that?' cried Laurie, with a startled face.

'Yes, it is; she don't know us, she don't even talk about the flocks of green doves, as she calls the vine leaves on the wall; she don't look like my Beth, and there's nobody to help us bear it; mother and father both gone, and God seems so far away I can't find Him.'

As the tears streamed fast down poor Jo's cheeks, she stretched out her hand in a helpless sort of way, as if groping in the dark, and Laurie took it in his, whispering, as well as he could, with a lump in his throat,—

'I'm here, hold on to me, Jo, dear!'

She could not speak, but she did 'hold on,' and the warm grasp of the friendly human hand comforted her sore heart, and seemed to lead her nearer to the Divine arm which alone could uphold her in her trouble. Laurie longed to say something tender and comfortable, but no fitting words came to him, so he stood silent, gently stroking her bent head as her mother used to do. It was the best thing he could have done; far more soothing than the most eloquent words, for Jo felt the unspoken sympathy, and, in the silence, learned the sweet solace which affection administers to sorrow. Soon she dried the tears which had relieved her, and looked up with a grateful face.

'Thank you, Teddy, I'm better now; I don't feel so forlorn, and will try to bear it if it comes.'

'Keep hoping for the best; that will help you lots, Jo. Soon your mother will be here, and then everything will be right.'

'I'm so glad father is better; now she won't feel so bad about leaving him. Oh, me! it does seem as if all the troubles came in a heap, and I got the heaviest part on my shoulders,' sighed Jo, spreading her wet handkerchief over her knees, to dry.

'Don't Meg pull fair?' asked Laurie, looking indignant.

'Oh, yes; she tries to, but she don't love Bethy as I do; and she won't miss her as I shall. Beth is my conscience, and I *can't* give her up; I can't! I can't!'

Down went Jo's face into the wet handkerchief, and she cried despairingly; for she had kept up bravely till now, and never shed a tear. Laurie drew his hand across his eyes, but could not speak till he had subdued the choky feeling in his throat, and steadied his lips. It might be unmanly, but he couldn't help it, and I am glad of it. Presently, as Jo's sobs quieted, he said, hopefully, 'I don't think she will die; she's so good, and we all love her so much, I don't believe God will take her away yet.'

'The good and dear people always do die,' groaned Jo, but she stopped crying, for her friend's words cheered her up, in spite of her own doubts and fears.

'Poor girl! you're worn out. It isn't like you to be forlorn. Stop a bit; I'll hearten you up in a jiffy.'

Laurie went off two stairs at a time, and Jo laid her wearied head down on Beth's little brown hood, which no one had thought of moving from the table where she left it. It must have possessed some magic, for the submissive spirit of its gentle owner seemed to enter into Jo; and, when Laurie came running down with a glass of wine, she took it with a smile, and said, bravely, 'I drink—Health to my Beth! You are a good doctor, Teddy, and *such* a comfortable friend; how can I ever pay you?' she added, as the wine refreshed her body, as the kind words had done her troubled mind.

'I'll send in my bill, by and by; and tonight I'll give

you something that will warm the cockles of your heart better than quarts of wine,' said Laurie, beaming at her with a face of suppressed satisfaction at something.

'What is it?' cried Jo, forgetting her woes for a minute, in her wonder.

'I telegraphed to your mother yesterday, and Brooke answered she'd come at once, and she'll be here tonight, and everything will be all right. Aren't you glad I did it?'

Laurie spoke very fast, and turned red and excited all in a minute, for he had kept his plot a secret, for fear of disappointing the girls or harming Beth. Jo grew quite white, flew out of her chair, and the moment he stopped speaking she electrified him by throwing her arms round his neck, and crying out, with a joyful cry, 'Oh, Laurie! oh, mother! I *am* so glad!' She did not weep again, but laughed hysterically, and trembled and clung to her friend as if she was a little bewildered by the sudden news. Laurie, though decidedly amazed, behaved with great presence of mind; he patted her back soothingly, and, finding that she was recovering, followed it up by a bashful kiss or two, which brought Jo round at once. Holding on to the banisters, she put him gently away, saying, breathless, 'Oh, don't! I didn't mean to; it was dreadful of me; but you were such a dear to go and do it in spite of Hannah, that I couldn't help flying at you. Tell me all about it, and don't give me wine again; it makes me act so.'

'I don't mind!' laughed Laurie, as he settled his tie. 'Why, you see I got fidgety, and so did grandpa. We thought Hannah was overdoing the authority business, and your mother ought to know. She'd never forgive us if Beth,—well, if anything happened, you know. So I got grandpa to say it was high time we did something, and off I pelted to the office yesterday, for the doctor looked sober, and Hannah most took my head off when I proposed a telegram. I never *can* bear to be "marmed over;" so that settled my mind, and I did it. Your mother will come, I know, and the late train is in at two, A.M. I shall go for her; and you've only got to bottle up your rapture, and keep Beth quiet, till that blessed lady gets here.'

'Laurie, you're an angel! How shall I ever thank you?'

'Fly at me again; I rather like it,' said Laurie, looking mischievous,—a thing he had not done for a fortnight.

'No, thank you. I'll do it by proxy, when your grandpa comes. Don't tease, but go home and rest, for you'll be up half the night. Bless you, Teddy; bless you!'

Jo had backed into a corner; and, as she finished her speech, she vanished precipitately into the kitchen, where she sat down upon a dresser, and told the assembled cats that she was 'happy, oh, *so* happy!' while Laurie departed, feeling that he had made rather a neat thing of it.

'That's the interferingest chap I ever see; but I forgive him, and do hope Mrs March is coming on right away,' said Hannah, with an air of relief, when Jo told the good news.

Meg had a quiet rapture, and then brooded over the letter, while Jo set the sick room in order, and Hannah 'knocked up a couple of pies in case of company unexpected.' A breath of fresh air seemed to blow through the house, and something better than sunshine brightened the quiet rooms; everything appeared to feel the hopeful change; Beth's bird began to chirp again, and a half-blown rose was discovered on Amy's bush in the window; the fires seemed to burn with unusual cheeriness, and every time the girls met their pale faces broke into smiles as they hugged one another, whispering, encouragingly, 'Mother's coming, dear! mother's coming!' Every one rejoiced but Beth; she lay in that heavy stupor, alike unconscious of hope and joy, doubt and danger. It was a piteous sight,—the once rosy face so changed and vacant,—the once busy hands so weak and wasted,—the once smiling lips quite dumb,—and the once pretty, well-kept hair scattered rough and tangled on the pillow. All day she lay so, only rousing now and then to mutter, 'Water!' with lips so parched they could hardly shape the word; all day Jo and Meg hovered over her, watching, waiting, hoping, and trusting in God and mother; and all day the snow fell, the bitter wind raged, and the hours dragged slowly by. But night came at last; and every time the clock struck the sisters, still sitting on either side of the bed, looked at each other with brightening eyes, for each hour brought help nearer. The doctor had been in to say that some change for better or worse would probably take place about midnight, at which time he would return.

Hannah, quite worn out, lay down on the sofa at the bed's foot, and fell fast asleep; Mr Laurence marched to and fro in the parlor, feeling that he would rather face a rebel battery than Mrs March's anxious countenance as she entered; Laurie lay on the rug, pretending to rest, but staring into the fire with the thoughtful look which made his black eyes beautifully soft and clear.

The girls never forgot that night, for no sleep came to them as they kept their watch, with that dreadful sense of powerlessness which comes to us in hours like those.

'If God spares Beth I never will complain again,' whispered Meg, earnestly.

'If God spares Beth I'll try to love and serve Him all my life,' answered Jo, with equal fervor.

'I wish 1 had no heart, it aches so,' sighed Meg, after a pause.

'If life is often as hard as this, I don't see how we ever shall get through it,' added her sister, despondently.

Here the clock struck twelve, and both forgot themselves in watching Beth, for they fancied a change passed over her wan face. The house was still as death, and nothing but the wailing of the wind broke the deep hush. Weary Hannah slept on, and no one but the sisters saw the pale shadow which seemed to fall upon the little bed. An hour went by, and nothing happened except Laurie's quiet departure for the station. Another hour,—still no one came; and anxious fears of delay in the storm, or accidents by the way, or, worst of all, a great grief at Washington, haunted the poor girls.

It was past two, when Jo, who stood at the window thinking how dreary the world looked in its winding-sheet of snow, heard a movement by the bed, and, turning quickly, saw Meg kneeling before their mother's easy-chair, with her face hidden. A dreadful fear passed coldly over Jo, as she thought, 'Beth is dead, and Meg is afraid to tell me.'

She was back at her post in an instant, and to her excited eyes a great change seemed to have taken place. The fever flush, and the look of pain, were gone, and the beloved little face looked so pale and peaceful in its utter repose, that Jo felt no desire to weep or lament. Leaning low over this dearest of her sisters, she kissed the damp forehead with her heart on her lips, and softly whispered, 'Good-by, my Beth; good-by!'

As if waked by the stir, Hannah started out of her sleep, hurried to the bed, looked at Beth, felt her hands, listened at her lips, and then, throwing her apron over her head, sat down to rock to and fro, exclaiming, under her breath, 'The fever's turned; she's sleepin' nat'ral; her skin's damp, and she breathes easy. Praise be given! Oh, my goodness me!'

Before the girls could believe the happy truth, the doctor came to confirm it. He was a homely man, but they thought his face quite heavenly when he smiled, and said, with a fatherly look at them, 'Yes, my dears; I think the little girl will pull through this time. Keep the house quiet; let her sleep, and when she wakes give her—'

What they were to give, neither heard; for both crept into the dark hall, and, sitting on the stairs, held each other close, rejoicing with hearts too full for words. When they went back to be kissed and cuddled by faithful Hannah, they found Beth lying, as she used to do, with her cheek pillowed on her hand, the dreadful pallor gone, and breathing quietly, as if just fallen asleep.

'If mother would only come now!' said Jo, as the winter night began to wane.

'See,' said Meg, coming up with a white, half-opened rose, 'I thought this would hardly be ready to lay in Beth's hand tomorrow if she—went away from us. But it has blossomed in the night, and now I mean to put it in my vase here, so that when the darling wakes, the first thing she sees will be the little rose, and mother's face.'

Never had the sun risen so beautifully, and never had the world seemed so lovely, as it did to the heavy eyes of Meg and Jo, as they looked out in the early morning, when their long, sad vigil was done.

'It looks like a fairy world,' said Meg, smiling to herself, as she stood behind the curtain watching the dazzling sight.

'Hark!' cried Jo, starting to her feet.

Yes, there was a sound of bells at the door below, a cry from Hannah, and then Laurie's voice, saying, in a joyful whisper, 'Girls! she's come! she's come!'

19

Amy's Will

WHILE these things were happening at home, Amy was having hard times at Aunt March's. She felt her exile deeply, and, for the first time in her life, realized how much she was beloved and petted at home. Aunt March never petted any one; she did not approve of it; but she meant to be kind, for the well-behaved little girl pleased her very much, and Aunt March had a soft place in her old heart for her nephew's children, though she didn't think proper to confess it. She really did her best to make Amy happy, but, dear me, what mistakes she made! Some old people keep young at heart in spite of wrinkles and gray hairs, can sympathize with children's little cares and joys, make them feel at home, and can hide wise lessons under pleasant plays, giving and receiving friendship in the sweetest way. But Aunt March had not this gift, and she worried Amy most to death with her rules and orders, her prim ways, and long, prosy talks. Finding the child more docile and amiable than her sister, the old lady felt it her duty to try and counteract, as far as possible, the bad effects of home freedom and indulgence. So she took Amy in hand, and taught her as she herself had been taught sixty years ago; a process which carried dismay to Amy's soul, and made her feel like a fly in the web of a very strict spider.

She had to wash the cups every morning, and polish up the old-fashioned spoons, the fat silver teapot, and the glasses, till they shone. Then she must dust the room, and what a trying job that was! Not a speck escaped Aunt March's eye, and all the furniture had claw legs, and much carving, which was never dusted to suit. Then Polly must be fed, the lap-dog combed, and a dozen trips upstairs and down, to get things or deliver orders, for the old lady was very lame, and seldom left her big chair. After these tiresome labors she must do her lessons, which was a daily trial of every virtue she possessed. Then she was allowed one hour for exercise or play, and didn't she enjoy it? Laurie came every day, and wheedled Aunt March till Amy was allowed to go out with him, when they walked and rode, and had capital times. After dinner she had to read aloud, and sit still while the old lady slept, which she usually did for an hour, as she dropped off over the first page. Then patch-work or towels appeared, and Amy sewed with outward meekness and inward rebellion till dusk, when she was allowed to amuse herself as she liked, till tea-time. The evenings were the worst of all, for Aunt March fell to telling long stories about her youth, which were so unutterably dull, that Amy was always ready to go to bed, intending to cry over her hard fate, but usually going to sleep before she had squeezed out more than a tear or two.

If it had not been for Laurie and old Esther, the maid, she felt that she never could have got through that dreadful time. The parrot alone was enough to drive her distracted, for he soon felt that she did not admire him, and revenged himself by being as mischievous as possible. He pulled her hair whenever she came near him, upset his bread and milk to plague her when she had newly cleaned his cage, made Mop bark by pecking at him while Madame dozed; called her names before company, and behaved in all respects like a reprehensible old bird. Then she could not endure the dog, a fat, cross beast, who snarled and yelped at her when she made his toilet, and who laid on his back with all his legs in the air, and a most idiotic expression of countenance, when he wanted something to eat, which was about a dozen times a day. The cook was bad-tempered, the old coachman deaf, and Esther the only one who ever took any notice of the young lady.

Esther was a French woman, who had lived with 'Madame,' as she called her mistress, for many years, and who rather tyrannized over the old lady, who could not get along without her. Her real name was Estelle; but Aunt March ordered her to change it, and she obeyed, on condition that she was never asked to change her religion. She took a fancy to Mademoiselle, and amused her very much, with odd stories of her life in France, when Amy sat with her while she got up Madame's laces. She also allowed her to roam about the great house, and examine the curious and pretty things stored away in the big wardrobes and the ancient chests; for Aunt March hoarded like a magpie. Amy's chief delight was an Indian cabinet full of queer drawers, little pigeon-holes, and secret places in which were kept all sorts of ornaments, some precious, some merely curious, all more or less antique. To examine and arrange these things gave Amy great satisfaction, especially the jewel cases; in which, on velvet cushions, reposed the ornaments which had adorned a belle forty years ago. There was the garnet set which Aunt March wore when she came out, the pearls her father gave her on her wedding day, her lover's diamonds, the jet mourning rings and pins, the queer lockets, with portraits of dead friends, and weeping willows made of hair inside, the baby bracelets her one little daughter had worn; Uncle March's big watch, with the red seal so many childish hands had played with, and in a box, all by itself, lay Aunt March's wedding ring, too small now for her fat finger, but put carefully away, like the most precious jewel of them all.

'Which would Mademoiselle choose if she had her will?' asked Esther, who always sat near to watch over and lock up the valuables.

'I like the diamonds best, but there is no necklace among them, and I'm fond of necklaces, they are so becoming. I should choose this if I might,' replied Amy, looking with great admiration at a string of gold and ebony beads, from which hung a heavy cross of the same.

'I, too, covet that, but not as a necklace; ah, no! to me it is a rosary, and as such I should use it like a good Catholic,' said Esther, eyeing the handsome thing wistfully.

'Is it meant to use as you use the string of good-smelling wooden beads hanging over your glass?' asked Amy.

'Truly, yes, to pray with. It would be pleasing to the saints if one used so fine a rosary as this, instead of wearing it as a vain bijou.'

'You seem to take a deal of comfort in your prayers, Esther, and always come down looking quiet and satisfied. I wish I could.'

'If Mademoiselle was a Catholic, she would find true comfort; but, as that is not to be, it would be well if you went apart each day to meditate, and pray, as did the good mistress whom I served before Madame. She had a little chapel, and in it found solacement for much trouble.'

'Would it be right for me to do so too?' asked Amy, who, in her loneliness, felt the need of help of some sort, and found that she was apt to forget her little book, now that Beth was not there to remind her of it.

'It would be excellent and charming; and I shall gladly arrange the little dressing-room for you, if you like it. Say nothing to Madame, but when she sleeps go you and sit alone a while to think good thoughts, and ask the dear God to preserve your sister.'

Esther was truly pious, and quite sincere in her advice; for she had an affectionate heart, and felt much for the sisters in their anxiety. Amy liked the idea, and gave her leave to arrange the light closet next her room, hoping it would do her good.

'I wish I knew where all these pretty things would go when Aunt March dies,' she said, as she slowly replaced the shining rosary, and shut the jewel cases one by one.

'To you and your sisters. I know it; Madame confides in me; I witnessed her will, and it is to be so,' whispered Esther, smiling.

'How nice! but I wish she'd let us have them now. Pro-cras-ti-nation is not agreeable,' observed Amy, taking a last look at the diamonds.

'It is too soon yet for the young ladies to wear these things. The first one who is affianced will have the pearls—Madame has said it; and I have a fancy that the little turquoise ring will be given to you when you do, for Madame approves your good behavior and charming manners.'

'Do you think so? Oh, I'll be a lamb, if I can only have that lovely ring! It's ever so much prettier than Kitty Bryant's. I do like Aunt March, after all;' and Amy tried on the blue ring with a delighted face, and a firm resolve to earn it.

From that day she was a model of obedience, and the old lady complacently admired the success of her training. Esther fitted up the closet with a little table, placed a footstool before it, and over it a picture, taken from one of the shut-up rooms. She thought it was of no great value, but, being appropriate, she borrowed it, well knowing that Madame would never know it, nor care if she did. It was, however, a very valuable copy of one of the famous pictures of the world, and Amy's beauty-loving eyes were never tired of looking up at the sweet face of the divine other, while tender thoughts of her own were busy at her heart. On the table she laid her little Testament and hymn-book, kept a vase always full of the best flowers Laurie brought her, and came every day to 'sit alone, thinking good thoughts, and praying the dear God to preserve her sister.' Esther had given her a rosary of black beads, with a silver cross, but Amy hung it up, and did not use it, feeling doubtful as to its fitness for Protestant prayers.

The little girl was very sincere in all this, for, being left alone outside the safe home-nest, she felt the need of some kind hand to hold by so sorely, that she instinctively turned to the strong and tender Friend, whose fatherly love most closely surrounds His little children. She missed her mother's help to understand and rule herself, but having been taught where to look, she did her best to find the way, and walk in it confidingly. But Amy was a young pilgrim, and just now her burden seemed very heavy. She tried to forget herself, to keep cheerful, and be satisfied with doing right, though no one saw or praised her for it. In her first effort at being very, very good, she decided to make her will, as Aunt March had done; so that if she *did* fall ill and die, her possessions might be justly and generously divided. It cost her a pang even to think of giving up the little treasures which in her eyes were as precious as the old lady's jewels.

During one of her play hours she wrote out the important document as well as she could, with some help from Esther as to certain legal terms; and, when the good-natured French woman had signed her name, Amy felt relieved, and laid it by to show Laurie, whom she wanted as a second witness. As it was a rainy day, she went upstairs to amuse herself in one of the large chambers, and took Polly with her for company. In this room there was a wardrobe full of old-fashioned costumes, with which Esther allowed her to play, and it was her favorite amusement to array herself in the faded brocades, and parade up and down before the long mirror, making stately courtesies, and sweeping her train about, with a rustle which delighted her ears. So busy was she on this day, that she did not hear Laurie's ring, nor see his face peeping in at her, as she gravely promenaded to and fro, flirting her fan and tossing her head, on which she wore a great pink turban, contrasting oddly with her blue brocade dress and yellow quilted petticoat. She was obliged to walk carefully, for she had on high-heeled shoes, and, as Laurie told Jo afterward, it was a comical sight to see her mince along in her gay suit, with Polly sidling and bridling just behind her, imitating her as well as he could, and occasionally stopping to laugh, or exclaim, 'Ain't we fine? Get along you fright! Hold your tongue! Kiss me, dear; ha! ha!'

Having with difficulty restrained an explosion of merriment, lest it should offend her majesty, Laurie tapped, and was graciously received.

'Sit down and rest while I put these things away; then I want to consult you about a very serious matter,' said Amy, when she had shown her splendor, and driven Polly into a corner. 'That bird is the trial of my life,' she continued, removing the pink mountain from her head, while Laurie seated himself astride of a chair. 'Yesterday, when aunt was asleep, and I was trying to be as still as a mouse, Polly began to squall and flap about in his cage; so I went to let him out, and found a big spider there. I poked it out, and it ran under the book-case; Polly marched straight after it, stooped down and peeped under the book-case, saying, in his funny way, with a cock of his eye, "Come out and take a walk, my dear." I *couldn't* help laughing, which made Poll swear, and aunt woke up and scolded us both.'

'Did the spider accept the old fellow's invitation?' asked Laurie, yawning.

'Yes; out it came, and away ran Polly, frightened to death, and scrambled up on aunt's chair, calling out, "Catch her! catch her! catch her!" as I chased the spider.'

'That's a lie! Oh lor!' cried the parrot, pecking at Laurie's toes.

'I'd wring your neck if you were mine, you old torment,' cried Laurie, shaking his fist at the bird; who put his head on one side, and gravely croaked, 'Allyluyer! bless your buttons, dear!'

'Now I'm ready,' said Amy, shutting the wardrobe, and taking a paper out of her pocket. 'I want you to read that, please, and tell me if it is legal and right. I felt that I ought to do it, for life is uncertain, and I don't want any ill-feeling over my tomb.'

Laurie bit his lips, and turning a little from the pensive speaker, read the following document, with praiseworthy gravity, considering the spelling:—

'MY LAST WILL AND TESTIMENT.

'I, Amy Curtis March, being in my sane mind, do give and bequeethe all my earthly property—viz. to wit:—namely

'To my father, my best pictures, sketches, maps, and works of art, including frames. Also my $100, to do what he likes with.

'To my mother, all my clothes, except the blue apron with pockets,—also my likeness, and my medal, with much love.

'To my dear sister Margaret, I give my turkquoise ring (if I get it), also my green box with the doves on it, also my piece of real lace for her neck, and my sketch of her as a memorial of her "little girl."

'To Jo I leave my breast-pin, the one mended with sealing wax, also my bronze inkstand—she lost the cover,—and my most precious plaster rabbit, because I am sorry I burnt up her story.

'To Beth (if she lives after me) I give my dolls and the little bureau, my fan, my linen collars and my new slippers if she can wear them being thin when she gets well. And I herewith also leave her my regret that I ever made fun of old Joanna.

'To my friend and neighbor Theodore Laurence I bequeethe my paper marshay portfolio, my clay model of a horse though he did say it hadn't any neck. Also in return for his great kindness in the hour of affliction any one of my artistic works he likes, Noter Dame is the best.

'To our venerable benefactor Mr Laurence I leave my purple box with a looking glass in the cover which will be nice for his pens and remind him of the departed girl who thanks him for his favors to her family, specially Beth.

'I wish my favorite playmate Kitty Bryant to have the blue silk apron and my gold-bead ring with a kiss.

'To Hannah I give the band-box she wanted and all the patch work I leave hoping she "will remember me, when it you see."

'And now having disposed of my most valuable property I hope all will be satisfied and not blame the dead. I forgive every one, and trust we may all meet when the trump shall sound. Amen.

'To this will and testiment I set my hand and seal on this 20th day of Nov. Anni Domino 1861.

'Amy Curtis March.

'*Witnesses:* Estelle Valnor, Theodore Laurence.'

The last name was written in pencil, and Amy explained that he was to rewrite it in ink, and seal it up for her properly.

'What put it into your head? Did any one tell you about Beth's giving away her things?' asked Laurie, soberly, as Amy laid a bit of red tape, with sealing-wax, a taper, and a standish before him.

She explained; and then asked, anxiously, 'What about Beth?'

'I'm sorry I spoke; but as I did, I'll tell you. She felt so ill one day, that she told Jo she wanted to give her piano to Meg, her bird to you, and the poor old doll to Jo, who would love it for her sake. She was sorry she had so little to give, and left locks of hair to the rest of us, and her best love to grandpa. *She* never thought of a will.'

Laurie was signing and sealing as he spoke, and did not look up till a great tear dropped on the paper. Amy's face was full of trouble; but she only said, 'Don't people put sort of postscripts to their wills, sometimes.'

'Yes; "codicils," they call them.'

'Put one in mine then—that I wish *all* my curls cut off, and given round to my friends. I forgot it; but I want it done, though it will spoil my looks.'

Laurie added it, smiling at Amy's last and greatest sacrifice. Then he amused her for an hour, and was much interested in all her trials. But when he came to go, Amy held him back to whisper, with trembling lips, 'Is there really any danger about Beth?'

'I'm afraid there is; but we must hope for the best, so don't cry, dear;' and Laurie put his arm about her with a brotherly gesture, which was very comforting.

When he had gone, she went to her little chapel, and, sitting in the twilight, prayed for Beth with streaming tears and an aching heart, feeling that a million turquoise rings would not console her for the loss of her gentle little sister.

20

Confidential

I DON'T think I have any words in which to tell the meeting of the mother and daughters; such hours are beautiful to live, but very hard to describe, so I will leave it to the imagination of my readers; merely saying that the house was full of genuine happiness, and that Meg's tender hope was realized; for when Beth woke from that long, healing sleep, the first objects on which her eyes fell *were* the little rose and mother's face. Too weak to wonder at anything, she only smiled, and nestled close into the loving arms about her, feeling that the hungry longing was satisfied at last. Then she slept again, and the girls waited upon their mother, for she would not unclasp the thin hand which clung to hers, even in sleep. Hannah had 'dished up' an astonishing breakfast for the traveller, finding it impossible to vent her excitement in any other way; and Meg and Jo fed their mother like dutiful young storks, while they listened to her whispered account of father's state, Mr Brooke's promise to stay and nurse him, the delays which the storm occasioned on the homeward journey, and the unspeakable comfort Laurie's hopeful face had given her when she arrived, worn out with fatigue, anxiety and cold.

What a strange, yet pleasant day that was! so brilliant and gay without, for all the world seemed abroad to welcome the first snow; so quiet and reposeful within, for every one slept, spent with watching, and a Sabbath stillness reigned through the house, while nodding Hannah mounted guard at the door. With a blissful sense of burdens lifted off, Meg and Jo closed their weary eyes, and lay at rest like storm-beaten boats, safe at anchor in a quiet harbor. Mrs March would not leave Beth's side, but rested in the big chair, waking often to look at, touch, and brood over her child, like a miser over some recovered treasure.

Laurie, meanwhile, posted off to comfort Amy, and told his story so well that Aunt March actually 'sniffed' herself, and never once said, 'I told you so.' Amy came out so strong on this occasion, that I think the good thoughts in the little chapel really began to bear fruit. She dried her tears quickly, restrained her impatience to see her mother, and never even thought of the turquoise ring, when the old lady heartily agreed in Laurie's opinion, that she behaved 'like a capital little woman.' Even Polly seemed impressed, for he called her 'good girl,' blessed her buttons, and begged her to 'come and take a walk, dear,' in his most affable tone. She would very gladly have gone out to enjoy the bright wintry weather; but, discovering that Laurie was dropping with sleep in spite of manful efforts to conceal the fact, she persuaded him to rest on the sofa, while she wrote a note to her mother. She was a long time about it; and, when returned, he was stretched out with both arms under his head, sound asleep, while Aunt March had pulled down the curtains, and sat doing nothing in an unusual fit of benignity.

After a while, they began to think he was not going to wake till night, and I'm not sure that he would, had he not been effectually roused by Amy's cry of joy at sight of her mother. There probably were a good many happy little girls in and about the city that day, but it is my private opinion that Amy was the happiest of all, when she sat in her mother's lap and told her trials, receiving consolation and compensation in the shape of approving smiles and fond caresses. They were alone together in the chapel, to which her mother did not object when its purpose was explained to her.

'On the contrary, I like it very much, dear,' she said, looking from the dusty rosary to the well-worn little book, and the lovely picture with its garland of evergreen. 'It is an excellent plan to have some place where we can go to be quiet, when things vex or grieve us. There are a good many hard times in this life of ours, but we can always bear them if we ask help in the right way. I think my little girl is learning this?'

'Yes, mother; and when I go home I mean to have a corner in the big closet to put my books, and the copy of that picture which I've tried to make. The woman's face is not good, it's too beautiful for me to draw, but the baby is done better, and I love it very much. I like to think He was a little child once, for then I don't seem so far away, and that helps me.'

As Amy pointed to the smiling Christ-child on his mother's knee, Mrs March saw something on the lifted hand that made her smile. She said nothing, but Amy understood the look, and, after a minute's pause, she added, gravely,—

'I wanted to speak to you about this, but I forgot it. Aunt gave me the ring today; she called me to her and kissed me, and put it on my finger, and said I was a credit to her, and she'd like to keep me always. She gave that funny guard to keep the turquoise on, as it's too big. I'd like to wear them, mother; can I?'

'They are very pretty, but I think you're rather too young for such ornaments, Amy,' said Mrs March, looking at the plump little hand, with the band of sky-blue stones on the forefinger, and the quaint guard, formed of two tiny, golden hands clasped together.

'I'll try not to be vain,' said Amy; 'I don't think I like it, only because it's so pretty; but I want to wear it as the girl in the story wore her bracelet, to remind me of something.'

'Do you mean Aunt March?' asked her mother, laughing.

'No, to remind me not to be selfish.' Amy looked so earnest and sincere about it, that her mother stopped laughing, and listened respectfully to the little plan.

'I've thought a great deal lately about "my bundle of naughties," and being selfish is the largest one in it; so I'm going to try hard to cure it, if I can. Beth isn't selfish, and that's the reason every one loves her, and feels so bad at the thoughts of losing her. People wouldn't feel half so bad about me if I was sick, and I don't deserve to have them; but I'd like to be loved and missed by a great many friends, so I'm going to try and be like Beth all I can. I'm apt to forget my resolutions; but, if I had something always about me to remind me, I guess I should do better. May I try this way?'

'Yes; but I have more faith in the corner of the big

closet. Wear your ring, dear, and do your best; I think you will prosper, for the sincere wish to be good is half the battle. Now, I must go back to Beth. Keep up your heart, little daughter, and we will soon have you home again.'

That evening, while Meg was writing to her father, to report the traveller's safe arrival, Jo slipped upstairs into Beth's room, and, finding her mother in her usual place, stood a minute twisting her fingers in her hair, with a worried gesture and an undecided look.

'What is it, deary?' asked Mrs March, holding out her hand with a face which invited confidence.

'I want to tell you something, mother.'

'About Meg?'

'How quick you guessed! Yes, it's about her, and though it's a little thing, it fidgets me.'

'Beth is asleep; speak low, and tell me all about it. That Moffat hasn't been here, I hope?' asked Mrs March, rather sharply.

'No; I should have shut the door in his face if he had,' said Jo, settling herself on the floor at her mother's feet. 'Last summer Meg left a pair of gloves over at the Laurences, and only one was returned. We forgot all about it, till Teddy told me that Mr Brooke had it. He kept it in his waistcoat pocket, and once it fell out, and Teddy joked him about it, and Mr Brooke owned that he liked Meg, but didn't dare say so, she was so young and he so poor. Now isn't it a *dreadful* state of things?'

'Do you think Meg cares for him?' asked Mrs March, with an anxious look.

'Mercy me! I don't know anything about love, and such nonsense!' cried Jo, with a funny mixture of interest and contempt. 'In novels, the girls show it by starting and blushing, fainting away, growing thin, and acting like fools. Now Meg don't do anything of the sort; she eats and drinks, and sleeps, like a sensible creature; she looks straight in my face when I talk about that man, and only blushes a little bit when Teddy jokes about lovers. I forbid him to do it, but he don't mind me as he ought.'

'Then you fancy that Meg is *not* interested in John?'

'Who?' cried Jo, staring.

'Mr Brooke; I call him "John" now; we fell into the way of doing so at the hospital, and he likes it.'

'Oh, dear! I know you'll take his part; he's been good to father, and you won't send him away, but let Meg marry him, if she wants to. Mean thing! to go petting pa and truckling to you, just to wheedle you into liking him;' and Jo pulled her hair again with a wrathful tweak.

'My dear, don't get angry about it, and I will tell you how it happened. John went with me at Mr Laurence's request, and was so devoted to poor father, that we couldn't help getting fond of him. He was perfectly open and honorable about Meg, for he told us he loved her; but would earn a comfortable home before he asked her to marry him. He only wanted our leave to love her and work for her, and the right to make her love him if he could. He is a truly excellent young man, and we could not refuse to listen to him; but I will not consent to Meg's engaging herself so young.'

'Of course not; it would be idiotic! I knew there was mischief brewing; I felt it; and now it's worse than I imagined. I just wish I could marry Meg myself, and keep her safe in the family.'

This odd arrangement made Mrs March smile; but she said, gravely, 'Jo, I confide in you, and don't wish you to say anything to Meg yet. When John comes back, and I see them together, I can judge better of her feelings toward him.'

'She'll see his in those handsome eyes that she talks about, and then it will be all up with her. She's got such a soft heart, it will melt like butter in the sun if any one looks sentimentally at her. She read the short reports he sent more than she did your letters, and pinched me when I spoke of it, and likes brown eyes, and don't think John an ugly name, and she'll go and fall in love, and there's an end of peace and fun, and cosy times, together. I see it all! they'll go lovering round the house, and we shall have to dodge; Meg will be absorbed, and no good to me any more; Brooke will scratch up a fortune somehow,—carry her off and make a hole in the family; and I shall break my heart, and everything will be abominably uncomfortable. Oh, deary me! why weren't we all boys? then there wouldn't be any bother!'

Jo leaned her chin on her knees, in a disconsolate attitude, and shook her fist at the reprehensible John. Mrs March sighed, and Jo looked up with an air of relief.

'You don't like it, mother? I'm glad of it; let's send him about his business, and not tell Meg a word of it, but all be jolly together as we always have been.'

'I did wrong to sigh, Jo. It is natural and right you should all go to homes of your own, in time; but I do want to keep my girls as long as I can; and I am sorry that this happened so soon, for Meg is only seventeen, and it will be some years before John can make a home for her. Your father and I have agreed that she shall not bind herself in any way, nor be married, before twenty. If she and John love one another, they can wait, and test the love by doing so. She is conscientious, and I have no fear of her treating him unkindly. My pretty, tender-hearted girl! I hope things will go happily with her.'

'Hadn't you rather have her marry a rich man?' asked

Jo, as her mother's voice faltered a little over the last words.

'Money is a good and useful thing, Jo; and I hope my girls will never feel the need of it too bitterly, nor be tempted by too much. I should like to know that John was firmly established in some good business, which gave him an income large enough to keep free from debt, and make Meg comfortable. I'm not ambitious for a splendid fortune, a fashionable position, or a great name for my girls. If rank and money come with love and virtue, also, I should accept them gratefully, and enjoy your good fortune; but I know, by experience, how much genuine happiness can be had in a plain little house, where the daily bread is earned, and some privations give sweetness to the few pleasures; I am content to see Meg begin humbly, for, if I am not mistaken, she will be rich in the possession of a good man's heart, and that is better than a fortune.'

'I understand, mother, and quite agree; but I'm disappointed about Meg, for I'd planned to have her marry Teddy by and by, and sit in the lap of luxury all her days. Wouldn't it be nice?' asked Jo, looking up with a brighter face.

'He is younger than she, you know,' began Mrs March; but Jo broke in,—

'Oh, that don't matter; he's old for his age, and tall;

and can be quite grown-up in his manners, if he likes. Then he's rich, and generous, and good, and loves us all; and I say it's a pity my plan is spoilt.'

'I'm afraid Laurie is hardly grown-up enough for Meg, and altogether too much of a weathercock, just now, for any one to depend on. Don't make plans, Jo; but let time and their own hearts mate your friends. We can't meddle safely in such matters, and had better not get "romantic rubbish," as you call it, into our heads, lest it spoil our friendship.'

'Well, I won't; but I hate to see things going all criss-cross, and getting snarled up, when a pull here, and a snip there, would straighten it out. I wish wearing flat-irons on our heads would keep us from growing up. But buds will be roses, and kittens, cats,—more's the pity!'

'What's that about flat-irons and cats?' asked Meg, as she crept into the room, with the finished letter in her hand.

'Only one of my stupid speeches. I'm going to bed; come on, Peggy,' said Jo, unfolding herself, like an animated puzzle.

'Quite right, and beautifully written. Please add that I send my love to John,' said Mrs March, as she glanced over the letter, and gave it back.

'Do you call him "John"?' asked Meg, smiling, with her innocent eyes looking down into her mother's.

'Yes; he has been like a son to us, and we are very fond of him,' replied Mrs March, returning the look with a keen one.

'I'm glad of that; he is so lonely. Good-night, mother, dear. It is so inexpressibly comfortable to have you here,' was Meg's quiet answer.

The kiss her mother gave her was a very tender one; and, as she went way, Mrs March said, with a mixture of satisfaction and regret, 'She does not love John yet, but will soon learn to.'

21

Laurie Makes Mischief, and Jo Makes Peace

JO'S face was a study next day, for the secret rather weighed upon her, and she found it hard not to look mysterious and important. Meg observed it, but did not trouble herself to make inquiries, for she had learned that the best way to manage Jo was by the law of contraries, so she felt sure of being told everything if she did not ask. She was rather surprised, therefore, when the silence remained unbroken, and Jo assumed a patronizing air, which decidedly aggravated Meg, who in her turn assumed an air of dignified reserve, and devoted herself to her mother. This left Jo to her own devices; for Mrs March had taken her place as nurse, and bid her rest, exercise, and amuse herself after her long confinement. Amy being gone, Laurie was her only refuge; and, much as she enjoyed his society, she rather dreaded him just then, for he was an incorrigible tease, and she feared he would coax her secret from her.

She was quite right; for the mischief-loving lad no sooner suspected a mystery, than he set himself to finding it out, and led Jo a trying life of it. He wheedled, bribed, ridiculed, threatened and scolded; affected indifference, that he might surprise the truth from her; declared he knew, then that he didn't care; and, at last, by dint of perseverance, he satisfied himself that it concerned Meg and Mr Brooke. Feeling indignant that he was not taken into his tutor's confidence, he set his wits to work to devise some proper retaliation for the slight.

Meg meanwhile had apparently forgotten the matter, and was absorbed in preparations for her father's return; but all of a sudden a change seemed to come over her, and, for a day or two, she was quite unlike herself. She started when spoken to, blushed when looked at, was very quiet, and sat over her sewing with a timid, troubled look on her face. To her mother's inquiries she answered that she was quite well, and Jo's she silenced by begging to be let alone.

'She feels it in the air—love, I mean—and she's going very fast. She's got most of the symptoms, is twittery and cross, don't eat, lies awake, and mopes in corners.

I caught her singing that song about "the silver-voiced brook," and once she said "John," as you do, and then turned as red as a poppy. Whatever shall we do?' said Jo, looking ready for any measures, however violent.

'Nothing but wait. Let her alone, be kind and patient, and father's coming will settle everything,' replied her mother.

'Here's a note to you, Meg, all sealed up. How odd! Teddy never seals mine,' said Jo, next day, as she distributed the contents of the little post-office.

Mrs March and Jo were deep in their own affairs, when a sound from Meg made them look up to see her staring at her note, with a frightened face.

'My child, what is it?' cried her mother, running to her, while Jo tried to take the paper which had done the mischief.

'It's all a mistake—he didn't send it—oh, Jo, how could you do it?' and Meg hid her face in her hands, crying as if her heart was quite broken.

'Me! I've done nothing! What's she talking about?' cried Jo, bewildered.

Meg's mild eyes kindled with anger as she pulled a crumpled note from her pocket, and threw it at Jo, saying, reproachfully,—

'You wrote it, and that bad boy helped you. How could you be so rude, so mean, and cruel to us both?'

Jo hardly heard her, for she and her mother were reading the note, which was written in a peculiar hand.

'My Dearest Margaret,—

'I can no longer restrain my passion, and must know my fate before I return. I dare not tell your parents yet, but I think they would consent if they knew that we adored one another. Mr Laurence will help me to some good place, and then, my sweet girl, you will make me happy. I implore you to say nothing to your family yet, but to send one word of hope through Laurie to

'Your devoted
'John.'

'Oh, the little villain! that's the way he meant to pay me for keeping my word to mother. I'll give him a hearty scolding, and bring him over to beg pardon,' cried Jo, burning to execute immediate justice. But her mother held her back, saying, with a look she seldom wore,—

'Stop, Jo, you must clear yourself first. You have played so many pranks, that I am afraid you have had a hand in this.'

'On my word, mother, I haven't! I never saw that note before, and don't know anything about it, as true as I live!' said Jo, so earnestly, that they believed her. 'If I *had* taken a part in it I'd have done it better than this, and have written a sensible note. I should think you'd have known Mr Brooke wouldn't write such stuff as that,' she added, scornfully tossing down the paper.

'It's like his writing,' faltered Meg, comparing it with the note in her hand.

'Oh, Meg, you didn't answer it?' cried Mrs March, quickly.

'Yes, I did!' and Meg hid her face again, overcome with shame.

'Here's a scrape! *Do* let me bring that wicked boy over to explain, and be lectured. I can't rest till I get hold of him;' and Jo made for the door again.

'Hush! let me manage this, for it is worse than I thought. Margaret, tell me the whole story,' commanded Mrs March, sitting down by Meg, yet keeping hold of Jo, lest she should fly off.

'I received the first letter from Laurie, who didn't look as if he knew anything about it,' began Meg, without looking up. 'I was worried at first, and meant to tell you; then I remembered how you liked Mr Brooke, so I thought you wouldn't mind if I kept my little secret for a few days. I'm so silly that I liked to think no one knew; and, while I was deciding what to say, I felt like the girls in books, who have such things to do. Forgive me, mother, I'm paid for my silliness now; I never can look him in the face again.'

'What did you say to him?' asked Mrs March.

'I only said I was too young to do anything about it yet; that I didn't wish to have secrets from you, and he must speak to father. I was very grateful for his kindness, and would be his friend, but nothing more, for a long while.'

Mrs March smiled, as if well pleased, and Jo clapped her hands, exclaiming, with a laugh,—

'You are almost equal to Caroline Percy, who was a pattern of prudence! Tell on, Meg. What did he say to that?'

'He writes in a different way entirely; telling me that he never sent any love-letter at all, and is very sorry that my roguish sister, Jo, should take such liberties with our names. It's very kind and respectful, but think how dreadful for me!'

Meg leaned against her mother, looking the image of despair, and Jo tramped about the room, calling Laurie names. All of a sudden she stopped, caught up the two notes, and, after looking at them closely, said, decidedly, 'I don't believe Brooke ever saw either of these letters. Teddy wrote both, and keeps yours to crow over me with, because I wouldn't tell him my secret.'

'Don't have any secrets, Jo; tell it to mother, and keep out of trouble, as I should have done,' said Meg, warningly.

'Bless you, child! mother told me.'

'That will do, Jo. I'll comfort Meg while you go and get Laurie. I shall sift the matter to the bottom, and put a stop to such pranks at once.'

Away ran Jo, and Mrs March gently told Meg Mr Brooke's real feelings. 'Now, dear, what are your own? Do you love him enough to wait till he can make a home for you, or will you keep yourself quite free for the present?'

'I've been so scared and worried, I don't want to have anything to do with lovers for a long while,—perhaps never,' answered Meg, petulantly. 'If John *doesn't* know anything about this nonsense, don't tell him, and make Jo and Laurie hold their tongues. I won't be deceived and plagued, and made a fool of,—it's a shame!'

Seeing that Meg's usually gentle temper was roused, and her pride hurt by this mischievous joke, Mrs March soothed her by promises of entire silence, and great discretion for the future. The instant Laurie's step was heard in the hall, Meg fled into the study, and Mrs March received the culprit alone. Jo had not told him why he was wanted, fearing he wouldn't come; but he knew the minute he saw Mrs March's face, and stood twirling his hat with a guilty air, which convicted him at once. Jo was dismissed, but chose to march up and down the hall like a sentinel, having some fear that the prisoner might bolt. The sound of voices in the parlor rose and fell for half an hour; but what happened during that interview the girls never knew.

When they were called in, Laurie was standing by their mother with such a penitent face, that Jo forgave him on the spot, but did not think it wise to betray the fact. Meg received his humble apology, and was much comforted by the assurance that Brooke knew nothing of the joke.

'I'll never tell him to my dying day,—wild horses shan't drag it out of me; so you'll forgive me, Meg, and I'll do anything to show how out-and-out sorry I am,' he added, looking very much ashamed of himself.

'I'll try; but it was a very ungentlemanly thing to do. I didn't think you could be so sly and malicious, Laurie,' replied Meg, trying to hide her maidenly confusion under a gravely reproachful air.

'It was altogether abominable, and I don't deserve to be spoken to for a month; but you will, though, won't you?' and Laurie folded his hands together, with such an imploring gesture, and rolled up his eyes in such a meekly repentant way, as he spoke in his irresistibly persuasive tone, that it was impossible to frown upon him, in spite of his scandalous behavior. Meg pardoned him, and Mrs March's grave face relaxed, in spite of her efforts to keep sober, when she heard him declare that he would atone for his sins by all sorts of penances, and abase himself like a worm before the injured damsel.

Jo stood aloof, meanwhile, trying to harden her heart against him, and succeeding only in primming up her face into an expression of entire disapprobation. Laurie looked at her once or twice, but, as she showed no sign of relenting, he felt injured, and turned his back on her till the others were done with him, when he made her a low bow, and walked off without a word.

As soon as he had gone, she wished she had been more forgiving; and, when Meg and her mother went upstairs, she felt lonely, and longed for Teddy. After resisting for some time, she yielded to the impulse, and, armed with a book to return, went over to the big house.

'Is Mr Laurence in?' asked Jo, of a housemaid, who was coming down stairs.

'Yes, miss; but I don't believe he's seeable just yet.'

'Why not; is he ill?'

'La, no, miss! but he's had a scene with Mr Laurie, who is in one of his tantrums about something, which vexes the old gentleman, so I dursn't go nigh him.'

'Where is Laurie?'

'Shut up in his room, and he won't answer, though I've been a tapping. I don't know what's to become of the dinner, for it's ready, and there's no one to eat it.'

'I'll go and see what the matter is. I'm not afraid of either of them.'

Up went Jo, and knocked smartly on the door of Laurie's little study.

'Stop that, or I'll open the door and make you!' called out the young gentleman, in a threatening tone.

Jo immediately pounded again; the door flew open, and in she bounced, before Laurie could recover from his surprise. Seeing that he really *was* out of temper, Jo, who knew how to manage him assumed a contrite expression, and, going artistically down upon her knees, said, meekly, 'Please forgive me for being so cross. I came to make it up, and can't go away till I have.'

'It's all right; get up, and don't be a goose, Jo,' was the cavalier reply to her petition.

'Thank you; I will. Could I ask what's the matter? You don't look exactly easy in your mind.'

'I've been shaken, and I won't bear it!' growled Laurie, indignantly.

'Who did it?' demanded Jo.

'Grandfather; if it had been any one else I'd have—' and the injured youth finished his sentence by an energetic gesture of the right arm.

'That's nothing; I often shake you, and you don't mind,' said Jo, soothingly.

'Pooh! you're a girl, and it's fun; but I'll allow no man to shake *me*.'

'I don't think any one would care to try it, if you looked as much like a thunder-cloud as you do now. Why were you treated so?'

'Just because I wouldn't say what your mother wanted me for. I'd promised not to tell, and of course I wasn't going to break my word.'

'Couldn't you satisfy your grandpa in any other way?'

'No; he *would* have the truth, the whole truth, and nothing but the truth. I'd have told my part of the scrape, if I could, without bringing Meg in. As I couldn't, I held my tongue, and bore the scolding till the old gentleman collared me. Then I got angry, and bolted, for fear I should forget myself.'

'It wasn't nice, but he's sorry, I know; so go down and make up. I'll help you.'

'Hanged if I do! I'm not going to be lectured and pummelled by every one, just for a bit of a frolic. I *was* sorry about Meg, and begged pardon like a man; but I won't do it again, when I wasn't in the wrong.'

'He didn't know that.'

'He ought to trust me, and not act as if I was a baby.

It's no use, Jo; he's got to learn that I'm able to take care of myself, and don't need any one's apron-string to hold on by.'

'What pepper-pots you are!' sighed Jo. 'How do you mean to settle this affair?'

'Well, he ought to beg pardon, and believe me when I say I can't tell him what the row's about.'

'Bless you! he won't do that.'

'I won't go down till he does.'

'Now, Teddy, be sensible; let it pass, and I'll explain what I can. You can't stay here, so what's the use of being melodramatic?'

'I don't intend to stay here long, any-way. I'll slip off and take a journey somewhere, and when grandpa misses me he'll come round fast enough.'

'I dare say; but you ought not to go and worry him.'

'Don't preach. I'll go to Washington and see Brooke; it's gay there, and I'll enjoy myself after the troubles.'

'What fun you'd have! I wish I could run off too!' said Jo, forgetting her part of Mentor in lively visions of martial life at the capital.

'Come on, then! Why not? You go and surprise your father, and I'll stir up old Brooke. It would be a glorious joke; let's do it, Jo! We'll leave a letter saying we are all right, and trot off at once. I've got money enough; it will do you good, and be no harm, as you go to your father.'

For a moment Jo looked as if she would agree; for, wild as the plan was, it just suited her. She was tired of care and confinement, longed for change, and thoughts of her father blended temptingly with the novel charms of camps and hospitals, liberty and fun. Her eyes kindled as they turned wistfully toward the window, but they fell on the old house opposite, and she shook her head with sorrowful decision.

'If I was a boy, we'd run away together, and have a capital time; but as I'm a miserable girl, I must be proper, and stop at home. Don't tempt me, Teddy, it's a crazy plan.'

'That's the fun of it!' began Laurie, who had got a wilful fit on him, and was possessed to break out of bounds in some way.

'Hold your tongue!' cried Jo, covering her ears. '"Prunes and prisms" are my doom, and I may as well make up my mind to it. I came here to moralize, not to hear about things that make me skip to think of.'

'I knew Meg would wet-blanket such a proposal, but I thought you had more spirit,' began Laurie, insinuatingly.

'Bad boy, be quiet. Sit down and think of your own sins, don't go making me add to mine. If I get your grandpa to apologize for the shaking, will you give up running away?' asked Jo, seriously.

'Yes, but you won't do it,' answered Laurie, who wished to 'make up,' but felt that his outraged dignity must be appeased first.

'If I can manage the young one I can the old one,' muttered Jo, as she walked away, leaving Laurie bent over a railroad map, with his head propped up on both hands.

'Come in!' and Mr Laurence's gruff voice sounded gruffer than ever, as Jo tapped at his door.

'It's only me, sir, come to return a book,' she said, blandly, as she entered.

'Want any more?' asked the old gentleman, looking grim and vexed, but trying not to show it.

'Yes, please, I like old Sam so well, I think I'll try the second volume,' returned Jo, hoping to propitiate him by accepting a second dose of 'Boswell's Johnson,' as he had recommended that lively work.

The shaggy eyebrows unbent a little, as he rolled the steps toward the shelf where the Johnsonian literature was placed. Jo skipped up, and, sitting on the top step, affected to be searching for her book, but was really wondering how best to introduce the dangerous object of her visit. Mr Laurence seemed to suspect that something was brewing in her mind; for, after taking several brisk turns about the room, he faced round on her, speaking so abruptly, that 'Rasselas' tumbled face downward on the floor.

'What has that boy been about? Don't try to shield him, now! I know he has been in mischief, by the way he acted when he came home. I can't get a word from him; and, when I threatened to shake the truth out of him, he bolted upstairs, and locked himself into his room.'

'He did do wrong, but we forgave him, and all promised not to say a word to any one,' began Jo, reluctantly.

'That won't do; he shall not shelter himself behind a promise from you soft-hearted girls. If he's done anything amiss, he shall confess, beg pardon, and be punished. Out with it, Jo! I won't be kept in the dark.'

Mr Laurence looked so alarming, and spoke so sharply, that Jo would have gladly run away, if she could, but she was perched aloft on the steps, and he stood at the foot, a lion in the path, so she had to stay and brave it out.

'Indeed, sir, I cannot tell, mother forbade it. Laurie has confessed, asked pardon, and been punished quite enough. We don't keep silence to shield him, but some one else, and it will make more trouble if you interfere. Please don't; it was partly my fault, but it's all right now, so let's forget it, and talk about the "Rambler," or something pleasant.'

'Hang the "Rambler!" come down and give me your

word that this harum-scarum boy of mine hasn't done anything ungrateful or impertinent. If he has, after all your kindness to him, I'll thrash him with my own hands.'

The threat sounded awful, but did not alarm Jo, for she knew the irascible old man would never lift a finger against his grandson, whatever he might say to the contrary. She obediently descended, and made as light of the prank as she could without betraying Meg, or forgetting the truth.

'Hum! ha! well, if the boy held his tongue because he'd promised, and not from obstinacy, I'll forgive him. He's a stubborn fellow, and hard to manage,' said Mr Laurence, rubbing up his hair till it looked as if he'd been out in a gale, and smoothing the frown from his brow with an air of relief.

'So am I; but a kind word will govern me when all the king's horses and all the king's men couldn't,' said Jo, trying to say a kind word for her friend, who seemed to get out of one scrape only to fall into another.

'You think I'm not kind to him, hey?' was the sharp answer.

'Oh, dear, no, sir; you are rather too kind sometimes, and then just a trifle hasty when he tries your patience. Don't you think you are?'

Jo was determined to have it out now, and tried to

look quite placid, though she quaked a little after her bold speech. To her great relief and surprise, the old gentleman only threw his spectacles on to the table with a rattle, and exclaimed, frankly,—

'You're right, girl, I am! I love the boy, but he tries my patience past bearing, and I don't know how it will end, if we go on so.'

'I'll tell you,—he'll run away.' Jo was sorry for that speech the minute it was made; she meant to warn him that Laurie would not bear much restraint, and hoped he would be more forbearing with the lad.

Mr Laurence's ruddy face changed suddenly, and he sat down with a troubled glance at the picture of a handsome man, which hung over his table. It was Laurie's father, who *had* run away in his youth, and married against the imperious old man's will. Jo fancied he remembered and regretted the past, and she wished she had held her tongue.

'He won't do it, unless he is very much worried, and only threatens it sometimes, when he gets tired of studying. I often think I should like to, especially since my hair was cut; so, if you ever miss us, you may advertise for two boys, and look among the ships bound for India.'

She laughed as she spoke, and Mr Laurence looked relieved, evidently taking the whole as a joke.

'You hussy, how dare you talk in that way? where's your respect for me, and your proper bringing up? Bless the boys and girls! what torments they are; yet we can't do without them,' he said, pinching her cheeks good-humoredly.

'Go and bring that boy down to his dinner, tell him it's all right, and advise him not to put on tragedy airs with his grandfather; I won't bear it.'

'He won't come, sir; he feels badly because you didn't believe him when he said he couldn't tell. I think the shaking hurt his feelings very much.'

Jo tried to look pathetic, but must have failed, for Mr Laurence began to laugh, and she knew the day was won.

'I'm sorry for that, and ought to thank him for not shaking *me*, I suppose. What the dickens does the fellow expect?' and the old gentleman looked a trifle ashamed of his own testiness.

'If I was you, I'd write him an apology, sir. He says he won't come down till he has one; and talks about Washington, and goes on in an absurd way. A formal apology will make him see how foolish he is, and bring him down quite amiable. Try it; he likes fun, and this way is better than talking. I'll carry it up, and teach him his duty.'

Mr Laurence gave her a sharp look, and put on his

spectacles, saying, slowly, 'You're a sly puss! but I don't mind being managed by you and Beth. Here, give me a bit of paper, and let us have done with this nonsense.'

The note was written in the terms which one gentleman would use to another after offering some deep insult. Jo dropped a kiss on the top of Mr Laurence's bald head, and ran up to slip the apology under Laurie's door, advising him, through the keyhole, to be submissive, decorous, and a few other agreeable impossibilities. Finding the door locked again, she left the note to do its work, and was going quietly away, when the young gentleman slid down the banisters, and waited for her at the bottom, saying, with his most virtuous expression of countenance, 'What a good fellow you are, Jo! Did you get blown up?' he added, laughing.

'No; he was pretty clever, on the whole.'

'Ah! I got it all around! even you cast me off over there, and I felt just ready to go to the deuce,' he began, apologetically.

'Don't talk in that way; turn over a new leaf and begin again, Teddy, my son.'

'I keep turning over new leaves, and spoiling them, as I used to spoil my copy-books; and I make so many beginnings there never will be an end,' he said, dolefully.

'Go and eat your dinner; you'll feel better after it. Men

always croak when they are hungry,' and Jo whisked out at the front door after that.

'That's a "label" on my "sect,"' answered Laurie, quoting Amy, as he went to partake of humble-pie dutifully with his grandfather, who was quite saintly in temper, and overwhelmingly respectful in manner, all the rest of the day.

Every one thought the matter ended, and the little cloud blown over; but the mischief was done, for, though others forgot it, Meg remembered. She never alluded to a certain person, but she thought of him a good deal, dreamed dreams more than ever; and, once, Jo, rummaging her sister's desk for stamps, found a bit of paper scribbled over with the words, 'Mrs John Brooke;' whereat she groaned tragically, and cast it into the fire, feeling that Laurie's prank had hastened the evil day for her.

22

Pleasant Meadows

LIKE sunshine after storm were the peaceful weeks which followed. The invalids improved rapidly, and Mr March began to talk of returning early in the new year. Beth was soon able to lie on the study sofa all day, amusing herself with the well-beloved cats, at first, and, in time, with doll's sewing, which had fallen sadly behindhand. Her once active limbs were so stiff and feeble that Jo took her a daily airing about the house, in her strong arms. Meg cheerfully blackened and burnt her white hands cooking delicate messes for 'the dear;' while Amy, a loyal slave of the ring, celebrated her return by giving away as many of her treasures as she could prevail on her sisters to accept.

As Christmas approached, the usual mysteries began

to haunt the house, and Jo frequently convulsed the family by proposing utterly impossible, or magnificently absurd ceremonies, in honor of this unusually merry Christmas. Laurie was equally impracticable, and would have had bonfires, sky-rockets, and triumphal arches, if he had had his own way. After many skirmishes and snubbings, the ambitious pair were considered effectually quenched, and went about with forlorn faces, which were rather belied by explosions of laughter when the two got together.

Several days of unusually mild weather fitly ushered in a splendid Christmas-day. Hannah 'felt in her bones that it was going to be an uncommonly plummy day,' and she proved herself a true prophetess, for everybody and everything seemed bound to produce a grand success. To begin with: Mr March wrote that he should soon be with them; then Beth felt uncommonly well that morning, and, being dressed in her mother's gift,—a soft crimson merino wrapper,—was borne in triumph to the window, to behold the offering of Jo and Laurie. The Unquenchables had done their best to be worthy of the name, for, like elves, they had worked by night, and conjured up a comical surprise. Out in the garden stood a stately snow-maiden, crowned with holly, bearing a basket of fruit and flowers in one hand, a great roll of new music in the other, a perfect rainbow of an Afghan round her chilly shoulders, and a Christmas carol issuing from her lips, on a pink paper streamer:—

'THE JUNGFRAU TO BETH.

'God bless you, dear Queen Bess!
    May nothing you dismay;
But health, and peace, and happiness,
    Be yours, this Christmas-day.

'Here's fruit to feed our busy bee,
    And flowers for her nose;
Here's music for her pianee,—
    An Afghan for her toes.

'A portrait of Joanna, see,
    By Raphael No. 2,
Who labored with great industry,
    To make it fair and true.

'Accept a ribbon red I beg,
    For Madam Purrer's tail;
And ice cream made by lovely Peg,—
    A Mont Blanc in a pail.

> *'Their dearest love my makers laid*
> *Within my breast of snow,*
> *Accept it, and the Alpine maid,*
> *From Laurie and from Jo.'*

How Beth laughed when she saw it! how Laurie ran up and down to bring in the gifts, and what ridiculous speeches Jo made as she presented them!

'I'm so full of happiness, that, if father was only here, I couldn't hold one drop more,' said Beth, quite sighing with contentment as Jo carried her off to the study to rest after the excitement, and to refresh herself with some of the delicious grapes the 'Jungfrau' had sent her.

'So am I,' added Jo, slapping the pocket wherein reposed the long-desired Undine and Sintram.

'I'm sure I am,' echoed Amy, poring over the engraved copy of the Madonna and Child, which her mother had given her, in a pretty frame.

'Of course I am,' cried Meg, smoothing the silvery folds of her first silk dress; for Mr Laurence had insisted on giving it.

'How can *I* be otherwise!' said Mrs March, gratefully, as her eyes went from her husband's letter to Beth's smiling face, and her hand caressed the brooch made of gray and golden, chestnut and dark brown hair, which the girls had just fastened on her breast.

Now and then, in this work-a-day world, things do happen in the delightful story-book fashion, and what a comfort that is. Half an hour after every one had said they were so happy they could only hold one drop more, the drop came. Laurie opened the parlor door, and popped his head in very quietly. He might just as well have turned a somersault, and uttered an Indian warwhoop; for his face was so full of suppressed excitement, and his voice so treacherously joyful, that every one jumped up, though he only said, in a queer, breathless voice, 'Here's another Christmas present for the March family.'

Before the words were well out of his mouth, he was whisked away somehow, and in his place appeared a tall man, muffled up to the eyes, leaning on the arm of another tall man, who tried to say something and couldn't. Of course there was a general stampede; and for several minutes everybody seemed to lose their wits, for the strangest things were done, and no one said a word. Mr March became invisible in the embrace of four pairs of loving arms; Jo disgraced herself by nearly fainting away, and had to be doctored by Laurie in the china closet; Mr Brooke kissed Meg entirely by mistake, as he somewhat incoherently explained; and Amy, the dignified, tumbled over a stool, and, never stopping to get up, hugged and cried over her father's boots in the most touching manner. Mrs March was the first to recover herself, and held up her hand with a warning, 'Hush! remember Beth!'

But it was too late; the study door flew open,—the little red wrapper appeared on the threshold,—joy put strength into the feeble limbs,—and Beth ran straight into her father's arms. Never mind what happened just after that; for the full hearts overflowed, washing away the bitterness of the past, and leaving only the sweetness of the present.

It was not at all romantic, but a hearty laugh set everybody straight again,—for Hannah was discovered behind the door, sobbing over the fat turkey, which she had forgotten to put down when she rushed up from the kitchen. As the laugh subsided, Mrs March began to thank Mr Brooke for his faithful care of her husband, at which Mr Brooke suddenly remembered that Mr March needed rest, and, seizing Laurie, he precipitately retired. Then the two invalids were ordered to repose, which they did, by both sitting in one big chair, and talking hard.

Mr March told how he had longed to surprise them, and how, when the fine weather came, he had been allowed by his doctor to take advantage of it; how devoted Brooke had been, and how he was altogether a most estimable and upright young man. Why Mr March paused a minute just there, and, after a glance at Meg, who was violently poking the fire, looked at his wife with an inquiring lift of the eyebrows, I leave you to imagine; also why Mrs March gently nodded her head, and asked, rather abruptly, if he wouldn't have something to eat. Jo saw and understood the look; and she stalked grimly away, to get wine and beef tea, muttering to herself, as she slammed the door, 'I hate estimable young men with brown eyes!'

There never *was* such a Christmas dinner as they had that day. The fat turkey was a sight to behold, when Hannah sent him up, stuffed, browned and decorated. So was the plum-pudding, which quite melted in one's mouth; likewise the jellies, in which Amy revelled like a fly in a honey-pot. Everything turned out well; which was a mercy, Hannah said, 'For my mind was that flustered, mum, that it's a merrycle I didn't roast the pudding and stuff the turkey with raisens, let alone bilin' of it in a cloth.'

Mr Laurence and his grandson dined with them; also Mr Brooke,—at whom Jo glowered darkly, to Laurie's infinite amusement. Two easy-chairs stood side by side at the head of the table, in which sat Beth and her father, feasting, modestly, on chicken and a little fruit. They drank healths, told stories, sang songs, 'reminisced,' as the old folks say, and had a thoroughly good time. A sleigh-ride had been planned, but the girls would not leave their father; so the guests departed early, and, as twilight gathered, the happy family sat together round the fire.

'Just a year ago we were groaning over the dismal Christmas we expected to have. Do you remember?' asked Jo, breaking a short pause, which had followed a long conversation about many things.

'Rather a pleasant year on the whole!' said Meg, smiling at the fire, and congratulating herself on having treated Mr Brooke with dignity.

'I think it's been a pretty hard one,' observed Amy, watching the light shine on her ring, with thoughtful eyes.

'I'm glad it's over, because we've got you back,' whispered Beth, who sat on her father's knee.

'Rather a rough road for you to travel, my little pilgrims, especially the latter part of it. But you have got on bravely; and I think the burdens are in a fair way to tumble off very soon,' said Mr March, looking, with fatherly satisfaction, at the four young faces gathered round him.

'How do you know? Did mother tell you?' asked Jo.

'Not much; straws show which way the wind blows; and I've made several discoveries today.'

'Oh, tell us what they are!' cried Meg, who sat beside him.

'Here is one!' and, taking up the hand which lay on the arm of his chair, he pointed to the roughened forefinger, a burn on the back, and two or three little hard spots on the palm. 'I remember a time when this hand was white and smooth, and your first care was to keep it so. It was very pretty then, but to me it is much prettier now,—for in these seeming blemishes I read a little history. A burnt offering has been made of vanity; this hardened palm has earned something better than blisters, and I'm sure the sewing done by these pricked fingers will last a long time, so much good-will went into the stitches. Meg, my dear, I value the womanly skill which keeps home happy, more than white hands or fashionable accomplishments; I'm proud to shake this good, industrious little hand, and hope I shall not soon be asked to give it away.'

If Meg had wanted a reward for hours of patient labor, she received it in the hearty pressure of her father's hand, and the approving smile he gave her.

'What about Jo? Please say something nice; for she has tried so hard, and been so very, very good to me,' said Beth, in her father's ear.

He laughed, and looked across at the tall girl who sat opposite, with an unusually mild expression in her brown face.

'In spite of the curly crop, I don't see the "son Jo" whom I left a year ago,' said Mr March. 'I see a young lady who pins her collar straight, laces her boots neatly, and neither whistles, talks slang, nor lies on the rug, as she used to do. Her face is rather thin and pale, just now, with watching and anxiety; but I like to look at it, for it has grown gentler, and her voice is lower; she doesn't bounce, but moves quietly, and takes care of a certain little person in a motherly way, which delights me. I rather miss my wild girl; but if I get a strong, helpful, tender-hearted woman in her place, I shall feel quite satisfied. I don't know whether the shearing sobered our black sheep, but I do know that in all Washington I couldn't find anything beautiful enough to be bought with the five-and-twenty dollars which my good girl sent me.'

Jo's keen eyes were rather dim for a minute, and her thin face grew rosy in the firelight, as she received her father's praise, feeling that she did deserve a portion of it.

'Now Beth;' said Amy, longing for her turn, but ready to wait.

'There's so little of her I'm afraid to say much, for fear she will slip away altogether, though she is not so shy as she used to be,' began their father, cheerfully; but, recollecting how nearly he *had* lost her, he held her close, saying, tenderly, with her cheek against his own, 'I've got you safe, my Beth, and I'll keep you so, please God.'

After a minute's silence, he looked down at Amy, who sat on the cricket at his feet, and said, with a caress of the shining hair,—

'I observed that Amy took drumsticks at dinner, ran errands for her mother all the afternoon, gave Meg her place tonight, and has waited on every one with patience and good-humor. I also observe that she does not fret much, nor prink at the glass, and has not even mentioned a very pretty ring which she wears; so I conclude that she has learned to think of other people more, and of herself less, and has decided to try and mould her character as carefully as she moulds her little clay figures. I am glad of this; for though I should be very proud of a graceful statue made by her, I shall be infinitely prouder of a lovable daughter, with a talent for making life beautiful to herself and others.'

'What are you thinking of, Beth?' asked Jo, when Amy had thanked her father, and told about her ring.

'I read in "Pilgrim's Progress" today, how, after many troubles, Christian and Hopeful came to a pleasant green meadow, where lilies bloomed all the year round, and there they rested happily, as we do now, before they went on to their journey's end,' answered Beth; adding, as she slipped out of her father's arms, and went slowly to the instrument, 'It's singing time now, and I want to be in my old place. I'll try to sing the song of the shepherd boy which the Pilgrims heard. I made the music for father, because he likes the verses.'

So, sitting at the dear little piano, Beth softly touched the keys, and, in the sweet voice they had never thought to hear again, sang, to her own accompaniment, the quaint hymn, which was a singularly fitting song for her:—

'He that is down need fear no fall;
    He that is low no pride;
He that is humble ever shall
    Have God to be his guide.

'I am content with what I have,
    Little be it or much;
And, Lord! contentment still I crave,
    Because Thou savest such.

'Fulness to them a burden is,
    That go on Pilgrimage;
Here little, and hereafter bliss,
    Is best from age to age!'

23

Aunt March Settles The Question

LIKE bees swarming after their queen, mother and daughters hovered about Mr March the next day, neglecting everything to look at, wait upon, and listen to, the new invalid, who was in a fair way to be killed by kindness. As he sat propped up in the big chair by Beth's sofa, with the other three close by, and Hannah popping in her head now and then, 'to peek at the dear man,' nothing seemed needed to complete their happiness. But something *was* needed, and the elder ones felt it, though none confessed the fact. Mr and Mrs March looked at one another with an anxious expression, as their eyes followed Meg. Jo had sudden fits of sobriety, and was seen to shake her fist at Mr Brooke's umbrella, which had been left in the hall; Meg was absent-minded,

382

shy and silent, started when the bell rang, and colored when John's name was mentioned; Amy said 'Every one seemed waiting for something, and couldn't settle down, which was queer, since father was safe at home,' and Beth innocently wondered why their neighbors didn't run over as usual.

Laurie went by in the afternoon, and, seeing Meg at the window, seemed suddenly possessed with a melodramatic fit, for he fell down upon one knee in the snow, beat his breast, tore his hair, and clasped his hands imploringly, as if begging some boon; and when Meg told him to behave himself, and go away, he wrung imaginary tears out of his handkerchief; and staggered round the corner as if in utter despair.

'What does the goose mean?' said Meg, laughing, and trying to look unconscious.

'He's showing you how your John will go on by and by. Touching, isn't it?' answered Jo, scornfully.

'Don't say *my John*, it isn't proper or true;' but Meg's voice lingered over the words as if they sounded pleasant to her. 'Please don't plague me, Jo; I've told you I don't care *much* about him, and there isn't to be anything said, but we are all to be friendly, and go on as before.'

'We can't for something *has* been said, and Laurie's mischief has spoilt you for me. I see it, and so does mother; you are not like your old self a bit, and seem ever so far away from me. I don't mean to plague you, and will bear it like a man, but I do wish it was all settled. I hate to wait; so if you mean ever to do it, make haste, and have it over quick,' said Jo, pettishly.

'*I* can't say or do anything till he speaks, and he won't, because father said I was too young,' began Meg, bending over her work with a queer little smile, which suggested that she did not quite agree with her father on that point.

'If he did speak, you wouldn't know what to say, but would cry or blush, or let him have his own way, instead of giving a good, decided, No.'

'I'm not so silly and weak as you think. I know just what I should say, for I've planned it all, so I needn't be taken unawares; there's no knowing what may happen, and I wished to be prepared.'

Jo couldn't help smiling at the important air which Meg had unconsciously assumed, and which was as becoming as the pretty color varying in her cheeks.

'Would you mind telling me what you'd say?' asked Jo, more respectfully.

'Not at all; you are sixteen now, quite old enough to be my confidant, and my experience will be useful to you by and by, perhaps, in your own affairs of this sort.'

'Don't mean to have any; it's fun to watch other people philander, but I should feel like a fool doing it myself,' said Jo, looking alarmed at the thought.

'I guess not, if you liked any one very much, and he liked you,' Meg spoke as if to herself, and glanced out at the lane where she had often seen lovers walking together in the summer twilight.

'I thought you were going to tell your speech to that man,' said Jo, rudely shortening her sister's little reverie.

'Oh, I should merely say, quite calmly and decidedly, "Thank you, Mr Brooke, you are very kind, but I agree with father, that I am too young to enter into any engagement at present; so please say no more, but let us be friends as we were."'

'Hum! that's stiff and cool enough. I don't believe you'll ever say it, and I know he won't be satisfied if you do. If he goes on like the rejected lovers in books, you'll give in, rather than hurt his feelings.'

'No I won't! I shall tell him I've made up my mind, and shall walk out of the room with dignity.'

Meg rose as she spoke, and was just going to rehearse the dignified exit, when a step in the hall made her fly into her seat, and begin to sew as if her life depended on finishing that particular seam in a given time. Jo smothered a laugh at the sudden change, and, when some one gave a modest tap, opened the door with a grim aspect, which was anything but hospitable.

'Good afternoon, I came to get my umbrella,—that is, to see how your father finds himself today,' said Mr Brooke, getting a trifle confused, as his eye went from one tell-tale face to the other.

'It's very well, he's in the rack, I'll get him, and tell it you are here,' and having jumbled her father and the umbrella well together in her reply, Jo slipped out of the room to give Meg a chance to make her speech, and air her dignity. But the instant she vanished, Meg began to sidle toward the door, murmuring,—

'Mother will like to see you, pray sit down, I'll call her.'

'Don't go; are you afraid of me, Margaret?' and Mr Brooke looked so hurt, that Meg thought she must have done something very rude. She blushed up to the little curls on her forehead, for he had never called her Margaret before, and she was surprised to find how natural and sweet it seemed to hear him say it. Anxious to appear friendly and at her ease, she put out her hand with a confiding gesture, and said, gratefully,—

'How can I be afraid when you have been so kind to father? I only wish I could thank you for it.'

'Shall I tell you how?' asked Mr Brooke, holding the

small hand fast in both his big ones, and looking down at Meg with so much love in the brown eyes, that her heart began to flutter, and she both longed to run away and to stop and listen.

'Oh no, please don't—I'd rather not,' she said, trying to withdraw her hand, and looking frightened in spite of her denial.

'I won't trouble you, I only want to know if you care for me a little, Meg, I love you so much, dear,' added Mr Brooke, tenderly.

This was the moment for the calm, proper speech, but Meg didn't make it, she forgot every word of it, hung her head, and answered, 'I don't know,' so softly, that John had to stoop down to catch the foolish little reply.

He seemed to think it was worth the trouble, for he smiled to himself as if quite satisfied, pressed the plump hand gratefully, and said, in his most persuasive tone, 'Will you try and find out? I want to know *so* much; for I can't go to work with any heart until I learn whether I am to have my reward in the end or not.'

'I'm too young,' faltered Meg, wondering why she was so fluttered, yet rather enjoying it.

'I'll wait; and, in the meantime, you could be learning to like me. Would it be a very hard lesson, dear?'

'Not if I chose to learn it, but—'

'Please choose to learn, Meg. I love to teach, and this is easier than German,' broke in John, getting possession of the other hand, so that she had no way of hiding her face, as he bent to look at it.

His tone was properly beseeching; but, stealing a shy look at him, Meg saw that his eyes were merry as well as tender, and that he wore the satisfied smile of one who had no doubt of his success. This nettled her; Annie Moffat's foolish lessons in coquetry came into her mind, and the love of power, which sleeps in the bosoms of the best of little women, woke up all of a sudden, and took possession of her. She felt excited and strange, and, not knowing what else to do, followed a capricious impulse, and, withdrawing her hands, said, petulantly, 'I *don't* choose; please go away, and let me be!'

Poor Mr Brooke looked as if his lovely castle in the air was tumbling about his ears, for he had never seen Meg in such a mood before, and it rather bewildered him.

'Do you really mean that?' he asked, anxiously, following her as she walked away.

'Yes, I do; I don't want to be worried about such things. Father says I needn't; it's too soon, and I'd rather not.'

'Mayn't I hope you'll change your mind by and by? I'll wait, and say nothing till you have had more time. Don't play with me, Meg. I didn't think that of you.'

'Don't think of me at all. I'd rather you wouldn't,' said

Meg, taking a naughty satisfaction in trying her lover's patience and her own power.

He was grave and pale now, and looked decidedly more like the novel heroes whom she admired; but he neither slapped his forehead nor tramped about the room, as they did; he just stood looking at her so wistfully, so tenderly, that she found her heart relenting in spite of her. What would have happened next I cannot say, if Aunt March had not come hobbling in at this interesting minute.

The old lady couldn't resist her longing to see her nephew; for she had met Laurie as she took her airing, and, hearing of Mr March's arrival, drove straight out to see him. The family were all busy in the back part of the house, and she had made her way quietly in, hoping to surprise them. She did surprise two of them so much, that Meg started as if she had seen a ghost, and Mr Brooke vanished into the study.

'Bless me! what's all this?' cried the old lady, with a rap of her cane, as she glanced from the pale young gentleman to the scarlet young lady.

'It's father's friend. I'm *so* surprised to see you!' stammered Meg, feeling that she was in for a lecture now.

'That's evident,' returned Aunt March, sitting down. 'But what is father's friend saying, to make you look like a peony? There's mischief going on, and I insist upon knowing what it is!' with another rap.

'We were merely talking. Mr Brooke came for his umbrella,' began Meg, wishing that Mr Brooke and the umbrella were safely out of the house.

'Brooke? That boy's tutor? Ah! I understand now. I know all about it. Jo blundered into a wrong message in one of your pa's letters, and I made her tell me. You haven't gone and accepted him, child?' cried Aunt March, looking scandalized.

'Hush! he'll hear! Shan't I call mother?' said Meg, much troubled.

'Not yet. I've something to say to you, and I must free my mind at once. Tell me, do you mean to marry this Cook? If you do, not one penny of my money ever goes to you. Remember that, and be a sensible girl,' said the old lady, impressively.

Now Aunt March possessed, in perfection, the art of rousing the spirit of opposition in the gentlest people, and enjoyed doing it. The best of us have a spice of perversity in us, especially when we are young, and in love. If Aunt March had begged Meg to accept John Brooke, she would probably have declared she couldn't think of it; but, as she was peremptorily ordered *not* to like him, she immediately made up her mind that she would. Inclination as well as perversity made the decision easy, and, being already much excited, Meg opposed the old lady with unusual spirit.

'I shall marry whom I please, Aunt March, and you can leave your money to any one you like,' she said, nodding her head with a resolute air.

'Highty tighty! Is that the way you take my advice, miss? You'll be sorry for it, by and by, when you've tried love in a cottage, and found it a failure.'

'It can't be a worse one than some people find in big houses,' retorted Meg.

Aunt March put on her glasses and took a look at the girl,—for she did not know her in this new mood. Meg hardly knew herself, she felt so brave and independent,—so glad to defend John, and assert her right to love him, if she liked. Aunt March saw that she had begun wrong, and, after a little pause, made a fresh start, saying, as mildly as she could, 'Now, Meg, my dear, be reasonable, and take my advice. I mean it kindly, and don't want you to spoil your whole life by making a mistake at the beginning. You ought to marry well, and help your family; it's your duty to make a rich match, and it ought to be impressed upon you.'

'Father and mother don't think so; they like John, though he *is* poor.'

'Your pa and ma, my dear, have no more worldly wisdom than two babies.'

'I'm glad of it,' cried Meg, stoutly.

Aunt March took no notice, but went on with her lecture. 'This Rook is poor, and hasn't got any rich relations, has he?'

'No; but he has many warm friends.'

'You can't live on friends; try it, and see how cool they'll grow. He hasn't any business, has he?'

'Not yet; Mr Laurence is going to help him.'

'That won't last long. James Laurence is a crotchety old fellow, and not to be depended on. So you intend to marry a man without money, position, or business, and go on working harder than you do now, when you might be comfortable all your days by minding me, and doing better? I thought you had more sense, Meg.'

'I couldn't do better if I waited half my life! John is good and wise; he's got heaps of talent; he's willing to work, and sure to get on, he's so energetic and brave. Every one likes and respects him, and I'm proud to think he cares for me, though I'm so poor, and young, and silly,' said Meg, looking prettier than ever in her earnestness.

'He knows *you* have got rich relations, child; that's the secret of his liking, I suspect.'

'Aunt March, how dare you say such a thing? John is above such meanness, and I won't listen to you a minute if you talk so,' cried Meg, indignantly, forgetting everything but the injustice of the old lady's suspicions. 'My John wouldn't marry for money, any more than I would. We are willing to work, and we mean to wait. I'm not afraid of being poor, for I've been happy so far, and I know I shall be with him, because he loves me, and I—'

Meg stopped there, remembering, all of a sudden, that she hadn't made up her mind; that she had told 'her John' to go away, and that he might be overhearing her inconsistent remarks.

Aunt March was very angry, for she had set her heart on having her pretty niece make a fine match, and something in the girl's happy young face made the lonely old woman feel both sad and sour.

'Well; I wash my hands of the whole affair! You are a wilful child, and you've lost more than you know by this piece of folly. No, I won't stop; I'm disappointed in you, and haven't spirits to see your pa now. Don't expect anything from me when you are married; your Mr Brooke's friends must take care of you. I'm done with you forever.'

And, slamming the door in Meg's face, Aunt March drove off in high dudgeon. She seemed to take all the girl's courage with her; for, when left alone, Meg stood a moment undecided whether to laugh or cry. Before she could make up her mind, she was taken possession of by Mr Brooke, who said, all in one breath, 'I couldn't help hearing, Meg. Thank you for defending me, and Aunt March for proving that you *do* care for me a little bit.'

'I didn't know how much, till she abused you,' began Meg.

'And I needn't go away, but may stay and be happy—may I, dear?'

Here was another fine chance to make the crushing speech and the stately exit, but Meg never thought of doing either, and disgraced herself forever in Jo's eyes, by meekly whispering, 'Yes, John,' and hiding her face on Mr Brooke's waistcoat.

Fifteen minutes after Aunt March's departure, Jo came softly down stairs, paused an instant at the parlor door, and, hearing no sound within, nodded and smiled, with a satisfied expression, saying to herself, 'She has sent him away as we planned, and that affair is settled. I'll go and hear the fun, and have a good laugh over it.'

But poor Jo never got her laugh, for she was transfixed upon the threshold by a spectacle which held her there, staring with her mouth nearly as wide open as her eyes. Going in to exult over a fallen enemy, and to praise a strong-minded sister for the banishment of an objectionable lover, it certainly *was* a shock to behold the aforesaid enemy serenely sitting on the sofa, with the strong-minded sister enthroned upon his knee, and wearing an expression of the most abject submission. Jo gave a sort of gasp, as if a cold shower-bath had suddenly fallen upon her,—for such an unexpected turning of the tables actually took her breath away. At the odd sound, the lovers turned and saw her. Meg jumped up, looking both proud and shy; but 'that man,' as Jo called him, actually laughed, and said, coolly, as he kissed the astonished new comer, 'Sister Jo, congratulate us!'

That was adding insult to injury! it was altogether too much! and, making some wild demonstration with her hands, Jo vanished without a word. Rushing upstairs, she startled the invalids by exclaiming, tragically, as she burst into the room, 'Oh, *do* somebody go down quick! John Brooke is acting dreadfully, and Meg likes it!'

Mr and Mrs March left the room with speed; and, casting herself upon the bed, Jo cried and scolded tempestuously as she told the awful news to Beth and Amy. The little girls, however, considered it a most agreeable and interesting event, and Jo got little comfort from them; so she went up to her refuge in the garret, and confided her troubles to the rats.

Nobody ever knew what went on in the parlor that afternoon; but a great deal of talking was done, and quiet Mr Brooke astonished his friends by the eloquence and spirit with which he pleaded his suit, told his plans, and persuaded them to arrange everything just as he wanted it.

The tea-bell rang before he had finished describing the paradise which he meant to earn for Meg, and he proudly took her into supper, both looking so happy, that Jo hadn't the heart to be jealous or dismal. Amy was very much impressed by John's devotion and Meg's dignity. Beth beamed at them from a distance, while Mr and Mrs March surveyed the young couple with such tender satisfaction, that it was perfectly evident Aunt March was right in calling them as 'unworldly as a pair of babies.' No one ate much, but every one looked very happy, and the old room seemed to brighten up amazingly when the first romance of the family began there.

'You can't say "nothing pleasant ever happens now," can you, Meg?' said Amy, trying to decide how she would group the lovers in the sketch she was planning to make.

'No, I'm sure I can't. How much has happened since I said that! It seems a year ago,' answered Meg, who was in a blissful dream, lifted far above such common things as bread and butter.

'The joys come close upon the sorrows this time, and I rather think the changes have begun,' said Mrs March.

'In most families there comes, now and then, a year full of events; this has been such an one, but it ends well, after all.'

'Hope the next will end better,' muttered Jo, who found it very hard to see Meg absorbed in a stranger before her face; for Jo loved a few persons very dearly, and dreaded to have their affection lost or lessened in any way.

'I hope the third year from this *will* end better; I mean it shall, if I live to work out my plans,' said Mr Brooke, smiling at Meg, as if everything had become possible to him now.

'Doesn't it seem very long to wait?' asked Amy, who was in a hurry for the wedding.

'I've got so much to learn before I shall be ready, it seems a short time to me,' answered Meg, with a sweet gravity in her face, never seen there before.

'You have only to wait. *I* am to do the work,' said John, beginning his labors by picking up Meg's napkin, with an expression which caused Jo to shake her head, and then say to herself, with an air of relief, as the front door banged, 'Here comes Laurie; now we shall have a little sensible conversation.'

But Jo was mistaken; for Laurie came prancing in, overflowing with spirits, bearing a great bridal-looking bouquet for 'Mrs John Brooke,' and evidently laboring under the delusion that the whole affair had been brought about by his excellent management.

'I knew Brooke would have it all his own way,—he always does; for when he makes up his mind to accomplish anything, it's done, though the sky falls,' said Laurie, when he had presented his offering and his congratulations.

'Much obliged for that recommendation. I take it as a good omen for the future, and invite you to my wedding on the spot,' answered Mr Brooke, who felt at peace with all mankind, even his mischievous pupil.

'I'll come if I'm at the ends of the earth; for the sight of Jo's face alone, on that occasion, would be worth a long journey. You don't look festive, ma'am; what's the matter?' asked Laurie, following her into a corner of the parlor, whither all had adjourned to greet Mr Laurence.

'I don't approve of the match, but I've made up my mind to bear it, and shall not say a word against it,' said Jo, solemnly. 'You can't know how hard it is for me to give up Meg,' she continued, with a little quiver in her voice.

'You don't give her up. You only go halves,' said Laurie, consolingly.

'It never can be the same again. I've lost my dearest friend,' sighed Jo.

'You've got me, anyhow. I'm not good for much, I know; but I'll stand by you, Jo, all the days of my life; upon my word I will!' and Laurie meant what he said.

'I know you will, and I'm ever so much obliged; you are always a great comfort to me, Teddy,' returned Jo, gratefully shaking hands.

'Well, now, don't be dismal, there's a good fellow. It's all right, you see. Meg is happy; Brooke will fly round and get settled immediately; grandpa will attend to him, and it will be very jolly to see Meg in her own little house. We'll have capital times after she is gone, for I shall be through college before long, and then we'll go abroad, or some nice trip or other. Wouldn't that console you?'

'I rather think it would; but there's no knowing what may happen in three years,' said Jo, thoughtfully.

'That's true! Don't you wish you could take a look forward, and see where we shall all be then? I do,' returned Laurie.

'I think not, for I might see something sad; and every one looks so happy now, I don't believe they could be much improved,' and Jo's eyes went slowly round the room, brightening as they looked, for the prospect was a pleasant one.

Father and mother sat together quietly re-living the first chapter of the romance which for them began some twenty years ago. Amy was drawing the lovers, who sat apart in a beautiful world of their own, the light of which touched their faces with a grace the little artist could not copy. Beth lay on her sofa talking cheerily with her old friend, who held her little hand as if he felt that it possessed the power to lead him along the peaceful ways she walked. Jo lounged in her favorite low seat, with the grave, quiet look which best became her; and Laurie, leaning on the back of her chair, his chin on a level with her curly head, smiled with his friendliest aspect, and nodded at her in the long glass which reflected them both.

So grouped the curtain falls upon Meg, Jo, Beth and Amy. Whether it ever rises again, depends upon the reception given to the first act of the domestic drama, called 'LITTLE WOMEN.'

LITTLE WOMEN

The Backstory

Learn all about the author's life and how it
inspired her famous story, and find out which
of the March girls you most resemble!

Who's Who in *Little Women*

Josephine March: Jo wishes she had been born a boy so she could go and fight with her father, and truthfully she's not very good at being a girl! She hopes to become rich and famous as an author one day, but in the meantime she amuses herself and her sisters by creating 'wild theatricals' and fun and imaginative games based on the books she reads like *Pilgrim's Progress* or *The Pickwick Papers*. Jo has a fiery temper which often gets her into trouble, but she is also loving and unfailingly generous – she impulsively sells her hair, her 'one beauty' to raise money for her father.

Margaret March: Meg is wise and sensible and a great help to her mother, but she remembers when the family were not so poor, and the beautiful dresses she used to have. Sometimes vanity gets the better of her – such as when she allows her fashionable friends to dress her up for a party. By the end of the novel she's learnt that she would rather marry a poor man, and be loved and respected, than be a 'doll' with all the finery money can bring.

Amy March: Amy is the youngest, and the little princess of the family with her proper manners, airs and graces. She is sociable and artistic and well-liked by her school friends.

Described as a 'snow queen' with her blond hair and blue eyes, she cares too much about her looks (she even wears a clothes peg to correct her snub nose!) and can be a little selfish, but like her sisters she is always trying to correct her vices. When she is sent away during Beth's illness, she learns that she loves her sisters far more than herself. Amy is particularly close to Meg, who understands her best.

Elizabeth March: Beth is called 'Mouse' by her sisters, and this nickname suits her sweet, quiet and shy character. She is naturally unselfish and considerate, and it's often Beth who restores peace and goodwill when her siblings argue. Beth is almost painfully afraid of strangers, but her music and friendship with the March's gruff old neighbour brings her out of herself. Beth's sweet and steady temper endears her particularly to Jo.

Marmee: Mrs March is a calm, warm-hearted woman with a keen sense of the importance of aiding and caring for others. Louisa May Alcott describes her as 'noble' with a 'can-I-help-you' look about her (do your best 'can-I-help-you' look to yourself in the mirror). Marmee is a devoted and supportive wife to Mr March, and she has cheerfully adapted to supporting her family in his absence. To her girls she is 'the most splendid mother in the world' and she teaches them to care more about fashioning their characters than fashion, and to speak out against injustice and cruelty.

Hannah: Hannah is the family's loyal domestic servant. Although she can sometimes be a little grumpy, she loves the girls dearly and is more of a friend to them than a hired hand.

The Hummels: The Hummels are a large German family who have emigrated to America and live in terrible poverty. The March family do their best to help them, giving them food and firewood, even their Christmas dinner! Could you give up a tasty feast as cheerfully as the March girls do?

Theodore Lawrence: Laurie, or Teddy, lives next door to the March family. His parents are dead, and he is lonely living with his aged grandfather until the girls befriend him. Laurie is very similar to Jo – outspoken, occasionally hot-tempered and stubborn, but full of fun, thoughtful and charming. He longs to run off to Italy and be a musician, but his grandfather expects him to study and become a man of business.

Aunt March: This 'peppery old lady' is a rich relative of the March family. She is lame, and Jo works as her companion and helper, though they both have short tempers and frequently fall out!

Old Mr Lawrence: Laurie's grandfather is rich and proud, and seems so fierce that the March girls think of him as a 'lion'. But they soon charm him (particularly shy little Beth) and discover that he is gentlemanly and generous despite his gruff exterior.

Annie and Belle Moffat: Rich and fashionable friends of Meg's, Annie and Belle represent the superficial world of finery and gossip that the March family have left behind.

Mr Brooke: Laurie's tutor is quiet and serious, with handsome brown eyes. He falls in love with Meg (who wouldn't!) and is a great help to the family when he escorts Mrs March to Washington when her husband is ill. He is poor, but energetic and brave and as Meg angrily tells her nosy Aunt March, she knows she will be happy with him.

The Vaughans: Kate, Fred, Frank and Grace are British friends of Laurie who come to stay with him. They are soon caught up in March family sport and games, and if you read on to the sequel of *Little Women, Good Wives*, you'll find out more about them.

Mr March: The girls' father is absent for most of the novel, but we learn through his letters that he is a very good man. His kindness is such that he lost his fortune trying to help a friend, and he is clearly a good father as his four daughters adore him and want to do their best to please him and make him proud.

Who are you?
Which of the four March girls do you most resemble? Take this quick quiz to find out!

1) **It's Sunday and all the chores are done. How do you use your spare time?**

   a) By sewing bows and ribbons on to your best bonnet, in keeping with the latest fashions.

   b) You shut yourself away in the attic and write wonderful stories of dastardly knights and damsels in distress, until your fingers are covered in ink.

   c) You'll sketch, or perhaps try and pinch your nose into a better shape.

   d) After playing with your stray kittens and dolls and making sure they are comfortable, you'll practise your sisters' favourite tunes on the piano.

2) **You want to be good like Marmee, but sometimes it's so hard! Which quality do you strive to conquer in yourself?**

   a) You envy other girls who have beautiful things you can't afford, which makes you bitter and cross sometimes.

b) Your terrible temper leads to fights and harsh words with the people you love.

c) You're so used to being petted and looked after that you can't stand it when you don't get your own way.

d) You hate social situations, too timid to make new friends who might benefit from your kindness.

3) **You've been invited to a fashionable party. How do you react?**

a) How exciting! But oh, whatever will you wear? Your old dress will look so dowdy compared to the silks and satins worn by the other girls.

b) Hang parties! You don't like to stand about and make small talk, you'd prefer to be off skating or running about like a boy, or still better, curled up with a good book.

c) A party is the perfect place to demonstrate your fine manners and show off your perfect curls.

d) Oh no, all those people! You'd much rather stay at home than spend one minute in a room full of frightening strangers.

4) **You're daydreaming about your castle in the air, what does it look like?**

a) Your castle is a lovely house full of luxurious things, pretty clothes and lots of servants so you never have to work again.

b) Your castle is full of horses, books and inkstands, and there you'll write of the marvellous deeds you've accomplished, whatever they might be.

c) In your castle you'd be an artist in Rome, famous and admired for your fine pictures.

d) Your castle is your own home, with your family and friends all about you.

Mostly As: You're Meg, and you'll always be admired for your mild and sweet temper as much as your pretty face.

Mostly Bs: You're topsy turvy Jo, with a wild imagination, always ready for adventure and fun.

Mostly Cs: You're Amy - with your dainty manners and funny way with words you are always good company.

Mostly Ds: You're shy but sunshiny Beth, always looking after people and keeping the peace.

Who was Louisa May Alcott?

Louisa May Alcott was born on 29 November 1832 in Pennsylvania, and she grew up with plenty of books to read but seldom enough to eat. Louisa went to work when she was very young as a paid companion and teacher, but she loved writing most of all, and like Jo March she started selling sensational stories in order to help provide financial support for her family. She worked as a nurse during the American Civil War but the experience made her extremely ill. *Little Women* was published in 1868 and she followed it with three sequels, *Good Wives* (1869), *Little Men* (1871) and *Jo's Boys* (1886). Louisa was a campaigner for women's rights and the abolition of the slave trade. She died on 6 March 1888.

Behind the Scenes of *Little Women*

Meg, Jo, Beth and Amy live in the town of Concord, which is a real town in America, in the state of Massachusetts. It is situated on the East Coast of the United States, not far from Boston and north of New York. Though it is a comparatively small town, several famous American writers lived in Concord, including Louisa May Alcott of course.

On the very first page of the novel we learn that the girls' father is 'far away, where the fighting was'. The 'fighting' is the American Civil War, which began in 1861 and ended in 1865. It started because Abraham Lincoln was elected President, and he wanted to ban slavery throughout the United States. Eleven states in the south of America did not want slavery to be banned, so they announced they no longer wanted to be part of the United States. These eleven states were called the 'Confederacy'. The President and American government said this rebellion was illegal and wrong, and so the twenty-five other American states who supported the government, called the 'Union', went to war against the Confederacy. The Civil War was not just about slavery, but it was an important factor, and when the Confederacy surrendered four years later, slavery was finally abolished throughout the country. Massachusetts was part of the Union, so Mr March is in the Union army, though he is not a soldier but a chaplain, which is a particular sort of clergyman.

Louisa May Alcott and her family supported Abraham Lincoln and the Union, because they believed slavery should indeed be banned. Like Jo, Louisa wanted to go and fight. But since women were not allowed to join the army, she became a nurse and went to Washington (like Mrs March) to care for wounded soldiers.

You can already see from these examples that Louisa May Alcott based much of *Little Women* on her real life. Louisa was also one of four sisters – the eldest was called Anna, and the two younger sisters were called Lizzie and Abba May. Aren't their names similar to Meg, Beth and Amy! Like Mr March, Louisa's father lost his money and her mother was head of the household, while Louisa wrote stories to earn money for her family.

Louisa lived with her family in Orchard House, which of course is also the name of the March family home. If you ever happen to be in Concord you can visit the house, which is still standing, and see where Louisa and her sisters lived. Over 50,000 people visit Orchard House every year, because *Little Women* has been read and loved by so many people all over the world.

Little Women was published in two parts, the first in 1868 and the second in 1869. At the end of the book the author hints that if the reception to her story is good there will be further stories of Meg, Jo, Beth and Amy. Readers did indeed love the book, and so Louisa May Alcott wrote three sequels. *Good Wives* tells of what happens when the girls grow up and fall in love. In *Jo's Boys* and *Little Men* we return to Concord to see new characters join our familiar friends for more adventures.

Can you guess what happens to the March family? Will Meg marry John Brooke? Will Jo become a great writer and Amy an artist? Will Beth ever leave her beloved family home? Can you imagine Laurie as a grown-up man of business? Quick, grab a copy of *Good Wives* and return to Orchard House to find out!

What does that word mean?

china-aster – a type of flower.

Vivan – this is short for 'a vivandière', which is a French term for a woman who visits regiments of soldiers to sell food and drink.

spandy – this means 'completely'.

piece-bags – these are bags holding scraps of cloth to be used for repairing clothes or in patchwork.

prink – this means to make little adjustments here and there to be sure your hairstyle and outfit is perfect.

rubbers – this is short for rubber shoes, which were worn over your existing footwear to keep them dry in the rain.

redowa – this is a type of lively dance.

The Old Man of the Sea – this is a character in the story 'Sinbad the Sailor'. The Old Man tricked Sinbad into helping him across a stream by carrying him on his shoulders, but then refused to let go and get down, and Sinbad had to carry him everywhere. To compare someone with the Old Man of the Sea means that they are a tiresome burden, hard work.

Petrea – this is a character in, a Swedish novel published in Louisa May Alcott's time.

Uncle Tom – this is a reference to *Uncle Tom's Cabin*, an important novel of the time by Harriet Beecher Stowe.

Dr Blimber – another character from literature, he is the headmaster in *Dombey and Son* by Charles Dickens.

Apollyon – is an evil figure from mythology, and appears in the girl's favourite book, *Pilgrim's Progress*.

Vanity Fair – this is also a reference to *Pilgrim's Progress*. 'Vanity Fair' is a place which symbolises self-indulgence and frivolity.

muslin, tarlatan, poplin – these are all different kinds of dress fabric.

soupçon – this French for 'a tiny amount'.

ruche – another French word, meaning a frill or pleat of fabric.

The Pickwick Club – this game of the March sisters is inspired by Charles Dickens' book *The Pickwick Papers*, which is a funny novel about four gentlemen and their comical misfortunes.

dewote – Laurie is pretending to be a character from *The Pickwick Papers* , 'Sam Weller', who had difficulty saying the letter v, and always pronounced it as a w – 'dewote' is therefore 'devote'.

Sairey Gamp – this is another character from a Dickens novel, this time the disgraceful nurse from *Martin Chuzzlewit* by Charles Dickens.

Flora McFlimsey – a character from an old children's book.

Miss Malaprop – Mrs Malaprop is a character in an eighteenth century play by Sheridan called *The Rivals*. She frequently uses words that sounded similar to the ones she intended but were actually wrong, just as Amy does in this book.

ennui – this is a French word meaning a feeling of weariness caused by boredom.

saleratus – this is another term for baking soda.

deaconed – this is an American expression for when the better quality food, or fruit in this case, is put on top in a dish to hide poor quality fruit underneath.

spirit of '76 – this refers to the period between 1776 and 1783 when Britain and America were enemies, and the thirteen American colonies were fighting for independence from Great Britain's control.

the Row – this refers to Rotten Row in Hyde Park, London, where fashionable people could ride horses.

a brake – this means a fern frond.

Atalanta – she is a Greek goddess who ran races against each of her suitors. The first to beat her would be allowed to marry her. One clever suitor threw down three golden apples, which delayed Atalanta as she stopped to pick them up, and so he won the race.

comme la fo – Amy means *comme il faut*, which is French for 'behaving correctly'.

hose – this means 'stockings'.

standish – this is a stand holding pens and ink.

paper marshay – Amy means papier mâché, a mixture of paper and glue which can be shaped into boxes, bowls, ornaments etc. and then becomes hard when dry.

Anni Domino – Amy has mixed up her letters; she means Anno Domini, which is Latin for 'the year of our Lord'.

Afghan – this refers to a particular kind of shawl or blanket, with a geometric design.

cricket – not a chirping insect in this case! Instead it means a low stool.

Visit **www.worldofstories.co.uk**

THIS BOOK
BELONGS TO

_____

_____

VINTAGE CLASSICS

OTHER BOOKS BY FRANCES HODGSON BURNETT

A Little Princess
The Making o f Marchioness
Little Lord Fauntleroy

Frances Hodgson Burnett

The
Secret
Garden

VINTAGE BOOKS
London

Published by Vintage 2012

Chapter illustrations copyright © Suyeon Noh

The Secret Garden was first published in 1911

Vintage
Random House, 20 Vauxhall Bridge Road,
London SW1V 2SA

www.vintage-classics.info

Addresses for companies within The Random House Group Limited can
be found at: www.randomhouse.co.uk/offices.htm

The Random House Group Limited Reg. No. 954009

A CIP catalogue record for this book
is available from the British Library

The Random House Group Limited supports The Forest Stewardship
Council (FSC®), the leading international forest certification organisation.
Our books carrying the FSC label are printed on FSC® certified paper.
FSC is the only forest certification scheme endorsed by the leading
environmental organisations, including Greenpeace. Our paper
procurement policy can be found at
www.randomhouse.co.uk/environment

Printed and bound in Great Britain by
CPI Group (UK) Ltd, Croydon CR0 4YY

Contents

1

There is No One Left

WHEN Mary Lennox was sent to Misselthwaite Manor to live with her uncle, everybody said she was the most disagreeable-looking child ever seen. It was true, too. She had a little thin face and a little thin body, thin light hair and a sour expression. Her hair was yellow, and her face was yellow because she had been born in India and had always been ill in one way or another. Her father had held a position under the English Government and had always been busy and ill himself, and her mother had been a great beauty who cared only to go to parties and amuse herself with gay people. She had not wanted a little girl at all, and when Mary was born she handed her over to the care of an Ayah, who was made to understand that if she wished to please the Memsahib she must keep the child out of sight as much as possible. So when she was a sickly, fretful, ugly little baby she was kept out of the way, and when she became a sickly, fretful, toddling thing she was kept out of the way also. She never remembered seeing familiarly anything but the dark faces of her Ayah and the other native servants, and as they always obeyed her and gave her her own way in everything, because the Memsahib would be angry if she was disturbed by her crying, by the time she was six years old she was as tyrannical and selfish a little pig as ever lived. The young English governess who came to teach her to read and write disliked her so much that she gave up her place in three months, and when other governesses came to try to fill it they always went away in a shorter time than the first one. So if Mary had not chosen really to want to know how to read books, she would never have learned her letters at all.

One frightfully hot morning, when she was about nine years old, she awakened feeling very cross, and she became crosser still when she saw that the servant who stood by her bedside was not her Ayah.

'Why did you come?' she said to the strange woman. 'I will not let you stay. Send my Ayah to me.'

The woman looked frightened, but she only stammered that the Ayah could not come, and when Mary threw herself into a passion and beat and kicked her, she looked only more frightened and repeated that it was not possible for the Ayah to come to Missie Sahib.

There was something mysterious in the air that morning. Nothing was done in its regular order and several of the native servants seemed missing, while those whom Mary saw slunk or hurried about with ashy and scared faces. But no one would tell her anything, and her Ayah did not come. She was actually left alone as the morning went on, and at last wandered out into the garden and began to play by herself under a tree near the veranda. She pretended that she was making a flower-bed, and she stuck big scarlet hibiscus blossoms into little heaps of earth, all the time growing more and more angry and muttering to herself the things she would say and the names she would call Saidie when she returned.

'Pig! Pig! Daughter of Pigs!' she said, because to call a native a pig is the worst insult of all.

She was grinding her teeth and saying this over and over again when she heard her mother come out on the veranda with someone. She was with a fair young man, and they stood talking together in low strange voices. Mary knew the fair young man who looked like a boy. She had heard that he was a very young officer who had just come from England. The child stared at him, but she stared most at her mother. She always did this when she had a chance to see her, because the Memsahib – Mary

3

used to call her that oftener than anything else – was such a tall, slim, pretty person and wore such lovely clothes. Her hair was like curly silk and she had a delicate little nose which seemed to be disdaining things, and she had large laughing eyes. All her clothes were thin and floating, and Mary said they were 'full of lace'. They looked fuller of lace than ever this morning, but her eyes were not laughing at all. They were large and scared and lifted imploringly to the fair boy officer's face.

'Is it so very bad? Oh, is it?' Mary heard her say.

'Awfully,' the young man answered in a trembling voice. 'Awfully, Mrs Lennox. You ought to have gone to the hills two weeks ago.'

The Memsahib wrung her hands.

'Oh, I know I ought!' she cried. 'I only stayed to go to that silly dinner-party. What a fool I was!'

At that very moment such a loud sound of wailing broke out from the servants' quarters that she clutched the young man's arm, and Mary stood shivering from head to foot. The wailing grew wilder and wilder.

'What is it? What is it?' Mrs Lennox gasped.

'Someone has died,' answered the boy officer. 'You did not say it had broken out among your servants.'

'I did not know!' the Memsahib said. 'Come with me! Come with me!' and she turned and ran into the house.

After that, appalling things happened, and the mysteriousness of the morning was explained to Mary. The cholera had broken out in its most fatal form and people were dying like flies. The Ayah had been taken ill in the night, and it was because she had just died that the servants had wailed in the huts. Before the next day three other servants were dead and others had run away in terror. There was panic on every side, and dying people in all the bungalows.

During the confusion and bewilderment of the second day Mary hid herself in the nursery and was forgotten by everyone. Nobody thought of her, nobody wanted her, and strange things happened of which she knew nothing. Mary alternately cried and slept through the hours. She only knew that people were ill and that she heard mysterious and frightening sounds. Once she crept into the dining-room and found it empty, though a partly finished meal was on the table and chairs and plates looked as if they had been hastily pushed back when the diners rose suddenly for some reason. The child ate some fruit and biscuits, and being thirsty she drank a glass of wine which stood nearly filled. It was sweet, and she did not know how strong it was. Very soon it made her intensely drowsy, and she went back to her nursery and shut herself in again, frightened by cries she heard in the huts and by the hurrying sound of feet. The wine made her so sleepy that she could scarcely keep her eyes open, and she lay down on her bed and knew nothing more for a long time.

Many things happened during the hours in which she slept so heavily, but she was not disturbed by the wails and the sound of things being carried in and out of the bungalow.

When she awakened she lay and stared at the wall. The house was perfectly still. She had never known it to be so silent before. She heard neither voices nor footsteps, and wondered if everybody had got well of the cholera and all the trouble was over. She wondered also who would take care of her now her Ayah was dead. There would be a new Ayah, and perhaps she would know some new stories. Mary had been rather tired of the old ones. She did not cry because her nurse had died. She was not an affectionate child and had never cared much for anyone. The noise and hurrying about and wailing over the cholera had frightened her, and she had been angry because no one seemed to remember that she was alive. Everyone was too panic-stricken to think of a little girl no one was fond of. When people had the cholera it seemed that they remembered nothing but themselves. But if everyone had got well again, surely someone would remember and come to look for her.

But no one came, and as she lay waiting the house

seemed to grow more and more silent. She heard something rustling on the matting, and when she looked down she saw a little snake gliding along and watching her with eyes like jewels. She was not frightened, because he was a harmless little thing who would not hurt her, and he seemed in a hurry to get out of the room. He slipped under the door as she watched him.

'How queer and quiet it is,' she said. 'It sounds as if there was no one in the bungalow but me and the snake.'

Almost the next minute she heard footsteps in the compound, and then on the veranda. They were men's footsteps, and the men entered the bungalow and talked in low voices. No one went to meet or speak to them, and they seemed to open doors and look into rooms.

'What desolation!' she heard one voice say. 'That pretty, pretty woman! I suppose the child, too. I heard there was a child, though no one ever saw her.'

Mary was standing in the middle of the nursery when they opened the door a few minutes later. She looked an ugly, cross little thing and was frowning because she was beginning to be hungry and feel disgracefully neglected. The first man who came in was a large officer she had once seen talking to her father. He looked tired and troubled, but when he saw her he was so startled that he almost jumped back.

'Barney!' he cried out. 'There is a child here! A child alone! In a place like this! Mercy on us, who is she?'

'I am Mary Lennox,' the little girl said, drawing herself up stiffly. She thought the man was very rude to call her father's bungalow 'A place like this!' 'I fell asleep when everyone had the cholera and I have only just wakened up. Why does nobody come?'

'It is the child no one ever saw!' exclaimed the man, turning to his companions. 'She has actually been forgotten!'

'Why was I forgotten?' Mary said, stamping her foot. 'Why does nobody come?'

The young man whose name was Barney looked at her very sadly. Mary even thought she saw him wink his eyes as if to wink tears away.

'Poor little kid!' he said. 'There is nobody left to come.'

It was in that strange and sudden way that Mary found out that she had neither father nor mother left; that they had died and been carried away in the night, and that the few native servants who had not died also had left the house as quickly as they could get out of it, none of them even remembering that there was a Missie Sahib. That was why the place was so quiet. It was true that there was no one in the bungalow but herself and the little rustling snake.

2

Mistress Mary Quite Contrary

M ARY had liked to look at her mother from a distance, and she had thought her very pretty, but as she knew very little of her, she could scarcely have been expected to love her or to miss her very much when she was gone. She did not miss her at all, in fact, and as she was a self-absorbed child she gave her entire thought to herself, as she had always done. If she had been older she would no doubt have been very anxious at being left alone in the world, but she was very young, and as she had always been taken care of, she supposed she always would be. What she thought was that she would like to know if she was going to nice people, who would be polite to her and give her her own way as her Ayah and the other native servants had done.

She knew that she was not going to stay at the English clergyman's house where she was taken at first. She did not want to stay. The English clergyman was poor and he had five children all nearly the same age and they wore shabby clothes and were always quarrelling and snatching toys from each other. Mary hated their untidy bungalow and was so disagreeable to them that after the first day or two nobody would play with her. By the second day they had given her a nickname which made her furious.

It was Basil who thought of it first. Basil was a little boy with impudent blue eyes and a turned-up nose, and Mary hated him. She was playing by herself under a tree, just as she had been playing the day the cholera broke out. She was making heaps of earth and paths for a garden and Basil came and stood near to watch her. Presently he got rather interested and suddenly made a suggestion.

'Why don't you put a heap of stones there and pretend it is a rockery?' he said. 'There in the middle,' and he leaned over her to point.

'Go away!' cried Mary. 'I don't want boys. Go away!'

For a moment Basil looked angry, and then he began to tease. He was always teasing his sisters. He danced round and round her and made faces and sang and laughed.

Mistress Mary, quite contrary,
How does your garden grow?
With silver bells, and cockle shells,
And marigolds all in a row.

He sang it until the other children heard and laughed, too; and the crosser Mary got, the more they sang 'Mistress Mary Quite Contrary'; and after that as long as she stayed with them they called her 'Mistress Mary Quite Contrary' when they spoke of her to each other, and often when they spoke to her.

'You are going to be sent home,' Basil said to her, 'at the end of the week. And we're glad of it.'

'I am glad of it, too,' answered Mary, 'Where is home?'

'She doesn't know where home is!' said Basil, with seven-year-old scorn. 'It's England, of course. Our grandmamma lives there, and our sister Mabel was sent to her last year. You are not going to your grandmamma. You have none. You are going to your uncle. His name is Mr Archibald Craven.'

'I don't know anything about him,' snapped Mary.

'I know you don't,' Basil answered. 'You don't know anything. Girls never do. I heard Father and Mother talking about him. He lives in a great, big, desolate old house in the country, and no one goes near him. He's so cross he won't let them, and they wouldn't come if he would let them. He's a hunchback, and he's horrid.'

'I don't believe you,' said Mary; and she turned her back and stuck her fingers in her ears, because she would not listen any more.

But she thought over it a great deal afterward; and when Mrs Crawford told her that night that she was going to sail away to England in a few days and going to her uncle, Mr Archibald Craven, who lived at Misselthwaite Manor, she looked so stony and stubbornly uninterested that they did not know what to think about her. They tried to be kind to her, but she only turned her face away when Mrs Crawford attempted to kiss her, and held herself stiffly when Mr Crawford patted her shoulder.

'She is such a plain child,' Mrs Crawford said pityingly afterward. 'And her mother was such a pretty creature. She had a very pretty manner, too, and Mary has the most unattractive ways I ever saw in a child. The children call her "Mistress Mary Quite Contrary", and though it's naughty of them, one can't help understanding it.'

'Perhaps if her mother had carried her pretty face and her pretty manners oftener into the nursery, Mary might have learned some pretty ways, too. It is very sad, now the poor beautiful thing is gone, to remember that many people never even knew that she had a child at all.'

'I believe she scarcely ever looked at her,' sighed Mrs Crawford. 'When her Ayah was dead there was no one to give a thought to the little thing. Think of the servants running away and leaving her all alone in that deserted bungalow. Colonel McGrew said he nearly jumped out of his skin when he opened the door and found her standing by herself in the middle of the room.'

Mary made the long voyage to England under the care of an officer's wife, who was taking her children to leave them in a boarding-school. She was very much absorbed in her own little boy and girl, and was rather glad to hand the child over to the woman Mr Archibald Craven sent to meet her in London. The woman was his housekeeper at Misselthwaite Manor, and her name was Mrs Medlock. She was a stout woman, with very red cheeks and sharp black eyes. She wore a very purple dress, a black silk mantle with jet fringes on it, and a black bonnet with purple velvet flowers which stuck up and trembled when she moved her head. Mary did not like her at all, but as she very seldom liked people, there was nothing remarkable in that; besides which it was very evident Mrs Medlock did not think much of her.

'My word! she's a plain little piece of goods!' she said. 'And we'd heard that her mother was a beauty. She hasn't handed much of it down, has she, ma'am?'

'Perhaps she will improve as she grows older,' the officer's wife said good-naturedly. 'If she were not so sallow and had a nicer expression, her features are rather good. Children alter so much.'

'She'll have to alter a good deal,' answered Mrs Medlock. 'And there's nothing likely to improve children at Misselthwaite – if you ask me!'

They thought Mary was not listening because she was standing a little apart from them at the window of the private hotel they had gone to. She was watching the passing buses and cabs and people, but she heard quite well and was made very curious about her uncle and the place he lived in. What sort of a place was it, and what would he be like? What was a hunchback? She had never seen one. Perhaps there were none in India.

Since she had been living in other people's houses and had had no Ayah, she had begun to feel lonely and to think queer thoughts which were new to her. She had begun to wonder why she had never seemed to belong to anyone even when her father and mother had been alive. Other children seemed to belong to their fathers and mothers, but she had never seemed to really be anyone's little girl. She had had servants, and food and clothes, but no one had taken any notice of her. She did not know that this was because she was a disagreeable child; but then, of course, she did not know she was disagreeable. She often thought that other people were, but she did not know that she was so herself.

She thought Mrs Medlock the most disagreeable person she had ever seen, with her common, highly coloured face and her common fine bonnet. When the next day they set out on their journey to Yorkshire, she walked through the station to the railway carriage with her head up and trying to keep as far away from her as she could, because she did not want to seem to belong to her. It would have made her very angry to think people imagined she was her little girl.

But Mrs Medlock was not in the least disturbed by her and her thoughts. She was the kind of woman who would 'stand no nonsense from young ones'. At least, that is what she would have said if she had been asked. She had not wanted to go to London just when her sister Maria's daughter was going to be married, but she had a comfortable, well-paid place as housekeeper at Misselthwaite Manor, and the only way in which she could keep it was to do at once what Mr Archibald Craven told her to do. She never dared even to ask a question.

'Captain Lennox and his wife died of the cholera,' Mr Craven had said in his short, cold way. 'Captain Lennox was my wife's brother and I am their daughter's guardian. The child is to be brought here. You must go to London and bring her yourself.'

So she packed her small trunk and made the journey.

Mary sat in her corner of the railway carriage and looked plain and fretful. She had nothing to read or to look at, and she had folded her thin little black-gloved hands in her lap. Her black dress made her look yellower than ever, and her limp light hair straggled from under her black crêpe hat.

'A more marred-looking young one I never saw in my life,' Mrs Medlock thought. (Marred is a Yorkshire word and means spoiled and pettish.) She had never seen a child who sat so still without doing anything; and at last she got tired of watching her and began to talk in a brisk, hard voice.

'I suppose I may as well tell you something about where you are going to,' she said. 'Do you know anything about your uncle?'

'No,' said Mary.

'Never heard your father and mother talk about him?'

'No,' said Mary, frowning. She frowned because she remembered that her father and mother had never talked to her about anything in particular. Certainly they had never told her things.

'Humph,' muttered Mrs Medlock, staring at her queer, unresponsive little face. She did not say any more for a few moments, and then she began again.

'I suppose you might as well be told something – to prepare you. You are going to a queer place.'

Mary said nothing at all, and Mrs Medlock looked rather discomfited by her apparent indifference, but after taking a breath, she went on.

'Not but that it's a grand big place in a gloomy way, and Mr Craven's proud of it in his way – and that's gloomy enough, too. The house is six hundred years old, and it's on the edge of the moor, and there's near a hundred rooms in it, though most of them's shut up and locked. And there's pictures and fine old furniture and things that's been there for ages, and there's a big park round it and gardens and trees with branches trailing to the ground – some of them.' She paused and took another breath. 'But there's nothing else,' she ended suddenly.

Mary had begun to listen in spite of herself. It all sounded so unlike India, and anything new rather attracted her. But she did not intend to look as if she were interested. That was one of her unhappy, disagreeable ways. So she sat still.

'Well,' said Mrs Medlock. 'What do you think of it?'

'Nothing,' she answered. 'I know nothing about such places.'

That made Mrs Medlock laugh a short sort of laugh.

'Eh!' she said. 'But you are like an old woman. Don't you care?'

'It doesn't matter,' said Mary, 'whether I care or not.'

'You are right enough there,' said Mrs Medlock. 'It doesn't. What you're to be kept at Misselthwaite Manor for I don't know, unless because it's the easiest way. *He's* not going to trouble himself about you, that's sure and certain. He never troubles himself about no one.'

She stopped herself as if she had just remembered something in time.

'He's got a crooked back,' she said. 'That set him wrong. He was a sour young man and got no good of all his money and big place till he was married.'

Mary's eyes turned towards her, in spite of her intention not to seem to care. She had never thought of the hunchback's being married, and she was a trifle surprised. Mrs Medlock saw this, and as she was a talkative woman, she continued with more interest. This was one way of passing some of the time, at any rate.

'She was a sweet, pretty thing, and he'd have walked the world over to get her a blade o' grass she wanted. Nobody thought she'd marry him, but she did, and people said she married him for his money. But she didn't – she didn't,' positively. 'When she died –'

Mary gave a little involuntary jump.

'Oh! did she die?' she exclaimed, quite without meaning to. She had just remembered a French fairy story she had once read called *Riquet à la Houppe*. It had been about a poor hunchback and a beautiful princess, and it had made her suddenly sorry for Mr Archibald Craven.

'Yes, she died,' Mrs Medlock answered. 'And it made him queerer than ever. He cares about nobody. He won't see people. Most of the time he goes away, and when he is at Misselthwaite he shuts himself up in the West Wing and won't let anyone but Pitcher see him. Pitcher's an old fellow, but he took care of him when he was a child and he knows his ways.'

It sounded like something in a book, and it did not make Mary feel cheerful. A house with a hundred rooms, nearly all shut up and with their doors locked – a house on the edge of a moor – whatsoever a moor was – sounded dreary. A man with a crooked back who shut himself up also! She stared out of the window with her lips pinched together, and it seemed quite natural that the rain should have begun to pour down in grey slanting lines and splash and stream down the window-panes. If the pretty wife had been alive, she might have made things cheerful by being something like her own mother and by running in and out and going to parties as she had done in frocks 'full of lace'. But she was not there any more.

'You needn't expect to see him, because ten to one you won't,' said Mrs Medlock. 'And you mustn't expect that there will be people to talk to you. You'll have to play about and look after yourself. You'll be told what rooms you can go into and what rooms you're to keep out of. There's gardens enough. But when you're in the house don't go wandering and poking about. Mr Craven won't have it.'

'I shall not want to go poking about,' said sour little Mary; and just as suddenly as she had begun to be rather sorry for Mr Archibald Craven, she began to cease to be sorry and to think he was unpleasant enough to deserve all that had happened to him.

And she turned her face towards the streaming panes of the window of the railway carriage and gazed out at the grey rain-storm which looked as if it would go on for ever and ever. She watched it so long and steadily that the greyness grew heavier and heavier before her eyes and she fell asleep.

3
Across the Moor

SHE slept a long time, and when she awakened Mrs Medlock had bought a lunch-basket at one of the stations, and they had some chicken and cold beef and bread-and-butter and some hot tea. The rain seemed to be streaming down more heavily than ever, and everybody in the station wore wet and glistening waterproofs. The guard lighted the lamps in the carriage, and Mrs Medlock cheered up very much over her tea and chicken and beef. She ate a great deal, and afterwards fell asleep herself, and Mary sat and stared at her and watched her fine bonnet slip on one side until she herself fell asleep once more in the corner of the carriage, lulled by the splashing of the rain against the windows. It was quite dark when she awakened again. The train had stopped at a station and Mrs Medlock was shaking her.

'You have had a sleep!' she said. 'It's time to open your eyes! We're at Thwaite Station, and we've got a long drive before us.'

Mary stood up and tried to keep her eyes open while Mrs Medlock collected her parcels. The little girl did not offer to help her, because in India native servants always picked up or carried things, and it seemed quite proper that other people should wait on one.

The station was a small one, and nobody but themselves seemed to be getting out of the train. The station-master spoke to Mrs Medlock in a rough, good-natured way, pronouncing his words in a queer broad fashion which Mary found out afterwards was Yorkshire.

'I see tha's got back,' he said. 'An' tha's browt th' young 'un with thee.'

'Aye, that's her,' answered Mrs Medlock, speaking with a Yorkshire accent herself and jerking her head over her shoulder towards Mary. 'How's thy missus?'

'Well enow. Th' carriage is waitin' outside for thee.'

A brougham stood on the road before the little outside platform. Mary saw that it was a smart carriage and that it was a smart footman who helped her in. His long waterproof coat and the waterproof covering of his hat were shining and dripping with rain as everything was, the burly station-master included.

When he shut the door, mounted the box with the coachman, and they drove off, the little girl found herself seated in a comfortably cushioned corner, but she was not inclined to go to sleep again. She sat and looked out of the window, curious to see something of the road over which she was being driven to the queer place Mrs Medlock had spoken of. She was not at all a timid child, and she was not exactly frightened, but she felt that there was no knowing what might happen in a house with a hundred rooms nearly all shut up – a house standing on the edge of a moor.

'What is a moor?' she said suddenly to Mrs Medlock.

'Look out of the window in about ten minutes and you'll see,' the woman answered. 'We've got to drive five miles across Missel Moor before we get to the Manor. You won't see much because it's a dark night, but you can see something.'

Mary asked no more questions, but waited in the darkness of her corner, keeping her eyes on the window. The carriage lamps cast rays of light a little distance ahead of them, and she caught glimpses of the things they passed. After they had left the station they had driven through a tiny village and she had seen whitewashed cottages and the lights of a public house. Then they had passed a church and a vicarage and a little shop window or so in a cottage with toys and sweets and odd things set out for sale. Then they were on the high road, and she saw hedges and trees. After that there seemed nothing different for a long time – or at least it seemed a long time to her.

At last the horses began to go more slowly, as if they were climbing up-hill, and presently there seemed to be no more hedges and no more trees. She could see nothing, in fact, but a dense darkness on either side. She leaned forward and pressed her face against the window just as the carriage gave a big jolt.

'Eh! We're on the moor now sure enough,' said Mrs Medlock.

The carriage lamps shed a yellow light on a rough-looking road which seemed to be cut through bushes and low-growing things which ended in the great expanse of dark apparently spread out before and around them. A wind was rising and making a singular, wild, low, rushing sound.

'It's – it's not the sea, is it?' said Mary, looking round at her companion.

'No, not it,' answered Mrs Medlock. 'Nor it isn't fields nor mountains, it's just miles and miles and miles of wild land that nothing grows on but heather and gorse and broom, and nothing lives on but wild ponies and sheep.'

'I feel as if it might be the sea, if there were water on it,' said Mary. 'It sounds like the sea just now.'

'That's the wind blowing through the bushes,' Mrs Medlock said. 'It's a wild, dreary enough place to my mind, though there's plenty that likes it – particularly when the heather's in bloom.'

On and on they drove through the darkness, and though the rain stopped, the wind rushed by and whistled and made strange sounds. The road went up and down, and several times the carriage passed over a little bridge beneath which water rushed very fast with a great deal of noise. Mary felt as if the drive would never come to an end, and that the wide, bleak moor was a wide expanse of black ocean through which she was passing on a strip of dry land.

'I don't like it,' she said to herself. 'I don't like it,' and she pinched her thin lips more tightly together.

The horses were climbing up a hilly piece of road when she first caught sight of a light. Mrs Medlock saw it as soon as she did, and drew a long sigh of relief.

'Eh, I am glad to see that bit o' light twinkling,' she exclaimed. 'It's the light in the lodge window. We shall get a good cup of tea after a bit, at all events.'

It was 'after a bit', as she said, for when the carriage passed through the park gates there was still two miles of avenue to drive through, and the trees (which nearly met overhead) made it seem as if they were driving through a long dark vault.

They drove out of the vault into a clear space and stopped before an immensely long but low-built house, which seemed to ramble round a stone court. At first Mary thought that there were no lights at all in the windows, but as she got out of the carriage she saw that one room in a corner upstairs showed a dull glow.

The entrance door was a huge one made of massive, curiously shaped panels of oak studded with big iron nails and bound with great iron bars. It opened into an enormous hall, which was so dimly lighted that the faces in the portraits on the walls and the figures in the suits of armour made Mary feel that she did not want to look at them. As she stood on the stone floor she looked a very small, odd little black figure, and she felt as small and lost and odd as she looked.

A neat, thin old man stood near the manservant who opened the door for them.

'You are to take her to her room,' he said in a husky voice. 'He doesn't want to see her. He's going to London in the morning.'

'Very well, Mr Pitcher,' Mrs Medlock answered. 'So long as I know what's expected of me, I can manage.'

'What's expected of you, Mrs Medlock,' Mr Pitcher

said, 'is that you make sure that he's not disturbed and that he doesn't see what he doesn't want to see.'

And then Mary Lennox was led up a broad staircase and down a long corridor and up a short flight of steps and through another corridor and another, until a door opened in a wall and she found herself in a room with a fire in it and a supper on a table.

Mrs Medlock said unceremoniously:

'Well, here you are! This room and the next are where you'll live – and you must keep to them. Don't you forget that!'

It was in this way Mistress Mary arrived at Misselthwaite Manor, and she had perhaps never felt quite so contrary in all her life.

4

Martha

WHEN she opened her eyes in the morning it was because a young housemaid had come into her room to light the fire and was kneeling on the hearth-rug raking out the cinders noisily. Mary lay and watched her for a few moments and then began to look about the room. She had never seen a room at all like it, and thought it curious and gloomy. The walls were covered with tapestry with a forest scene embroidered on it. There were fantastically dressed people under the trees, and in the distance there was a glimpse of the turrets of a castle. There were hunters and horses and dogs and ladies. Mary felt as if she were in the forest with them. Out of a deep window she could see a great climbing stretch of land which seemed to have no trees on it, and to look rather like an endless, dull, purplish sea.

'What is that?' she said, pointing out of the window.

Martha, the young housemaid, who had just risen to her feet, looked, and pointed also.

'That there?' she said.

'Yes.'

'That's th' moor,' with a good-natured grin. 'Does tha' like it?'

'No,' answered Mary. 'I hate it.'

'That's because tha'rt not used to it,' Martha said, going back to her hearth. 'Tha' thinks it's too big an' bare now. But tha' will like it.'

'Do you?' inquired Mary.

'Aye, that I do,' answered Martha, cheerfully polishing away at the grate. 'I just love it. It's none bare. It's covered wi' growin' things as smells sweet. It's fair lovely in spring an' summer when th' gorse an' broom an' heather's in flower. It smells o' honey an' there's such a lot o' fresh air – an' th' sky looks so high an' th' bees an' skylarks makes such a nice noise hummin' an' singin'. Eh! I wouldn't live away from th' moor for anythin'.'

Mary listened to her with a grave, puzzled expression. The native servants she had been used to in India were not in the least like this. They were obsequious and servile and did not presume to talk to their masters as if they were their equals. They made salaams and called them 'protector of the poor' and names of that sort.

Indian servants were commanded to do things, not asked. It was not the custom to say 'Please' and 'Thank you', and Mary had always slapped her Ayah in the face when she was angry. She wondered a little what this girl would do if one slapped her in the face. She was a round, rosy, good-natured looking creature, but she had a sturdy way which made Mistress Mary wonder if she might not even slap back – if the person who slapped her was only a little girl.

'You are a strange servant,' she said from her pillows, rather haughtily.

Martha sat up on her heels, with her blacking-brush in her hand, and laughed, without seeming the least out of temper.

'Eh! I know that,' she said. 'If there was a grand missus at Misselthwaite I should never have been even one of th' under-housemaids. I might have been let to be scullery-maid, but I'd never have been let upstairs. I'm too common an' I talk too much Yorkshire. But this is a funny house for all it's so grand. Seems like there's neither master nor mistress except Mr Pitcher and Mrs Medlock. Mr Craven, he won't be troubled about any-thin' when he's here, an' he's nearly always away. Mrs Medlock gave me th' place out o' kindness. She told me she could never have done it if Misselthwaite had been like other big houses.'

'Are you going to be my servant?' Mary asked, still in her imperious little Indian way.

Martha began to rub her grate again.

'I'm Mrs Medlock's servant,' she said stoutly. 'And she's Mr Craven's – but I'm to do the housemaid's work up here an' wait on you a bit. But you won't need much waitin' on.'

'Who is going to dress me?' demanded Mary.

Martha sat up on her heels again and stared. She spoke in broad Yorkshire in her amazement.

'Canna' tha' dress thysen?' she said.

'What do you mean? I don't understand your language,' said Mary.

'Eh! I forgot,' Martha said. 'Mrs Medlock told me I'd have to be careful or you wouldn't know what I was sayin'. I mean can't you put on your own clothes?'

'No,' answered Mary, quite indignantly. 'I never did in my life. My Ayah dressed me, of course.'

'Well,' said Martha, evidently not in the least aware that she was impudent, 'it's time tha' should learn. Tha' cannot begin younger. It'll do thee good to wait on thysen a bit. My mother always said she couldn't see why grand people's children didn't turn out fair fools – what with nurses an' bein' washed an' dressed an' took out to walk as if they was puppies!'

31

...ent in India,' said Mistress Mary disdainfully.
...d scarcely stand this.

...Martha was not at all crushed.

'Eh! I can see it's different,' she answered almost sympathetically. 'I dare say it's because there's such a lot o' blacks there instead o' respectable white people. When I heard you was comin' from India I thought you was a black too.'

Mary sat up in bed, furious.

'What!' she said. 'What! You thought I was a native. You – you daughter of a pig!'

Martha stared and looked hot.

'Who are you callin' names?' she said. 'You needn't be so vexed. That's not th' way for a young lady to talk. I've nothin' against th' blacks. When you read about 'em in tracts they're always very religious. You always read as a black's a man an' a brother. I've never seen a black, an' I was fair pleased to think I was goin' to see one close. When I come in to light your fire this mornin' I crep' up to your bed an' pulled th' cover back careful to look at you. An' there you was,' disappointedly, 'no more black than me – for all you're so yeller.'

Mary did not even try to control her rage and humiliation.

'You thought I was a native! You dared! You don't know anything about natives! They are not people – they're servants who must salaam to you. You know nothing about India. You know nothing about anything!'

She was in such a rage and felt so hopeless before the girl's simple stare, and somehow she suddenly felt so horribly lonely and far away from everything she understood and which understood her, that she threw herself face downward on the pillows and burst into passionate sobbing. She sobbed so unrestrainedly that good-natured Yorkshire Martha was a little frightened and quite sorry for her. She went to the bed and bent over her.

'Eh! you mustn't cry like that there!' she begged. 'You mustn't for sure. I didn't know you'd be vexed. I don't know anythin' about anythin' – just like you said. I beg your pardon, miss. Do stop cryin'.'

There was something comforting and really friendly in her queer Yorkshire speech and sturdy way which had a good effect on Mary. She gradually ceased crying and became quiet. Martha looked relieved.

'It's time for thee to get up now,' she said. 'Mrs Medlock said I was to carry tha's breakfast an' tea an' dinner into th' room next to this. It's been made into a nursery for thee. I'll help thee on with thy clothes if tha'll get out of bed. If th' buttons are at th' back tha' cannot button them up tha'self.'

When Mary at last decided to get up, the clothes

Martha took from the wardrobe were not the ones she had worn when she arrived the night before with Mrs Medlock.

'Those are not mine,' she said. 'Mine are black.'

She looked the thick white wool coat and dress over, and added with cool approval:

'Those are nicer than mine.'

'These are th' ones tha' must put on,' Martha answered. 'Mr Craven ordered Mrs Medlock to get 'em in London. He said, "I won't have a child dressed in black wanderin' about like a lost soul," he said. "It'd make the place sadder than it is. Put colour on her." Mother she said she knew what he meant. Mother always knows what a body means. She doesn't hold with black hersel'.'

'I hate black things,' said Mary.

The dressing process was one which taught them both something. Martha had 'buttoned up' her little sisters and brothers, but she had never seen a child who stood still and waited for another person to do things for her as if she had neither hands nor feet of her own.

'Why doesn't tha' put on tha' own shoes?' she said when Mary quietly held out her foot.

'My Ayah did it,' answered Mary, staring. 'It was the custom.'

She said that very often – 'It was the custom.' The native servants were always saying it. If one told them to do a thing their ancestors had not done for a thousand years they gazed at one mildly and said, 'It is not the custom' and one knew that was the end of the matter.

It had not been the custom that Mistress Mary should do anything but stand and allow herself to be dressed like a doll, but before she was ready for breakfast she began to suspect that her life at Misselthwaite Manor would end by teaching her a number of things quite new to her – things such as putting on her own shoes and stockings, and picking up things she let fall. If Martha had been a well-trained fine young lady's-maid she would have been more subservient and respectful and would have known that it was her business to brush hair, and button boots, and pick things up and lay them away. She was, however, only an untrained Yorkshire rustic who had been brought up in a moorland cottage with a swarm of little brothers and sisters who had never dreamed of doing anything but waiting on themselves and on the younger ones who were either babies in arms or just learning to totter about and tumble over things.

If Mary Lennox had been a child who was ready to be amused she would perhaps have laughed at Martha's readiness to talk, but Mary only listened to her coldly and wondered at her freedom of manner. At first she was not at all interested, but gradually, as the girl rattled on in her good-tempered, homely way, Mary began to notice what she was saying.

'Eh! you should see 'em all,' she said. There's twelve of us an' my father only gets sixteen shilling a week. I can tell you my mother's put to it to get porridge for 'em all. They tumble about on th' moor an' play there all day, an' mother says th' air of th' moor fattens 'em. She says she believes they eat th' grass same as th' wild ponies do. Our Dickon, he's twelve years old and he's got a young pony he calls his own.'

'Where did he get it?' asked Mary.

'He found it on th' moor with its mother when it was a little one, an' he began to make friends with it an' give it bits o' bread an' pluck young grass for it. And it got to like him so it follows him about an' it lets him get on its back. Dickon's a kind lad an' animals like him.'

Mary had never possessed an animal pet of her own and had always thought she should like one. So she began to feel a slight interest in Dickon, and as she had never been interested in anyone but herself, it was the dawning of a healthy sentiment. When she went into the room which had been made into a nursery for her, she found that it was rather like the one she had slept in. It was not a child's room, but a grown-up person's room, with gloomy old pictures on the walls and heavy old oak chairs. A table in the centre was set with a good, substantial breakfast. But she had always had a very small appetite, and she looked with something more than indifference at the first plate Martha set before her.

'I don't want it,' she said.

'Tha' doesn't want thy porridge!' Martha exclaimed incredulously.

'No.'

'Tha' doesn't know how good it is. Put a bit o' treacle on it or a bit o' sugar.'

'I don't want it,' repeated Mary.

'Eh!' said Martha. 'I can't abide to see good victuals go to waste. If our children was at this table they'd clean it bare in five minutes.'

'Why?' asked Mary coldly.

'Why!' echoed Martha. 'Because they scarce ever had their stomachs full in their lives. They're as hungry as young hawks an' foxes.'

'I don't know what it is to be hungry,' said Mary with the indifference of ignorance.

Martha looked indignant.

'Well, it would do thee good to try it. I can see that plain enough,' she said outspokenly. 'I've no patience with folks as sits an' just stares at good bread an' meat. My word! don't I wish Dickon and Phil an' Jane an' th' rest of 'em had what's here under their pinafores.'

'Why don't you take it to them?' suggested Mary.

'It's not mine,' answered Martha stoutly. 'An' this isn't my day out. I get my day out once a month same as the rest. Then I go home an' clean up for mother an' give her a day's rest.'

Mary drank some tea and ate a little toast and some marmalade.

'You wrap up warm an' run out an' play you,' said Martha. 'It'll do you good and give you some stomach for your meat.'

Mary went to the window. There were gardens and paths and big trees, but everything looked dull and wintry.

'Out? Why should I go out on a day like this?'

'Well, if tha' doesn't go out tha'lt have to stay in, an' what has tha' got to do?'

Mary glanced about her. There was nothing to do. When Mrs Medlock had prepared the nursery she had not thought of amusement. Perhaps it would be better to go and see what the gardens were like.

'Who will go with me?' she inquired.

Martha stared.

'You'll go by yourself,' she answered. 'You'll have to learn to play like other children does when they haven't got sisters and brothers. Our Dickon goes off on th' moor by himself an' plays for hours. That's how he made friends with th' pony. He's got sheep on th' moor that knows him, an' birds as comes an' eats out of his hand. However little there is to eat, he always saves a bit o' his bread to coax his pets.'

It was really this mention of Dickon which made Mary decide to go out, though she was not aware of it. There would be birds outside, though there would not be ponies or sheep. They would be different from the birds in India, and it might amuse her to look at them.

Martha found her coat and hat for her and a pair of stout little boots and she showed her her way downstairs.

'If tha' goes round that way tha'll come to th' gardens,' she said, pointing to a gate in a wall of shrubbery. 'There's lots o' flowers in summer-time, but there's nothin' bloomin' now.' She seemed to hesitate a second before she added, 'One of th' gardens is locked up. No one has been in it for ten years.'

'Why?' asked Mary in spite of herself. Here was another locked door that added to the hundred in the strange house.

'Mr Craven had it shut when his wife died so sudden. He won't let no one go inside. It was her garden. He locked th' door an' dug a hole and buried th' key. There's Mrs Medlock's bell ringing – I must run.'

After she was gone Mary turned down the walk which

led to the door in the shrubbery. She could not help thinking about the garden which no one had been into for ten years. She wondered what it would look like and whether there were any flowers still alive in it. When she had passed through the shrubbery gate she found herself in great gardens, with wide lawns and winding walks with clipped borders. There were trees, and flower-beds, and evergreens clipped into strange shapes, and a large pool with an old grey fountain in its midst. But the flower-beds were bare and wintry and the fountain was not playing. This was not the garden which was shut up. How could a garden be shut up? You could always walk into a garden.

She was just thinking this, when she saw that, at the end of the path she was following, there seemed to be a long wall, with ivy growing over it. She was not familiar enough with England to know that she was coming upon the kitchen-gardens where the vegetables and fruit were growing. She went towards the wall and found that there was a green door in the ivy, and that it stood open. This was not the closed garden evidently, and she could go into it.

She went through the door and found that it was a garden with walls all around it and that it was only one of several walled gardens which seemed to open into one another. She saw another open green door, revealing bushes and pathways between beds containing winter vegetables. Fruit-trees were trained flat against the wall, and over some of the beds there were glass frames. The place was bare and ugly enough, Mary thought, as she stood and stared about her. It might be nicer in summer, when things were green, but there was nothing pretty about it now.

Presently an old man with a spade over his shoulder walked through the door leading from the second garden. He looked startled when he saw Mary, and then touched his cap. He had a surly old face, and did not seem at all pleased to see her – but then she was displeased with his garden and wore her 'quite contrary' expression, and certainly did not seem at all pleased to see him.

'What is this place?' she asked.

'One 'o th' kitchen-gardens,' he answered.

'What is that?' said Mary, pointing through the other green door.

'Another of 'em,' shortly. 'There's another on t'other side o' th' wall an' there's th' orchard t'other side o' that.'

'Can I go in them?' asked Mary.

'If tha' likes. But there's nowt to see.'

Mary made no response. She went down the path and through the second green door. There she found more walls and winter vegetables and glass frames, but in the second wall there was another green door and it was not open. Perhaps it led into the garden which no one had seen for ten years. As she was not at all a timid child and always did what she wanted to do, Mary went to the green door and turned the handle. She hoped the door would not open, because she wanted to be sure she had found the mysterious garden – but it did open quite easily and she walked through it and found herself in an orchard. There were walls all around it also and trees trained against them, and there were bare fruit-trees growing in the winter-browned grass – but there was no green door to be seen anywhere. Mary looked for it, and yet when she had entered the upper end of the garden she had noticed that the wall did not seem to end with the orchard, but to extend beyond it as if it enclosed a place at the other side. She could see the tops of trees above the wall, and when she stood still she saw a bird with a bright red breast sitting on the topmost branch of one of them, and suddenly he burst into his winter song – almost as if he had caught sight of her and was calling to her.

She stopped and listened to him, and somehow his cheerful, friendly little whistle gave her a pleased feeling – even a disagreeable little girl may be lonely, and the big closed house and big bare moor and big bare gardens had made this one feel as if there was no one left in the world but herself. If she had been an affectionate child, who had been used to being loved, she would have broken her heart, but even though she was 'Mistress Mary Quite Contrary' she was desolate, and the bright-breasted little bird brought a look into her sour little face which was almost a smile. She listened to him until he flew away. He was not like an Indian bird, and she liked him and wondered if she should ever see him again. Perhaps he lived in the mysterious garden and knew all about it.

Perhaps it was because she had nothing whatever to do that she thought so much of the deserted garden. She was curious about it, and wanted to see what it was like. Why had Mr Archibald Craven buried the key? If he had liked his wife so much why did he hate her garden? She wondered if she should ever see him, but she knew that if she did she should not like him, and he would not like her, and that she should only stand and stare at him and say nothing, though she should be wanting dreadfully to ask him why he had done such a queer thing.

'People never like me and I never like people,' she thought. 'And I can never talk as the Crawford children could. They were always talking and laughing and making noises.'

She thought of the robin and of the way he seemed to sing his song at her, and as she remembered the tree-top he perched on she stopped rather suddenly on the path.

'I believe that tree was in the secret garden – I feel sure it was,' she said. 'There was a wall round the place and there was no door.'

She walked back into the first kitchen-garden she had entered and found the old man digging there. She went and stood beside him and watched him a few moments in her cold little way. He took no notice of her, and so at last she spoke to him.

'I have been into the other gardens,' she said.

'There was nothin' to prevent thee,' he answered crustily.

'I went into the orchard.'

'There was no dog at th' door to bite thee,' he answered.

'There was no door there into the other garden,' said Mary.

'What garden?' he said in a rough voice, stopping his digging for a moment.

'The one on the other side of the wall,' answered Mistress Mary. 'There were trees there – I saw the tops of them. A bird with a red breast was sitting on one of them, and he sang.'

To her surprise the surly old weather-beaten face actually changed its expression. A slow smile spread over it and the gardener looked quite different. It made her think that it was curious how much nicer a person looked when he smiled. She had not thought of it before.

He turned about to the orchard side of his garden and began to whistle – a low, soft whistle. She could not understand how such a surly man could make such a coaxing sound.

Almost the next moment a wonderful thing happened. She heard a soft little rushing flight through the air – and it was the bird with the red breast flying to them, and he actually alighted on the big clod of earth quite near to the gardener's foot.

'Here he is,' chuckled the old man, and then he spoke to the bird as if he were speaking to a child.

'Where has tha' been, tha' cheeky little beggar?' he said. 'I've not seen thee before today. Has tha' begun tha' courtin' this early in th' season? Tha'rt too for'ard.'

The bird put his tiny head on one side and looked up at him with his soft bright eye, which was like a black dewdrop. He seemed quite familiar and not the least afraid. He hopped about and pecked the earth briskly, looking for seeds and insects. It actually gave Mary a queer feeling in her heart, because he was so pretty and cheerful and seemed so like a person. He had a tiny plump body and a delicate beak, and slender delicate legs.

'Will he always come when you call him?' she asked almost in a whisper.

'Aye, that he will. I've knowed him ever since he was a fledgling. He come out of th' nest in th' other garden, an' when first he flew over th' wall he was too weak to fly back for a few days an' we got friendly. When he went over th' wall again th' rest of th' brood was gone an' he was lonely an' he come back to me.'

'What kind of a bird is he?' Mary asked.

'Doesn't tha' know? He's a robin redbreast, an' they're th' friendliest, curiousest birds alive. They're almost as friendly as dogs – if you know how to get on with 'em. Watch him peckin' about there an' lookin' round at us now an' again. He knows we're talkin' about him.'

It was the queerest thing in the world to see the old fellow. He looked at the plump little scarlet-waistcoated bird as if he were both proud and fond of him.

'He's a conceited one,' he chuckled. 'He likes to hear folk talk about him. An' curious – bless me, there never was his like for curiosity an' meddlin'. He's always comin' to see what I'm plantin'. He knows all th' things Mester Craven never troubles hissel' to find out. He's th' head gardener, he is.'

The robin hopped about, busily pecking the soil, and now and then stopped and looked at them a little. Mary thought his black dewdrop eyes gazed at her with great curiosity. It really seemed as if he were finding out all about her. The queer feeling in her heart increased.

'Where did the rest of the brood fly to?' she asked.

'There's no knowin'. The old ones turn 'em out o' their nest an' make 'em fly, an' they're scattered before you know it. This one was a knowin' one an' he knew he was lonely.'

Mistress Mary went a step nearer to the robin and looked at him very hard.

'I'm lonely,' she said.

She had not known before that this was one of the things which made her feel sour and cross. She seemed to find it out when the robin looked at her and she looked at the robin.

The old gardener pushed his cap back on his bald head and stared at her a minute.

'Art tha' th' little wench from India?' he asked.

Mary nodded.

'Then no wonder tha'rt lonely. Tha'lt be lonelier before tha's done,' he said.

He began to dig again, driving his spade deep into the rich black garden soil, while the robin hopped about, very busily employed.

'What is your name?' Mary inquired.

He stood up to answer her.

'Ben Weatherstaff,' he answered, and then he added with a surly chuckle, 'I'm lonely mysel' except when he's with me,' and he jerked his thumb towards the robin. 'He's th' only friend I've got.'

'I have no friends at all,' said Mary. 'I never had. My Ayah didn't like me and I never played with anyone.'

It is a Yorkshire habit to say what you think with blunt frankness, and old Ben Weatherstaff was a Yorkshire moor man.

'Tha' an' me are a good bit alike,' he said. 'We was wove out of th' same cloth. We're neither of us good-lookin' an' we're both of us as sour as we look. We've got the same nasty tempers, both of us, I'll warrant.'

This was plain speaking, and Mary Lennox had never heard the truth about herself in her life. Native servants always salaamed and submitted to you, whatever you did. She had never thought much about her looks, but she wondered if she was as unattractive as Ben Weatherstaff, and she also wondered if she looked as sour as he had looked before the robin came. She actually began to wonder also if she was 'nasty-tempered'. She felt uncomfortable.

Suddenly a clear rippling little sound broke out near her and she turned round. She was standing a few feet from a young apple-tree, and the robin had flown on to one of its branches and had burst out into a scrap of a song. Ben Weatherstaff laughed outright.

'What did he do that for?' asked Mary.

'He's made up his mind to make friends with thee,' replied Ben. 'Dang me if he hasn't took a fancy to thee.'

'To me?' said Mary, and she moved towards the little tree softly and looked up.

'Would you make friends with me?' she said to the robin, just as if she were speaking to a person. 'Would you?' And she did not say it either in her hard little voice or in her imperious Indian voice, but in a tone so soft and eager and coaxing that Ben Weatherstaff was as surprised as she had been when she heard him whistle.

'Why,' he cried out, 'tha' said that as nice an' human as if tha' was a real child instead of a sharp old woman. Tha' said it almost like Dickon talks to his wild things on th' moor.'

'Do you know Dickon?' Mary asked, turning round rather in a hurry.

'Everybody knows him. Dickon's wanderin' about everywhere. Th' very blackberries an' heather-bells knows him. I warrant th' foxes shows him where their cubs lies an' th' skylarks doesn't hide their nests from him.'

Mary would have liked to ask some more questions. She was almost as curious about Dickon as she was about the deserted garden. But just at that moment the robin, who had ended his song, gave a little shake of his wings, spread them, and flew away. He had made his visit and had other things to do.

'He has flown over the wall!' Mary cried out, watching him. 'He has flown into the orchard – he has flown across the other wall – into the garden where there is no door!'

'He lives there,' said old Ben. 'He came out o' th' egg there. If he's courtin', he's makin' up to some young madam of a robin that lives among th' old rose-trees there.'

'Rose-trees,' said Mary. 'Are there rose-trees?'

Ben Weatherstaff took up his spade again and began to dig.

'There was ten year' ago,' he mumbled.

'I should like to see them,' said Mary. 'Where is the green door? There must be a door somewhere.'

Ben drove his spade deep and looked as uncompanionable as he had looked when she first saw him.

'There was ten year' ago, but there isn't now,' he said.

'No door!' cried Mary. 'There must be.'

'None as anyone can find, an' none as is anyone's business. Don't be a meddlesome wench an' poke your nose where it's no cause to go. Here, I must go on with my work. Get you gone an' play you. I've no more time.'

And he actually stopped digging, threw his spade over his shoulder, and walked off, without even glancing at her or saying good-bye.

5

The Cry in the Corridor

AT FIRST each day which passed by for Mary Lennox was exactly like the others. Every morning she awoke in her tapestried room and found Martha kneeling upon the hearth building her fire; every morning she ate her breakfast in the nursery which had nothing amusing in it; and after each breakfast she gazed out of the window across to the huge moor, which seemed to spread out on all sides and climb up to the sky, and after she had stared for a while she realised that if she did not go out she would have to stay in and do nothing – and so she went out. She did not know that this was the best thing she could have done, and she did not know that, when she began to walk quickly or even run along the paths and down the avenue, she was stirring her slow blood and making herself stronger by fighting with the wind which swept down from the moor. She ran only to make herself warm, and she hated the wind which rushed at her face and roared and held her back as if it were some giant she could not see. But the big breaths of rough fresh air blown over the heather filled her lungs with something which was good for her whole thin body and whipped some red colour into her cheeks and brightened her dull eyes when she did not know anything about it.

But after a few days spent almost entirely out of doors, she wakened one morning knowing what it was to be hungry, and when she sat down to her breakfast she did not glance disdainfully at her porridge and push it away, but took up her spoon and began to eat it and went on eating it until her bowl was empty.

'Tha' got on well enough with that this mornin', didn't tha'?' said Martha.

'It tastes nice today,' said Mary, feeling a little surprised herself.

'It's th' air of th' moor that's givin' thee stomach for tha' victuals,' answered Martha. 'It's lucky for thee that tha's got victuals as well as an appetite. There's been twelve in our cottage as had th' stomach an' nothing to put in it. You go on playin' you out o' doors every day an' you'll get some flesh on your bones an' you won't be so yeller.'

'I don't play,' said Mary. 'I have nothing to play with.'

'Nothin' to play with!' exclaimed Martha. 'Our children play with sticks and stones. They just runs about an' shouts an' looks at things.'

Mary did not shout, but she looked at things. There was nothing else to do. She walked round and round the gardens and wandered about the paths in the park. Sometimes she looked for Ben Weatherstaff, but though several times she saw him at work he was too busy to look at her or was too surly. Once when she was walking towards him he picked up his spade and turned away, as if he did it on purpose.

One place she went to oftener than to any other. It was the long walk outside the gardens with the walls round them. There were bare flower-beds on either side of it and against the walls ivy grew thickly. There was one part of the wall where the creeping dark green leaves were more bushy than elsewhere. It seemed as if for a long time that part had been neglected. The rest of it had been clipped and made to look neat, but at this lower end of the walk it had not been trimmed at all.

A few days after she had talked to Ben Weatherstaff, Mary stopped to notice this and wondered why it was so. She had just paused and was looking up at a long spray of ivy swinging in the wind, when she saw a gleam of scarlet and heard a brilliant chirp, and there, on the top of the wall, perched Ben Weatherstaff's robin redbreast, tilting forward to look at her with his small head on one side.

'Oh!' she cried out, 'is it you – is it you?' And it did not seem at all queer to her that she spoke to him as if she was sure that he would understand and answer her.

He did answer. He twittered and chirped and hopped along the wall, as if he were telling her all sorts of things. It seemed to Mistress Mary as if she understood him, too, though he was not speaking in words. It was as if he said:

'Good morning! Isn't the wind nice? Isn't the sun nice? Isn't everything nice? Let us both chirp and hop and twitter. Come on! Come on!'

Mary began to laugh, and as he hopped and took little flights along the wall she ran after him. Poor little thin, sallow, ugly Mary – she actually looked almost pretty for a moment.

'I like you! I like you!' she cried out, pattering down the walk; and she chirped and tried to whistle, which last she did not know how to do in the least. But the robin seemed to be quite satisfied and chirped and whistled back at her. At last he spread his wings and made a darting flight to the top of a tree, where he perched and sang loudly.

That reminded Mary of the first time she had seen him. He had been swinging on a tree-top then and she had been standing in the orchard. Now she was on the other side of the orchard and standing in the path outside a wall – much lower down – and there was the same tree inside.

'It's the garden no one can go into,' she said to herself. 'It's the garden without a door. He lives in there. How I wish I could see what it is like!'

She ran up the walk to the green door she had entered the first morning. Then she ran down the path through the other door and then into the orchard, and when she stood and looked up there was the tree on the other side of the wall, and there was the robin just finishing his song and beginning to preen his feathers with his beak.

'It is the garden,' she said. 'I am sure it is.'

She walked round and looked closely at that side of the orchard wall, but she only found what she had found before – that there was no door in it. Then she ran through the kitchen-gardens again and out into the walk outside the long ivy-covered wall, and she walked to the end of it and looked at it, but there was no door; and then she walked to the other end, looking again, but there was no door.

'It's very queer,' she said. 'Ben Weatherstaff said there

was no door and there is no door. But there must have been one ten years ago, because Mr Craven buried the key.'

This gave her so much to think of that she began to be quite interested and feel that she was not sorry that she had come to Misselthwaite Manor. In India she had always felt hot and too languid to care much about anything. The fact was that the fresh wind from the moor had begun to blow the cobwebs out of her young brain and to waken her up a little.

She stayed out of doors nearly all day, and when she sat down to her supper at night she felt hungry and drowsy and comfortable. She did not feel cross when Martha chattered away. She felt as if she rather liked to hear her, and at last she thought she would ask her a question. She asked it after she had finished her supper and had sat down on the hearth-rug before the fire.

'Why did Mr Craven hate the garden?' she said.

She had made Martha stay with her and Martha had not objected at all. She was very young, and used to a crowded cottage full of brothers and sisters, and she found it dull in the great servants' hall downstairs, where the footman and upper-housemaids made fun of her Yorkshire speech and looked upon her as a common little thing, and sat and whispered among themselves. Martha liked to talk, and the strange child who had lived in India, and been waited upon by 'blacks', was novelty enough to attract her.

She sat down on the hearth herself without waiting to be asked.

'Art tha' thinkin' about that garden yet?' she said. 'I knew tha' would. That was just the way with me when I first heard about it.'

'Why did he hate it?' Mary persisted.

Martha tucked her feet under her and made herself quite comfortable.

'Listen to th' wind wutherin' round the house,' she said. 'You could bare stand up on the moor if you was out on it tonight.'

Mary did not know what 'wutherin'' meant until she listened, and then she understood. It must mean that hollow, shuddering sort of roar which rushed round and round the house, as if the giant no one could see were buffeting it and beating at the walls and windows to try to break in. But one knew he could not get in, and somehow it made one feel very safe and warm inside a room with a red coal fire.

'But why did he hate it so?' she asked, after she had listened. She intended to know if Martha did.

Then Martha gave up her store of knowledge.

'Mind,' she said, 'Mrs Medlock said it's not to be talked about. There's lots o' things in this place that's not to be talked over. That's Mr Craven's orders. His troubles are none servants' business, he says. But for th' garden he wouldn't be like he is. It was Mrs Craven's garden that she had made when first they were married an' she just loved it, an' they used to 'tend the flowers themselves. An' none o' th' gardeners was ever let to go in. Him an' her used to go in an' shut th' door an' stay there hours an' hours, readin' an' talkin'. An' she was just a bit of a girl an' there was an old tree with a branch bent like a seat on it. An' she made roses grow over it an' she used to sit there. But one day when she was sittin' there th' branch broke an' she fell on th' ground an' was hurt so bad that next day she died. Th' doctors thought he'd go out o' his mind an' die, too. That's why he hates it. No one's never gone in since, an' he won't let anyone talk about it.'

Mary did not ask any more questions. She looked at the fire and listened to the wind 'wutherin' '. It seemed to be 'wutherin' ' louder than ever.

At that moment a very good thing was happening to her. Four good things had happened to her, in fact, since she came to Misselthwaite Manor. She had felt as if she had understood a robin and that he had understood her; she had run in the wind until her blood had grown warm; she had been healthily hungry for the first time in her life; and she had found out what it was to be sorry for someone. She was getting on.

But as she was listening to the wind she began to listen to something else. She did not know what it was, because at first she could scarcely distinguish it from the wind itself. It was a curious sound – it seemed almost as if a child were crying somewhere. Sometimes the wind sounded rather like a child crying, but presently Mistress Mary felt quite sure that this sound was inside the house; not outside it. It was far away, but it was inside. She turned round and looked at Martha.

'Do you hear anyone crying?' she said.

Martha suddenly looked confused.

'No,' she answered. 'It's th' wind. Sometimes it sounds as if someone was lost on th' moor an' wailin'. It's got all sorts o' sounds.'

'But listen,' said Mary. 'It's in the house – down one of those long corridors.'

And at that very moment a door must have been opened somewhere downstairs; for a great rushing draught blew along the passage and the door of the room they sat in was blown open with a crash, and as they both jumped to their feet the light was blown out and the crying sound was swept down the far corridor, so that it was to be heard more plainly than ever.

'There!' said Mary. 'I told you so! It is someone crying – and it isn't a grown-up person.'

Martha ran and shut the door and turned the key, but before she did it they both heard the sound of a door in some far passage shutting with a bang, and then everything was quiet, for even the wind ceased 'wutherin'' for a few moments.

'It was th' wind,' said Martha stubbornly. 'An' if it wasn't, it was little Betty Butterworth, th' scullery-maid. She's had th' toothache all day.'

But something troubled and awkward in her manner made Mistress Mary stare very hard at her. She did not believe she was speaking the truth.

6

'There Was Someone Crying – There Was!'

THE next day the rain poured down in torrents again, and when Mary looked out of her window the moor was almost hidden by grey mist and cloud. There could be no going out today.

'What do you do in your cottage when it rains like this?' she asked Martha.

'Try to keep from under each other's feet mostly,' Martha answered. 'Eh! there does seem a lot of us then. Mother's a good-tempered woman, but she gets fair moithered. The biggest ones goes out in th' cow-shed and plays there. Dickon he doesn't mind th' wet. He goes out just th' same as if th' sun was shinin'. He says he sees things on rainy days as doesn't show when it's fair weather. He once found a little fox cub half drowned in its hole and he brought it home in th' bosom of his shirt to keep it warm. Its mother had been killed near by an' th' hole was swum out an' th' rest o' th' litter was dead. He's got it at home now. He found a half-drowned young crow another time an' he brought it home, too, an' tamed it. It's named Soot, because it's so black an' it hops an' flies about with him everywhere.'

The time had come when Mary had forgotten to resent Martha's familiar talk. She had even begun to find it interesting and to be sorry when she stopped or went away. The stories she had been told by her Ayah when she lived in India had been quite unlike those Martha had to tell about the moorland cottage which held fourteen people who lived in four little rooms and never had quite enough to eat. The children seemed to tumble about and amuse themselves like a litter of rough, good-natured collie puppies. Mary was most attracted by the mother and Dickon. When Martha told stories of what 'mother' said or did they always sounded comfortable.

'If I had a raven or a fox cub I could play with it,' said Mary. 'But I have nothing.'

Martha looked perplexed.

'Can tha' knit?' she asked.

'No,' answered Mary.

'Can tha' sew?'

'No.'

63

'Can tha' read?'

'Yes.'

'Then why doesn't tha' read somethin' or learn a bit o' spellin'? Tha'st old enough to be learnin' thy book a good bit now.'

'I haven't any books,' said Mary. 'Those I had were left in India.'

'That's a pity,' said Martha. 'If Mrs Medlock'd let thee go int' th' library, there's thousands o' books there.'

Mary did not ask where the library was, because she was suddenly inspired by a new idea. She made up her mind to go and find it herself. She was not troubled about Mrs Medlock. Mrs Medlock seemed always to be in her comfortable housekeeper's sitting-room downstairs. In this queer place one scarcely ever saw anyone at all. In fact, there was no one to see but the servants, and when their master was away they lived a luxurious life below stairs, where there was a huge kitchen hung about with shining brass and pewter, and a large servants' hall where there were four or five abundant meals eaten every day, and where a great deal of lively romping went on when Mrs Medlock was out of the way.

Mary's meals were served regularly, and Martha waited on her, but no one troubled themselves about her in the least. Mrs Medlock came and looked at her every day or two, but no one inquired what she did or told her what to do. She supposed that perhaps this was the English way of treating children. In India she had always been attended by her Ayah, who had followed her about and waited on her, hand and foot. She had often been tired of her company. Now she was followed by nobody and was learning to dress herself, because Martha looked as though she thought she was silly and stupid when she wanted to have things handed to her and put on.

'Hasn't tha' got good sense?' she said once, when Mary had stood waiting for her to put on her gloves for her. 'Our Susan Ann is twice as sharp as thee an' she's only four year' old. Sometimes tha' looks fair soft in th' head.'

Mary had worn her contrary scowl for an hour after that, but it made her think several entirely new things.

She stood at the window for about ten minutes this morning after Martha had swept up the hearth for the last time and gone downstairs. She was thinking over the new idea which had come to her when she heard of the library. She did not care very much about the library itself, because she had read very few books; but to hear of it brought back to her mind the hundred rooms with closed doors. She wondered if they were all really locked and what she would find if she could get into any of them. Were there a hundred really? Why shouldn't she go and see how many doors she could count? It would be something to do on this morning when she could not go out. She had never been taught to ask permission to do things, and she knew nothing at all about authority, so she would not have thought it necessary to ask Mrs Medlock if she might walk about the house, even if she had seen her.

She opened the door of the room and went into the corridor, and then she began her wanderings. It was a long corridor and it branched into other corridors and it led her up short flights of steps which mounted to others again. There were doors and doors, and there were pictures on the walls. Sometimes they were pictures of dark, curious landscapes, but oftenest they were portraits of men and women in queer, grand costumes made of satin and velvet. She found herself in one long gallery whose walls were covered with those portraits. She had never thought there could be so many in any house. She walked slowly down this place and stared at the faces, which also seemed to stare at her. She felt as if they were wondering what a little girl from India was doing in their house. Some were pictures of children – little girls in thick satin frocks which reached to their feet and stood out about them, and boys with puffed sleeves and lace collars and long hair, or with big ruffs around their necks. She always stopped to look at the children, and wonder what their names were, and where they had gone, and why they wore such odd clothes. There was a stiff, plain little girl rather like herself. She wore a green brocade dress and held a green parrot on her finger. Her eyes had a sharp, curious look.

'Where do you live now?' said Mary aloud to her. 'I wish you were here.'

Surely no other little girl ever spent such a queer morning. It seemed as if there was no one in all the huge, rambling house but her own small self, wandering about upstairs and down, through narrow passages and wide ones, where it seemed to her that no one but herself had ever walked. Since so many rooms had been built, people must have lived in them, but it all seemed so empty that she could not quite believe it true.

It was not until she climbed to the second floor that she thought of turning the handle of a door. All the doors were shut, as Mrs Medlock had said they were, but at last she put her hand on the handle of one of them and turned it. She was almost frightened for a moment when she felt that it turned without difficulty and that when she pushed upon the door itself it slowly and heavily opened. It was a massive door and opened into a big bedroom. There were embroidered hangings on the wall, and inlaid furniture such as she had seen in India stood about the room. A broad window with leaded panes looked out upon the moor; and over the mantel was another portrait of the stiff, plain little girl who seemed to stare at her more curiously than ever.

'Perhaps she slept here once,' said Mary. 'She stares at me so that she makes me feel queer.'

After that she opened more doors and more. She saw so many rooms that she became quite tired and began to think there must be a hundred, though she had not counted them. In all of them there were old pictures or old tapestries with strange scenes worked on them. There were curious pieces of furniture and curious ornaments in nearly all of them.

In one room, which looked like a lady's sitting-room, the hangings were all embroidered velvet, and in a cabinet were about a hundred little elephants made of ivory. They were of different sizes, and some had their mahouts or palanquins on their backs. Some were much bigger than the others and some were so tiny that they seemed only babies. Mary had seen carved ivory in India and she knew all about the elephants. She opened the door of the cabinet and stood on a footstool and played with these for quite a long time. When she got tired she set the elephants in order and shut the door of the cabinet.

In all her wanderings through the long corridors and the empty rooms she had seen nothing alive; but in this room she saw something. Just after she had closed the cabinet door she heard a tiny rustling sound. It made her jump and she looked around at the sofa by the fireplace, from which it seemed to come. In the corner of the sofa there was a cushion, and in the velvet which covered it there was a hole, and out of the hole peeped a tiny head with a pair of frightened eyes in it.

Mary crept softly across the room to look. The bright eyes belonged to a little grey mouse, and the mouse had eaten into the cushion and made a comfortable nest there. Six baby mice were cuddled up asleep near her. If there was no one else alive in the hundred rooms there were seven mice who did not look lonely at all.

'If they wouldn't be so frightened I would take them back with me,' said Mary.

She had wandered about long enough to feel too tired to wander any further, and she turned back. Two or three times she lost her way by turning down the wrong corridor and was obliged to ramble up and down until she found the right one; but at last she reached her own floor again, though she was some distance from her own room and did not know exactly where she was.

'I believe I have taken a wrong turning again,' she said, standing still at what seemed the end of a short passage with tapestry on the wall. 'I don't know which way to go. How still everything is!'

It was while she was standing here and just after she had said this that the stillness was broken by a sound. It was another cry, but not quite like the one she had heard last night; it was only a short one, a fretful, childish whine muffled by passing through walls.

'It's nearer than it was,' said Mary, her heart beating rather faster. 'And it *is* crying.'

She put her hand accidentally upon the tapestry near her, and then sprang back, feeling quite startled. The tapestry was the covering of a door which fell open and showed her that there was another part of the corridor behind it, and Mrs Medlock was coming up it with her bunch of keys in her hand and a very cross look on her face.

'What are you doing here?' she said, and she took Mary by the arm and pulled her away. 'What did I tell you?'

'I turned round the wrong corner,' explained Mary. 'I didn't know which way to go and I heard someone crying.'

She quite hated Mrs Medlock at the moment, but she hated her more the next.

'You didn't hear anything of the sort,' said the house-keeper. 'You come along back to your own nursery or I'll box your ears.'

And she took her by the arm and half pushed, half

pulled her up one passage and down another, until she pushed her in at the door of her own room.

'Now,' she said, 'you stay where you're told to stay or you'll find yourself locked up. The master had better get you a governess, same as he said he would. You're one that needs someone to look sharp after you. I've got enough to do.'

She went out of the room and slammed the door after her, and Mary went and sat on the hearth-rug, pale with rage. She did not cry, but ground her teeth.

'There *was* someone crying – there *was* – there *was!*' she said to herself.

She had heard it twice now, and some time she would find out. She had found out a great deal this morning. She felt as if she had been on a long journey, and at any rate she had had something to amuse her all the time, and she had played with the ivory elephants and had seen the grey mouse and its babies in their nest in the velvet cushion.

7

The Key of the Garden

TWO days after this, when Mary opened her eyes she sat upright in bed immediately, and called to Martha.

'Look at the moor! Look at the moor!'

The rain-storm had ended and the grey mist and clouds had been swept away in the night by the wind. The wind itself had ceased and a brilliant, deep blue sky arched high over the moorland. Never, never had Mary dreamed of a sky so blue. In India skies were hot and blazing; this was of a deep, cool blue, which almost seemed to sparkle like the waters of some lovely, bottomless lake, and here and there, high, high in the arched blueness, floated small clouds of snow-white fleece. The far-reaching world of the moor itself looked softly blue instead of gloomy purple-black or awful dreary grey.

'Aye,' said Martha, with a cheerful grin. 'Th' storm's over for a bit. It does like this at this time o' th' year. It goes off in a night like it was pretendin' it had never been here an' never meant to come again. That's because th' springtime's on its way. It's a long way off yet, but it's comin'.'

'I thought perhaps it always rained or looked dark in England,' Mary said.

'Eh! no!' said Martha, sitting up on her heels among her black-lead brushes. 'Nowt o' th' soart!'

'What does that mean?' asked Mary seriously. In India the natives spoke different dialects which only a few people understood, so she was not surprised when Martha used words she did not know.

Martha laughed as she had done the first morning.

'There now,' she said. 'I've talked broad Yorkshire again like Mrs Medlock said I mustn't. "Nowt o' th' soart" means "nothin' of the sort",' slowly and carefully, 'but it takes so long to say it. Yorkshire's th' sunniest place on earth when it is sunny. I told thee tha'd like th' moor after a bit. Just you wait till you see th' gold-coloured gorse blossoms an' th' blossoms o' th' broom, an' th' heather flowerin', all purple bells, an' hundreds o' butterflies flutterin' an' bees hummin' an' skylarks soarin' up an' singin'. You'll want to get out on it at sunrise an' live out on it all day like Dickon does.'

'Could I ever get there?' asked Mary wistfully, looking through her window at the far-off blue. It was so new and big and wonderful and such a heavenly colour.

'I don't know,' answered Martha. 'Tha's never used tha' legs since tha' was born, it seems to me. Tha' couldn't walk five mile. It's five mile to our cottage.'

'I should like to see your cottage.'

Martha stared at her a moment curiously before she took up her polishing brush and began to rub the grate again. She was thinking that the small plain face did not look quite as sour at this moment as it had done the first morning she saw it. It looked just a trifle like little Susan Ann's when she wanted something very much.

'I'll ask my mother about it,' she said. 'She's one o' them that nearly always sees a way to do things. It's my day out today an' I'm goin' home. Eh! I am glad. Mrs Medlock thinks a lot o' mother. Perhaps she could talk to her.'

'I like your mother,' said Mary.

'I should think tha' did,' agreed Martha, polishing away.

'I've never seen her,' said Mary.

'No, tha' hasn't,' replied Martha.

She sat up on her heels again and rubbed the end of

her nose with the back of her hand, as if puzzled for a moment, but she ended quite positively.

'Well, she's that sensible an' hard workin' an' good-natured an' clean that no one could help likin' her, whether they'd seen her or not. When I'm going home to her on my day out I just jump for joy when I'm crossin' th' moor.'

'I like Dickon,' added Mary. 'And I've never seen him.'

'Well,' said Martha stoutly. 'I've told thee that th' very birds like him an' th' rabbits an' wild sheep an' ponies, an' th' foxes themselves. I wonder,' staring at her reflectively, 'what Dickon would think of thee?'

'He wouldn't like me,' said Mary in her stiff, cold little way. 'No one does.'

Martha looked reflective again.

'How does tha' like thysel'?' she inquired, really quite as if she were curious to know.

Mary hesitated a moment and thought it over.

'Not at all – really,' she answered. 'But I never thought of that before.'

Martha grinned a little as if at some homely recollection.

'Mother said that to me once,' she said. 'She was at her wash-tub an' I was in a bad temper an' talkin' ill of folk an' she turns round on me an' says: "Tha' young vixen, tha'! There tha' stands sayin' tha' doesn't like this one an' tha' doesn't like that one. How does tha' like thysel'?" It made me laugh an' it brought me to my senses in a minute.'

She went away in high spirits as soon as she had given Mary her breakfast. She was going to walk five miles across the moor to the cottage, and she was going to help her mother with the washing and do the week's baking and enjoy herself thoroughly.

Mary felt lonelier than ever when she knew she was no longer in the house. She went out into the garden as quickly as possible, and the first thing she did was to run round and round the fountain flower garden ten times. She counted the times carefully and when she had finished she felt in better spirits. The sunshine made the whole place look different. The high, deep, blue sky arched over Misselthwaite, as well as over the moor, and she kept lifting her face and looking up into it, trying to imagine what it would be like to lie down on one of the little snow-white clouds and float about. She went into the first kitchen-garden and found Ben Weatherstaff working there with two other gardeners. The change in the weather seemed to have done him good. He spoke to her of his own accord.

'Springtime's coming,' he said. 'Cannot tha' smell it?'

Mary sniffed and thought she could.

'I smell something nice and fresh and damp,' she said.

'That's th' good rich earth,' he answered, digging away. 'It's in a good humour makin' ready to grow things. It's glad when plantin' time comes. It's dull in th' winter when it's got nowt to do. In th' flower gardens out there things will be stirrin' down below in th' dark. Th' sun's warmin' 'em. You'll see bits o' green spikes stickin' out o' th' black earth after a bit.'

'What will they be?' asked Mary.

'Crocuses an' snowdrops an' daffydowndillys. Has tha' never seen them?'

'No. Everything is hot, and wet, and green after the rains in India,' said Mary. 'And I think things grow up in a night.'

'These won't grow up in a night,' said Weatherstaff. 'Tha'll have to wait for 'em. They'll poke up a bit higher here, and push out a spike more there, an' uncurl a leaf this day an' another that. You watch 'em.'

'I am going to,' answered Mary.

Very soon she heard the soft rustling flight of wings again and she knew at once that the robin had come again. He was very pert and lively, and hopped about so close to her feet, and put his head on one side and looked at her so shyly that she asked Ben Weatherstaff a question.

'Do you think he remembers me?' she said.

'Remembers thee!' said Weatherstaff indignantly. 'He knows every cabbage stump in th' gardens, let alone th' people. He's never seen a little wench here before, an' he's bent on findin' out all about thee. Tha's no need to try to hide anything from *him*.'

'Are things stirring down below in the dark in that garden where he lives?' Mary inquired.

'What garden?' grunted Weatherstaff, becoming surly again.

'The one where the old rose-trees are.' She could not help asking, because she wanted so much to know. 'Are all the flowers dead, or do some of them come again in the summer? Are there ever any roses?'

'Ask him,' said Ben Weatherstaff, hunching his shoulders towards the robin. 'He's the only one as knows. No one else has seen inside it for ten year.'

Ten years was a long time, Mary thought. She had been born ten years ago.

She walked away, slowly thinking. She had begun to like the garden just as she had begun to like the robin and Dickon and Martha's mother. She was beginning to like Martha, too. That seemed a good many people to like – when you were not used to liking. She thought of the robin as one of the people. She went to her walk outside the long, ivy-covered wall over which she could see the tree-tops; and the second time she walked up and down the most interesting and exciting thing happened to her, and it was all through Ben Weatherstaff's robin.

She heard a chirp and a twitter, and when she looked at the bare flower-bed at her left side there he was hopping about and pretending to peck things out of the earth to persuade her that he had not followed her. But she knew he had followed her, and the surprise so filled her with delight that she almost trembled a little.

'You do remember me!' she cried. 'You do! You are prettier than anything else in the world!'

She chirped, and talked, and coaxed and he hopped and flirted his tail and twittered. It was as if he were talking. His red waistcoat was like satin, and he puffed his tiny breast out and was so fine and so grand and so pretty that it was really as if he were showing her how important and like a human person a robin could be. Mistress Mary forgot that she had ever been contrary in her life when he allowed her to draw closer and closer to him, and bend down and talk and try to make something like robin sounds.

Oh! to think that he should actually let her come as near to him as that! He knew nothing in the world would make her put out her hand towards him or startle him in the least tiniest way. He knew it because he was a real person – only nicer than any other person in the world. She was so happy that she scarcely dared to breathe.

The flower-bed was not quite bare. It was bare of flowers because the perennial plants had been cut down for their winter rest, but there were tall shrubs and low ones which grew together at the back of the bed, and as the robin hopped about under them she saw him hop over a small pile of freshly turned-up earth. He stopped on it to look for a worm. The earth had been turned up because a dog had been trying to dig up a mole and he had scratched quite a deep hole.

Mary looked at it, not really knowing why the hole was there, and as she looked she saw something almost buried in the newly turned soil. It was something like a ring of rusty iron or brass, and when the robin flew up into a tree near by she put out her hand and picked the ring up. It was more than a ring, however; it was an old key which looked as if it had been buried a long time.

Mistress Mary stood up and looked at it with an almost frightened face as it hung from her finger.

'Perhaps it has been buried for ten years,' she said in a whisper. 'Perhaps it is the key to the garden!'

8

The Robin Who Showed the Way

S HE looked at the key quite a long time. She turned it over and over, and thought about it. As I have said before, she was not a child who had been trained to ask permission or consult her elders about things. All she thought about the key was that if it was the key to the closed garden, and she could find out where the door was, she could perhaps open it and see what was inside the walls, and what had happened to the old rose-trees. It was because it had been shut up so long that she wanted to see it. It seemed as if it must be different from other places and that something strange must have happened to it during ten years. Besides that, if she liked it she could go into it every day and shut the door behind her, and she could make up some play of her own and play it quite alone, because nobody would ever know where she was, but would think the door was still locked and the key buried in the earth. The thought of that pleased her very much.

Living, as it were, all by herself in a house with a hundred mysteriously closed rooms and having nothing whatever to do to amuse herself, had set her inactive brain to work and was actually awakening her imagination. There is no doubt that the fresh, strong, pure air from the moor had a great deal to do with it. Just as it had given her an appetite, and fighting with the wind had stirred her blood, so the same things had stirred in her mind. In India she had always been too hot and languid and weak to care much about anything, but in this place she was beginning to care and to want to do new things. Already she felt less 'contrary', though she did not know why.

She put the key in her pocket and walked up and down her walk.No one but herself ever seemed to come there, so she could walk slowly and look at the wall, or rather, at the ivy growing on it. The ivy was the baffling thing. Howsoever carefully she looked, she could see nothing but thickly growing, glossy, dark green leaves. She was very much disappointed. Something of her contrariness came back to her as she paced the wall and looked over it at the tree-tops inside. It seemed so silly, she said to herself, to be near it and not be able to get in. She took the key in her pocket when she went back to the house, and she made up her mind that she would always carry it with her when she went out, so that if she ever should find the hidden door she would be ready.

Mrs Medlock had allowed Martha to sleep all night at the cottage, but she was back at her work in the morning with cheeks redder than ever and in the best of spirits.

'I got up at four o'clock,' she said. 'Eh! It was pretty on th' moor with th' birds gettin' up an' th' rabbits scamperin' about an' th' sun risin'. I didn't walk all th' way. A man gave me a ride in his cart an' I can tell you I did enjoy myself.'

She was full of stories of the delights of her day out. Her mother had been glad to see her, and they had got the baking and washing all out of the way. She had even made each of the children a dough-cake with a bit of brown sugar in it.

'I had 'em all pipin' hot when they came in from playin' on th' moor. An' th' cottage all smelt o' nice, clean, hot bakin' an' there was a good fire, an' they just shouted for joy. Our Dickon, he said our cottage was good enough for a king to live in.'

In the evening they had all sat round the fire, and Martha and her mother had sewed patches on torn clothes and mended stockings, and Martha had told them about the little girl who had come from India and who had been waited on all her life by what Martha called 'blacks' until she didn't know how to put on her own stockings.

'Eh! they did like to hear about you,' said Martha. 'They wanted to know all about th' blacks an' about th' ship you came in. I couldn't tell 'em enough.'

Mary reflected a little.

'I'll tell you a great deal more before your next day out,' she said, 'so that you will have more to talk about. I dare say they would like to hear about riding on elephants and camels, and about the officers going to hunt tigers.'

'My word!' cried delighted Martha. 'It would set 'em clean off their heads. Would tha' really do that, Miss? It would be the same as a wild beast show like we heard they had in York once.'

'India is quite different from Yorkshire,' Mary said slowly, as she thought the matter over. 'I never thought of that. Did Dickon and your mother like to hear you talk about me?'

'Why, our Dickon's eyes nearly started out o' his head, they got that round,' answered Martha. 'But Mother, she was put out about your seemin' to be all by yourself like. She said: "Hasn't Mr Craven got no governess for her, nor no nurse?" and I said: "No, he hasn't, though Mrs

84

Medlock says he will when he thinks of it, but she says he mayn't think of it for two or three years." '

'I don't want a governess,' said Mary sharply.

'But Mother says you ought to be learnin' your book by this time an' you ought to have a woman to look after you, an' she says: "Now, Martha, you just think how you'd feel yourself, in a big place like that, wanderin' about alone, an' no mother. You do your best to cheer her up," she says, an' I said I would.'

Mary gave her a long, steady look.

'You do cheer me up,' she said. 'I like to hear you talk.'

Presently Martha went out of the room and came back with something held in her hands under her apron.

'What does tha' think,' she said, with a cheerful grin. 'I've brought thee a present.'

'A present!' exclaimed Mistress Mary. How could a cottage full of fourteen hungry people give anyone a present!

'A man was drivin' across the moor peddlin',' Martha explained. 'An' he stopped his cart at our door. He had pots an' pans an' odds an' ends, but Mother had no money to buy anythin'. Just as he was goin' away our 'Lizbeth Ellen called out: "Mother, he's got skippin'-ropes with red an' blue handles." An' Mother, she calls out quite sudden: "Here, stop, mister! How much are they?" An' he says "Tuppence," an' Mother she began fumblin' in her pocket, an' she says to me: "Martha, tha's brought thee thy wages like a good lass, an' I've got four places to put every penny, but I'm just goin' to take tuppence out of it to buy that child a skippin'-rope," an' she bought one, an' here it is.'

She brought it out from under her apron and exhibited it quite proudly. It was a strong, slender rope with a striped red and blue handle at each end, but Mary Lennox had never seen a skipping-rope before. She gazed at it with a mystified expression.

'What is it for?' she asked curiously.

'For!' cried out Martha. 'Does tha' mean that they've not got skippin'-ropes in India, for all they've got elephants and tigers and camels? No wonder most of 'em's black. This is what it's for; just watch me.'

And she ran into the middle of the room and, taking a handle in each hand, began to skip, and skip, and skip, while Mary turned in her chair to stare at her, and the queer faces in the old portraits seemed to stare at her, too, and wonder what on earth this common little cottager had the impudence to be doing under their very noses. But Martha did not even see them. The interest and curiosity in Mistress Mary's face delighted her, and she went on skipping and counted as she skipped until she had reached a hundred.

'I could skip longer than that,' she said when she stopped. 'I've skipped as much as five hundred when I was twelve, but I wasn't as fat then as I am now, an' I was in practice.'

Mary got up from her chair beginning to feel excited herself.

'It looks nice,' she said. 'Your mother is a kind woman. Do you think I could ever skip like that?'

'You just try it,' urged Martha, handing her the skipping-rope. 'You can't skip a hundred at first, but if you practise you'll mount up. That's what Mother said. She says: "Nothin' will do her more good than skippin'-rope. It's th' sensiblest toy a child can have. Let her play out in th' fresh air skippin' an' it'll stretch her legs an' arms an' give her some strength in 'em."'

It was plain that there was not a great deal of strength in Mistress Mary's arms and legs when she first began to skip. She was not very clever at it, but she liked it so much that she did not want to stop.

'Put on tha' things and run an' skip out o' doors,' said Martha. 'Mother said I must tell you to keep out o' doors as much as you could, even when it rains a bit, so as tha' wrap up warm.'

Mary put on her coat and hat and took her skipping-rope over her arm. She opened the door to go out, and then suddenly thought of something and turned back rather slowly.

'Martha,' she said, 'they were your wages. It was your twopence really. Thank you.' She said it stiffly because she was not used to thanking people or noticing that they did things for her. 'Thank you,' she said, and held out her hand because she did not know what else to do.

Martha gave her hand a clumsy little shake, as if she was not accustomed to this sort of thing either. Then she laughed.

'Eh! tha' art a queer, old-womanish thing,' she said. 'If tha'd been our 'Lizabeth Ellen tha'd have given me a kiss.'

Mary looked stiffer than ever.

'Do you want me to kiss you?'

Martha laughed again.

'Nay, not me,' she answered. 'If tha' was different, p'raps tha'd want to thysel'. But th' isn't. Run off outside an' play with thy rope.'

Mistress Mary felt a little awkward as she went out of the room. Yorkshire people seemed strange, and Martha was always rather a puzzle to her. At first she had disliked her very much, but now she did not.

The skipping-rope was a wonderful thing. She counted and skipped, and skipped and counted, until her cheeks were quite red, and she was more interested than she had ever been since she was born. The sun was shining and a little wind was blowing – not a rough wind, but one which came in delightful little gusts and brought a fresh scent of newly turned earth with it. She skipped round the fountain garden, and up one walk and down another. She skipped at last into the kitchen-garden and saw Ben Weatherstaff digging and talking to his robin, which was hopping about him. She skipped down the walk towards him and he lifted his head and looked at her with a curious expression. She had wondered if he would notice her. She really wanted him to see her skip.

'Well!' he exclaimed. 'Upon my word! P'raps tha' art a young 'un, after all, an' p'raps tha's got child's blood in thy veins instead of sour buttermilk. Tha's skipped red into thy cheeks as sure as my name's Ben Weatherstaff. I wouldn't have believed tha' could do it.'

'I never skipped before,' Mary said. 'I'm just beginning. I can only go up to twenty.'

'Tha' keep on,' said Ben. 'Tha' shapes well enough at it for a young 'un that's lived with heathen. Just see how he's watchin' thee,' jerking his head towards the robin. 'He followed after thee yesterday. He'll be at it again today. He'll be bound to find out what th' skippin'-rope is. He's never seen one. Eh!' shaking his head at the bird, 'tha' curiosity will be th' death of thee some time if tha' doesn't look sharp.'

Mary skipped round all the gardens and round the orchard, resting every few minutes. At length she went to her own special walk and made up her mind to try if she could skip the whole length of it. It was a good long skip, and she began slowly, but before she had gone half-way down the path she was so hot and breathless that she was obliged to stop. She did not mind much, because she had already counted up to thirty. She stopped with a little laugh of pleasure, and there, lo and behold, was the robin swaying on a long branch of ivy. He had followed her, and he greeted her with a chirp. As Mary had skipped towards him she felt something heavy in her pocket strike against her at each jump, and when she saw the robin she laughed again.

'You showed me where the key was yesterday,' she said. 'You ought to show me the door today; but I don't believe you know!'

The robin flew from his swinging spray of ivy on to the top of the wall and he opened his beak and sang a loud, lovely trill, merely to show off. Nothing in the world is quite as adorably lovely as a robin when he shows off – and they are nearly always doing it.

Mary Lennox had heard a great deal about Magic in

her Ayah's stories, and she always said what happened almost at that moment was Magic.

One of the nice little gusts of wind rushed down the walk, and it was a stronger one than the rest. It was strong enough to wave the branches of the trees, and it was more than strong enough to sway the trailing sprays of untrimmed ivy hanging from the wall. Mary had stepped close to the robin, and suddenly the gust of wind swung aside some loose ivy trails, and more suddenly still she jumped towards it and caught it in her hand. This she did because she had seen something under it – a round knob which had been covered by the leaves hanging over it. It was the knob of a door.

She put her hands under the leaves and began to pull and push them aside. Thick as the ivy hung, it nearly all was a loose and swinging curtain, though some had crept over wood and iron. Mary's heart began to thump and her hands to shake a little in her delight and excitement. The robin kept singing and twittering away and tilting his head on one side, as if he were as excited as she was. What was this under her hands which was square and made of iron and which her fingers found a hole in?

It was the lock of the door which had been closed ten years, and she put her hand in her pocket, drew out the key, and found it fitted the keyhole. She put the key in and turned it. It took two hands to do it, but it did turn.

And then she took a long breath and looked behind her up the long walk to see if anyone was coming. No one was coming. No one ever did come, it seemed, and she took another long breath, because she could not help it, and she held back the swinging curtain of ivy and pushed back the door which opened slowly – slowly.

Then she slipped through it, and shut it behind her, and stood with her back against it, looking about her and breathing quite fast with excitement, and wonder, and delight.

She was standing *inside* the secret garden.

9

The Strangest House Anyone Ever Lived In

I T WAS the sweetest, most mysterious-looking place
anyone could imagine. The high walls which shut it
in were covered with the leafless stems of climbing roses,
which were so thick that they were matted together.
Mary Lennox knew they were roses because she had
seen a great many roses in India. All the ground was
covered with grass of a wintry brown, and out of it
grew clumps of bushes which were surely rose-bushes
if they were alive. There were numbers of standard roses
which had so spread their branches that they were like
little trees. There were other trees in the garden, and
one of the things which made the place look strangest
and loveliest was that climbing roses had run all over
them and swung down long tendrils which made light

swaying curtains, and here and there they had caught at each other or at a far-reaching branch and had crept from one tree to another and made lovely bridges of themselves. There were neither leaves nor roses on them now, and Mary did not know whether they were dead or alive, but their thin grey or brown branches and sprays looked like a sort of hazy mantle spreading over everything, walls, and trees, and even brown grass, where they had fallen from their fastenings and run along the ground. It was this hazy tangle from tree to tree which made it look so mysterious. Mary had thought it must be different from other gardens which had not been left all by themselves so long; and, indeed, it was different from any other place she had ever seen in her life.

'How still it is!' she whispered. 'How still!'

Then she waited a moment and listened at the stillness. The robin, who had flown to his tree-top, was still as all the rest. He did not even flutter his wings; he sat without stirring, and looked at Mary.

'No wonder it is still,' she whispered again. 'I am the first person who has spoken in here for ten years.'

She moved away from the door, stepping as softly as if she were afraid of awakening someone. She was glad that there was grass under her feet and that her steps made no sounds. She walked under one of the fairy-like arches between the trees and looked up at the sprays and tendrils which formed them.

'I wonder if they are all quite dead,' she said. 'Is it all a quite dead garden? I wish it wasn't.'

If she had been Ben Weatherstaff she could have told whether the wood was alive by looking at it, but she could only see that there were only grey or brown sprays and branches, and none showed any signs of even a tiny leaf-bud anywhere.

But she was *inside* the wonderful garden, and she could come through the door under the ivy any time, and she felt as if she had found a world all her own.

The sun was shining inside the four walls and the high arch of blue sky over this particular piece of Misselthwaite seemed even more brilliant and soft than it was over the moor. The robin flew down from his tree-top and hopped about or flew after her from one bush to another. He chirped a good deal and had a very busy air, as if he were showing her things. Everything was strange and silent, and she seemed to be hundreds of miles away from anyone, but somehow she did not feel lonely at all. All that troubled her was her wish that she knew whether all the roses were dead, or if perhaps some of them had lived and might put out leaves and buds as the weather got warmer. She did not want it to be a quite dead garden. If it were a quite alive garden, how wonderful it would be, and what thousands of roses would grow on every side!

Her skipping-rope had hung over her arm when she came in, and after she had walked about for a while she thought she would skip round the whole garden, stopping when she wanted to look at things. There seemed to have been grass paths here and there, and in one or two corners there were alcoves of evergreen with stone seats or all moss-covered flower-urns in them.

As she came near the second of these alcoves she stopped skipping. There had once been a flower-bed in it, and she thought she saw something sticking out of the black earth – some sharp little pale green points. She remembered what Ben Weatherstaff had said, and she knelt down to look at them.

'Yes, they are tiny growing things and they *might* be crocuses or snowdrops or daffodils,' she whispered.

She bent very close to them and sniffed the fresh scent of the damp earth. She liked it very much.

'Perhaps there are some other ones coming up in other places,' she said. 'I will go all over the garden and look.'

She did not skip, but walked. She went slowly and kept her eyes on the ground. She looked in the old border-beds and among the grass, and after she had gone round, trying to miss nothing, she had found ever so many more sharp, pale green points, and she had become quite excited again.

'It isn't a quite dead garden,' she cried out softly to herself. 'Even if the roses are dead, there are other things alive.'

She did not know anything about gardening, but the grass seemed so thick in some of the places where the green points were pushing their way through that she thought they did not seem to have room enough to grow. She searched about until she found a rather sharp piece of wood and knelt down and dug and weeded out the weeds and grass until she made nice little clear places around them.

'Now they look as if they could breathe,' she said, after she had finished with the first ones. 'I am going to do ever so many more. I'll do all I can see. If I haven't time today I can come tomorrow.'

She went from place to place, and dug and weeded, and enjoyed herself so immensely that she was led on from bed to bed and into the grass under the trees. The exercise made her so warm that she first threw her coat off, and then her hat, and without knowing it she was smiling down on to the grass and the pale green points all the time.

The robin was tremendously busy. He was very much pleased to see gardening begun on his own estate. He had often wondered at Ben Weatherstaff. Where gardening is done all sorts of delightful things to eat are turned up with the soil. Now here was this new kind of creature who was not half Ben's size and yet had the sense to come into his garden and begin at once.

Mistress Mary worked in her garden until it was time to go to her midday dinner. In fact she was rather late in remembering, and when she put on her coat and hat and picked up her skipping-rope, she could not believe that she had been working two or three hours. She had been actually happy all the time; and dozens and dozens of the tiny, pale green points were to be seen in cleared places, looking twice as cheerful as they had looked before when the grass and weeds had been smothering them.

'I shall come back this afternoon,' she said, looking all round at her new kingdom, and speaking to the trees and rose-bushes as if they heard her.

Then she ran lightly across the grass, pushed open the slow old door, and slipped through it under the ivy. She had such red cheeks and such bright eyes and ate such a dinner that Martha was delighted.

'Two pieces o' meat an' two helps o' rice-puddin'!' she said. 'Eh! Mother will be pleased when I tell her what th' skippin'-rope's done for thee.'

In the course of her digging with her pointed stick,

Mistress Mary had found herself digging up a sort of white root rather like an onion. She had put it back in its place and patted the earth carefully down on it, and just now she wondered if Martha could tell her what it was.

'Martha,' she said, 'what are those white roots that look like onions?'

'They're bulbs,' answered Martha. 'Lots o' spring flowers grow from 'em. Th' very little ones are snowdrops an' crocuses an' th' big ones are narcissuses an' jonquils an' daffydowndillys. Th' biggest of all is lilies an' purple flags. Eh! they are nice. Dickon's got a whole lot of 'em planted in our bit o' garden.'

'Does Dickon know all about them?' asked Mary, a new idea taking possession of her.

'Our Dickon can make a flower grow out of a brick wall. Mother says he just whispers things out o' th' ground.'

'Do bulbs live a long time? Would they live years and years if no one helped them?' inquired Mary anxiously.

'They're things as helps themselves,' said Martha. 'That's why poor folk can afford to have 'em. If you don't trouble 'em, most of 'em'll work away underground for a lifetime an' spread out an' have little 'uns. There's a place in th' park woods here where there's snowdrops by thousands. They're the prettiest sight in Yorkshire when th' spring comes. No one knows when they was first planted.'

'I wish the spring was here now,' said Mary. 'I want to see all the things that grow in England.'

She had finished her dinner and gone to her favourite seat on the hearth-rug.

'I wish – I wish I had a little spade,' she said.

'Whatever does tha' want a spade for?' asked Martha laughing. 'Art tha' goin' to take to diggin'? I must tell Mother that, too.'

Mary looked at the fire and pondered a little. She must be careful if she meant to keep her secret kingdom. She wasn't doing any harm, but if Mr Craven found out about the open door, he would be fearfully angry and get a new key and lock it up for ever more. She really could not bear that.

'This is such a big, lonely place,' she said slowly, as if she were turning matters over in her mind. 'The house is lonely, and the park is lonely, and the gardens are lonely. So many places seem shut up. I never did many things in India, but there were more people to look at – natives and soldiers marching by – and sometimes bands playing, and my Ayah told me stories. There is no one to talk to here except you and Ben Weatherstaff. And you have to do your work and Ben Weatherstaff won't speak to me often. I thought if I had a little spade I could dig somewhere as he does, and I might make a little garden if he would give me some seeds.'

Martha's face lighted up.

'There now!' she exclaimed, 'if that wasn't one of the things Mother said. She says: "There's such a lot o' room in that big place, why don't they give her a bit for herself, even if she doesn't plant nothin' but parsley an' radishes? She'd dig an' rake away an' be right down happy over it." Them was the very words she said.'

'Were they?' said Mary. 'How many things she knows, doesn't she?'

'Eh!' said Martha. 'It's like she says: "A woman as brings up twelve children learns something besides her A. B. C. Children's as good as 'rithmetic to set you findin' out things."'

'How much would a spade cost – a little one?' Mary asked.

'Well,' was Martha's reflective answer, 'at Thwaite village there's a shop or so an' I saw little garden sets with a spade an' a rake an' a fork all tied together for two shillings. An' they was stout enough to work with, too.'

'I've got more than that in my purse,' said Mary. 'Mrs Morrison gave me five shillings, and Mrs Medlock gave me some money from Mr Craven.'

'Did he remember thee that much?' exclaimed Martha.

'Mrs Medlock said I was to have a shilling a week to spend. She gives me one every Saturday. I didn't know what to spend it on.'

'My word! that's riches,' said Martha. 'Tha' can buy anything in th' world tha' wants. The rent of our cottage is only one an' threepence, an' it's like pulling eye-teeth to get it. Now I've just thought of somethin',' putting her hands on her hips.

'What?' said Mary eagerly.

'In the shop at Thwaite they sell packages o' flower-seeds for a penny each, and our Dickon, he knows which is th' prettiest ones an' how to make 'em grow. He walks over to Thwaite many a day just for th' fun of it. Does tha' know how to print letters?' suddenly.

'I know how to write,' Mary answered.

Martha shook her head.

'Our Dickon can only read printin'. If tha' could print we could write a letter to him an' ask him to go an' buy th' garden tools an' th' seeds at th' same time.'

'Oh! you're a good girl!' Mary cried. 'You are, really. I didn't know you were so nice. I know I can print letters if I try. Let's ask Mrs Medlock for a pen and ink and some paper.'

'I've got some of my own,' said Martha. 'I brought 'em

so I could print a bit of a letter to Mother of a Sunday. I'll go and get it.'

She ran out of the room, and Mary stood by the fire and twisted her thin little hands together with sheer pleasure.

'If I have a spade,' she whispered, 'I can make the earth nice and soft and dig up weeds. If I have seeds and can make flowers grow, the garden won't be dead at all – it will come alive.'

She did not go out again that afternoon because when Martha returned with her pen and ink and paper she was obliged to clear the table and carry the plates and dishes downstairs, and when she got into the kitchen Mrs Medlock was there, and told her to do something, so Mary waited for what seemed to her a long time before she came back. Then it was a serious piece of work to write to Dickon. Mary had been taught very little because her governesses had disliked her too much to stay with her. She could not spell particularly well, but she found that she could print letters when she tried. This was the letter Martha dictated to her:

My dear Dickon,

This comes hoping to find you well as it leaves me at present. Miss Mary has plenty of money and will you go to Thwaite and buy her some flower seeds and a set of garden tools to make a flower-bed. Pick the prettiest ones and easy to grow because she has never done it before and lived in India which is different. Give my love to mother and every one of you. Miss Mary is going to tell me a lot more so that on my next day out you can hear about elephants and camels and gentlemen going hunting lions and tigers.

Your loving sister,
Martha Phoebe Sowerby

'We'll put the money in th' envelope an' I'll get th' butcher's boy to take it in his cart. He's a great friend o' Dickon's,' said Martha.

'How shall I get the things when Dickon buys them?' asked Mary.

'He'll bring 'em to you himself. He'll like to walk over this way.'

'Oh!' exclaimed Mary, 'then I shall see him! I never thought I should see Dickon.'

'Does tha' want to see him?' asked Martha suddenly, she had looked so pleased.

'Yes, I do. I never saw a boy foxes and crows loved. I want to see him very much.'

Martha gave a little start, as if she suddenly remembered something.

'Now to think,' she broke out, 'to think o' me forgettin' that there; an' I thought I was goin' to tell you first thing this mornin'. I asked Mother – and she said she'd ask Mrs Medlock her own self.'

'Do you mean –' Mary began.

'What I said Tuesday. Ask her if you might be driven over to our cottage some day and have a bit o' Mother's hot oat cake, an' butter, an' a glass o' milk.'

It seemed as if all the interesting things were happening in one day. To think of going over the moor in the daylight and when the sky was blue! To think of going into the cottage which held twelve children!

'Does she think Mrs Medlock would let me go?' she asked, quite anxiously.

'Aye, she thinks she would. She knows what a tidy woman Mother is and how clean she keeps the cottage.'

'If I went I should see your mother as well as Dickon,' said Mary, thinking it over and liking the idea very much. 'She doesn't seem to be like the mothers in India.'

Her work in the garden and the excitement of the afternoon ended by making her feel quiet and thoughtful. Martha stayed with her until tea-time, but they sat in comfortable quiet and talked very little. But just before Martha went downstairs for the tea-tray, Mary asked a question.

'Martha,' she said, 'has the scullery-maid had the toothache again today?'

Martha certainly started slightly.

'What makes thee ask that?' she said.

'Because when I waited so long for you to come back I opened the door and walked down the corridor to see if you were coming. And I heard that far-off crying again, just as we heard it the other night. There isn't a wind today, so you see it couldn't have been the wind.'

'Eh!' said Martha restlessly. 'Tha' mustn't go walkin' about in corridors an' listenin'. Mr Craven would be that there angry there's no knowin' what he'd do.'

'I wasn't listening,' said Mary. 'I was just waiting for you – and I heard it. That's three times.'

'My word! There's Mrs Medlock's bell,' said Martha, and she almost ran out of the room.

'It's the strangest house anyone ever lived in,' said Mary drowsily, as she dropped her head on the cushioned seat of the arm-chair near her. Fresh air, and digging, and skipping-rope had made her feel so comfortably tired that she fell asleep.

10

Dickon

THE sun shone down for nearly a week on the secret garden. The Secret Garden was what Mary called it when she was thinking of it. She liked the name, and she liked still more the feeling that when its beautiful old walls shut her in, no one knew where she was. It seemed almost like being shut out of the world in some fairy place. The few books she had read and liked had been fairy-story books, and she had read of secret gardens in some of the stories. Sometimes people went to sleep in them for a hundred years, which she had thought must be rather stupid. She had no intention of going to sleep, and, in fact, she was becoming wider awake every day which passed at Misselthwaite. She was beginning to like to be out of doors; she no longer hated the wind, but enjoyed it. She could run faster, and longer, and she could skip up to a hundred. The bulbs in the secret garden must have been much astonished. Such nice clear spaces were made round them that they had all the breathing space they wanted, and really, if Mistress Mary had known it, they began to cheer up under the dark earth and work tremendously. The sun could get at them and warm them, and when the rain came down it could reach them at once, so they began to feel very much alive.

Mary was an odd, determined little person, and, now she had something interesting to be determined about, she was very much absorbed indeed. She worked and dug and pulled up weeds steadily, only becoming more pleased with her work every hour instead of tiring of it. It seemed to her like a fascinating sort of play. She found many more of the sprouting pale green points than she had ever hoped to find. They seemed to be starting up everywhere, and each day she was sure she found tiny new ones, some so tiny that they barely peeped above the earth. There were so many that she remembered what Martha had said about the 'snowdrops by the thousands', and about bulbs spreading and making new ones. These had been left to themselves for ten years and perhaps they had spread, like the snowdrops, into thousands. She wondered how long it would be before they showed that they were flowers. Sometimes she stopped digging to look at the garden and try to imagine what it would be like when it was covered with thousands of lovely things in bloom.

During that week of sunshine, she became more intimate with Ben Weatherstaff. She surprised him several times by seeming to start up beside him as if she sprang out of the earth. The truth was that she was afraid that he would pick up his tools and go away if he saw her coming, so she always walked towards him as silently as possible. But, in fact, he did not object to her as strongly as he had at first. Perhaps he was secretly rather flattered by her evident desire for his elderly company. Then, also, she was more civil than she had been. He did not know that when she first saw him she spoke to him as she would have spoken to a native, and had not known that a cross, sturdy old Yorkshireman was not accustomed to salaam to his masters, and be merely commanded by them to do things.

'Tha'rt like th' robin,' he said to her one morning when he lifted his head and saw her standing by him. 'I never knows when I shall see thee or which side tha'll come from.'

'He's friends with me now!' said Mary.

'That's like him,' snapped Ben Weatherstaff. 'Makin' up to th' women-folk just for vanity an' flightiness. There's nothin' he wouldn't do for th' sake o' showin' off an' flirtin' his tail-feathers. He's as full o' pride as an egg's full o' meat.'

He very seldom talked much and sometimes did not even answer Mary's questions except by a grunt, but this morning he said more than usual. He stood up and rested one hobnailed boot on the top of his spade while he looked her over.

'How long has tha' been here?' he jerked out.

'I think it's about a month,' she answered.

'Tha's beginnin' to do Misselthwaite credit,' he said. 'Tha's a bit fatter than tha' was an' tha's not quite so yeller. Tha' looked like a young plucked crow when tha' first came into this garden. Thinks I to myself I never set eyes on an uglier, sourer-faced young 'un.'

Mary was not vain, and as she had never thought much of her looks, she was not greatly disturbed.

'I know I'm fatter,' she said. 'My stockings are getting tighter. They used to make wrinkles. There's the robin, Ben Weatherstaff.'

There, indeed, was the robin, and she thought he looked nicer than ever. His red waistcoat was as glossy as satin and he flirted his wings and tail and tilted his head and hopped about with all sorts of lively graces. He seemed determined to make Ben Weatherstaff admire him. But Ben was sarcastic.

'Aye, there tha' art!' he said. 'Tha' can put up with me

for a bit sometimes when tha's got no one better. Tha's been reddenin' up thy waistcoat an' polishin' thy feathers this two weeks. I know what tha's up to. Tha's courtin' some bold young madam somewhere, tellin' thy lies to her about bein' th' finest cock robin on Missel Moor an' ready to fight all th' rest of 'em.'

'Oh! look at him!' exclaimed Mary.

The robin was evidently in a fascinating, bold mood. He hopped closer and closer and looked at Ben Weatherstaff more and more engagingly. He flew on to the nearest currant-bush and tilted his head and sang a little song right at him.

'Tha' thinks tha'll get over me by doin' that,' said Ben, wrinkling his face up in such a way that Mary felt sure he was trying not to look pleased. 'Tha' thinks no one can stand out against thee – that's what tha' thinks.'

The robin spread his wings – Mary could scarcely believe her eyes. He flew right up to the handle of Ben Weatherstaff's spade and alighted on the top of it. Then the old man's face wrinkled itself slowly into a new expression. He stood still as if he were afraid to breathe – as if he would not have stirred for the world, lest his robin should start away. He spoke quite in a whisper.

'Well, I'm danged!' he said as softly as if he were saying something quite different. 'Tha' does know how to get at a chap – tha' does! Tha's fair unearthly, tha's so knowin'.'

And he stood without stirring – almost without drawing his breath – until the robin gave another flirt to his wings and flew away. Then he stood looking at the handle of the spade as if there might be Magic in it, and then he began to dig again and said nothing for several minutes.

But because he kept breaking into a slow grin now and then, Mary was not afraid to talk to him.

'Have you a garden of your own?' she asked.

'No. I'm a bachelder an' lodge with Martin at th' gate.'

'If you had one,' said Mary, 'what would you plant?'

'Cabbages an' 'taters an' onions.'

'But if you wanted to make a flower-garden,' persisted Mary, 'what would you plant?'

'Bulbs an' sweet-smellin' things – but mostly roses.'

Mary's face lighted up.

'Do you like roses?' she said.

Ben Weatherstaff rooted up a weed and threw it aside before he answered.

'Well, yes, I do. I was learned that by a young lady I was gardener to. She had a lot in a place she was fond of, an' she loved 'em like they was children – or robins. I've seen her bend over an' kiss 'em.' He dragged out another weed and scowled at it. 'That were as much as ten year' ago.'

'Where is she now?' asked Mary, much interested.

'Heaven,' he answered, and drove his spade deeply into the soil, ''cording to what parson says.'

'What happened to the roses?' Mary asked again, more interested than ever.

'They was left to themselves.'

Mary was becoming quite excited.

'Did they quite die? Do roses quite die when they are left to themselves?' she ventured.

'Well, I'd got to like 'em – an' I liked her – an' she liked 'em,' Ben Weatherstaff admitted reluctantly. 'Once or twice a year I'd go an' work at 'em a bit – prune 'em an' dig about th' roots. They run wild, but they was in rich soil, so some of 'em lived.'

'When they have no leaves and look grey and brown and dry, how can you tell whether they are dead or alive?' inquired Mary.

'Wait till th' spring gets at 'em – wait till th' sun shines on th' rain an' th' rain falls on the sunshine an' then tha'll find out.'

'How – how?' cried Mary, forgetting to be careful.

'Look along th' twigs an' branches an' if tha' sees a bit of a brown lump swelling here an' there, watch it after th' warm rain an' see what happens.' He stopped suddenly and looked curiously at her eager face. 'Why does tha' care so much about roses an' such, all of a sudden?' he demanded.

Mistress Mary felt her face grow red. She was almost afraid to answer.

'I – I want to play that – that I have a garden of my own,' she stammered. 'I – there is nothing for me to do. I have nothing – and no one.'

'Well,' said Ben Weatherstaff slowly, as he watched her, 'that's true. Tha' hasn't.'

He said it in such an odd way that Mary wondered if he was actually a little sorry for her. She had never felt sorry for herself; she had only felt tired and cross, because she disliked people and things so much. But now the world seemed to be changing and getting nicer. If no one found out about the secret garden, she should enjoy herself always.

She stayed with him for ten or fifteen minutes longer and asked him as many questions as she dared. He answered every one of them in his queer, grunting way, and he did not seem really cross and did not pick up his spade and leave her. He said something about roses just as she was going away, and it reminded her of the ones he had said he had been fond of.

'Do you go and see those other roses now?' she asked.

'Not been this year. My rheumatics has made me too stiff in th' joints.'

He said it in his grumbling voice, and then quite suddenly he seemed to get angry with her, though she did not see why he should.

'Now look here!' he said sharply. 'Don't tha' ask so many questions. Tha'rt th' worst wench for askin' questions I've ever come across. Get thee gone an' play thee. I've done talkin' for today.'

And he said it so crossly that she knew there was not the least use in staying another minute. She went skipping slowly down the outside walk, thinking him over and saying to herself that, queer as it was, here was another person whom she liked, in spite of his crossness. She liked old Ben Weatherstaff. Yes, she did like him. She always wanted to try to make him talk to her. Also she began to believe that he knew everything in the world about flowers.

There was a laurel-hedged walk which curved round the secret garden and ended at a gate which opened into a wood in the park. She thought she would skip round this walk and look into the wood and see if there were any rabbits hopping about. She enjoyed the skipping very much, and when she reached the little gate she opened it and went through because she heard a low, peculiar whistling sound and wanted to find out what it was.

It was a very strange thing indeed. She quite caught her breath as she stopped to look at it. A boy was sitting under a tree, with his back against it, playing on a rough wooden pipe. He was a funny-looking boy about twelve. He looked very clean and his nose turned up and his cheeks were as red as poppies, and never had Mistress Mary seen such round and such blue eyes in any boy's face. And on the trunk of the tree he leaned against, a brown squirrel was clinging and watching him, and from behind a bush near by a cock pheasant was delicately stretching his neck to peep out, and quite near him were two rabbits sitting up and sniffing with tremulous noses – and actually it appeared as if they were all drawing near to watch him and listen to the strange, low, little call his pipe seemed to make.

When he saw Mary he held up his hand and spoke to her in a voice almost as low as and rather like his piping.

'Don't tha' move,' he said. 'It'd flight 'em.'

Mary remained motionless. He stopped playing his pipe and began to rise from the ground. He moved so slowly that it scarcely seemed as though he were moving at all, but at last he stood on his feet and then the squirrel scampered back up into the branches of his tree, the pheasant withdrew his head, and the rabbits dropped on all fours and began to hop away, though not at all as if they were frightened.

'I'm Dickon,' the boy said. 'I know tha'rt Miss Mary.'

Then Mary realised that somehow she had known at first that he was Dickon. Who else could have been charming rabbits and pheasants as the natives charm snakes in India? He had a wide, red, curving mouth and his smile spread all over his face.

'I got up slow,' he explained, 'because if tha' makes a quick move it startles 'em. A body 'as to move gentle an' speak low when wild things is about.'

He did not speak to her as if they had never seen each other before, but as if he knew her quite well. Mary knew nothing about boys, and she spoke to him a little stiffly because she felt rather shy.

'Did you get Martha's letter?' she asked.

He nodded his curly, rust-coloured head.

'That's why I come.'

He stooped to pick up something which had been lying on the ground beside him when he piped.

'I've got th' garden tools. There's a little spade an' rake an' a fork an' hoe. Eh! they are good 'uns. There's a trowel, too. An' th' woman in th' shop threw in a packet o' white poppy an' one o' blue larkspur when I bought th' other seeds.'

'Will you show the seeds to me?' Mary said.

She wished she could talk as he did. His speech was so quick and easy. It sounded as if he liked her and was not the least afraid she would not like him, though he was only a common moor boy, in patched clothes and with a funny face and a rough, rusty-red head. As she came closer to him she noticed that there was a clean fresh scent of heather and grass and leaves about him, almost as if he were made of them. She liked it very much, and when she looked into his funny face with the red cheeks and round blue eyes she forgot that she had felt shy.

'Let us sit down on this log and look at them,' she said.

They sat down and he took a clumsy little brown-paper package out of his coat pocket. He untied the string and inside there were ever so many neater and small packages, with a picture of a flower on each one.

'There's a lot o' mignonette an' poppies,' he said. 'Mignonette's th' sweetest smellin' thing as grows an' it'll grow wherever you cast it, same as poppies will. Them as'll come up an' bloom if you just whistle to 'em, them's th' nicest of all.'

He stopped and turned his head quickly, his poppy-cheeked face lighting up.

'Where's that robin as is callin' us?' he said.

The chirp came from a thick holly bush, bright with

scarlet berries, and Mary thought she knew whose it was.

'Is it really calling us?' she asked.

'Aye,' said Dickon, as if it was the most natural thing in the world, 'he's callin' someone he's friends with. That's same as sayin' "Here I am. Look at me. I want a bit of a chat." There he is in the bush. Whose is he?'

'He's Ben Weatherstaff's, but I think he knows me a little,' answered Mary.

'Aye, he knows thee,' said Dickon in his low voice again. 'An' he likes thee. He's took thee on. He'll tell me all about thee in a minute.'

He moved quite close to the bush with the slow movement Mary had noticed before and then he made a sound almost like the robin's own twitter. The robin listened a few seconds, intently, and then answered quite as if he were replying to a question.

'Aye, he's a friend o' yours,' chuckled Dickon.

'Do you think he is?' cried Mary eagerly. She did so want to know. 'Do you think he really likes me?'

'He wouldn't come near thee if he didn't,' answered Dickon. 'Birds is rare choosers an' a robin can flout a body worse than a man. See, he's making up to thee now. "Cannot tha' see a chap?" he's sayin'.'

And it really seemed as if it must be true. He so sidled and twittered and tilted as he hopped on his bush.

'Do you understand everything birds say?' said Mary.

Dickon's grin spread until he seemed all wide, red, curving mouth, and he rubbed his rough head.

'I think I do, and they think I do,' he said. 'I've lived on th' moor with 'em so long. I've watched 'em break shell and come out an' fledge an' learn to fly an' begin to sing, till I think I'm one of 'em. Sometimes I think p'raps I'm a bird, or a fox, or a rabbit, or a squirrel, or even a beetle, an' I don't know it.'

He laughed and came back to the log and began to talk about the flower seeds again. He told her what they looked like when they were flowers; he told her how to plant them, and watch them, and feed and water them.

'See here,' he said suddenly, turning round to look at her. 'I'll plant them for thee myself. Where is tha' garden?'

Mary's thin hands clutched each other as they lay on her lap. She did not know what to say, so for a whole minute she said nothing. She had never thought of this. She felt miserable. And she felt as if she went red and then pale.

'Tha's got a bit o' garden, hasn't tha?' Dickon said.

It was true that she had turned red and then pale. Dickon saw her do it, and as she still said nothing, he began to be puzzled.

'Wouldn't they give thee a bit?' he asked. 'Hasn't tha' got any yet?'

She held her hands even tighter and turned her eyes towards him.

'I don't know anything about boys,' she said slowly. 'Could you keep a secret, if I told you one? It's a great secret, I don't know what I should do if anyone found it out. I believe I should die!' She said the last sentence quite fiercely.

Dickon looked more puzzled than ever and even rubbed his hand over his rough head again, but he answered good-humouredly.

'I'm keepin' secrets all th' time,' he said. 'If I couldn't keep secrets from th' other lads, secrets about foxes' cubs, an' birds' nests, an' wild things' holes, there'd be naught safe on th' moor. Aye, I can keep secrets.'

Mistress Mary did not mean to put out her hand and clutch his sleeve, but she did it.

'I've stolen a garden,' she said very fast. 'It isn't mine. It isn't anybody's. Nobody wants it, nobody cares for it, nobody ever goes into it. Perhaps everything is dead in it already; I don't know.'

She began to feel hot and as contrary as she had ever felt in her life.

'I don't care, I don't care! Nobody has any right to take

it from me when I care about it and they don't. They're letting it die, all shut in by itself,' she ended passionately, and she threw her arms over her face and burst out crying – poor little Mistress Mary.

Dickon's curious blue eyes grew rounder and rounder.

'Eh-h-h!' he said, drawing his exclamation out slowly, and the way he did it meant both wonder and sympathy.

'I've nothing to do,' said Mary. 'Nothing belongs to me. I found it myself and I got into it myself. It was only just like the robin, and they wouldn't take it from the robin.'

'Where is it?' asked Dickon in a dropped voice.

Mistress Mary got up from the log at once. She knew she felt contrary again, and obstinate, and she did not care at all. She was imperious and Indian, and at the same time hot and sorrowful.

'Come with me and I'll show you,' she said.

She led him round the laurel path and to the walk where the ivy grew so thickly. Dickon followed her with a queer, almost pitying, look on his face. He felt as if he were being led to look at some strange bird's nest and must move softly. When she stepped to the wall and lifted the hanging ivy he started. There was a door and Mary pushed it slowly open and they passed in together, and then Mary stood and waved her hand round defiantly.

'It's this,' she said. 'It's a secret garden, and I'm the only one in the world who wants it to be alive.'

Dickon looked round and round about it, and round and round again.

'Eh!' he almost whispered, 'it is a queer, pretty place. It's like as if a body was in a dream.'

11

The Nest of the Missel Thrush

FOR two or three minutes he stood looking round him, while Mary watched him, and then he began to walk about softly, even more lightly than Mary had walked the first time she had found herself inside the four walls. His eyes seemed to be taking in everything – the grey trees with the grey creepers climbing over them and hanging from their branches, the tangle on the wall and among the grass, the evergreen alcoves with the stone seats and tall flower urns standing in them.

'I never thought I'd see this place,' he said at last in a whisper.

'Did you know about it?' asked Mary.

She had spoken aloud and he made a sign to her.

'We must talk low,' he said, 'or someone'll hear us an' wonder what's to do in here.'

'Oh! I forgot!' said Mary, feeling frightened and putting her hand quickly against her mouth. 'Did you know about the garden?' she asked again when she had recovered herself.

Dickon nodded.

'Martha told me there was one as no one ever went inside,' he answered. 'Us used to wonder what it was like.'

He stopped and looked round at the lovely grey tangle about him, and his round eyes looked queerly happy.

'Eh! The nests as'll be here come springtime,' he said. 'It'd be th' safest nestin' place in England. No one ever comin' near an' tangles o' trees an' roses to build in. I wonder all th' birds on th' moor don't build here.'

Mistress Mary put her hand on his arm again without knowing it.

'Will there be roses?' she whispered. 'Can you tell? I thought perhaps they were all dead.'

'Eh! No! Not them – not all of 'em!' he answered. 'Look here!'

He stepped over to the nearest tree – an old, old one with grey lichen all over its bark, but upholding a curtain of tangled sprays and branches. He took a thick knife out of his pocket and opened one of its blades.

'There's lots o' dead wood as ought to be cut out,'

he said. 'An' there's a lot o' old wood, but it made some new last year. This here's a new bit,' and he touched a shoot which looked brownish-green instead of hard, dry grey.

Mary touched it herself in an eager, reverent way.

'That one?' she said. 'Is that one quite alive – quite?'

Dickon curved his wide, smiling mouth.

'It's as wick as you or me,' he said; and Mary remembered that Martha had told her that 'wick' meant 'alive' or 'lively'.

'I'm glad it's wick!' she cried out in her whisper. 'I want them all to be wick. Let us go round the garden and count how many wick ones there are.'

She quite panted with eagerness and Dickon was as eager as she was. They went from tree to tree and from bush to bush. Dickon carried his knife in his hand and showed her things which she thought wonderful.

'They're run wild,' he said, 'but th' strongest ones has fair thrived on it. The delicatest ones has died out, but the others has growed an' growed, an' spread an' spread, till they's a wonder. See here!' and he pulled down a thick, grey, dry-looking branch. 'A body might think this was dead wood, but I don't believe it is – down to th' root. I'll cut it low down an' see.'

He knelt and with his knife cut the lifeless-looking branch through, not far above the earth.

'There!' he said exultantly. 'I told thee so. There's green in that wood yet. Look at it.'

Mary was down on her knees before he spoke, gazing with all her might.

'When it looks a bit greenish an' juicy like that, it's wick,' he explained. 'When th' inside is dry an' breaks easy, like this here piece I've cut off, it's done for. There's a big root here as all this live wood sprung out of, an' if th' old wood's cut off an' it's dug round, an' took care of there'll be' – he stopped and lifted his face to look up at the climbing and hanging sprays about him – 'there'll be a fountain o' roses here this summer.'

They went from bush to bush and from tree to tree. He was very strong and clever with his knife and knew how to cut the dry and dead wood away, and could tell when an unpromising bough or twig had still green life in it. In the course of half an hour, Mary thought she could tell too, and when he cut through a lifeless-looking branch she would cry out joyfully under her breath when she caught sight of the least shade of moist green. The spade, and hoe, and fork were very useful. He showed her how to use a fork while he dug about the roots with the spade and stirred the earth and let the air in.

They were working industriously round one of the biggest standard roses when he caught sight of something which made him utter an exclamation of surprise.

'Why!' he cried, pointing to the grass a few feet away. 'Who did that?'

It was one of Mary's own little clearings round the pale green points.

'I did it,' said Mary.

'Why, I thought tha' didn't know nothin' about gardenin',' he exclaimed.

'I don't,' she answered, 'but they were so little and the grass was so thick and strong, and they looked as if they had no room to breathe. So I made a place for them. I don't even know what they are.'

Dickon went and knelt down by them, smiling his wide smile.

'Tha' was right,' he said. 'A gardener couldn't have told thee better. They'll grow now like Jack's beanstalk. They're crocuses an' snowdrops, an' these here is narcissuses,' turning to another patch, 'an' here's daffydowndillys. Eh! They will be a sight.'

He ran from one clearing to another.

'Tha' has done a lot o' work for such a little wench,' he said, looking her over.

'I'm growing fatter,' said Mary, 'and I'm growing stronger. I used always to be tired. When I dig I'm not tired at all. I like to smell the earth when it's turned up.'

'It's rare good for thee,' he said, nodding his head wisely. 'There's naught as nice as th' smell o' good clean earth, except th' smell o' fresh growin' things when th' rain falls on 'em. I get out on th' moor many a day when it's rainin' an' I lie under a bush an' listen to th' soft swish o' drops on th' heather an' I just sniff an' sniff. My nose end fair quivers like a rabbit's, Mother says.'

'Do you never catch cold?' inquired Mary, gazing at him wonderingly. She had never seen such a funny boy, or such a nice one.

'Not me,' he said, grinning. 'I never ketched cold since I was born. I wasn't brought up nesh enough. I've chased about th' moor in all weathers, same as th' rabbits does. Mother says I've sniffed too much fresh air for twelve year' to ever get to sniffin' with cold. I'm as tough as a whitethorn knobstick.'

He was working all the time he was talking and Mary was following him and helping him with her fork or the trowel.

'There's a lot of work to do here!' he said once, looking about quite exultantly.

'Will you come again and help me to do it?' Mary begged. 'I'm sure I can help, too. I can dig and pull up weeds, and do whatever you tell me. Oh! do come, Dickon!'

'I'll come every day if tha' wants me, rain or shine,' he answered stoutly. 'It's th' best fun I ever had in my life – shut in here an' wakenin' up a garden.'

'If you will come,' said Mary, 'if you will help me to make it alive I'll – I don't know what I'll do,' she ended helplessly. What could you do for a boy like that?

'I'll tell thee what tha'll do,' said Dickon, with his happy grin. 'Tha'll get fat an' tha'll get as hungry as a young fox an' tha'll learn how to talk to th' robin same as I do. Eh! We'll have a lot o' fun.'

He began to walk about, looking up in the trees and at the walls and bushes with a thoughtful expression.

'I wouldn't want to make it look like a gardener's garden, all clipped an' spick an' span, would you?' he said. 'It's nicer like this with things runnin' wild, an' swingin' an' catchin' hold of each other.'

'Don't let us make it tidy,' said Mary anxiously. 'It wouldn't seem like a secret garden if it was tidy.'

Dickon stood rubbing his rusty-red head with a rather puzzled look.

'It's a secret garden sure enough,' he said, 'but seems like someone besides th' robin must have been in it since it was shut up ten year' ago.'

'But the door was locked and the key was buried,' said Mary. 'No one could get in.'

'That's true,' he answered. 'It's a queer place. Seems to me as if there'd been a bit o' prunin' done here an' there, later than ten year' ago.'

'But how could it have been done?' said Mary.

He was examining a branch of a standard rose and he shook his head.

'Aye! How could it!' he murmured. 'With th' door locked an' th' key buried.'

Mistress Mary always felt that however many years she lived she should never forget that first morning when her garden began to grow. Of course, it did seem to begin to grow for her that morning. When Dickon began to clear places to plant seeds, she remembered what Basil had sung at her when he wanted to tease her.

'Are there any flowers that look like bells?' she inquired.

'Lilies o' th' valley does,' he answered, digging away with the trowel, 'an' there's Canterbury bells, an' campanulas.'

'Let us plant some,' said Mary.

'There's lilies o' th' valley here already; I saw 'em. They'll have growed too close an' we'll have to separate 'em, but there's plenty. Th' other ones take two years to bloom from seed, but I can bring you some bits o' plants from our cottage garden. Why does tha' want 'em?'

Then Mary told him about Basil and his brothers and sisters in India and of how she had hated them, and of their calling her 'Mistress Mary Quite Contrary'.

'They used to dance round and sing at me. They sang:

> *Mistress Mary, quite contrary,*
> *How does your garden grow?*
> *With silver bells and cockle shells,*
> *And marigolds all in a row.*

I just remembered it and it made me wonder if there were really flowers like silver bells.'

She frowned a little and gave her trowel a rather spiteful dig into the earth.

'I wasn't as contrary as they were.'

But Dickon laughed.

'Eh!' he said, and as he crumpled the rich black soil she saw he was sniffing up the scent of it, 'there doesn't seem to be no need for no one to be contrary when there's flowers an' such like, an' such lots o' friendly wild things runnin' about makin' homes for themselves, or buildin' nests an' singin' an' whistlin', does there?'

Mary, kneeling by him holding the seeds, looked at him and stopped frowning.

'Dickon,' she said. 'You are as nice as Martha said you were. I like you, and you make the fifth person. I never thought I should like five people.'

Dickon sat up on his heels as Martha did when she was polishing the grate. He did look funny and delightful, Mary thought, with his round blue eyes and red cheeks and happy-looking turned-up nose.

'Only five folks as tha' likes?' he said. 'Who is th' other four?'

'Your mother and Martha,' Mary checked them off on her fingers, 'and the robin and Ben Weatherstaff.'

Dickon laughed, so that he was obliged to stifle the sound by putting his arm over his mouth. 'I know tha' thinks I'm a queer lad,' he said, 'but I think tha' art th' queerest little lass I ever saw.'

Then Mary did a strange thing. She leaned forward and asked him a question she had never dreamed of asking anyone before. And she tried to ask it in Yorkshire because that was his language, and in India a native was always pleased if you knew his speech.

'Does tha' like me?' she said.

'Eh!' he answered heartily, 'that I does. I likes thee wonderful, an' so does th' robin, I do believe!'

'That's two, then,' said Mary. 'That's two for me.'

And then they began to work harder than ever and more joyful. Mary was startled and sorry when she heard the big clock in the courtyard strike the hour of her midday dinner.

'I shall have to go,' she said mournfully. 'And you will have to go too, won't you?'

Dickon grinned.

'My dinner's easy to carry about with me,' he said. 'Mother always lets me put a bit o' somethin' in my pocket.'

He picked up his coat from the grass and brought out of a pocket a lumpy little bundle tied up in a quite clean, coarse, blue and white handkerchief. It held two thick pieces of bread with a slice of something laid between them.

'It's oftenest naught but bread,' he said, 'but I've got a fine slice o' fat bacon with it today.'

Mary thought it looked a queer dinner, but he seemed ready to enjoy it.

'Run on an' get thy victuals,' he said. 'I'll be done with mine first. I'll get some more work done before I start back home.'

He sat down with his back against a tree.

'I'll call th' robin up,' he said, 'and give him th' rind o' th' bacon to peck at. They likes a bit o' fat wonderful.'

Mary could scarcely bear to leave him. Suddenly it seemed as if he might be a sort of wood fairy who might be gone when she came into the garden again. He seemed too good to be true. She went slowly half-way to the door in the wall and then she stopped and went back.

'Whatever happens, you – you never would tell?' she said.

His poppy-coloured cheeks were distended with his first big bite of bread and bacon, but he managed to smile encouragingly.

'If tha' was a missel thrush an' showed me where thy nest was, does tha' think I'd tell anyone? Not me,' he said. 'Tha' art as safe as a missel thrush.'

And she was quite sure she was.

12

'Might I Have a Bit of Earth?'

MARY ran so fast that she was rather out of breath when she reached her room. Her hair was ruffled on her forehead and her cheeks were bright pink. Her dinner was waiting on the table, and Martha was waiting near it.

'Tha's a bit late,' she said. 'Where has tha' been?'

'I've seen Dickon!' said Mary. 'I've seen Dickon!'

'I knew he'd come,' said Martha exultantly. 'How does tha' like him?'

'I think – I think he's beautiful!' said Mary in a determined voice.

Martha looked rather taken aback, but she looked pleased, too.

'Well,' she said, 'he's th' best lad as ever was born, but

us never thought he was handsome. His nose turns up too much.'

'I like it to turn up,' said Mary.

'An' his eyes is so round,' said Martha, a trifle doubtful. 'Though they're a nice colour.'

'I like them round,' said Mary. 'And they are exactly the colour of the sky over the moor.'

Martha beamed with satisfaction.

'Mother says he made 'em that colour with always lookin' up at th' birds an' th' clouds. But he has got a big mouth, hasn't he, now?'

'I love his big mouth,' said Mary obstinately. 'I wish mine were just like it.'

Martha chuckled delightedly.

'It'd look rare an' funny in thy bit of a face,' she said. 'But I knowed it would be that way when tha' saw him. How did tha' like th' seeds an' th' garden tools?'

'How did you know he brought them?' asked Mary.

'Eh! I never thought of his not bringin' 'em. He'd be sure to bring 'em if they was in Yorkshire. He's such a trusty lad.'

Mary was afraid that she might begin to ask difficult questions, but she did not. She was very much interested in the seeds and gardening tools, and there was only one moment when Mary was frightened. This was when she began to ask where the flowers were to be planted.

'Who did tha' ask about it?' she inquired.

'I haven't asked anybody yet,' said Mary, hesitatingly.

'Well, I wouldn't ask th' head gardener. He's too grand, Mr Roach is.'

'I've never seen him,' said Mary. 'I've only seen under-gardeners and Ben Weatherstaff.'

'If I was you, I'd ask Ben Weatherstaff,' advised Martha. 'He's not half as bad as he looks, for all he's so crabbed. Mr Craven lets him do what he likes, because he was here when Mrs Craven was alive, an' he used to make her laugh. She liked him. Perhaps he'd find you a corner somewhere out o' the way'.

'If it was out of the way and no one wanted it, no one *could* mind my having it, could they?' Mary said anxiously.

'There wouldn't be no reason,' answered Martha. 'You wouldn't do no harm.'

Mary ate her dinner as quickly as she could, and when she rose from the table she was going to run to her room to put on her hat again, but Martha stopped her.

'I've got somethin' to tell you,' she said. 'I thought I'd let you eat your dinner first. Mr Craven came back this mornin' and I think he wants to see you.'

Mary turned quite pale.

'Oh!' she said. 'Why? Why? He didn't want to see me when I came. I heard Pitcher say he didn't.'

'Well,' explained Martha. 'Mrs Medlock says it's because o' Mother. She was walkin' to Thwaite village an' she met him. She'd never spoke to him before, but Mrs Craven had been to our cottage two or three times. He'd forgot, but Mother hadn't, an' she made bold to stop him. I don't know what she said to him about you, but she said somethin' as put him in th' mind to see you before he goes away again, tomorrow.'

'Oh!' cried Mary, 'is he going away tomorrow? I'm so glad!'

'He's goin' for a long time. He mayn't come back till autumn or winter. He's goin' to travel in foreign places. He's always doin' it.'

'Oh! I'm so glad – so glad!' said Mary thankfully.

If he did not come back until winter, or even autumn, there would be time to watch the secret garden come alive. Even if he found out then and took it away from her, she would have had that much at least.

'When do you think he will want to see –'

She did not finish the sentence, because the door opened, and Mrs Medlock walked in. She had on her best black dress and cap, and her collar was fastened with a large brooch with a picture of a man's face on it. It was a coloured photograph of Mr Medlock, who had died years ago, and she always wore it when she was dressed up. She looked nervous and excited.

'Your hair's rough,' she said quickly. 'Go and brush it. Martha, help her to slip on her best dress. Mr Craven sent me to bring her to him in his study.'

All the pink left Mary's cheeks. Her heart began to thump and she felt herself changing into a stiff, plain, silent child again. She did not even answer Mrs Medlock, but turned and walked into her bedroom, followed by Martha. She said nothing while her dress was changed, and her hair brushed, and after she was quite tidy she followed Mrs Medlock down the corridors, in silence. What was there for her to say? She was obliged to go and see Mr Craven, and he would not like her, and she would not like him. She knew what he would think of her.

She was taken to a part of the house she had not been into before. At last Mrs Medlock knocked at a door, and when someone said, 'Come in,' they entered the room together. A man was sitting in an arm-chair before the fire, and Mrs Medlock spoke to him.

'This is Miss Mary, sir,' she said.

'You can go and leave her here. I will ring for you when I want you to take her away,' said Mr Craven.

When she went out and closed the door, Mary could only stand waiting, a plain little thing, twisting her thin hands together. She could see that the man in the chair was not so much a hunchback as a man with high, rather crooked shoulders, and he had black hair streaked with white. He turned his head over his high shoulders and spoke to her.

'Come here!' he said.

Mary went to him.

He was not ugly. His face would have been handsome if it had not been so miserable. He looked as if the sight of her worried and fretted him and as if he did not know what in the world to do with her.

'Are you well?' he asked.

'Yes,' answered Mary.

'Do they take good care of you?'

'Yes.'

He rubbed his forehead fretfully as he looked her over.

'You are very thin,' he said.

'I am getting fatter,' Mary answered, in what she knew was her stiffest way.

What an unhappy face he had! His black eyes seemed as if they scarcely saw her, as if they were seeing something else, and he could hardly keep his thoughts upon her.

'I forgot you,' he said. 'How could I remember you? I intended to send you a governess or nurse or someone of that sort, but I forgot.'

'Please,' began Mary. 'Please –' and then the lump in her throat choked her.

'What do you want to say?' he inquired.

'I am – I am too big for a nurse,' said Mary. 'And please – please don't make me have a governess yet.'

He rubbed his forehead again and stared at her.

'That was what the Sowerby woman said,' he muttered absent-mindedly.

Then Mary gathered a scrap of courage.

'Is she – is she Martha's mother?' she stammered.

'Yes, I think so,' he replied.

'She knows about children,' said Mary. 'She has twelve. She knows.'

He seemed to rouse himself.

'What do you want to do?'

'I want to play out of doors,' Mary answered, hoping that her voice did not tremble. 'I never liked it in India. It makes me hungry here, and I am getting fatter.'

He was watching her.

'Mrs Sowerby said it would do you good. Perhaps it will,' he said. 'She thought you had better get stronger before you had a governess.'

'It makes me feel strong when I play and the wind comes over the moor,' argued Mary.

'Where do you play?' he asked next.

'Everywhere,' gasped Mary. 'Martha's mother sent me a skipping-rope. I skip and run – and I look about to see if things are beginning to stick up out of the earth. I don't do any harm.'

'Don't look so frightened,' he said in a worried voice. 'You could not do any harm, a child like you! You may do what you like.'

Mary put her hand up to her throat because she was afraid he might see the excited lump which she felt jump into it. She came a step nearer to him.

'May I?' she said tremulously.

Her anxious little face seemed to worry him more than ever.

'Don't look so frightened,' he exclaimed. 'Of course you may. I am your guardian, though I am a poor one for any child. I cannot give you time or attention. I am too ill, and wretched and distracted; but I wish you to be happy and comfortable. I don't know anything about children, but Mrs Medlock is to see that you have all you need. I sent for you today because Mrs Sowerby said I ought to see you. Her daughter had talked about you. She thought you needed fresh air and freedom and running about.'

'She knows all about children,' Mary said again in spite of herself.

'She ought to,' said Mr Craven. 'I thought her rather bold to stop me on the moor, but she said Mrs Craven had been kind to her.' It seemed hard for him to speak his dead wife's name. 'She is a respectable woman. Now I have seen you I think she said sensible things. Play out

143

of doors as much as you like. It's a big place, and you may go where you like and amuse yourself as you like. Is there anything you want?' As if a sudden thought had struck him. 'Do you want toys, books, dolls?'

'Might I,' quavered Mary, 'might I have a bit of earth?'

In her eagerness she did not realise how queer the words would sound and that they were not the ones she had meant to say. Mr Craven looked quite startled.

'Earth!' he repeated. 'What do you mean?'

'To plant seeds in – to make things grow – to see them come alive,' Mary faltered.

He gazed at her a moment and then passed his hand quickly over his eyes.

'Do you – care about gardens so much?' he said slowly.

'I didn't know about them in India,' said Mary. 'I was always ill and tired, and it was so hot. I sometimes made little beds in the sand and stuck flowers in them. But here it is different.'

Mr Craven got up and began to walk slowly across the room.

'A bit of earth,' he said to himself and Mary thought that somehow she must have reminded him of something. When he stopped and spoke to her his dark eyes looked almost soft and kind.

'You can have as much earth as you want,' he said. 'You remind me of someone else who loved the earth and things that grow. When you see a bit of earth you want,' with something like a smile, 'take it, child, and make it come alive.'

'May I take it from anywhere – if it's not wanted?'

'Anywhere,' he answered. 'There! You must go now, I am tired.' He touched the bell to call Mrs Medlock. 'Good-bye. I shall be away all summer.'

Mrs Medlock came so quickly that Mary thought she must have been waiting in the corridor.

'Mrs Medlock,' Mr Craven said to her, 'now I have seen the child I understand what Mrs Sowerby meant. She must be less delicate before she begins lessons. Give her simple, healthy food. Let her run wild in the garden. Don't look after her too much. She needs liberty and fresh air and romping about. Mrs Sowerby is to come and see her now and then, and she may sometimes go to the cottage.'

Mrs Medlock looked pleased. She was relieved to hear that she need not 'look after' Mary too much. She had felt her a tiresome charge, and had, indeed, seen as little of her as she dared. In addition to this, she was fond of Martha's mother.

'Thank you, sir,' she said. 'Susan Sowerby and me went to school together, and she's as sensible and good-hearted a woman as you'd find in a day's walk. I never had any children myself and she's had twelve, and there never was healthier or better ones. Miss Mary can get no harm from them. I'd always take Susan Sowerby's advice about children myself. She's what you might call healthy-minded – if you understand me.'

'I understand,' Mr Craven answered. 'Take Miss Mary away now and send Pitcher to me.'

When Mrs Medlock left her at the end of her own corridor Mary flew back to her room. She found Martha waiting there. Martha had, in fact, hurried back after she had removed the dinner service.

'I can have my garden!' cried Mary. 'I may have it where I like! I am not going to have a governess for a long time! Your mother is coming to see me and I may go to your cottage. He says a little girl like me could not do any harm and I may do what I like – anywhere!'

'Eh!' said Martha, delighted, 'that was nice of him, wasn't it?'

'Martha,' said Mary solemnly, 'he is really a nice man, only his face is so miserable and his forehead is all drawn together.'

She ran as quickly as she could to the garden. She had been away so much longer than she had thought she should, and she knew Dickon would have to set out early on his five-mile walk. When she slipped through the door under the ivy, she saw he was not working where she had left him. The gardening tools were laid together under a tree. She ran to them, looking all round the place, but there was no Dickon to be seen. He had gone away and the secret garden was empty – except for the robin, who had just flown across the wall and sat on a standard rose-bush watching her.

'He's gone,' she said woefully. 'Oh! Was he – was he – was he only a wood fairy?'

Something white fastened to the standard rose-bush caught her eye. It was a piece of paper – in fact, it was a piece of the letter she had printed for Martha to send to Dickon. It was fastened on the bush with a long thorn, and in a minute she knew Dickon had left it there. There were some roughly printed letters on it and a sort of picture. At first she could not tell what it was. Then she saw it was meant for a nest with a bird sitting on it. Underneath were the printed letters, and they said:

'I will cum bak.'

13

'*I Am Colin*'

MARY took the picture back to the house when she went to her supper and she showed it to Martha. 'Eh!' said Martha with great pride. 'I never knew our Dickon was as clever as that. That there's a picture of a missel thrush on her nest, as large as life an' twice as natural.'

Then Mary knew Dickon had meant the picture to be a message. He had meant that she might be sure he would keep her secret. Her garden was her nest and she was like a missel thrush. Oh, how she did like that queer, common boy!

She hoped he would come back the very next day, and she fell asleep looking forward to the morning.

But you never know what the weather will do in Yorkshire, particularly in the springtime. She was awakened in the night by the sound of rain beating with heavy drops against her window. It was pouring down in torrents and the wind was 'wuthering' round the corners and in the chimneys of the huge old house. Mary sat up in bed and felt miserable and angry.

'The rain is as contrary as I ever was,' she said. 'It came because it knew I did not want it.'

She threw herself back on her pillow and buried her face. She did not cry, but she lay and hated the sound of the heavily beating rain, she hated the wind and its 'wuthering'. She could not go to sleep again. The mournful sound kept her awake, because she felt mournful herself. If she had felt happy it would probably have lulled her to sleep. How it 'wuthered' and how the big raindrops poured down and beat against the pane!

'It sounds just like a person lost on the moor and wandering on and on crying,' she said.

*

She had been lying awake, turning from side to side for about an hour, when suddenly something made her sit up in bed and turn her head towards the door listening. She listened and she listened.

'It isn't the wind now,' she said in a loud whisper. 'That isn't the wind. It is different. It is that crying I heard before.'

The door of her room was ajar and the sound came

down the corridor, a far-off faint sound of fretful crying. She listened for a few minutes and each minute she became more and more sure. She felt as if she must find out what it was. It seemed even stranger than the secret garden and the buried key. Perhaps the fact that she was in a rebellious mood made her bold. She put her foot out of bed and stood on the floor.

'I am going to find out what it is,' she said. 'Everybody is in bed and I don't care about Mrs Medlock – I don't care!'

There was a candle by her bedside and she took it up and went softly out of the room. The corridor looked very long and dark, but she was too excited to mind that. She thought she remembered the corners she must turn to find the short corridor with the door covered with tapestry – the one Mrs Medlock had come through the day she lost herself. The sound had come up that passage. So she went on with her dim light, almost feeling her way, her heart beating so loud that she fancied she could hear it. The far-off, faint crying went on and led her. Sometimes it stopped for moment or so and then began again. Was this the right corner to turn? She stopped and thought. Yes, it was. Down this passage and then to the left, and then up two broad steps, and then to the right again. Yes, there was the tapestry door.

She pushed it open very gently and closed it behind

her, and she stood in the corridor and could hear the crying quite plainly, though it was not loud. It was on the other side of the wall at her left and a few yards farther on there was a door. She could see a glimmer of light coming from beneath it. The Someone was crying in that room, and it was quite a young Someone.

So she walked to the door and pushed it open, and there she was standing in the room!

It was a big room with ancient, handsome furniture in it. There was a low fire glowing faintly on the hearth and a night-light burning by the side of a carved, four-poster bed hung with brocade, and on the bed was lying a boy, crying pitifully.

Mary wondered if she was in a real place or if she had fallen asleep again and was dreaming without knowing it.

The boy had a sharp, delicate face, the colour of ivory, and he seemed to have eyes too big for it. He had also a lot of hair which tumbled over his forehead in heavy locks and made his thin face seem smaller. He looked like a boy who had been ill, but he was crying more as if he were tired and cross than as if he were in pain.

Mary stood near the door with her candle in her hand, holding her breath. Then she crept across the room, and as she drew nearer the light attracted the boy's attention and he turned his head on his pillow and stared at her, his grey eyes opening so wide that they seemed immense.

'Who are you?' he said at last in a half-frightened whisper. 'Are you a ghost?'

'No, I am not,' Mary answered, her own whisper sounding half-frightened. 'Are you one?'

He stared and stared and stared. Mary could not help noticing what strange eyes he had. They were agate-grey and they looked too big for his face because they had black lashes all round them.

'No,' he replied, after waiting a moment or so. 'I am Colin.'

'Who is Colin?' she faltered.

'I am Colin Craven. Who are you?'

'I am Mary Lennox. Mr Craven is my uncle.'

'He is my father,' said the boy.

'Your father!' gasped Mary. 'No one ever told me he had a boy! Why didn't they?'

'Come here,' he said, still keeping his strange eyes fixed on her with an anxious expression.

She came close to the bed and he put out his hand and touched her.

'You are real, aren't you?' he said. 'I have such real dreams very often. You might be one of them.'

Mary had slipped on a woollen wrapper before she

left her room and she put a piece of it between his fingers.

'Rub that and see how thick and warm it is,' she said. 'I will pinch you a little if you like, to show you how real I am. For a minute I thought you might be a dream, too.'

'Where did you come from?' he asked.

'From my own room. The wind wuthered so I couldn't go to sleep and I heard someone crying and wanted to find out who it was. What were you crying for?'

'Because I couldn't go to sleep either, and my head ached. Tell me your name again.'

'Mary Lennox. Did no one ever tell you I had come to live here?'

He was still fingering the fold of her wrapper, but he began to look a little more as if he believed in her reality.

'No,' he answered. 'They daren't.'

'Why?' asked Mary.

'Because I should have been afraid you would see me. I won't let people see me and talk me over.'

'Why?' Mary asked again, feeling more mystified every moment.

'Because I am like this always, ill and having to lie down. My father won't let people talk me over, either. The servants are not allowed to speak about me. If I live

I may be a hunchback, but I shan't live. My father hates to think I may be like him.'

'Oh, what a queer house this is!' Mary said. 'What a queer house! Everything is a kind of secret. Rooms are locked up and gardens are locked up – and you! Have you been locked up?'

'No. I stay in this room because I don't want to be moved out of it. It tires me too much.'

'Does your father come and see you?' Mary ventured.

'Sometimes. Generally when I am asleep. He doesn't want to see me.'

'Why?' Mary could not help asking again.

A sort of angry shadow passed over the boy's face.

'My mother died when I was born and it makes him wretched to look at me. He thinks I don't know, but I've heard people talking. He almost hates me.'

'He hates the garden, because she died,' said Mary, half speaking to herself.

'What garden?' the boy asked.

'Oh! Just – just a garden she used to like,' Mary stammered. 'Have you been here always?'

'Nearly always. Sometimes I have been taken to places at the seaside, but I won't stay because people stare at me. I used to wear an iron thing to keep my back straight, but a grand doctor came from London to see me and said it was stupid. He told them to take it off and keep me out in the fresh air. I hate fresh air and I don't want to go out.'

'I didn't when first I came here,' said Mary. 'Why do you keep looking at me like that?'

'Because of the dreams that are so real,' he answered rather fretfully. 'Sometimes when I open my eyes I don't believe I'm awake.'

'We're both awake,' said Mary. She glanced round the room with its high ceiling and shadowy corners and dim firelight. 'It looks quite like a dream, and it's the middle of the night, and everybody in the house is asleep – everybody but us. We are wide awake.'

'I don't want it to be a dream,' the boy said restlessly.

Mary thought of something all at once.

'If you don't like people to see you,' she began, 'do you want me to go away?'

He still held the fold of her wrapper and he gave it a little pull.

'No,' he said. 'I should be sure you were a dream if you went. If you are real, sit down on that big footstool and talk. I want to hear about you.'

Mary put down her candle on the table near the bed and sat down on the cushioned stool. She did not want to go away at all. She wanted to stay in the mysterious, hidden-away room and talk to the mysterious boy.

'What do you want me to tell you?' she said.

He wanted to know how long she had been at Misselthwaite; he wanted to know which corridor her room was on; he wanted to know what she had been doing; if she disliked the moor as he disliked it; where she had lived before she came to Yorkshire. She answered all these questions and many more, and he lay back on his pillow and listened. He made her tell him a great deal about India and about her voyage across the ocean. She found out that because he had been an invalid he had not learned things as other children had. One of his nurses had taught him to read when he was quite little and he was always reading and looking at pictures in splendid books.

Though his father rarely saw him when he was awake, he was given all sorts of wonderful things to amuse himself with. He never seemed to have been amused, however. He could have anything he asked for and was never made to do anything he did not like to do.

'Everyone is obliged to do what pleases me,' he said indifferently. 'It makes me ill to be angry. No one believes I shall live to grow up.'

He said it as if he was so accustomed to the idea that it had ceased to matter to him at all. He seemed to like the sound of Mary's voice. As she went on talking he listened in a drowsy, interested way. Once or twice she wondered if he were not gradually falling into a doze. But at last he asked a question which opened up a new subject.

'How old are you?' he asked.

'I am ten,' answered Mary, forgetting herself for the moment, 'and so are you.'

'How do you know that?' he demanded in a surprised voice.

'Because when you were born the garden door was locked and the key was buried. And it has been locked for ten years.'

Colin half sat up, turning towards her, leaning on his elbows.

'What garden door was locked? Who did it? Where was the key buried?' he exclaimed, as if he were suddenly very much interested.

'It – it was the garden Mr Craven hates,' said Mary nervously. 'He locked the door. No one – no one knew where he buried the key.'

'What sort of a garden is it?' Colin persisted eagerly.

'No one has been allowed to go into it for ten years,' was Mary's careful answer.

But it was too late to be careful. He was too much like herself. He, too, had had nothing to think about, and the idea of a hidden garden attracted him as it had attracted her. He asked question after question. Where was it? Had she never looked for the door? Had she never asked the gardeners?

'They won't talk about it,' said Mary. 'I think they have been told not to answer questions.'

'I would make them,' said Colin.

'Could you?' Mary faltered, beginning to feel frightened. If he could make people answer questions, who knew what might happen?

'Everyone is obliged to please me. I told you that,' he said. 'If I were to live, this place would some time belong to me. They all know that. I would make them tell me.'

Mary had not known that she herself had been spoiled, but she could see quite plainly that this mysterious boy had been. He thought that the whole world belonged to him. How peculiar he was and how coolly he spoke of not living.

'Do you think you won't live?' she asked, partly because she was curious and partly in hope of making him forget the garden.

'I don't suppose I shall,' he answered as indifferently as he had spoken before. 'Ever since I remember anything I have heard people say I shan't. At first they thought I was too little to understand, and now they think I don't hear. But I do. My doctor is my father's cousin. He is quite poor and if I die he will have all Misselthwaite when my father is dead. I should think he wouldn't want me to live.'

'Do you want to live?' inquired Mary.

'No,' he answered, in a cross, tired fashion. 'But I don't want to die. When I feel ill I lie here and think about it until I cry and cry.'

'I have heard you crying three times,' Mary said, 'but I did not know who it was. Were you crying about that?' She did so want him to forget the garden.

'I dare say,' he answered. 'Let us talk about something else. Talk about that garden. Don't you want to see it?'

'Yes,' answered Mary in quite a low voice.

'I do,' he went on persistently. 'I don't think I ever really wanted to see anything before, but I want to see that garden. I want the key dug up. I want the door unlocked. I would let them take me there in my chair. That would be getting fresh air. I am going to make them open the door.'

He had become quite excited and his strange eyes began to shine like stars and looked more immense than ever.

'They have to please me,' he said. 'I will make them take me there and I will let you go, too.'

Mary's hands clutched each other. Everything would be spoiled – everything. Dickon would never come back.

She would never again feel like a missel thrush with a safe-hidden nest.

'Oh, don't – don't – don't – don't do that!' she cried out.

He stared as if he thought she had gone crazy!

'Why?' he exclaimed. 'You said you wanted to see it.'

'I do,' she answered, almost with a sob in her throat, 'but if you make them open the door and take you in like that it will never be a secret again.'

He leaned still farther forward.

'A secret,' he said. 'What do you mean? Tell me.'

Mary's words almost tumbled over one another.

'You see – you see,' she panted, 'if no one knows but ourselves – if there was a door, hidden somewhere under the ivy – if there was – and we could find it; and if we could slip through it together and shut it behind us, and no one knew anyone was inside and we called it our garden and pretended that – that we were missel thrushes and it was our nest, and if we played there almost every day and dug and planted seeds and made it all come alive –'

'Is it dead?' he interrupted her.

'It soon will be if no one cares for it,' she went on. 'The bulbs will live but the roses –'

He stopped her again as excited as she was herself.

'What are bulbs?' he put in quickly.

'They are daffodils and lilies and snowdrops. They are working in the earth now – pushing up pale green points because the spring is coming.'

'Is the spring coming?' he said. 'What is it like? You don't see it in rooms if you are ill.'

'It is the sun shining on the rain and the rain falling on the sunshine, and things pushing up and working under the earth,' said Mary. 'If the garden was a secret and we could get into it we could watch the things grow bigger every day, and see how many roses are alive. Don't you see? Oh, don't you see how much nicer it would be if it was a secret?'

He dropped back on his pillow and lay there with an odd expression on his face.

'I never had a secret,' he said, 'except that one about not living to grow up. They don't know I know that, so it is a sort of secret. But I like this kind better.'

'If you won't make them take you to the garden,' pleaded Mary, 'perhaps – I feel almost sure I can find out how to get in some time. And then – if the doctor wants you to go out in your chair, and if you can always do what you want to do, perhaps – perhaps we might find some boy who would push you, and we could go alone and it would always be a secret garden.'

'I should – like – that,' he said very slowly, his eyes

looking dreamy. 'I should like that. I should not mind fresh air in a secret garden.'

Mary began to recover her breath and feel safer, because the idea of keeping the secret seemed to please him. She felt almost sure that if she kept on talking and could make him see the garden in his mind as she had seen it, he would like it so much that he could not bear to think that everybody might tramp into it when they chose.

'I'll tell you what I *think* it would be like, if you could go into it,' she said. 'It has been shut up so long things have grown into a tangle perhaps.'

He lay quite still and listened while she went on talking about the roses which *might* have clambered from tree to tree and hung down – about the many birds which *might* have built their nests there because it was so safe. And then she told him about the robin and Ben Weatherstaff, and there was so much to tell about the robin and it was so easy and safe to talk about it that she ceased to feel afraid. The robin pleased him so much that he smiled until he looked almost beautiful, and at first Mary had thought that he was even plainer than herself, with his big eyes and heavy locks of hair.

'I did not know birds could be like that,' he said. 'But if you stay in a room you never see things. What a lot of things you know. I feel as if you had been inside that garden.'

She did not know what to say, so she did not say anything. He evidently did not expect an answer and the next moment he gave her a surprise.

'I am going to let you look at something,' he said. 'Do you see that rose-coloured silk curtain hanging on the wall over the mantelpiece?'

Mary had not noticed it before, but she looked up and saw it. It was a curtain of soft silk hanging over what seemed to be some picture.

'Yes,' she answered.

'There is a cord hanging from it,' said Colin. 'Go and pull it.'

Mary got up, much mystified, and found the cord. When she pulled it the silk curtain ran back on rings and when it ran back it uncovered a picture. It was the picture of a girl with a laughing face. She had bright hair tied up with a blue ribbon and her gay, lovely eyes were exactly like Colin's unhappy ones, agate-grey and looking twice as big as they really were, because of the black lashes all round them.

'She is my mother,' said Colin complainingly. 'I don't see why she died. Sometimes I hate her for doing it.'

'How queer!' said Mary.

'If she had lived I believe I should not have been ill always,' he grumbled. 'I dare say I should have lived, too. And my father would not have hated to look at me. I dare say I should have had a strong back. Draw the curtain again.'

Mary did as she was told and returned to her footstool.

'She is much prettier than you,' she said, 'but her eyes are just like yours – at least they are the same shape and colour. Why is the curtain drawn over her?'

He moved uncomfortably.

'I made them do it,' he said. 'Sometimes I don't like to see her looking at me. She smiles too much when I am ill and miserable. Besides, she is mine, and I don't want everyone to see her.'

There were a few moments of silence and then Mary spoke. 'What would Mrs Medlock do if she found out that I had been here?' she inquired.

'She would do as I told her to do,' he answered. 'And I should tell her that I wanted you to come here and talk to me every day. I am glad you came.'

'So am I,' said Mary. 'I will come as often as I can, but' – she hesitated – 'I shall have to look every day for the garden door.'

'Yes, you must,' said Colin, 'and you can tell me about it afterwards.'

He lay thinking a few minutes, as he had done before, and then he spoke again.

'I think you shall be a secret, too,' he said. 'I will not tell them until they find out. I can always send the nurse out of the room and say that I want to be by myself. Do you know Martha?'

'Yes, I know her very well,' said Mary. 'She waits on me.'

He nodded his head towards the outer corridor.

'She is the one who is asleep in the other room. The nurse went away yesterday to stay all night with her sister and she always makes Martha attend to me when she wants to go out. Martha shall tell you when to come here.'

Then Mary understood Martha's troubled look when she had asked questions about the crying.

'Martha knew about you all the time?' she said.

'Yes; she often attends to me. The nurse likes to get away from me and then Martha comes.'

'I have been here a long time,' said Mary. 'Shall I go away now? Your eyes look sleepy.'

'I wish I could go to sleep before you leave me,' he said rather shyly.

'Shut your eyes,' said Mary, drawing her footstool closer, 'and I will do what my Ayah used to do in India.

I will pat your hand and stroke it and sing something quite low.'

'I should like that perhaps,' he said drowsily.

Somehow she was sorry for him and did not want him to lie awake, so she leaned against the bed and began to stroke and pat his hand and sing a very low little charming song in Hindustani.

'That is nice,' he said more drowsily still, and she went on chanting and stroking, but when she looked at him again his black lashes were lying close against his cheeks, for his eyes were shut and he was fast asleep. She got up softly, took her candle, and crept away without making a sound.

14

A Young Rajah

THE moor was hidden in mist when the morning came, and the rain had not stopped pouring down. There could be no going out of doors. Martha was so busy that Mary had no opportunity of talking to her, but in the afternoon she asked her to come and sit with her in the nursery. She came, bringing the stocking she was always knitting when she was doing nothing else.

'What's the matter with thee?' she asked as soon as they sat down. 'Tha' looks as if tha'd somethin' to say.'

'I have. I have found out what the crying was,' said Mary.

Martha let her knitting drop on her knee and gazed at her with startled eyes.

'Tha' hasn't!' she exclaimed. 'Never!'

'I heard it in the night,' Mary went on. 'And I got up

and went to see where it came from. It was Colin. I found him.'

Martha's face became red with fright.

'Eh! Miss Mary!' she said, half crying. 'Tha' shouldn't have done it – tha' shouldn't. Tha'll get me in trouble. I never told thee nothin' about him – but tha'll get me in trouble. I shall lose my place and what'll Mother do!'

'You won't lose your place,' said Mary. 'He was glad I came. We talked and talked and he said he was glad I came.'

'Was he?' cried Martha. 'Art tha' sure? Tha' doesn't know what he's like when anything vexes him. He's a big lad to cry like a baby, but when he's in a passion he'll fair scream just to frighten us. He knows us daren't call our souls our own.'

'He wasn't vexed,' said Mary. 'I asked him if I should go away and he made me stay. He asked me questions and I sat on a big footstool and talked to him about India and about the robin and gardens. He wouldn't let me go. He let me see his mother's picture. Before I left him I sang him to sleep.'

Martha fairly gasped with amazement.

'I can scarcely believe thee!' she protested. 'It's as if tha'd walked straight into a lion's den. If he'd been like he is most times he'd have throwed himself into

168

one of his tantrums and roused th' house. He won't let strangers look at him.'

'He let me look at him. I looked at him all the time and he looked at me. We stared!' said Mary.

'I don't know what to do!' cried agitated Martha. 'If Mrs Medlock finds out, she'll think I broke orders and told thee and I shall be packed back to Mother.'

'He is not going to tell Mrs Medlock anything about it yet. It's to be a sort of secret just at first,' said Mary firmly. 'And he says everybody is obliged to do as he pleases.'

'Aye, that's true enough – th' bad lad!' sighed Martha, wiping her forehead with her apron.

'He says Mrs Medlock must. And he wants me to come and talk to him every day. And you are to tell me when he wants me.'

'Me!' said Martha; 'I shall lose my place – I shall for sure!'

'You can't if you are doing what he wants you to do and everybody is ordered to obey him,' Mary argued.

'Does tha' mean to say,' cried Martha with wide-open eyes, 'that he was nice to thee?'

'I think he almost liked me,' Mary answered.

'Then tha' must have bewitched him!' decided Martha, drawing a long breath.

'Do you mean Magic?' inquired Mary. 'I've heard about Magic in India, but I can't make it. I just went into his room and I was so surprised to see him I stood and stared. And then he turned round and stared at me. And he thought I was a ghost or a dream and I thought perhaps he was. And it was so queer being there alone together in the middle of the night and not knowing about each other. And we began to ask each other questions. And when I asked him if I must go away he said I must not.'

'Th' world's comin' to an end!' gasped Martha.

'What is the matter with him?' asked Mary.

'Nobody knows for sure and certain,' said Martha. 'Mr Craven went off his head like when he was born. Th' doctors thought he'd have to be put in a 'sylum. It was because Mrs Craven died like I told you. He wouldn't set eyes on th' baby. He just raved and said it'd be another hunchback like him and it'd better die.'

'Is Colin a hunchback?' Mary asked. 'He didn't look like one.'

'He isn't yet,' said Martha. 'But he began all wrong. Mother said that there was enough trouble raging in th' house to set any child wrong. They was afraid his back was weak an' they've always been takin' care of it – keepin' him lyin' down and not lettin' him walk. Once they made him wear a brace, but he fretted so he was downright ill. Then a big doctor came to see him an' made them take it off. He talk'd to th' other doctor quite rough – in a polite way. He said there'd been too much medicine and too much lettin' him have his own way.'

'I think he's a very spoiled boy,' said Mary.

'He's th' worst young nowt as ever was!' said Martha. 'I won't say as he hasn't been ill a good bit. He's had coughs an' colds that's nearly killed him two or three times. Once he had rheumatic fever an' once he had typhoid. Eh! Mrs Medlock did get a fright then. He'd been out of his head an' she was talkin' to th' nurse, thinkin' he didn't know nothin', an' she said: "He'll die this time sure enough, an' best thing for him an' for everybody." An' she looked at him, an' there he was with his big eyes open, starin' at her as sensible as she was herself. She didn't know what'd happen, but he just stared at her an' says: "You give me some water an' stop talkin'." '

'Do you think he will die?' asked Mary.

'Mother says there's no reason why any child should live that gets no fresh air an' doesn't do nothin' but lie on his back an' read picture-books an' take medicine. He's weak and hates th' trouble o' bein' taken out o' doors, an' he gets cold so easy he says it makes him ill.'

Mary sat and looked at the fire.

'I wonder,' she said slowly, 'if it would not do him good to go out into a garden and watch things growing. It did me good.'

'One of th' worst fits he ever had,' said Martha, 'was one time they took him out where the roses is by the fountain. He'd been readin' in a paper about people gettin' somethin' he called "rose cold", an' he began to sneeze an' said he'd got it, an' then a new gardener as didn't know th' rules passed by an' looked at him curious. He threw himself into a passion an' he said he'd looked at him because he was going to be a hunchback. He cried himself into a fever an' was ill all night.'

'If he ever gets angry at me, I'll never go and see him again,' said Mary.

'He'll have thee if he wants thee,' said Martha. 'Tha' may as well know that at th' start.'

Very soon afterwards a bell rang, and she rolled up her knitting.

'I dare say th' nurse wants me to stay with him a bit,' she said. 'I hope he's in a good temper.'

She was out of the room about ten minutes and then she came back with a puzzled expression.

'Well, tha' has bewitched him,' she said. 'He's up on his sofa with his picture-books. He's told the nurse to stay away until six o'clock. I'm to wait in the next room. Th' minute she was gone he called me to him an' says: "I want Mary Lennox to come and talk to me, and remember you're not to tell anyone." You'd better go as quick as you can.'

Mary was quite willing to go quickly. She did not want to see Colin as much as she wanted to see Dickon, but she wanted to see him very much.

There was a bright fire on the hearth when she entered his room, and in the daylight she saw it was a very beautiful room indeed. There were rich colours in the rugs and hangings and pictures and books on the walls, which made it look glowing and comfortable even in spite of the grey sky and falling rain. Colin looked rather like a picture himself. He was wrapped in a velvet dressing-gown and sat against a big brocaded cushion. He had a red spot on each cheek.

'Come in,' he said. 'I've been thinking about you all the morning.'

'I've been thinking about you, too,' answered Mary. 'You don't know how frightened Martha is. She says Mrs Medlock will think she told me about you and then she will be sent away.'

He frowned.

'Go and tell her to come here,' he said. 'She is in the next room.'

Mary went and brought her back. Poor Martha was shaking in her shoes. Colin was still frowning.

'Have you to do what I please or have you not?' he demanded.

'I have to do what you please, sir,' Martha faltered, turning quite red.

'Has Medlock to do what I please?'

'Everybody has, sir,' said Martha.

'Well, then, if I order you to bring Miss Mary to me, how can Medlock send you away if she finds it out?'

'Please don't let her, sir,' pleaded Martha.

'I'll send *her* away if she dares to say a word about such a thing,' said Master Craven grandly. 'She wouldn't like that, I can tell you.'

'Thank you, sir,' bobbing a curtsy. 'I want to do my duty, sir.'

'What I want is your duty,' said Colin, more grandly still. 'I'll take care of you. Now go away.'

When the door closed behind Martha, Colin found Mistress Mary gazing at him as if he had set her wondering.

'Why do you look at me like that?' he asked her. 'What are you thinking about?'

'I am thinking about two things.'

'What are they? Sit down and tell me.'

'This is the first one,' said Mary, seating herself on the big stool. 'Once in India I saw a boy who was a rajah. He had rubies and emeralds and diamonds stuck all over him. He spoke to his people just as you spoke to Martha. Everybody had to do everything he told them –

in a minute. I think they would have been killed if they hadn't.'

'I shall make you tell me about rajahs presently,' he said, 'but first tell me what the second thing was.'

'I was thinking,' said Mary, 'how different you are from Dickon.'

'Who is Dickon?' he said. 'What a queer name!'

She might as well tell him, she thought. She could talk about Dickon without mentioning the secret garden. She had liked to hear Martha talk about him. Besides, she longed to talk about him. It would seem to bring him nearer.

'He is Martha's brother. He is twelve years old,' she explained. 'He is not like anyone else in the world. He can charm foxes and squirrels and birds just as the natives in India charm snakes. He plays a very soft tune on a pipe and they come and listen.'

There were some big books on a table at his side, and he dragged one suddenly towards him.

'There is a picture of a snake-charmer in this,' he exclaimed. 'Come and look at it.'

The book was a beautiful one with superb coloured illustrations, and he turned to one of them.

'Can he do that?' he asked eagerly.

'He played on his pipe and they listened,' Mary explained. 'But he doesn't call it Magic. He says it's because he lives on the moor so much and he knows their ways. He says he feels sometimes as if he was a bird or a rabbit himself, he likes them so. I think he asked the robin questions. It seemed as if they talked to each other in soft chirps.'

Colin lay back on his cushion and his eyes grew larger and larger and the spots on his cheeks burned.

'Tell me some more about him,' he said.

'He knows all about eggs and nests,' Mary went on. 'And he knows where foxes and badgers and otters live. He keeps them secret so that other boys won't find their holes and frighten them. He knows about everything that grows or lives on the moor.'

'Does he like the moor?' said Colin. 'How can he when it's such a great, bare, dreary place?'

'It's the most beautiful place,' protested Mary. 'Thousands of lovely things grow on it, and there are thousands of little creatures all busy building nests and making holes and burrows and chippering or singing or squeaking to each other. They are so busy and having such fun under the earth or in the trees or heather. It's their world.'

'How do you know all that?' said Colin, turning on his elbow to look at her.

'I have never been there once, really,' said Mary, suddenly remembering. 'I only drove over it in the dark. I thought it was hideous. Martha told me about it first, and then Dickon. When Dickon talks about it you feel as if you saw things and heard them, and as if you were standing in the heather with the sun shining and the gorse smelling like honey – and all full of bees and butterflies.'

'You never see anything if you are ill,' said Colin restlessly. He looked like a person listening to a new sound in the distance and wondering what it was.

'You can't if you stay in a room,' said Mary.

'I couldn't go on the moor,' he said in a resentful tone.

Mary was silent for a minute, and then she said something bold.

'You might – some time.'

He moved as if he were startled.

'Go on the moor! How could I? I am going to die.'

'How do you know?' said Mary unsympathetically. She didn't like the way he had of talking about dying. She did not feel very sympathetic. She felt rather as if he almost boasted about it.

'Oh, I've heard it ever since I remember,' he answered crossly. 'They are always whispering about it and thinking I don't notice. They wish I would, too.'

Mistress Mary felt quite contrary. She pinched her lips together.

'If they wished I would,' she said, 'I wouldn't. Who wishes you would?'

'The servants – and, of course, Dr Craven, because he would get Misselthwaite and be rich instead of poor. He daren't say so, but he always looks cheerful when I am worse. When I had typhoid fever his face got quite fat. I think my father wishes it, too.'

'I don't believe he does,' said Mary quite obstinately.

That made Colin turn and look at her again.

'Don't you?' he said.

And then he lay back on his cushion and was still, as if he were thinking. And there was quite a long silence. Perhaps they were both of them thinking strange things children do not usually think of.

'I like the grand doctor from London, because he made them take the iron thing off,' said Mary at last. 'Did he say you were going to die?'

'No.'

'What did he say?'

'He didn't whisper,' Colin answered. 'Perhaps he knew I hated whispering. I heard him say one thing quite aloud. He said: "The lad might live if he would make up his mind to it. Put him in the humour." It sounded as if he was in a temper.'

'I'll tell you who would put you in the humour, perhaps,' said Mary, reflecting. She felt as if she would like this thing to be settled one way or the other. 'I believe Dickon would. He's always talking about live things. He never talks about dead things or things that are ill. He's always looking up in the sky to watch birds flying – or looking down at the earth to see something growing. He has such round blue eyes and they are so wide open with looking about. And he laughs such a big laugh with his wide mouth – and his cheeks are as red – as red as cherries.'

She pulled her stool nearer to the sofa and her expression quite changed at the remembrance of the wide, curving mouth and wide open eyes.

'See here,' she said. 'Don't let us talk about dying; I don't like it. Let us talk about living. Let us talk and talk about Dickon. And then we will look at your pictures.'

It was the best thing she could have said. To talk about Dickon meant to talk about the moor and about the cottage and the fourteen people who lived in it on sixteen shillings a week – and the children who got fat on the moor grass like the wild ponies. And about Dickon's mother – and the skipping-rope – and the moor with the sun on it – and about pale green points sticking up out of the black sod. And it was all so alive that Mary talked more than she had ever talked before – and Colin both talked and listened as he had never done either before. And they both began to laugh over nothing as children will when they are happy together. And they laughed so that in the end they were making as much noise as if they had been two ordinary, healthy, natural, ten-year-old creatures – instead of a hard, little, unloving girl and a sickly boy who believed that he was going to die.

They enjoyed themselves so much that they forgot the pictures and they forgot about the time. They had been laughing quite loudly over Ben Weatherstaff and his robin, and Colin was actually sitting up as if he had forgotten about his weak back when he suddenly remembered something.

'Do you know there is one thing we have never once thought of?' he said. 'We are cousins.'

It seemed so queer that they had talked so much and never remembered this simple thing that they laughed more than ever, because they had got into the humour to laugh at anything. And in the midst of the fun the door opened and in walked Dr Craven and Mrs Medlock.

Dr Craven started in actual alarm and Mrs Medlock almost fell back because he had accidentally bumped against her.

'Good Lord!' exclaimed poor Mrs Medlock, with her eyes almost starting out of her head. 'Good Lord!'

'What is this?' said Dr Craven, coming forward. 'What does it mean?'

Then Mary was reminded of the boy rajah again.

Colin answered as if neither the doctor's alarm nor Mrs Medlock's terror were of the slightest consequence. He was as little disturbed or frightened as if an elderly cat and dog had walked into the room.

'This is my cousin, Mary Lennox,' he said. 'I asked her to come and talk to me. I like her. She must come and talk to me whenever I send for her.'

Dr Craven turned reproachfully to Mrs Medlock.

'Oh, sir,' she panted. 'I don't know how it's happened. There's not a servant on the place that'd dare to talk – they all have their orders.'

'Nobody told her anything,' said Colin. 'She heard me crying and found me herself. I am glad she came. Don't be silly, Medlock.'

Mary saw that Dr Craven did not look pleased, but it was quite plain that he dare not oppose his patient. He sat down by Colin and felt his pulse.

'I am afraid there has been too much excitement. Excitement is not good for you, my boy,' he said.

'I should be excited if she kept away,' answered Colin, his eyes beginning to look dangerously sparkling. 'I am better. She makes me better. The nurse must bring up her tea with mine. We will have tea together.'

Mrs Medlock and Dr Craven looked at each other in a troubled way, but there was evidently nothing to be done.

'He does look rather better, sir,' ventured Mrs Medlock. 'But' – thinking the matter over – 'he looked better this morning before she came into the room.'

'She came into the room last night. She stayed with me a long time. She sang a Hindustani song to me and it made me go to sleep,' said Colin. 'I was better when I wakened up. I wanted my breakfast. I want my tea now. Tell nurse, Medlock.'

Dr Craven did not stay very long. He talked to the nurse for a few minutes when she came into the room and said a few words of warning to Colin. He must not talk too much; he must not forget that he was ill; he must not forget that he was very easily tired. Mary thought that there seemed to be a number of uncomfortable things he was not to forget.

Colin looked fretful and kept his strange, black-lashed eyes fixed on Dr Craven's face.

'I *want* to forget it,' he said at last. 'She makes me forget it. That is why I want her.'

Dr Craven did not look happy when he left the room. He gave a puzzled glance at the little girl sitting on the large stool. She had become a stiff, silent child again as soon as he entered, and he could not see what the attraction was. The boy actually did look brighter, however – and he sighed rather heavily as he went down the corridor.

They are always wanting me to eat things when I don't want to,' said Colin, as the nurse brought in the tea and put it on the table by the sofa. 'Now, if you'll eat I will. Those muffins look so nice and hot. Tell me about rajahs.'

15

Nest Building

AFTER another week of rain, the high arch of blue sky appeared again and the sun which poured down was quite hot. Though there had been no chance to see either the secret garden or Dickon, Mistress Mary had enjoyed herself very much. The week had not seemed long. She had spent hours of every day with Colin in his room, talking about rajahs or gardens or Dickon and the cottage on the moor. They had looked at the splendid books and pictures, and sometimes Mary had read things to Colin, and sometimes he had read a little to her. When he was amused and interested she thought he scarcely looked like an invalid at all, except that his face was so colourless and he was always on the sofa.

'You are a sly young one to listen and get out of your bed to go following things up like you did that night,'

Mrs Medlock said once. 'But there's no saying it's not been a sort of blessing to the lot of us. He's not had a tantrum or a whining fit since you made friends. The nurse was just going to give up the case because she was so sick of him, but she says she doesn't mind staying now you've gone on duty with her,' laughing a little.

In her talks with Colin, Mary had tried to be very cautious about the secret garden. There were certain things she wanted to find out from him, but she felt that she must find them out without asking him direct questions. In the first place, as she began to like to be with him, she wanted to discover whether he was the kind of boy you could tell a secret to. He was not in the least like Dickon, but he was evidently so pleased with the idea of a garden no one knew anything about that she thought perhaps he could be trusted. But she had not known him long enough to be sure. The second thing she wanted to find out was this: If he could be trusted – if he really could – wouldn't it be possible to take him to the garden without having anyone find it out? The grand doctor had said that he must have fresh air, and Colin had said that he would not mind fresh air in a secret garden. Perhaps if he had a great deal of fresh air and knew Dickon and the robin and saw things growing, he might not think so much about dying. Mary had seen herself in the glass sometimes lately when she had realised that she looked quite a different creature from the child she had seen when she arrived from India. This child looked nicer. Even Martha had seen a change in her.

'Th' air from th' moor has done thee good already,' she had said. 'Tha'rt not nigh so yeller and tha'rt not nigh so scrawny. Even tha' hair doesn't slamp down on tha' head so flat. It's got some life in it so as it sticks out a bit.'

'It's like me,' said Mary. 'It's growing stronger and fatter. I'm sure there's more of it.'

'It looks it, for sure,' said Martha, ruffling it up a little round her face. 'Tha'rt not half so ugly when it's that way an' there's a bit o' red in tha' cheeks.'

If gardens and fresh air had been good for her, perhaps they would be good for Colin. But then, if he hated people to look at him, perhaps he would not like to see Dickon.

'Why does it make you angry when you are looked at?' she inquired one day.

'I always hated it,' he answered, 'even when I was very little. Then when they took me to the seaside and I used to lie in my carriage, everybody used to stare and ladies would stop and talk to my nurse and then they would begin to whisper, and I knew then they were saying I shouldn't live to grow up. Then sometimes the ladies would pat my cheeks and say "Poor child!" Once when a lady did that I screamed out loud and bit her hand. She was so frightened she ran away.'

'She thought you had gone mad like a dog,' said Mary, not at all admiringly.

'I don't care what she thought,' said Colin, frowning.

'I wonder why you didn't scream and bite me when I came into your room?' said Mary. Then she began to smile slowly.

'I thought you were a ghost or a dream,' he said. 'You can't bite a ghost or a dream, and if you scream they don't care.'

'Would you hate it if – if a boy looked at you?' Mary asked uncertainly.

He lay back on his cushion and paused thoughtfully.

'There's one boy,' he said quite slowly, as if he were thinking over every word, 'there's one boy I believe I shouldn't mind. It's that boy who knows where the foxes live – Dickon.'

'I'm sure you wouldn't mind him,' said Mary.

'The birds don't and other animals,' he said, still thinking it over, 'perhaps that's why I shouldn't. He's a sort of animal-charmer and I am a boy animal.'

Then he laughed and she laughed, too; in fact, it ended in their both laughing a great deal and finding the idea of a boy animal hiding in his hole very funny indeed.

What Mary felt afterwards was that she need not fear about Dickon.

*

On that first morning when the sky was blue again, Mary wakened very early. The sun was pouring in slanting rays through the blinds and there was something so joyous in the sight of it that she jumped out of bed and ran to the window. She drew up the blinds and opened the window itself, and a great waft of fresh, scented air blew in upon her. The moor was blue and the whole world looked as if something Magic had happened to it. There were tender little fluting sounds here and there and everywhere, as if scores of birds were beginning to tune up for a concert. Mary put her hand out of the window and held it in the sun.

'It's warm – warm!' she said. 'It will make the green points push up and up and up, and it will make the bulbs and roots work and struggle with all their might under the earth.'

She kneeled down and leaned out of the window as far as she could, breathing big breaths and sniffing the air until she laughed because she remembered what Dickon's mother had said about the end of his nose quivering like a rabbit's.

'It must be very early,' she said. 'The little clouds are all pink and I've never seen the sky look like this. No one is up. I don't even hear the stable-boys.'

A sudden thought made her scramble to her feet.

'I can't wait! I am going to see the garden!'

She had learned to dress herself by this time, and she put on her clothes in five minutes. She knew a small side door which she could unbolt herself, and she flew downstairs in her stocking feet and put on her shoes in the hall. She unchained and unbolted and unlocked, and when the door was open she sprang across the step with one bound, and there she was standing on the grass, which seemed to have turned green, and with the sun pouring down on her and warm, sweet wafts about her and the fluting and twittering and singing coming from every bush and tree. She clasped her hands for pure joy and looked up in the sky, and it was so blue and pink and pearly and white and flooded with springtime light that she felt as if she must flute and sing aloud herself, and knew that thrushes and robins and skylarks could not possibly help it. She ran around the shrubs and paths towards the secret garden.

'It is all different already,' she said. 'The grass is greener and things are sticking up everywhere and things are uncurling and green buds of leaves are showing. This afternoon I am sure Dickon will come.'

The long warm rain had done strange things to the

herbaceous beds which bordered the walk by the lower wall. There were things sprouting and pushing out from the roots of clumps of plants and there were actually here and there glimpses of royal purple and yellow unfurling among the stems of crocuses. Six months before Mistress Mary would not have seen how the world was waking up, but now she missed nothing.

When she had reached the place where the door hid itself under the ivy, she was startled by a curious loud sound. It was the caw-caw of a crow, and it came from the top of the wall, and when she looked up, there sat a big, glossy-plumaged, blue-black bird, looking down at her very wisely indeed. She had never seen a crow so close before, and he made her a little nervous, but the next moment he spread his wings and flapped away across the garden. She hoped he was not going to stay inside, and she pushed the door open wondering if he would. When she got fairly into the garden she saw that he probably did intend to stay, because he had alighted on a dwarf apple-tree, and under the apple-tree was lying a little reddish animal with a busy tail, and both of them were watching the stooping body and the rust-red head of Dickon, who was kneeling on the grass working hard.

Mary flew across the grass to him.

'Oh, Dickon! Dickon!' she cried out. 'How could you

get here so early! How could you! The sun has only just got up!' He got up himself, laughing and glowing, and tousled; his eyes like a bit of the sky.

'Eh!' he said. 'I was up long before him. How could I have stayed abed! Th' world's all fair begun again this morning', it has. An' it's workin' an' hummin' an' scratchin' an' pipin' an' nest-buildin' an' breathin' out scents, till you've got to be out on it 'stead o' lyin' on your back. When th' sun did jump up, th' moor went mad for joy, an' I was in the midst of th' heather, an' I run like mad myself, shoutin' an' singin'. An' I come straight here. I couldn't have stayed away. Why, th' garden was lyin' here waitin'!'

Mary put her hands on her chest, panting, as if she had been running herself.

'Oh, Dickon! Dickon!' she said. 'I'm so happy I can scarcely breathe!'

Seeing him talking to a stranger, the little bushy-tailed animal rose from its place under the tree and came to him, and the rook, cawing once, flew down from its branch and settled quietly on his shoulder.

'This is th' little fox cub,' he said, rubbing the little reddish animal's head. 'It's named Captain. An' this here's Soot. Soot, he flew across th' moor with me, an' Captain he run same as if th' hounds had been after him. They both felt same as I did.'

Neither of the creatures looked as if they were the least afraid of Mary. When Dickon began to walk about, Soot stayed on his shoulder and Captain trotted quietly close to his side.

'See here!' said Dickon. 'See how these has pushed up, an' these an' these! An' eh! look at these here!'

He threw himself upon his knees and Mary went down beside him. They had come upon a whole clump of crocuses burst into purple and orange and gold. Mary bent her face down and kissed and kissed them.

'You never kiss a person in that way,' she said when she lifted her head. 'Flowers are so different.'

He looked puzzled, but smiled.

'Eh!' he said, 'I've kissed Mother many a time that way when I come in from th' moor after a day's roamin' an' she stood there at th' door in th' sun, lookin' so glad an' comfortable.'

They ran from one part of the garden to another and found so many wonders that they were obliged to remind themselves that they must whisper or speak low. He showed her swelling leaf-buds on rose branches which had seemed dead. He showed her ten thousand new green points pushing through the mould. They put their eager young noses close to the earth and sniffed its warmed springtime breathing; they dug and pulled and laughed low with rapture until Mistress Mary's hair was as tumbled as Dickon's and her cheeks were almost as poppy red as his.

There was every joy on earth in the secret garden that morning, and in the midst of them came a delight more delightful than all, because it was more wonderful. Swiftly something flew across the wall and darted through the trees to a close-grown corner, a little flare of red-breasted bird with something hanging from its beak. Dickon stood quite still and put his hand on Mary almost as if they had suddenly found themselves laughing in a church.

'We munnot stir,' he whispered in broad Yorkshire. 'We munnot scarce breathe. I knowed he was mate-huntin' when I seed him last. It's Ben Weatherstaff's robin. He's buildin' his nest. He'll stay here if us don't flight him.'

They settled down softly upon the grass and sat there without moving.

'Us mustn't seem as if us was watchin' him too close,' said Dickon. 'He'd be out with us for good if he got th' notion us was interferin' now. He'll be a good bit different till all this is over. He's settin' up housekeepin'. He'll be shyer an' readier to take things ill. He's got no time for visitin' an' gossipin'. Us must keep still a bit an' try to look as if us was grass an' trees an' bushes. Then when he's got used to seein' us I'll chirp a bit an' he'll know us'll not be in his way.'

Mistress Mary was not at all sure that she knew, as Dickon seemed to, how to try to look like grass and trees and bushes. But he had said the queer thing as if it were the simplest and most natural thing in the world, and she felt it must be quite easy to him, and, indeed, she watched him for a few minutes carefully, wondering if it was possible for him to turn quietly green and put out branches and leaves. But he only sat wonderfully still, and when he spoke dropped his voice to such a softness that it was curious that she could hear him, but she could.

'It's part o' th' springtime, this nest-buildin' is,' he said. 'I warrant it's been goin' on in th' same way every year since th' world was begun. They've got their way o' thinkin' and doin' things, an' a body had better not meddle. You can lose a friend in springtime easier than any other season if you're too curious.'

'If we talk about him I can't help looking at him,' Mary said as softly as possible. 'We must talk of something else. There is something I want to tell you.'

'He'll like it better if us talks o' somethin' else,' said Dickon. 'What is it tha's got to tell me?'

'Well – do you know about Colin?' she whispered.

He turned his head to look at her.

'What does tha' know about him?' he asked.

'I've seen him. I have been to talk to him every day this week. He wants me to come. He says I'm making him forget about being ill and dying,' answered Mary.

Dickon looked actually relieved as soon as the surprise died away from his round face.

'I am glad o' that,' he exclaimed. 'I'm right down glad. It makes me easier. I knowed I must say nothin' about him an' I don't like havin' to hide things.'

'Don't you like hiding the garden?' said Mary.

'I'll never tell about it,' he answered. 'But I says to Mother: "Mother," I says, "I got a secret to keep. It's not a bad 'un, tha' knows that. It's no worse than hidin' where a bird's nest is. Tha' doesn't mind it, does tha'?"'

Mary always wanted to hear about Mother.

'What did she say?' she asked, not at all afraid to hear.

Dickon grinned sweet-temperedly.

'It was just like her, what she said,' he answered. 'She give my head a bit of a rub an' laughed an' she says: "Eh, lad, tha' can have all th' secrets tha' likes. I've knowed thee twelve year."'

'How did you know about Colin?' asked Mary.

'Everybody as knowed about Mester Craven knowed there was a little lad as was like to be a cripple, an' they knowed Mester Craven didn't like him to be talked about. Folks is sorry for Mester Craven because Mrs Craven was such a pretty young lady an' they was so fond of each other. Mrs Medlock stops in our cottage whenever she goes to Thwaite an' she doesn't mind talkin' to Mother before us children, because she knows us has been brought up to be trusty. How did tha' find out about him? Martha was in fine trouble th' last time she came home. She said tha'd heard him frettin' an' tha' was askin' questions an' she didn't know what to say.'

Mary told him her story about the midnight wuthering of the wind which had wakened her and about the faint, far-off sounds of the complaining voice which had led her down the dark corridors with her candle and had ended with her opening of the door of the dimly lighted room with the carven four-poster bed in the corner. When she described the small, ivory-white face and the strange black-rimmed eyes, Dickon shook his head.

'Them's just like his mother's eyes, only hers was always laughin', they say,' he said. 'They say as Mr Craven can't bear to see him when he's awake, an' it's because his eyes is so like his mother's an' yet looks so different in his miserable bit of a face.'

'Do you think he wants him to die?' whispered Mary.

'No, but he wishes he'd never been born. Mother, she says that's th' worst thing on earth for a child. Them as is not wanted scarce ever thrives. Mester Craven, he'd buy anythin' as money could buy for th' poor lad, but he'd like to forget he's on earth. For one thing, he's afraid he'll look at him some day and find he's growed hunchback.'

'Colin's so afraid of it himself that he won't sit up,' said Mary. 'He says he's always thinking that if he should feel a lump coming he should go crazy and scream himself to death.'

'Eh! he oughtn't to lie there thinkin' things like that,' said Dickon. 'No lad could get well as thought them sort o' things.'

The fox was lying on the grass close by him looking up to ask for a pat now and then, and Dickon bent down and rubbed his neck softly and thought a few minutes in silence. Presently he lifted his head and looked round the garden.

'When first we got in here,' he said, 'it seemed like everything was grey. Look round now and tell me if tha' doesn't see a difference.'

Mary looked and caught her breath a little.

'Why!' she cried, 'the grey wall is changing. It is as if a green mist were creeping over it. It's almost like a green gauze veil.'

'Aye,' said Dickon, 'an' it'll be greener and greener till th' grey's all gone. Can tha' guess what I was thinkin'?'

'I know it was something nice,' said Mary eagerly. 'I believe it was something about Colin.'

'I was thinkin' that if he was out here he wouldn't be watchin' for lumps to grow on his back; he'd be watchin' for buds to break on th' rose-bushes, an' he'd likely be healthier,' explained Dickon. 'I was wonderin' if us could ever get him in th' humour to come out here an' lie under th' trees in his carriage.'

'I've been wondering that myself. I've thought of it almost every time I've talked to him,' said Mary. 'I've wondered if he could keep a secret and I've wondered if we could bring him here without anyone seeing us. I thought perhaps you could push his carriage. The doctor said he must have fresh air, and if he wants us to take him out, no one dare disobey him. He won't go out for other people, and perhaps they will be glad if he will go out with us. He could order the gardeners to keep away so they wouldn't find out.'

Dickon was thinking very hard as he scratched Captain's back.

'It'd be good for him, I'll warrant,' he said. 'Us'd not be thinkin' he'd better never been born. Us'd be just two children watchin' a garden grow, an' he'd be another. Two lads an' a little lass just lookin' on at th' springtime. I warrant it'd be better than doctor's stuff.'

'He's been lying in his room so long and he's always been so afraid of his back that it has made him queer,' said Mary. 'He knows a good many things out of books, but he doesn't know anything else. He says he has been too ill to notice things, and he hates going out of doors and hates gardens and gardeners. But he likes to hear about this garden because it is a secret. I daren't tell him much, but he said he wanted to see it.'

'Us'll have him out here some time for sure,' said Dickon. 'I could push his carriage well enough. Has tha' noticed how th' robin an' his mate has been workin' while we've been sittin' here? Look at him perched on that branch wonderin' where it'd be best to put that twig he's got in his beak.'

He made one of his low, whistling calls, and the robin turned his head and looked at him inquiringly, still holding his twig. Dickon spoke to him as Ben Weatherstaff did, but Dickon's tone was one of friendly advice.

'Wheres'ever tha' puts it,' he said, 'it'll be all right. Tha' knew how to build tha' nest before tha' came out o' th' egg. Get on with thee, lad. Tha'st got no time to lose.'

'Oh! I do like to hear you talk to him!' Mary said laughing delightedly. 'Ben Weatherstaff scolds him and makes fun of him, but he hops about and looks as if he understood every word, and I know he likes it. Ben

Weatherstaff says he is so conceited he would rather have stones thrown at him than not be noticed.'

Dickon laughed too, and went on talking.

'Tha' knows us won't trouble thee,' he said to the robin. 'Us is near bein' wild things ourselves. Us is nest-buildin' too, bless thee. Look out tha' doesn't tell on us.'

And though the robin did not answer, because his beak was occupied, Mary knew that when he flew away with his twig to his own corner of the garden, the darkness of his dew-bright eye meant that he would not tell their secret for the world.

16

'I Won't!' Said Mary

THEY found a great deal to do that morning, and Mary was late in returning to the house and was also in such a hurry to get back to her work that she quite forgot Colin until the last moment.

'Tell Colin that I can't come and see him yet,' she said to Martha. 'I'm very busy in the garden.'

Martha looked rather frightened.

'Eh! Miss Mary,' she said, 'it may put him all out of humour when I tell him that.'

But Mary was not as afraid of him as other people were, and she was not a self-sacrificing person.

'I can't stay,' she answered. 'Dickon's waiting for me'; and she ran away.

The afternoon was even lovelier and busier than the morning had been. Already nearly all the weeds were cleared out of the garden and most of the roses and trees had been pruned or dug about. Dickon had brought a spade of his own, and he had taught Mary to use all her tools, so that by this time it was plain that though the lovely wild place was not likely to become a 'gardener's garden', it would be a wilderness of growing things before the springtime was over.

'There'll be apple-blossoms an' cherry-blossoms overhead,' Dickon said, working away with all his might. 'An' there'll be peach an' plum trees in bloom against th' walls, an' th' grass'll be a carpet o' flowers'.

The little fox and the rook were as happy and busy as they were, and the robin and his mate flew backwards and forwards like tiny streaks of lightning. Sometimes the rook flapped his black wings and soared away over the tree-tops in the park. Each time he came back and perched near Dickon and cawed several times as if he were relating his adventures, and Dickon talked to him just as he had talked to the robin. Once when Dickon was so busy that he did not answer him at first, Soot flew on to his shoulder and gently tweaked his ear with his large beak. When Mary wanted to rest a little, Dickon sat down with her under a tree, and once he took his pipe out of his pocket and played the soft, strange little notes, and two squirrels appeared on the wall and looked and listened.

'Tha's a good bit stronger than tha' was,' Dickon said, looking at her as she was digging. 'Tha's beginnin' to look different, for sure.'

Mary was glowing with exercise and good spirits.

'I'm getting fatter and fatter every day,' she said quite exultantly. 'Mrs Medlock will have to get me some bigger dresses. Martha says my hair is growing thicker. It isn't so flat and stringy.'

The sun was beginning to set and sending deep gold-coloured rays slanting under the trees when they parted.

'It'll be fine tomorrow,' said Dickon. 'I'll be at work by sunrise.'

'So will I,' said Mary.

*

She ran back to the house as quickly as her feet would carry her. She wanted to tell Colin about Dickon's fox cub and the rook and about what the springtime had been doing. She felt sure he would like to hear. So it was not very pleasant when she opened the door of her room to see Martha standing waiting for her with a doleful face.

'What is the matter?' she asked. 'What did Colin say when you told him I couldn't come?'

'Eh!' said Martha, 'I wish tha'd gone. He was nigh

goin' into one o' his tantrums. There's been a nice to do all afternoon to keep him quiet. He would watch the clock all th' time.'

Mary's lips pinched themselves together. She was no more used to considering other people than Colin was, and she saw no reason why an ill-tempered boy should interfere with the thing she liked best. She knew nothing about the pitifulness of people who had been ill and nervous and who did not know that they could control their tempers and need not make other people ill and nervous, too. When she had had a headache in India, she had done her best to see that everybody else also had a headache or something quite as bad. And she felt she was quite right; but, of course, now she felt that Colin was quite wrong.

He was not on his sofa when she went into his room. He was lying flat on his back in bed, and he did not turn his head towards her as she came in. This was a bad beginning, and Mary marched up to him with her stiff manner.

'Why didn't you get up?' she said.

'I did get up this morning when I thought you were coming,' he answered, without looking at her. 'I made them put me back in bed this afternoon. My back ached and my head ached and I was tired. Why didn't you come?'

'I was working in the garden with Dickon,' said Mary.

Colin frowned and condescended to look at her.

'I won't let that boy come here if you go and stay with him instead of coming to talk to me,' he said.

Mary flew into a fine passion. She could fly into a passion without making a noise. She just grew sour and obstinate and did not care what happened.

'If you send Dickon away, I'll never come into this room again,' she retorted.

'You'll have to if I want you,' said Colin.

'I won't!' said Mary.

'I'll make you,' said Colin. 'They shall drag you in.'

'Shall they, Mr Rajah!' said Mary fiercely. 'They may drag me in, but they can't make me talk when they get me here. I'll sit and clench my teeth and never tell you one thing. I won't even look at you. I'll stare at the floor!'

They were a nice agreeable pair as they glared at each other. If they had been two little street boys they would have sprung at each other and had a rough-and-tumble fight. As it was, they did the next thing to it.

'You are a selfish thing!' cried Colin.

'What are you?' said Mary. 'Selfish people always say that. Anyone is selfish who doesn't do what they want.

You're more selfish than I am. You're the most selfish boy I ever saw.'

'I'm not!' snapped Colin. 'I'm not as selfish as your fine Dickon is! He keeps you playing in the dirt when he knows I am all by myself. He's selfish, if you like!'

Mary's eyes flashed fire.

'He's nicer than any other boy that ever lived!' she said. 'He's – he's like an angel!' It might sound rather silly to say that, but she did not care.

'A nice angel!' Colin sneered ferociously. 'He's a common cottage boy off the moor!'

'He's better than a common rajah!' retorted Mary. 'He's a thousand times better!'

Because she was the stronger of the two, she was beginning to get the better of him. The truth was that he had never had a fight with anyone like himself in his life, and, upon the whole, it was rather good for him, though neither he nor Mary knew anything about that. He turned his head on his pillow and shut his eyes and a big tear was squeezed out and ran down his cheek. He was beginning to feel pathetic and sorry for himself – not for anyone else.

'I'm not as selfish as you, because I'm always ill, and I'm sure there is a lump coming on my back,' he said. 'And I am going to die besides.'

'You're not!' contradicted Mary unsympathetically.

He opened his eyes quite wide with indignation. He had never heard such a thing said before. He was at once furious and slightly pleased, if a person could be both at the same time.

'I'm not?' he cried. 'I am! You know I am! Everybody says so.'

'I don't believe it!' said Mary sourly. 'You just say that to make people sorry. I believe you're proud of it. I don't believe it! If you were a nice boy it might be true – but you're too nasty!'

In spite of his invalid back, Colin sat up in bed in quite a healthy rage.

'Get out of the room!' he shouted, and he caught hold of his pillow and threw it at her. He was not strong enough to throw it far, and it only fell at her feet, but Mary's face looked as pinched as a nut-cracker.

'I'm going,' she said. 'And I won't come back!'

She walked to the door, and when she reached it she turned round and spoke again.

'I was going to tell you all sorts of nice things,' she said. 'Dickon brought his fox and his rook and I was going to tell you all about them. Now I won't tell you a single thing!'

She marched out of the door and closed it behind her, and there to her great astonishment she found the trained nurse standing as if she had been listening and, more amazing still – she was laughing. She was a big, handsome young woman, who ought not to have been a trained nurse at all, as she could not bear invalids, and she was always making excuses to leave Colin to Martha or anyone else who would take her place. Mary had never liked her, and she simply stood and gazed up at her as she stood giggling into her handkerchief.

'What are you laughing at?' she asked her.

'At you two young ones,' said the nurse. 'It's the best thing that could happen to the sickly, pampered thing to have someone to stand up to him that's as spoiled as himself'; and she laughed into her handkerchief again. 'If he'd had a young vixen of a sister to fight with, it would have been the saving of him.'

'Is he going to die?'

'I don't know and I don't care,' said the nurse. 'Hysterics and temper are half what ails him.'

'What are hysterics?' asked Mary.

'You'll find out if you work him into a tantrum after this – but at any rate, you've given him something to have hysterics about, and I am glad of it.'

Mary went back to her room not feeling at all as she had felt when she had come in from the garden. She was cross and disappointed, but not at all sorry for Colin. She had looked forward to telling him a great many things, and she had meant to try to make up her mind whether it would be safe to trust him with the great secret. She had been beginning to think it would be, but now she had changed her mind entirely. She would never tell him and he could stay in his room and never get any fresh air and die if he liked! It would serve him right! She felt so sour and unrelenting that for a few minutes she almost forgot about Dickon and the green veil creeping over the world and the soft wind blowing down from the moor.

Martha was waiting for her, and the trouble in her face had been temporarily replaced by interest and curiosity. There was a wooden box on the table and its cover had been removed and revealed that it was full of neat packages.

'Mr Craven sent it to you,' said Martha. 'It looks as if it had picture-books in it.'

Mary remembered what he had asked her the day she had gone to his room. 'Do you want anything – dolls – toys – books?' She opened the package wondering if he had sent a doll, and also wondering what she should do with it if he had. But he had not sent one. There were several beautiful books such as Colin had, and two of them were about gardens and were full of pictures. There were two or three games and there was a beautiful little writing-case with a gold monogram on it and a gold pen and ink-stand.

Everything was so nice that her pleasure began to crowd her anger out of her mind. She had not expected him to remember her at all, and her hard little heart grew quite warm.

'I can write better than I can print,' she said, 'and the first thing I shall write with that pen will be a letter to tell him I am much obliged.'

If she had been friends with Colin she would have run to show him her presents at once, and they would have looked at the pictures and read some of the gardening books and perhaps tried playing the games, and he would have enjoyed himself so much he would never once have thought he was going to die or have put his hand on his spine to see if there was a lump coming. He had a way of doing that which she could not bear. It gave her an uncomfortable, frightened feeling because he always looked so frightened himself. He said that if he felt even quite a little lump some day he should know his hunch had begun to grow. Something he had heard Mrs Medlock whispering to the nurse had given him the idea, and he had thought over it in secret until it was quite firmly fixed in his mind. Mrs Medlock had said his father's back had begun to show its crookedness in that way when he was a child. He had never told anyone but Mary that most of his 'tantrums', as they called them, grew out of his hysterical hidden fear. Mary had been sorry for him when he had told her.

'He always began to think about it when he was cross or tired,' she said to herself. 'And he has been cross today. Perhaps – perhaps he had been thinking about it all the afternoon.'

She stood still, looking down at the carpet and thinking.

'I said I would never go back again – ' she hesitated, knitting her brows – 'but perhaps, just perhaps, I will go and see – if he wants me – in the morning. Perhaps he'll try to throw his pillow at me again, but – I think – I'll go.'

17

A Tantrum

S HE had got up very early in the morning and had worked hard in the garden, and she was tired and sleepy, so as soon as Martha had brought her supper and she had eaten it, she was glad to go to bed. As she laid her head on the pillow, she murmured to herself:

'I'll go out before breakfast and work with Dickon and then afterwards – I believe – I'll go to see him.'

She thought it was the middle of the night when she was awakened by such dreadful sounds that she jumped out of bed in an instant. What was it – what was it? The next minute she felt quite sure she knew. Doors were opened and shut and there were hurrying feet in the corridors and someone was crying and screaming at the same time, screaming and crying in a horrible way.

'It's Colin,' she said. 'He's having one of those tantrums the nurse calls hysterics. How awful it sounds.'

As she listened to the sobbing screams she did not wonder that people were so frightened that they gave him his own way in everything rather than hear them. She put her hands over her ears and felt sick and shivering.

'I don't know what to do. I don't know what to do,' she kept saying. 'I can't bear it.'

Once she wondered if he would stop if she dared go to him, and then she remembered how he had driven her out of the room and thought that perhaps the sight of her might make him worse. Even when she pressed her hands more tightly over her ears she could not keep the awful sounds out. She hated them so and was so terrified by them that suddenly they began to make her angry, and she felt as if she should like to fly into a tantrum herself and frighten him as he was frightening her. She was not used to anyone's temper but her own. She took her hands from her ears and sprang up and stamped her foot.

'He ought to be stopped! Somebody ought to make him stop! Somebody ought to beat him!' she cried out.

Just then she heard feet almost running down the corridor, and her door opened and the nurse came in. She was not laughing now by any means. She even looked rather pale.

'He's working himself into hysterics,' she said in a great hurry. 'He'll do himself harm. No one can do anything with him. You come and try, like a good child. He likes you.'

'He turned me out of the room this morning,' said Mary, stamping her foot in excitement.

The stamp rather pleased the nurse. The truth was that she had been afraid she might find Mary crying and hiding her head under the bed-clothes.

'That's right,' she said. 'You're in the right humour. You go and scold him. Give him something new to think of. Do go, child, as quick as ever you can.'

It was not until afterwards that Mary realised that the thing had been funny as well as dreadful – that it was funny that all the grown-up people were so frightened that they came to a little girl just because they guessed she was almost as bad as Colin himself.

She flew along the corridor, and the nearer she got to the screams the higher her temper mounted. She felt quite wicked by the time she reached the door. She slapped it open with her hand and ran across the room to the four-poster bed.

'You stop!' she almost shouted. 'You stop! I hate you! Everybody hates you! I wish everybody would run out of the house and let you scream yourself to death! You *will* scream yourself to death in a minute, and I wish you would!'

A nice, sympathetic child could neither have thought nor said such things, but it just happened that the shock of hearing them was the best possible thing for this hysterical boy whom no one had ever dared to restrain or contradict.

He had been lying on his face beating his pillow with his hands, and he actually almost jumped around, he turned so quickly at the sound of the furious little voice. His face looked dreadful, white and red, and swollen, and he was gasping and choking; but savage little Mary did not care an atom.

'If you scream another scream,' she said, 'I'll scream too – and I can scream louder than you can, and I'll frighten you, I'll frighten you!'

He actually had stopped screaming because she had startled him so. The scream which had been coming almost choked him. The tears were streaming down his face and he shook all over.

'I can't stop!' he gasped, and sobbed. 'I can't – I can't!'

'You can!' shouted Mary. 'Half that ails you is hysterics and temper – just hysterics – hysterics – hysterics!' and she stamped each time she said it.

'I felt the lump – I felt it,' choked out Colin. 'I knew I

should. I shall have a hunch on my back and then I shall die,' and he began to writhe again and turned on his face and sobbed and wailed, but he didn't scream.

'You didn't feel a lump!' contradicted Mary fiercely. 'If you did it was only a hysterical lump. Hysterics makes lumps. There's nothing the matter with your horrid back – nothing but hysterics! Turn over and let me look at it.'

She liked the word 'hysterics', and felt somehow as if it had an effect on him. He was probably like herself and had never heard it before.

'Nurse,' she commanded, 'come here and show me his back this minute!'

The nurse, Mrs Medlock, and Martha had been standing huddled together near the door staring at her, their mouths half open. All three had gasped with fright more than once. The nurse came forward as if she were half afraid. Colin was heaving with great breathless sobs.

'Perhaps he – he won't let me,' she hesitated, in a low voice.

Colin heard her, however, and he gasped out between two sobs:

'Sh-show her! She-she'll see then!'

It was a poor, thin back to look at when it was bared. Every rib could be counted and every joint of the spine, though Mistress Mary did not count them as she bent over and examined them with a solemn, savage little face. She looked so sour and old-fashioned that the nurse turned her head aside to hide the twitching of her mouth. There was just a minute's silence, for even Colin tried to hold his breath while Mary looked up and down his spine, and down and up, as intently as if she had been the great doctor from London.

'There's not a single lump there!' she said at last. 'There's not a lump as big as a pin – except backbone lumps, and you can only feel them because you're thin. I've got backbone lumps myself, and they used to stick out as much as yours do, until I began to get fatter, and I am not fat enough yet to hide them. There's not a lump as big as a pin. If you ever say there is again, I shall laugh!'

No one but Colin himself knew what effect those crossly spoken childish words had on him. If he had ever had anyone to talk to about his secret terrors – if he had ever dared to let himself ask questions – if he had had childish companions and had not lain on his back in the huge closed house, breathing an atmosphere heavy with the fears of people who were most of them ignorant and tired of him, he would have found out that most of his fright and illness was created by himself. But he had lain and thought of himself and his aches and weariness for hours and days and months and years. And now that an angry, unsympathetic little girl insisted obstinately that he was not at all as he thought he was, he actually felt as if she might be speaking the truth.

'I didn't know,' ventured the nurse, 'that he thought he had a lump on his spine. His back is weak because he won't try to sit up. I could have told him there was no lump there.' Colin gulped and turned his face a little to look at her.

'C-could you?' he said pathetically.

'Yes, sir.'

'There!' said Mary, and she gulped, too.

Colin turned on his face again, and but for his long-drawn broken breaths, which were the dying down of his storm of sobbing, he lay still for a minute, though great tears streamed down his face and wet the pillow. Actually the tears meant that a curious great relief had come to him. Presently he turned and looked at the nurse again, and strangely enough he was not like a rajah at all as he spoke to her.

'Do you think – I could – live to grow up?' he said.

The nurse was neither clever nor soft-hearted, but she could repeat some of the London doctor's words.

'You probably will if you will do what you are told to do, and not give way to your temper, and stay out a great deal in the fresh air.'

Colin's tantrum had passed and he was weak and worn out with crying, and this perhaps made him feel gentle. He put out his hand a little towards Mary, and I am glad to say that, her own tantrum having passed, she was softened too, and met him half-way with her hand, so that it was a sort of making up.

'I'll – I'll go out with you, Mary,' he said. 'I shan't hate fresh air if we can find –' He remembered just in time to stop himself from saying 'if we can find the secret garden,' and he ended: 'I shall like to go out with you if Dickon will come and push my chair. I do so want to see Dickon and the fox and the crow.'

The nurse remade the tumbled bed and shook and straightened the pillows. Then she made Colin a cup of beef-tea and gave a cup to Mary, who really was very glad to get it after her excitement. Mrs Medlock and Martha gladly slipped away, and after everything was neat and calm and in order, the nurse looked as if she would very gladly slip away also. She was a healthy young woman who resented being robbed of her sleep, and she yawned quite openly as she looked at Mary, who had pushed her big footstool close to the four-poster bed and was holding Colin's hand.

'You must go back and get your sleep out,' she said. 'He'll drop off after a while – if he's not too upset. Then I'll lie down myself in the next room.'

'Would you like me to sing you that song I learned from my Ayah?' Mary whispered to Colin. His hand pulled hers gently and he turned his tired eyes on her appealingly.

'Oh, yes!' he answered. 'It's such a soft song. I shall go to sleep in a minute.'

'I will put him to sleep,' Mary said to the yawning nurse. 'You can go if you like.'

'Well,' said the nurse, with an attempt at reluctance. 'If he doesn't go to sleep in half an hour you must call me.'

'Very well,' answered Mary.

The nurse was out of the room in a minute, and as soon as she was gone Colin pulled Mary's hand again.

'I almost told,' he said: 'but I stopped myself in time. I won't talk and I'll go to sleep, but you said you had a whole lot of nice things to tell me. Have you – do you think you have found out anything at all about the way into the secret garden?'

Mary looked at his poor little tired face and swollen eyes and her heart relented.

'Ye-es,' she answered, 'I think I have. And if you will go to sleep I will tell you tomorrow.'

His hand quite trembled.

'Oh, Mary!' he said. 'Oh, Mary! If I could go into it I think I should live to grow up! Do you suppose that instead of singing the Ayah song – you could just tell me softly as you did that first day what you imagine it looks like inside? I am sure it will make me go to sleep.'

'Yes,' answered Mary. 'Shut your eyes.'

He closed his eyes and lay quite still and she held his hand and began to speak very slowly and in a very low voice.

'I think it has been left alone so long – that it has grown all into a lovely tangle. I think the roses have climbed and climbed and climbed until they hang from the branches and walls and creep over the ground – almost like a strange grey mist. Some of them have died, but many – are alive, and when the summer comes there will be curtains and fountains of roses. I think the ground is full of daffodils and snowdrops and lilies and iris working their way out of the dark. Now the spring has begun – perhaps – perhaps –'

The soft drone of her voice was making him stiller and stiller, and she saw it and went on.

'Perhaps they are coming up through the grass – perhaps there are clusters of purple crocuses and gold ones – even now. Perhaps the leaves are beginning to break out and uncurl – and perhaps – the grey is changing and a green gauze veil is creeping – and creeping over – everything. And the birds are coming to look at it – because it is – so safe and still. And perhaps – perhaps – perhaps –' very softly and slowly indeed, 'the robin has found a mate – and is building a nest.'

And Colin was asleep.

18

'Tha' Munnot Waste No Time'

OF COURSE, Mary did not waken early the next morning. She slept late because she was tired, and when Martha brought her breakfast she told her that though Colin was quite quiet, he was ill and feverish, as he always was after he had worn himself out with a fit of crying. Mary ate her breakfast slowly as she listened.

'He says he wishes tha' would please go and see him as soon as tha' can,' Martha said. 'It's queer what a fancy he's took to thee. Tha' did give it him last night for sure – didn't tha'? Nobody else would have dared to do it. Eh! poor lad! He's been spoiled till salt won't save him. Mother says as th' two worst things as can happen to a child is never to have his own way – or always to have it. She doesn't know which is th' worst. Tha' was in a fine temper tha'self, too. But he says to me when I went into his room: "Please ask Miss Mary if she'll please come an' talk to me?" Think o' him saying please! Will you go, Miss?'

'I'll run and see Dickon first,' said Mary. 'No, I'll go and see Colin first and tell him – I know what I'll tell him,' with a sudden inspiration.

She had her hat on when she appeared in Colin's room, and for a second he looked disappointed. He was in bed, and his face was pitifully white and there were dark circles round his eyes.

'I'm glad you came,' he said. 'My head aches and I ache all over because I'm so tired. Are you going somewhere?'

Mary went and leaned against his bed.

'I won't be long,' she said. 'I'm going to Dickon, but I'll come back. Colin, it's – it's something about the secret garden.'

His whole face brightened and a little colour came into it.

'Oh! is it?' he cried out. 'I dreamed about it all night. I heard you say something about grey changing into green, and I dreamed I was standing in a place all filled with trembling little green leaves – and there were birds on nests everywhere and they looked so soft and still. I'll lie and think about it until you come back.'

In five minutes Mary was with Dickon in their garden.

The fox and the crow were with him again, and this time he had brought two tame squirrels.

'I came over on the pony this mornin,' he said. 'Eh! he is a good little chap – Jump is! I brought these two in my pockets. This here one he's called Nut an' this here other one's called Shell.'

When he said 'Nut' one squirrel leaped on to his right shoulder, and when he said 'Shell' the other one leaped on to his left shoulder.

When they sat down on the grass with Captain curled at their feet, Soot solemnly listening on a tree and Nut and Shell nosing about close to them, it seemed to Mary that it would be scarcely bearable to leave such delightfulness, but when she began to tell her story somehow the look in Dickon's funny face gradually changed her mind. She could see he felt sorrier for Colin than she did. He looked up at the sky and all about him.

'Just listen to them birds – th' world seems full of 'em – all whistlin' an' pipin,' he said. 'Look at 'em dartin' about, an' hearken at 'em callin' to each other. Come springtime seems like as if all th' world's callin.' The leaves is uncurlin' so you can see 'em – an', my word, th' nice smells there is about!' sniffing with his happy turned-up nose. 'An' that poor lad lyin' shut up an' seein' so little that he gets to thinkin' o' things as sets him screamin'. Eh! my! we mun get him out here – we mun get him watchin' an' listenin' an' sniffin' up th' air an' get him just soaked through wi' sunshine. An' we munnot lose no time about it.'

When he was very much interested he often spoke quite broad Yorkshire, though at other times he tried to modify his dialect so that Mary could better understand. But she loved his broad Yorkshire, and had, in fact, been trying to learn to speak it herself. So she spoke a little now.

'Aye, that we mun,' she said (which meant 'Yes, indeed, we must'). 'I'll tell thee what us'll do first,' she proceeded, and Dickon grinned, because when the little wench tried to twist her tongue into speaking Yorkshire it amused him very much. 'He's took a graidely fancy to thee. He wants to see thee and he wants to see Soot an' Captain. When I go back to the house to talk to him I'll ax him if tha' canna come an' see him tomorrow mornin' – an' bring tha' creatures wi' thee – an' then – in a bit, when there's more leaves out an' happen a bud or two, we'll get him to come out an' tha' shall push him in his chair an' we'll bring him here an' show him everything.'

When she stopped she was quite proud of herself. She had never made a long speech in Yorkshire before, and she had remembered very well.

'Tha' mun talk a bit o' Yorkshire like that to Mester Colin,' Dickon chuckled. 'Tha'll make him laugh an' there's nowt as good for ill folk as laughin' is. Mother says she believes as half a hour's good laugh every mornin' 'ud cure a chap as was making ready for typhus fever.'

'I'm going to talk Yorkshire to him this very day,' said Mary, chuckling herself.

The garden had reached the time when every day and every night it seemed as if Magicians were passing through it drawing loveliness out of the earth and the boughs with wands. It was hard to go away and leave it all, particularly as Nut had actually crept on to her dress and Shell had scrambled down the trunk of the apple-tree they sat under and stayed there looking at her with inquiring eyes. But she went back to the house and when she sat down close to Colin's bed he began to sniff as Dickon did, though not in such an experienced way.

'You smell like flowers and – and fresh things,' he cried out quite joyously. 'What is it you smell of? It's cool and warm and sweet all at the same time.'

'It's th' wind from th' moor,' said Mary. 'It comes o' sittin' on th' grass under a tree wi' Dickon an' wi' Captain an' Soot an' Nut an' 'Shell. It's th' springtime an' out o' doors an' sunshine as smells so graidely.'

She said it as broadly as she could, and you do not

know how broadly Yorkshire sounds until you have heard someone speak it. Colin began to laugh.

'What are you doing?' he said. 'I never heard you talk like that before. How funny it sounds.'

'I'm givin' thee a bit o' Yorkshire,' answered Mary triumphantly. 'I canna talk as graidely as Dickon an' Martha can, but tha' sees I can shape a bit. Doesn't tha' understand a bit o' Yorkshire when tha' hears it? An' tha' a Yorkshire lad thysel' bred an' born! Eh! I wonder tha'rt not ashamed o' thy face.'

And then she began to laugh too, and they both laughed until they could not stop themselves, and they laughed until the room echoed and Mrs Medlock opening the door to come in drew back into the corridor and stood listening, amazed.

'Well, upon my word!' she said, speaking rather broad Yorkshire herself because there was no one to hear her, and she was so astonished. 'Whoever heard th' like! Whoever on earth would ha' thought it!'

There was so much to talk about. It seemed as if Colin could never hear enough of Dickon and Captain and Soot and Nut and Shell and the pony whose name was Jump. Mary had run round into the wood with Dickon to see Jump. He was a tiny little shaggy moor pony with thick locks hanging over his eyes and with a pretty face and a nuzzling velvet nose. He was rather thin with living on moor grass, but he was as tough and wiry as if the muscle in his little legs had been made of steel springs. He had lifted his head and whinnied softly the moment he saw Dickon, and he had trotted up to him and put his head across his shoulder, and then Dickon had talked into his ear and Jump had talked back in odd little whinnies and puffs and snorts. Dickon had made him give Mary his small front hoof and kiss her on the cheek with his velvet muzzle.

'Does he really understand everything Dickon says?' Colin asked.

'It seems as if he does,' answered Mary. 'Dickon says anything will understand if you're friends with it for sure, but you have to be friends for sure.'

Colin lay quiet a little while, and his strange grey eyes seemed to be staring at the wall, but Mary saw he was thinking.

'I wish I was friends with things,' he said at last, 'but I'm not. I never had anything to be friends with, and I can't bear people.'

'Can't you bear me?' asked Mary.

'Yes, I can,' he answered. 'It's very funny, but I even like you.'

'Ben Weatherstaff said I was like him,' said Mary. 'He said he'd warrant we'd both got the same nasty tempers. I think you are like him, too. We are all three alike – you and I and Ben Weatherstaff. He said we were neither of us much to look at, and we were as sour as we looked. But I don't feel as sour as I used to before I knew the robin and Dickon.'

'Did you feel as if you hated people?'

'Yes,' answered Mary, without any affectation. 'I should have detested you if I had seen you before I saw the robin and Dickon.'

Colin put out his thin hand and touched her.

'Mary,' he said, 'I wish I hadn't said what I did about sending Dickon away. I hated you when you said he was like an angel and I laughed at you, but – but perhaps he is.'

'Well, it was rather funny to say it,' she admitted frankly, 'because his nose does turn up and he has a big mouth and his clothes have patches all over them and he talks broad Yorkshire, but – but if an angel did come to Yorkshire and live on the moor – if there was a Yorkshire angel – I believe he'd understand the green things and know how to make them grow and he would know how to talk to the wild creatures as Dickon does, and they'd know he was friends for sure.'

'I shouldn't mind Dickon looking at me,' said Colin; 'I want to see him.'

'I'm glad you said that,' answered Mary, 'because – because –'

Quite suddenly it came into her mind that this was the minute to tell him. Colin knew something new was coming.

'Because what?' he cried eagerly.

Mary was so anxious that she got up from her stool and came to him and caught hold of both his hands.

'Can I trust you? I trusted Dickon because birds trusted him. Can I trust you – for sure – *for sure?*' she implored.

Her face was so solemn that he almost whispered his answer.

'Yes – yes!'

'Well, Dickon will come to see you tomorrow morning and he'll bring his creatures with him.'

'Oh! Oh!' Colin cried out in delight.

'But that's not all,' Mary went on, almost pale with solemn excitement. 'The rest is better. There is a door into the garden. I found it. It is under the ivy on the wall.'

If he had been a strong, healthy boy, Colin would probably have shouted, 'Hooray! Hooray! Hooray!' but he was weak and rather hysterical; his eyes grew bigger and bigger and he gasped for breath.

'Oh! Mary!' he cried out, with a half sob. 'Shall I see it? Shall I get into it? Shall I *live* to get into it?' and he clutched her hands and dragged her towards him.

'Of course you'll see it!' snapped Mary indignantly. 'Of course you'll live to get into it! Don't be silly!'

And she was so un-hysterical and natural and childish that she brought him to his senses and he began to laugh at himself, and a few minutes afterwards she was sitting on her stool again telling him not what she imagined the secret garden to be like, but what it really was, and Colin's aches and tiredness were forgotten and he was listening enraptured.

'It is just what you thought it would be,' he said at last. 'It sounds just as if you had really seen it. You know I said that when you told me first.'

Mary hesitated about two minutes and then boldly spoke the truth.

'I had seen it – and I had been in,' she said. 'I found the key and got in weeks ago. But I daren't tell you – I daren't because I was so afraid I couldn't trust you – *for sure!*'

19

'It Has Come!'

OF COURSE, Dr Craven had been sent for the morning after Colin had had his tantrum. He was always sent for at once when such a thing occurred, and he always found, when he arrived, a white, shaken boy lying on his bed, sulky and still so hysterical that he was ready to break into fresh sobbing at the least word. In fact, Dr Craven dreaded and detested the difficulties of these visits. On this occasion he was away from Misselthwaite Manor until afternoon.

'How is he?' he asked Mrs Medlock rather irritably when he arrived. 'He will break a blood-vessel in one of those fits some day. The boy is half insane with hysteria and self-indulgence.'

'Well, sir,' answered Mrs Medlock, 'you'll scarcely believe your eyes when you see him. That plain, sour-faced child that's almost as bad as himself has just bewitched him. How she's done it there's no telling. The Lord knows, she's nothing to look at and you scarcely ever hear her speak, but she did what none of us dare do. She just flew at him like a little cat last night, and stamped her feet and ordered him to stop screaming, and somehow she startled him so that he actually did stop, and this afternoon – well, just come up and see, sir. It's past crediting.'

The scene which Dr Craven beheld when he entered his patient's room was indeed rather astonishing to him. As Mrs Medlock opened the door he heard laughing and chattering. Colin was on his sofa in his dressing-gown and he was sitting up quite straight looking at a picture in one of the garden books and talking to the plain child who at that moment could scarcely be called plain at all because her face was so glowing with enjoyment.

'Those long spires of blue ones – we'll have a lot of those,' Colin was announcing. 'They're called Del-phin-iums.'

'Dickon says they're larkspurs made big and grand,' cried Mistress Mary. 'There are clumps there already.'

Then they saw Dr Craven and stopped. Mary became quite still and Colin looked fretful.

'I am sorry to hear you were ill last night, my boy,' Dr

Craven said, a trifle nervously. He was rather a nervous man.

'I'm better now – much better,' Colin answered, rather like a rajah. 'I'm going out in my chair in a day or two if it is fine. I want some fresh air.'

Dr Craven sat down by him and felt his pulse and looked at him curiously.

'It must be a very fine day,' he said, 'and you must be very careful not to tire yourself.'

'Fresh air won't tire me,' said the young rajah.

As there had been occasions when this same young gentleman had shrieked aloud with rage and had insisted that fresh air would give him cold and kill him, it is not to be wondered at that his doctor felt somewhat startled.

'I thought you did not like fresh air,' he said.

'I don't when I am by myself,' replied the rajah; 'but my cousin is going out with me.'

'And the nurse, of course?' suggested Dr Craven.

'No, I will not have the nurse,' so magnificently that Mary could not help remembering how the young native prince had looked with his diamonds and emeralds and pearls stuck all over him and the great rubies on the small dark hand he had waved to command his servants to approach with salaams and receive his orders.

'My cousin knows how to take care of me. I am always

better when she is with me. She made me better last night. A very strong boy I know will push my carriage.'

Dr Craven felt rather alarmed. If this tiresome, hysterical boy should chance to get well, he himself would lose all chance of inheriting Misselthwaite; but he was not an unscrupulous man, though he was a weak one, and he did not intend to let him run into actual danger.

'He must be a strong boy and a steady boy,' he said. 'And I must know something about him. Who is he? What is his name?'

'It's Dickon,' Mary spoke up suddenly. She felt somehow that everyone who knew the moor must know Dickon. And she was right, too. She saw that in a moment Dr Craven's serious face relaxed into a relieved smile.

'Oh, Dickon,' he said. 'If it is Dickon you will be safe enough. He's as strong as a moor pony, is Dickon.'

'And he's trusty,' said Mary. 'He's th' trustiest lad i' Yorkshire.' She had been talking Yorkshire to Colin and she forgot herself.

'Did Dickon teach you that?' asked Dr Craven, laughing outright.

'I'm learning it as if it was French,' said Mary, rather coldly. 'It's like a native dialect in India. Very clever people try to learn them. I like it and so does Colin.'

'Well, well,' he said. 'If it amuses you perhaps it won't do you any harm. Did you take your bromide last night, Colin?'

'No,' Colin answered. 'I wouldn't take it at first, and after Mary made me quiet she talked me to sleep – in a low voice – about the spring creeping into a garden.'

'That sounds soothing,' said Dr Craven, more perplexed than ever and glancing sideways at Mistress Mary sitting on her stool and looking down silently at the carpet. 'You are evidently better, but you must remember –'

'I don't want to remember,' interrupted the rajah, appearing again. 'When I lie by myself and remember I begin to have pains everywhere, and I think of things that make me begin to scream because I hate them so. If there was a doctor anywhere who could make you forget you were ill instead of remembering it, I would have him brought here.' And he waved a thin hand which ought really to have been covered with royal signet rings made of rubies. 'It is because my cousin makes me forget that she makes me better.'

Dr Craven had never made such a short stay after a 'tantrum'; usually he was obliged to remain a very long time and do a great many things. This afternoon he did not give any medicine or leave any new orders, and he was spared any disagreeable scenes. When he went downstairs he looked very thoughtful, and when he talked to Mrs Medlock in the library she felt that he was a much puzzled man.

'Well, sir,' she ventured, 'could you have believed it?'

'It is certainly a new state of affairs,' said the doctor. 'And there's no denying it is better than the old one.'

'I believe Susan Sowerby's right – I do that,' said Mrs Medlock. 'I stopped in her cottage on my way to Thwaite yesterday, and had a bit of talk with her. And she says to me: "Well, Sarah Ann, she mayn't be a good child, an' she mayn't be a pretty one, but she's a child, an' children needs children." We went to school together, Susan Sowerby and me.'

'She's the best sick nurse I know,' said Dr Craven. 'When I find her in a cottage I know the chances are that I shall save my patient.'

Mrs Medlock smiled. She was fond of Susan Sowerby.

'She's got a way with her, has Susan,' she went on quite volubly. 'I've been thinking all morning of one thing she said yesterday. She says: "Once when I was givin' th' children a bit of a preach after they'd been fightin' I ses to 'em all, 'When I was at school my jography told as th' world was shaped like a orange an' I found out before I was ten that th' whole orange doesn't belong to nobody. No one owns more than his bit of a quarter an' there's times it seems like there's not enow quarters to go round. But don't you – none o' you – think as you own th' whole orange or you'll find out you're mistaken, an' you won't find it out without hard knocks.' What children learns from children," she says, "is that there's no sense in grabbin' at th' whole orange – peel an' all. If you do, you'll likely not get even th' pips, an' them's too bitter to eat." '

'She's a shrewd woman,' said Dr Craven, putting on his coat.

'Well, she's got a way of saying things,' ended Mrs Medlock, much pleased. 'Sometimes I've said to her, "Eh, Susan, if you was a different woman an' didn't talk such broad Yorkshire I've seen the times when I should have said you was clever." '

*

That night Colin slept without once awakening, and when he opened his eyes in the morning he lay still and smiled without knowing it – smiled because he felt so curiously comfortable. It was actually nice to be awake, and he turned over and stretched his limbs luxuriously. He felt as if tight strings which had held him had loosened themselves and let him go. He did not know that Dr Craven would have said that his nerves had relaxed and rested themselves. Instead of lying and staring at the wall and wishing he had not awakened, his mind was full of the plans he and Mary had made yesterday, of pictures of the garden and of Dickon and his wild creatures. It was so nice to have things to think about. And he had not been awake more than ten minutes when he heard feet running along the corridor and Mary was at the door. The next minute she was in the room and had run across to his bed, bringing with her a waft of fresh air full of the scent of the morning.

'You've been out! You've been out! There's that nice smell of leaves!' he cried.

She had been running and her hair was loose and blown, and she was bright with the air and pink-cheeked, though he could not see it.

'It's so beautiful!' she said, a little breathless with her speed. 'You never saw anything so beautiful! It has *come!* I thought it had come that other morning, but it was only coming. It is here now! It has come, the Spring! Dickon says so!'

'Has it?' cried Colin, and though he really knew nothing about it, he felt his heart beat. He actually sat up in bed.

'Open the window!' he added, laughing half with joyful excitement and half at his own fancy. 'Perhaps we may hear golden trumpets!'

And though he laughed, Mary was at the window in a moment and in a moment more it was opened wide and freshness and softness and scents and birds' songs were pouring through.

'That's fresh air,' she said. 'Lie on your back and draw in long breaths of it. That's what Dickon does when he's lying on the moor. He says he feels it in his veins and it makes him strong and he feels as if he could live for ever and ever. Breathe it and breathe it.'

She was only repeating what Dickon had told her, but she caught Colin's fancy.

' "For ever and ever!" Does it make him feel like that?' he said, and he did as she told him, drawing in long deep breaths over and over again, until he felt that something quite new and delightful was happening to him.

Mary was at his bedside again.

'Things are crowding up out of the earth,' she ran on in a hurry. 'And there are flowers uncurling and buds on everything and the green veil has covered nearly all the grey and the birds are in such a hurry about their nests for fear they may be too late, that some of them are even fighting for places in the secret garden. And the rose-bushes look as wick as wick can be, and there are primroses in the lanes and woods, and the seeds we planted are up, and Dickon has brought the fox and the crow and the squirrels and a new-born lamb.'

And then she paused for breath. The new-born lamb Dickon had found three days before lying by its dead mother among the gorse bushes on the moor. It was not the first motherless lamb he had found and he knew what to do with it. He had taken it to the cottage wrapped in his jacket and he had let it lie near the fire and had fed it with warm milk. It was a soft thing, with a darling silly baby face and legs rather long for its body. Dickon had carried it over the moor in his arms, and its feeding-bottle was in his pocket with a squirrel, and when Mary had sat under a tree with its limp warmness huddled on her lap, she had felt as if she were too full of strange joy to speak. A lamb – a lamb! a living lamb who lay on your lap like a baby!

She was describing it with great joy and Colin was listening and drawing in long breaths of air when the nurse entered. She started a little at the sight of the open window. She had sat stifling in the room many a warm day because her patient was sure that open windows gave people cold.

'Are you sure you are not chilly, Master Colin?' she inquired.

'No,' was the answer. 'I am breathing long breaths of fresh air. It makes you strong. I am going to get up to the sofa for breakfast and my cousin will have breakfast with me.'

The nurse went away, concealing a smile, to give the order for two breakfasts. She found the servants' hall a more amusing place than the invalid's chamber, and just now everybody wanted to hear the news from upstairs. There was a great deal of joking about the unpopular young recluse who, as the cook said, 'had found his master, and good for him'. The servants' hall had been very tired of the tantrums, and the butler, who was a man with a family, had more than once expressed his opinion that the invalid would be all the better 'for a good hiding'.

When Colin was on his sofa and the breakfast for two was put upon the table, he made an announcement to the nurse in his most rajah-like manner.

'A boy, and a fox, and a crow, and two squirrels, and a new-born lamb, are coming to see me this morning. I want them brought upstairs as soon as they come,' he said. 'You are not to begin playing with the animals in the servants' hall and keep them there. I want them here.'

The nurse gave a little gasp and tried to conceal it with a cough.

'Yes, sir,' she answered.

'I'll tell you what you can do,' added Colin, waving his hand. 'You can tell Martha to bring them here. The boy is Martha's brother. His name is Dickon and he is an animal charmer.'

'I hope the animals won't bite, Master Colin,' said the nurse.

'I told you he was a charmer,' said Colin austerely. 'Charmers' animals never bite.'

'There are snake-charmers in India,' said Mary; 'and they can put their snakes' heads in their mouths.'

'Goodness!' shuddered the nurse.

They ate their breakfast with the morning air pouring in upon them. Colin's breakfast was a very good one, and Mary watched him with serious interest.

'You will begin to get fatter just as I did,' she said. 'I never wanted my breakfast when I was in India, and now I always want it.'

'I wanted mine this morning,' said Colin. 'Perhaps it was the fresh air. When do you think Dickon will come?'

He was not long in coming. In about ten minutes Mary held up her hand.

'Listen!' she said. 'Did you hear a caw?'

Colin listened and heard it, the oddest sound in the world to hear inside a house, a hoarse 'caw-caw'.

'Yes,' he answered.

'That's Soot,' said Mary. 'Listen again! Do you hear a bleat – a tiny one?'

'Oh, yes!' cried Colin, quite flushing.

'That's the new-born lamb,' said Mary. 'He's coming.'

Dickon's moorland boots were thick and clumsy, and

though he tried to walk quietly they made a clumping sound as he walked through the long corridors. Mary and Colin heard him marching – marching, until he passed through the tapestry door on to the soft carpet of Colin's own passage.

'If you please, sir,' announced Martha, opening the door, 'if you please, sir, here's Dickon an' his creatures.'

Dickon came in smiling his nicest wide smile. The new-born lamb was in his arms and the little red fox trotted by his side. Nut sat on his left shoulder and Soot on his right, and Shell's head and paws peeped out of his coat pocket.

Colin slowly sat up and stared and stared – as he had stared when he first saw Mary; but this was a stare of wonder and delight. The truth was that in spite of all he had heard he had not in the least understood what this boy would be like and that his fox and his crow and his squirrels and his lamb were so near to him and his friendliness that they seemed almost to be part of himself. Colin had never talked to a boy in his life, and he was so overwhelmed by his own pleasure and curiosity that he did not even think of speaking.

But Dickon did not feel the least shy or awkward. He had not felt embarrassed because the crow had not known his language and had only stared and had not spoken to him the first time they met. Creatures were always like that until they found out about you. He walked over to Colin's sofa and put the new-born lamb quietly on his lap, and immediately the little creature turned to the warm velvet dressing-gown and began to nuzzle and nuzzle into its folds and butt its tight-curled head with soft impatience against his side. Of course, no boy could have helped speaking then.

'What is it doing?' cried Colin. 'What does it want?'

'It wants its mother,' said Dickon, smiling more and more. 'I brought it to thee a bit hungry because I knowed tha'd like to see it feed.'

He knelt down by the sofa and took a feeding-bottle from his pocket.

'Come on, little 'un,' he said, turning the small, woolly, white head with a gentle brown hand. 'This is what tha's after. Tha'll get more out o' this than tha' will out o' silk velvet coats. There now,' and he pushed the rubber tip of the bottle into the nuzzling mouth and the lamb began to suck it with ravenous ecstasy.

After that there was no wondering what to say. By the time the lamb fell asleep questions poured forth, and Dickon answered them all. He told them how he had found the lamb just as the sun was rising three mornings ago. He had been standing on the moor listening to a skylark and watching him swing higher and higher into the blue, until he was only a speck in the heights of blue.

'I'd almost lost him but for his song an' I was wonderin' how a chap could hear it when it seemed as if he'd get out o' th' world in a minute – an' just then I heard somethin' else far off among th' gorse bushes. It was a weak bleatin', an' I knowed it was a new lamb as was hungry an' I knowed it wouldn't be hungry, if it hadn't lost its mother somehow, so I set off searchin'. Eh! I did have a look for it. I went in an' out among th' gorse bushes an' round an' round an' I always seemed to take th' wrong turnin'. But at last I seed a bit o' white by a rock on top o' th' moor an' I climbed up an' found th' little 'un half dead wi' cold an' clemmin'.'

While he talked, Soot flew solemnly in and out of the open window and cawed remarks about the scenery, while Nut and Shell made excursions into the big trees outside and ran up and down trunks and explored branches. Captain curled up near Dickon, who sat on the hearth-rug from preference.

They looked at the pictures in the gardening books and Dickon knew all the flowers by their country names and knew exactly which ones were already growing in the secret garden.

'I couldna' say that there name,' he said, pointing to one under which was written 'Aquilegia', 'but us calls that a columbine, an' that there one it's a snapdragon and they both grow wild in hedges, but these is garden ones an' they're bigger and grander. There's some big clumps o' columbine in th' garden. They'll look like a bed o' blue an' white butterflies flutterin' when they're out.'

'I'm going to see them,' cried Colin. 'I am going to see them!'

'Aye, that tha' mun,' said Mary quite seriously. 'An' tha' munnot lose no time about it.'

20

'I Shall Live for Ever – and Ever – and Ever!'

BUT they were obliged to wait more than a week because first there came some very windy days and then Colin was threatened with a cold, which two things happening one after the other would no doubt have thrown him into a rage, but that there was so much careful and mysterious planning to do and almost every day Dickon came in, if only for a few minutes, to talk about what was happening on the moor and in the lanes and hedges and on the borders of streams. The things he had to tell about otters' and badgers' and water-rats' houses, not to mention birds' nests and field-mice and their burrows, were enough to make you almost tremble with excitement when you heard all the intimate details from an animal charmer and realised with what thrilling eagerness and anxiety the whole busy underworld was working.

'They're same as us,' said Dickon, 'only they have to build their homes every year. An' it keeps 'em so busy they fair scuffle to get 'em done.'

The most absorbing thing, however, was the preparations to be made before Colin could be transported with sufficient secrecy to the garden. No one must see the chair-carriage and Dickon and Mary after they turned a certain corner of the shrubbery and entered upon the walk outside the ivied walls. As each day passed, Colin had become more and more fixed in his feelings that the mystery surrounding the garden was one of its greatest charms. Nothing must spoil that. No one must ever suspect that they had a secret. People must think that he was simply going out with Mary and Dickon because he liked them and did not object to their looking at him. They had long and quite delightful talks about their route. They would go up this path and down that one and cross the other and go round among the fountain flower-beds as if they were looking at the 'bedding-out plants' the head gardener, Mr Roach, had been having arranged. That would seem such a rational thing to do that no one would think it at all mysterious. They would turn into the shrubbery walks and lose themselves until they came to the long walls. It was almost as seriously and elaborately thought out as the plans of a march made by great generals in time of war.

Rumours of the new and curious things which were occurring in the invalid's apartments had, of course, filtered through the servants' hall into the stableyards and out among the gardeners, but, notwithstanding this, Mr Roach was startled one day when he received orders from Master Colin's room to the effect that he must report himself in the apartment no outsider had ever seen, as the invalid himself desired to speak to him.

'Well, well,' he said to himself, as he hurriedly changed his coat, 'what's to do now? His Royal Highness that wasn't to be looked at calling up a man he's never set eyes on.'

Mr Roach was not without curiosity. He had never caught even a glimpse of the boy and had heard a dozen exaggerated stories about his uncanny looks and ways and his insane tempers. The thing he had heard oftenest was that he might die at any moment and there had been numerous fanciful descriptions of a humped back and helpless limbs, given by people who had never seen him.

'Things are changing in this house, Mr Roach,' said Mrs Medlock, as she led him up the back staircase to the corridor on to which opened the hitherto mysterious chamber.

'Let's hope they're changing for the better, Mrs Medlock,' he answered.

'They couldn't well change for the worse,' she continued; 'and queer as it all is, there's them as finds their duties made a lot easier to stand up under. Don't you be surprised, Mr Roach, if you find yourself in the middle of a menagerie and Martha Sowerby's Dickon more at home than you or me could ever be.'

There really was a sort of Magic about Dickon as Mary always privately believed. When Mr Roach heard his name he smiled quite leniently.

'He'd be at home in Buckingham Palace or at the bottom of the coal mine,' he said. 'And yet it's not impudence, either. He's just fine, is that lad.'

It was perhaps well he had been prepared or he might have been startled. When the bedroom door was opened a large crow, which seemed quite at home perched on the high back of a carven chair, announced the entrance of a visitor by saying 'Caw-caw' quite loudly. In spite of Mrs Medlock's warning, Mr Roach only just escaped being sufficiently undignified to jump backwards.

The young rajah was neither in bed nor on his sofa. He was sitting in an arm-chair and a young lamb was standing by him shaking its tail in feeding-lamb fashion as Dickon knelt giving it milk from its bottle. A squirrel was perched on Dickon's bent back attentively nibbling a nut. The little girl from India was sitting on a big footstool looking on.

'Here is Mr Roach, Master Colin,' said Mrs Medlock. The young rajah turned and looked his servitor over – at least that was what the head gardener felt happened.

'Oh, you are Roach, are you?' he said. 'I sent for you to give you some very important orders.'

'Very good, sir,' answered Roach, wondering if he was to receive instructions to fell all the oaks in the park or to transform the orchards into water-gardens.

'I am going out in my chair this afternoon,' said Colin. 'If the fresh air agrees with me I may go out every day. When I go, none of the gardeners are to be anywhere near the Long Walk by the garden walls. No one is to be there. I shall go out about two o'clock and everyone must keep away until I send word that they may go back to their work.'

'Very good, sir,' replied Mr Roach, much relieved to hear that the oaks might remain and that the orchards were safe.

'Mary,' said Colin, turning to her, 'what is that thing you say in India when you have finished talking and want people to go?'

'You say, "You have my permission to go," ' answered Mary.

The rajah waved his hand.

'You have my permission to go, Roach,' he said. 'But remember, this is very important.'

'Caw-caw!' remarked the crow hoarsely, but not impolitely.

'Very good, sir. Thank you, sir,' said Mr Roach, and Mrs Medlock took him out of the room.

Outside in the corridor, being a rather good-natured man, he smiled until he almost laughed.

'My word!' he said, 'he's got a fine, lordly way with him, hasn't he? You'd think he was a whole Royal Family rolled into one – Prince Consort and all.'

'Eh!' protested Mrs Medlock, 'we've had to let him trample all over every one of us ever since he had feet, and he thinks that's what folks was born for.'

'Perhaps he'll grow out of it, if he lives,' suggested Mr Roach.

'Well, there's one thing pretty sure,' said Mrs Medlock. 'If he does live and that Indian child stays here, I'll warrant she teaches him that the whole orange does not belong to him, as Susan Sowerby says. And he'll be likely to find out the size of his own quarter.'

Inside the room Colin was leaning back on his cushions.

'It's all safe now,' he said. 'And this afternoon I shall see it – this afternoon I shall be in it!'

Dickon went back to the garden with his creatures, and Mary stayed with Colin. She did not think he looked tired, but he was very quiet before their lunch came, and he was quiet while they were eating it. She wondered why, and asked him about it.

'What big eyes you've got, Colin,' she said. 'When you are thinking they get as big as saucers. What are you thinking about now?'

'I can't help thinking about what it will look like,' he answered.

'The garden?' asked Mary.

'The springtime,' he said. 'I was thinking that I've really never seen it before. I scarcely ever went out, and when I did go I never looked at it. I didn't even think about it.'

'I never saw it in India, because there wasn't any,' said Mary.

Shut in and morbid as his life had been, Colin had more imagination than she had, and at least he had spent a good deal of time looking at wonderful books and pictures.

'That morning when you ran in and said "It's come! It's come!" you made me feel quite queer. It sounded as if things were coming with a great procession and big bursts and wafts of music. I've a picture like it in one of my books – crowds of lovely people and children with garlands and branches with blossoms on them, everyone laughing and dancing and crowding and playing on pipes. That was why I said, "Perhaps we shall hear golden trumpets," and told you to throw open the window.'

'How funny!' said Mary. 'That's really just what it feels like. And if all the flowers and leaves and green things and birds, and wild creatures danced past at once, what a crowd it would be! I'm sure they'd dance and sing and flute and that would be the wafts of music.'

They both laughed, but it was not because the idea was laughable, but because they both so liked it.

A little later the nurse made Colin ready. She noticed that instead of lying like a log while his clothes were put on, he sat up and made some efforts to help himself, and he talked and laughed with Mary all the time.

'This is one of his good days, sir,' she said to Dr Craven, who dropped in to inspect him. 'He's in such good spirits that it makes him stronger.'

'I'll call in again later in the afternoon, after he has come in,' said Dr Craven. 'I must see how the going out agrees with him. I wish,' in a very low voice, 'that he would let you go with him.'

'I'd rather give up the case this moment, sir, than even

stay here while it's suggested,' answered the nurse with sudden firmness.

'I hadn't really decided to suggest it,' said the doctor, with his slight nervousness. 'We'll try the experiment. Dickon's a lad I'd trust with a new-born child.'

The strongest footman in the house carried Colin downstairs and put him in his wheeled-chair, near which Dickon waited outside. After the manservant had arranged his rugs and cushions, the rajah waved his hand to him and to the nurse.

'You have my permission to go,' he said, and they both disappeared quickly, and it must be confessed, giggled, when they were safely inside the house.

Dickon began to push the wheeled-chair slowly and steadily. Mistress Mary walked beside it and Colin leaned back and lifted his face to the sky. The arch of it looked very high and the small snowy clouds seemed like white birds floating on outspread wings below its crystal blueness. The wind swept in soft big breaths down from the moor and was strange with a wild clear-scented sweetness. Colin kept lifting his thin chest to draw it in, and his big eyes looked as if it were they which were listening – listening, instead of his ears.

'There are so many sounds of singing and humming and calling out,' he said. 'What is that scent the puffs of wind bring?'

'It's gorse on th' moor that's openin' out,' answered Dickon. 'Eh! th' bees are at it wonderful today.'

Not a human creature was to be caught sight of in the paths they took. In fact every gardener or gardener's lad had been witched away. But they wound in and out among the shrubbery and out and round the fountain beds, following their carefully planned route for the mere mysterious pleasure of it. But when at last they turned into the Long Walk by the ivied walls, the excited sense of an approaching thrill made them, for some curious reason they could not have explained, begin to speak in whispers.

'This is it,' breathed Mary. 'This is where I used to walk up and down and wonder and wonder.'

'Is it?' cried Colin, and his eyes began to search the ivy with eager curiousness. 'But I can see nothing,' he whispered. 'There is no door.'

'That's what I thought,' said Mary.

Then there was a lovely, breathless silence and the chair wheeled on.

'That is the garden where Ben Weatherstaff works,' said Mary.

'Is it?' said Colin.

A few yards more and Mary whispered again.

'This is where the robin flew over the wall,' she said.

'Is it?' cried Colin. 'Oh! I wish he'd come again!'

'And that,' said Mary with solemn delight, pointing under a big lilac bush, 'is where he perched on the little heap of earth and showed me the key.'

Then Colin sat up.

'Where? Where? There?' he cried, and his eyes were as big as the wolf's in Red Hiding Hood, when Red Riding Hood felt called upon to remark on them. Dickon stood still and the wheeled-chair stopped.

'And this,' said Mary, stepping on to the bed close to the ivy, 'is where I went to talk to him when he chirped at me from the top of the wall. And this is the ivy the wind blew back,' and she took hold of the hanging green curtain.

'Oh! is it – ' gasped Colin.

'And here is the handle, and here is the door. Dickon, push him in – push him in quickly!'

And Dickon did it with one strong, steady, splendid push.

But Colin had actually dropped back against his cushions, even though he gasped with delight, and he had covered his eyes with his hands and held them there, shutting out everything until they were inside and the chair stopped as if by magic and the door was closed. Not till then did he take them away and look round and round and round as Dickon and Mary had done. And over walls and earth and trees and swinging sprays and tendrils the fair green veil of tender little leaves had crept, and in the grass under the trees and the grey urns in the alcoves and here and there everywhere, were touches or splashes of gold and purple and white and the trees were showing pink and snow above his head, and there were flutterings of wings and faint sweet pipes and humming and scents and scents. And the sun fell warm upon his face like a hand with a lovely touch. And in wonder Mary and Dickon stood and stared at him. He looked so strange and different because a pink glow of colour had actually crept all over him – ivory face and neck and hands and all.

'I shall get well! I shall get well!' he cried out. 'Mary! Dickon! I shall get well! And I shall live for ever and ever and ever!'

21

Ben Weatherstaff

ONE of the strange things about living in the world is that it is only now and then one is quite sure one is going to live for ever and ever and ever. One knows it sometimes when one gets up at the tender, solemn dawntime and goes out and stands alone and throws one's head far back and looks up and up and watches the pale sky slowly changing and flushing and marvellous unknown things happening until the East almost makes one cry out and one's heart stands still at the strange, unchanging majesty of the rising of the sun – which has been happening every morning for thousands and thousands and thousands of years. One knows it then for a moment or so. And one knows it sometimes when one stands by oneself in a wood at sunset and the mysterious deep gold stillness slanting through and under the branches seems to be saying slowly again and again something one cannot quite hear, however much one tries. Then sometimes the immense quiet of the dark-blue at night with millions of stars waiting and watching makes one sure; and sometimes a sound of far-off music makes it true; and sometimes a look in someone's eyes.

And it was like that with Colin when he first saw and heard and felt the springtime inside the four high walls of a hidden garden. That afternoon the whole world seemed to devote itself to being perfect and radiantly beautiful and kind to one boy. Perhaps out of pure heavenly goodness the spring came and crowded everything it possibly could into that one place. More than once, Dickon paused in what he was doing and stood still with a sort of growing wonder in his eyes, shaking his head softly.

'Eh! It is graidely,' he said. 'I'm twelve goin' on thirteen an' there's a lot o' afternoons in thirteen years, but seems to me like I never seed one as graidely as this 'ere.'

'Aye, it is a graidely one,' said Mary, and she sighed for mere joy. 'I'll warrant it's th' graideliest one as ever was in this world.'

'Does tha' think' said Colin, with dreamy carefulness, 'as happen it was made loike this 'ere all o' purpose for me?'

'My word!' cried Mary admiringly, 'that there is a bit o' good Yorkshire. Tha'rt shapin' first rate – that – tha' art.'

And delight reigned.

They drew the chair under the plum-tree, which was snow-white with blossoms and musical with bees. It was like a king's canopy, a fairy king's. There were flowering cherry-trees near and apple-trees whose buds were pink and white, and here and there one had burst open wide. Between the blossoming branches of the canopy bits of blue sky looked down like wonderful eyes.

Mary and Dickon worked a little here and there and Colin watched them. They brought him things to look at – buds which were opening, buds which were tight closed, bits of twig whose leaves were just showing green, the feather of a woodpecker which had dropped on the grass, the empty shell of some bird early hatched. Dickon pushed the chair slowly round and round the garden, stopping every other moment to let him look at wonders springing out of the earth or trailing down from trees. It was like being taken in state round the country of a magic king and queen and shown all the mysterious riches it contained.

'I wonder if we shall see the robin?' said Colin.

'Tha'll see him often enow after a bit,' answered Dickon. 'When th' eggs hatches out th' little chap he'll be kep' so busy it'll make his head swim. Tha'll see him flyin' backward an' for'ard carryin' worms nigh as big as himsel' an' that much noise goin' on in th' nest when he gets there as fair flusters him so as he scarce knows which big mouth to drop th' first piece in. An' gapin' beaks an' squawks on every side. Mother says as when she sees th' work a robin has to keep them gapin' beaks filled, she feels like she was a lady with nothin' to do. She says she's seen th' little chaps when it seemed like th' sweat must be droppin' off 'em, though folk can't see it.'

This made them giggle so delightedly that they were obliged to cover their mouths with their hands, remembering that they must not be heard. Colin had been instructed as to the law of whispers and low voices several days before. He liked the mysteriousness of it and did his best, but in the midst of excited enjoyment it is rather difficult never to laugh above a whisper.

Every moment of the afternoon was full of new things and every hour the sunshine grew more golden. The wheeled-chair had been drawn back under the canopy and Dickon had sat down on the grass and had just drawn out his pipe when Colin saw something he had not had time to notice before.

'That's a very old tree over there, isn't it?' he said.

Dickon looked across the grass at the tree and Mary looked and there was a brief moment of stillness.

'Yes,' answered Dickon, after it, and his low voice had a very gentle sound.

Mary gazed at the tree and thought.

'The branches are quite grey and there's not a single leaf anywhere,' Colin went on. 'It's quite dead, isn't it?'

'Aye,' admitted Dickon. 'But them roses as has climbed all over it will near hide every bit o' th' dead wood when they're full o' leaves an' flowers. It won't look dead then. It'll be th' prettiest of all.'

Mary still gazed at the tree and thought.

'It looks as if a big branch had been broken off,' said Colin. 'I wonder how it was done.'

'It's been done many a year,' answered Dickon. 'Eh!' with a sudden relieved start and laying his hand on Colin, 'look at that robin! There he is! He's been foragin' for his mate.'

Colin was almost too late, but he just caught sight of him, the flash of red-breasted bird with something in his beak. He darted through the greenness and into the close-grown corner and out of sight. Colin leaned back on his cushion again, laughing a little.

'He's taking her tea to her. Perhaps it's five o'clock. I think I'd like some tea myself.'

And so they were safe.

'It was Magic which sent the robin,' said Mary secretly to Dickon afterwards. 'I know it was Magic.' For both she and Dickon had been afraid Colin might ask something about the tree whose branch had broken off ten years ago, and they had talked it over together and Dickon had stood and rubbed his head in a troubled way.

'We mun look as if it wasn't no different from th' other trees,' he had said. 'We couldn't never tell him how it broke, poor lad. If he says anything about it we mun – we mun try to look cheerful.'

'Aye, that we mun,' had answered Mary.

But she had not felt as if she looked cheerful when she gazed at the tree. She wondered and wondered in those few moments if there was any reality in that other thing Dickon had said. He had gone on rubbing his rust-red hair in a puzzled way, but a nice comforted look had begun to grow in his blue eyes.

'Mrs Craven was a very lovely young lady,' he had gone on rather hesitatingly. 'An' Mother she thinks maybe she's about Misselthwaite many a time lookin' after Mester Colin, same as all mothers do when they're took out o' th' world. They have to come back, tha' sees. Happen she's been in the garden an' happen it was her set us to work, an' told us to bring him here.'

Mary had thought he meant something about Magic. She was a great believer in Magic. Secretly she quite believed that Dickon worked Magic, of course, good Magic, on everything near him and that was why people liked him so much and wild creatures knew he was their friend. She wondered, indeed, if it were not possible that his gift had brought the robin just at the right moment when Colin asked that dangerous question. She felt that his Magic was working all the afternoon and making Colin look an entirely different boy. It did not seem possible that he could be the crazy creature who had screamed and beaten and bitten his pillow. Even his ivory whiteness seemed to change. The faint glow of colour which had shown on his face and neck and hands when he first got inside the garden really never quite died away. He looked as if he were made of flesh instead of ivory or wax.

They saw the robin carry food to his mate two or three times, and it was so suggestive of afternoon tea that Colin felt they must have some.

'Go and make one of the menservants bring some in a basket to the rhododendron walk,' he said. 'And then you and Dickon can bring it here.'

It was an agreeable idea; easily carried out, and when the white cloth was spread upon the grass, with hot tea and buttered toast and crumpets, a delightfully hungry meal was eaten, and several birds on domestic errands paused to inquire what was going on and were led into investigating crumbs with great activity. Nut and Shell whisked up trees with pieces of cake, and Soot took the entire half of a buttered crumpet into a corner and pecked at and examined and turned it over and made hoarse remarks about it until he decided to swallow it all joyfully in one gulp.

The afternoon was dragging towards its mellow hour. The sun was deepening the gold of its lances, the bees were going home and the birds were flying past less often. Dickon and Mary were sitting on the grass, the tea-basket was repacked ready to be taken back to the house, and Colin was lying against his cushions with his heavy locks pushed back from his forehead and his face looking quite a natural colour.

'I don't want this afternoon to go,' he said; 'but I shall come back tomorrow, and the day after, and the day after, and the day after.'

'You'll get plenty of fresh air, won't you?' said Mary.

'I'm going to get nothing else,' he answered. 'I've seen the spring now and I'm going to see the summer. I'm going to see everything grow here. I'm going to grow here myself.'

'That tha' will,' said Dickon. 'Us'll have thee walkin' about here an' diggin' same as other folk afore long.'

Colin flushed tremendously.

'Walk!' he said. 'Dig! Shall I?'

Dickon's glance at him was delicately cautious. Neither

he nor Mary had ever asked if anything was the matter with his legs.

'For sure tha' will,' he said stoutly. 'Tha' – tha's got legs o' thine own, same as other folks!'

Mary was rather frightened until she heard Colin's answer.

'Nothing really ails them,' he said, 'but they are so thin and weak. They shake so that I'm afraid to try to stand on them.'

Both Mary and Dickon drew a relieved breath.

'When tha' stops bein' afraid tha'lt stand on 'em,' Dickon said with renewed cheer. 'An' tha'lt stop bein' afraid in a bit.'

'I shall?' said Colin, and he lay still, as if he were wondering about things.

They were really very quiet for a little while. The sun was dropping lower. It was that hour when everything stills itself, and they really had had a busy and exciting afternoon. Colin looked as if he were resting luxuriously. Even the creatures had ceased moving about and had drawn together and were resting near them. Soot had perched on a low branch and drawn up one leg and dropped the grey film drowsily over his eyes. Mary privately thought he looked as if he might snore in a minute.

In the midst of this stillness it was rather startling

when Colin half lifted his head and exclaimed in a loud, suddenly alarmed whisper:

'Who is that man?'

Dickon and Mary scrambled to their feet.

'Man?' they both cried in low, quick voices.

Colin pointed to the high wall.

'Look!' he whispered excitedly. 'Just look!'

Mary and Dickon wheeled about and looked. There was Ben Weatherstaff's indignant face glaring at them over the wall from the top of a ladder! He actually shook his fist at Mary.

'If I wasn't a bachelder, an' tha' was a wench o' mine,' he cried, 'I'd give thee a hidin'!'

He mounted another step threateningly, as if it were his energetic intention to jump down and deal with her; but as she came towards him he evidently thought better of it and stood on the top step of his ladder shaking his fist down at her.

'I never thowt much o' thee!' he harangued, 'I couldna' abide thee th' first time I set eyes on thee. A scrawny, buttermilk-faced young besom, allus askin' questions an' pokin' tha' nose where it wasna' wanted. I never knowed how tha' got so thick wi' me. If it hadna' been for th' robin – drat him –'

'Ben Weatherstaff,' called out Mary, finding her breath. She stood below him and called up to him with a sort of gasp. 'Ben Weatherstaff, it was the robin who showed me the way!'

Then it did seem as if Ben really would scramble down on her side of the wall, he was so outraged.

'Tha' young bad 'un!' he called down to her. 'Layin' tha' badness on a robin – not but what he's impidint enow for anythin'. Him showin' thee th' way! Him! Eh! tha' young nowt' – she could see his next words burst out because he was overpowered by curiosity – 'however i' this world did tha' get in?'

'It was the robin who showed me the way,' she protested obstinately. 'He didn't know he was doing it, but he did. And I can't tell you from here, while you're shaking your fist at me.'

He stopped shaking his fist very suddenly at that very moment and his jaw actually dropped as he stared over her head at something he saw coming over the grass towards him.

At the first sound of his torrent of words Colin had been so surprised that he had only sat up and listened as if he were spellbound. But in the midst of it he had recovered himself and beckoned imperiously to Dickon.

'Wheel me over there!' he commanded. 'Wheel me quite close and stop right in front of him!'

And this if you please, this is what Ben Weatherstaff

beheld and which made his jaw drop. A wheeled-chair with luxurious cushions and robes which came towards him looking rather like some sort of state coach because a young rajah leaned back in it with royal command in his great black-rimmed eyes and a thin white hand extended haughtily towards him. And it stopped right under Ben Weatherstaff's nose. It was really no wonder his mouth dropped open.

'Do you know who I am?' demanded the rajah.

How Ben Weatherstaff stared! His red old eyes fixed themselves on what was before him as if he were seeing a ghost. He gazed and gazed and gulped a lump down his throat and did not say a word.

'Do you know who I am?' demanded Colin still more imperiously. 'Answer!'

Ben Weatherstaff put his gnarled hand up and passed it over his eyes and over his forehead and then he did answer in a queer, shaky voice.

'Who tha' art?' he said. 'Aye, that I do – wi' tha' mother's eyes starin' at me out o' tha' face. Lord knows how tha' come here. But tha'rt th' poor cripple.'

Colin forgot that he had ever had a back. His face flushed scarlet and he sat bolt upright.

'I'm not a cripple!' he cried out furiously. 'I'm not!'

'He's not!' cried Mary, almost shouting up the wall in

her fierce indignation. 'He's not got a lump as big as a pin! I looked and there was none there – not one!'

Ben Weatherstaff passed his hand over his forehead again and gazed as if he could never gaze enough. His hand shook and his mouth shook and his voice shook. He was an ignorant old man and a tactless old man and he could only remember the things he had heard.

'Tha' – tha' hasn't got a crooked back?' he said hoarsely.

'No!' shouted Colin.

'Tha' – tha' hasn't got crooked legs?' quavered Ben more hoarsely yet.

It was too much. The strength which Colin usually threw into his tantrums rushed through him now in a new way. Never yet had he been accused of crooked legs – even in whispers – and the perfectly simple belief in their existence which was revealed by Ben Weatherstaff's voice was more than rajah flesh and blood could endure. His anger and insulted pride made him forget everything but this one moment, and filled him with power he had never known before, an almost unnatural strength.

'Come here!' he shouted to Dickon, and he actually began to tear the coverings off his lower limbs and disentangle himself. 'Come here! Come here! This minute!'

Dickon was by his side in a second. Mary caught her breath in a short gasp and felt herself turn pale.

'He can do it! He can do it! He can do it! He can!' she gabbled over to herself under her breath as fast as she could.

There was a brief, fierce scramble, the rugs were tossed on the ground, Dickon held Colin's arm, the thin legs were out, the thin feet were on the grass. Colin was standing upright – upright – as straight as an arrow and looking strangely tall – his head thrown back and his strange eyes flashing lightning.

'Look at me!' he flung up at Ben Weatherstaff. 'Just look at me – you! Just look at me!'

'He's as straight as I am,' cried Dickon. 'He's as straight as any lad i' Yorkshire!'

What Ben Weatherstaff did Mary thought queer beyond measure. He choked and gulped and suddenly tears ran down his weather-wrinkled cheeks as he struck his old hands together.

'Eh!' he burst forth, 'th' lies folk tells! Tha'rt as thin as a lath an' as white as a wraith, but there's not a knob on thee. Tha'lt make a mon yet. God bless thee!'

Dickon held Colin's arms strongly, but the boy had not begun to falter. He stood straighter and straighter and looked Ben Weatherstaff in the face.

'I'm your master,' he said, 'when my father is away.

And you are to obey me. This is my garden. Don't dare to say a word about it! You get down from that ladder and go out to the Long Walk and Miss Mary will meet you and bring you here. I want to talk to you. We did not want you, but now you will have to be in the secret. Be quick!'

Ben Weatherstaff's crabbed old face was still wet with that one queer rush of tears. It seemed as if he could not take his eyes from thin, straight Colin standing on his feet with his head thrown back.

'Eh! lad,' he almost whispered. 'Eh! my lad!' And then remembering himself he suddenly touched his hat gardener fashion and said, 'Yes, sir! Yes, sir!' and obediently disappeared as he descended the ladder.

22

When the Sun Went Down

WHEN his head was out of sight, Colin turned to Mary.

'Go and meet him,' he said, and Mary flew across the grass to the door under the ivy.

Dickon was watching him with sharp eyes. There were scarlet spots on his cheeks and he looked amazing, but he showed no signs of falling.

'I can stand,' he said, and his head was still held up and he said it quite grandly.

'I told thee tha' could as soon as tha' stopped bein' afraid,' answered Dickon. 'An' tha's stopped.'

'Yes, I've stopped,' said Colin.

Then suddenly he remembered something Mary had said.

'Are you making Magic?' he asked sharply.

Dickon's curly mouth spread in a cheerful grin.

'Tha's doin' Magic thysel',' he said. 'It's same Magic as made these 'ere work out o' th' earth,' and he touched with his thick boot a clump of crocuses in the grass.

Colin looked down at them.

'Aye,' he said slowly, 'there couldna' be bigger Magic than that there – there couldna' be.'

He drew himself up straighter than ever.

'I'm going to walk to that tree,' he said, pointing to one a few feet away from him. 'I'm going to be standing when Weatherstaff comes here. I can rest against the tree if I like. When I want to sit down I will sit down, but not before. Bring a rug from the chair.'

He walked to the tree, and though Dickon held his arm he was wonderfully steady. When he stood against the tree trunk it was not too plain that he supported himself against it, and he still held himself so straight that he looked tall.

When Ben Weatherstaff came through the door in the wall he saw him standing there and he heard Mary muttering something under her breath.

'What art sayin'?' he asked rather testily, because he did not want his attention distracted from the long, thin, straight boy figure and proud face.

But she did not tell him. What she was saying was this:

'You can do it! You can do it! I told you you could! You can do it! You can do it! You *can!*'

She was saying it to Colin because she wanted to make Magic and keep him on his feet looking like that. She could not bear that he should give in before Ben Weatherstaff. He did not give in. She was uplifted by a sudden feeling that he looked quite beautiful in spite of his thinness. He fixed his eyes on Ben Weatherstaff in his funny, imperious way.

'Look at me!' he commanded. 'Look at me all over! Am I a hunchback? Have I got crooked legs?'

Ben Weatherstaff had not quite got over his emotion, but he had recovered a little and answered almost in his usual way.

'Not tha',' he said. 'Nowt o' th' sort. What's tha' been doin' with thysel' – hidin' out o' sight an' lettin' folk think tha' was cripple an' half-witted?'

'Half-witted!' said Colin angrily. 'Who thought that?'

'Lots o' fools,' said Ben. 'Th' world's full o' jackasses brayin' an' they never bray nowt but lies. What did tha' shut thysel' up for?'

'Everyone thought I was going to die,' said Colin shortly. 'I'm not!'

And he said it with such decision Ben Weatherstaff looked him over, up and down, down and up.

'Tha' die!' he said with dry exultation. 'Nowt o' th' sort. Tha's got too much pluck in thee. When I seed thee put tha' legs on th' ground in such a hurry I knowed tha' was all right. Sit thee down on th' rug a bit, young Mester, an' give me thy orders.'

There was a queer mixture of crabbed tenderness and shrewd understanding in his manner. Mary had poured out speech as rapidly as she could as they had come down the Long Walk. The chief thing to be remembered, she had told him, was that Colin was getting well – getting well. The garden was doing it. No one must let him remember about having humps and dying.

The rajah condescended to seat himself on a rug under the tree.

'What work do you do in the gardens, Weatherstaff?' he inquired.

'Anythin' I'm told to do,' answered old Ben. 'I'm kep' on by favour – because she liked me.'

'She?' said Colin.

'Tha' mother,' answered Ben Weatherstaff.

'My mother?' said Colin, and he looked about him quietly. 'This was her garden, wasn't it?'

'Aye, it was that!' and Ben Weatherstaff looked about him too. 'She were main fond of it.'

'It is my garden now. I am fond of it. I shall come here every day,' announced Colin. 'But it is to be a secret. My orders are that no one is to know that we come here. Dickon and my cousin have worked and made it come alive. I shall send for you sometimes to help – but you must come when no one can see you.'

Ben Weatherstaff's face twisted itself in a dry old smile.

'I've come here before when no one saw me,' he said.

'What!' exclaimed Colin. 'When?'

'Th' last time I was here,' rubbing his chin and looking round, 'was about two year' ago.'

'But no one had been in it for ten years!' cried Colin. 'There was no door!'

'I'm no one,' said old Ben dryly. 'An' I didn't come through th' door, I come over th' wall. Th' rheumatics held me back th' last two year.'

'Tha' come an' did a bit o' prunin'!' cried Dickon. 'I couldn't make out how it had been done.'

'She was so fond of it – she was!' said Ben Weatherstaff slowly. 'An' she was such a pretty young thing. She says to me once, "Ben," says she laughin', "if ever I'm ill or if I go away you must take care of my roses." When she did go away th' orders was no one was ever to come nigh. But I come,' with grumpy obstinacy. 'Over th' wall I come – until th' rheumatics stopped me – an' I did a bit o' work once a year. She'd gave her order first.'

'It wouldn't have been as wick as it is if tha' hadn't done it,' said Dickon. 'I did wonder.'

'I'm glad you did it, Weatherstaff,' said Colin. 'You'll know how to keep the secret.'

'Aye, I'll know, sir,' answered Ben. 'An' it'll be easier for a man wi' rheumatics to come in at th' door.'

On the grass near the tree Mary had dropped her trowel. Colin stretched out his hand and took it up. An odd expression came into his face and he began to scratch at the earth. His thin hand was weak enough, but presently as they watched him – Mary with quite breathless interest – he drove the end of the trowel into the soil and turned some over.

'You can do it! You can do it!' said Mary to herself. 'I tell you, you can!'

Dickon's round eyes were full of eager curiousness, but he said not a word. Ben Weatherstaff looked on with an interested face.

Colin persevered. After he had turned a few trowelfuls of soil he spoke exultantly to Dickon in his best Yorkshire.

'Tha' said as tha'd have me walkin' about here same as other folk – an' tha' said tha'd have me diggin'. I thowt tha' was just leein' to please me. This is only th' first day an' I've walked – an' here I am diggin'.'

Ben Weatherstaff's mouth fell open again when he heard him, but he ended by chuckling.

'Eh!' he said, 'that sounds as if tha'd got wits enow. Tha'rt a Yorkshire lad for sure. An' tha'rt diggin', too. How'd tha' like to plant a bit o' somethin? I can get thee a rose in a pot.'

'Go and get it!' said Colin, digging excitedly. 'Quick! Quick!'

It was done quickly enough indeed. Ben Weatherstaff went his way forgetting rheumatics. Dickon took his spade and dug the hole deeper and wider than a new digger with thin hands could make it. Mary slipped out to run and bring back a watering-can. When Dickon had deepened the hole, Colin went on turning the soft earth over and over. He looked up at the sky, flushed and glowing with the strangely new exercise, slight as it was.

'I want to do it before the sun goes quite – quite down,' he said.

Mary thought that perhaps the sun held back a few minutes just on purpose. Ben Weatherstaff brought the rose in its pot from the greenhouse. He hobbled over the grass as fast as he could. He had begun to be excited, too. He knelt down by the hole and broke the pot from the mould.

'Here, lad,' he said, handing the plant to Colin. 'Set it

in the earth thysel' same as th' king does when he goes to a new place.'

The thin white hands shook a little and Colin's flush grew deeper as he set the rose in the mould and held it while old Ben made firm the earth. It was filled in and pressed down and made steady. Mary was leaning forward on her hands and knees. Soot had flown down and marched forward to see what was being done. Nut and Shell chattered about it from a cherry-tree.

'It's planted!' said Colin at last. 'And the sun is only slipping over the edge. Help me up, Dickon. I want to be standing when it goes. That's part of the Magic.'

And Dickon helped him, and the Magic – or whatever it was – so gave him strength that when the sun did slip over the edge and end the strange, lovely afternoon for them, there he actually stood on his two feet – laughing.

23

Magic

D R CRAVEN had been waiting some time at the house when they returned to it. He had indeed begun to wonder if it might not be wise to send someone out to explore the garden paths. When Colin was brought back to his room, the poor man looked him over seriously.

'You should not have stayed so long,' he said. 'You must not over-exert yourself.'

'I am not tired at all,' said Colin. 'It has made me well. Tomorrow I am going out in the morning as well as in the afternoon.'

'I am not sure that I can allow it,' answered Dr Craven. 'I am afraid it would not be wise.'

'It would not be wise to try to stop me,' said Colin quite seriously. 'I am going.'

Even Mary had found out that one of Colin's chief peculiarities was that he did not know in the least what a rude little brute he was with his way of ordering people about. He had lived on a sort of desert island all his life and as he had been the king of it he had made his own manners and had had no one to compare himself with. Mary had indeed been rather like him herself, and since she had been at Misselthwaite had gradually discovered that her own manners had not been of the kind which is usual or popular. Having made this discovery, she naturally thought it of enough interest to communicate to Colin. So she sat and looked at him curiously for a few minutes after Dr Craven had gone. She wanted to make him ask her why she was doing it, and of course she did.

'What are you looking at me for?' he said.

'I'm thinking that I am rather sorry for Dr Craven.'

'So am I,' said Colin calmly, but not without an air of some satisfaction. 'He won't get Misselthwaite at all now I'm not going to die.'

'I'm sorry for him because of that, of course,' said Mary, 'but I was thinking just then that it must have been very horrid to have had to be polite for ten years to a boy who was always rude. I would never have done it.'

'Am I rude?' Colin inquired undisturbedly.

'If you had been his own boy and he had been a

slapping sort of man,' said Mary, 'he would have slapped you.'

'But he daren't,' said Colin.

'No, he daren't,' answered Mistress Mary, thinking the thing out quite without prejudice. 'Nobody ever dared to do anything you didn't like – because you were going to die and things like that. You were such a poor thing.'

'But,' announced Colin stubbornly, 'I am not going to be a poor thing. I won't let people think I'm one. I stood on my feet this afternoon.'

'It is always having your own way that has made you so queer,' Mary went on, thinking aloud.

Colin turned his head, frowning.

'Am I queer?' he demanded.

'Yes,' answered Mary, 'very. But you needn't be cross,' she added impartially, 'because so am I queer – and so is Ben Weatherstaff. But I am not as queer as I was before I began to like people and before I found the garden.'

'I don't want to be queer,' said Colin. 'I am not going to be,' and he frowned again with determination.

He was a very proud boy. He lay thinking for a while and then Mary saw his beautiful smile begin and gradually change his whole face.

'I shall stop being queer,' he said, 'if I go every day to the garden. There is Magic in there – good Magic, you know, Mary, I am sure there is.'

'So am I,' said Mary.

'Even if it isn't real Magic,' Colin said, 'we can pretend it is. *Something* is there – *something!*'

'It's Magic,' said Mary, 'but not black. It's as white as snow.'

They always called it Magic, and indeed it seemed like it in the months that followed – the wonderful months – the radiant months – the amazing ones. Oh! the things which happened in that garden! If you have never had a garden, you cannot understand, and if you have had a garden, you will know that it would take a whole book to describe all that came to pass there. At first it seemed that green things would never cease pushing their way through the earth, in the grass, in the beds, even in the crevices of the walls. Then the green things began to show buds, and the buds began to unfurl and show colour, every shade of blue, every shade of purple, every tint and hue of crimson. In its happy days flowers had been tucked away into every inch and hole and corner. Ben Weatherstaff had seen it done and had himself scraped out mortar from between the bricks of the wall and made pockets of earth for lovely clinging things to grow on. Iris and white lilies rose out of the grass in sheaves, and the green alcoves filled themselves with amazing armies of the blue and white flower lances of tall delphiniums or columbines or campanulas.

'She was main fond o' them – she was,' Ben Weatherstaff said. 'She liked them things as was allus pointin' up to th' blue sky, she used to tell. Not as she was one o' them as looked down on th' earth – not her. She just loved it, but she said as th' blue sky allus looked so joyful.'

The seeds Dickon and Mary had planted grew as if fairies had tended them. Satiny poppies of all tints danced in the breeze by the score, gaily defying flowers which had lived in the garden for years, and which it might be confessed seemed rather to wonder how such new people had got there. And the roses – the roses! Rising out of the grass, tangled round the sun-dial, wreathing the tree-trunks, and hanging from their branches, climbing up the walls and spreading over them with long garlands falling in cascades – they came alive day by day, hour by hour. Fair, fresh leaves, and buds – and buds – tiny at first, but swelling and working Magic until they burst and uncurled into cups of scent delicately spilling themselves over their brims and filling the garden air.

Colin saw it all, watching each change as it took place. Every morning he was brought out and every hour of each day, when it didn't rain, he spent in the garden. Even grey days pleased him. He would lie on the grass 'watching things growing', he said. If you watched long enough, he declared, you could see buds unsheathe themselves. Also you could make the acquaintance of strange, busy insect things running about on various unknown but evidently serious errands, sometimes carrying tiny scraps of straw or feather or food, or climbing blades of grass as if they were trees from whose tops one could look out to explore the country. A mole throwing up its mound at the end of its burrow and making its way out at last with the long-nailed paws, which looked so like elfish hands, had absorbed him one whole morning. Ants' ways, beetles' ways, bees' ways, frogs' ways, birds' ways, plants' ways, gave him a new world to explore, and when Dickon revealed them all and added foxes' ways, otters' ways, ferrets' ways, squirrels' ways, and trouts' and water-rats' and badgers' ways, there was no end to the things to talk about and think over.

And this was not the half of the Magic. The fact that he had really once stood on his feet had set Colin thinking tremendously, and when Mary told him of the spell she had worked, he was excited and approved of it greatly. He talked of it constantly.

'Of course, there must be lots of Magic in the world,' he said wisely one day, 'but people don't know what it is like or how to make it. Perhaps the beginning is just to say nice things are going to happen until you make them happen. I am going to try an experiment.'

The next morning when they went to the secret garden, he sent at once for Ben Weatherstaff. Ben came as quickly as he could, and found the rajah standing on his feet under a tree and looking very grand, but also very beautifully smiling.

'Good morning, Ben Weatherstaff,' he said. 'I want you and Dickon and Miss Mary to stand in a row and listen to me because I am going to tell you something very important.'

'Aye, aye, sir!' answered Ben Weatherstaff, touching his forehead. (One of the long-concealed charms of Ben Weatherstaff was that in his boyhood he had once run away to sea and had made voyages. So he could reply like a sailor.)

'I am going to try a scientific experiment,' explained the rajah. 'When I grow up I am going to make great scientific discoveries and I am going to begin now with this experiment.'

'Aye, aye, sir!' said Ben Weatherstaff promptly, though this was the first time he had heard of great scientific discoveries.

It was the first time Mary had heard of them, either, but even at this stage she had begun to realise that, queer as he was, Colin had read about a great many singular things and was somehow a very convincing sort of boy. When he held up his head and fixed his strange eyes on you, it seemed as if you believed him almost in spite of yourself, though he was only ten years old – going on eleven. At this moment he was especially convincing because he suddenly felt the fascination of actually making a sort of speech like a grown-up person.

'The great scientific discoveries I am going to make,' he went on, 'will be about Magic. Magic is a great thing, and scarcely anyone knows anything about it except a few people in old books – and Mary a little, because she was born in India, where there are fakirs. I believe Dickon knows some Magic, but perhaps he doesn't know he knows it. He charms animals and people. I would never have let him come to see me if he had not been an animal-charmer – which is a boy-charmer, too, because a boy is an animal. I am sure there is Magic in everything, only we have not sense enough to get hold of it and make it do things for us – like electricity and horses and steam.'

This sounded so imposing that Ben Weatherstaff became quite excited and really could not keep still.

'Aye, aye, sir,' he said, and he began to stand up quite straight.

'When Mary found this garden it looked quite dead,' the orator proceeded. 'Then something began pushing things up out of the soil and making things out of nothing. One day things weren't there and another they were. I had never watched things before, and it made me feel very curious. Scientific people are always curious, and I am going to be scientific. I keep saying to myself: "What is it? What is it?" It's something. It can't be nothing! I don't know its name, so I call it Magic. I have never seen the sun rise, but Mary and Dickon have, and from what they tell me I am sure that is Magic, too. Something pushes it up and draws it. Sometimes since I've been in the garden I've looked up through the trees at the sky and I have had a strange feeling of being happy as if something were pushing and drawing in my chest and making me breathe fast. Magic is always pushing and drawing and making things out of nothing. Everything is made out of Magic, leaves and trees, flowers and birds, badgers and foxes and squirrels and people. So it must be all around us. In this garden – in all the places. The Magic in this garden has made me stand up and know I am going to live to be a man. I am going to make the scientific experiment of trying to get some and put it in myself and make it push and draw me and make me strong. I don't know how to do it, but I think that if you keep thinking about it and calling it, perhaps it will come. Perhaps that is the first baby way to get it. When I was going to try to stand that first time, Mary kept saying to herself as fast as she could, "You can do it! You can do it!" and I did. I had to try myself at the same time, of course, but her Magic helped me – and so did Dickon's. Every morning and evening and as often in the day-time as I can remember I am going to say, "Magic is in me! Magic is making me well! I am going to be as strong as Dickon, as strong as Dickon!" And you must all do it, too. That is my experiment. Will you help, Ben Weatherstaff?'

'Aye, aye, sir!' said Ben Weatherstaff. 'Aye, aye!'

'If you keep doing it every day as regularly as soldiers go through drill, we shall see what will happen and find out if the experiment succeeds. You learn things by saying them over and over and thinking about them until they stay in your mind for ever, and I think it will be the same with Magic. If you keep calling it to come to you and help you, it will get to be part of you and it will stay and do things.'

'I once heard an officer in India tell my mother that there were fakirs who said words over and over thousands of times,' said Mary.

'I've heard Jem Fettleworth's wife say th' same thing over thousands o' times – callin' Jem a drunken brute,' said Ben Weatherstaff dryly. 'Summat allus comes o' that, sure enough. He gave her a good hidin' an' went to th' Blue Lion an' got as drunk as a lord.'

Colin drew his brows together and thought a few minutes. Then he cheered up.

'Well,' he said, 'you see something did come of it. She

used the wrong Magic until she made him beat her. If she'd used the right Magic and had said something nice, perhaps he wouldn't have got as drunk as a lord and perhaps – perhaps he might have brought her a new bonnet.'

Ben Weatherstaff chuckled and there was shrewd admiration in his little old eyes.

'Tha'rt a clever lad as well as a straight-legged one, Mester Colin,' he said. 'Next time I see Bess Fettleworth I'll give her a bit of a hint o' what Magic will do for her. She'd be rare an' pleased if th' sinetifik 'speriment worked – an' so 'ud Jem.'

Dickon had stood listening to the lecture, his round eyes shining with curious delight. Nut and Shell were on his shoulders, and he held a long-eared, white rabbit in his arm and stroked and stroked it softly while it laid its ears along its back and enjoyed itself.

'Do you think the experiment will work?' Colin asked him, wondering what he was thinking. He so often wondered what Dickon was thinking when he saw him looking at him or at one of his 'creatures' with his happy, wide smile.

He smiled now, and his smile was wider than usual.

'Aye,' he answered, 'that I do. It'll work same as th' seeds do when th' sun shines on 'em. It'll work for sure. Shall us begin it now?'

Colin was delighted and so was Mary. Fired by recollections of fakirs and devotees in illustrations, Colin suggested that they should all sit cross-legged under the tree, which made a canopy.

'It will be like sitting in a sort of temple,' said Colin. 'I'm rather tired and I want to sit down.'

'Eh!' said Dickon, 'tha' mustn't begin by sayin' tha'rt tired. Tha' might spoil th' Magic.'

Colin turned and looked at him – into his innocent, round eyes.

'That's true,' he said slowly. 'I must only think of the Magic.'

It all seemed most majestic and mysterious when they sat down in their circle. Ben Weatherstaff felt as if he had somehow been led into appearing at a prayer-meeting. Ordinarily he was very fixed in being what he called 'agen' prayer-meetin's', but this being the rajah's affair, he did not resent it, and was, indeed, inclined to be gratified at being called upon to assist. Mistress Mary felt solemnly enraptured. Dickon held his rabbit in his arm, and perhaps he made some charmer's signal no one heard, for when he sat down, cross-legged like the rest, the crow, the fox, the squirrels, and the lamb slowly drew near and made part of the circle, settling each into a place of rest as if of their own desire.

'The "creatures" have come,' said Colin gravely. 'They want to help us.'

Colin really looked quite beautiful, Mary thought. He held his head high as if he felt like a sort of priest, and his strange eyes had a wonderful look in them. The light shone on him through the tree canopy.

'Now we will begin,' he said. 'Shall we sway backwards and forwards, Mary, as if we were dervishes?'

'I canna' do no swayin' back'ard and for'ard,' said Ben Weatherstaff. 'I've got th' rheumatics.'

'The Magic will take them away,' said Colin in a High Priest tone, 'but we won't sway until it has done it. We will only chant.'

'I canna' do no chantin',' said Ben Weatherstaff, a trifle testily. 'They turned me out o' th' church choir th' only time I ever tried it.'

No one smiled. They were all too much in earnest. Colin's face was not even crossed by a shadow. He was thinking only of the Magic.

'Then I will chant,' he said. And he began, looking like a strange boy spirit. 'The sun is shining – the sun is shining. That is the Magic. The flowers are growing – the roots are stirring. That is the Magic. Being alive is the Magic – being strong is the Magic. The Magic is in me – the Magic is in me. It is in me – it is in me. It's in every one of us. It's in Ben Weatherstaff's back. Magic!

Magic! Come and help!' He said it a great many times – not a thousand times, but quite a goodly number. Mary listened entranced. She felt as if it were at once queer and beautiful and she wanted him to go on and on. Ben Weatherstaff began to feel soothed into a sort of dream which was quite agreeable. The humming of the bees in the blossoms mingled with the chanting voice and drowsily melted into a doze. Dickon sat cross-legged with his rabbit asleep on his arm and a hand resting on the lamb's back. Soot had pushed away a squirrel and huddled close to him on his shoulder; the grey film dropped over his eyes. At last Colin stopped.

'Now I am going to walk round the garden,' he announced.

Ben Weatherstaff's head had just dropped forward and he lifted it with a jerk.

'You have been asleep,' said Colin.

'Nowt o' th' sort,' mumbled Ben. 'Th' sermon was good enow – but I'm bound to get out afore th' collection.'

He was not quite awake yet.

'You're not in church,' said Colin.

'Not me,' said Ben, straightening himself. 'Who said I were? I heard every bit of it. You said th' Magic was in my back. Th' doctor calls it rheumatics.'

The rajah waved his hand.

'That was the wrong Magic,' he said. 'You will get

better. You have my permission to go to your work. But come back tomorrow.'

'I'd like to see thee walk round the garden,' grunted Ben.

It was not an unfriendly grunt, but it was a grunt. In fact, being a stubborn old party and not having entire faith in Magic, he made up his mind that if he were sent away he would climb his ladder and look over the wall so that he might be ready to hobble back if there were any stumbling.

The rajah did not object to his staying, and so the procession was formed. It really did look like a procession. Colin was at its head with Dickon on one side and Mary on the other. Ben Weatherstaff walked behind, and the 'creatures' trailed after them, the lamb and the fox cub keeping close to Dickon, the white rabbit hopping along or stopping to nibble and Soot following with the solemnity of a person who felt himself in charge.

It was a procession which moved slowly, but with dignity. Every few yards it stopped to rest. Colin leaned on Dickon's arm and privately Ben Weatherstaff kept a sharp look-out, but now and then Colin took his hand from its support and walked a few steps alone. His head was held up all the time and he looked very grand.

'The Magic is in me!' he kept saying. 'The Magic is making me strong! I can feel it! I can feel it!'

It seemed very certain that something was upholding and uplifting him. He sat on the seats in the alcoves and once or twice he sat down on the grass and several times he paused in the path and leaned on Dickon, but he would not give up until he had gone all round the garden. When he returned to the canopy tree his cheeks were flushed and he looked triumphant.

'I did it! The Magic worked!' he cried. 'That is my first scientific discovery.'

'What will Dr Craven say?' broke out Mary.

'He won't say anything,' Colin answered, 'because he will not be told. This is to be the biggest secret of all. No one is to know anything about it until I have grown so strong that I can walk and run like any other boy. I shall come here every day in my chair and I shall be taken back in it. I won't have people whispering and asking questions and I won't let my father hear about it until the experiment has quite succeeded. Then some time when he comes back to Misselthwaite I shall just walk into his study and say: "Here I am: I am like any other boy. I am quite well and I shall live to be a man. It has been done by a scientific experiment."'

'He will think he is in a dream,' cried Mary. 'He won't believe his eyes.'

Colin flushed triumphantly. He had made himself believe that he was going to get well, which was really more than half the battle, if he had been aware of it. And the thought which stimulated him more than any other was this imagining what his father would look like when he saw that he had a son who was as straight and strong as other fathers' sons. One of his darkest miseries in the unhealthy, morbid past days had been his hatred of being a sickly, weak-backed boy, whose father was afraid to look at him.

'He'll be obliged to believe them,' he said. 'One of the things I am going to do, after the Magic works and before I begin to make scientific discoveries, is to be an athlete.'

'We shall have thee takin' to boxin' in a week or so,' said Ben Weatherstaff. "Tha'lt end wi' winnin' th' Belt an' bein' champion prize-fighter of all England.'

Colin fixed his eyes on him sternly.

'Weatherstaff,' he said, 'that is disrespectful. You must not take liberties because you are in the secret. However much the Magic works, I shall not be a prize-fighter. I shall be a Scientific Discoverer.'

'Ax pardon – ax pardon, sir,' answered Ben, touching his forehead in salute. 'I ought to have seed it wasn't a jokin' matter,' but his eyes twinkled and secretly he was immensely pleased. He really did not mind being snubbed, since the snubbing meant that the lad was gaining strength and spirit.

24

'Let Them Laugh'

THE secret garden was not the only one Dickon worked in. Round the cottage on the moor there was a piece of ground enclosed by a low wall of rough stones. Early in the morning and late in the fading twilight and on all the days Colin and Mary did not see him, Dickon worked there planting or tending potatoes and cabbages, turnips and carrots and herbs for his mother. In the company of his 'creatures' he did wonders there and was never tired of doing them, it seemed. While he dug or weeded he whistled or sang bits of Yorkshire moor songs or talked to Soot or Captain or the brothers and sisters he had taught to help him.

'We'd never get on as comfortable as we do,' Mrs Sowerby said, 'if it wasn't for Dickon's garden. Anything'll grow for him. His 'taters and cabbages is twice th' size of anyone else's an' they've got a flavour with 'em as nobody's has.'

When she found a moment to spare she liked to go out and talk to him. After supper there was still a long clear twilight to work in, and that was her quiet time. She could sit upon the low rough wall and look on and hear stories of the day. She loved this time. There were not only vegetables in this garden. Dickon had bought penny packages of flower seeds now and then and sown bright, sweet-scented things among gooseberry bushes and even cabbages and he grew borders of mignonette and pinks and pansies and things, whose seeds he could save year after year or whose roots would bloom each spring and spread in time into fine clumps. The low wall was one of the prettiest things in Yorkshire because he had tucked moorland foxglove and ferns and rock-cress and hedgerow flowers into every crevice until only here and there glimpses of the stones were to be seen.

'All a chap's got to do to make 'em thrive, Mother,' he would say, 'is to be friends with 'em for sure. They're just like th' "creatures". If they're thirsty give 'em a drink, and if they're hungry give 'em a bit o' food. They want to live same as we do. If they died I should feel as if I'd been a bad lad and somehow treated them heartless.'

It was in these twilight hours that Mrs Sowerby heard

of all that happened at Misselthwaite Manor. At first she was only told that 'Mester Colin' had taken a fancy to going out into the grounds with Miss Mary and that it was doing him good. But it was not long before it was agreed between the two children that Dickon's mother might 'come into the secret'. Somehow it was not doubted that she was 'safe for sure'.

So one beautiful, still evening, Dickon told the whole story, with all the thrilling details of the buried key and the robin and the grey haze which had seemed like deadness and the secret Mistress Mary had planned never to reveal. The coming of Dickon and how it had been told to him, the doubt of Mester Colin and the final drama of his introduction to the hidden domain, combined with the incident of Ben Weatherstaff's angry face peering over the wall and Mester Colin's sudden indignant strength, made Mrs Sowerby's nice-looking face quite change colour several times.

'My word!' she said. 'It was a good thing that little lass came to th' Manor. It's been th' makin' o' her an' th' savin' o' him. Standin' on his feet! An' us all thinkin' he was a poor, half-witted lad with not a straight bone in him.'

She asked a great many questions and her blue eyes were full of deep thinking.

'What do they make of it at th' Manor – him being so well an' cheeful an' never complainin'?' she inquired.

'They don't know what to make of it,' answered Dickon. 'Every day as comes round his face looks different. It's fillin' out and doesn't look so sharp an' th' waxy colour is goin'. But he has to do his bit o' complainin',' with a highly entertained grin.

'What for, i' Mercy's name?' asked Mrs Sowerby.

Dickon chuckled.

'He does it to keep them from guessin' what's happened. If the doctor knew he'd found out he could stand on his feet, he'd likely write and tell Mester Craven. Mester Colin's savin' th' secret to tell himself. He's goin' to practise his Magic on his legs every day till his father comes back an' then he's goin' to march into his room an' show him he's as straight as other lads. But him an' Miss Mary thinks it's best plan to do a bit o' groanin' and frettin' now an' then to throw off th' scent.'

Mrs Sowerby was laughing a low, comfortable laugh long before he had finished his last sentence.

'Eh!' she said, 'that pair's enjoyin' theirselves, I'll warrant. They'll get a good bit o' play actin' out of it, an' there's nothin' children likes as much as play actin'. Let's hear what they do, Dickon, lad.'

Dickon stopped weeding and sat up on his heels to tell her. His eyes were twinkling with fun.

'Mester Colin is carried down to his chair every time he goes out,' he explained. 'An' he flies out at John, th' footman, for not carryin' him careful enough. He makes himself as helpless-lookin' as he can an' never lifts his head until we're out o' sight o' th' house. An' he grunts an' frets a good bit when he's bein' settled into his chair. Him an' Miss Mary's both got to enjoyin' it, an' when he groans an' complains she'll say: "Poor Colin! Does it hurt you so much? Are you so weak as that, poor Colin?" – but th' trouble is that sometimes they can scarce keep from burstin' out laughin'. When we get safe into the garden they laugh till they've no breath left to laugh with. An' they have to stuff their faces into Mester Colin's cushions to keep the gardeners from hearin', if any of 'em's about.'

'Th' more they laugh th' better for 'em!' said Mrs Sowerby, still laughing herself. 'Good, healthy child laughin's better than pills any day o' th' year. That pair'll plump up for sure.'

'They are plumpin' up,' said Dickon. 'They're that hungry they don't know how to get enough to eat without makin' talk. Mester Colin says if he keeps sendin' for more food, they won't believe he's an invalid at all. Miss Mary says she'll let him eat her share, but he says that if she goes hungry she'll get thin an' they mun both get fat at once.'

Mrs Sowerby laughed so heartily at the revelation of this difficulty that she quite rocked backwards and forwards in her blue cloak, and Dickon laughed with her.

'I'll tell thee what, lad,' Mrs Sowerby said when she could speak. 'I've thought of a way to help 'em. When tha' goes to 'em in th' mornin's tha' shall take a pail o' good new milk an' I'll bake 'em a crusty cottage loaf or some buns wi' currants in 'em, same as you children like. Nothin's so good as fresh milk an' bread. Then they could take off th' edge o' their hunger while they were in their garden an' th' fine food they get indoors 'ud polish off th' corners.'

'Eh! Mother!' said Dickon admiringly, 'what a wonder tha' art! Tha' always sees a way out o' things. They was quite in a pother yesterday. They didn't see how they was to manage without orderin' up more food – they felt that empty inside.'

'They're two young 'uns growin' fast, and health's comin' back to both of 'em. Children like that feels like young wolves an' food's flesh an' blood to 'em,' said Mrs Sowerby. Then she smiled Dickon's own curving smile. 'Eh! but they're enjoyin' their selves for sure,' she said.

She was quite right, the comfortable, wonderful mother creature – and she had never been more so than when she said their 'play actin'' would be their joy. Colin and Mary found it one of their most thrilling sources of entertainment. The idea of protecting themselves from suspicion had been unconsciously suggested to them first by the puzzled nurse and then by Dr Craven himself.

'Your appetite is improving very much, Master Colin,' the nurse had said one day. 'You used to eat nothing, and so many things disagreed with you.'

'Nothing disagrees with me now,' replied Colin, and then seeing the nurse looking at him curiously, he suddenly remembered that perhaps he ought not to appear too well just yet. 'At least, things don't so often disagree with me. It's the fresh air.'

'Perhaps it is,' said the nurse, still looking at him with a mystified expression. 'But I must talk to Dr Craven about it.'

'How she stared at you!' said Mary when she went away. 'As if she thought there must be something to find out.'

'I won't have her finding out things,' said Colin. 'No one must begin to find out yet.'

When Dr Craven came that morning he seemed puzzled, too. He asked a number of questions, to Colin's great annoyance.

'You stay out in the garden a great deal,' he suggested. 'Where do you go?'

Colin put on his favourite air of dignified indifference to opinion.

'I will not let anyone know where I go,' he answered. 'I go to a place I like. Everyone has orders to keep out of the way. I won't be watched and stared at. You know that!'

'You seem to be out all day, but I do not think it has done you harm – I do not think so. The nurse says that you eat much more than you have ever done before.'

'Perhaps,' said Colin, prompted by a sudden inspiration, 'perhaps it is an unnatural appetite.'

'I do not think so, as your food seems to agree with you,' said Dr Craven. 'You are gaining flesh rapidly and your colour is better.'

'Perhaps – perhaps I am bloated and feverish,' said Colin, assuming a discouraging air of gloom. 'People who are not going to live are often – different.'

Dr Craven shook his head. He was holding Colin's wrist, and he pushed up his sleeve and felt his arm.

'You are not feverish,' he said thoughtfully, 'and such flesh as you have gained is healthy. If we can keep this up, my boy, we need not talk of dying. Your father will be very happy to hear of this remarkable improvement.'

'I won't have him told!' Colin broke forth fiercely. 'It will only disappoint him if I get worse again – and I may get worse this very night. I might have a raging fever. I feel as if I might be beginning to have one now. I won't have letters written to my father – I won't – I won't! You are making me angry, and you know that is bad for me. I feel hot already. I hate being written about and being talked over as much as I hate being stared at!'

'Hush-h! my boy,' Dr Craven soothed him. 'Nothing shall be written without your permission. You are too sensitive about things. You must not undo the good which has been done.'

He said no more about writing to Mr Craven, and when he saw the nurse he privately warned her that such a possibility must not be mentioned to the patient.

'The boy is extraordinarily better,' he said. 'His advance seems almost abnormal. But, of course, he is doing now of his own free will what we could not make him do before. Still, he excites himself very easily and nothing must be said to irritate him.'

Mary and Colin were much alarmed and talked together anxiously. From this time dated their plan of 'play actin'.'

'I may be obliged to have a tantrum,' said Colin regretfully. 'I don't want to have one and I'm not miserable enough now to work myself into a big one. Perhaps I couldn't have one at all. That lump doesn't come in my throat now, and I keep thinking of nice things instead of horrible ones. But if they talk about writing to my father, I shall have to do something.'

He made up his mind to eat less, but unfortunately

it was not possible to carry out this brilliant idea when he wakened each morning with an amazing appetite and the table near his sofa was set with a breakfast of home-made bread and fresh butter, snow-white eggs, raspberry jam, and clotted cream. Mary always breakfasted with him, and when they found themselves at the table – particularly if there were delicate slices of sizzling ham sending forth tempting odours from under a hot silver cover – they would look into each other's eyes in desperation.

'I think we shall have to eat it all this morning, Mary,' Colin always ended by saying. 'We can send away some of the lunch and a great deal of the dinner.'

But they never found they could send away anything, and the highly polished condition of the empty plates returned to the pantry awakened much comment.

'I do wish,' Colin would say also, 'I do wish the slices of ham were thicker, and one muffin each is not enough for anyone.'

'It's enough for a person who is going to die,' answered Mary when first she heard this, 'but it's not enough for a person who is going to live. I sometimes feel as if I could eat three when those nice fresh heather and gorse smells from the moor come pouring in at the open window.'

The morning that Dickon – after they had been enjoying themselves in the garden for about two hours

– went behind a big rose-bush and brought forth two tin pails and revealed that one was full of rich new milk with cream on the top of it, and that the other held cottage-made currant buns folded in a clean blue and white napkin, buns so carefully tucked in that they were still hot, there was a riot of surprised joyfulness. What a wonderful thing for Mrs Sowerby to think of! What a kind, clever woman she must be! How good the buns were! And what delicious fresh milk!

'Magic is in her just as it is in Dickon,' said Colin. 'It makes her think of ways to do things – nice things. She is a Magic person. Tell her we are grateful, Dickon – extremely grateful.'

He was given to using rather grown-up phrases at times.

He enjoyed them. He liked this so much that he improved upon it.

'Tell her she has been most bounteous and our gratitude is extreme.'

And then forgetting his grandeur he fell to and stuffed himself with buns and drank milk out of the pail in copious draughts in the manner of any hungry little boy who had been taking unusual exercise and breathing in moorland air and whose breakfast was more than two hours behind him.

This was the beginning of many agreeable incidents

of the same kind. They actually awoke to the fact that as Mrs Sowerby had fourteen people to provide food for she might not have enough to satisfy two extra appetites every day. So they asked her to let them send some of their shillings to buy things.

Dickon made the stimulating discovery that in the wood in the park outside the garden where Mary had first found him piping to the wild creatures, there was a deep little hollow where you could build a sort of tiny oven with stones and roast potatoes and eggs in it. Roasted eggs were a previously unknown luxury, and very hot potatoes with salt and fresh butter in them were fit for a woodland king besides being deliciously satisfying. You could buy both potatoes and eggs and eat as many as you liked without feeling as if you were taking food out of the mouths of fourteen people.

Every beautiful morning the Magic was worked by the mystic circle under the plum-tree which provided a canopy of thickening green leaves after its brief blossom-time was ended. After the ceremony Colin always took his walking exercise, and throughout the day he exercised his newly found power at intervals. Each day he grew stronger and could walk more steadily and cover more ground. And each day his belief in the Magic grew stronger – as well it might. He tried one experiment after another as he felt himself gaining strength, and it was Dickon who showed him the best things of all.

'Yesterday,' he said one morning after an absence, 'I went to Thwaite for Mother, an' near th' Blue Cow Inn I seed Bob Haworth. He's the strongest chap on th' moor. He's the champion wrestler an' he can jump higher than any other chap an' throw th' hammer farther. He's gone all th' way to Scotland for th' sports some years. He's knowed me ever since I was a little 'un an' he's a friendly sort an' I axed him some questions. Th' gentry calls him an athlete and I thought o' thee, Mester Colin, and I says: "How did tha' make tha' muscles stick out that way, Bob? Did tha' do anythin' extra to make thysel' so strong?" An' he says: "Well, yes, lad, I did. A strong man in a show that came to Thwaite once showed me how to exercise my arms an' legs an' every muscle in my body." An' I says: "Could a delicate chap make himself stronger with 'em, Bob?" an' he laughed an' says, "Art tha' th' delicate chap?" an' I says, "No, but I knows a young gentleman that's gettin' well of a long illness an' I wish I knowed some o' them tricks to tell him about." I didn't say no names an' he didn't ask none. He's friendly same as I said, an' he stood up an' showed me good-natured like, an' I imitated what he did till I knowed it by heart.'

Colin had been listening excitedly.

'Can you show me?' he cried. 'Will you?'

'Aye, to be sure,' Dickon answered, getting up. 'But he says tha' mun do 'em gentle at first an' be careful not to tire thysel'. Rest in between times an' take deep breaths an' don't overdo.'

'I'll be careful,' said Colin. 'Show me! Show me! Dickon, you are the most Magic boy in the world!'

Dickon stood up on the grass and slowly went through a carefully practical but simple series of muscle exercises. Colin watched them with widening eyes. He could do a few while he was sitting down. Presently he did a few gently while he stood upon his already steadied feet. Mary began to do them also. Soot, who was watching the performance, became much disturbed and left his branch and hopped about restlessly because he could not do them too.

From that time the exercises were part of the day's duties as much as the Magic was. It became possible for both Colin and Mary to do more of them each time they tried, and such appetites were the result that but for the basket Dickon put down behind the bush each morning when he arrived, they would have been lost. But the little oven in the hollow and Mrs Sowerby's bounties were so satisfying that Mrs Medlock and the nurse and Dr Craven became mystified again. You can trifle with your breakfast and seem to disdain your dinner if you are full to the brim with roasted eggs and potatoes and richly frothed new milk and oat-cakes and buns and heather honey and clotted cream.

'They are eating next to nothing,' said the nurse. 'They'll die of starvation if they can't be persuaded to take some nourishment. And yet see how they look.'

'Look!' exclaimed Mrs Medlock indignantly. 'Eh! I'm moithered to death with them. They're a pair of young Satans. Bursting their jackets one day and the next turning up their noses at the best meals Cook can tempt them with. Not a mouthful of that lovely young fowl and bread sauce did they set a fork into yesterday – and the poor woman fair *invented* a pudding for them – and back it's sent. She almost cried. She's afraid she'll be blamed if they starve themselves into their graves.'

Dr Craven came and looked at Colin long and carefully. He wore an extremely worried expression when the nurse talked with him and showed him the almost untouched tray of breakfast she had saved for him to look at – but he was even more worried when he sat down by Colin's sofa and examined him. He had been called to London on business and had not seen the boy for nearly two weeks. When young things begin to gain health they gain it rapidly. The waxen tinge had left Colin's skin and a warm rose showed through it; his beautiful eyes were clear and the hollows under them and in his cheeks and temples had filled out. His once dark, heavy locks had begun to look as if they sprang healthily from his forehead and were soft and warm with life. His lips were fuller and of a normal colour. In fact, as an imitation of a boy who was a confirmed invalid he was a disgraceful sight. Dr Craven held his chin in his hand and thought him over.

'I am sorry to hear that you do not eat anything,' he said. 'That will not do. You will lose all you have gained – and you have gained amazingly. You ate so well a short time ago.'

'I told you it was an unnatural appetite,' answered Colin.

Mary was sitting on her stool near by and she suddenly made a very queer sound which she tried so violently to repress that she ended by almost choking.

'What is the matter?' said Dr Craven, turning to look at her.

Mary became quite severe in her manner.

'It was something between a sneeze and a cough,' she replied, with reproachful dignity, 'and it got into my throat.'

'But,' she said afterwards to Colin, 'I couldn't stop myself. It just burst out because all at once I couldn't help remembering that last big potato you ate and the way your mouth stretched when you bit through that thick, lovely crust with jam and clotted cream on it.'

'Is there any way in which those children can get food secretly?' Dr Craven inquired of Mrs Medlock.

'There's no way unless they dig it out of the earth or pick it off the trees,' Mrs Medlock answered. 'They stay out in the grounds all day and see no one but each other. And if they want anything different to eat from what's sent up to them, they need only ask for it.'

'Well,' said Dr Craven, 'so long as going without food agrees with them, we need not disturb ourselves. The boy is a new creature.'

'So is the girl,' said Mrs Medlock. 'She's begun to be downright pretty since she's filled out and lost her ugly little sour look. Her hair's grown thick and healthy looking and she's got a bright colour. The glummest, ill-natured little thing she used to be, and now her and Master Colin laugh together like a pair of crazy young ones. Perhaps they're growing fat on that.'

'Perhaps they are,' said Dr Craven. 'Let them laugh.'

25

The Curtain

AND the secret garden bloomed and bloomed and every morning revealed new miracles. In the robin's nest there were eggs and the robin's mate sat upon them, keeping them warm with her feathery little breast and careful wings. At first she was very nervous, and the robin himself was indignantly watchful. Even Dickon did not go near the close-grown corner in those days, but waited until by the quiet working of some mysterious spell he seemed to have conveyed to the soul of the little pair that in the garden there was nothing which was not quite like themselves – nothing which did not understand the wonderfulness of what was happening to them – the immense, tender, terrible, heart-breaking beauty and solemnity of Eggs. If there had been one person in that garden who had not known through all his or her innermost being that if an Egg were taken away or hurt the whole world would whirl round and crash through space and come to an end – if there had been even one who did not feel it and act accordingly there could have been no happiness even in that golden springtime air. But they all knew it and felt it and the robin and his mate knew they knew it.

At first the robin watched Mary and Colin with sharp anxiety. For some mysterious reason he knew he need not watch Dickon. The first moment he set his dew-bright black eye on Dickon he knew he was not a stranger, but a sort of robin without beak or feathers. He could speak robin (which is quite a distinct language not to be mistaken for any other). To speak robin to a robin is like speaking French to a Frenchman. Dickon always spoke it to the robin himself, so the queer gibberish he used when he spoke to humans did not matter in the least. The robin thought he spoke this gibberish to them because they were not intelligent enough to understand feathered speech. His movements also were robin. They never startled one by being sudden enough to seem dangerous or threatening. Any robin could understand Dickon, so his presence was not even disturbing.

But at the outset it seemed necessary to be on guard against the other two. In the first place the boy creature did not come into the garden on his legs. He was pushed in on a thing with wheels and the skins of wild animals were thrown over him. That in itself was doubtful. Then when he began to stand up and move about he did it in a queer, unaccustomed way, and the others seemed to have to help him. The robin used to secrete himself in a bush and watch this anxiously, his head tilted first to one side and then on the other. He thought that the slow movements might mean that he was preparing to pounce, as cats do. When cats are preparing to pounce they creep over the ground very slowly. The robin talked this over with his mate a great deal for a few days, but after that he decided not to speak of the subject because her terror was so great that he was afraid it might be injurious to the eggs.

When the boy began to walk by himself and even to move more quickly, it was an immense relief. But for a long time – or it seemed a long time to the robin – he was a source of some anxiety. He did not act as the other humans did. He seemed very fond of walking, but he had a way of sitting or lying down for a while and then getting up in a disconcerting manner to begin again.

One day the robin remembered that when he himself had been made to learn to fly by his parents he had done much the same sort of thing. He had taken short flights of a few yards and then had been obliged to rest. So it occurred to him that this boy was learning to fly

– or rather to walk. He mentioned this to his mate, and when he told her that the Eggs would probably conduct themselves in the same way after they were fledged, she was quite comforted and even became eagerly interested and derived great pleasure from watching the boy over the edge of her nest – though she always thought that the Eggs would be much cleverer and learn more quickly. But then she said indulgently that humans were always more clumsy and slow than Eggs, and most of them never seemed really to learn to fly at all. You never met them in the air or on tree-tops.

After a while the boy began to move about as the others did, but all three of the children at times did unusual things. They would stand under the trees and move their arms and legs and heads about in a way which was neither walking nor running nor sitting down. They went through these movements at intervals every day, and the robin was never able to explain to his mate what they were doing or trying to do. He could only say that he was sure that the Eggs would never flap about in such a manner, but as the boy who could speak robin fluently was doing the thing with them, birds could be quite sure that the actions were not of a dangerous nature. Of course, neither the robin nor his mate had ever heard of the champion wrestler, Bob Haworth, and his exercises for making the muscles stand out like lumps. Robins are not like human beings; their muscles are always exercised from the first, and so they develop themselves in a natural manner. If you have to fly about to find every meal you eat, your muscles do not become atrophied (atrophied means wasted away through want of use).

When the boy was walking and running about and digging and weeding like the others, the nest in the corner was brooded over by a great peace and content. Fears for the Eggs became things of the past. Knowing that your Eggs were as safe as if they were locked in a bank vault and the fact that you could watch so many curious things going on made sitting a most entertaining occupation. On wet days the Eggs' mother sometimes felt even a little dull because the children did not come into the garden.

But even on wet days it could not be said that Mary and Colin were dull. One morning when the rain streamed down unceasingly and Colin was beginning to feel a little restive, as he was obliged to remain on his sofa because it was not safe to get up and walk about, Mary had an inspiration.

'Now that I am a real boy,' Colin had said, 'my legs and arms and all my body are so full of Magic that I can't keep them still. They want to be doing things all the time. Do you know that when I waken in the morning,

Mary, when it's quite early and the birds are just shouting outside and everything seems just shouting for joy – even the trees and things we can't really hear – I feel as if I must jump out of bed and shout myself. And if I did it, just think what would happen!'

Mary giggled inordinately.

'The nurse would come running and Mrs Medlock would come running and they would be sure you had gone crazy and they'd send for the doctor,' she said.

Colin giggled himself. He could see how they would all look – how horrified by his outbreak and how amazed to see him standing upright.

'I wish my father would come home,' he said. 'I want to tell him myself. I'm always thinking about it – but we couldn't go on like this much longer. I can't stand lying still and pretending, and besides, I look too different. I wish it wasn't raining today.'

It was then Mistress Mary had her inspiration.

'Colin,' she began mysteriously, 'do you know how many rooms there are in this house?'

'About a thousand, I suppose,' he answered.

'There's about a hundred no one ever goes into,' said Mary. 'And one rainy day I went and looked into ever so many of them. No one ever knew, though Mrs Medlock nearly found me out. I lost my way when I was coming back, and I stopped at the end of your corridor. That was the second time I heard you crying.'

Colin started up on his sofa.

'A hundred rooms no one goes into,' he said. 'It sounds almost like a secret garden. Suppose we go and look at them. You could wheel me in my chair and nobody would know where we went.'

'That's what I was thinking,' said Mary. 'No one would dare to follow us. There are galleries where you could run. We could do our exercises. There is a little Indian room where there is a cabinet full of ivory elephants. There are all sorts of rooms.'

'Ring the bell,' said Colin.

When the nurse came in he gave his orders.

'I want my chair,' he said. 'Miss Mary and I are going to look at the part of the house which is not used. John can push me as far as the picture-gallery because there are some stairs. Then he must go away and leave us alone until I send for him again.'

Rainy days lost their terrors that morning. When the footman had wheeled the chair into the picture-gallery and left the two together in obedience to orders, Colin and Mary looked at each other delighted. As soon as Mary had made sure that John was really on his way back to his own quarters below stairs, Colin got out of his chair.

'I am going to run from one end of the gallery to the other,' he said, 'and then I am going to jump and then we will do Bob Haworth's exercises.'

And they did all these things and many others. They looked at the portraits and found the plain little girl dressed in green brocade and holding the parrot on her finger.

'All these,' said Colin, 'must be my relations. They lived a long time ago. That parrot one, I believe, is one of my great, great, great, great-aunts. She looks rather like you, Mary – not as you look now, but as you looked when you came here. Now you are a great deal fatter and better-looking.'

'So are you,' said Mary, and they both laughed.

They went to the Indian room and amused themselves with the ivory elephants. They found the rose-coloured brocade boudoir and the hole in the cushion the mouse had left, but the mice had grown up and run away and the hole was empty. They saw more rooms and made more discoveries than Mary had made on her first pilgrimage. They found new corridors and corners and flights of steps and new old pictures they liked and weird old things they did not know the use of. It was a curiously entertaining morning, and the feeling of wandering about in the same house with other people, but at the same time feeling as if one were miles away from them was a fascinating thing.

'I'm glad we came,' Colin said. 'I never knew I lived in such a big, queer old place. I like it. We will ramble about every rainy day. We shall always be finding new queer corners and things.'

That morning they had found among other things such good appetites that when they returned to Colin's room it was not possible to send the luncheon away untouched.

When the nurse carried the tray downstairs she slapped it down on the kitchen dresser so that Mrs Loomis, the cook, could see the highly polished dishes and plates.

'Look at that!' she said. 'This is a house of mystery, and those two children are the greatest mysteries in it.'

'If they keep that up every day,' said the strong young footman, John, 'there'd be small wonder that he weighs twice as much today as he did a month ago. I should have to give up my place in time, for fear of doing my muscles an injury.'

That afternoon Mary noticed that something new had happened in Colin's room. She had noticed it the day before, but had said nothing because she thought the change might have been made by chance. She said nothing today, but she sat and looked fixedly at the picture over the mantel. She could look at it because the curtain had been drawn aside. That was the change she noticed.

'I know what you want me to tell you,' said Colin, after she had stared a few minutes. 'I always know when you want me to tell you something. You are wondering why the curtain is drawn back. I am going to keep it like that.'

'Why?' asked Mary.

'Because it doesn't make me angry any more to see her laughing. I wakened when it was bright moonlight two nights ago and felt as if the Magic was filling the room and making everything so splendid that I couldn't lie still. I got up and looked out of the window. The room was quite light and there was a patch of moonlight on the curtain, and somehow that made me go and pull the cord. She looked right down at me as if she were laughing because she was glad I was standing there. It made me like to look at her. I want to see her laughing like that all the time. I think she must have been a sort of Magic person perhaps.'

'You are so like her now,' said Mary, 'that sometimes I think perhaps you are her ghost made into a boy.'

That idea seemed to impress Colin. He thought it over and then answered her slowly.

'If I were her ghost – my father would be fond of me,' he said.

'Do you want him to be fond of you?' inquired Mary.

'I used to hate it because he was not fond of me. If he grew fond of me I think I should tell him about the Magic. It might make him more cheerful.'

26

'It's Mother!'

THEIR belief in the Magic was an abiding thing. After the morning's incantations Colin sometimes gave them Magic lectures.

'I like to do it,' he explained, 'because when I grow up and make great scientific discoveries I shall be obliged to lecture about them, and so this is practice. I can only give short lectures now because I am very young, and, besides, Ben Weatherstaff would feel as if he was in church and he would go to sleep.'

'T' best thing about lecturin',' said Ben, 'is that a chap can get up an' say aught he pleases an' no other chap can answer him back. I wouldn't be agin' lecturin' a bit mysel' sometimes.'

But when Colin held forth under his tree old Ben fixed devouring eyes on him and kept them there. He looked him over with critical affection. It was not so much the lecture which interested him as the legs which looked straighter and stronger each day, the boyish head which held itself up so well, the once sharp chin and hollow cheeks which had filled and rounded out, and the eyes which had begun to hold the light he remembered in another pair. Sometimes when Colin felt Ben's earnest gaze meant that he was much impressed he wondered what he was reflecting on, and once, when he had seemed quite entranced, he questioned him.

'What are you thinking about, Ben Weatherstaff?' he asked.

'I was thinkin',' answered Ben, 'as I'd warrant tha's gone up three or four pound this week. I was lookin' at tha' calves an' tha' shoulders. I'd like to get thee on a pair o' scales.'

'It's the Magic and — and Mrs Sowerby's buns and milk and things,' said Colin. 'You see, the scientific experiment has succeeded.'

That morning Dickon was too late to hear the lecture. When he came he was ruddy with running and his funny face looked more twinkling than usual. As they had a good deal of weeding to do after the rains, they fell to work. They always had plenty to do after a warm, deep sinking rain. The moisture which was good for the flowers was also good for the weeds, which thrust up tiny blades of grass and points of leaves which must be pulled up before their roots took too firm hold. Colin was as good at weeding as anyone in these days, and he could lecture while he was doing it.

'The Magic works best when you work yourself,' he said this morning. 'You can feel it in your bones and muscles. I am going to read books about bones and muscles, but I am going to write a book about Magic. I am making it up now. I keep finding out things.'

It was not very long after he had said this that he laid down his trowel and stood up on his feet. He had been silent for several minutes, and they had seen that he was thinking out lectures, as he often did. When he dropped his trowel and stood upright it seemed to Mary and Dickon as if a sudden strong thought had made him do it. He stretched himself out to his tallest height and he threw out his arms exultantly. Colour glowed in his face and his strange eyes widened with joyfulness. All at once he had realised something to the full.

'Mary! Dickon!' he cried. 'Just look at me!'

They stopped their weeding and looked at him.

'Do you remember that first morning you brought me in here?' he demanded.

Dickon was looking at him very hard. Being an animal-charmer, he could see more things than most people could, and many of them were things he never talked about. He saw some of them now in this boy.

'Aye, that we do,' he answered.

Mary looked hard, too, but she said nothing.

'Just this minute,' said Colin, 'all at once I remembered it myself – when I looked at my hand digging with the trowel – and I had to stand up on my feet to see if it was real. And it is real! I'm *well* – I'm *well*!'

'Aye, that tha' art!' said Dickon.

'I'm well! I'm well!' said Colin again, and his face went quite red all over.

He had known it before in a way, he had hoped it and felt it and thought about it, but just at that minute something had rushed all through him – a sort of rapturous belief and realisation, and it had been so strong that he could not help calling out.

'I shall live for ever and ever and ever!' he cried grandly. 'I shall find out thousands and thousands of things. I shall find out about people and creatures and everything that grows – like Dickon – and I shall never stop making Magic. I'm well! I'm well! I feel – I feel as if I want to shout out something – something thankful, joyful!'

Ben Weatherstaff, who had been working near a rose-bush, glanced round at him.

'Tha' might sing th' Doxology,' he suggested in his

dryest grunt. He had no opinion of the Doxology, and he did not make the suggestion with any particular reverence.

But Colin was of an exploring mind, and he knew nothing about the Doxology.

'What is that?' he inquired.

'Dickon can sing it for thee, I'll warrant,' replied Ben Weatherstaff.

Dickon answered with his all-perceiving animal-charmer's smile.

'They sing it i' church,' he said. 'Mother says she believes th' skylarks sings it when they gets up i' th' mornin'.'

'If she says that, it must be a nice song,' Colin answered. 'I've never been in a church myself. I was always too ill. Sing it, Dickon. I want to hear it.'

Dickon was quite simple and unaffected about it. He understood what Colin felt better than Colin did himself. He understood by a sort of instinct so natural that he did not know it was understanding. He pulled off his cap and looked round still smiling.

'Tha' must take off tha' cap,' he said to Colin, 'an' so mun tha', Ben – an' tha' mun stand up, tha' knows.'

Colin took off his cap and the sun shone on and warmed his thick hair as he watched Dickon intently. Ben Weatherstaff scrambled up from his knees and bared his head, too, with a sort of puzzled, half-resentful look on his face, as if he didn't know exactly why he was doing this remarkable thing.

Dickon stood out among the trees and rose-bushes and began to sing in quite a simple, matter-of-fact way, and in a nice strong boy's voice:

> *Praise God from whom all blessings flow,*
> *Praise Him all creatures here below,*
> *Praise Him above ye Heavenly Host,*
> *Praise Father, Son, and Holy Ghost. Amen.*

When he had finished, Ben Weatherstaff was standing quite still with his jaws set obstinately, but with a disturbed look in his eyes fixed on Colin. Colin's face was thoughtful and appreciative.

'It is a very nice song,' he said. 'I like it. Perhaps it means just what I mean when I want to shout that I am thankful to the Magic.' He stopped and thought in a puzzled way. 'Perhaps they are both the same thing. How can we know the exact names of everything? Sing it again, Dickon. Let us try, Mary. I want to sing it, too. It's my song. How does it begin? "Praise God from whom all blessings flow"?'

And they sang it again, and Mary and Colin lifted their voices as musically as they could, and Dickon's swelled quite loud and beautiful – and at the second line Ben Weatherstaff raspingly cleared his throat, and at the third he joined in with such vigour that it seemed almost savage, and when the 'Amen' came to an end, Mary observed that the very same thing had happened to him which had happened when he found out that Colin was not a cripple – his chin was twitching and he was staring and winking, and his leathery old cheeks were wet.

'I never seed no sense in th' Doxology afore,' he said hoarsely, 'but I may change my mind i' time. I should say tha's gone up five pound this week, Mester Colin – five on 'em!'

Colin was looking across the garden at something attracting his attention, and his expression had become a startled one.

'Who is coming in here?' he said quickly. 'Who is it?'

The door in the ivied wall had been pushed gently open and a woman had entered. She had come in with the last line of their song and she had stood still listening and looking at them. With the ivy behind her, the sunlight drifting through the trees and dappling her long blue cloak, and her nice fresh face smiling across the greenery, she was rather like a softly coloured illustration in one of Colin's books. She had wonderful affectionate eyes which seemed to take everything in –

all of them, even Ben Weatherstaff and the 'creatures' and every flower that was in bloom. Unexpectedly as she had appeared, not one of them felt that she was an intruder at all. Dickon's eyes lighted like lamps.

'It's Mother – that's who it is!' he cried, and he went across the grass at a run.

Colin began to move towards her, too, and Mary went with him. They both felt their pulses beat faster.

'It's Mother!' Dickon said again when they met halfway. 'I knowed tha' wanted to see her an' I told her where th' door was hid.'

Colin held out his hand with a sort of flushed royal shyness, but his eyes quite devoured her face.

'Even when I was ill I wanted to see you,' he said, 'you and Dickon and the secret garden. I'd never wanted to see anyone or anything before.'

The sight of his uplifted face brought about a sudden change in her own. She flushed and the corners of her mouth shook and a mist seemed to sweep over her eyes.

'Eh! dear lad!' she broke out tremulously. 'Eh! dear lad!' as if she had not known she were going to say it. She did not say, 'Mester Colin', but just 'dear lad' quite suddenly. She might have said it to Dickon in the same way if she had seen something in his face which touched her. Colin liked it.

'Are you surprised because I am so well?' he asked.

She put her hand on his shoulder and smiled the mist out of her eyes.

'Aye, that I am!' she said; 'but tha'rt so like thy mother tha' made my heart jump.'

'Do you think,' said Colin a little awkwardly, 'that will make my father like me?'

'Aye, for sure, dear lad,' she answered, and she gave his shoulder a soft, quick pat. 'He mun come home – he mun come home.'

'Susan Sowerby,' said Ben Weatherstaff, getting close to her. 'Look at th' lad's legs, wilt tha'? They was like drumsticks i' stockin' two month' ago – an' I heard folk tell as they was bandy an' knock-kneed both at th' same time. Look at 'em now!'

Susan Sowerby laughed a comfortable laugh.

'They're goin' to be fine strong lad's legs in a bit,' she said. 'Let him go playing', an' workin' in th' garden an' eatin' hearty an' drinkin' plenty o' good sweet milk an' there'll not be a finer pair i' Yorkshire, thank God for it.'

She put both hands on Mistress Mary's shoulders and looked her little face over in a motherly fashion.

'An' thee, too!' she said. 'Tha'rt grown near as hearty as our 'Lizabeth Ellen. I'll warrant tha'rt like thy mother, too. Our Martha told me as Mrs Medlock heard she was a pretty woman. Tha'lt be like a blush-rose when tha' grows up, my little lass, bless thee.'

She did not mention that when Martha came home on her 'day out' and described the plain, sallow child she had said that she had no confidence whatever in what Mrs Medlock had heard. 'It doesn't stand to reason that a pretty woman could be th' mother o' such a fou' little lass,' she had added obstinately.

Mary had not had time to pay much attention to her changing face. She had only known that she looked 'different' and seemed to have a great deal more hair and that it was growing very fast. But remembering her pleasure in looking at the Memsahib in the past, she was glad to hear that she might some day look like her.

Susan Sowerby went round their garden with them and was told the whole story of it and shown every bush and tree which had come alive. Colin walked on one side of her and Mary on the other. Each of them kept looking up at her comfortable, rosy face, secretly curious about the delightful feeling she gave them – a sort of warm, supported feeling. It seemed as if she understood them as Dickon understood his 'creatures'. She stooped over the flowers and talked about them as if they were children. Soot followed her and once or twice cawed at her and flew upon her shoulder as if it were Dickon's.

When they told her about the robin and the first flight of the young ones, she laughed a motherly little mellow laugh in her throat.

'I suppose learnin' 'em to fly is like learnin' children to walk, but I'm feared I should be all in a worrit if mine had wings instead o' legs,' she said.

It was because she seemed such a wonderful woman in her nice moorland cottage way that at last she was told about the Magic.

'Do you believe in Magic?' asked Colin, after he had explained about Indian fakirs. 'I do hope you do.'

'That I do, lad,' she answered. 'I never knowed it by that name, but what does th' name matter? I warrant they call it a different name i' France an' a different one i' Germany. Th' same thing as set th' seeds swellin' an' th' sun shinin' made thee a well lad an' it's th' Good Thing. It isn't like us poor fools as think it matters if us is called out of our names. Th' Big Good Thing doesn't stop to worrit, bless thee. It goes on makin' worlds by th' million – worlds like us. Never thee stop believin' in th' Big Good Thing an' knowin' th' world's full of it – an' call it what tha' likes. Tha' wert singin' to it when I come into th' garden.'

'I felt so joyful,' said Colin, opening his beautiful, strange eyes at her. 'Suddenly, I felt how different I was – how strong my arms and legs were, you know – and how

I could dig and stand – and I jumped up and wanted to shout out something to anything that would listen.'

'Th' Magic listened when tha' sung th' Doxology. It would ha' listened to anything tha'd sung. It was th' joy that mattered. Eh! lad, lad – what's names to th' Joy Maker,' and she gave his shoulders a quick, soft pat again.

She had packed a basket which held a regular feast this morning, and when the hungry hour came and Dickon brought it out from its hiding place, she sat down with them under their tree and watched them devour their food, laughing and quite gloating over their appetites. She was full of fun and made them laugh at all sorts of odd things. She told them stories in broad Yorkshire and taught them new words. She laughed as if she could not help it when they told her of the increasing difficulty there was in pretending that Colin was still a fretful invalid.

'You see we can't help laughing nearly all the time when we are together,' explained Colin. 'And it doesn't sound ill at all. We try to choke it back, but it will burst out and that sounds worse than ever.'

'There's one thing that comes into my mind so often,' said Mary, 'and I can scarcely ever hold in when I think of it suddenly. I keep thinking suppose Colin's face should get to look like a full moon. It isn't like one yet, but he gets a tiny bit fatter every day – and suppose some morning it should look like one – what should we do!'

'Bless us all, I can see tha' has a good bit o' play actin' to do,' said Susan Sowerby. 'But tha' won't have to keep it up much longer. Mester Craven'll come home.'

'Do you think he will?' asked Colin. 'Why?'

Susan Sowerby chuckled softly.

'I suppose it 'ud nigh break thy heart if he found out before tha' told him in tha' own way,' she said. 'Tha's laid awake nights plannin' it.'

'I couldn't bear anyone else to tell him,' said Colin. 'I think about different ways every day. I think now I just want to run into his room.'

'That'd be a fine start for him,' said Susan Sowerby. 'I'd like to see his face, lad. I would that! He mun come back – that he mun.'

One of the things they talked of was the visit they were to make to her cottage. They planned it all. They were to drive over the moor and lunch out of doors among the heather. They would see all the twelve children and Dickon's garden and would not come back until they were tired.

Susan Sowerby got up at last to return to the house and Mrs Medlock. It was time for Colin to be wheeled back also. But before he got into his chair he stood quite close to Susan and fixed his eyes on her with a kind of bewildered adoration and he suddenly caught hold of the fold of her blue cloak and held it fast.

'You were just what I – what I wanted,' he said. 'I wish you were my mother – as well as Dickon's!'

All at once Susan Sowerby bent down and drew him with her warm arms close against the bosom under the blue cloak – as if he had been Dickon's brother. The quick mist swept over her eyes.

'Eh! dear lad!' she said. 'Thy own mother's in this 'ere very garden, I do believe. She couldna' keep out of it. Thy father mun come back to thee – he mun!'

27

In the Garden

IN EACH century since the beginning of the world wonderful things have been discovered. In the last century more amazing things were found out than in any century before. In this new century hundreds of things still more astounding will be brought to light. At first people refuse to believe that a strange new thing can be done, then they begin to hope it can't be done, then they see it can be done – then it is done and all the world wonders why it was not done centuries ago. One of the new things people began to find out in the last century was that thoughts – just mere thoughts – are as powerful as electric batteries – as good for one as sunlight is, or as bad for one as poison. To let a sad thought or a bad one get into your mind is as dangerous as letting a scarlet fever germ get into your body. If you let it stay there after it has got in you may never get over it as long as you live.

So long as Mistress Mary's mind was full of disagreeable thoughts about her dislikes and sour opinions of people and her determination not to be pleased by or interested in anything, she was a yellow-faced, sickly, bored and wretched child. Circumstances, however, were very kind to her, though she was not at all aware of it. They began to push her about for her own good. When her mind gradually filled itself with robins, and moorland cottages crowded with children, with queer, crabbed old gardeners and common little Yorkshire housemaids, with springtime and with secret gardens coming alive day by day, and also with a moor boy and his 'creatures', there was no room left for the disagreeable thoughts which affected her liver and her digestion and made her yellow and tired.

So long as Colin shut himself up in his room and thought only of his fears and weakness and his detestation of people who looked at him and reflected hourly on humps and early death, he was a hysterical, half-crazy little hypochondriac who knew nothing of the sunshine and the spring, and also did not know that he could get well and stand upon his feet if he tried to do it. When new, beautiful thoughts began to push out the old, hideous ones, life began to come back to him, his blood ran healthily through his veins, and strength poured into him like a flood. His scientific experiment was quite practical and simple and there was nothing weird about it at all. Much more surprising things can happen to anyone who, when a disagreeable or discouraged thought comes into his mind, just has the sense to remember in time and push it out by putting in an agreeable, determinedly courageous one. Two things cannot be in one place.

> *Where you tend a rose, my lad,*
> *A thistle cannot grow.*

While the secret garden was coming alive and two children were coming alive with it, there was a man wandering about certain far-away beautiful places in the Norwegian fjords, and the valleys and mountains of Switzerland, and he was a man who for ten years had kept his mind filled with dark and heartbroken thinking. He had not been courageous; he had never tried to put any other thoughts in the place of the dark ones. He had wandered by blue lakes and thought them; he had lain on mountain-sides with sheets of deep-blue gentians blooming all about him and flower breaths filling all the air and he had thought them. A terrible sorrow had fallen upon him when he had been happy and he had let his soul fill itself with blackness and had refused obstinately to allow any rift of light to pierce through. He had forgotten and deserted his home and his duties. When he travelled about, darkness so brooded over him that the sight of him was a wrong done to other people because it was as if he poisoned the air about him with gloom. Most strangers thought he must be either half mad or a man with some hidden crime on his soul. He was a tall man with a drawn face and crooked shoulders, and the name he always entered on hotel registers was 'Archibald Craven, Misselthwaite Manor, Yorkshire, England'.

He had travelled far and wide since the day he saw Mistress Mary in his study and told her she might have her 'bit of earth'. He had been in the most beautiful places in Europe, though he had remained nowhere more than a few days. He had chosen the quietest and remotest spots. He had been on the tops of mountains whose heads were in the clouds and had looked down on other mountains when the sun rose and touched them with such light as made it seem as if the world were just being born.

But the light had never seemed to touch himself until one day when he realised that for the first time in ten years a strange thing had happened. He was in a wonderful valley in the Austrian Tyrol and he had been walking alone through such beauty as might have lifted any man's soul out of shadow. He had walked a long way and it had not lifted his. But at last he had felt tired and had thrown himself down to rest on a carpet of moss by a stream. It was a clear little stream which ran quite merrily along on its narrow way through the luscious damp greenness. Sometimes it made a sound rather like very low laughter as it bubbled over and round stones. He saw birds come and dip their heads to drink it in and then flick their wings and fly away. It seemed like a thing alive and yet its tiny voice made the stillness seem deeper. The valley was very, very still.

As he sat gazing into the clear running of the water, Archibald Craven gradually felt his mind and body both grow quiet, as quiet as the valley itself. He wondered if he were going to sleep, but he was not. He sat and gazed at the sunlit water and his eyes began to see things growing at its edge. There was one lovely mass of blue forget-me-nots growing so close to the stream that its leaves were wet and at these he found himself looking as he remembered he had looked at such things years ago. He was actually thinking tenderly how lovely it was and what wonders of blue its hundreds of little blossoms were. He did not know that just that simple thought was slowly filling his mind – filling and filling it until other things were softly pushed aside. It was as if a sweet, clear spring had begun to rise in a stagnant pool and had risen and risen until at last it swept the dark water away. But of course he did not think of this himself. He only knew that the valley seemed to grow quieter and quieter as he sat and stared at the bright, delicate blueness. He did not know how long he sat there or what was happening to him, but at last he moved as if he were awakening and he got up slowly and stood on the moss carpet, drawing a long, deep, soft breath and wondering at himself. Something seemed to have been unbound and released in him, very quietly.

'What is it?' he said, almost in a whisper, and he passed his hand over his forehead. 'I almost feel as if – I were alive!'

I do not know enough about the wonderfulness of undiscovered things to be able to explain how this had happened to him. Neither does anyone else yet. He did not understand at all himself – but he remembered this strange hour months afterwards when he was at Misselthwaite again and he found out quite by accident that on this very day Colin had cried out as he went into the secret garden:

'I am going to live for ever and ever and ever!'

The singular calmness remained with him the rest of the evening, and he slept a new, reposeful sleep; but it was not with him very long. He did not know that it could be kept. By the next night he had opened the doors wide to his dark thoughts, and they had come trooping and rushing back. He left the valley and went on his wandering way again. But, strange as it seemed to him, there were minutes – sometimes half-hours – when, without his knowing why, the black burden seemed to lift itself again and he knew he was a living man and not a dead one. Slowly – slowly – for no reason that he knew of – he was 'coming alive' with the garden.

As the golden summer changed into the deeper golden autumn he went to the Lake of Como. There he found the loveliness of a dream. He spent his days upon the crystal blueness of the lake or he walked back into the soft, thick verdure of the hills and tramped until he was tired, so that he might sleep. But by this time he had begun to sleep better, he knew, and his dreams had ceased to be a terror to him.

'Perhaps,' he thought, 'my body is growing stronger.'

It was growing stronger but – because of the rare, peaceful hours when his thoughts were changed – his soul was slowly growing stronger, too. He began to think of Misselthwaite and wonder if he should not go home. Now and then he wondered vaguely about his boy and asked himself what he should feel when he went and stood by the carved four-poster bed again and looked down at the sharply chiselled, ivory-white face while it slept and the black lashes rimmed so startlingly the close-shut eyes. He shrank from it.

One marvel of a day he had walked so far that when he returned the moon was high and full and all the world was purple shadow and silver. The stillness of lake and shore and wood was so wonderful that he did not go into the villa he lived in. He walked down to a little bowered terrace at the water's edge and sat upon a seat and breathed in all the heavenly scents of the night. He felt the strange calmness stealing over him and it grew deeper and deeper until he fell asleep.

He did not know when he fell asleep and when he began to dream; his dream was so real that he did not feel as if he were dreaming. He remembered afterwards how intensely wide awake and alert he had thought he was. He thought that as he sat and breathed in the scent of the late roses and listened to the lapping of the water at his feet, he heard a voice calling. It was sweet and clear and happy and far away. It seemed very far, but he heard it as distinctly as if it had been at his very side.

'Archie! Archie! Archie!' it said, and then again, sweeter and clearer than before, 'Archie! Archie!'

He thought he sprang to his feet not even startled.

It was such a real voice and it seemed so natural that he should hear it.

'Lilias! Lilias!' he answered. 'Lilias! where are you?'

'In the garden,' it came back like a sound from a golden flute. 'In the garden!'

And then the dream ended. But he did not awaken. He slept soundly and sweetly all through the lovely night. When he did awake at last it was brilliant morning and a servant was standing staring at him. He was an Italian servant and was accustomed, as all the servants of the villa were, to accepting without question any strange thing his foreign master might do. No one ever knew when he would go out or come in or where he would choose to sleep or if he would roam about the garden or lie in the boat on the lake all night. The man held a salver with some letters on it and he waited quietly until Mr Craven took them. When he had gone away Mr Craven sat a few moments holding them in his hand and looking at the lake. His strange calm was still upon him and something more – a lightness, as if the cruel thing which had been done had not happened as he thought – as if something had changed. He was remembering the dream – the real – real dream.

'In the garden!' he said, wondering at himself. 'In the garden! But the door is locked and the key is buried deep.'

When he glanced at the letters a few minutes later, he saw that the one lying at the top of the rest was an English letter and came from Yorkshire. It was directed in a plain woman's hand, but it was not a hand he knew. He opened it, scarcely thinking of the writer, but the first words attracted his attention at once.

Dear Sir,

I am Susan Sowerby that made bold to speak to you once on the moor. It was about Miss Mary I spoke. I will make bold to speak again. Please, sir, I would come home if I was you. I think you would be glad to come and – if you will excuse me, sir – I think your lady would ask you to come if she was here,

Your obedient servant,
Susan Sowerby

Mr Craven read the letter twice before he put it back in its envelope. He kept thinking about the dream.

'I will go back to Misselthwaite,' he said. 'Yes, I'll go at once.'

And he went through the garden to the villa and ordered Pitcher to prepare for his return to England.

In a few days he was in Yorkshire again, and on his long railroad journey he found himself thinking of his boy as he had never thought in all the ten years past. During those years he had only wished to forget him. Now, though he did not intend to think about him, memories of him constantly drifted into his mind. He remembered the black days when he had raved like a madman because the child was alive and the mother was dead. He had refused to see it, and when he had gone to look at it at last it had been such a weak wretched thing that everyone had been sure it would die in a few days. But to the surprise of those who took care of it the days passed and it lived, and then everyone believed it would be a deformed and crippled creature.

He had not meant to be a bad father, but he had not felt like a father at all. He had supplied doctors and nurses and luxuries, but he had shrunk from the mere thought of the boy and had buried himself in his own misery. The first time after a year's absence he returned to Misselthwaite and the small miserable-looking thing languidly and indifferently lifted to his face the great grey eyes with black lashes round them, so like and yet so horribly unlike the happy eyes he had adored, he could not bear the sight of them and turned away pale as death. After that he scarcely ever saw him except when he was asleep, and all he knew of him was that he was a confirmed invalid, with a vicious, hysterical, half-insane temper. He could only be kept from furies dangerous to himself by being given his own way in every detail.

All this was not an uplifting thing to recall, but as the train whirled him through the mountain passes and golden plains, the man who was 'coming alive' began to think in a new way and he thought long and steadily and deeply.

'Perhaps I have been all wrong for ten years,' he said to himself. 'Ten years is a long time. It may be too late to do anything – quite too late. What have I been thinking of!'

Of course this was the wrong Magic – to begin by saying 'too late'. Even Colin could have told him that. But he knew nothing of Magic – either black or white. This he had yet to learn. He wondered if Susan Sowerby had taken courage and written to him only because the motherly creature had realised that the boy was much worse – was fatally ill. If he had not been under the spell of the curious calmness which had taken possession of him he would have been more wretched than ever. But the calm had brought a sort of courage and hope with it. Instead of giving way to thoughts of the worst he actually found he was trying to believe in better things.

'Could it be possible that she sees that I may be able to do him good and control him?' he thought. 'I will go and see her on my way to Misselthwaite.'

But when on his way across the moor he stopped the carriage at the cottage, seven or eight children who were playing about gathered in a group and bobbing seven or eight friendly and polite curtsies, told him that their mother had gone to the other side of the moor early in the morning to help a woman who had a new baby. 'Our Dickon', they volunteered, was over at the manor working in one of the gardens, where he spent several days each week.

Mr Craven looked over the collection of sturdy little bodies and round, red-cheeked faces, each one grinning in its own particular way, and he awoke to the fact that they were a healthy, likeable lot. He smiled to their friendly grins, and took a golden sovereign from his pocket and gave it to 'our 'Lizabeth Ellen', who was the oldest.

'If you divide that into eight parts there will be half a crown for each of you,' he said.

Then amid grins and chuckles and bobbing of curtsies, he drove away, leaving ecstasy and nudging elbows and little jumps of joy behind.

The drive across the wonderfulness of the moor was a soothing thing. Why did it seem to give him a sense of homecoming which he had been sure he could never feel again – that sense of the beauty of land and sky and purple bloom of distance, and a warming of the heart at drawing nearer to the great old house which had held those of his blood for six hundred years? How he had driven away from it the last time shuddering to think of its closed rooms and the boy living in the four-poster bed with the brocaded hangings. Was it possible that perhaps he might find him changed a little for the better, and that he might overcome his shrinking from him? How real that dream had been – how wonderful and clear the voice which had called back to him, 'In the garden – In the garden!'

'I will try to find the key,' he said. 'I will try to open the door. I must – though I don't know why.'

When he arrived at the Manor the servants who received him with the usual ceremony, noticed that he looked better, and that he did not go to the remote rooms where he usually lived, attended by Pitcher. He went into the library and sent for Mrs Medlock. She came to him somewhat excited, and curious and flustered.

'How is Master Colin, Medlock?' he inquired.

'Well, sir,' Mrs Medlock answered, 'he's – he's different, in a manner of speaking.'

'Worse?' he suggested.

Mrs Medlock really was flushed.

'Well, you see, sir,' she tried to explain, 'neither Dr Craven, nor the nurse, nor me can exactly make him out.'

'Why is that?'

'To tell the truth, sir, Master Colin might be better and he might be changing for the worse. His appetite, sir, is past understanding – and his ways – '

'Has he become more – more peculiar?' her master asked, knitting his brows anxiously.

'That's it, sir. He's growing very peculiar – when you compare him with what he used to be. He used to eat nothing, and then suddenly he began to eat something enormous – and then he stopped again all at once and the meals were sent back just as they used to be. You never knew, sir, perhaps, that out of doors he never would let himself be taken. The things we've gone through to get him to go out in his chair would leave a body trembling like a leaf. He'd throw himself into such a state that Dr Craven said he couldn't be responsible for forcing him. Well, sir, just without warning – not long after one of his worst tantrums, he suddenly insisted on being taken out every day by Miss Mary and Susan Sowerby's boy, Dickon, that could push his chair. He took a fancy to both Miss Mary and Dickon, and Dickon brought his tame animals, and, if you'll credit it, sir, out of doors he will stay from morning until night.'

'How does he look?' was the next question.

'If he took his food natural, sir, you'd think he was putting on flesh – but we're afraid it may be a sort of bloat. He laughs sometimes in a queer way when he's alone with Miss Mary. He never used to laugh at all. Dr Craven is coming to see you at once, if you'll allow him. He never was as puzzled in his life.'

'Where is Master Colin now?' Mr Craven asked.

'In the garden, sir. He's always in the garden – though not a human creature is allowed to go near for fear they'll look at him.'

Mr Craven scarcely heard her last words.

'In the garden!' he said, and after he had sent Mrs Medlock away, he stood and repeated it again and again. 'In the garden!'

He had to make an effort to bring himself back to the place he was standing in, and when he felt he was on earth again he turned and went out of the room. He took his way, as Mary had done, through the door in the shrubbery and among the laurels and the fountain beds. The fountain was playing now, and was encircled by beds of brilliant autumn flowers. He crossed the lawn and turned into the Long Walk by the ivied walls. He did not walk quickly, but slowly, and his eyes were on the path. He felt as if he were being drawn back to the place he had so long forsaken, and he did not know why. As he drew near to it his step became still more slow. He knew where the door was, even though the ivy hung over it – but he did not know exactly where it lay – that buried key.

So he stopped and stood still, looking about him, and almost the moment after he paused he started and listened – asking himself if he were walking in a dream.

The ivy hung thick over the door, the key was buried under the shrubs, no human being had passed that portal for ten lonely years – and yet inside the garden there were sounds. They were the sounds of running, scuffling feet seeming to chase round and round under the trees, they were strange sounds of lowered, suppressed voices – exclamations and smothered, joyous cries. It seemed actually like the laughter of young things, the uncontrollable laughter of children who were trying not to be heard, but who in a moment or so – as their excitement mounted – would burst forth. What in heaven's name was he dreaming of – what in heaven's name did he hear? Was he losing his reason and thinking he heard things which were not for human ears? Was it that the far, clear voice had meant?

And then the moment came, the uncontrollable moment when the sounds forgot to hush themselves. The feet ran faster and faster – they were nearing the garden door – there was quick, strong, young breathing and a wild outbreak of laughing shouts which could not be contained – and the door in the wall was flung wide open, the sheet of ivy swinging back, and a boy burst through it at full speed and, without seeing the outsider, dashed almost into his arms.

Mr Craven had extended them just in time to save him from falling as a result of his unseeing dash against him, and when he held him away to look at him in amazement at his being there he truly gasped for breath.

He was a tall boy and a handsome one. He was glowing with life, and his running had sent splendid colour leaping to his face. He threw the thick hair back from his forehead and lifted a pair of strange grey eyes – eyes full of boyish laughter and rimmed with black lashes like a fringe. It was the eyes which made Mr Craven gasp for breath.

'Who – What? Who?' he stammered.

This was not what Colin had expected – this was not what he had planned. He had never thought of such a meeting. And yet to come dashing out – winning a race – perhaps it was even better. He drew himself up to his very tallest. Mary, who had been running with him and had dashed through the door too, believed that he managed to make himself look taller than he had ever looked before – inches taller.

'Father,' he said, 'I'm Colin. You can't believe it. I scarcely can myself. I'm Colin.'

Like Mrs Medlock, he did not understand what his father meant when he said hurriedly:

'In the garden! In the garden!'

'Yes,' hurried on Colin. 'It was the garden that did it – and Mary and Dickon and the creatures – and the

360

Magic. No one knows. We kept it to tell you when you came. I'm well; I can beat Mary in a race. I'm going to be an athlete.'

He said it all so like a healthy boy – his face flushed, his words tumbling over each other in his eagerness – that Mr Craven's soul shook with unbelieving joy.

Colin put out his hand and laid it on his father's arm.

'Aren't you glad, Father?' he ended. 'Aren't you glad? I'm going to live for ever and ever and ever!'

Mr Craven put his hands on both the boy's shoulders and held him still. He knew he dared not even try to speak for a moment.

'Take me into the garden, my boy,' he said at last. 'And tell me all about it.'

And so they led him in.

The place was a wilderness of autumn gold and purple and violet and flaming scarlet, and on every side were sheaves of late lilies standing together – lilies which were white or white and ruby. He remembered well when the first of them had been planted that just at this season of the year their late glories should reveal themselves. Late roses climbed and hung and clustered, and the sunshine deepening the hue of the yellowing trees made one feel that one stood in an embowered temple of gold. The newcomer stood silent just as the children had done when they came into its greyness. He looked round and round.

'I thought it would be dead,' he said.

'Mary thought so at first,' said Colin. 'But it came alive.'

Then they sat down under their tree – all but Colin, who wanted to stand while he told the story.

It was the strangest thing he had ever heard, Archibald Craven thought, as it was poured forth in headlong boy fashion. Mystery and Magic and wild creatures, the weird midnight meeting – the coming of the spring – the passion of insulted pride which had dragged the young rajah to his feet to defy old Ben Weatherstaff to his face. The odd companionship, the play-acting, the great secret so carefully kept. The listener laughed until tears came into his eyes, and sometimes tears came into his eyes when he was not laughing. The Athlete, the Lecturer, the Scientific Discoverer was a laughable, lovable, healthy young human thing.

'Now,' he said at the end of the story, 'it need not be a secret any more. I dare say it will frighten them nearly into fits when they see me – but I am never going to get into the chair again. I shall walk back with you, Father – to the house.'

*

Ben Weatherstaff's duties rarely took him away from the gardens, but on this occasion he made an excuse to carry some vegetables to the kitchen, and being invited into the servants' hall by Mrs Medlock to drink a glass of beer, he was on the spot – as he had hoped to be – when the most dramatic event Misselthwaite Manor had seen during the present generation actually took place.

One of the windows looking upon the courtyard gave also a glimpse of the lawn. Mrs Medlock, knowing Ben had come from the gardens, hoped that he might have caught sight of his master, and even by chance of his meeting with Master Colin.

'Did you see either of them, Weatherstaff?' she asked.

Ben took his beer-mug from his mouth and wiped his lips with the back of his hand.

'Aye, that I did,' he answered with a shrewdly significant air.

'Both of them?' suggested Mrs Medlock.

'Both of 'em,' returned Ben Weatherstaff. 'Thank ye kindly, ma'am, I could sup up another mug of it.'

'Together?' said Mrs Medlock, hastily overfilling his beer-mug in her excitement.

'Together, ma'am,' and Ben gulped down half of his new mug at one gulp.

'Where was Master Colin? How did he look? What did they say to each other?'

'I didna' hear that,' said Ben, 'along o' only bein' on th' step-ladder lookin' over th' wall. But I'll tell thee this. There's been things goin' on outside as you house people knows nowt about. An' what tha'll find out tha'll find out soon.'

And it was not two minutes before he swallowed the last of his beer and waved his mug solemnly towards the window which took in through the shrubbery a piece of the lawn.

'Look there,' he said, 'if tha's curious. Look what's comin' across th' grass.'

When Mrs Medlock looked she threw up her hands and gave a little shriek, and every man and woman servant within hearing bolted across the servants' hall and stood looking through the window with their eyes almost starting out of their heads.

Across the lawn came the Master of Misselthwaite, and he looked as many of them had never seen him. And by his side, with his head up in the air and his eyes full of laughter, walked as strongly and steadily as any boy in Yorkshire – Master Colin!

The Secret Garden

The Backstory

Find out about the real secret garden, the plucky author and more…

VINTAGE CLASSICS

Who's Who in *The Secret Garden*

Mary Lennox: Mary is ten years old. She has neither father nor mother and is an orphan. She's not pretty, she's sour and she's cross. It is no wonder she is known as 'Mistress Mary Quite Contrary'! But much like the secret garden itself which has been neglected, she begins to blossom.

Dickon Sowerby: Dickon is twelve years old and he is Martha Sowerby's younger brother. He spends time roaming the Yorkshire moors and he makes friends with all the wildlife, from ponies to sheep, even the birds come and eat out of his hand.

Colin Craven: Colin is ten years old. His mother died when she gave birth to him and his father spends a lot of time abroad. He is ill and never goes outside. He is bad tempered, spoiled and he thinks he won't live to grow up.

Archibald Craven: the owner of the queer Misselthwaite Manor. He is Mary's uncle and Colin's father. His wife, Lilian Craven, died ten years ago. He seems miserable and distracted.

Martha Sowerby: a young, tender-hearted housemaid who looks after Mary and eventually becomes friends with her.

Ben Weatherstaff: the old and sharp tongued gardener of Misselthwaite Manor.

Susan Sowerby: Martha and Dickon's mother. She has twelve children and is respected in the community as a sensible and good-hearted woman. She is kind and takes interest in the care of Mary and Colin.

The Robin: a pretty and cheerful bird that seems so like a little person that Mary makes friends with him instantly. He is a curious creature and he helps Mary uncover the secrets of Misselthwaite Manor.

Mrs Medlock: the no-nonsense housekeeper at Misselthwaite Manor.

Dr Craven: Archibald Craven's cousin and Colin's doctor.

Who are you?
Which inhabitant of Misselthwaite Manor do you most resemble? Take this quiz to find out!

1) **What do you most dislike?**
   a) Other people.
   b) Being indoors.
   c) Fresh air.

2) **What are your worst and best qualities?**
   a) You are bad tempered sometimes, but you can be thoughtful, you love gardens and you try to help your friends.
   b) You don't have any bad qualities, you are kind, you love animals and you can keep secrets.
   c) You are selfish, throw tantrums and order people about. You can also be grateful, plucky and loyal to your friends.

3) **You see a robin, do you:**
   a) Get a queer feeling in your heart, like him enormously and feel quite sure he is looking at you and finding out all about you.

b) Make a twittering sound almost like the robin's own and have a good old chat.

c) Robins? You don't see robins because you rarely go outside.

4) **Your favourite way to spend your time is**
   a) Skipping and gardening.
   b) Rambling over the moors, watching wildlife.
   c) Moaning.

Mostly As: You're Mary Lennox.
Mostly Bs: You're Dickon Sowerby.
Mostly Cs: You're Colin Craven.

Test yourself on your knowledge of *The Secret Garden*
(Turn to the back for answers. No cheating!)

1) What is the name of the disease that Mary's parents die of in India?

2) Where in England is Misselthwaite Manor?

3) Who first tells Mary about the Secret Garden?

4) How long has the garden been locked?

5) Who shows Mary the door to the Secret Garden?

6) Who is in the picture that Colin keeps in his room behind a curtain?

7) What type of animals are Captain and Soot?

8) What does Ben Weatherstaff help Colin to plant in the Secret Garden?

Is there a *real* secret garden?

Almost! Frances moved to Great Maytham Hall in Kent in 1897. She set to work on the garden immediately. When she arrived it was one big orchard and overgrown with brambles so she cleared it up and created a rose garden.

She always said, 'As long as one has a garden, one has a future, and if one has a future, one is alive.'

The gardens at Great Maytham Hall are open to the visit once a year as part of the National Gardens Scheme. If you look at www.ngs.org.uk you can find out the details and plan your visit.

Who was Frances Hodgson Burnett?

She was energetic, warm-hearted and generous.

She was born in 1849 in Manchester but when her father died Frances's mother emigrated with her sons and daughters to Tennessee in the United States. Life there was harsh and they were quite poor but the young Frances would entertain herself and her siblings with stories. And then in 1868, at the age of eighteen, she went out with her sister to pick grapes and made enough money from that job to buy paper and stamps. She wrote out one romantic tale and sent the story off to a magazine. Marvellously, her story was accepted and from that day forward she became the breadwinner in her family, writing up to six stories a month.

When she married a man called Swan Burnett in 1872, she kept up her writing. Frances's two sons, Lionel and Vivian, would sleep beneath her desk as toddlers.

It was unusual for a woman to earn her own money and support her family in the way that Frances did so people in nineteenth-century England and America were very surprised and interested in her. Many newspapers and magazines were interested in her private life and wrote about her much like they do about celebrities today.

In 1890, something very sad happened: Frances's son, Lionel, died at the age of sixteen. When she wrote about Colin in *The Secret Garden* Frances might have been thinking about her own son and wishing that his sickness could have been cured. Her other son, Vivian, lived and Frances once made him a real velvet suit. The sight of him in his smart suit inspired her to write her book *Little Lord Fauntleroy*.

Because of her own difficult childhood, Frances was known for treating children kindly. Sometimes she would collect gifts from the First Class passengers on transatlantic boats and give them to the poorer immigrants making the same journey.

What would life be like if you had lived in the time of *The Secret Garden*?

You wouldn't have had central heating. Houses were kept warm with open fireplaces which people like Martha would have had to make in the mornings and sweep clean later in the day.

You wouldn't have had a television, computer games or even a playground to entertain you. Children would sing, play games like tag and entertain themselves with puzzles, toy trains, dolls' houses, toy animals and rocking horses.

Trainers, hoodies and jeans were yet to be invented and boys were dressed in suits with trousers that came to their knees. Girls wore dresses and boots.

There were no books about Harry Potter or Tracy Beaker but they did have wonderful books like *Alice's Adventures in Wonderland*, the fairytales of Hans Christian Andersen and the Brothers Grimm, *The Arabian Nights*, and of course, the very book you have in your hands!

What can I do if I don't have a secret garden on my doorstep?

Mary Lennox was very lucky to find the secret garden but every garden has a great many fascinating and lovely creatures, flowers and plants just waiting to be discovered.

Next time you are in your own garden or at a local garden play this game and take a closer look at what lurks all around you:

What you'll need:

A pencil and paper to record your findings

A friend or two if you'd like to make it a competition and see who can find the list below first (or we'd love to see drawings of what you find so do email us pictures of your discoveries to worldofstories@randomhouse.co.uk)

A dry day!

How long will it take?

As much time as you like

What should I do?

As Dickon says, 'There's naught as nice as th' smell o' good clean earth, except the smell o' fresh growin things when th' rain falls on 'em… I just sniff an sniff'. Can you find something fragrant? And what about something smelly? Something prickly and something smooth? Something tall and something tiny?

'What are Bulbs?' asks Colin. Daffodils, tulips, crocuses, lilies and snowdrops grow out of bulbs. Can you spot any in your garden? Or maybe just the spring-time pale-green points?

Can you find leaves with 1/2/3/4/5/6/7 points?

Gardens seem very green don't they? But what other colours are there? Can you find an example of all the colours in the rainbow?

Can you find something beginning with each letter of the alphabet? (We'll let you off XYZ).

What is that strange word?

The book takes place in India and Yorkshire so there are a few words that might be new to you:

ayah – nursemaid

aye – yes

browt – brought

cholera – Mary's parents die of cholera which is a dangerous disease caught from infected food or water

graidely – good

lass – girl

marred – spoiled

Missie Sahib – Sahib was a word that was used in India to mean mistress or master. Mary is called Missie Sahib and Mary's mother is called Memsahib

moithered – annoyed

mun(not) – must (not)

nesh – delicate

now o' th' soart – nothing of the sort

rajah – a prince, chief, or ruler in india

salaamed – a respectful act of greeting, often a low bow. 'Salaam' means 'Peace'

theysen – yourself

wick – alive, lively

wuthering – blowing with a shuddering, roaring sound

Answers to *The Secret Garden* quiz – how did you do?

1) Cholera

2) Yorkshire

3) Martha

4) Ten years

5) The robin

6) His mother, Lilias Craven

7) Fox cub and a crow

8) A rose

THIS BOOK
BELONGS TO

_____

_____

OTHER BOOKS BY LEWIS CARROLL

Lewis Carroll

Alice's Adventures in Wonderland

and

Through the Looking Glass

VINTAGE BOOKS
London

Published by Vintage 2012

Alice's Adventures in Wonderland was first published in 1865
Through the Looking-Glass was first published in 1871

Illustrations by John Tenniel

Vintage
Random House, 20 Vauxhall Bridge Road,
London SW1V 2SA

www.vintage-classics.info

Addresses for companies within The Random House Group Limited can
be found at: www.randomhouse.co.uk/offices.htm

The Random House Group Limited Reg. No. 954009

A CIP catalogue record for this book
is available from the British Library

The Random House Group Limited supports The Forest Stewardship
Council (FSC®), the leading international forest certification organisation.
Our books carrying the FSC label are printed on FSC® certified paper.
FSC is the only forest certification scheme endorsed by the leading
environmental organisations, including Greenpeace. Our paper
procurement policy can be found at
www.randomhouse.co.uk/environment

Printed and bound in Great Britain by
CPI Group (UK) Ltd, Croydon, CR0 4YY

Contents

Contents

Alice's Adventures
in Wonderland

All in the golden afternoon
    Full leisurely we glide;
For both our oars, with little skill,
    By little arms are plied,
While little hands make vain pretence
    Our wanderings to guide.

Ah, cruel Three! In such an hour,
    Beneath such dreamy weather,
To beg a tale of breath too weak
    To stir the tiniest feather!
Yet what can one poor voice avail
    Against three tongues together?

Imperious Prima flashes forth
    Her edict 'to begin it' –
In gentler tone Secunda hopes
    'There will be nonsense in it!'
While Tertia interrupts the tale
    Not *more* than once a minute.

Anon, to sudden silence won,
    In fancy they pursue
The dream-child moving through a land
    Of wonders wild and new,
In friendly chat with bird or beast –
    And half believe it true.

And ever, as the story drained
 The wells of fancy dry,
And faintly strove that weary one
 To put the subject by,
'The rest next time –' 'It *is* next time!'
 The happy voices cry.

Thus grew the tale of Wonderland:
 Thus slowly, one by one,
Its quaint events were hammered out –
 And now the tale is done,
And home we steer, a merry crew,
 Beneath the setting sun.

Alice! a childish story take,
 And with a gentle hand
Lay it where Childhood's dreams are twined
 In Memory's mystic band,
Like pilgrim's wither'd wreath of flowers
 Pluck'd in a far-off land.

1

Down the Rabbit-Hole

A LICE was beginning to get very tired of sitting by her sister on the bank, and of having nothing to do: once or twice she had peeped into the book her sister was reading, but it had no pictures or conversations in it, 'and what is the use of a book,' thought Alice, 'without pictures or conversation?'

So she was considering in her own mind (as well as she could, for the hot day made her feel very sleepy and stupid), whether the pleasure of making a daisy-chain would be worth the trouble of getting up and picking the daisies, when suddenly a White Rabbit with pink eyes ran close by her.

There was nothing so *very* remarkable in that; nor did Alice think it so *very* much out of the way to hear the Rabbit say to itself, 'Oh dear! Oh dear! I shall be too late!' (when she thought it over afterwards, it occurred to her that she ought to have wondered at this, but at the time it all seemed quite natural); but when the Rabbit actually *took a watch out of its waistcoat-pocket*, and looked at it, and then hurried on, Alice started to her feet, for it flashed across her mind that she had never before seen a rabbit with either waistcoat-pocket, or a watch to take out of it, and burning with curiosity, she ran across the field after it, and fortunately was just in time to see it pop down a large rabbit-hole under the hedge.

In another moment down went Alice after it, never once considering how in the world she was to get out again.

The rabbit-hole went straight on like a tunnel for some way, and then dipped suddenly down, so suddenly that Alice had not a moment to think about stopping herself before she found herself falling down a very deep well.

Either the well was very deep or she fell very slowly, for she had plenty of time as she went down to look about her, and to wonder what was going to happen next. First, she tried to look down and make out what she was coming to, but it was too dark to see anything; then she looked at the sides of the well, and noticed that they were filled with cupboards and pictures hung upon pegs. She took down a jar from one of the shelves as she passed; it was labelled 'orange marmalade', but to her great disappointment it was empty: she did not like to drop the jar for fear of killing somebody, so managed to put it into one of the cupboards as she fell past it.

'Well!' thought Alice to herself, 'after such a fall as this, I shall think nothing of tumbling down stairs! How brave they'll all think me at home! Why, I wouldn't say anything about it, even if I fell off the top of the house!' (Which was very likely true.)

Down, down, down. Would the fall *never* come to an end! 'I wonder how many miles I've fallen by this time?' she said aloud. 'I must be getting somewhere near the centre of the earth. Let me see: that would be four thousand miles down, I think –' (for, you see, Alice had learnt several things of this sort in her lessons in the schoolroom, and though this was not a *very* good opportunity for showing off her knowledge, as there was no one to listen to her, still it was good practice to say it over) '– yes, that's about the right distance – but then I wonder what Latitude or Longitude I've got to?' (Alice had no idea what Latitude was, or Longitude either, but thought they were nice grand words to say.)

Presently she began again. 'I wonder if I shall fall right *through* the earth! How funny it'll seem to come out among the people that walk with their heads downwards! The Antipathies, I think –' (she was rather glad there *was* no one listening, this time, as it didn't sound at all the right word) '– but I shall have to ask them what the name of the country is, you know. Please, Ma'am, is this New Zealand or Australia?' (and she tried to curtsey as she spoke – fancy *curtseying* as you're falling through the air! Do you think you could manage it!) 'And what an ignorant little girl she'll think me for asking! No, it'll never do to ask: perhaps I shall see it written up somewhere.'

Down, down, down. There was nothing else to do, so Alice soon began talking again. 'Dinah'll miss me very much to-night, I should think!' (Dinah was the cat.) 'I hope they'll remember her saucer of milk at tea-time. Dinah, my dear! I wish you were down here with me! There are no mice in the air, I'm afraid, but you might catch a bat, and that's very like a mouse, you know. But do cats eat bats, I wonder?' And here Alice began to get rather sleepy, and went on saying to herself, in a dreamy sort of way, 'Do cats eat bats? Do cats eat bats?' and sometimes, 'Do bats eat cats?' for, you see, as she couldn't answer either question, it didn't much matter which way she put it. She felt that she was dozing off, and had just begun to dream that she was walking hand in hand with Dinah, and saying to her very earnestly, 'Now, Dinah, tell me the truth: did you ever eat a bat?' when suddenly, thump! thump! down she came upon a heap of sticks and dry leaves, and the fall was over.

Alice was not a bit hurt, and she jumped up on to her feet in a moment: she looked up, but it was all dark overhead; before her was another long passage, and the White Rabbit was still in sight, hurrying down it. There was not a moment to be lost: away went Alice like the wind, and was just in time to hear it say, as it turned a corner, 'Oh my ears and whiskers, how late it's getting!' She was close behind it when she turned the corner, but the Rabbit was no longer to be seen: she found herself in a long, low hall, which was lit up by a row of lamps hanging from the roof.

There were doors all round the hall, but they were all locked; and when Alice had been all the way down one side and up the other, trying every door, she walked sadly down the middle, wondering how she was ever to get out again.

Suddenly she came upon a little three-legged table, all made of solid glass; there was nothing on it except a tiny golden key, and Alice's first thought was that it might belong to one of the doors of the hall; but, alas! either the locks were too large, or the key was too small, but at any rate it would not open any of them. However, on the second time round, she came upon a low curtain she had not noticed before, and behind it was a little door about fifteen inches high: she tried the little golden key in the lock, and to her great delight it fitted!

Alice opened the door and found that it led into a small passage, not much larger than a rat-hole: she knelt down and looked along the passage into the loveliest garden you ever saw.

How she longed to get out of that dark hall, and wander about among those beds of bright flowers and those cool fountains, but she could not even get her head through the doorway; 'and even if my head would go through,' thought poor Alice, 'it would be of very little use without my shoulders. Oh, how I wish I could shut up like a telescope! I think I could, if I only knew how to begin.' For, you see, so many out-of-the-way things had happened lately, that Alice had begun to think that very few things indeed were really impossible.

There seemed to be no use in waiting by the little door, so she went back to the table, half hoping she might find another key on it, or at any rate a book of rules for shutting people up like telescopes: this time she found a little bottle on it, ('which certainly was not here before,' said Alice,) and round the neck of the bottle was a paper label, with the words 'DRINK ME' beautifully printed on it in large letters.

It was all very well to say 'Drink me,' but the wise little Alice was not going to do *that* in a hurry. 'No, I'll look first,' she said, 'and see whether it's marked "*poison*" or not'; for she had read several nice little histories about children who had got burnt, and eaten up by wild beasts and other unpleasant things, all because they *would* not remember the simple rules their friends had taught them: such as, that a red-hot poker will burn you if

you hold it too
long; and that
if you cut your
finger *very*
deeply with a
knife, it usually
bleeds; and
she had never
forgotten that,
if you drink
much from a
bottle marked
'poison,' it is
almost certain
to disagree with
you, sooner or
later.

However, the bottle was *not* marked 'poison,' so Alice
ventured to taste it, and finding it very nice, (it had,
in fact, a sort of mixed flavour of cherry-tart, custard,
pineapple, roast turkey, toffee, and hot buttered toast,)
she very soon finished it off.

*　　　*　　　*　　　*

*　　　*　　　*

*　　　*　　　*　　　*

'What a curious feeling!' said Alice; 'I must be shutting up like a telescope.'

And so it was indeed: she was now only ten inches high, and her face brightened up at the thought that she was now the right size for going through the little door into that lovely garden. First, however, she waited for a few minutes to see if she was going to shrink any further: she felt a little nervous about this; 'for it might end, you know,' said Alice to herself, 'in my going out altogether, like a candle. I wonder what I should be like then?' And she tried to fancy what the flame of a candle is like after the candle is blown out, for she could not remember ever having seen such a thing.

After a while, finding that nothing more happened, she decided on going into the garden at once; but, alas for poor Alice! when she got to the door, she found she had forgotten the little golden key, and when she went back to the table for it, she found she could not possibly reach it: she could see it quite plainly through the glass, and she tried her best to climb up one of the legs of the table, but it was too slippery; and when she had tired herself out with trying, the poor little thing sat down and cried.

'Come, there's no use in crying like that!' said Alice to herself, rather sharply; 'I advise you to leave off this minute!' She generally gave herself very good advice, (though she very seldom followed it), and sometimes she scolded herself so severely as to bring tears into her eyes; and once she remembered trying to box her own ears for having cheated herself in a game of croquet she was playing against herself, for this curious child was very fond of pretending to be two people. 'But it's no use now,' thought poor Alice, 'to pretend to be two people! Why, there's hardly enough of me left to make *one* respectable person!'

Soon her eye fell on a little glass box that was lying under the table: she opened it, and found in it a very small cake, on which the words 'eat me' were beautifully marked in currants. 'Well, I'll eat it,' said Alice, 'and if it makes me grow larger, I can reach the key; and if it makes me grow smaller, I can creep under the door; so either way I'll get into the garden, and I don't care which happens!'

She ate a little bit, and said anxiously to herself, 'Which way? Which way?' holding her hand on the top of her head to feel which way it was growing, and she was quite surprised to find that she remained the same size: to be sure, this generally happens when one eats cake, but Alice had got so much into the way of expecting nothing but out-of-the-way things to happen, that it seemed quite dull and stupid for life to go on in the common way.

So she set to work, and very soon finished off the cake.

*   *   *   *
*   *   *
*   *   *   *

2

The Pool of Tears

'CURIOUSER and curiouser!' cried Alice (she was so much surprised, that for the moment she quite forgot how to speak good English); 'now I'm opening out like the largest telescope that ever was! Good-bye, feet!' (for when she looked down at her feet, they seemed to be almost out of sight, they were getting so far off). 'Oh, my poor little feet, I wonder who will put on your shoes and stockings for you now, dears? I'm sure *I* shan't be able! I shall be a great deal too far off to trouble myself about you: you must manage the best way you can; – but I must be kind to them,' thought Alice, 'or perhaps they won't walk the way I want to go! Let me see: I'll give them a new pair of boots every Christmas.'

And she went on planning to herself how she would manage it. 'They must go by the carrier,' she thought; 'and how funny it'll seem, sending presents to one's own feet! And how odd the directions will look!

> *Alice's Right Foot, Esq.*
> *Hearthrug,*
> *near the Fender,*
> *(with Alice's love).*

O dear, what nonsense I'm talking!'

Just then her head struck against the roof of the hall: in fact she was now more than nine feet high, and she at once took up the little golden key and hurried off to the garden door.

Poor Alice! It was as much as she could do, lying down on one side, to look through into the garden with one eye; but to get through was more hopeless than ever: she sat down and began to cry again.

'You ought to be ashamed of yourself,' said Alice, 'a great girl like you,' (she might well say this), 'to go on crying in this way! Stop this moment, I tell you!' But she went on all the same, shedding gallons of tears, until there was a large pool all round her, about four inches deep and reaching half down the hall.

After a time she heard a little pattering of feet in the distance, and she hastily dried her eyes to see what was coming. It was the White Rabbit returning, splendidly dressed, with a pair of white kid gloves in one hand and a large fan in the other: he came trotting along in a great hurry, muttering to himself as he came, 'Oh! the Duchess, the Duchess! Oh! won't she be savage if I've kept her waiting!' Alice felt so desperate that she was ready to ask help of any one; so, when the Rabbit came near her, she began, in a low, timid voice, 'If you please, sir –' The Rabbit started violently, dropped the white kid gloves and the fan, and skurried away into the darkness as hard as he could go.

Alice took up the fan and gloves, and, as the hall was very hot, she kept fanning herself all the time she went on talking: 'Dear, dear! How queer everything is today! And yesterday things went on just as usual. I wonder if I've been changed in the night? Let me think: was I the same when I got up this morning? I almost think I can remember feeling a little different. But if I'm not the same, the next question is, Who in the world am I? Ah *that's* the great puzzle!' And she began thinking over all the children she knew that were of the same age as herself, to see if she could have been changed for any of them.

'I'm sure I'm not Ada,' she said, 'for her hair goes in such long ringlets, and mine doesn't go in ringlets at all; and I'm sure I can't be Mabel, for I know all sorts of things, and she, oh! she knows such a very little! Besides, *she's* she, and *I'm* I, and – oh dear, how puzzling it all is! I'll try if I know all the things I used to know. Let me see: four times five is twelve, and four times six is thirteen, and four times seven is – oh dear! I shall never get to twenty at that rate! However, the Multiplication Table doesn't signify: let's try Geography. London is the capital of Paris, and Paris is the capital of Rome, and Rome – no, *that's* all wrong, I'm certain! I must have been changed for Mabel! I'll try and say "*How doth the little –*"' and she crossed her hands on her lap as if she were saying lessons, and began to repeat it, but her voice sounded hoarse and strange, and the words did not come the same as they used to do:

> '*How doth the little crocodile*
>   *Improve his shining tail,*
> *And pour the waters of the Nile*
>   *On every golden scale!*
>
> '*How cheerfully he seems to grin,*
>   *How neatly spread his claws,*

And welcome little fishes in
With gently smiling jaws!'

'I'm sure those are not the right words,' said poor Alice, and her eyes filled with tears again as she went on, 'I must be Mabel after all, and I shall have to go and live in that poky little house, and have next to no toys to play with, and oh! ever so many lessons to learn! No, I've made up my mind about it; if I'm Mabel, I'll stay down here! It'll be no use their putting their heads down and saying "Come up again, dear!" I shall only look up and say "Who am I then? Tell me that first, and then, if I like being that person, I'll come up: if not, I'll stay down here till I'm somebody else" – but, oh dear!' cried Alice, with a sudden burst of tears, 'I do wish they *would* put their heads down! I am so *very* tired of being all alone here!'

As she said this she looked down at her hands, and was surprised to see that she had put on one of the Rabbit's little white kid gloves while she was talking. 'How *can* I have done that?' she thought. 'I must be growing small again.' She got up and went to the table to measure herself by it, and found that, as nearly as she could guess, she was now about two feet high, and was going on shrinking rapidly: she soon found out that the cause of this was the fan she was holding, and she dropped it hastily, just in time to avoid shrinking away altogether.

'That *was* a narrow escape!' said Alice, a good deal frightened at the sudden change, but very glad to find herself still in existence; 'and now for the garden!' and she ran with all speed back to the little door: but, alas! the little door was shut again, and the little golden key was lying on the glass table as before, 'and things are worse than ever,' thought the poor child, 'for I never was so small as this before, never! And I declare it's too bad, that it is!'

As she said these words her foot slipped, and in another moment, splash! she was up to her chin in salt water. Her first idea was that she had somehow fallen into the sea, 'and in that case I can go back by railway,' she said to herself. (Alice had been to the seaside once in her life, and had come to the general conclusion, that wherever you go to on the English coast you find a number of bathing machines in the sea, some children digging in the sand with wooden spades, then a row of lodging houses, and behind them a railway station.) However, she soon made out that she was in the pool of tears which she had wept when she was nine feet high.

'I wish I hadn't cried so much!' said Alice, as she swam about, trying to find her way out. 'I shall be punished for it now, I suppose, by being drowned in my own tears! That *will* be a queer thing, to be sure! However, everything is queer today.'

Just then she heard something splashing about in the pool a little way off, and she swam nearer to make out what it was: at first she thought it must be a walrus or hippopotamus, but then she remembered how small she was now, and she soon made out that it was only a mouse that had slipped in like herself.

'Would it be of any use, now,' thought Alice, 'to speak to this mouse? Everything is so out-of-the-way down here, that I should think very likely it can talk: at any rate, there's no harm in trying.' So she began: 'O Mouse, do you know the way out of this pool? I am very tired of swimming about here, O Mouse!' (Alice thought this must be the right way of speaking to a mouse: she had never done such a thing before, but she remembered having seen in her brother's Latin Grammar, 'A mouse – of a mouse – to a mouse – a mouse – O mouse!') The Mouse looked at her rather inquisitively, and seemed to her to wink with one of its little eyes, but it said nothing.

'Perhaps it doesn't understand English,' thought Alice; 'I daresay it's a French mouse, come over with William the Conqueror.' (For, with all her knowledge of history, Alice had no very clear notion how long ago anything had happened.) So she began again: 'Où est ma chatte?' which was the first sentence in her French lesson-book. The Mouse gave a sudden leap out of the water, and seemed to quiver all over with fright. 'Oh, I beg your pardon!' cried Alice hastily, afraid that she had hurt the poor animal's feelings. 'I quite forgot you didn't like cats.'

'Not like cats!' cried the Mouse, in a shrill, passionate voice. 'Would you like cats if you were me?'

'Well, perhaps not,' said Alice in a soothing tone: 'don't be angry about it. And yet I wish I could show you our cat Dinah: I think you'd take a fancy to cats if you could only see her. She is such a dear quiet thing,' Alice went on, half to herself, as she swam lazily about in the pool, 'and she sits purring so nicely by the fire, licking her paws and washing her face – and she is such a nice soft thing to nurse and she's such a capital one for catching mice – oh, I beg your pardon!' cried Alice again, for this time the Mouse was bristling all over, and she felt certain it must be really offended. 'We won't talk about her any more if you'd rather not.'

'We, indeed!' cried the Mouse, who was trembling down to the end of his tail. As if *I* would talk on such a subject! Our family always *hated* cats: nasty, low, vulgar things! Don't let me hear the name again!'

'I won't indeed!' said Alice, in a great hurry to change the subject of conversation. 'Are you – are you fond – of – of dogs?' The Mouse did not answer, so Alice went on eagerly: 'There is such a nice little dog near our house I should like to show you! A little bright-eyed terrier, you know, with oh, such long curly brown hair! And it'll fetch things when you throw them, and it'll sit up and beg for its dinner, and all sorts of things – I can't remember half of them – and it belongs to a farmer, you know, and he says it's so useful, it's worth a hundred pounds! He says it kills all the rats and – oh dear!' cried Alice in a sorrowful tone, 'I'm afraid I've offended it again!' For the Mouse was swimming away from her as hard as it could go, and making quite a commotion in the pool as it went.

So she called softly after it, 'Mouse dear! Do come back again, and we won't talk about cats or dogs either, if you don't like them!' When the Mouse heard this, it turned round and swam slowly back to her: its face was quite pale (with passion, Alice thought), and it said in a low trembling voice, 'Let us get to the shore, and then I'll tell you my history, and you'll understand why it is I hate cats and dogs.'

It was high time to go, for the pool was getting quite crowded with the birds and animals that had fallen into it: there were a Duck and a Dodo, a Lory and an Eaglet, and several other curious creatures. Alice led the way, and the whole party swam to the shore.

A Caucus-race and a Long Tale

T HEY were indeed a queer-looking party that assembled on the bank – the birds with draggled feathers, the animals with their fur clinging close to them, and all dripping wet, cross, and uncomfortable.

The first question of course was, how to get dry again: they had a consultation about this, and after a few minutes it seemed quite natural to Alice to find herself talking familiarly with them, as if she had known them all her life. Indeed, she had quite a long argument with the Lory, who at last turned sulky, and would only say, 'I am older than you, and must know better'; and this Alice would not allow without knowing how old it was, and, as the Lory positively refused to tell its age, there was no more to be said.

At last the Mouse, who seemed to be a person of authority among them, called out, 'Sit down, all of you, and listen to me! *I'll* soon make you dry enough!' They all sat down at once, in a large ring, with the Mouse in the middle. Alice kept her eyes anxiously fixed on it, for she felt sure she would catch a bad cold if she did not get dry very soon.

'Ahem!' said the Mouse with an important air, 'are you all ready? This is the driest thing I know. Silence all round, if you please! "William the Conqueror, whose cause was favoured by the pope, was soon submitted to by the English, who wanted leaders, and had been of late much accustomed to usurpation and conquest. Edwin and Morcar, the earls of Mercia and Northumbria —"'

'Ugh!' said the Lory, with a shiver.

'I beg your pardon!' said the Mouse, frowning, but very politely: 'Did you speak?'

'Not I!' said the Lory hastily.

'I thought you did,' said the Mouse. '— I proceed. "Edwin and Morcar, the earls of Mercia and Northumbria, declared for him, and even Stigand, the patriotic archbishop of Canterbury, found it advisable —"'

'Found *what*?' said the Duck.

'Found *it*,' the Mouse replied rather crossly: 'of course you know what "it" means.'

'I know what "it" means well enough, when *I* find a

thing,' said the Duck: 'it's generally a frog or a worm. The question is, what did the archbishop find?'

The Mouse did not notice this question, but hurriedly went on, '"– found it advisable to go with Edgar Atheling to meet William and offer him the crown. William's conduct at first was moderate. But the insolence of his Normans –" How are you getting on now, my dear?' it continued, turning to Alice as it spoke.

'As wet as ever,' said Alice in a melancholy tone: 'it doesn't seem to dry me at all.'

'In that case,' said the Dodo solemnly, rising to its feet, 'I move that the meeting adjourn, for the immediate adoption of more energetic remedies –'

'Speak English!' said the Eaglet. 'I don't know the meaning of half those long words, and, what's more, I don't believe you do either!' And the Eaglet bent down its head to hide a smile: some of the other birds tittered audibly.

'What I was going to say,' said the Dodo in an offended tone, 'was, that the best thing to get us dry would be a Caucus-race.'

'What *is* a Caucus-race?' said Alice; not that she wanted much to know, but the Dodo had paused as if it thought that *somebody* ought to speak, and no one else seemed inclined to say anything.

'Why,' said the Dodo, 'the best way to explain it is to do it.' (And, as you might like to try the thing yourself, some winter day, I will tell you how the Dodo managed it.)

First it marked out a race-course, in a sort of circle, ('the exact shape doesn't matter,' it said,) and then all the party were placed along the course, here and there. There was no 'One, two, three, and away,' but they began running when they liked, and left off when they liked, so that it was not easy to know when the race was over. However, when they had been running half an hour or so, and were quite dry again, the Dodo suddenly called out 'The race is over!' and they all crowded round it, panting, and asking, 'But who has won?'

This question the Dodo could not answer without a great deal of thought, and it sat for a long time with one finger pressed upon its forehead (the position in which you usually see Shakespeare, in the pictures of him), while the rest waited in silence. At last the Dodo said, '*Everybody* has won, and all must have prizes.'

'But who is to give the prizes?' quite a chorus of voices asked.

'Why, *she*, of course,' said the Dodo, pointing to Alice with one finger; and the whole party at once crowded round her, calling out in a confused way, 'Prizes! Prizes!'

Alice had no idea what to do, and in despair she put her hand in her pocket, and pulled out a box of comfits, (luckily the salt water had not got into it), and handed them round as prizes. There was exactly one a-piece all round.

'But she must have a prize herself, you know,' said the Mouse.

'Of course,' the Dodo replied very gravely. 'What else have you got in your pocket?' he went on, turning to Alice.

'Only a thimble,' said Alice sadly.

'Hand it over here,' said the Dodo.

Then they all crowded round her once more, while the Dodo solemnly presented the thimble, saying 'We beg your acceptance of this elegant thimble'; and, when it had finished this short speech, they all cheered.

Alice thought the whole thing very absurd, but they all looked so grave that she did not dare to laugh; and, as she could not think of anything to say, she simply bowed, and took the thimble, looking as solemn as she could.

The next thing was to eat the comfits: this caused some noise and confusion, as the large birds complained that they could not taste theirs, and the small ones choked and had to be patted on the back. However, it was over at last, and they sat down again in a ring, and begged the Mouse to tell them something more.

'You promised to tell me your history, you know,' said Alice, 'and why it is you hate – C and D,' she added in a whisper, half afraid that it would be offended again.

'Mine is a long and a sad tale!' said the Mouse, turning to Alice, and sighing.

'It *is* a long tail, certainly,' said Alice, looking down with wonder at the Mouse's tail; 'but why do you call it sad?' And she kept on puzzling about it while the Mouse was speaking, so that her idea of the tale was something like this:–

'Fury said to a
mouse, That he
met in the
house,
"Let us
both go to
law: *I* will
prosecute
you. – Come,
I'll take no
denial; We
must have a
trial: For
really this
morning I've
nothing
to do."
Said the
mouse to the
cur, "Such
a trial,
dear Sir,
With
no jury
or judge,
would be
wasting
our
breath."
"I'll be
judge, I'll
be jury "
Said
cunning
old Fury:
"I'll
try the
whole
cause,
and
condemn
you
to
death."'

'You are not attending!' said the Mouse to Alice
severely. 'What are you thinking of?'

'I beg your pardon,' said Alice very humbly: 'you had got to the fifth bend, I think?'

'I had *not*!' cried the Mouse, sharply and very angrily.

'A knot!' said Alice, always ready to make herself useful, and looking anxiously about her, 'Oh, do let me help to undo it!'

'I shall do nothing of the sort,' said the Mouse, getting up and walking away. 'You insult me by talking such nonsense!'

'I didn't mean it!' pleaded poor Alice. 'But you're so easily offended, you know!'

The Mouse only growled in reply.

'Please come back and finish your story!' Alice called after it; and the others all joined in chorus, 'Yes, please do!' but the Mouse only shook its head impatiently, and walked a little quicker.

'What a pity it wouldn't stay!' sighed the Lory, as soon as it was quite out of sight; and an old Crab took the opportunity of saying to her daughter 'Ah, my dear! Let this be a lesson to you never to lose *your* temper!' 'Hold your tongue, Ma!' said the young Crab, a little snappishly. 'You're enough to try the patience of an oyster!'

'I wish I had our Dinah here, I know I do!' said Alice aloud, addressing nobody in particular. 'She'd soon fetch it back!'

'And who is Dinah, if I might venture to ask the question?' said the Lory.

Alice replied eagerly, for she was always ready to talk about her pet: 'Dinah's our cat. And she's such a capital one for catching mice you can't think! And oh, I wish you could see her after the birds! Why, she'll eat a little bird as soon as look at it!'

This speech caused a remarkable sensation among the party. Some of the birds hurried off at once: one old Magpie began wrapping itself up very carefully, remarking, 'I really must be getting home; the night-air doesn't suit my throat!' and a Canary called out in a trembling voice to its children, 'Come away, my dears! It's high time you were all in bed!' On various pretexts they all moved off, and Alice was soon left alone.

'I wish I hadn't mentioned Dinah!' she said to herself in a melancholy tone. 'Nobody seems to like her, down here, and I'm sure she's the best cat in the world! Oh, my dear Dinah! I wonder if I shall ever see you any more!' And here poor Alice began to cry again, for she felt very lonely and low-spirited. In a little while, however, she again heard a little pattering of footsteps in the distnce, and she looked up eagerly, half hoping that the Mouse had changed his mind, and was coming back to finish his story.

4

The Rabbit Sends in a Little Bill

IT was the White Rabbit, trotting slowly back again, and looking anxiously about as it went, as if it had lost something; and she heard it muttering to itself 'The Duchess! The Duchess! Oh my dear paws! Oh my fur and whiskers! She'll get me executed, as sure as ferrets are ferrets! Where *can* I have dropped them, I wonder?' Alice guessed in a moment that it was looking for the fan and the pair of white kid gloves, and she very good-naturedly began hunting about for them, but they were nowhere to be seen – everything seemed to have changed since her swim in the pool, and the great hall, with the glass table and the little door, had vanished completely.

Very soon the Rabbit noticed Alice, as she went hunting about, and called out to her in an angry tone,

'Why, Mary Ann, what *are* you doing out here? Run home this moment, and fetch me a pair of gloves and a fan! Quick, now!' And Alice was so much frightened that she ran off at once in the direction it pointed to, without trying to explain the mistake it had made.

'He took me for his housemaid,' she said to herself as she ran. 'How surprised he'll be when he finds out who I am! But I'd better take him his fan and gloves – that is, if I can find them.' As she said this, she came upon a neat little house, on the door of which was a bright brass plate with the name 'w. RABBIT' engraved upon it. She went in without knocking, and hurried upstairs, in great fear lest she should meet the real Mary Ann, and be turned out of the house before she had found the fan and gloves.

'How queer it seems,' Alice said to herself, 'to be going messages for a rabbit! I suppose Dinah'll be sending me on messages next!' And she began fancying the sort of thing that would happen: '"Miss Alice! Come here directly, and get ready for your walk!" "Coming in a minute, nurse! But I've got to watch this mouse-hole till Dinah comes back, and see that the mouse doesn't get out." Only I don't think,' Alice went on, 'that they'd let Dinah stop in the house if it began ordering people about like that!'

By this time she had found her way into a tidy little

room with a table in the window, and on it (as she had hoped) a fan and two or three pairs of tiny white kid gloves: she took up the fan and a pair of the gloves, and was just going to leave the room, when her eye fell upon a little bottle that stood near the looking-glass. There was no label this time with the words 'DRINK ME,' but nevertheless she uncorked it and put it to her lips. 'I know *something* interesting is sure to happen,' she said to herself, 'whenever I eat or drink anything; so I'll just see what this bottles does. I do hope it'll make me grow large again, for really I'm quite tired of being such a tiny little thing!'

It did so indeed, and much sooner than she had expected: before she had drunk half the bottle, she found her head pressing against the ceiling, and had to stoop to save her neck from being broken. She hastily put down the bottle, saying to herself 'That's quite enough – I hope I shan't grow any more – As it is, I can't get out at the door – I do wish I hadn't drunk quite so much!'

Alas! It was too late to wish that! She went on growing, and growing, and very soon had to kneel down on the floor: in another minute there was not even room for this, and she tried the effect of lying down with one elbow against the door, and the other arm curled round her head. Still she went on growing, and as a last resource, she put one arm out of the window, and one foot up the chimney, and said to herself 'Now I can do no more, whatever happens. What *will* become of me?'

Luckily for Alice, the little magic bottle had now had its full effect, and she grew no larger: still it was very uncomfortable, and, as there seemed to be no sort of chance of her ever getting out of the room again, no wonder she felt unhappy.

'It was much pleasanter at home,' thought poor Alice, 'when one wasn't always growing larger and smaller, and being ordered about by mice and rabbits. I almost wish I hadn't gone down that rabbit-hole – and yet – and yet – it's rather curious, you know, this sort of life! I do wonder what *can* have happened to me! When I used to read fairytales, I fancied that kind of thing never happened, and now here I am in the middle of one! There ought to be a book written about me, that there ought! And when I grow up, I'll write one – but I'm grown up now,' she added in a sorrowful tone; 'at least there's no room to grow up any more *here*.'

'But then,' thought Alice, 'shall I *never* get any older than I am now? That'll be a comfort, one way – never to be an old woman – but then – always to have lessons to learn! Oh, I shouldn't like *that*!'

'Oh, you foolish Alice!' she answered herself. 'How can you learn lessons in here? Why, there's hardly room for *you*, and no room at all for any lesson-books!'

And so she went on, taking first one side and then the other, and making quite a conversation of it altogether; but after a few minutes she heard a voice outside, and stopped to listen.

'Mary Ann! Mary Ann!' said the voice. 'Fetch me my gloves this moment!' Then came a little pattering of feet on the stairs. Alice knew it was the Rabbit coming to look for her, and she trembled till she shook the house, quite forgetting that she was now about a thousand times as large as the Rabbit, and had no reason to be afraid of it.

Presently the Rabbit came up to the door, and tried

to open it; but, as the door opened inwards, and Alice's elbow was pressed hard against it, that attempt proved a failure. Alice heard it say to itself 'Then I'll go round and get in at the window.'

'*That* you won't!' thought Alice, and, after waiting till she fancied she heard the Rabbit just under the window, she suddenly spread out her hand, and made a snatch in the air. She did not get hold of anything, but she heard a little shriek and a fall, and a crash of broken glass, from which she concluded that it was just possible it had fallen into a cucumber-frame, or something of the sort.

Next came an angry voice – the Rabbit's – 'Pat! Pat! Where are you?' And then a voice she had never heard before, 'Sure then I'm here! Digging for apples, yer honour!'

'Digging for apples, indeed!' said the Rabbit angrily. 'Here! Come and help me out of *this*!' (Sounds of more broken glass.)

'Now tell me, Pat, what's that in the window?'

'Sure, it's an arm, yer honour!' (He pronounced it 'arrum.')

'An arm, you goose! Who ever saw one that size? Why, it fills the whole window!'

'Sure, it does, yer honour: but it's an arm for all that.'

'Well, it's got no business there, at any rate: go and take it away!'

There was a long silence after this, and Alice could only hear whispers now and then; such as, 'Sure, I don't like it, yer honour, at all, at all!' 'Do as I tell you, you coward!' and at last she spread out her hand again, and made another snatch in the air. This time there were *two* little shrieks, and more sounds of broken glass. 'What a number of cucumber-frames there must be!' thought Alice. 'I wonder what they'll do next! As for pulling me

43

out of the window, I only wish they *could*! I'm sure *I* don't want to stay in here any longer!'

She waited for some time without hearing anything more: at last came a rumbling of little cartwheels, and the sound of a good many voices all talking together: she made out the words: 'Where's the other ladder? – Why, I hadn't to bring but one; Bill's got the other – Bill! fetch it here, lad! – Here, put 'em up at this corner – No, tie 'em together first – they don't reach half high enough yet – Oh! they'll do well enough; don't be particular – Here, Bill! catch hold of this rope – Will the roof bear? – Mind that loose slate – Oh, it's coming down! Heads below!' (a loud crash) – 'Now, who did that? – It was Bill, I fancy – Who's to go down the chimney? – Nay, *I* shan't! *You* do it! – *That* I won't, then! – Bill's to go down – Here, Bill! the master says you're to go down the chimney!'

'Oh! So Bill's got to come down the chimney, has he?' said Alice to herself. 'Why, they seem to put everything upon Bill! I wouldn't be in Bill's place for a good deal: this fireplace is narrow, to be sure; but I *think* I can kick a little!'

She drew her foot as far down the chimney as she could, and waited till she heard a little animal (she couldn't guess of what sort it was) scratching and scrambling about in the chimney close above her: then, saying to herself 'This is Bill,' she gave one sharp kick, and waited

to see what would
happen next.

The first thing she
heard was a general
chorus of 'There goes
Bill!' then the Rabbit's
voice alone – 'Catch
him, you by the
hedge!' then silence,
and then another
confusion of voices
– 'Hold up his head –
Brandy now – Don't
choke him – How was
it, old fellow? What
happened to you? Tell
us all about it!'

Last came a little
feeble, squeaking
voice, ('That's Bill,'
thought Alice,) 'Well,
I hardly know – No
more, thank ye; I'm
better now – but I'm
a deal too flustered to
tell you – all I know is,

something comes at me like a Jack-in-the-box, and up I goes like a sky-rocket!'

'So you did, old fellow!' said the others.

'We must burn the house down!' said the Rabbit's voice; and Alice called out as loud as she could, 'If you do, I'll set Dinah at you!'

There was a dead silence instantly, and Alice thought to herself, 'I wonder what they *will* do next! If they had any sense, they'd take the roof off.' After a minute or two, they began moving about again, and Alice heard the Rabbit say, 'A barrowful will do, to begin with.'

'A barrowful of *what*?' thought Alice; but she had not long to doubt, for the next moment a shower of little pebbles came rattling in at the window, and some of them hit her in the face. 'I'll put a stop to this,' she said to herself, and shouted out, 'You'd better not do that again!' which produced another dead silence.

Alice noticed with some surprise that the pebbles were all turning into little cakes as they lay on the floor, and a bright idea came into her head. 'If I eat one of these cakes,' she thought, 'it's sure to make *some* change in my size; and as it can't possibly make me larger, it must make me smaller, I suppose.'

So she swallowed one of the cakes, and was delighted to find that she began shrinking directly. As soon as she was small enough to get through the door, she ran out of the house, and found quite a crowd of little animals and birds waiting outside. The poor little Lizard, Bill, was in the middle, being held up by two guinea-pigs, who were giving it something out of a bottle. They all made a rush at Alice the moment she appeared; but she ran off as hard as she could, and soon found herself safe in a thick wood.

'The first thing I've got to do,' said Alice to herself, as she wandered about in the wood, 'is to grow to my right size again; and the second thing is to find my way into that lovely garden. I think that will be the best plan.'

It sounded an excellent plan, no doubt, and very neatly and simply arranged; the only difficulty was, that she had not the smallest idea how to set about it; and while she was peering about anxiously among the trees, a little sharp bark just over her head made her look up in a great hurry.

An enormous puppy was looking down at her with large round eyes, and feebly stretching out one paw, trying to touch her. 'Poor little thing!' said Alice, in a coaxing tone, and she tried hard to whistle to it; but she was terribly frightened all the time at the thought that it might be hungry, in which case it would be very likely to eat her up in spite of all her coaxing.

Hardly knowing what she did, she picked up a little bit of stick, and held it out to the puppy; whereupon the puppy jumped into the air off all its feet at once, with a yelp of delight, and rushed at the stick, and made believe to worry it; then Alice dodged behind a great thistle, to keep herself from being run over; and the moment she appeared on the other side, the puppy made another rush at the stick, and tumbled head over heels in its hurry to get hold of it; then Alice, thinking it was very like having a game of play with a cart-horse, and expecting every moment to be trampled under its feet, ran round the thistle again; then the puppy began a series of short charges at the stick, running a very little way forwards each time and a long way back, and barking hoarsely all the while, till at last it sat down a good way off, panting, with its tongue hanging out of its mouth, and its great eyes half shut.

This seemed to Alice a good opportunity for making her escape; so she set off at once, and ran till she was quite tired and out of breath, and till the puppy's bark sounded quite faint in the distance.

'And yet what a dear little puppy it was!' said Alice, as she leant against a buttercup to rest herself, and fanned herself with one of the leaves: 'I should have liked teaching it tricks very much, if – if I'd only been the right size to do it! Oh dear! I'd nearly forgotten that I've got to grow up again! Let me see – how is it to be managed? I suppose I ought to eat or drink something or other; but the great question is, what?'

The great question certainly was, what? Alice looked all round her at the flowers and the blades of grass, but she could not see anything that looked like the right thing to eat or drink under the circumstances. There was a large mushroom growing near her, about the same height as herself; and when she had looked under it, and on both sides of it, and behind it, it occurred to her that she might as well look and see what was on top of it.

She stretched herself up on tiptoe, and peeped over the edge of the mushroom, and her eyes immediately met those of a large blue caterpillar, that was sitting on the top with its arms folded, quietly smoking a long hookah, and taking not the smallest notice of her or anything else.

5

Advice from a Caterpillar

THE Caterpillar and Alice looked at each other for some time in silence: at last the Caterpillar took the hookah out of its mouth, and addressed her in a languid, sleepy voice.

'Who are *you*?' said the Caterpillar.

This was not an encouraging opening for a conversation. Alice replied, rather shyly, 'I-I hardly know, sir, just at present – at least I know who I *was* when I got up this morning, but I think I must have been changed several times since then.'

'What do you mean by that?' said the Caterpillar sternly. 'Explain yourself!'

'I can't explain *myself*, I'm afraid, sir,' said Alice, 'because I'm not myself, you see.'

'I don't see,' said the Caterpillar.

'I'm afraid I can't put it more clearly,' Alice replied very politely, 'for I can't understand it myself to begin with; and being so many different sizes in a day is very confusing.

'It isn't,' said the Caterpillar.

'Well, perhaps you haven't found it so yet,' said Alice; 'but when you have to turn into a chrysalis – you will some day, you know – and then after that into a butterfly, I should think you'll feel it a little queer, won't you?'

'Not a bit,' said the Caterpillar.

'Well, perhaps your feelings may be different,' said Alice; 'all I know is, it would feel very queer to *me*.'

'You!' said the Caterpillar contemptuously. 'Who are *you*?'

Which brought them back again to the beginning

of the conversation. Alice felt a little irritated at the Caterpillar 's making such *very* short remarks, and she drew herself up and said, very gravely, 'I think you ought to tell me who *you* are, first.'

'Why?' said the Caterpillar.

Here was another puzzling question; and as Alice could not think of any good reason, and as the Caterpillar seemed to be in a *very* unpleasant state of mind, she turned away.

'Come back!' the Caterpillar called after her. 'I've something important to say!'

This sounded promising, certainly: Alice turned and came back again.

'Keep your temper,' said the Caterpillar.

'Is that all?' said Alice, swallowing down her anger as well as she could.

'No,' said the Caterpillar.

Alice thought she might as well wait, as she had nothing else to do, and perhaps after all it might tell her something worth hearing. For some minutes it puffed away without speaking, but at last it unfolded its arms, took the hookah out of its mouth again, and said, 'So you think you're changed, do you?'

'I'm afraid I am, sir,' said Alice; 'I can't remember things as I used – and I don't keep the same size for ten minutes together!'

'Can't remember *what* things?' said the Caterpillar.
'Well, I've tried to say "*How doth the little busy bee*," but
it all came different!' Alice replied in a very melancholy
voice.

'Repeat, "*You are old, Father William*,"' said the
Caterpillar.

Alice folded her hands, and began:–

'You are old, Father William,' *the young man said,*
'*And your hair has become very white;*
And yet you incessantly stand on your head –
Do you think, at your age, it is right?'

'In my youth,' Father William replied to his son,
'I feared it might injure the brain;
But, now that I'm perfectly sure I have none,
Why, I do it again and again.'

'You are old, said the youth, 'as I mentioned before,
And have grown most uncommonly fat;
Yet you turned a back-somersault in at the door –
Pray, what is the reason of that?'

'In my youth,' said the sage, as he shook his grey locks,
'I kept all my limbs very supple
By the use of this ointment – one shilling the box –
Allow me to sell you a couple?'

'You are old,' said the youth, 'and your jaws are too weak
For anything tougher than suet;
Yet you finished the goose, with the bones and the beak –
Pray how did you manage to do it?'

'In my youth,' said his father, 'I took to the law,
And argued each case with my wife;
And the muscular strength, which it gave to my jaw,
Has lasted the rest of my life.'

'You are old,' said the youth, 'one would hardly suppose
That your eye was as steady as ever;
Yet you balanced an eel on the end of your nose –
What made you so awfully clever?'

'*I have answered three questions, and that is enough,*'
Said his father; 'don't give yourself airs!
Do you think I can listen all day to such stuff?
Be off, or I'll kick you down stairs!'

'That is not said right,' said the Caterpillar.

'Not *quite* right, I'm afraid,' said Alice, timidly; 'some of the words have got altered.'

'It is wrong from beginning to end,' said the Caterpillar decidedly, and there was silence for some minutes.

The Caterpillar was the first to speak.

'What size do you want to be?' it asked.

'Oh, I'm not particular as to size,' Alice hastily replied; 'only one doesn't like changing so often, you know.'

'I *don't* know,' said the Caterpillar.

Alice said nothing: she had never been so much contradicted in all her life before, and she felt that she was losing her temper.

'Are you content now?' said the Caterpillar.

'Well, I should like to be a *little* larger, sir, if you wouldn't mind,' said Alice: 'three inches is such a wretched height to be.'

'It is a very good height indeed!' said the Caterpillar angrily, rearing itself upright as it spoke (it was exactly three inches high).

'But I'm not used to it!' pleaded poor Alice in a piteous tone. And she thought to herself, 'I wish the creatures wouldn't be so easily offended!'

'You'll get used to it in time,' said the Caterpillar; and put the hookah into its mouth and began smoking again.

This time Alice waited patiently until it chose to speak again. In a minute or two the Caterpillar took the hookah out of its mouth and yawned once or twice, and shook itself. Then it got down off the mushroom, and crawled away into the grass, merely remarking as it went, 'One side will make you grow taller, and the other side will make you grow shorter.'

'One side of *what*? The other side of *what*?' thought Alice to herself.

'Of the mushroom,' said the Caterpillar, just as if she had asked it aloud; and in another moment it was out of sight.

Alice remained looking thoughtfully at the mushroom for a minute, trying to make out which were the two sides of it; and as it was perfectly round, she found this a very difficult question. However, at last she stretched her arms round it as far as they would go, and broke off a bit of the edge with each hand.

'And now which is which?' she said to herself, and nibbled a little of the right-hand bit to try the effect: the next moment she felt a violent blow underneath her chin: it had struck her foot!

She was a good deal frightened by this very sudden change, but she felt that there was no time to be lost, as she was shrinking rapidly; so she set to work at once to eat some of the other bit. Her chin was pressed so closely against her foot, that there was hardly room to open her mouth; but she did it at last, and managed to swallow a morsel of the left-hand bit.

        *   *   *   *
           *   *   *
        *   *   *   *

'Come, my head's free at last!' said Alice in a tone of delight, which changed into alarm in another moment, when she found that her shoulders were nowhere to be found: all she could see, when she looked down, was an immense length of neck, which seemed to rise like a stalk out of a sea of green leaves that lay far below her.

'What *can* all that green stuff be?' said Alice. 'And where *have* my shoulders got to? And oh, my poor hands, how is it I can't see you?' She was moving them about as she spoke, but no result seemed to follow, except a little shaking among the distant green leaves.

As there seemed to be no chance of getting her hands up to her head, she tried to get her head down to them, and was delighted to find that her neck would bend about easily in any direction, like a serpent. She had just succeeded in curving it down into a graceful zigzag, and was going to dive in among the leaves, which she found to be nothing but the tops of the trees under which she had been wandering, when a sharp hiss made her draw back in a hurry: a large pigeon had flown into her face, and was beating her violently with its wings.

'Serpent!' screamed the Pigeon.

'I'm *not* a serpent!' said Alice indignantly. 'Let me alone!'

'Serpent, I say again!' repeated the Pigeon, but in a more subdued tone, and added with a kind of sob, 'I've tried every way, and nothing seems to suit them!'

'I haven't the least idea what you're talking about,' said Alice.

'I've tried the roots of trees, and I've tried banks, and I've tried hedges,' the Pigeon went on without attending to her; 'but those serpents! There's no pleasing them!'

Alice was more and more puzzled, but she thought there was no use in saying anything more till the Pigeon had finished.

'As if it wasn't trouble enough hatching the eggs,' said the Pigeon; 'but I must be on the look-out for serpents night and day! Why, I haven't had a wink of sleep these three weeks!'

'I'm very sorry you've been annoyed,' said Alice, who was beginning to see its meaning.

'And just as I'd taken the highest tree in the wood,' continued the Pigeon, raising its voice to a shriek, 'and just as I was thinking I should be free of them at last, they must needs come wriggling down from the sky! Ugh, Serpent!'

'But I'm *not* a serpent, I tell you!' said Alice. 'I'm a – I'm a –'

'Well, *what* are you?' said the Pigeon. 'I can see you're trying to invent something!'

'I-I'm a little girl,' said Alice, rather doubtfully, as

she remembered the number of changes she had gone through that day.

'A likely story indeed!' said the Pigeon in a tone of the deepest contempt. 'I've seen a good many little girls in my time, but never *one* with such a neck as that! No, no! You're a serpent; and there's no use denying it. I suppose you'll be telling me next that you never tasted an egg!'

'I *have* tasted eggs, certainly,' said Alice, who was a very truthful child; 'but little girls eat eggs quite as much as serpents do, you know.'

'I don't believe it,' said the Pigeon; 'but if they do, why then they're a kind of serpent, that's all I can say.'

This was such a new idea to Alice, that she was quite silent for a minute or two, which gave the Pigeon the opportunity of adding, 'You're looking for eggs, I know *that* well enough; and what does it matter to me whether you're a little girl or a serpent?'

'It matters a good deal to *me*,' said Alice hastily; 'but I'm not looking for eggs, as it happens; and if I was, I shouldn't want *yours*: I don't like them raw.'

'Well, be off, then!' said the Pigeon in a sulky tone, as it settled down again into its nest. Alice crouched down among the trees as well as she could, for her neck kept getting entangled among the branches, and every now and then she had to stop and untwist it. After a while she remembered that she still held the pieces of mushroom in her hands, and she set to work very carefully, nibbling first at one and then at the other, and growing sometimes taller and sometimes shorter, until she had succeeded in bringing heself down to her usual height.

It was so long since she had been anything near the right size, that it felt quite strange at first; bur she got used to it in a few minutes, and began talking to herself, as usual. 'Come, there's half my plan done now! How puzzling all these changes are! I'm never sure what I'm going to be, from one minute to another! However, I've got back to my right size: the next thing is, to get into that beautiful garden – how *is* that to be done, I wonder?' As she said this, she came suddenly upon an open place, with a little house in it about four feet high. 'Whoever lives there,' thought Alice, 'it'll never do to come upon them *this* size: why, I should frighten them out of their wits!' So she began nibbling at the right-hand bit again, and did not venture to go near the house till she had brought herself down to nine inches high.

6

Pig and Pepper

FOR a minute or two she stood looking at the house, and wondering what to do next, when suddenly a footman in livery came running out of the wood – (she considered him to be a footman because he was in livery: otherwise, judging by his face only, she would have called him a fish) – and rapped loudly at the door with his knuckles. It was opened by another footman in livery, with a round face, and large eyes like a frog; and both footmen, Alice noticed, had powdered hair that curled all over their heads. She felt very curious to know what it was all about, and crept a little way out of the wood to listen.

The Fish-Footman began by producing from under his arm a great letter, nearly as large as himself, and this he handed over to the other, saying, in a solemn tone,

'For the Duchess. An invitation from the Queen to play croquet.' The Frog-Footman repeated, in the same solemn tone, only changing the order of the words a little, 'From the Queen. An invitation for the Duchess to play croquet.'

Then they both bowed low, and their curls got entangled together.

Alice laughed so much as this, that she had to run back into the wood for fear of their hearing her; and when she next peeped out the Fish-Footman was gone, and the other was sitting on the ground near the door, staring stupidly up into the sky.

Alice went timidly up to the door, and knocked.

'There's no sort of use in knocking,' said the Footman, 'and that for two reasons. First, because I'm on the same side of the door as you are; secondly, because they're making such a noise inside, no one could possibly hear you.' And certainly there was a most extraordinary noise going on within – a constant howling and sneezing, and every now and then a great crash, as if a dish or kettle had been broken to pieces.

'Please, then,' said Alice, 'how am I to get in?'

'There might be some sense in your knocking,' the Footman went on without attending to her, 'if we had the door between us. For instance, if you were *inside*, you might knock, and I could let you out, you know.' He was looking up into the sky all the time he was speaking, and this Alice thought decidedly uncivil. 'But perhaps he can't help it,' she said to herself; 'his eyes are so *very* nearly at the top of his head. But at any rate he might answer questions. – How am I to get in?' she repeated, aloud.

'I shall sit here,' the Footman remarked, 'till

tomorrow –'

At this moment the door of the house opened, and a large plate came skimming out, straight at the Footman's head: it just grazed his nose, and broke to pieces against one of the trees behind him.

'– or next day, maybe,' the Footman continued in the same tone, exactly as if nothing had happened.

'How am I to get in?' asked Alice again, in a louder tone.

'*Are* you to get in at all?' said the Footman. 'That's the first question, you know.'

It was, no doubt: only Alice did not like to be told so. 'It's really dreadful,' she muttered to herself, 'the way all the creatures argue. It's enough to drive one crazy!'

The Footman seemed to think this a good opportunity for repeating his remark, with variations. 'I shall sit here,' he said, 'on and off, for days and days.'

'But what am *I* to do?' said Alice.

'Anything you like,' said the Footman, and began whistling.

'Oh, there's no use in talking to him,' said Alice desperately: 'he's perfectly idiotic!' And she opened the door and went in.

The door led right into a large kitchen, which was full of smoke from one end to the other: the Duchess was sitting on a three-legged stool in the middle, nursing a baby; the cook was leaning over the fire, stirring a large cauldron which seemed to be full of soup.

'There's certainly too much pepper in that soup!' Alice said to herself, as well as she could for sneezing.

There was certainly too much of it in the air. Even the Duchess sneezed occasionally; and as for the baby, it was sneezing and howling alternately without a moment's pause. The only things in the kitchen that did not sneeze, were the cook, and a large cat which was sitting on the hearth and grinning from ear to ear.

'Please would you tell me,' said Alice, a little timidly, for she was not quite sure whether it was good manners for her to speak first, 'why your cat grins like that?'

'It's a Cheshire cat,' said the Duchess, 'and that's why. Pig!'

She said the last word with such sudden violence that Alice quite jumped; but she saw in another moment that it was addressed to the baby, and not to her, so she took courage, and went on again:–

'I didn't know that Cheshire cats always grinned; in fact, I didn't know that cats *could* grin.'

'They all can,' said the Duchess; 'and most of 'em do.'

'I don't know of any that do,' Alice said very politely, feeling quite pleased to have got into a conversation.

'You don't know much,' said the Duchess; 'and that's a fact.'

Alice did not at all like the tone of this remark, and thought it would be as well to introduce some other subject of conversation. While she was trying to fix on one, the cook took the cauldron of soup off the fire, and at once set to work throwing everything within her reach at the Duchess and the baby – the fire-irons came first; then followed a shower of saucepans, plates, and dishes. The Duchess took no notice of them even when they hit her; and the baby was howling so much already, that it was quite impossible to say whether the blows hurt it or not.

'Oh, *please* mind what you're doing!' cried Alice, jumping up and down in an agony of terror. 'Oh, there goes his *precious* nose'; as an unusually large saucepan flew close by it, and very nearly carried it off.

'If everybody minded their own business,' the Duchess said in a hoarse growl, 'the world would go round a deal faster than it does.'

'Which would *not* be an advantage,' said Alice, who felt very glad to get an opportunity of showing off a little of her knowledge. 'Just think of what work it would make with the day and night! You see the earth takes twenty-four hours to turn round on its axis –'

'Talking of axes,' said the Duchess, 'chop off her head!'

Alice glanced rather anxiously at the cook, to see if she meant to take the hint; but the cook was busily stirring the soup, and seemed not to be listening, so she went on again: 'Twenty-four hours, I *think*; or is it twelve? I –'

'Oh, don't bother *me*,' said the Duchess; 'I never could abide figures!' And with that she began nursing her child again, singing a sort of lullaby to it as she did so, and giving it a violent shake at the end of every line:

> *Speak roughly to your little boy,*
> *And beat him when he sneezes:*

> *He only does it to annoy,*
> *Because he knows it teases.'*

CHORUS

(in which the cook and the baby joined):–

'Wow! wow! wow!'

While the Duchess sang the second verse of the song, she kept tossing the baby violently up and down, and the poor little thing howled so, that Alice could hardly hear the words:–

> *'I speak severely to my boy,*
> *I beat him when he sneezes;*
> *For he can thoroughly enjoy*
> *The pepper when he pleases!'*

CHORUS

'Wow! wow! wow!'

'Here! you may nurse it a bit, if you like!' the Duchess said to Alice, flinging the baby at her as she spoke. 'I must go and get ready to play croquet with the Queen,' and she hurried out of the room. The cook threw a frying-pan after her as she went out, but it just missed her.

Alice caught the baby with some difficulty, as it was a queer-shaped little creature, and held out its arms and legs in all directions, 'just like a star-fish,' thought Alice. The poor little thing was snorting like a steam-engine when she caught it, and kept doubling itself up and straightening itself out again, so that altogether, for the first minute or two, it was as much as she could do to hold it.

As soon as she had made out the proper way of nursing it, (which was to twist it up into a sort of knot, and then keep tight hold of its right ear and left foot, so as to prevent its undoing itself,) she carried it out into the open air. 'If I don't take this child away with me,' thought Alice, 'they're sure to kill it in a day or two: wouldn't it be murder to leave it behind?' She said the last words out loud, and the little thing grunted in reply (it had left off sneezing by this time). 'Don't grunt,' said Alice; 'that's not at all a proper way of expressing yourself.'

The baby grunted again, and Alice looked very anxiously into its face to see what was the matter with it. There could be no doubt that it had a *very* turn-up nose, much more like a snout than a real baby: altogether Alice did not like the look of the thing at all. 'But perhaps it was only sobbing,' she thought, and looked into its eyes again, to see if there were any tears.

No, there were no tears. 'If you're going to turn into

a pig, my dear,' said Alice, seriously, 'I'll have nothing more to do with you. Mind now!' The poor little thing sobbed again (or grunted, it was impossible to say which), and they went on for some while in silence.

Alice was just beginning to think to herself, 'Now, what am I to do with this creature when I get it home?' when it grunted again, so violently, that she looked down into its face in some alarm. This time there could be *no* mistake about it: it was neither more nor less than a pig, and she felt that it would be quite absurd for her to carry it any further.

So she set the little creature down, and felt quite relieved to see it trot away quietly into the wood. 'If it had grown up,' she said to herself, 'it would have made a dreadfully ugly child: but it makes rather a handsome pig, I think.' And she began thinking over other children she knew, who might do very well as pigs, and was just saying to herself, 'if one only knew the right way to change them –' when she was a little startled by seeing the Cheshire Cat sitting on a bough of a tree a few yards off.

The Cat only grinned when it saw Alice. It looked good-natured, she thought: still it had *very* long claws and a great many teeth, so she felt that it ought to be treated with respect.

'Cheshire Puss,' she began, rather timidly, as she did not at all know whether it would like the name: however, it only grinned a little wider. 'Come, it's pleased so far,' thought Alice, and she went on. 'Would you tell me, please, which way I ought to go from here?'

'That depends a good deal on where you want to get to,' said the Cat.

'I don't much care where –' said Alice.

'Then it doesn't matter which way you go,' said the Cat.

'– so long as I get *somewhere*,' Alice added as an explanation.

'Oh, you're sure to do that,' said the Cat, 'if you only walk long enough.'

Alice felt this could not be denied, so she tried another question. 'What sort of people live about here?'

'In *that* direction,' the Cat said, waving its right paw round, 'lives a Hatter: and in *that* direction,' waving the other paw, 'lives a March Hare. Visit either you like: they're both mad.'

'But I don't want to go among mad people,' Alice remarked.

'Oh, you can't help that,' said the Cat: 'we're all mad here. I'm mad. You're mad.'

'How do you know I'm mad?' said Alice.

'You must be,' said the Cat, 'or you wouldn't have come here.'

Alice didn't think that proved it at all; however, she went on 'And how do you know that you're mad?'

'To begin with,' said the Cat, 'a dog's not mad. You grant that?'

'I suppose so,' said Alice.

'Well, then,' the Cat went on, 'you see, a dog growls when it's angry, and wags its tail when it's pleased. Now *I* growl when I'm pleased, and wag my tail when I'm angry. Therefore I'm mad.'

'*I* call it purring, not growling,' said Alice.

'Call it what you like,' said the Cat. 'Do you play

croquet with the Queen today?'

'I should like it very much,' said Alice, 'but I haven't been invited yet.'

'You'll see me there,' said the Cat, and vanished.

Alice was not much surprised at this, she was getting so used to queer things happening. While she was looking at the place where it had been, it suddenly appeared again.

'By-the-bye, what became of the baby?' said the Cat. 'I'd nearly forgotten to ask.'

'It turned into a pig,' Alice quietly said, just as if it had come back in a natural way.

'I thought it would,' said the Cat, and vanished again.

Alice waited a little, half expecting to see it again, but it did not appear, and after a minute or two she walked on in the direction in which the March Hare was said to live. 'I've seen hatters before,' she said to herself; 'the March Hare will be much the most interesting, and perhaps as this is May it won't be raving mad – at least not so mad as it was in March.' As she said this, she looked up, and there was the Cat again, sitting on a branch of a tree.

'Did you say pig, or fig?' said the Cat.

'I said pig,' replied Alice; 'and I wish you wouldn't keep appearing and vanishing so suddenly: you make one quite giddy.'

'All right,' said the Cat; and this time it vanished quite slowly, beginning with the end of the tail, and ending with the grin, which remained some time after the rest of it had gone.

'Well! I've often seen a cat without a grin,' thought Alice; 'but a grin without a cat! It's the most curious thing I ever saw in all my life!'

She had not gone much farther before she came in sight of the house of the March Hare: she thought it must be the right house, because the chimneys were shaped like ears and the roof was thatched with fur. It was so large a house, that she did not like to go nearer till she had nibbled some more of the left-hand bit of mushroom, and raised herself to about two feet high: even then she walked up towards it rather timidly, saying to herself 'Suppose it should be raving mad after all! I almost wish I'd gone to see the Hatter instead!'

7

A Mad Tea-Party

THERE was a table set out under a tree in front of the house, and the March Hare and the Hatter were having tea at it: a Dormouse was sitting between them, fast asleep, and the other two were using it as a cushion, resting their elbows on it, and talking over its head. 'Very uncomfortable for the Dormouse,' thought Alice; 'only, as it's asleep, I suppose it doesn't mind.'

The table was a large one, but the three were all crowded together at one corner of it: 'No room! No room!' they cried out when they saw Alice coming. 'There's *plenty* of room!' said Alice indignantly, and she sat down in a large arm-chair at one end of the table.

'Have some wine,' the March Hare said in an encouraging rone.

Alice looked all round the table, but there was nothing on it but tea. 'I don't see any wine,' she remarked.

'There isn't any,' said the March Hare.

Then it wasn't very civil of you to offer it,' said Alice angrily.

'It wasn't very civil of you to sit down without being invited,' said the March Hare.

'I didn't know it was *your* table,' said Alice; 'it's laid for a great many more than three.'

'Your hair wants cutting,' said the Hatter. He had been looking at Alice for some time with great curiosity, and this was his first speech.

'You should learn not to make personal remarks,' Alice said with some severity; 'it's very rude.'

The Hatter opened his eyes very wide on hearing this; but all he *said* was, 'Why is a raven like a writing-desk?'

'Come, we shall have some fun now!' thought Alice. 'I'm glad they've begun asking riddles. – I believe I can guess that,' she added aloud.

'Do you mean that you think you can find out the answer to it?' said the March Hare.

'Exactly so,' said Alice.

'Then you should say what you mean,' the March Hare went on.

'I do,' Alice hastily replied; 'at least – at least I mean what I say – that's the same thing, you know.'

'Not the same thing a bit!' said the Hatter. 'You might just as well say that "I see what I eat" is the same thing as "I eat what I see"!'

'You might just as well say,' added the March Hare, 'that "I like what I get" is the same thing as "I get what I like"!'

'You might just as well say,' added the Dormouse, who seemed to be talking in his sleep, 'that "I breathe when I sleep" is the same thing as "I sleep when I breathe"!'

'It *is* the same thing with you,' said the Hatter, and here the conversation dropped, and the party sat silent for a minute, while Alice thought over all she could remember about ravens and writing-desks, which wasn't much.

The Hatter was the first to break the silence.

'What day of the month is it?' he said, turning to Alice: he had taken his watch out of his pocket, and was looking at it uneasily, shaking it every now and then, and holding it to his ear.

Alice considered a little, and then said 'The fourth.'

'Two days wrong!' sighed the Hatter. 'I told you butter wouldn't suit the works!' he added, looking angrily at the March Hare.

'It was the *best* butter,' the March Hare meekly replied.

'Yes, but some crumbs must have got in as well,' the Hatter grumbled: 'you shouldn't have put it in with the bread-knife.'

The March Hare took the watch and looked at it gloomily: then he dipped it into his cup of tea, and looked at it again: but he could think of nothing better to say than his first remark, 'It was the *best* butter, you know.'

Alice had been looking over his shoulder with some curiosity. 'What a funny watch!' she remarked. 'It tells the day of the month, and doesn't tell what o'clock it is!'

'Why should it?' muttered the Hatter. 'Does *your* watch tell you what year it is?'

'Of course not,' Alice replied very readily: 'but that's because it stays the same year for such a long time together.'

'Which is just the case with *mine*,' said the Hatter.

Alice felt dreadfully puzzled. The Hatter's remark seemed to have no sort of meaning in it, and yet it was certainly English. 'I don't quite understand you,' she said, as politely as she could.

'The Dormouse is asleep again,' said the Hatter, and he poured a little hot tea upon its nose.

The Dormouse shook its head impatiently, and said, without opening its eyes, 'Of course, of course; just what I was going to remark myself.'

'Have you guessed the riddle yet?' the Hatter said, turning to Alice again.

'No, I give it up,' Alice replied: 'what's the answer?'

'I haven't the slightest idea,' said the Hatter.

'Nor I,' said the March Hare.

Alice sighed wearily. 'I think you might do something better with the time,' she said, 'than waste it in asking riddles that have no answers.'

'If you knew Time as well as I do,' said the Hatter, 'you wouldn't talk about wasting *it*. It's *him*.'

'I don't know what you mean,' said Alice.

'Of course you don't!' the Hatter said, tossing his head contemptuously. 'I dare say you never even spoke to Time!'

'Perhaps not,' Alice cautiously replied: 'but I know I have to beat time when I learn music.'

'Ah! that accounts for it,' said the Hatter. 'He won't stand beating. Now, if you only kept on good terms with him, he'd do almost anything you liked with the clock. For instance, suppose it were nine o'clock in the morning, just time to begin lessons: you'd only have to whisper a hint to Time, and round goes the clock in a twinkling! Half-past one, time for dinner!'

('I only wish it was,' the March Hare said to itself in a whisper.)

'That would be grand, certainly,' said Alice thoughtfully: 'but then – I shouldn't be hungry for it, you know.'

'Not at first, perhaps,' said the Hatter: 'but you could keep it to half-past one as long as you liked.'

'Is that the way *you* manage?' Alice asked.

The Hatter shook his head mournfully. 'Not I!' he replied. 'We quarrelled last March – just before *he* went mad, you know –' (pointing with his teaspoon at the March Hare,) '– it was at the great concert given by the Queen of Hearts, and I had to sing

> "Twinkle, twinkle, little bat!
> How I wonder what you're at!"

You know the song, perhaps?'

'I've heard something like it,' said Alice.

'It goes on, you know,' the Hatter continued, 'in this way:—

> "Up above the world you fly,
> Like a tea-tray in the sky.
>   Twinkle, twinkle —"'

Here the Dormouse shook itself, and began singing in its sleep '*Twinkle, twinkle, twinkle, twinkle* –' and went on so long that they had to pinch it to make it stop.

'Well, I'd hardly finished the first verse,' said the Hatter, 'when the Queen jumped up and bawled out, "He's murdering the time! Off with his head!"'

'How dreadfully savage!' exclaimed Alice.

'And ever since that,' the Hatter went on in a mournful tone, 'he won't do a thing I ask! It's always six o'clock now.'

A bright idea came into Alice's head. 'Is that the reason so many tea-things are put out here?' she asked.

'Yes, that's it,' said the Hatter with a sigh: 'it's always tea-time, and we've no time to wash the things between whiles.'

'Then you keep moving round, I suppose?' said Alice.

'Exactly so,' said the Hatter: 'as the things get used up.'

'But what happens when you come to the beginning again?' Alice ventured to ask.

'Suppose we change the subject,' the March Hare interrupted, yawning. 'I'm getting tired of this. I vote the young lady tells us a story.'

'I'm afraid I don't know one,' said Alice, rather alarmed at the proposal.

'Then the Dormouse shall!' they both cried. 'Wake up, Dormouse!' And they pinched it on both sides at once.

The Dormouse slowly opened his eyes. 'I wasn't asleep,' he said in a hoarse, feeble voice: 'I heard every word you fellows were saying.'

'Tell us a story!' said the March Hare.

'Yes, please do!' pleaded Alice.

'And be quick about it,' added the Hatter, 'or you'll be asleep again before it's done.'

'Once upon a time there were three little sisters,' the Dormouse began in a great hurry; 'and their names were Elsie, Lacie, and Tillie; and they lived at the bottom of a well —'

'What did they live on?' said Alice, who always took a great interest in questions of eating and drinking.

'They lived on treacle,' said the Dormouse, after thinking a minute or two.

'They couldn't have done that, you know,' Alice gently remarked; 'they'd have been ill.'

'So they were,' said the Dormouse; '*very* ill.'

Alice tried to fancy to herself what such an extraordinary way of living would be like, but it puzzled her too much, so she went on: 'But why did they live at the bottom of a well?'

'Take some more tea,' the March Hare said to Alice, very earnestly.

'I've had nothing yet,' Alice replied in an offended tone, 'so I can't take more.'

'You mean you can't take *less*,' said the Hatter: 'it's very easy to take *more* than nothing.'

'Nobody asked *your* opinion,' said Alice.

'Who's making personal remarks now?' the Hatter asked triumphantly.

Alice did not quite know what to say to this: so she helped herself to some tea and bread-and-butter, and then turned to the Dormouse, and repeated her question. 'Why did they live at the bottom of a well?'

The Dormouse again took a minute or two to think about it, and then said, 'It was a treacle-well.'

'There's no such thing!' Alice was beginning very angrily, but the Hatter and the March Hare went 'Sh! sh!' and the Dormouse sulkily remarked, 'If you can't be civil, you'd better finish the story for yourself.'

'No, please go on!' Alice said very humbly: 'I won't interrupt again. I dare say there may be *one*.'

'One, indeed!' said the Dormouse indignantly. However, he consented to go on. And so these three little sisters – they were learning to draw, you know –'

'What did they draw?' said Alice, quite forgetting her promise.

'Treacle,' said the Dormouse, without considering at all this time.

'I want a clean cup,' interrupted the Hatter: 'let's all move one place on.'

He moved on as he spoke, and the Dormouse followed him: the March Hare moved into the Dormouse's place, and Alice rather unwillingly took the place of the March Hare. The Hatter was the only one who got any advantage from the change: and Alice was a good deal worse off than before, as the March Hare had just upset the milk-jug into his plate.

Alice did not wish to offend the Dormouse again, so she began very cautiously: 'But I don't understand. Where did they draw the treacle from?'

'You can draw water out of a water-well,' said the Hatter; 'so I should think you could draw treacle out of a treacle-well – eh, stupid?'

'But they were *in* the well,' Alice said to the Dormouse, not choosing to notice this last remark.

'Of course they were,' said the Dormouse; '– well in.'

This answer so confused poor Alice, that she let the Dormouse go on for some time without interrupting it.

'They were learning to draw,' the Dormouse went on, yawning and rubbing its eyes, for it was getting very sleepy; 'and they drew all manner of things – everything that begins with an M –'

'Why with an M?' said Alice.

'Why not?' said the March Hare.

Alice was silent.

The Dormouse had closed its eyes by this time, and was going off into a doze; but, on being pinched by the Hatter, it woke up again with a little shriek, and went on: '– that begins with an M, such as mouse-traps, and the moon, and memory, and muchness – you know you say things are "much of a muchness" – did you ever see such a thing as a drawing of a muchness?'

'Really, now you ask me,' said Alice, very much confused, 'I don't think –'

'Then you shouldn't talk,' said the Hatter.

This piece of rudeness was more than Alice could bear: she got up in great disgust, and walked off; the Dormouse fell asleep instantly, and neither of the others took the least notice of her going, though she looked back once or twice, half hoping that they would call after her: the last time she saw them, they were trying to put the Dormouse into the teapot.

At any rate I'll never go *there* again!' said Alice as she picked her way through the wood. 'It's the stupidest tea-party I ever was at in all my life!'

Just as she said this, she noticed that one of the trees had a door leading right into it. 'That's very curious!' she thought. 'But everything's curious today. I think I may as well go in at once.' And in she went.

Once more she found herself in the long hall, and close to the little glass table. 'Now, I'll manage better this time,' she said to herself, and began by taking the little golden key, and unlocking the door that led into the garden. Then she set to work nibbling at the mushroom (she had kept a piece of it in her pocket) till she was about a foot high: then she walked down the little passage: and *then* – she found herself at last in the beautiful garden, among the bright flower-beds and the cool fountains.

8

The Queen's Croquet-Ground

A LARGE rose-tree stood near the entrance of the garden: the roses growing on it were white, but there were three gardeners at it, busily painting them red. Alice thought this a very curious thing, and she went nearer to watch them, and just as she came up to them she heard one of them say, 'Look out now, Five! Don't go splashing paint over me like that!'

'I couldn't help it,' said Five in a sulky tone; 'Seven jogged my elbow.'

On which Seven looked up and said, 'That's right, Five! Always lay the blame on others!'

'*You'd* better not talk!' said Five. 'I heard the Queen say only yesterday you deserved to be beheaded!'

'What for?' said the one who had spoken first.

'That's none of *your* business, Two!' said Seven.

'Yes it *is* his business!' said Five, 'and I'll tell him – it was for bringing the cook tulip-roots instead of onions.'

Seven flung down his brush, and had just begun 'Well, of all the unjust things –' when his eye chanced to fall upon Alice, as she stood watching them, and he checked himself suddenly: the others looked round also, and all of them bowed low.

'Would you tell me,' said Alice, a little timidly 'why you are painting those roses?'

Five and Seven said nothing, but looked at Two. Two began in a low voice, 'Why the fact is, you see, Miss, this here ought to have been a *red* rose-tree, and we put a white one in by mistake; and if the Queen was to find out, we should all have our heads cut off, you know. So you see, Miss, we're doing our best, afore she comes, to –' At this moment Five, who had been anxiously looking across the garden, called out 'The Queen! The Queen!' and the three gardeners instantly threw themselves flat upon their faces. There was a sound of many footsteps, and Alice looked round, eager to see the Queen.

First came ten soldiers carrying clubs; these were all shaped like the three gardeners, oblong and flat, with their hands and feet at the corners: next the ten courtiers; these were ornamented all over with diamonds, and walked two and two, as the soldiers did. After these came the royal children; there were ten of them, and the little dears came jumping merrily along hand in hand, in couples: they were all ornamented with hearts. Next came the guests, mostly Kings and Queens, and among them Alice recognised the White Rabbit: it was talking in a hurried nervous manner, smiling at everything that was said, and went by without noticing her. Then followed the Knave of Hearts, carrying the King's crown on a crimson velvet cushion; and, last of all this procession, came THE KING AND QUEEN OF HEARTS.

Alice was rather doubtful whether she ought not to lie down on her face like the three gardeners, but she could not remember ever having heard of such a rule at processions; 'and besides, what would be the use of a procession,' thought she, 'if people had all to lie down upon their faces, so that they couldn't see it?' So she stood still where she was, and waited.

When the procession came opposite to Alice, they all stopped and looked at her, and the Queen said severely 'Who is this?' She said it to the Knave of Hearts, who only bowed and smiled in reply.

'Idiot!' said the Queen, tossing her head impatiently; and, turning to Alice, she went on, 'What's your name, child?'

'My name is Alice, so please your Majesty,' said Alice very politely; but she added, to herself, 'Why, they're only a pack of cards, after all. I needn't be afraid of them!'

'And who are *these*?' said the Queen, pointing to the three gardeners who were lying round the rose-tree; for, you see, as they were lying on their faces, and the pattern on their backs was the same as the rest of the pack, she could not tell whether they were gardeners, or soldiers, or courtiers, or three of her own children.

'How should *I* know?' said Alice, surprised at her own courage. 'It's no business of *mine*.'

The Queen turned crimson with fury, and, after glaring at her for a moment like a wild beast, screamed 'Off with her head! Off —'

'Nonsense!' said Alice, very loudly and decidedly, and the Queen was silent.

The King laid his hand upon her arm, and timidly said 'Consider, my dear: she is only a child!'

The Queen turned angrily away from him, and said to the Knave 'Turn them over!'

The Knave did so, very carefully, with one foot.

'Get up!' said the Queen, in a shrill, loud voice, and the three gardeners instantly jumped up, and began bowing to the King, the Queen, the royal children, and everybody else.

'Leave off that!' screamed the Queen. 'You make me giddy.' And then, turning to the rose-tree, she went on, 'What *have* you been doing here?'

'May it please your Majesty,' said Two, in a very humble tone, going down on one knee as he spoke, 'we were trying —'

'*I* see!' said the Queen, who had meanwhile been examining the roses. 'Off with their heads!' and the procession moved on, three of the soldiers remaining behind to execute the unfortunate gardeners, who ran to Alice for protection.

'You shan't be beheaded!' said Alice, and she put them into a large flower-pot that stood near. The three soldiers wandered about for a minute or two, looking for them, and then quietly marched off after the others.

'Are their heads off?' shouted the Queen.

'Their heads are gone, if it please your Majesty!' the soldiers shouted in reply.

'That's right!' shouted the Queen. 'Can you play croquet?'

The soldiers were silent, and looked at Alice, as the question was evidently meant for her.

'Yes!' shouted Alice.

'Come on, then!' roared the Queen, and Alice joined the procession, wondering very much what would happen next.

'It's – it's a very fine day!' said a timid voice at her side. She was walking by the White Rabbit, who was peeping anxiously into her face.

'Very,' said Alice: '– where's the Duchess?'

'Hush! Hush!' said the Rabbit in a low, hurried tone. He looked anxiously over his shoulder as he spoke, and then raised himself upon tiptoe, put his mouth close to her ear, and whispered 'She's under sentence of execution.'

'What for?' said Alice.

'Did you say "What a pity!"?' the Rabbit asked.

'No, I didn't,' said Alice: 'I don't think it's at all a pity. I said "What for?"'

'She boxed the Queen's ears –' the Rabbit began. Alice gave a little scream of laughter. 'Oh, hush!' the Rabbit whispered in a frightened tone. 'The Queen will hear you! You see, she came rather late, and the Queen said –'

'Get to your places!' shouted the Queen in a voice of thunder, and people began running about in all directions, tumbling up against each other; however, they got settled down in a minute or two, and the game began. Alice thought she had never seen such a curious croquet-ground in all her life; it was all ridges and furrows; the balls were live hedgehogs, the mallets live flamingoes, and the soldiers had to double themselves up and to stand on their hands and feet, to make the arches.

The chief difficulty Alice found at first was in managing her flamingo: she succeeded in getting its body tucked away, comfortably enough, under her arm, with its legs hanging down, but generally, just as she had got its neck nicely straightened out, and was going to give the hedgehog a blow with its head, it *would* twist itself round and look up in her face, with such a puzzled expression that she could not help bursting out laughing: and when she had got its head down, and was going to begin again, it was very provoking to find that the hedgehog had unrolled itself, and was in the act of crawling away: besides all this, there was generally a ridge or furrow in the way wherever she wanted to send the hedgehog to, and, as the doubled-up soldiers were always getting up and walking off to other parts of the ground, Alice soon came to the conclusion that it was a very difficult game indeed.

The players all played at once without waiting for turns, quarrelling all the while, and fighting for the hedgehogs; and in a very short time the Queen was in a furious passion, and went stamping about, and shouting 'Off with his head!' or 'Off with her head!' about once in a minute.

Alice began to feel very uneasy: to be sure, she had not as yet had any dispute with the Queen, but she knew that it might happen any minute, 'and then,' thought she, 'what would become of me? They're dreadfully fond of beheading people here; the great wonder is, that there's any one left alive!'

She was looking about for some way of escape, and wondering whether she could get away without being seen, when she noticed a curious appearance in the air: it puzzled her very much at first, but, after watching it a minute or two, she made it out to be a grin, and she said to herself 'It's the Cheshire Cat: now I shall have somebody to talk to.'

'How are you getting on?' said the Cat, as soon as there was mouth enough for it to speak with.

Alice waited till the eyes appeared, and then nodded. 'It's no use speaking to it,' she thought, 'till its ears have come, or at least one of them.' In another minute the whole head appeared, and then Alice put down her flamingo, and began an account of the game, feeling very glad she had someone to listen to her. The Cat seemed to think that there was enough of it now in sight, and no more of it appeared.

'I don't think they play at all fairly,' Alice began, in rather a complaining tone, 'and they all quarrel so dreadfully one can't hear oneself speak – and they don't seem to have any rules in particular; at least, if there are, nobody attends to them – and you've no idea how confusing it is all the things being alive; for instance, there's the arch I've got to go through next walking about at the other end of the ground – and I should have croqueted the Queen's hedgehog just now, only it ran away when it saw mine coming!'

'How do you like the Queen?' said the Cat in a low voice.

'Not at all, 'said Alice: 'she's so extremely –' Just then she noticed that the Queen was close behind her, listening: so she went on, '– likely to win, that it's hardly worth while finishing the game.'

The Queen smiled and passed on.

'Who *are* you talking to?' said the King, coming up to Alice, and looking at the Cat's head with great curiosity.

'It's a friend of mine – a Cheshire Cat,' said Alice: 'allow me to introduce it.'

'I don't like the look of it at all,' said the King: 'however, it may kiss my hand if it likes.'

'I'd rather not,' the Cat remarked.

'Don't be impertinent,' said the King, 'and don't look at me like that!' He got behind Alice as he spoke.

'A cat may look at a king,' said Alice. 'I've read that in some book, but I don't remember where.'

'Well, it must be removed,' said the King very decidedly, and he called to the Queen, who was passing at the moment, 'My dear! I wish you would have this cat removed!'

The Queen had only one way of settling all difficulties, great or small. 'Off with his head!' she said, without even looking round.

'I'll fetch the executioner myself,' said the King eagerly, and he hurried off.

Alice thought she might as well go back, and see how the game was going on, as she heard the Queen's voice in the distance, screaming with passion. She had already heard her sentence three of the players to be executed for having missed their turns, and she did not like the look of things at all, as the game was in such confusion that she never knew whether it was her turn or not. She she went in search of her hedgehog.

The hedgehog was engaged in a fight with another hedgehog, which seemed to Alice an excellent opportunity for croqueting one of them with the other: the only difficulty was, that her flamingo was gone across to the other side of the garden, where Alice could see it trying in a helpless sort of way to fly up into a tree.

By the time she had caught the flamingo and brought it back, the fight was over, and both the hedgehogs were out of sight: 'but it doesn't matter much,' thought Alice, 'as all the arches are gone from this side of the ground.' So she tucked it away under her arm, that it might not escape again, and went back for a little more conversation with her friend.

When she got back to the Cheshire Cat, she was surprised to find quite a large crowd collected round it:

there was a dispute going on between the executioner, the King, and the Queen, who were all talking at once, while all the rest were quite silent, and looked very uncomfortable.

The moment Alice appeared, she was appealed to by all three to settle the question, and they repeated their arguments to her, though, as they all spoke at once, she found it very hard indeed to make out exactly what they said.

The executioner's argument was, that you couldn't cut off a head unless there was a body to cut it off from: that he had never had to do such a thing before, and he wasn't going to begin at *his* time of life.

The King's argument was, that anything that had a head could be beheaded, and that you weren't to talk nonsense.

The Queen's argument was, that if something wasn't done about it in less than no time she'd have everybody executed, all round. (It was this last remark that had made the whole party look so grave and anxious.)

Alice could think of nothing else to say but 'It belongs to the Duchess: you'd better ask *her* about it.'

'She's in prison,' the Queen said to the executioner: 'fetch her here.' And the executioner went off like an arrow.

The Cat's head began fading away the moment he was gone, and, by the time he had come back with the Duchess, it had entirely disappeared; so the King and the executioner ran wildly up and down looking for it, while the rest of the party went back to the game.

9

The Mock Turtle's Story

'YOU can't think how glad I am to see you again, you dear old thing!' said the Duchess, as she tucked her arm affectionately into Alice's, and they walked off together.

Alice was very glad to find her in such a pleasant temper, and thought to herself that perhaps it was only the pepper that had made her so savage when they met in the kitchen.

'When *I'm* a Duchess,' she said to herself, (not in a very hopeful tone though), 'I won't have any pepper in my kitchen *at all*. Soup does very well without – Maybe it's always pepper that makes people hot-tempered,' she went on, very much pleased at having found out a new kind of rule, 'and vinegar that makes them sour – and camomile that makes them bitter – and – and barley-sugar and such things that make children sweet-tempered. I only wish people knew *that*: then they wouldn't be so stingy about it, you know –'

She had quite forgotten the Duchess by this time, and was a little startled when she heard her voice close to her ear. 'You're thinking about something, my dear, and that makes you forget to talk. I can't tell you just now what the moral of that is, but I shall remember it in a bit.'

'Perhaps it hasn't one,' Alice ventured to remark.

'Tut, tut, child!' said the Duchess. 'Everything's got a moral, if only you can find it.' And she squeezed herself up closer to Alice's side as she spoke.

Alice did not much like keeping so close to her: first, because the Duchess was *very* ugly; and secondly, because she was exactly the right height to rest her chin upon Alice's shoulder, and it was an uncomfortably sharp chin. However, she did not like to be rude, so she bore it as well as she could.

'The game's going on rather better now,' she said, by way of keeping up the conversation a little.

''Tis so,' said the Duchess: 'and the moral of that is – "Oh, 'tis love, 'tis love, that makes the world go round!"'

'Somebody said,' Alice whispered, 'that it's done by everybody minding their own business!'

'Ah, well! It means much the same thing,' said the Duchess, digging her sharp little chin into Alice's shoulder as she added, 'and the moral of *that* is – "Take care of the sense, and the sounds will take care of themselves."'

'How fond she is of finding morals in things!' Alice thought to herself.

'I dare say you're wondering why I don't put my arm round your waist,' the Duchess said after a pause: 'the reason is, that I'm doubtful about the temper of your flamingo. Shall I try the experiment?'

'He might bite,' Alice cautiously replied, not feeling at all anxious to have the experiment tried.

'Very true,' said the Duchess: 'flamingoes and mustard both bite. And the moral of that is – "Birds of a feather flock together."'

'Only mustard isn't a bird,' Alice remarked.

'Right, as usual,' said the Duchess: 'what a clear way you have of putting things!'

'It's a mineral, I *think*,' said Alice.

'Of course it is,' said the Duchess, who seemed ready to agree to everything that Alice said; 'there's a large mustard-mine near here. And the moral of that is – "The more there is of mine, the less there is of yours."'

'Oh, I know!' exclaimed Alice, who had not attended to this last remark, 'it's a vegetable. It doesn't look like one, but it is.'

'I quite agree with you,' said the Duchess; 'and the moral of that is – "Be what you would seem to be" – or if you'd like it put more simply – "Never imagine yourself not to be otherwise than what it might appear to others that what you were or might have been was not otherwise than what you had been would have appeared to them to be otherwise."'

'I think I should understand that better,' Alice said very politely, 'if I had it written down: but I can't quite follow it as you say it.'

'That's nothing to what I could say if I chose,' the Duchess replied, in a pleased tone.

'Pray don't trouble yourself to say it any longer than that,' said Alice.

'Oh, don't talk about trouble!' said the Duchess. 'I make you a present of everything I've said as yet.'

'A cheap sort of present!' thought Alice. 'I'm glad they don't give birthday presents like that!' But she did not venture to say it out loud.

'Thinking again?' the Duchess asked, with another dig of her sharp little chin.

'I've a right to think,' said Alice sharply, for she was beginning to feel a little worried.

'Just about as much right,' said the Duchess, 'as pigs have to fly; and the m –'

But here, to Alice's great surprise, the Duchess's voice died away, even in the middle of her favourite word 'moral,' and the arm that was linked into hers began to tremble. Alice looked up, and there stood the Queen in front of them, with her arms folded, frowning like a thunderstorm.

'A fine day, your Majesty!' the Duchess began in a low, weak voice.

'Now, I give you fair warning,' shouted the Queen, stamping on the ground as she spoke; 'either you or your head must be off, and that in about half no time! Take your choice!'

The Duchess took her choice, and was gone in a moment.

'Let's go on with the game,' the Queen said to Alice; and Alice was too much frightened to say a word, but slowly followed her back to the croquet-ground.

The other guests had taken advantage of the Queen's absence, and were resting in the shade: however, the moment they saw her, they hurried back to the game, the Queen merely remarking that a moment's delay would cost them their lives.

All the time they were playing the Queen never left off quarrelling with the other players, and shouting 'Off with his head!' or 'Off with her head!' Those whom she sentenced were taken into custody by the soldiers, who of course had to leave off being arches to do this, so that by the end of half an hour or so there were no arches left, and all the players, except the King, the Queen, and Alice, were in custody and under sentence of execution.

Then the Queen left off, quite out of breath, and said to Alice, 'Have you seen the Mock Turtle yet?'

'No,' said Alice. 'I don't even know what a Mock Turtle is.'

'It's the thing Mock Turtle Soup is made from,' said the Queen.

'I never saw one, or heard of one,' said Alice.

'Come on, then,' said the Queen, 'and he shall tell you his history.'

As they walked off together, Alice heard the King say in a low voice, to the company generally, 'You are all pardoned.' 'Come, *that's* a good thing!' she said to herself, for she had felt quite unhappy at the number of executions the Queen had ordered.

They very soon came upon a Gryphon, lying fast asleep in the sun. (If you don't know what a Gryphon is, look at the picture.) 'Up, lazy thing!' said the Queen, 'and take this young lady to see the Mock Turtle, and to hear his history. I must go back and see after some executions I have ordered'; and she walked off, leaving Alice alone with the Gryphon. Alice did not quite like the look of the creature, but on the whole she thought it would be quite as safe to stay with it as to go after that savage Queen: so she waited.

The Gryphon sat up and rubbed its eyes: then it watched the Queen till she was out of sight: then it chuckled. 'What fun!' said the Gryphon, half to itself, half to Alice.

'What *is* the fun?' said Alice.

'Why, *she*,' said the Gryphon. 'It's all her fancy, that: they never executes nobody, you know. Come on!'

'Everybody says "come on!" here,' thought Alice, as she went slowly after it: 'I never was so ordered about in all my life, never!'

They had not gone far before they saw the Mock Turtle in the distance, sitting sad and lonely on a little ledge of rock, and, as they came nearer, Alice could hear him sighing as if his heart would break. She pitied him deeply. 'What is his sorrow?' she asked the Gryphon, and the Gryphon answered, very nearly in the same words as before, 'It's all his fancy, that: he hasn't got no sorrow, you know. Come on!'

So they went up to the Mock Turtle, who looked at them with large eyes full of tears, but said nothing.

'This here young lady,' said the Gryphon, 'she wants for to know your history, she do.'

'I'll tell it her,' said the Mock Turtle in a deep, hollow

tone: 'sit down, both of you, and don't speak a word till I've finished.'

So they sat down, and nobody spoke for some minutes. Alice thought to herself, 'I don't see how he can *ever* finish, if he doesn't begin.' But she waited patiently.

'Once,' said the Mock Turtle at last, with a deep sigh, 'I was a real Turtle.'

These words were followed by a very long silence, broken only by an occasional exclamation of 'Hjckrrh!' from the Gryphon, and the constant heavy sobbing of the Mock Turtle. Alice was very nearly getting up and saying, 'Thank you, sir, for your interesting story,' but she could not help thinking there must be more to come, so she sat still and said nothing.

'When we were little,' the Mock Turtle went on at last, more calmly, though still sobbing a little now and then, 'we went to school in the sea. The master was an old Turtle – we used to call him Tortoise –'

'Why did you call him Tortoise, if he wasn't one?' Alice asked.

'We called him Tortoise because he taught us,' said the Mock Turtle angrily: 'really you are very dull!'

'You ought to be ashamed of yourself for asking such a simple question,' added the Gryphon; and then they both sat silent and looked at poor Alice, who felt ready to sink into the earth. At last the Gryphon said to the Mock

Turtle, 'Drive on, old fellow! Don't be all day about it!'
and he went on in these words:

'Yes, we went to school in the sea, though you mayn't
believe it –'

'I never said I didn't!' interrupted Alice.

'You did,' said the Mock Turtle.

'Hold your tongue!' added the Gryphon, before Alice could speak again. The Mock Turtle went on.

'We had the best of educations – in fact, we went to school every day –'

'*I've* been to a day-school, too,' said Alice; 'you needn't be so proud as all that.'

'With extras?' asked the Mock Turtle a little anxiously.

'Yes,' said Alice, 'we learned French and music.'

'And washing?' said the Mock Turtle.

'Certainly not!' said Alice indignantly.

'Ah! then yours wasn't a really good school,' said the Mock Turtle in a tone of great relief. 'Now at *ours* they had at the end of the bill, "French, music, *and washing* – extra."'

'You couldn't have wanted it much,' said Alice; 'living at the bottom of the sea.'

'I couldn't afford to learn it,' said the Mock Turtle with a sigh. 'I only took the regular course.'

'What was that?' inquired Alice.

'Reeling and Writhing, of course, to begin with,' the Mock Turtle replied; 'and then the different branches of Arithmetic – Ambition, Distraction, Uglification, and Derision.'

'I never heard of "Uglification,"' Alice ventured to say. 'What is it?'

The Gryphon lifted up both its paws in surprise. 'What! Never heard of uglifying!' it exclaimed. 'You know what to beautify is, I suppose?'

'Yes,' said Alice doubtfully: 'it means – to – make – anything – prettier.'

'Well, then,' the Gryphon went on, 'if you don't know what to uglify is, you *are* a simpleton.'

Alice did not feel encouraged to ask any more questions about it, so she turned to the Mock Turtle, and said 'What else had you to learn?'

'Well, there was Mystery,' the Mock Turtle replied, counting off the subjects on his flappers, '– Mystery, ancient and modern, with Seaography: then Drawling – the Drawling-master was an old conger-eel, that used to come once a week: *he* taught us Drawling, Stretching, and Fainting in Coils.'

'What was *that* like?' said Alice.

'Well, I can't show it you myself,' the Mock Turtle said: 'I'm too stiff. And the Gryphon never learnt it.'

'Hadn't time,' said the Gryphon: 'I went to the Classical master, though. He was an old crab, *he* was.'

'I never went to him,' the Mock Turtle said with a sigh: 'he taught Laughing and Grief, they used to say.'

'So he did, so he did,' said the Gryphon, sighing in his turn; and both creatures hid their faces in their paws.

'And how many hours a day did you do lessons?' said Alice, in a hurry to change the subject.

'Ten hours the first day,' said the Mock Turtle: 'nine the next, and so on.'

'What a curious plan!' exclaimed Alice.

'That's the reason they're called lessons,' the Gryphon remarked: 'because they lessen from day to day.'

This was quite a new idea to Alice, and she thought it over a little before she made her next remark. 'Then the eleventh day must have been a holiday?'

'Of course it was,' said the Mock Turtle.

'And how did you manage on the twelfth?' Alice went on eagerly.

'That's enough about lessons,' the Gryphon interrupted in a very decided tone: 'tell her something about the games now.'

10

The Lobster Quadrille

THE Mock Turtle sighed deeply, and drew the back of one flapper across his eyes. He looked at Alice, and tried to speak, but for a minute or two sobs choked his voice. 'Same as if he had a bone in his throat,' said the Gryphon: and it set to work shaking him and punching him in the back. At last the Mock Turtle recovered his voice, and, with tears running down his cheeks, he went on again:–

'You may not have lived much under the sea –' ('I haven't,' said Alice) – 'and perhaps you were never even introduced to a lobster –' (Alice began to say 'I once tasted –' but checked herself hastily, and said 'No, never') '– so you can have no idea what a delightful thing a Lobster Quadrille is!'

'No, indeed,' said Alice. 'What sort of a dance is it?'

'Why,' said the Gryphon, 'you first form into a line along the sea-shore –'

'Two lines!' cried the Mock Turtle. 'Seals, turtles, salmon, and so on; then, when you've cleared all the jellyfish out of the way –'

'*That* generally takes some time,' interrupted the Gryphon.

'– you advance twice –'

'Each with a lobster as a partner!' cried the Gryphon.

'Of course,' the Mock Turtle said: 'advance twice, set to partners –'

'– change lobsters, and retire in same order,' continued the Gryphon.

'Then, you know,' the Mock Turtle went on, 'you throw the –'

'The lobsters!' shouted the Gryphon, with a bound into the air.

'– as far out to sea as you can –'

'Swim after them!' screamed the Gryphon.

'Turn a somersault in the sea!' cried the Mock Turtle, capering wildly about.

'Change lobsters again!' yelled the Gryphon.

'Back to land again, and that's all the first figure,' said the Mock Turtle, suddenly dropping his voice; and the two creatures, who had been jumping about like mad things all this time. sat down again very sadly and quietly, and looked at Alice.

'It must be a very pretty dance,' said Alice timidly.

'Would you like to see a little of it?' said the Mock Turtle.

'Very much indeed,' said Alice.

'Come, let's try the first figure!' said the Mock Turtle to the Gryphon. 'We can do without lobsters, you know. Which shall sing?'

'Oh, *you* sing,' said the Gryphon. 'I've forgotten the words.'

So they began solemnly dancing round and round Alice, every now and then treading on her toes when they passed too close, and waving their forepaws to mark the time, while the Mock Turtle sang this, very slowly and sadly:

> '"*Will you walk a little faster?" said a whiting to a snail.*
> *"There's a porpoise close behind us, and he's treading on my tail.*
> *See how eagerly the lobsters and the turtles all advance!*
> *They are waiting on the shingle – will you come and join the dance?*
> *Will you, won't you, will you, won't you, will you join the dance?*
> *Will you, won't you, will you, won't you, won't you join the dance?*

> '"*You can really have no notion how delightful it will be*
> *When they take us up and throw us, with the lobsters, out to sea!"*

But the snail replied "Too far, too far!" and gave a
     look askance –
Said he thanked the whiting kindly, but he would not
     join the dance.
Would not, could not, would not, could not, would
     not join the dance.
Would not, could not, would not, could not, could not
     join the dance.

'"What matters it how far we go?" his scaly friend
     replied.
"There is another shore, you know, upon the other
     side.
The further off from England the nearer is to
     France –
Then turn not pale, beloved snail, but come and join
     the dance.
Will you, won't you, will you, won't you, will you join
     the dance?
Will you, won't you, will you, won't you, won't you
     join the dance?"'

'Thank you, it's a very interesting dance to watch,' said
Alice, feeling very glad that it was over at last: 'and I do
so like that curious song about the whiting!'

'Oh, as to the whiting,' said the Mock Turtle, 'they –

you've seen them, of course?'

'Yes,' said Alice, 'I've often seen them at dinn –' she checked herself hastily.

'I don't know where Dinn may be,' said the Mock Turtle, 'but if you've seen them so often, of course you know what they're like.'

'I believe so,' Alice replied thoughtfully. 'They have their tails in their mouths – and they're all over crumbs.'

'You're wrong about the crumbs,' said the Mock Turtle: 'crumbs would all wash off in the sea. But they *have* their tails in their mouths; and the reason is –' here the Mock Turtle yawned and shut his eyes. – 'Tell her about the reason and all that,' he said to the Gryphon.

'The reason is,' said the Gryphon, 'that they *would* go with the lobsters to the dance. So they got thrown out to sea. So they had to fall a long way. So they got their tails fast in their mouths. So they couldn't get them out again. That's all.'

'Thank you,' said Alice, 'it's very interesting. I never knew so much about a whiting before.'

'I can tell you more than that, if you like,' said the Gryphon. 'Do you know why it's called a whiting?'

'I never thought about it,' said Alice. 'Why?'

'*It does the boots and shoes,*' the Gryphon replied very solemnly.

Alice was thoroughly puzzled. 'Does the boots and shoes!' she repeated in a wondering tone.

'Why, what are *your* shoes done with?' said the Gryphon. 'I mean what makes them so shiny?'

Alice looked down at them, and considered a little before she gave her answer. 'They're done with blacking, I believe.'

'Boots and shoes under the sea,' the Gryphon went on in a deep voice, 'are done with whiting. Now you know.'

'And what are they made of?' Alice asked in a tone of great curiosity.

'Soles and eels, of course,' the Gryphon replied rather impatiently: 'any shrimp could have told you that.'

'If I'd been the whiting,' said Alice, whose thoughts were still running on the song, 'I'd have said to the porpoise, "Keep back, please: we don't want *you* with us!"'

'They were obliged to have him with them,' the Mock Turtle said: 'no wise fish would go anywhere without a porpoise.'

'Wouldn't it really?' said Alice in a tone of great surprise.

'Of course not,' said the Mock Turtle: 'why, if a fish came to *me*, and told me he was going a journey, I should say "With what porpoise?"'

'Don't you mean "purpose"?' said Alice.

'I mean what I say,' the Mock Turtle replied in an offended tone. And the Gryphon added 'Come, let's hear some of *your* adventures.'

'I could tell you my adventures – beginning from this morning,' said Alice a little timidly: 'but it's no use going back to yesterday, because I was a different person then.'

'Explain all that,' said the Mock Turtle.

'No, no! The adventures first,' said the Gryphon in an impatient tone: 'explanations take such a dreadful time.'

So Alice began telling them her adventures from the time when she first saw the White Rabbit. She was a little nervous about it just at first, the two creatures got so close to her, one on each side, and opened their eyes and mouths so *very* wide, but she gained courage as she went on. Her listeners were perfectly quiet till she got to the part about her repeating '*You are old, Father William,*' to the Caterpillar, and the words all coming different, and then the Mock Turtle drew a long breath, and said 'That's very curious.'

'It's all about as curious as it can be,' said the Gryphon.

'It all came different!' the Mock Turtle repeated thoughtfully. 'I should like to hear her try and repeat something now. Tell her to begin.' He looked at the Gryphon as if he thought it had some kind of authority over Alice.

'Stand up and repeat '"*Tis the voice of the sluggard,*"' said the Gryphon.

'How the creatures order one about, and make one repeat lessons!' thought Alice; 'I might as well be at school at once.' However, she got up, and began to repeat it, but her head was so full of the Lobster Quadrille, that she hardly knew what she was saying, and the words came very queer indeed:–

''Tis the voice of the Lobster; I heard him declare,
"You have baked me too brown, I must sugar my hair."
As a duck with its eyelids, so he with his nose
Trims his belt and his buttons, and turns out his toes.'

'That's different from what *I* used to say when I was a child,' said the Gryphon.

'Well, I never heard it before,' said the Mock Turtle; 'but it sounds uncommon nonsense.'

Alice said nothing; she had sat down with her face in her hands, wondering if anything would *ever* happen in a natural way again.

'I should like to have it explained,' said the Mock Turtle.

'She can't explain it,' said the Gryphon hastily. 'Go on with the next verse.'

'But about his toes?' the Mock Turtle persisted. 'How *could* he turn them out with his nose, you know?'

'It's the first position in dancing,' Alice said; but was dreadfully puzzled by the whole thing, and longed to change the subject.

'Go on with the next verse,' the Gryphon repeated impatiently: 'it begins "*I passed by his garden.*"'

Alice did not dare to disobey, though she felt sure it would all come wrong, and she went on in a trembling voice:–

> '*I passed by his garden, and marked, with one eye,*
> *How the Owl and the Panther were sharing a pie –*'

'What *is* the use of repeating all that stuff,' the Mock Turtle interrupted, 'if you don't explain it as you go on? It's by far the most confusing thing *I* ever heard!'

'Yes, I think you'd better leave off,' said the Gryphon: and Alice was only too glad to do so.

'Shall we try another figure of the Lobster Quadrille?' the Gryphon went on. 'Or would you like the Mock Turtle to sing you a song?'

'Oh, a song, please, if the Mock Turtle would be so kind,' Alice replied, so eagerly that the Gryphon said, in a rather offended tone, 'Hm! No accounting for tastes! Sing her "*Turtle Soup*," will you, old fellow?'

The Mock Turtle sighed deeply, and began, in a voice sometimes choked with sobs, to sing this:–

> '*Beautiful Soup, so rich and green,*
> *Waiting in a hot tureen!*

Who for such dainties would not stoop?
Soup of the evening, beautiful Soup!
Soup of the evening, beautiful Soup!
 Beau – ootiful Soo – oop!
 Beau – ootiful Soo – oop!
Soo – oop of the e – e – evening,
 Beautiful, beautiful Soup!

'Beautiful Soup! Who cares for fish,
Game, or any other dish?
Who would not give all else for two p
ennyworth only of beautiful Soup?
Pennyworth only of beautiful Soup?
 Beau – ootiful Soo – oop!
 Beau – ootiful Soo – oop!
Soo – oop of the e – e – evening,
 Beautiful, beauti – FUL SOUP!'

'Chorus again!' cried the Gryphon, and the Mock Turtle had just begun to repeat it, when a cry of 'The trial's beginning!' was heard in the distance.

'Come on!' cried the Gryphon, and, taking Alice by the hand, it hurried off, without waiting for the end of the song.

'What trial is it?' Alice panted as she ran; but the Gryphon only answered 'Come on!' and ran the faster, while more and more faintly came, carried on the breeze that followed them, the melancholy words:–

> '*Soo – oop of the e – e – evening,*
> *Beautiful, beautiful Soup!*'

11

Who Stole the Tarts?

THE King and Queen of Hearts were seated on their throne when they arrived, with a great crowd assembled about them – all sorts of little birds and beasts, as well as the whole pack of cards: the Knave was standing before them, in chains, with a soldier on each side to guard him; and near the King was the White Rabbit, with a trumpet in one hand, and a scroll of parchment in the other. In the very middle of the court was a table, with a large dish of tarts upon it: they looked so good, that it made Alice quite hungry to look at them – 'I wish they'd get the trial done,' she thought, 'and hand round the refreshments!' But there seemed to be no chance of this, so she began looking at everything about her, to pass away the time.

Alice had never been in a court of justice before,

but she had read about them in books, and she was quite pleased to find that she knew the name of nearly everything there. 'That's the judge,' she said to herself, 'because of his great wig.'

The judge, by the way, was the King; and as he wore his crown over the wig, (look at the frontispiece if you want to see how he did it,) he did not look at all comfortable, and it was certainly not becoming.

'And that's the jury-box,' thought Alice, 'and those twelve creatures,' (she was obliged to say 'creatures' you see, because some of them were animals, and some were birds,) 'I suppose they are the jurors.' She said this last word two or three times over to herself, being rather proud of it: for she thought and rightly too, that very few little girls of her age knew the meaning of it at all. However, 'jury-men' would have done just as well.

The twelve jurors were all writing very busily on slates. 'What are they doing?' Alice whispered to the Gryphon. 'They can't have anything to put down yet, before the trial's begun.'

'They're putting down their names,' the Gryphon whispered in reply, 'for fear they should forget them before the end of the trial.'

'Stupid things!' Alice began in a loud, indignant voice, but she stopped hastily, for the White Rabbit cried out, 'Silence in the court!' and the King put on his spectacles and looked anxiously round, to make out who was talking.

Alice could see, as well as if she were looking over their shoulders, that all the jurors were writing down 'stupid things!' on their slates, and she could even make out that one of them didn't know how to spell 'stupid,' and that he had to ask his neighbour to tell him. 'A nice muddle their slates'll be in before the trial's over!' thought Alice.

One of the jurors had a pencil that squeaked. This of course, Alice could *not* stand, and she went round the court and got behind him, and very soon found an opportunity of taking it away. She did it so quickly that the poor little juror (it was Bill, the Lizard) could not make out at all what had become of it; so, after hunting all about for it, he was obliged to write with one finger for the rest of the day; and this was of very little use, as it left no mark on the slate.

'Herald, read the accusation!' said the King.

On this the White Rabbit blew three blasts on the trumpet, and then unrolled the parchment scroll, and read as follows:–

> *'The Queen of Hearts, she made some tarts,*
>   *All on a summer day:*
> *The Knave of Hearts, he stole those tarts,*
>   *And took them quite away!'*

'Consider your verdict,' the King said to the jury.

'Not yet, not yet!' the Rabbit hastily interrupted. 'There's a great deal to come before that!'

'Call the first witness,' said the King; and the White Rabbit blew three blasts on the trumpet, and called out, 'First witness!'

The first witness was the Hatter. He came in with a

teacup in one hand and a piece of bread-and-butter in the other. 'I beg pardon, your Majesty,' he began, 'for bringing these in: but I hadn't quite finished my tea when I was sent for.'

'You ought to have finished,' said the King. 'When did you begin?'

The Hatter looked at the March Hare, who had followed him into the court, arm-in-arm with the Dormouse. 'Fourteenth of March, I *think* it was,' he said.

'Fifteenth,' said the March Hare.

'Sixteenth,' added the Dormouse.

'Write that down,' the King said to the jury, and the jury eagerly wrote down all three dates on their slates, and then added them up, and reduced the answer to shillings and pence.

'Take off your hat,' the King said to the Hatter.

'It isn't mine,' said the Hatter.

'*Stolen!*' the King exclaimed, turning to the jury, who instantly made a memorandum of the fact.

'I keep them to sell,' the Hatter added as an explanation: 'I've none of my own. I'm a hatter.'

Here the Queen put on her spectacles, and began staring at the Hatter, who turned pale and fidgeted.

'Give your evidence,' said the King; 'and don't be nervous, or I'll have you executed on the spot.'

This did not seem to encourage the witness at all: he kept shifting from one foot to the other, looking uneasily at the Queen, and in his confusion he bit a large piece out of his teacup instead of the bread-and-butter.

Just at this moment Alice felt a very curious sensation, which puzzled her a good deal until she made out what it was: she was beginning to grow larger again, and she thought at first she would get up and leave the court; but on second thoughts she decided to remain where she was as long as there was room for her.

'I wish you wouldn't squeeze so,' said the Dormouse, who was sitting next to her. 'I can hardly breathe.'

'I can't help it,' said Alice very meekly: 'I'm growing.'

'You have no right to grow *here*,' said the Dormouse.

'Don't talk nonsense,' said Alice more boldly: 'you know you're growing too.'

'Yes, but I grow at a reasonable pace,' said the Dormouse: 'not in that ridiculous fashion.' And he got up very sulkily and crossed over to the other side of the court.

All this time the Queen had never left off staring at the Hatter, and, just as the Dormouse crossed the court, she said to one of the officers of the court, 'Bring me the list of the singers in the last concert!' on which the wretched Hatter trembled so, that he shook both his shoes off.

'Give your evidence,' the King repeated angrily, 'or I'll have you executed. whether you're nervous or not.'

'I'm a poor man, your Majesty,' the Hatter began, in a trembling voice, '– and I hadn't begun my tea – not above a week or so – and what with the bread-and-butter getting so thin – and the twinkling of the tea –'

'The twinkling of the *what*?' said the King.

'It *began* with the tea,' the Hatter replied.

'Of course twinkling begins with a T!' said the King sharply. 'Do you take me for a dunce? Go on!'

'I'm a poor man,' the Hatter went on, 'and most things twinkled after that – only the March Hare said –'

'I didn't!' the March Hare interrupted in a great hurry.

'You did!' said the Hatter.

'I deny it!' said the March Hare.

'He denies it,' said the King: 'leave out that part.'

'Well, at any rate, the Dormouse said –' the Hatter went on, looking anxiously round to see if he would deny it too: but the Dormouse denied nothing, being fast asleep.

'After that,' continued the Hatter, 'I cut some more bread-and-butter –'

'But what did the Dormouse say?' one of the jury asked.

'That I can't remember,' said the Hatter.

'You *must* remember,' remarked the King, 'or I'll have you executed.'

The miserable Hatter dropped his teacup and bread-and-butter, and went down on one knee. 'I'm a poor man, your Majesty,' he began.

'You're a *very* poor *speaker*,' said the King.

Here one of the guinea-pigs cheered, and was immediately suppressed by the officers of the court. (As that is rather a hard word, I will just explain to you how it was done. They had a large canvas bag, which tied up at the mouth with strings: into this they slipped the guinea-pig, head first, and then sat upon it.)

'I'm glad I've seen that done,' thought Alice. 'I've so often read in the newspapers, at the end of trials, "There was some attempt at applause, which was immediately suppressed by the officers of the court," and I never understood what it meant till now.'

'If that's all you know about it, you may stand down,' continued the King.

'I can't go no lower,' said the Hatter: 'I'm on the floor as it is.'

'Then you may *sit* down,' the King replied.

Here the other guinea-pig cheered, and was suppressed.

'Come, that finishes the guinea-pigs!' thought Alice. 'Now we shall get on better.'

'I'd rather finish my tea,' said the Hatter, with an anxious look at the Queen, who was reading the list of singers.

'You may go,' said the King, and the Hatter hurriedly left the court, without even waiting to put his shoes on.

'– and just take his head off outside,' the Queen added to one of the officers: but the Hatter was out of sight before the officer could get to the door.

'Call the next witness!' said the King.

The next witness was the Duchess's cook. She carried the pepper-box in her hand, and Alice guessed who it was, even before she got into the court, by the way people near the door began sneezing all at once.

'Give your evidence,' said the King.

'Shan't,' said the cook.

The King looked anxiously at the White Rabbit, who said in a low voice, 'Your Majesty must cross-examine *this* witness.'

'Well, if I must, I must,' the King said, with a melancholy air, and, after folding his arms and frowning at the cook till his eyes were nearly out of sight, he said in a deep voice, 'What are tarts made of?'

'Pepper, mostly,' said the cook.

'Treacle,' said a sleepy voice behind her.

'Collar that Dormouse,' the Queen shrieked out. 'Behead that Dormouse! Turn that Dormouse out of court! Suppress him! Pinch him! Off with his whiskers!'

For some minutes the whole court was in confusion, getting the Dormouse turned out, and, by the time they had settled down again, the cook had disappeared.

'Never mind!' said the King, with an air of great relief. 'Call the next witness.' And he added in an undertone to the Queen, 'Really, my dear, *you* must cross-examine the next witness. It quite makes my forehead ache!'

Alice watched the White Rabbit as he fumbled over the list, feeling very curious to see what the next witness would be like, '– for they haven't got much evidence *yet*,' she said to herself. Imagine her surprise, when the White Rabbit read out, at the top of his shrill little voice, the name 'Alice!'

12

Alice's Evidence

'HERE!' cried Alice, quite forgetting in the flurry of the moment how large she had grown in the last few minutes, and she jumped up in such a hurry that she tipped over the jury-box with the edge of her skirt, upsetting all the jurymen on to the heads of the crowd below, and there they lay sprawling about, reminding her very much of a globe of goldfish she had accidentally upset the week before.

'Oh, I *beg* your pardon!' she exclaimed in a tone of great dismay, and began picking them up again as quickly as she could, for the accident of the goldfish kept running in her head, and she had a vague sort of idea that they must be collected at once and put back into the jury-box, or they would die.

'The trial cannot proceed,' said the King in a very

grave voice, 'until all the jurymen are back in their proper places – *all*,' he repeated with great emphasis, looking hard at Alice as he said so.

Alice looked at the jury-box, and saw that, in her haste,

she had put the Lizard in head downwards, and the poor little thing was waving its tail about in a melancholy way, being quite unable to move. She soon got it out again, and put it right; 'not that it signifies much,' she said to herself; 'I should think it would be *quite* as much use in the trial one way up as the other.'

As soon as the jury had a little recovered from the shock of being upset, and their slates and pencils had been found and handed back to them, they set to work very diligently to write out a history of the accident, all except the Lizard, who seemed too much overcome to do anything but sit with its mouth open, gazing up into the roof of the court.

'What do you know about this business?' the King said to Alice.

'Nothing,' said Alice.

'Nothing *whatever*?' persisted the King.

'Nothing whatever,' said Alice.

'That's very important,' the King said, turning to the jury. They were just beginning to write this down on their slates, when the White Rabbit interrupted: '*Un*important, your Majesty means, of course,' he said in a very respectful tone, but frowning and making faces at him as he spoke.

'*Un*important, of course, I meant,' the King hastily said, and went on to himself in an undertone, 'important

– unimportant – unimportant – important –' as if he were trying which word sounded best.

Some of the jury wrote it down 'important,' and some 'unimportant.' Alice could see this, as she was near enough to look over their slates; 'but it doesn't matter a bit,' she thought to herself.

At this moment the King, who had been for some time busily writing in his note-book, called out 'Silence!' and read out from his book, 'Rule Forty-two. *All persons more than a mile high to leave the court.*'

Everybody looked at Alice.

'*I'm* not a mile high,' said Alice.

'You are,' said the King.

'Nearly two miles high,' added the Queen.

'Well, I shan't go, at any rate,' said Alice: 'besides, that's not a regular rule: you invented it just now.'

'It's the oldest rule in the book,' said the King.

'Then it ought to be Number One,' said Alice.

The King turned pale, and shut his note-book hastily. 'Consider your verdict,' he said to the jury, in a low trembling voice.

'There's more evidence to come yet, please your Majesty,' said the White Rabbit, jumping up in a great hurry; 'this paper has just been picked up.'

'What's in it?' said the Queen.

'I haven't opened it yet,' said the White Rabbit, 'but

it seems to be a letter, written by the prisoner to – to somebody.'

'It must have been that,' said the King, 'unless it was written to nobody, which isn't usual, you know.'

'Who is it directed to?' said one of the jurymen.

'It isn't directed at all,' said the White Rabbit; 'in fact, there's nothing written on the *outside*.' He unfolded the paper as he spoke, and added 'It isn't a letter, after all: it's a set of verses.'

'Are they in the prisoner's handwriting?' asked another of the jurymen.

'No, they're not,' said the White Rabbit, 'and that's the queerest thing about it.' (The jury all looked puzzled.)

'He must have imitated somebody else's hand,' said the King. (The jury all brightened up again.)

'Please your Majesty,' said the Knave; 'I didn't write it, and they can't prove I did: there's no name signed at the end.'

'If you didn't sign it,' said the King, 'that only makes the matter worse. You *must* have meant some mischief, or else you'd have signed your name like an honest man.'

There was a general clapping of hands at this: it was the first really clever thing the King had said that day.

'That *proves* his guilt,' said the Queen.

'It proves nothing of the sort!' said Alice. 'Why, you don't even know what they're about!'

'Read them,' said the King.

The White Rabbit put on his spectacles. 'Where shall I begin, please your Majesty?' he asked.

'Begin at the beginning,' the King said gravely, 'and go on till you come to the end: then stop.'

These were the verses the White Rabbit read:–

'They told me you had been to her,
And mentioned me to him:
She gave me a good character,
But said I could not swim.

He sent them word I had not gone
(We know it to be true):
If she should push the matter on,
What would become of you?

I gave her one, they gave him two,
You gave us three or more;
They all returned from him to you,
Though they were mine before.

If I or she should chance to be
Involved in this affair,
He trusts to you to set them free,
Exactly as we were.

My notion was that you had been
(Before she had this fit)
An obstacle that came between
Him, and ourselves, and it.

Don't let him know she liked them best,
For this must ever be
A secret, kept from all the rest,
Between yourself and me.'

'That's the most important piece of evidence we've heard yet,' said the King, rubbing his hands; 'so now let the jury –'

'If any one of them can explain it,' said Alice, (she had grown so large in the last few minutes that she wasn't a bit afraid of interrupting him,) 'I'll give him sixpence. *I* don't believe there's an atom of meaning in it.'

The jury all wrote down on their slates, '*She* doesn't believe there's an atom of meaning in it,' but none of them attempted to explain the paper.

'If there's no meaning in it,' said the King, 'that

saves a world of trouble, you know, as we needn't try to find any. And yet I don't know,' he went on, spreading out the verses on his knee, and looking at them with one eye; 'I seem to see some meaning in them, after all. "– *said I could not swim –*" you can't swim, can you?' he added, turning to the Knave.

The Knave shook his head sadly. 'Do I look like it?' he said. (Which he certainly did *not*, being made entirely of cardboard.)

'All right, so far,' said the King, and he went on muttering over the verses to himself: '"*We know it to be true –*" that's the jury, of course – "*I gave her one, they gave him two –*" why, that must be what he did with the tarts, you know –'

'But, it goes on "*they all returned from him to you*,"' said Alice.

'Why, there they are!' said the King triumphantly, pointing to the tarts on the table. 'Nothing can be clearer than *that*. Then again – "*before she had this fit –*" you never had fits, my dear, I think?' he said to the Queen.

'Never!' said the Queen furiously, throwing an inkstand at the Lizard as she spoke. (The unfortunate little Bill had left off writing on his slate with one finger, as he found it made no mark; but he now hastily began again, using the ink, that was trickling down his face, as long as it lasted.)

'Then the words don't *fit* you,' said the King, looking round the court with a smile. There was a dead silence.

'It's a pun!' the King added in an offended tone, and everybody laughed. 'Let the jury consider their verdict,' the King said, for about the twentieth time that day.

'No, no!' said the Queen. 'Sentence first – verdict afterwards.'

'Stuff and nonsense!' said Alice loudly. 'The idea of having the sentence first!'

'Hold your tongue!' said the Queen, turning purple.

'I won't!' said Alice.

'Off with her head!' the Queen shouted at the top of her voice. Nobody moved.

'Who cares for you?' said Alice, (she had grown to her full size by this time.) 'You're nothing but a pack of cards!'

At this the whole pack rose up into the air, and came flying down upon her: she gave a little scream, half of fright and half of anger, and tried to beat them off, and found herself lying on the bank, with her head in the lap of her sister, who was gently brushing away some dead leaves that had fluttered down from the trees upon her face.

'Wake up, Alice dear!' said her sister; 'Why, what a long sleep you've had!'

'Oh, I've had such a curious dream!' said Alice, and she told her sister, as well as she could remember them, all these strange Adventures of hers that you have just been reading about; and when she had finished, her sister kissed her, and said, 'It *was* a curious dream, dear, certainly: but now run in to your tea; it's getting late.' So Alice got up and ran off, thinking while she ran, as well she might, what a wonderful dream it had been.

———

But her sister sat still just as she left her, leaning her head on her hand, watching the setting sun, and thinking of little Alice and all her wonderful Adventures, till she too began dreaming after a fashion, and this was her dream:–

First, she dreamed of little Alice herself, and once again the tiny hands were clasped upon her knee, and the bright eager eyes were looking up into hers – she could hear the very tones of her voice, and see that queer little toss of her head to keep back the wandering hair that *would* always get into her eyes – and still as she listened, or seemed to listen, the whole place around her became alive with the strange creatures of her little sister's dream.

The long grass rustled at her feet as the White Rabbit hurried by – the frightened Mouse splashed his way through the neighbouring pool – she could hear the rattle of the teacups as the March Hare and his friends shared their never-ending meal, and the shrill voice of the Queen ordering off her unfortunate guests to execution – once more the pig-baby was sneezing on the Duchess's knee, while plates and dishes crashed around it – once more the shriek of the Gryphon, the squeaking of the Lizard's slate-pencil, and the choking of the suppressed guinea-pigs, filled the air, mixed up with the distant sobs of the miserable Mock Turtle.

So she sat on, with closed eyes, and half believed herself in Wonderland, though she knew she had but to open them again, and all would change to dull reality – the grass would be only rustling in the wind, and the pool rippling to the waving of the reeds – the rattling teacups would change to tinkling sheep-bells, and the Queen's shrill cries to the voice of the shepherd boy – and the sneeze of the baby, the shriek of the Gryphon, and all the other queer noises, would change (she knew) to the confused clamours of the busy farm-yard – while the lowing of the cattle in the distance would take the place of the Mock Turtle's heavy sobs.

Lastly, she pictured to herself how this same little sister of hers would, in the after-time, be herself a grown woman; and how she would keep, through all her riper years, the simple and loving heart of her childhood: and how she would gather about her other little children, and make their eyes bright and eager with many a strange tale, perhaps even with the dream of Wonderland of long ago: and how she would feel with all their simple sorrows, and find a pleasure in all their simple joys, remembering her own child-life, and the happy summer days.

THE END

13

An Easter Greeting
to
Every Child Who Loves
Alice

DEAR CHILD

Please to fancy, if you can, that you are reading a real letter, from a real friend whom you have seen, and whose voice you can seem to yourself to hear wishing you, as I do now with all my heart, a happy Easter.

Do you know that delicious dreamy feeling when one first wakes on a summer morning, with the twitter of birds in the air, and the fresh breeze coming in at the open window – when, lying lazily with eyes half-shut, one sees as in a dream green boughs waving, or waters rippling in a golden light? It is a pleasure very near to sadness, bringing tears to one's eyes like a beautiful picture or poem. And is not that a Mother's gentle hand that undraws your curtains, and a Mother's sweet voice that summons you to rise? To rise and forget, in the bright sunlight, the ugly dreams that frightened you so when all was dark – to rise and enjoy another happy day, first kneeling to thank that unseen Friend, who sends you the beautiful sun?

Are these strange words from a writer of such tales as 'Alice'? And is this a strange letter to find in a book of nonsense? It may be so. Some perhaps may blame me for thus mixing together things grave and gay; others may smile and think it odd that any one should speak of solemn things at all, except in church and on a Sunday: but I think – nay, I am sure – that some children will read this gently and lovingly, and in the spirit in which I have written it.

For I do not believe God means us thus to divide life into two halves – to wear a grave face on Sunday, and to think it out-of-place to even so much as mention Him on a week-day. Do you think He cares to see only kneeling figures, and to hear only tones of prayer – and that He does not also love to see the lambs leaping in the sunlight, and to hear the merry voices of the children, as they roll among the hay? Surely their innocent laughter is as sweet in His ears as the grandest anthem that ever rolled up from the 'dim religious light' of some solemn cathedral?

And if I have written anything to add to those stories of innocent and healthy amusement that are laid up in books for the children I love so well, it is surely something I may hope to look back upon without shame and sorrow (as how much of life must then be recalled!) when my turn comes to walk through the valley of shadows.

This Easter sun will rise on you, dear child, feeling your 'life in every limb', and eager to rush out into the fresh morning air – and many an Easter-day will come and go, before it finds you feeble and gray-headed, creeping wearily out to bask once more in the sunlight – but it is good, even now, to think sometimes of that great morning when the 'Sun of Righteousness shall arise with healing in his wings'.

Surely your gladness need not be the less for the thought that you will one day see a brighter dawn than this – when lovelier sights will meet your eyes than any waving trees or rippling waters – when angel-hands shall undraw your curtains, and sweeter tones than ever loving Mother breathed shall wake you to a new and glorious day – and when all the sadness, and the sin, that darkened life on this little earth, shall be forgotten like the dreams of a night that is past!

Your affectionate friend,
LEWIS CARROLL

Easter, 1876

14

Christmas Greetings
From a Fairy to a Child

LADY dear, if Fairies may
    For a moment lay aside
Cunning tricks and elfish play,
    'Tis at happy Christmas-tide.

We have heard the children say –
    Gentle children, whom we love –
Long ago, on Christmas Day,
    Came a message from above.

Still, as Christmas-tide comes round,
    They remember it again –
Echo still the joyful sound,
    'Peace on earth, good-will to men.'

Yet the hearts must child-like be
    Where such heavenly guests abide.
Unto children, in their glee,
    All the year is Christmas-tide.

Thus, forgetting tricks and play
    For a moment, Lady dear,
We would wish you, if we may,
    Merry Christmas, glad New Year.

Christmas, 1887

Through the
Looking-Glass
and what Alice found there

DRAMATIS PERSONÆ
(*As arranged before commencement of game*)

WHITE			RED
PIECES	PAWNS	PAWNS	PIECES
Tweedledee	Daisy	Daisy	Humpty Dumpty
Unicorn	Haigha	Messenger	Carpenter
Sheep	Oyster	Oyster	Walrus
W.Queen	'Lily'	Tiger-lily	R.Queen
W.King	Fawn	Rose	R.King
Aged man	Oyster	Oyster	Crow
W.Knight	Hatta	Frog	R.Knight
Tweedledum	Daisy	Daisy	Lion

RED

WHITE

White Pawn (Alice) to play, and win in eleven moves

Preface

As the chess-problem, given on a previous page, has puzzled some of my readers, it may be well to explain that it is correctly worked out, so far as the *moves* are concerned. The *alternation* of Red and White is perhaps not so strictly observed as it might be, and the 'castling' of the three Queens is merely a way of saying that they entered the palace: but the 'check' of the White King at move 6, the capture of the Red Knight at move 7, and the final 'checkmate' of the Red King, will be found, by any one who will take the trouble to set the pieces and play the moves as directed, to be strictly in accordance with the laws of the game.

The new words, in the poem *Jabberwocky* (see p. 186), have given rise to some differences of opinion as to their pronunciation: so it may be well to give instructions on *that* point also. Pronounce 'slithy' as if it were the two words 'sly, the': make the 'g' *hard* in 'gyre' and 'gimble': and pronounce 'rath' to rhyme with 'bath.'

Child of the pure unclouded brow
And dreaming eyes of wonder!
Though time be fleet, and I and thou
Are half a life asunder,
Thy loving smile will surely hail
The love-gift of a fairy-tale.

I have not seen thy sunny face,
Nor heard thy silver laughter;
No thought of me shall find a place
In thy young life's hereafter –
Enough that now thou wilt not fail
To listen to my fairy-tale.

A tale begun in other days,
When summer suns were glowing –
A simple chime, that served to time
The rhythm of our rowing –
Whose echoes live in memory yet,
Though envious years would say 'forget.'

Come, hearken then, ere voice of dread,
With bitter tidings laden,
Shall summon to unwelcome bed
A melancholy maiden!
We are but older children, dear,
Who fret to find our bedtime near.

Without, the frost, the blinding snow,
The storm-wind's moody madness —
Within, the firelight's ruddy glow,
And childhood's nest of gladness.
The magic words shall hold thee fast:
Thou shalt not heed the raving blast.

And though the shadow of a sigh
May tremble through the story,
For 'happy summer days' gone by,
And vanish'd summer glory —
It shall not touch with breath of bale
The pleasance of our fairy-tale.

1

Looking-Glass House

ONE thing was certain, that the *white* kitten had had nothing to do with it: – it was the black kitten's fault entirely. For the white kitten had been having its face washed by the old cat for the last quarter of an hour (and bearing it pretty well, considering); so you see that it *couldn't* have had any hand in the mischief.

The way Dinah washed her children's faces was this: first she held the poor thing down by its ear with one paw, and then with the other paw she rubbed its face all over, the wrong way, beginning at the nose: and just now, as I said, she was hard at work on the white kitten, which was lying quite still and trying to purr – no doubt feeling that it was all meant for its good.

But the black kitten had been finished with earlier in the afternoon, and so, while Alice was sitting curled up in a corner of the great arm-chair, half talking to herself and half asleep, the kitten had been having a grand game of romps with the ball of worsted Alice had been trying to wind up, and had been rolling it up and down till it had all come undone again; and there it was, spread over the hearth-rug, all knots and tangles, with the kitten running after its own tail in the middle.

'Oh, you wicked wicked little thing!' cried Alice, catching up the kitten, and giving it a little kiss to make it understand that it was in disgrace. 'Really, Dinah ought to have taught you better manners! You *ought*, Dinah, you know you ought!' she added, looking reproachfully at the old cat, and speaking in as cross a voice as she could manage – and then she scrambled back into the arm-chair, taking the kitten and the worsted with her, and began winding up the ball again. But she didn't get on very fast, as she was talking all the time, sometimes to the kitten, and sometimes to herself. Kitty sat very demurely on her knee, pretending to watch the progress of the winding, and now and then putting out one paw and gently touching the ball, as if it would be glad to help if it might.

'Do you know what tomorrow is, Kitty?' Alice began. 'You'd have guessed if you'd been up in the window with me – only Dinah was making you tidy, so you couldn't. I was watching the boys getting in sticks for the bonfire – and it wants plenty of sticks, Kitty! Only it got so cold, and it snowed so, they had to leave off. Never mind, Kitty, we'll go and see the bonfire tomorrow.' Here Alice wound two or three turns of the worsted round the kitten's neck, just to see how it would look: this led to a scramble, in which the ball rolled down upon the floor, and yards and yards of it got unwound again.

'Do you know, I was so angry, Kitty,' Alice went on as soon as they were comfortably settled again, 'when I saw all the mischief you had been doing, I was very nearly opening the window, and putting you out into the snow! And you'd have deserved it, you little mischievous darling! What have you got to say for yourself? Now don't interrupt me!' she went on, holding up one finger. 'I'm going to tell you all your faults. Number one: you squeaked twice while Dinah was washing your face this morning. Now you can't deny it, Kitty: I heard you! What's that you say?' (pretending that the kitten was speaking.) 'Her paw went into your eye? Well, that's *your* fault, for keeping your eyes open – if you'd shut them tight up, it wouldn't have happened. Now don't make any more excuses, but listen! Number two: you pulled Snowdrop away by the tail just as I had put down the saucer of milk before her! What, you were thirsty, were you? How do you know she wasn't thirsty too? Now for Number three: you unwound every bit of the worsted while I wasn't looking!

'That's three faults, Kitty, and you've not been punished for any of them yet. You know I'm saving up all your punishments for Wednesday week – Suppose they had saved up all *my* punishments!' she went on, talking more to herself than the kitten. 'What *would* they do at the end of the year? I should be sent to prison, I suppose, when the day came. Or – let me see – suppose each punishment was to be going without a dinner: then, when the miserable day came, I should have to go without fifty dinners at once! Well, I shouldn't mind *that* much! I'd far rather go without them than eat them!

'Do you hear the snow against the window-panes, Kitty? How nice and soft it sounds! Just as if some one was kissing the window all over outside. I wonder if the snow *loves* the trees and fields, that it kisses them so gently? And then it covers them up snug, you know, with a white quilt; and perhaps it says, "Go to sleep, darlings, till the summer comes again." And when they wake up in the summer, Kitty, they dress themselves all in green, and dance about – whenever the wind blows – oh, that's very pretty!' cried Alice, dropping the ball of worsted to clap her hands. 'And I do so *wish* it was true! I'm sure the woods look sleepy in the autumn, when the leaves are getting brown.

'Kitty, can you play chess? Now, don't smile, my dear, I'm asking it seriously. Because, when we were playing just now, you watched just as if you understood it: and when I said "Check!" you purred! Well, it *was* a nice check, Kitty, and really I might have won, if it hadn't been for that nasty Knight, that came wriggling down among my pieces. Kitty, dear, let's pretend –' And here I wish I could tell you half the things Alice used to say, beginning with her favourite phrase 'Let's pretend.' She had had quite a long argument with her sister only the day before – all because Alice had begun with 'Let's pretend we're kings and queens;' and her sister, who liked being very exact, had argued that they couldn't, because there were only two of them, and Alice had been reduced at last to say, 'Well, *you* can be one of them then, and *I'll* be all the rest.' And once she had really frightened her old nurse by shouting suddenly in her ear, 'Nurse! Do let's pretend that I'm a hungry hyæna, and you're a bone!'

But this is taking us away from Alice's speech to the kitten. 'Let's pretend that you're the Red Queen, Kitty! Do you know, I think if you sat up and folded your arms, you'd look exactly like her. Now do try, there's a dear!' And Alice got the Red Queen off the table, and set it up before the kitten as a model for it to imitate: however, the thing didn't succeed, principally, Alice said, because the kitten wouldn't fold its arms properly. So, to punish it, she held it up to the Looking-glass, that it might see how sulky it was – 'and if you're not good directly,' she added, 'I'll put you through the Looking-glass House. How would you like *that*?

'Now, if you'll only attend, Kitty, and not talk so much, I'll tell you all my ideas about Looking-glass House. First, there's the room you can see through the glass – that's just the same as our drawing-room, only the things go the other way. I can see all of it when I get upon a chair – all but the bit just behind the fireplace. Oh! I do so wish I could see *that* bit! I want so much to know whether they've a fire in the winter: you never *can* tell, you know, unless our fire smokes, and then smoke comes up in that room too – but that may be only pretence, just to make it look as if they had a fire. Well then, the books are something like our books, only the words go the wrong way; I know that, because I've held up one of our books to the glass, and then they hold up one in the other room.

'How would you like to live in Looking-glass House, Kitty? I wonder if they'd give you milk in there? Perhaps

Looking-glass milk isn't good to drink – But oh, Kitty! now we come to the passage. You can just see a little *peep* of the passage in Looking-glass House, if you leave the door of our drawing-room wide open: and it's very

like our passage as far as you can see, only you know it
may be quite different on beyond. Oh, Kitty! how nice
it would be if we could only get through into Looking-
glass House! I'm sure it's got, oh! such beautiful things
in it! Let's pretend there's a way of getting through into
it, somehow, Kitty. Let's pretend the glass has got all soft

like gauze, so that we can get through. Why, it's turning into a sort of mist now, I declare! It'll be easy enough to get through –' She was up on the chimney-piece while she said this, though she hardly knew how she had got there. And certainly the glass was beginning to melt away, just like a bright silvery mist.

In another moment Alice was through the glass, and had jumped lightly down into the Looking-glass room. The very first thing she did was to look whether there was a fire in the fireplace, and she was quite pleased to find that there was a real one, blazing away as brightly as the one she had left behind. 'So I shall be as warm here as I was in the old room,' thought Alice: 'warmer, in fact, because there'll be no one here to scold me away from the fire. Oh, what fun it'll be, when they see me through the glass in here, and can't get at me!'

Then she began looking about and noticed that what could be seen from the old room was quite common and uninteresting, but that all the rest was as different as possible. For instance, the pictures on the wall next the fire seemed to be all alive, and the very clock on the chimney-piece (you know you can only see the back of it in the Looking-glass) had got the face of a little old man, and grinned at her.

'They don't keep this room so tidy as the other,' Alice thought to herself, as she noticed several of the chessmen down in the hearth among the cinders: but in another moment, with a little 'Oh!' of surprise, she was down on her hands and knees watching them. The chessmen were walking about, two and two!

'Here are the Red King and the Red Queen,' Alice said (in a whisper, for fear of frightening them), 'and there are the White King and the White Queen sitting on the edge of the shovel – and here are two Castles walking arm in arm – I don't think they can hear me,' she went on, as she put her head closer down, 'and I'm nearly sure they can't see me. I feel somehow as if I were invisible –'

Here something began squeaking on the table behind Alice, and made her turn her head just in time to see one of the White Pawns roll over and begin kicking: she watched it with great curiosity to see what would happen next.

'It is the voice of my child!' the White Queen cried out as she rushed past the King, so violently that she knocked him over among the cinders. 'My precious Lily! My imperial kitten!' and she began scrambling wildly up the side of the fender.

'Imperial fiddlestick!' said the King, rubbing his nose, which had been hurt by the fall. He had a right to be a *little* annoyed with the Queen, for he was covered with ashes from head to foot.

Alice was very anxious to be of use, and, as the poor little Lily was nearly screaming herself into a fit, she hastily picked up the Queen and set her on the table by the side of her noisy little daughter.

The Queen gasped, and sat down: the rapid journey through the air had quite taken away her breath and for a minute or two she could do nothing but hug the little Lily in silence. As soon as she had recovered her breath a little, she called out to the White King, who was sitting sulkily among the ashes, 'Mind the volcano!'

'What volcano?' said the King, looking up anxiously

into the fire, as if he thought that was the most likely place to find one.

'Blew – me – up,' panted the Queen, who was still a little out of breath. 'Mind you come up – the regular way – don't get blown up!'

Alice watched the White King as he slowly struggled up from bar to bar, till at last she said, 'Why, you'll be hours and hours getting to the table, at that rate. I'd far better help you, hadn't I?' But the King took no notice of the question: it was quite clear that he could neither hear her nor see her.

So Alice picked him up very gently, and lifted him across more slowly than she had lifted the Queen, that she mightn't take his breath away: but, before she put him on the table, she thought she might as well dust him a little, he was so covered in ashes.

She said afterwards that she had never seen in all her life such a face as the King made, when he found himself held in the air by an invisible hand, and being dusted: he was far too much astonished to cry out, but his eyes and mouth went on getting larger and larger, and rounder and rounder, till her hand shook so with laughing that she nearly let him drop upon the floor.

'Oh! *please* don't make such faces, my dear!' she cried out, quite forgetting that the King couldn't hear her. 'You make me laugh so that I can hardly hold you! And don't keep your mouth so wide open! All the ashes will get into it – there, now I think you're tidy enough!' she added, as she smoothed his hair, and set him upon the table near the Queen.

The King immediately fell flat on his back, and lay perfectly still: and Alice was a little alarmed at what she had done, and went round the room to see if she could find any water to throw over him. However, she could find nothing but a bottle of ink, and when she got back with it she found he had recovered, and he and the Queen were talking together in a frightened whisper – so low, that Alice could hardly hear what they said.

The King was saying, 'I assure you, my dear, I turned cold to the very ends of my whiskers!'

To which the Queen replied, 'You haven't got any whiskers.'

'The horror of that moment,' the King went on, 'I shall never, *never* forget!'

'You will, though,' the Queen said, 'if you don't make a memorandum of it.'

Alice looked on with great interest as the King took an enormous memorandum-book out of his pocket, and began writing. A sudden thought struck her, and she took hold of the end of the pencil, which came some way over his shoulder, and began writing for him.

The poor King looked puzzled and unhappy, and struggled with the pencil for some time without saying anything; but Alice was too strong for him, and at last he panted out, 'My dear! I really *must* get a thinner pencil. I can't manage this one a bit; it writes all manner of things that I don't intend –'

'What manner of things?' said the Queen, looking over the book (in which Alice had put '*The White Knight is sliding down the poker. He balances very badly*'). 'That's not a memorandum of *your* feelings!'

There was a book lying near Alice on the table, and while she sat watching the White King (for she was still a little anxious about him, and had the ink all ready to throw over him, in case he fainted again), she turned over the leaves, to find some part that she could read, '– for it's all in some language I don't know,' she said to herself.

It was like this.

JABBERWOCKY

'Twas brillig, and the slithy toves
Did gyre and gimble in the wabe;
All mimsy were the borogoves,
And the mome raths outgrabe

186

She puzzled over this for some time, but at last a bright thought struck her. 'Why, it's a Looking-glass book, of course! And if I hold it up to a glass, the words will all go the right way again.'

This was the poem that Alice read.

JABBERWOCKY

'Twas brillig, and the slithy toves
  Did gyre and gimble in the wabe;
All mimsy were the borogoves,
  And the mome raths outgrabe.

'Beware the Jabberwock, my son!
The jaws that bite, the claws that catch!
Beware the Jubjub bird, and shun
The frumious Bandersnatch!'

He took his vorpal sword in hand:
Long time the manxome foe he sought –
So rested he by the Tumtum tree,
And stood awhile in thought.

And as in uffish thought he stood,
The Jabberwock, with eyes of flame,
Came whiffling through the tulgey wood,
And burbled as it came!

One, two! One, two! And through and through
The vorpal blade went snicker-snack!
He left it dead, and with its head
He went galumphing back.

'And has thou slain the Jabberwock?
Come to my arms, my beamish boy!
A frabjous day! Callooh! Callay!'
He chortled in his joy.

'Twas brillig, and the slithy toves
Did gyre and gimble in the wabe;
All mimsy were the borogoves,
And the mome raths outgrabe.

'It seems very pretty,' she said when she had finished it, 'but it's *rather* hard to understand!' (You see she didn't like to confess, even to herself, that she couldn't make it out at all.) 'Somehow it seems to fill my head with ideas – only I don't exactly know what they are! However, *somebody* killed *something*: that's clear, at any rate –'

'But oh!' thought Alice, suddenly jumping up, 'if I don't make haste I shall have to go back through the Looking-glass, before I've seen what the rest of the house is like! Let's have a look at the garden first!' She was out of the room in a moment, and ran down stairs –

or, at least, it wasn't exactly running, but a new invention for getting down stairs quickly and easily, as Alice said to herself. She just kept the tips of her fingers on the hand-rail, and floated gently down without even touching the stairs with her feet; then she floated on through the hall, and would have gone straight out at the door in the same way, if she hadn't caught hold of the door-post. She was getting a little giddy with so much floating in the air, and was rather glad to find herself walking again in the natural way.

2

The Garden of Live Flowers

'I SHOULD see the garden far better,' said Alice to herself, 'if I could get to the top of that hill: and here's a path that leads straight to it – at least, no, it doesn't do that –' (after going a few yards along the path, and turning several sharp corners), 'but I suppose it will at last. But how curiously it twists! It's more like a corkscrew than a path! Well, *this* turn goes to the hill, I suppose – no, it doesn't! This goes straight back to the house! Well then, I'll try it the other way.'

And so she did: wandering up and down, and trying turn after turn, but always coming back to the house, do what she would. Indeed, once, when she turned a corner rather more quickly than usual, she ran against it before she could stop herself.

'It's no use talking about it,' Alice said, looking up at the house and pretending it was arguing with her. 'I'm not going in again yet. I know I should have to get through the Looking-glass again – back into the old room – and there'd be an end of all my adventures!'

So, resolutely turning her back upon the house, she set out once more down the path, determined to keep straight on till she got to the hill. For a few minutes all went on well, and she was just saying, 'I really *shall* do it this time –' when the path gave a sudden twist and shook itself (as she described it afterwards), and the next moment she found herself actually walking in at the door.

'Oh, it's too bad!' she cried. 'I never saw such a house for getting in the way! Never!'

However, there was the hill full in sight, so there was nothing to be done but start again. This time she came upon a large flower-bed, with a border of daisies, and a willow-tree growing in the middle.

'O Tiger-lily,' said Alice, addressing herself to one that was waving gracefully about in the wind, 'I *wish* you could talk!'

'We *can* talk,' said the Tiger-lily: 'when there's anybody worth talking to.'

Alice was so astonished that she could not speak for a minute: it quite seemed to take her breath away. At length, as the Tiger-lily only went on waving about, she spoke again, in a timid voice – almost in a whisper. 'And can *all* the flowers talk?'

'As well as *you* can,' said the Tiger-lily. 'And a great deal louder.'

'It isn't manners for us to begin, you know,' said the Rose, 'and I really was wondering when you'd speak! Said

I to myself, "Her face has got *some* sense in it, though it's not a clever one!" Still, you're the right colour, and that goes a long way.'

'I don't care about the colour,' the Tiger-lily remarked. 'If only her petals curled up a little more, she'd be all right.'

Alice didn't like being criticised, so she began asking questions. 'Aren't you sometimes frightened at being planted out here, with nobody to take care of you?'

'There's the tree in the middle,' said the Rose: 'what else is it good for?'

'But what could it do, if any danger came?' Alice asked.

'It could bark,' said the Rose.

'It says "Bough-wough!"' cried a Daisy: 'that's why its branches are called boughs!'

'Didn't you know *that*?' cried another Daisy, and here they all began shouting together, till the air seemed quite full of little shrill voices. 'Silence, every one of you!' cried the Tiger-lily, waving itself passionately from side to side, and trembling with excitement. 'They know I can't get at them!' it panted, bending its quivering head towards Alice, 'or they wouldn't dare to do it!'

'Never mind!' Alice said in a soothing tone, and stooping down to the daisies, who were just beginning again, she whispered, 'If you don't hold your tongues, I'll pick you!'

There was silence in a moment, and several of the pink daisies turned white.

'That's right!' said the Tiger-lily. 'The daisies are worst of all. When one speaks, they all begin together, and it's enough to make one wither to hear the way they go on!'

'How is it you can all talk so nicely?' Alice said, hoping to get it into a better temper by a compliment. 'I've been in many gardens before, but none of the flowers could talk.'

'Put your hand down, and feel the ground,' said the Tiger-lily. 'Then you'll know why.'

Alice did so. 'It's very hard,' she said, 'but I don't see what that has to do with it.'

'In most gardens,' the Tiger-lily said, 'they make the beds too soft – so that the flowers are always asleep.'

This sounded a very good reason, and Alice was quite pleased to know it. 'I never thought of that before!' she said.

'It's *my* opinion that you never think *at all*,' the Rose said in a rather severe tone.

'I never saw anybody looked stupider,' a Violet said, so suddenly, that Alice quite jumped; for it hadn't spoken before.

'Hold *your* tongue!' cried the Tiger-lily. 'As if *you* ever saw anybody! You keep your head under the leaves, and snore away there, till you know no more what's going on in the world, than if you were a bud!'

'Are there any more people in the garden besides me?' Alice said, not choosing to notice the Rose's last remark.

'There's one other flower in the garden that can move about like you,' said the Rose. 'I wonder how you do it –' ('You're always wondering,' said the Tiger-lily), 'but she's more bushy than you are.'

'Is she like me?' Alice asked eagerly, for the thought crossed her mind, 'There's another little girl in the garden, somewhere!'

'Well, she has the same awkward shape as you,' the Rose said, 'but she's redder – and her petals are shorter, I think.'

'Her petals are done up close, almost like a dahlia,' the Tiger-lily interrupted: 'not tumbled about anyhow, like yours.'

'But that's not *your* fault,' the Rose added kindly: 'you're beginning to fade, you know – and then one can't help one's petals getting a little untidy.'

Alice didn't like this idea at all: so, to change the subject, she asked 'Does she ever come out here?'

'I daresay you'll see her soon,' said the Rose. 'She's

one of the thorny kind.'

'Where does she wear the thorns?' Alice asked with some curiosity.

'Why, all round her head, of course,' the Rose replied. 'I was wondering *you* hadn't got some too. I thought it was the regular rule.'

'She's coming!' cried the Larkspur. 'I hear her footstep, thump, thump, along the gravel-walk!'

Alice looked round eagerly, and found that it was the Red Queen. 'She's grown a good deal!' was her first remark. She had indeed: when Alice first found her in the ashes, she had been only three inches high – and here she was, half a head taller than Alice herself!

'It's the fresh air that does it,' said the Rose: 'wonderfully fine air it is, out here.'

'I think I'll go and meet her,' said Alice, for though the flowers were interesting enough, she felt that it would be far grander to have a talk with a real Queen.

'You can't possibly do that,' said the Rose, '*I* should advise you to walk the other way.'

This sounded nonsense to Alice, so she said nothing, but set off at once towards the Red Queen. To her surprise, she lost sight of her in a moment, and found herself walking in at the front-door again.

A little provoked, she drew back, and after looking everywhere for the Queen (whom she spied out at last, a long way off), she thought she would try the plan, this time, of walking in the opposite direction.

It succeeded beautifully. She had not been walking a minute before she found herself face to face with the Red Queen, and full in sight of the hill she had been so long aiming at.

'Where do you come from?' said the Red Queen. 'And where are you going? Look up, speak nicely, and don't twiddle your fingers all the time.'

Alice attended to all these directions, and explained, as well as she could, that she had lost her way.

'I don't know what you mean by *your* way,' said the Queen: 'all the ways about here belong to *me* – but why did you come out here at all?' she added in a kinder tone. 'Curtsey while you're thinking what to say, it saves time.'

Alice wondered a little at this, but she was too much in awe of the Queen to disbelieve it. 'I'll try it when I go home,' she thought to herself, 'the next time I'm a little late for dinner.'

'It's time for you to answer now,' the Queen said, looking at her watch: 'open your mouth a *little* wider when you speak, and always say "your Majesty."'

'I only wanted to see what the garden was like, your Majesty –'

'That's right,' said the Queen, patting her on the head,

which Alice didn't like at all, 'though, when you say "garden," – *I've* seen gardens, compared with which this would be a wilderness.'

Alice didn't dare to argue the point, but went on: '– and I thought I'd try and find my way to the top of that hill –'

'When you say "hill,"' the Queen interrupted, 'I could show you hills, in comparison with which you'd call that a valley.'

'No, I couldn't,' said Alice, surprised into contradicting her at last: 'a hill *can't* be a valley, you know. That would be nonsense –'

The Red Queen shook her head. 'You may call it "nonsense" if you like,' she said, 'but *I've* heard nonsense, compared with which that would be as sensible as a dictionary!'

Alice curtseyed again, as she was afraid from the Queen's tone that she was a *little* offended: and they walked on in silence till they got to the top of the little hill.

For some minutes Alice stood without speaking, looking out in all directions over the country – and a most curious country it was. There were a number of tiny little brooks running straight across it from side to side, and the ground between was divided up into squares by a number of little green hedges, that reached from brook to brook.

'I declare it's marked out just like a large chessboard!' Alice said at last. 'There ought to be some men moving about somewhere – and so there are!' she added in a tone of delight, and her heart began to beat quick with excitement as she went on. 'It's a great huge game of chess that's being played – all over the world – if this is the world at all, you know. Oh, what fun it is! How I *wish* I was one of them! I wouldn't mind being a Pawn, if only I might join – though of course I should *like* to be a Queen, best.'

She glanced rather shyly at the real Queen as she said this, but her companion only smiled pleasantly, and said, 'That's easily managed. You can be the White Queen's Pawn, if you like, as Lily's too young to play: and you're in the Second Square to begin with: when you get to the Eighth Square you'll be a Queen –' Just at this moment, somehow or other, they began to run.

Alice never could quite make out, in thinking it over afterwards, how it was that they began: all she remembers is, that they were running hand in hand, and the Queen went so fast that it was all she could do to keep up with her: and still the Queen kept crying 'Faster! Faster!' but Alice felt she *could not* go faster, though she had no breath left to say so.

The most curious part of the thing was, that the trees and other things round them never changed their places at all: however fast they went, they never seemed to pass anything. 'I wonder if all the things move along with us?' thought poor puzzled Alice. And the Queen seemed to guess her thoughts, for she cried, 'Faster! Don't try to talk!'

Not that Alice had any idea of doing *that*. She felt as if she would never be able to talk again, she was getting so much out of breath: and still the Queen cried 'Faster!

Faster!' and dragged her along. 'Are we nearly there?' Alice managed to pant out at last.

'Nearly there!' the Queen repeated. 'Why, we passed it ten minutes ago! Faster!' And they ran on for a time in silence, with the wind whistling in Alice's ears, and almost blowing her hair off her head, she fancied.

'Now! Now!' cried the Queen. 'Faster! Faster!' And they went so fast that at last they seemed to skim through the air, hardly touching the ground with their feet, till suddenly, just as Alice was getting quite exhausted, they stopped, and she found herself sitting on the ground, breathless and giddy.

The Queen propped her up against a tree, and said kindly, 'You may rest a little now.'

Alice looked round her in great surprise. 'Why, I do believe we've been under this tree the whole time! Everything's just as it was!'

'Of course it is,' said the Queen: 'what would you have it?'

'Well, in *our* country,' said Alice, still panting a little, 'you'd generally get to somewhere else – if you ran very fast for a long time, as we've been doing.'

'A slow sort of country!' said the Queen. 'Now, *here*, you see, it takes all the running *you* can do, to keep in the same place. If you want to get somewhere else, you must run at least twice as fast as that!'

'I'd rather not try, please!' said Alice. 'I'm quite content to stay here – only I *am* so hot and thirsty!'

'I know what *you'd* like!' the Queen said good-naturedly, taking a little box out of her pocket. 'Have a biscuit?'

Alice thought it would not be civil to say 'No,' though it wasn't at all what she wanted. So she took it, and ate it as well as she could: and it was *very* dry; and she thought she had never been so nearly choked in all her life.

'While you're refreshing yourself,' said the Queen, 'I'll just take the measurements.' And she took a ribbon out of her pocket, marked in inches, and began measuring the ground, and sticking little pegs in here and there.

'At the end of two yards,' she said, putting in a peg to mark the distance, 'I shall give you your directions – have another biscuit?'

'No, thank you,' said Alice: 'one's *quite* enough!'

'Thirst quenched, I hope?' said the Queen.

Alice did not know what to say to this, but luckily the Queen did not wait for an answer, but went on. 'At the end of *three* yards I shall repeat them – for fear of your forgetting them. At the end of *four*, I shall say good-bye. And at the end of *five*, I shall go!'

She had got all the pegs put in by this time, and Alice looked on with great interest as she returned to the tree, and then began slowly walking down the row.

At the two-yard peg she faced round, and said, 'A pawn goes two squares in its first move, you know. So you'll go *very* quickly through the Third Square – by railway, I should think – and you'll find yourself in the Fourth Square in no time. Well, *that* square belongs to Tweedledum and Tweedledee – the Fifth is mostly water – the Sixth belongs to Humpty Dumpty – But you make no remark?'

'I – I didn't know I had to make one – just then,' Alice faltered out.

'You *should* have said,' the Queen went on in a tone of grave reproof, '"It's extremely kind of you to tell me all this" – however, we'll suppose it said – the Seventh Square is all forest – however, one of the Knights will show you the way – and in the Eighth Square we shall be Queens together, and it's all feasting and fun!' Alice got up and curtseyed, and sat down again.

At the next peg the Queen turned again, and this time she said, 'Speak in French when you can't think of the English for a thing – turn out your toes as you walk – and remember who you are!' She did not wait for Alice to curtsey this time, but walked on quickly to the next peg, where she turned for a moment to say 'good-bye,' and then hurried on to the last.

How it happened, Alice never knew, but exactly as she came to the last peg, she was gone. Whether she vanished into the air, or whether she ran quickly into the wood ('and she *can* run very fast!' thought Alice), there was no way of guessing, but she was gone, and Alice began to remember that she was a Pawn, and that it would soon be time for her to move.

3

Looking-Glass Insects

OF course the first thing to do was to make a grand survey of the country she was going to travel through. 'It's something very like learning geography,' thought Alice, as she stood on tiptoe in hopes of being able to see a little further. 'Principal rivers – there *are* none. Principal mountains – I'm on the only one, but I don't think it's got any name. Principal towns – why, what *are* those creatures, making honey down there? They can't be bees – nobody ever saw bees a mile off, you know –' and for some time she stood silent, watching one of them that was bustling about among the flowers, poking its proboscis into them, 'just as if it was a regular bee,' thought Alice.

However, this was anything but a regular bee: in fact, it was an elephant – as Alice soon found out, though the idea quite took her breath away at first. 'And what enormous flowers they must be!' was her next idea. 'Something like cottages with the roofs taken off, and stalks put to them – and what quantities of honey they must make! I think I'll go down and – no, I won't go *just* yet,' she went on, checking herself just as she was beginning to run down the hill, and trying to find some excuse for turning shy so suddenly. 'It'll never do to go down among them without a good long branch to brush them away – and what fun it'll be when they ask me how I liked my walk. I shall say – "Oh, I liked it well enough –"' (here came the favourite little toss of the head), '"only it was so dusty and hot, and the elephants did tease so!"'

'I think I'll go down the other way,' she said after a pause: 'and perhaps I may visit the elephants later on. Besides, I do so want to get into the Third Square!'

So with this excuse she ran down the hill and jumped over the first of the six little brooks.

'Tickets, please!' said the Guard, putting his head in at the window. In a moment everybody was holding out a ticket: they were about the same size as the people, and quite seemed to fill the carriage.

'Now then! Show your ticket, child!' the Guard went on, looking angrily at Alice. And a great many voices all said together ('like the chorus of a song,' thought Alice), 'Don't keep him waiting, child! Why, his time is worth a thousand pounds a minute!'

'I'm afraid I haven't got one,' Alice said in a frightened tone: 'there wasn't a ticket-office where I came from.' And again the chorus of voices went on. 'There wasn't room for one where she came from. The land there is worth a thousand pounds an inch!'

'Don't make excuses,' said the Guard: 'you should have bought one from the engine-driver.' And once more the chorus of voices went on with 'The man that drives the engine. Why, the smoke alone is worth a thousand pounds a puff!'

Alice thought to herself, 'Then there's no use in speaking.' The voices didn't join in this time, as she hadn't spoken, but, to her great surprise, they all *thought* in chorus (I hope you understand what *thinking in chorus* means – for I must confess that *I* don't), 'Better say nothing at all. Language is worth a thousand pounds a word!'

'I shall dream about a thousand pounds to-night, I know I shall!' thought Alice.

All this time the Guard was looking at her, first through a telescope, then through a microscope, and then through an opera-glass. At last he said, 'You're travelling the wrong way,' and shut up the window and went away.

'So young a child,' said the gentleman sitting opposite to her (he was dressed in white paper), 'ought to know which way she's going, even if she doesn't know her own name!'

A Goat, that was sitting next to the gentleman in white, shut his eyes and said in a loud voice, 'She ought to know her way to the ticket-office, even if she doesn't know her alphabet!'

There was a Beetle sitting next the Goat (it was a very queer carriage-full of passengers altogether), and, as the rule seemed to be that they should all speak in turn, *he* went on with 'She'll have to go back from here as luggage!'

Alice couldn't see who was sitting beyond the Beetle, but a hoarse voice spoke next. 'Change engines –' it said, and there it choked and was obliged to leave off.

'It sounds like a horse,' Alice thought to herself. And an extremely small voice, close to her ear, said,

'You might make a joke on that – something about "horse" and "hoarse," you know.'

Then a very gentle voice in the distance said, 'She must be labelled "Lass, with care," you know –'

And after that other voices went on ('What a number of people there are in the carriage!' thought Alice), saying, 'She must go by post, as she's got a head on her –' 'She must be sent as a message by the telegraph –' 'She must draw the train herself the rest of the way –,' and so on.

But the gentleman dressed in white paper leaned forwards and whispered in her ear, 'Never mind what they all say, my dear, but take a return-ticket every time the train stops.'

'Indeed I shan't!' Alice said rather impatiently. 'I don't

belong to this railway journey at all – I was in a wood just now – and I wish I could get back there!'

'You might make a joke on *that*,' said the little voice close to her ear: 'something about "you *would* if you could," you know.'

'Don't tease so,' said Alice, looking about in vain to see where the voice came from; 'if you're so anxious to have a joke made, why don't you make one yourself?'

The little voice sighed deeply: it was *very* unhappy, evidently, and Alice would have said something pitying to comfort it, 'if it would only sigh like other people!' she thought. But this was such a wonderfully small sigh, that she wouldn't have heard it at all, if it hadn't come *quite* close to her ear. The consequence of this was that it tickled her ear very much, and quite took off her thoughts from the unhappiness of the poor little creature.

'I know you are a friend,' the little voice went on; 'a dear friend, and an old friend. And you won't hurt me, though I *am* an insect.'

'What kind of insect?' Alice inquired a little anxiously. What she really wanted to know was, whether it could sting or not, but she thought this wouldn't be quite a civil question to ask.

'What, then you don't –' the little voice began, when it was drowned by a shrill scream from the engine, and everybody jumped up in alarm, Alice among the rest.

The Horse, who had put his head out of the window, quietly drew it in and said, 'It's only a brook we have to jump over.' Everybody seemed satisfied with this, though Alice felt a little nervous at the idea of trains jumping at all. 'However, it'll take us into the Fourth Square, that's some comfort!' she said to herself. In another moment she felt the carriage rise straight up into the air, and in her fright she caught at the thing nearest to her hand, which happened to be the Goat's beard.

*   *   *   *

*   *   *

*   *   *   *

But the beard seemed to melt away as she touched it, and she found herself sitting quietly under a tree – while the Gnat (for that was the insect she had been talking to) was balancing itself on a twig just over her head, and fanning her with its wings.

It certainly was a *very* large Gnat: 'about the size of a chicken,' Alice thought. Still, she couldn't feel nervous with it, after they had been talking together so long.

'– then you don't like all insects?' the Gnat went on, as quietly as if nothing had happened.

'I like them when they can talk,' Alice said. 'None of them ever talk, where *I* come from.'

'What sort of insects do you rejoice in, where *you* come from?' the Gnat inquired.

'I don't *rejoice* in insects at all,' Alice explained, 'because I'm rather afraid of them – at least the large kinds. But I can tell you the names of some of them.'

'Of course they answer to their names?' the Gnat remarked carelessly.

'I never knew them do it.'

'What's the use of their having names,' the Gnat said, 'if they won't answer to them?'

'No use to *them*,' said Alice; 'but it's useful to the people that name them, I suppose. If not, why do things have names at all?'

'I can't say,' the Gnat replied. 'Further on, in the wood down there, they've got no names – however, go on with your list of insects: you're wasting time.'

'Well, there's the Horse-fly,' Alice began, counting off the names on her fingers.

'All right,' said the Gnat: 'half way up that bush, you'll see a Rocking-horse-fly, if you look. It's made entirely of wood, and gets about by swinging itself from branch to branch.'

'What does it live on?' Alice asked, with great curiosity.

'Sap and sawdust,' said the Gnat. 'Go on with the list.'

Alice looked at the Rocking-horse-fly with great interest, and made up her mind that it must have been just repainted, it looked so bright and sticky; and then she went on.

'And there's the Dragon-fly.'

'Look on the branch above your head,' said the Gnat, 'and there you'll find a Snap-dragan-fly. Its body is made of plum-pudding, its wings of holly-leaves, and its head is a raisin burning in brandy.'

'And what does it live on?' Alice asked, as before.

'Frumenty and mince-pie,' the Gnat replied; 'and it makes its nest in a Christmas-box.'

'And then there's the Butterfly,' Alice went on, after she had taken a good look at the insect with its head on fire, and had thought to herself, 'I wonder if that's the reason insects are so fond of flying into candles – because they want to turn into Snap-dragon-flies!'

'Crawling at your feet,' said the Gnat (Alice drew her feet back in some alarm), 'you may observe a Bread-and-Butterfly. Its wings are thin slices of Bread-and-butter, its body is a crust, and its head is a lump of sugar.'

'And what does *it* live on?'

'Weak tea with cream in it.'

A new difficulty came into Alice's head. 'Supposing it couldn't find any?' she suggested.

'Then it would die, of course.'

'But that must happen very often,' Alice remarked thoughtfully.

'It always happens,' said the Gnat.

After this, Alice was silent for a minute or two, pondering. The Gnat amused itself meanwhile by humming round and round her head: at last it settled again and remarked, 'I suppose you don't want to lose your name?'

'No, indeed,' Alice said, a little anxiously.

'And yet I don't know,' the Gnat went on in a careless tone: 'only think how convenient it would be if you could manage to go home without it! For instance, if the governess wanted to call you to your lessons, she would call out "Come here –," and there she would have to leave off, because there wouldn't be any name for her to call, and of course you wouldn't have to go, you know.'

'That would never do, I'm sure,' said Alice: 'the governess would never think of excusing me lessons for that. If she couldn't remember my name, she'd call me "Miss!" as the servants do.'

'Well, if she said "Miss," and didn't say anything more,' the Gnat remarked, 'of course you'd miss your lessons. That's a joke. I wish *you* had made it.'

'Why do you wish *I* had made it?' Alice asked. 'It's a very bad one.'

But the Gnat only sighed deeply, while two large tears came rolling down its cheeks.

'You shouldn't make jokes,' Alice said, 'if it makes you so unhappy.'

Then came another of those melancholy little sighs, and this time the poor Gnat really seemed to have sighed itself away, for, when Alice looked up, there was nothing whatever to be seen on the twig, and, as she was getting quite chilly with sitting still so long, she got up and walked on.

She very soon came to an open field, with a wood on the other side of it: it looked much darker than the last wood, and Alice felt a *little* timid about going into it. However, on second thoughts, she made up her mind to go on: 'for I certainly won't go *back*,' she thought to herself, and this was the only way to the Eighth Square.

'This must be the wood,' she said thoughtfully to herself, 'where things have no names. I wonder what'll become of *my* name when I go in? I shouldn't like to lose it at all – because they'd have to give me another, and it would be almost certain to be an ugly one. But then the fun would be, trying to find the creature that had got my old name! That's just like the advertisements, you know, when people lose dogs – "*answers to the name of 'Dash:'* *had on a brass collar*" – just fancy calling everything you met "Alice," till one of them answered! Only they wouldn't answer at all, if they were wise.'

She was rambling on in this way when she reached the wood: it looked very cool and shady. 'Well, at any rate it's a great comfort,' she said as she stepped under the trees, 'after being so hot, to get into the – into the – into *what*?' she went on, rather surprised at not being able to think of the word. 'I mean to get under the – under the – under *this*, you know!' putting her hand on the trunk of the tree. 'What *does* it call itself, I wonder? I do believe it's got no name – why, to be sure it hasn't!'

She stood silent for a minute, thinking: then she suddenly began again. 'Then it really *has* happened, after all! And now, who am I? I *will* remember, if I can! I'm determined to do it!' But being determined didn't help her much, and all she could say, after a great deal of puzzling, was, 'L, I *know* it begins with L!'

Just then a Fawn came wandering by: it looked at Alice with its large gentle eyes, but didn't seem at all frightened. 'Here then! Here then!' Alice said, as she held out her hand and tried to stroke it; but it only started back a little, and then stood looking at her again.

'What do you call yourself?' the Fawn said at last. Such a soft sweet voice it had!

'I wish I knew!' thought poor Alice. She answered, rather sadly, 'Nothing, just now.'

'Think again,' it said: 'that won't do.'

Alice thought, but nothing came of it. 'Please, would you tell me what *you* call yourself?' she said timidly. 'I think that might help a little.'

'I'll tell you, if you'll come a little further on,' the Fawn said. 'I can't remember here.'

So they walked on together through the wood, Alice with her arms clasped lovingly round the soft neck of the Fawn, till they came out into another open field, and here the Fawn gave a sudden bound into the air, and shook itself free from Alice's arms. 'I'm a Fawn!' it cried out in a voice of delight, 'and, dear me! you're a human child!' A sudden look of alarm came into its beautiful brown eyes, and in another moment it had darted away at full speed.

Alice stood looking after it, almost ready to cry with vexation at having lost her dear little fellow-traveller so suddenly. 'However, I know my name now,' she said, 'that's *some* comfort. Alice – Alice – I won't forget it again. And now, which of these finger-posts ought I to follow, I wonder?'

It was not a very difficult question to answer, as there was only one road through the wood, and the two fingerposts both pointed along it. 'I'll settle it,' Alice said to herself, 'when the road divides and they point different ways.'

But this did not seem likely to happen. She went on and on, a long way, but wherever the road divided there were sure to be two finger-posts pointing the same way, one marked 'TO TWEEDLEDUM'S HOUSE, and the other 'TO THE HOUSE OF TWEEDLEDEE.'

'I do believe,' said Alice at last, 'that they live in the

same house! I wonder I never thought of that before – But I can't stay there long. I'll just call and say "How d'you do?" and ask them the way out of the wood. If I could only get to the Eighth Square before it gets dark!' So she wandered on, talking to herself as she went, till, on turning a sharp corner, she came upon two fat little men, so suddenly that she could not help starting back, but in another moment she recovered herself, feeling sure that they must be

4

Tweedledum and Tweedledee

THEY were standing under a tree, each with an arm round the other's neck, and Alice knew which was which in a moment, because one of them had 'DUM' embroidered on his collar, and the other 'DEE.' 'I suppose they've each got "TWEEDLE" round at the back of the collar,' she said to herself.

They stood so still that she quite forgot they were alive, and she was just looking round to see if the word 'TWEEDLE' was written at the back of each collar, when she was startled by a voice coming from the one marked 'DUM.'

'If you think we're wax-works,' he said, 'you ought to pay, you know. Wax-works weren't made to be looked at for nothing. Nohow!'

'Contrariwise,' added the one marked 'DEE,' 'if you think we're alive, you ought to speak.'

'I'm sure I'm very sorry,' was all Alice could say; for the words of the old song kept ringing through her head like the ticking of a clock, and she could hardly help saying them out loud:–

> 'Tweedledum and Tweedledee
>   Agreed to have a battle;
> For Tweedledum said Tweedledee
>   Had spoiled his nice new rattle.
>
> Just then flew down a monstrous crow,
>   As black as a tar-barrel;
> Which frightened both the heroes so,
>   They quite forgot their quarrel.'

'I know what you're thinking about,' said Tweedledum: 'but it isn't so, nohow.'

'Contrariwise,' continued Tweedledee, 'if it was so, it might be; and if it were so, it would be; but as it isn't, it ain't. That's logic.'

'I was thinking,' Alice said very politely, 'which is the best way out of this wood: it's getting so dark. Would you tell me, please?'

But the fat little men only looked at each other and grinned.

They looked so exactly like a couple of great schoolboys, that Alice couldn't help pointing her finger at Tweedledum, and saying 'First Boy!'

'Nohow!' Tweedledum cried out briskly, and shut his mouth up again with a snap.

'Next Boy!' said Alice, passing on to Tweedledee, though she felt quite certain he would only shout out 'Contrariwise!' and so he did.

'You've begun wrong!' cried Tweedledum. 'The first thing in a visit is to say "How d'ye do?" and shake hands!' And here the two brothers gave each other a hug, and then they held out the two hands that were free, to shake hands with her.

Alice did not like shaking hands with either of them first, for fear of hurting the other one's feelings; so, as the best way out of the difficulty, she took hold of both hands at once: the next moment they were dancing round in a ring. This seemed quite natural (she remembered afterwards), and she was not even surprised to hear music playing: it seemed to come from the tree under which they were dancing and it was done (as well as she could make it out) by the branches rubbing one across the other, like fiddles and fiddle-sticks.

'But it certainly *was* funny,' (Alice said afterwards, when she was telling her sister the history of all this,) 'to find myself singing "*Here we go round the mulberry bush.*" I don't know when I began it, bur somehow I felt as if I'd been singing it a long long time!'

The other two dancers were fat, and very soon out of breath. 'Four times round is enough for one dance,' Tweedledum panted out, and they left off dancing as suddenly as they had begun: the music stopped at the same moment.

Then they let go of Alice's hands, and stood looking at her for a minute: there was a rather awkward pause, as Alice didn't know how to begin a conversation with people she had just been dancing with. 'It would never do to say "How d'ye do?" *now*,' she said to herself: 'we seem to have got beyond that, somehow!'

'I hope you're not much tired?' she said at last.

'Nohow. And thank you *very* much for asking,' said Tweedledum.

'So *much* obliged!' added Tweedledee. 'You like poetry?'

'Ye-es, pretty well – *some* poetry,' Alice said doubtfully. 'Would you tell me which road leads out of the wood?'

'What shall I repeat to her?' said Tweedledee, looking round at Tweedledum with great solemn eyes, and not noticing Alice's question.

'"*The Walrus and the Carpenter*" is the longest,' Tweedledum replied, giving his brother an affectionate hug.

Tweedledee began instantly:

    'The sun was shining –'

Here Alice ventured to interrupt him. 'If it's *very* long,' she said, as politely as she could, 'would you please tell me first which road –'

Tweedledee smiled gently, and began again:

> *'The sun was shining on the sea,*
>   *Shining with all his might:*
> *He did his very best to make*
>   *The billows smooth and bright –*
> *And this was odd, because it was*
>   *The middle of the night.*

The moon was shining sulkily,
    Because she thought the sun
Had got no business to be there
    After the day was done –
"It's very rude of him," she said,
    "To come and spoil the fun!"

The sea was wet as wet could be,
    The sands were dry as dry.
You could not see a cloud, because
    No cloud was in the sky:
No birds were flying overhead -
    There were no birds to fly.

The Walrus and the Carpenter
    Were walking close at hand;
They wept like anything to see
    Such quantities of sand:
"If this were only cleared away,"
    They said, "it would be grand!"

"If seven maids with seven mops
    Swept it for half a year,
Do you suppose," the Walrus said,
    "That they could get it clear?"

"I doubt it," said the Carpenter,
    And shed a bitter tear.

"O Oysters, come and walk with us!"
    The Walrus did beseech.
"A pleasant walk, a pleasant talk,
    Along the briny beach:
We cannot do with more than four,
    To give a hand to each."

The eldest Oyster looked at him.
    But never a word he said:
The eldest Oyster winked his eye,
    And shook his heavy head —

Meaning to say he did not choose
    To leave the oyster-bed.

But four young oysters hurried up,
    All eager for the treat:
Their coats were brushed, their faces washed,
    Their shoes were clean and neat –
And this was odd, because, you know,
    They hadn't any feet.

Four other Oysters followed them,
    And yet another four;
And thick and fast they came at last,
    And more, and more, and more –
All hopping through the frothy waves,
    And scrambling to the shore.

The Walrus and the Carpenter
    Walked on a mile or so,
And then they rested on a rock
    Conveniently low:
And all the little Oysters stood
    And waited in a row.

"The time has come," the Walrus said,
    "To talk of many things:

Of shoes – and ships – and sealing wax –
    Of cabbages – and kings –
And why the sea is boiling hot –
    And whether pigs have wings."

"But wait a bit," the Oysters cried,
    "Before we have our chat;
For some of us are out of breath,
    And all of us are fat!"
"No hurry!" said the Carpenter.
    They thanked him much for that.

"A loaf of bread," the Walrus said,
    "Is what we chiefly need:

Pepper and vinegar besides
　　Are very good indeed –
Now if you're ready, Oysters dear,
　　We can begin to feed."

"But not on us!" the Oysters cried,
　　Turning a little blue,
"After such kindness, that would be
　　A dismal thing to do!"
"The night is fine," the Walrus said.
　　"Do you admire the view?"

"It was so kind of you to come!
　　And you are very nice!"
The Carpenter said nothing but
　　"Cut us another slice:
I wish you were not quite so deaf –
　　I've had to ask you twice!"

"It seems a shame," the Walrus said,
　　"To play them such a trick,
After we've brought them out so far,
　　And made them trot so quick!"
The Carpenter said nothing but
　　"The butter's spread too thick!"

"I weep for you," the Walrus said,
　"I deeply sympathize."
With sobs and tears he sorted out
　Those of the largest size,
Holding his pocket-handkerchief
　Before his streaming eyes.

"O Oysters," said the Carpenter.
　"You've had a pleasant run!
Shall we be trotting home again?"
　But answer came there none –
And this was scarcely odd, because
　They'd eaten every one.'

'I like the Walrus best,' said Alice: 'because you see he was a *little* sorry for the poor oysters.'

'He ate more than the Carpenter, though,' said Tweedledee. 'You see he held his handkerchief in front, so that the Carpenter couldn't count how many he took: contrariwise.'

'That was mean!' Alice said indignantly. 'Then I like the Carpenter best – if he didn't eat so many as the Walrus.'

'But he ate as many as he could get,' said Tweedledum.

This was a puzzler. After a pause, Alice began, 'Well! They were *both* very unpleasant characters –' Here she checked herself in some alarm, at hearing something that sounded to her like the puffing of a large steam-engine in the wood near them, though she feared it was more likely to be a wild beast. 'Are there any lions or tigers about here?' she asked timidly.

'It's only the Red King snoring,' said Tweedledee.

'Come and look at him!' the brothers cried, and they took each one of Alice's hands, and led her up to where the King was sleeping.

'Isn't he a *lovely* sight?' said Tweedledum.

Alice couldn't say honestly that he was. He had a tall red night-cap on, with a tassel, and he was lying crumpled up into a sort of untidy heap, and snoring loud

– 'fit to snore his head off!' as Tweedledum remarked.

'I'm afraid he'll catch cold with lying on the damp grass,' said Alice, who was a very thoughtful little girl.

'He's dreaming now,' said Tweedledee: 'and what do you think he's dreaming about?'

Alice said 'Nobody can guess that.'

'Why, about *you*!' Tweedledee exclaimed, clapping his hands triumphantly. 'And if he left off dreaming about you, where do you suppose you'd be?'

'Where I am now, of course,' said Alice.

'Not you!' Tweedledee retorted contemptuously. 'You'd be nowhere. Why, you're only a sort of thing in his dream!'

'If that there King was to wake,' added Tweedledum, 'you'd go out – bang! – just like a candle!'

'I shouldn't!' Alice exclaimed indignantly. 'Besides, if *I'm* only a sort of thing in his dream, what are *you*, I should like to know?'

'Ditto,' said Tweedledum.

'Ditto, ditto!' cried Tweedledee.

He shouted this so loud that Alice couldn't help saying, 'Hush! You'll be waking him, I'm afraid, if you make so much noise.'

'Well, it's no use *your* talking about waking him,' said Tweedledum, 'when you're only one of the things in his dream. You know very well you're not real.'

'I *am* real!' said Alice, and began to cry.

'You won't make yourself a bit realler by crying,' Tweedledee remarked: 'there's nothing to cry about.'

'If I wasn't real,' Alice said – half-laughing through her tears, it all seemed so ridiculous – 'I shouldn't be able to cry.'

'I hope you don't suppose those are real tears?' Tweedledum interrupted in a tone of great contempt.

'I know they're talking nonsense,' Alice thought to herself: 'and it's foolish to cry about it.' So she brushed away her tears, and went on as cheerfully as she could, 'At any rate I'd better be getting out of the wood, for really it's coming on very dark. Do you think it's going to rain?'

Tweedledum spread a large umbrella over himself

and his brother, and looked up into it. 'No, I don't think it is,' he said: 'at least – not under *here*. Nohow.'

'But it may rain *outside*?'

'It may – if it chooses,' said Tweedledee: 'we've no objection. Contrariwise.'

'Selfish things!' thought Alice, and she was just going to say 'Good-night' and leave them, when Tweedledum sprang out from under the umbrella, and seized her by the wrist.

'Do you see *that*?' he said, in a voice choking with passion, and his eyes grew large and yellow all in a moment, as he pointed with a trembling finger at a small white thing lying under the tree.

'It's only a rattle,' Alice said, after a careful examination of the little white thing. 'Not a rattle-*snake*, you know,' she added hastily, thinking that he was frightened: 'only an old rattle – quite old and broken.'

'I knew it was!' cried Tweedledum, beginning to stamp about wildly and tear his hair. 'It's spoilt, of course!' Here he looked at Tweedledee, who immediately sat down on the ground, and tried to hide himself under the umbrella.

Alice laid her hand upon his arm, and said in a soothing tone, 'You needn't be so angry about an old rattle.'

'But it isn't old!' Tweedledum cried, in a greater fury

than ever. 'It's new, I tell you – I bought it yesterday – my nice new RATTLE!' and his voice rose to a perfect scream.

All this time Tweedledee was trying his best to fold up the umbrella, with himself in it: which was such an extraordinary thing to do, that it quite took off Alice's attention from the angry brother. But he couldn't quite succeed, and it ended in his rolling over, bundled up in the umbrella, with only his head out: and there he lay, opening and shutting his mouth and his large eyes – 'looking more like a fish than anything else,' Alice thought.

'Of course you agree to have a battle?' Tweedledum said in a calmer tone.

'I suppose so,' the other sulkily replied, as he crawled out of the umbrella: 'only *she* must help us to dress up, you know.'

So the two brothers went off hand-in-hand into the wood, and returned in a minute with their arms full of things – such as bolsters, blankets, hearth-rugs, table-cloths, dish-covers and coal-scuttles. 'I hope you're a good hand at pinning and tying strings?' Tweedledum remarked. 'Every one of these things has got to go on, somehow or other.'

Alice said afterwards she had never seen such a fuss made about anything in all her life – the way those two bustled about – and the quantity of things they put on – and the trouble they gave her in tying strings and fastening buttons – 'Really they'll be more like bundles of old clothes than anything else, by the time they're ready!' she said to herself, as she arranged a bolster round the neck of Tweedledee, 'to keep his head from being cut off,' as he said.

'You know,' he added very gravely, 'it's one of the most serious things that can possibly happen to one in a battle – to get one's head cut off.'

Alice laughed loud: but she managed to turn it into a cough, for fear of hurting his feelings.

'Do I look very pale?' said Tweedledum, coming up to have his helmet tied on. (He *called* it a helmet, though it certainly looked much more like a saucepan.)

'Well – yes – a *little*,' Alice replied gently.

'I'm very brave generally,' he went on in a low voice: 'only today I happen to have a headache.'

'And *I've* got a toothache!' said Tweedledee, who had overheard the remark. 'I'm far worse than you!'

'Then you'd better not fight today,' said Alice thinking it a good opportunity to make peace.

'We *must* have a bit of a fight, but I don't care about going on long,' said Tweedledum. 'What's the time now?'

Tweedledee looked at his watch, and said 'Half-past four.'

'Let's fight till six, and then have dinner,' said Tweedledum.

'Very well,' the other said, rather sadly: 'and *she* can watch us – only you'd better not come *very* close,' he added: 'I generally hit everything I can see – when I get really excited.'

'And *I* hit everything within reach,' cried Tweedledum, 'whether I can see it or not.'

Alice laughed. 'You must hit the *trees* pretty often, I should think,' she said.

Tweedledum looked round him with a satisfied smile. 'I don't suppose,' he said, 'there'll be a tree left standing, for ever so far round, by the time we've finished!'

'And all about a rattle!' said Alice still hoping to make them a *little* ashamed of fighting for such a trifle.

'I shouldn't have minded it so much,' said Tweedledum, 'if it hadn't been a new one.'

'I wish the monstrous crow would come!' thought Alice.

'There's only one sword, you know,' Tweedledum said to his brother: 'but you can have the umbrella – it's quite as sharp. Only we must begin quick. It's getting as dark as it can.'

'And darker,' said Tweedledee.

It was getting dark so suddenly that Alice thought there must be a thunderstorm coming on. 'What a thick black cloud that is!' she said. 'And how fast it comes! Why, I do believe it's got wings!'

'It's the crow!' Tweedledum cried out in a shrill voice of alarm: and the two brothers took to their heels and were out of sight in a moment.

Alice ran a little way into the wood, and stopped under a large tree. 'It can never get at me *here*,' she thought: 'it's far too large to squeeze itself in among the trees. But I wish it wouldn't flap its wings so – it makes quite a hurricane in the wood – here's somebody's shawl being blown away!'

5

Wool and Water

SHE caught the shawl as she spoke, and looked about for the owner: in another moment the White Queen came running wildly through the wood, with both arms stretched out wide, as if she were flying, and Alice very civilly went to meet her with the shawl.

'I'm very glad I happened to be in the way,' Alice said, as she helped her to put on her shawl again.

The White Queen only looked at her in a helpless frightened sort of way, and kept repeating something in a whisper to herself that sounded like 'Bread-and-butter, bread-and butter,' and Alice felt that if there was to be any conversation at all, she must manage it herself. So she began rather timidly: 'Am I addressing the White Queen?'

'Well, yes, if you call that a-dressing,' the Queen said.

'It isn't *my* notion of the thing, at all.'

Alice thought it would never do to have an argument at the very beginning of their conversation, so she smiled and said, 'If your Majesty will only tell me the right way to begin, I'll do it as well as I can.'

'But I don't want it done at all!' groaned the poor Queen. 'I've been a-dressing myself for the last two hours.'

It would have been all the better, as it seemed to Alice, if she had got some one else to dress her, she was so dreadfully untidy. 'Every single thing's crooked,' Alice thought to herself, 'and she's all over pins! – May I put your shawl straight for you?' she added aloud.

'I don't know what's the matter with it!' the Queen said, in a melancholy voice. 'It's out of temper, I think. I've pinned it here, and I've pinned it there, but there's no pleasing it!'

'It *can't* go straight, you know, if you pin it all on one side,' Alice said, as she gently put it right for her; 'and, dear me, what a state your hair is in!'

'The brush has got entangled in it!' the Queen said with a sigh. 'And I lost the comb yesterday.'

Alice carefully released the brush, and did her best to get the hair into order. 'Come, you look rather better now!' she said, after altering most of the pins. 'But really you should have a lady's-maid!'

'I'm sure I'll take you with pleasure!' the Queen said. 'Twopence a week, and jam every other day.'

Alice couldn't help laughing, as she said, 'I don't want you to hire *me* – and I don't care for jam.'

'It's very good jam,' said the Queen.

'Well, I don't want any *today*, at any rate.'

'You couldn't have if it you *did* want it,' the Queen said. 'The rule is, jam tomorrow and jam yesterday – but never jam today.'

'It *must* come sometimes to "jam today,"' Alice objected.

'No, it can't,' said the Queen. 'It's jam every other day: today isn't any *other* day, you know.'

'I don't understand you,' said Alice. 'It's dreadfully confusing!'

'That's the effect of living backwards,' the Queen said kindly: 'it always makes one a little giddy at first –'

'Living backwards!' Alice repeated in great astonishment. 'I never heard of such a thing!'

'– but there's one great advantage in it, that one's memory works both ways.'

'I'm sure *mine* only works one way,' Alice remarked. 'I can't remember things before they happen.'

'It's a poor sort of memory that only works backwards,' the Queen remarked.

'What sorts of things do *you* remember best?' Alice ventured to ask.

'Oh, things that happened the week after next,' the Queen replied in a careless tone. 'For instance, now,' she went on, sticking a large piece of plaster on her finger as she spoke, 'there's the King's Messenger. He's in prison now, being punished; and the trial doesn't even begin till next Wednesday: and of course the crime comes last of all.'

'Suppose he never commits the crime?' said Alice.

'That would be all the better, wouldn't it?' the Queen said, as she bound the plaster round her finger with a bit of ribbon.

Alice felt there was no denying *that*. 'Of course it would be all the better,' she said: 'but it wouldn't be all the better his being punished.'

'You're wrong *there*, at any rate,' said the Queen: 'were *you* ever punished?'

'Only for faults,' said Alice.

'And you were all the better for it, I know!' the Queen said triumphantly.

'Yes, but then I *had* done the things I was punished for,' said Alice: 'that makes all the difference.'

'But if you *hadn't* done them,' the Queen said, 'that would have been better still; better, and better, and better!' Her voice went higher with each 'better,' till it got quite to a squeak at last.

Alice was just beginning to say 'There's a mistake somewhere –', when the Queen began screaming so loud that she had to leave the sentence unfinished. 'Oh, oh, oh!' shouted the Queen, shaking her hand about as if she wanted to shake it off. 'My finger's bleeding! Oh, oh, oh, oh!'

Her screams were so exactly like the whistle of a steam-engine, that Alice had to hold both her hands over her ears.

'What is the matter?' she said, as soon as there was a chance of making herself heard. 'Have you pricked your finger?'

'I haven't pricked it *yet*,' the Queen said, 'but I soon shall – oh, oh, oh!'

'When do you expect to do it?' Alice asked, feeling very much inclined to laugh.

'When I fasten my shawl again,' the poor Queen groaned out: 'the brooch will come undone directly. Oh, oh!' As she said the words the brooch flew open, and the Queen clutched wildly at it, and tried to clasp it again.

'Take care!' cried Alice. 'You're holding it all crooked!' And she caught at the brooch: but it was too late: the pin had slipped, and the Queen had pricked her finger.

'That accounts for the bleeding, you see,' she said to Alice with a smile. 'Now you understand the way things happen here.'

'But why don't you scream now?' Alice asked, holding her hands ready to put over her ears again.

'Why, I've done all the screaming already,' said the Queen. 'What would be the good of having it all over again?'

By this time it was getting light. 'The crow must have flown away, I think,' said Alice: 'I'm so glad it's gone. I thought it was the night coming on.'

'I wish *I* could manage to be glad!' the Queen said. 'Only I never can remember the rule. You must be very happy, living in this wood, and being glad whenever you like!'

'Only it is so *very* lonely here!' Alice said in a melancholy voice; and at the thought of her loneliness two large tears came rolling down her cheeks.

'Oh, don't go on like that!' cried the poor Queen, wringing her hands in despair. 'Consider what a great girl you are. Consider what a long way you've come today. Consider what o'clock it is. Consider anything, only don't cry!'

Alice could not help laughing at this, even in the midst of her tears. 'Can *you* keep from crying by considering things?' she asked.

'That's the way it's done,' the Queen said with great decision: 'nobody can do two things at once, you know. Let's consider your age to begin with – how old are you?'

'I'm seven and a half exactly.'

'You needn't say "exactually,"' the Queen remarked: 'I can believe it without that. Now I'll give *you* something to believe. I'm just one hundred and one, five months and a day.'

'I can't believe *that!*' said Alice.

'Can't you?' the Queen said in a pitying tone. 'Try again: draw a long breath, and shut your eyes.'

Alice laughed. 'There's no use trying,' she said: 'one *can't* believe impossible things.'

'I daresay you haven't had much practice,' said the Queen. 'When I was your age, I always did it for half-an-hour a day. Why, sometimes I've believed as many as six impossible things before breakfast. There goes the shawl again!'

The brooch had come undone as she spoke, and a sudden gust of wind blew the Queen's shawl across a little brook. The Queen spread out her arms again, and went flying after it, and this time she succeeded in catching it for herself. 'I've got it!' she cried in a triumphant tone. 'Now you shall see me pin it on again, all by myself!'

'Then I hope your finger is better now?' Alice said very politely, as she crossed the little brook after the Queen.

*   *   *   *
    *   *   *
*   *   *   *

'Oh, much better!' cried the Queen, her voice rising into a squeak as she went on. 'Much be-etter! Be-etter! Be-e-e-etter! Be-e-ehh!' The last word ended in a long bleat, so like a sheep that Alice quite started.

She looked at the Queen, who seemed to have suddenly wrapped herself up in wool. Alice rubbed her eyes, and looked again. She couldn't make out what had happened at all. Was she in a shop? And was that really – was it really a *sheep* that was sitting on the other side of the counter? Rub as she would, she could make nothing more of it: she was in a little dark shop, leaning with her elbows on the counter, and opposite to her was an old Sheep, sitting in an arm-chair knitting, and every now and then leaving off to look at her through a great pair of spectacles.

'What is it you want to buy?' the Sheep said at last, looking up for a moment from her knitting.

'I don't *quite* know yet,' Alice said, very gently. 'I should like to look all round me first, if I might.'

'You may look in front of you, and on both sides, if you like,' said the Sheep: 'but you can't look *all* round you – unless you've got eyes at the back of your head.'

But these, as it happened, Alice had *not* got: so she contented herself with turning round, looking at the shelves as she came to them.

The shop seemed to be full of all manner of curious things – but the oddest part of it all was, that whenever she looked hard at any shelf, to make out exactly what it had on it, that particular shelf was always quite empty: though the others round it were crowded as full as they could hold.

'Things flow about so here!' she said at last in a plaintive tone, after she had spent a minute or so in vainly pursuing a large bright thing, that looked sometimes like a doll and sometimes like a work-box, and was always in the shelf next above the one she was looking at. 'And this one is the most provoking of all – but I'll tell you what –' she added, as a sudden thought struck her, 'I'll follow it up to the very top shelf of all. It'll puzzle it to go through the ceiling, I expect!'

But even this plan failed: the 'thing' went through the ceiling as quietly as possible, as if it were quite used to it.

'Are you a child or a teetotum?' the Sheep said, as she took up another pair of needles. 'You'll make me giddy soon, if you go on turning round like that.' She was now working with fourteen pairs at once, and Alice couldn't help looking at her in great astonishment.

'How *can* she knit with so many?' the puzzled child thought to herself. 'She gets more and more like a porcupine every minute!'

'Can you row?' the Sheep asked, handing her a pair of knitting-needles as she spoke.

'Yes, a little – but not on land – and not with needles –' Alice was beginning to say, when suddenly the needles turned into oars in her hands, and she found they were in a little boat, gliding along between banks: so there was nothing for it but to do her best.

'Feather!' cried the Sheep, as she took up another pair of needles.

This didn't sound like a remark that needed any answer, so Alice said nothing, but pulled away. There was something very queer about the water, she thought, as every now and then the oars got fast in it, and would hardly come out again.

'Feather! Feather!' the Sheep cried again, taking more needles. 'You'll be catching a crab directly.'

'A dear little crab!' thought Alice. 'I should like that.'

'Didn't you hear me say "Feather"?' the Sheep cried angrily, taking up quite a bunch of needles.

'Indeed I did,' said Alice: 'you've said it very often – and very loud. Please, where *are* the crabs?'

'In the water, of course!' said the Sheep, sticking

some of the needles into her hair, as her hands were full. 'Feather, I say!'

'*Why* do you say "Feather" so often?' Alice asked at last, rather vexed. 'I'm not a bird!'

'You are,' said the Sheep: 'You're a little goose.'

This offended Alice a little, so there was no more conversation for a minute or two, while the boat glided gently on, sometimes among beds of weeds (which made the oars stick fast in the water, worse than ever), and sometimes under trees, but always with the same tall riverbanks frowning over their heads.

'Oh, please! There are some scented rushes!' Alice cried in a sudden transport of delight. 'There really are – and *such* beauties!'

'You needn't say "please" to *me* about 'em,' the Sheep said, without looking up from her knitting: 'I didn't put 'em there, and I'm not going to take 'em away.'

'No, but I meant – please, may we wait and pick some?' Alice pleaded. 'If you don't mind stopping the boat for a minute.'

'How am *I* to stop it?' said the Sheep. 'If you leave off rowing, it'll stop of itself.'

So the boat was left to drift down the stream as it would, till it glided gently in among the waving rushes. And then the little sleeves were carefully rolled up, and the little arms were plunged in elbow-deep, to get hold of the rushes a good long way down before breaking them off – and for a while Alice forgot all about the Sheep and the knitting, as she bent over the side of the boat, with just the ends of her tangled hair dipping in the water – while with bright eager eyes she caught at one bunch after another of the darling scented rushes.

'I only hope the boat won't tipple over!' she said to

herself. 'Oh, *what* a lovely one! Only I couldn't quite reach it.' And it certainly *did* seem a little provoking ('almost as if it happened on purpose,' she thought) that, though she managed to pick plenty of beautiful rushes as the boat glided by, there was always a more lovely one that she couldn't reach.

'The prettiest are always further!' she said at last, with a sigh at the obstinacy of the rushes in growing so far off, as, with flushed cheeks and dripping hair and hands, she scrambled back into her place, and began to arrange her new-found treasures.

What mattered it to her just then that the rushes had begun to fade, and to lose all their scent and beauty, from the very moment that she picked them? Even real scented rushes, you know, last only a very little while – and these, being dream-rushes, melted away almost like snow, as they lay in heaps at her feet – but Alice hardly noticed this, there were so many other curious things to think about.

They hadn't gone much farther before the blade of one of the oars got fast in the water and *wouldn't* come out again (so Alice explained it afterwards), and the consequence was that the handle of it caught her under the chin, and, in spite of a series of little shrieks of 'Oh, oh, oh!' from poor Alice, it swept her straight off the seat, and down among the heap of rushes.

However, she wasn't a bit hurt, and was soon up again: the Sheep went on with her knitting all the while, just as if nothing had happened. 'That was a nice crab you caught!' she remarked, as Alice got back into her place, very much relieved to find herself still in the boat.

'Was it? I didn't see it,' said Alice, peeping cautiously over the side of the boat into the dark water. 'I wish it hadn't let go – I should so like a little crab to take home with me!' But the Sheep only laughed scornfully, and went on with her knitting.

'Are there many crabs here?' said Alice.

'Crabs, and all sorts of things,' said the Sheep: 'plenty of choice, only make up your mind. Now, what *do* you want to buy?'

'To buy!' Alice echoed in a tone that was half astonished and half frightened – for the oars, and the boat, and the river, had vanished all in a moment, and she was back again in the little dark shop.

'I should like to buy an egg, please,' she said timidly. 'How do you sell them?'

'Fivepence farthing for one – twopence for two,' the Sheep replied.

'Then two are cheaper than one?' Alice said in a surprised tone, taking out her purse.

'Only you *must* eat them both, if you buy two,' said the Sheep.

'Then I'll have *one* please,' said Alice, as she put the money down on the counter. For she thought to herself, 'They mightn't be at all nice, you know.'

The Sheep took the money, and put it away in a box: then she said 'I never put things into people's hands – that would never do – you must get it for yourself.' And so saying, she went off to the other end of the shop, and set the egg upright on a shelf.

'I wonder *why* it wouldn't do?' thought Alice, as she groped her way among the tables and chairs, for the shop was very dark towards the end. 'The egg seems to get further away the more I walk towards it. Let me see, is this a chair? Why, it's got branches, I declare! How very odd to find trees growing here! And actually here's a little brook! Well, this is the very queerest shop I ever saw!'

So she went on, wondering more and more at every step, as everything turned into a tree the moment she came up to it, and she quite expected the egg to do the same.

6

Humpty Dumpty

HOWEVER, the egg only got larger and larger, and more and more human: when she had come within a few yards of it, she saw that it had eyes and a nose and mouth; and when she had come close to it, she saw clearly that it was HUMPTY DUMPTY himself. 'It can't be anybody else!' she said to herself. 'I'm as certain of it, as if his name were written all over his face.'

It might have been written a hundred times, easily, on that enormous face. Humpty Dumpty was sitting with his legs crossed, like a lurk, on the top of a high wall – such a narrow one that Alice quite wondered how he could keep his balance – and, as his eyes were steadily fixed in the opposite direction, and he didn't take the least notice of her, she thought he must be a stuffed figure after all.

'And how exactly like an egg he is!' she said aloud, standing with her hands ready to catch him, for she was every moment expecting him to fall.

'It's *very* provoking,' Humpty Dumpty said after a long silence, looking away from Alice as he spoke, 'to be called an egg – *very!*'

'I said you *looked* like an egg, Sir,' Alice gently explained. 'And some eggs are very pretty, you know,' she added, hoping to turn her remark into a sort of compliment.

'Some people,' said Humpty Dumpty, looking away from her as usual, 'have no more sense than a baby!'

Alice didn't know what to say to this: it wasn't at all like conversation, she thought, as he never said anything to *her*; in fact, his last remark was evidently addressed to a tree – so she stood and softly repeated to herself:–

> '*Humpty Dumpty sat on a wall:*
> *Humpty Dumpty had a great fall.*
> *All the King's horses and all the King's men*
> *Couldn't put Humpty Dumpty in his place again.*'

'That last line is much too long for the poetry,' she added, almost out loud, forgetting that Humpty Dumpty would hear her.

'Don't stand chattering to yourself like that,' Humpty

Dumpty said, looking at her for the first time, 'but tell me your name and your business.'

'My *name* is Alice, but –'

'It's a stupid name enough!' Humpty Dumpty interrupted impatiently. 'What does it mean?'

'*Must* a name mean something?' Alice asked doubtfully.

'Of course it must,' Humpty Dumpty said with a short laugh: '*my* name means the shape I am – and a good handsome shape it is, too. With a name like yours, you might be any shape, almost.'

'Why do you sit out here all alone?' said Alice, not wishing to begin an argument.

'Why, because there's nobody with me!' cried Humpty Dumpty. 'Did you think I didn't know the answer to *that*? Ask another.'

'Don't you think you'd be safer down on the ground?' Alice went on, not with any idea of making another riddle, but simply in her good-natured anxiety for the queer creature. 'That wall is so *very* narrow!'

'What tremendously easy riddles you ask!' Humpty Dumpty growled out. 'Of course I don't think so! Why, if ever I *did* fall off – which there's no chance of – but *if* I did –' Here he pursed up his lips and looked so solemn and grand that Alice could hardly help laughing. '*If* I did fall,' he went on, '*the King has promised me* – ah, you may turn pale, if you like! You didn't think I was going to say that, did you? *The King has promised me – with his very own mouth* to – to –'

'To send all his horses and all his men,' Alice interrupted, rather unwisely.

'Now I declare that's too bad!' Humpty Dumpty cried, breaking into a sudden passion. 'You've been listening at doors – and behind trees – and down chimneys – or you couldn't have known it!'

'I haven't, indeed!' Alice said very gently. 'It's in a book.'

'Ah, well! They may write such things in a *book*,' Humpty Dumpty said in a calmer tone. 'That's what you call a History of England, that is. Now, take a good look at me! I'm one that has spoken to a King, *I* am: mayhap you'll never see such another: and to show you I'm not proud, you may shake hands with me!' And he grinned almost from ear to ear, as he leant forwards (and as nearly as possible fell off the wall in doing so) and offered Alice his hand. She watched him a little anxiously as she took it. 'If he smiled much more, the ends of his mouth might meet behind,' she thought: 'and then I don't know what would happen to his head! I'm afraid it would come off!'

'Yes, all his horses and all his men,' Humpty Dumpty went on. 'They'd pick me up again in a minute, *they* would! However, this conversation is going on a little too fast: let's go back to the last remark but one.'

'I'm afraid I can't quite remember it,' Alice said very politely.

'In that case we start fresh,' said Humpty Dumpty, 'and it's my turn to choose a subject —' ('He talks about it just as if it was a game!' thought Alice.) 'So here's a question for you. How old did you say you were?'

Alice made a short calculation, and said 'Seven years and six months.'

'Wrong!' Humpty Dumpty exclaimed triumphantly. 'You never said a word like it!'

'I thought you meant "How old *are* you?"' Alice explained.

'If I'd meant that, I'd have said it,' said Humpty Dumpty.

Alice didn't want to begin another argument, so she said nothing.

'Seven years and six months!' Humpty Dumpty repeated thoughtfully. 'An uncomfortable sort of age. Now if you'd asked *my* advice, I'd have said "Leave off at seven" – but it's too late now.'

'I never ask advice about growing,' Alice said indignantly.

'Too proud?' the other enquired.

Alice felt even more indignant at this suggestion. 'I mean,' she said, 'that one can't help growing older.'

'*One* can't, perhaps,' said Humpty Dumpty, 'but *two* can. With proper assistance, you might have left off at seven.'

'What a beautiful belt you've got on!' Alice suddenly remarked. (They had had quite enough of the subject of age, she thought: and if they really were to take turns in choosing subjects, it was her turn now.) 'At least,' she corrected herself on second thoughts, 'a beautiful cravat, I should have said – no, a belt, I mean – I beg your pardon!' she added in dismay, for Humpty Dumpty looked thoroughly offended, and she began to wish she hadn't chosen that subject. 'If only I knew,' she thought to herself, 'which was neck and which was waist!'

Evidently Humpty Dumpty was very angry, though he said nothing for a minute or two. When he *did* speak again, it was in a deep growl.

'It is a – *most* – *provoking* – thing,' he said at last, 'when a person doesn't know a cravat from a belt!'

'I know it's very ignorant of me,' Alice said, in so humble a tone that Humpty Dumpty relented.

'It's a cravat, child, and a beautiful one, as you say. It's a present from the White King and Queen. There now!'

'Is it really?' said Alice, quite pleased to find that she *had* chosen a good subject, after all.

'They gave it me,' Humpty Dumpty continued thoughtfully, as he crossed one knee over the other and clasped his hands round it, 'they gave it me – for an un-birthday present.'

'I beg your pardon?' Alice said with a puzzled air.

'I'm not offended,' said Humpty Dumpty.

'I mean, what *is* an un-birthday present?'

'A present given when it isn't your birthday, of course.'

Alice considered a little. 'I like birthday presents best,' she said at last.

'You don't know what you're talking about!' cried Humpty Dumpty. 'How many days are there in a year?'

'Three hundred and sixty-five,' said Alice.

'And how many birthdays have you?'

'One.'

'And if you take one from three hundred and sixty-five, what remains?'

'Three hundred and sixty-four, of course.'

Humpty Dumpty looked doubtful. 'I'd rather see that done on paper,' he said.

Alice couldn't help smiling as she took out her memorandum-book, and worked the sum for him:

$$\begin{array}{r} 365 \\ \underline{1} \\ \underline{364} \end{array}$$

Humpty Dumpty took the book, and looked at it carefully. 'That seems to be done right –' he began.

'You're holding it upside down!' Alice interrupted.

'To be sure I was!' Humpty Dumpty said gaily, as she turned it round for him. 'I thought it looked a little queer. As I was saying, that *seems* to be done right –

though I haven't time to look it over thoroughly just now – and that shows that there are three hundred and sixty-four days when you might get un-birthday presents –'

'Certainly,' said Alice.

'And only *one* for birthday presents, you know. There's glory for you!'

'I don't know what you mean by "glory,"' Alice said.

Humpty Dumpty smiled contemptuously. 'Of course you don't – till I tell you. I meant "there's a nice knock-down argument for you!"'

'But "glory" doesn't mean "a nice knock-down argument,"' Alice objected.

'When *I* use a word,' Humpty Dumpty said in rather a scornful tone, 'it means just what I choose it to mean – neither more nor less.'

'The question is,' said Alice, 'whether you *can* make words mean so many different things.'

'The question is,' said Humpty Dumpty, 'which is to be master – that's all.'

Alice was too much puzzled to say anything, so after a minute Humpty Dumpty began again. 'They've a temper, some of them – particularly verbs, they're the proudest – adjectives you can do anything with, but not verbs – however, *I* can manage the whole lot of them! Impenetrability! That's what *I* say!'

'Would you tell me, please,' said Alice, 'what that means?'

'Now you talk like a reasonable child,' said Humpty Dumpty, looking very much pleased. 'I meant by "impenetrability" that we've had enough of that subject, and it would be just as well if you'd mention what you mean to do next, as I suppose you don't mean to stop here all the rest of your life.'

'That's a great deal to make one word mean,' Alice said in a thoughtful tone.

'When I make a word do a lot of work like that,' said Humpty Dumpty, 'I always pay it extra.'

'Oh!' said Alice. She was too much puzzled to make any other remark.

'Ah, you should see 'em come round me of a Saturday night,' Humpty Dumpty went on, wagging his head gravely from side to side: 'for to get their wages, you know.'

(Alice didn't venture to ask what he paid them with; and so you see I can't tell *you*.)

'You seem very clever at explaining words, Sir,' said Alice. 'Would you kindly tell me the meaning of the poem called "Jabberwocky"?'

'Let's hear it,' said Humpty Dumpty. 'I can explain all the poems that ever were invented – and a good many that haven't been invented just yet.'

This sounded very hopeful, so Alice repeated the first verse:

> ''Twas brillig, and the slithy toves
>   Did gyre and gimble in the wabe:
> All mimsy were the borogoves,
>   And the mome raths outgrabe.'

'That's enough to begin with,' Humpty Dumpty interrupted: 'there are plenty of hard words there. "*Brillig*" means four o'clock in the afternoon – the time when you begin *broiling* things for dinner.'

'That'll do very well,' said Alice: 'and "*slithy*"?'

'Well, "*slithy*" means "lithe and slimy." "Lithe" is the same as "active." You see it's like a portmanteau – there are two meanings packed up into one word.'

'I see it now,' Alice remarked thoughtfully: 'and what are "*toves*"?'

'Well, "toves" are something like badgers – they're something like lizards – and they're something like corkscrews.'

'They must be very curious-looking creatures.'

'They are that,' said Humpty Dumpty: 'also they make their nests under sun-dials – also they live on cheese.'

'And what's to "*gyre*" and to "*gimble*"?'

'To "*gyre*" is to go round and round like a gyroscope.
To "*gimble*" is to make holes like a gimblet.'

'And "*the wabe*" is the grass-plot round a sun-dial I
suppose?' said Alice, surprised at her own ingenuity.

'Of course it is. It's called "*wabe*" you know, because
it goes a long way before it, and a long way behind it –'

'And a long way beyond it on each side,' Alice added.

'Exactly so. Well then, "*mimsy*" is "flimsy and miserable" (there's another portmanteau for you). And a "*borogove*" is a thin shabby-looking bird with its feathers sticking out all round – something like a live mop.'

'And then "*mome raths*"?' said Alice. 'I'm afraid I'm giving you a great deal of trouble.'

'Well, a "*rath*" is a sort of green pig: but "*mome*" I'm not certain about. I think it's short for "from home" – meaning that they'd lost their way, you know.'

'And what does "*outgrabe*" mean?'

'Well, "*outgribing*" is something between bellowing and whistling, with a kind of sneeze in the middle: however, you'll hear it done, maybe – down in the wood yonder – and when you've once heard it you'll be *quite* content. Who's been repeating all that hard stuff to you?'

'I read it in a book,' said Alice. 'But I had some poetry repeated to me, much easier than that, by – Tweedledee, I think it was.'

'As to poetry, you know,' said Humpty Dumpty, stretching out one of his great hands, '*I* can repeat poetry as well as other folk, if it comes to that –'

'Oh, it needn't come to that!' Alice hastily said, hoping to keep him from beginning.

'The piece I'm going to repeat,' he went on without noticing her remark, 'was written entirely for your amusement.'

Alice felt that in that case she really *ought* to listen to it, so she sat down, and said 'Thank you' rather sadly.

> *'In winter, when the fields are white,*
> *I sing this song for your delight –*

only I don't sing it,' he added, as an explanation.

'I see you don't,' said Alice.

'If you can *see* whether I'm singing or not, you've sharper eyes than most,' Humpty Dumpty remarked severely. Alice was silent.

> *'In spring, when woods are getting green,*
> *I'll try and tell you what I mean.'*

'Thank you very much,' said Alice.

> *'In summer, when the days are long;*
> *Perhaps you'll understand the song:*
>
> *In autumn, when the leaves are brown,*
> *Take pen and ink, and write it down.*

'I will, if I can remember it so long,' said Alice.

'You needn't go on making remarks like that,' Humpty Dumpty said: 'they're not sensible, and they put me out.

> *'I sent a message to the fish:*
> *I told them "This is what I wish."*
>
> *The little fishes of the sea,*
> *They sent an answer back to me.*
>
> *The little fishes' answer was*
> *"We cannot do it, Sir, because —"'*

'I'm afraid I don't quite understand,' said Alice.

'It gets easier further on,' Humpty Dumpty replied.

> *'I sent to them again to say*
> *"It will be better to obey."*
>
> *The fishes answered with a grin,*
> *"Why, what a temper you are in!"*
>
> *I told them once, I told them twice:*
> *They would not listen to advice.*

I took a kettle large and new,
Fit for the deed I had to do.

My heart went hop, my heart went thump;
I filled the kettle at the pump.

Then some one came to me and said,
"The little fishes are in bed."

I said to him, I said it plain,
"Then you must wake them up again."

I said it very loud and clear;
I went and shouted in his ear.'

Humpty Dumpty raised his voice almost to a scream as he repeated this verse, and Alice thought with a shudder, 'I wouldn't have been the messenger for anything!'

'But he was very stiff and proud;
He said "You needn't shout so loud!"

And he was very proud and stiff;
He said "I'd go and wake them, if –"

I took a corkscrew from the shelf:
I went to wake them up myself.

275

And when I found the door was locked,
I pulled and pushed and kicked and knocked.

And when I found the door was shut,
I tried to turn the handle, but –'

There was a long pause.

'Is that all?' Alice timidly asked.

'That's all,' said Humpty Dumpty. 'Good-bye.'

This was rather sudden, Alice thought: but, after such

a *very* strong hint that she ought to be going, she felt that it would hardly be civil to stay. So she got up, and held out her hand. 'Good-bye, till we meet again!' she said as cheerfully as she could.

'I shouldn't know you again if we *did* meet,' Humpty Dumpty replied in a discontented tone, giving her one of his fingers to shake; 'you're so exactly like other people.'

'The face is what one goes by, generally,' Alice remarked in a thoughtful tone.

'That's just what I complain of,' said Humpty Dumpty. 'Your face is the same as everybody has – the two eyes, so –' (marking their places in the air with his thumb) 'nose in the middle, mouth under. It's always the same. Now if you had the two eyes on the same side of the nose, for instance – or the mouth at the top – that would be *some* help.'

'It wouldn't look nice,' Alice objected. But Humpty Dumpty only shut his eyes and said 'Wait till you've tried.'

Alice waited a minute to see if he would speak again, but as he never opened his eyes or took any further notice of her, she said 'Good-bye!' once more, and, getting no answer to this, she quietly walked away: but she couldn't help saying to herself as she went, 'Of all the unsatisfactory –' (she repeated this aloud, as it was a great comfort to have such a long word to say) 'of all the unsatisfactory people I *ever* met –' She never finished the sentence, for at this moment a heavy crash shook the forest from end to end.

The Lion and the Unicorn

THE next moment soldiers came running through the wood, at first in twos and threes, then ten or twenty together, and at last in such crowds that they seemed to fill the whole forest. Alice got behind a tree, for fear of being run over, and watched them go by.

She thought that in all her life she had never seen soldiers so uncertain on their feet: they were always tripping over something or other, and whenever one went down, several more always fell over him, so that the ground was soon covered with little heaps of men.

Then came the horses. Having four feet, these managed rather better than the foot-soldiers: but even *they* stumbled now and then; and it seemed to be a regular rule that, whenever a horse stumbled, the rider fell off instantly. The confusion got worse every moment, and Alice was very glad to get out of the wood into an open place, where she found the White King seated on the ground, busily writing in his memorandum-book.

'I've sent them all!' the King cried in a tone of delight, on seeing Alice. 'Did you happen to meet any soldiers, my dear, as you came through the wood?'

'Yes, I did,' said Alice: 'several thousand, I should think.'

'Four thousand two hundred and seven, that's the exact number,' the King said, referring to his book. 'I couldn't send all the horses, you know, because two of them are wanted in the game. And I haven't sent the two Messengers, either. They're both gone to the town. Just look along the road, and tell me if you can see either of them.'

'I see nobody on the road,' said Alice.

'I only wish *I* had such eyes,' the King remarked in a fretful tone. 'To be able to see Nobody! And at that distance too! Why, it's as much as *I* can do to see real people, by this light!'

All this was lost on Alice, who was still looking intently along the road, shading her eyes with one hand. 'I see somebody now!' she exclaimed at last. 'But he's coming very slowly – and what curious attitudes he goes into!' (For the Messenger kept skipping up and down, and wriggling like an eel, as he came along, with his great hands spread out like fans on each side.)

'Not at all,' said the King. 'He's an Anglo-Saxon Messenger – and those are Anglo-Saxon attitudes. He only does them when he's happy. His name is Haigha.' (He pronounced it so as to rhyme with 'mayor.')

'I love my love with an H,' Alice couldn't help

beginning, 'because he is Happy. I hate him with an H, because he is Hideous. I fed him with – with – with Ham sandwiches and Hay. His name is Haigha, and he lives –'

'He lives on the Hill,' the King remarked simply, without the least idea that he was joining in the game, while Alice was still hesitating for the name of a town beginning with H. 'The other Messenger's called Hatta. I must have *two*, you know – to come and go. One to come, and one to go.'

'I beg your pardon?' said Alice.

'It isn't respectable to beg,' said the King.

'I only meant that I didn't understand,' said Alice. 'Why one to come and one to go?'

'Don't I tell you?' the King repeated impatiently. 'I must have *two* – to fetch and carry. One to fetch, and one to carry.'

At this moment the Messenger arrived: he was far too much out of breath to say a word, and could only wave his hands about, and make the most fearful faces at the poor King.

'This young lady loves you with an H,' the King said, introducing Alice in the hope of turning off the Messenger's attention from himself – but it was no use – the Anglo-Saxon attitudes only got more extraordinary every moment, while the great eyes rolled wildly from side to side.

'You alarm me!' said the King. 'I feel faint – Give me a ham sandwich!'

On which the Messenger, to Alice's great amusement, opened a bag that hung round his neck, and handed a sandwich to the King, who devoured it greedily.

'Another sandwich!' said the King.

'There's nothing but hay left now,' the Messenger said, peeping into the bag.

'Hay, then,' the King murmured in a faint whisper.

Alice was glad to see that it revived him a good deal. 'There's nothing like eating hay when you're faint,' he remarked to her, as he munched away.

'I should think throwing cold water over you would be better,' Alice suggested: '– or some sal-volatile.'

'I didn't say there was nothing *better*,' the King replied. 'I said there was nothing *like* it.' Which Alice did not venture to deny.

'Who did you pass on the road?' the King went on, holding out his hand to the Messenger for some more hay.

'Nobody,' said the Messenger.

'Quite right,' said the King: 'this young lady saw him too. So of course Nobody walks slower than you.'

'I do my best,' the Messenger said in a sulky tone. 'I'm sure Nobody walks much faster than I do!'

'He can't do that,' said the King, 'or else he'd have been here first. However, now you've got your breath, you may tell us what's happened in the town.'

'I'll whisper it,' said the Messenger, putting his hands to his mouth in the shape of a trumpet, and stooping so as to get close to the King's ear. Alice was sorry for this, as she wanted to hear the news too. However, instead of whispering, he simply shouted at the top of his voice 'They're at it again!'

'Do you call *that* a whisper?' cried the poor King, jumping up and shaking himself. 'If you do such a thing again, I'll have you buttered! It went through and through my head like an earthquake!'

'It would have to be a very tiny earthquake!' thought Alice. 'Who are at it again?' she ventured to ask.

'Why, the Lion and the Unicorn, of course,' said the King.

'Fighting for the crown?'

'Yes, to be sure,' said the King: 'and the best of the joke is, that it's *my* crown all the while! Let's run and see them.' And they trotted off, Alice repeating to herself, as she ran, the words of the old song:

'The Lion and the Unicorn were fighting for the crown:
The Lion beat the Unicorn all round the town.

Some gave them white bread, some gave them brown;
Some gave them plum-cake and drummed them out of town.'

'Does – the one – that wins – get the crown?' she asked, as well as she could, for the run was putting her quite out of breath.

'Dear me, no!' said the King. 'What an idea!'

'Would you – be good enough,' Alice panted out, after running a little further, 'to stop a minute – just to get – one's breath again?'

'I'm *good* enough,' the King said, 'only I'm not strong

enough. You see, a minute goes by so fearfully quick. You might as well try to stop a Bandersnatch!'

Alice had no more breath for talking, so they trotted on in silence, till they came in sight of a great crowd, in the middle of which the Lion and Unicorn were fighting. They were in such a cloud of dust, that at first Alice could not make out which was which: but she soon managed to distinguish the Unicorn by his horn.

They placed themselves close to where Hatta, the other Messenger, was standing watching the fight, with a cup of tea in one hand and a piece of bread-and-butter in the other.

'He's only just out of prison, and he hadn't finished his tea when he was sent in,' Haigha whispered to Alice: 'and they only give them oyster-shells in there – so you see he's very hungry and thirsty. How are you, dear child?' he went on, putting his arm affectionately round Hatta's neck.

Hatta looked round and nodded, and went on with his bread-and-butter.

'Were you happy in prison, dear child?' said Haigha.

Hatta looked round once more, and this time a tear or two trickled down his cheek: but not a word would he say.

'Speak, can't you!' Haigha cried impatiently. But Hatta only munched away, and drank some more tea.

'Speak, won't you!' cried the King. 'How are they getting on with the fight?'

Hatta made a desperate effort, and swallowed a large piece of bread-and-butter. 'They're getting on very well,' he said in a choking voice: 'each of them has been down about eighty-seven times.'

'Then I suppose they'll soon bring the white bread and the brown?' Alice ventured to remark.

'It's waiting for 'em now,' said Hatta: 'This is a bit of it as I'm eating.'

There was a pause in the fight just then, and the Lion and the Unicorn sat down, panting, while the King called out 'Ten minutes allowed for refreshments!' Haigha and

Hatta set to work at once, carrying round trays of white and brown bread. Alice took a piece to taste, but it was *very* dry.

'I don't think they'll fight any more today,' the King said to Hatta: 'go and order the drums to begin.' And Hatta went bounding away like a grasshopper.

For a minute or two Alice stood silent, watching him. Suddenly she brightened up. 'Look, look!' she cried, pointing eagerly. 'There's the White Queen running across the country! She came flying out of the wood over yonder – How fast those Queens *can* run!'

'There's some enemy after her, no doubt,' the King said, without even looking round. 'That wood's full of them.'

'But aren't you going to run and help her?' Alice asked, very much surprised at his taking it so quietly.

'No use, no use!' said the King. 'She runs so fearfully quick. You might as well try to catch a Bandersnatch! But I'll make a memorandum about her, if you like – She's a dear good creature,' he repeated softly to himself, as he opened his memorandum-book. 'Do you spell "creature" with a double "e"?'

At this moment the Unicorn sauntered by them, with his hands in his pockets. 'I had the best of it this time?' he said to the King, just glancing at him as he passed.

'A little – a little,' the King replied, rather nervously. 'You shouldn't have run him through with your horn, you know.'

'It didn't hurt him,' the Unicorn said carelessly, and he was going on, when his eye happened to fall upon Alice: he turned round instantly, and stood for some time looking at her with an air of the deepest disgust.

'What – is – this?' he said at last.

'This is a child!' Haigha replied eagerly, coming in front of Alice to introduce her, and spreading out both his hands towards her in an Anglo-Saxon attitude. 'We only found it today. It's as large as life, and twice as natural!'

'I always thought they were fabulous monsters!' said the Unicorn. 'Is it alive?'

'It can talk,' said Haigha, solemnly.

The Unicorn looked dreamily at Alice, and said 'Talk, child.'

Alice could not help her lips curling up into a smile as she began: 'Do you know, I always thought Unicorns were fabulous monsters, too! I never saw one alive before!'

'Well, now that we *have* seen each other,' said the Unicorn, 'if you'll believe in me, I'll believe in you. Is that a bargain?'

'Yes, if you like,' said Alice.

'Come, fetch out the plum-cake, old man!' the Unicorn went on, turning from her to the King. 'None of your brown bread for me!'

'Certainly – certainly!' the King muttered, and beckoned to Haigha. 'Open the bag!' he whispered. 'Quick! Not that one – that's full of hay!'

Haigha took a large cake out of the bag, and gave it to Alice to hold, while he got out a dish and carving-knife. How they all came out of it Alice couldn't guess. It was just like a conjuring-trick, she thought.

The Lion had joined them while this was going on: he looked very tired and sleepy, and his eyes were half shut. 'What's this!' he said, blinking lazily at Alice, and speaking in a deep hollow tone that sounded like the tolling of a great bell.

'Ah, what *is* it, now?' the Unicorn cried eagerly. 'You'll never guess! *I* couldn't.'

The Lion looked at Alice wearily. 'Are you animal – or vegetable – or mineral?' he said, yawning at every other word.

'It's a fabulous monster!' the Unicorn cried out, before Alice could reply.

'Then hand round the plum-cake, Monster,' the Lion said, lying down and putting his chin on his paws. 'And sit down, both of you,' (to the King and the Unicorn): 'fair play with the cake, you know!'

The King was evidently very uncomfortable at having to sit down between the two great creatures; but there was no other place for him.

'What a fight we might have for the crown, now!' the Unicorn said, looking slyly up at the crown, which the poor King was nearly shaking off his head, he trembled so much.

'I should win easy,' said the Lion.

'I'm not so sure of that,' said the Unicorn.

'Why, I beat you all round the town, you chicken!' the Lion replied angrily, half getting up as he spoke.

Here the King interrupted, to prevent the quarrel going on: he was very nervous, and his voice quite quivered. 'All round the town?' he said. 'That's a good long way. Did you go by the old bridge, or the market-place? You get the best view by the old bridge.'

'I'm sure I don't know,' the Lion growled out as he lay down again. 'There was too much dust to see anything. What a time the Monster is, cutting up that cake!'

Alice had seated herself on the bank of a little brook, with the great dish on her knees, and was sawing very diligently with the knife. 'It's very provoking!' she said, in reply to the Lion (she was getting quite used to being called 'the Monster'). 'I've cut several slices already, but they always join on again!'

'You don't know how to manage Looking-glass cakes,' the Unicorn remarked. 'Hand it round first, and cut it afterwards.'

This sounded nonsense, but Alice very obediently got up, and carried the dish round, and the cake divided itself into three pieces as she did so. '*Now* cut it up,' said the Lion, as she returned to her place with the empty dish.

'I say, this isn't fair!' cried the Unicorn, as Alice sat with the knife in her hand, very much puzzled how to begin. 'The Monster has given the Lion twice as much as me.'

'She's kept none for herself, anyhow,' said the Lion. 'Do you like plum-cake, Monster?'

But before Alice could answer him, the drums began.

Where the noise came from, she couldn't make out: the air seemed full of it, and it rang through and through her head till she felt quite deafened. She started to her feet and sprang across the little brook in terror,

$$* \quad * \quad * \quad *$$
$$* \quad * \quad *$$
$$* \quad * \quad * \quad *$$

and had just time to see the Lion and the Unicorn rise to their feet, with angry looks at being interrupted in their feast, before she dropped to her knees, and put her hands over her ears, vainly trying to shut out the dreadful uproar.

'If *that* doesn't "drum them out of town,"' she thought to herself, 'nothing ever will!'

8

'It's My Own Invention'

AFTER a while the noise seemed gradually to die away, till all was dead silence, and Alice lifted up her head in some alarm. There was no one to be seen, and her first thought was that she must have been dreaming about the Lion and the Unicorn and those queer Anglo-Saxon Messengers. However, there was the great dish still lying at her feet, on which she had tried to cut the plum-cake, 'So I wasn't dreaming, after all,' she said to herself, 'unless – unless we're all part of the same dream. Only I do hope it's *my* dream, and not the Red King's! I don't like belonging to another person's dream,' she went on in a rather complaining tone: 'I've a great mind to go and wake him, and see what happens!'

At this moment her thoughts were interrupted by a loud shouting of 'Ahoy! Ahoy! Check!' and a Knight, dressed in crimson armour, came galloping down upon her, brandishing a great club. Just as he reached her, the horse stopped suddenly: 'You're my prisoner!' the Knight cried, as he tumbled off his horse.

Startled as she was, Alice was more frightened for him than for herself at the moment, and watched him with some anxiety as he mounted again. As soon as he was comfortably in the saddle, he began once more 'You're my –' but here another voice broke in 'Ahoy! Ahoy! Check!' and Alice looked round in some surprise for the new enemy.

This time it was a White Knight. He drew up at Alice's side, and tumbled off his horse just as the Red Knight had done: then he got on again, and the two Knights sat and looked at each other for some time without speaking. Alice looked from one to the other in some bewilderment.

'She's *my* prisoner, you know!' the Red Knight said at last.

'Yes, but then *I* came and rescued her!' the White Knight replied.

'Well, we must fight for her, then,' said the Red Knight, as he took up his helmet (which hung from the saddle, and was something the shape of a horse's head), and put it on.

'You will observe the Rules of Battle, of course?' the

White Knight remarked, putting on his helmet too.

'I always do,' said the Red Knight, and they began banging away at each other with such fury that Alice got behind a tree to be out of the way of the blows.

'I wonder, now, what the Rules of Battle are,' she said to herself, as she watched the fight, timidly peeping out from her hiding-place: 'one Rule seems to be, that if one Knight hits the other, he knocks him off his horse, and if he misses, he tumbles off himself – and another Rule seems to be that they hold their clubs with their arms, as if they were Punch and Judy – What a noise they make when they tumble! Just like a whole set of fire-irons falling into the fender! And how quiet the horses are! They let them get on and off them just as if they were tables!'

Another Rule of Battle, that Alice had not noticed, seemed to be that they always fell on their heads, and the battle ended with their both falling off in this way, side by side: when they got up again, they shook hands, and then the Red Knight mounted and galloped off.

'It was a glorious victory, wasn't it?' said the White Knight, as he came up panting.

'I don't know,' Alice said doubtfully. 'I don't want to be anybody's prisoner. I want to be a Queen.'

'So you will, when you've crossed the next brook,' said the White Knight. 'I'll see you safe to the end of the wood – and then I must go back, you know. That's the end of my move.'

'Thank you very much,' said Alice. May I help you off with your helmet?' It was evidently more than he could manage by himself; however, she managed to shake him out of it at last.

'Now one can breathe more easily,' said the Knight, putting back his shaggy hair with both hands, and turning his gentle face and large mild eyes to Alice.

She thought she had never seen such a strange-looking soldier in all her life.

He was dressed in tin armour, which seemed to fit him very badly, and he had a queer-shaped little deal box fastened across his shoulders, upside-down, and with the lid hanging open. Alice looked at it with great curiosity.

'I see you're admiring my little box,' the Knight said in a friendly tone. 'It's my own invention – to keep clothes and sandwiches in. You see I carry it upside-down, so that the rain can't get in.'

'But the things can get *out*', Alice gently remarked. 'Do you know the lid's open?'

'I didn't know it,' the Knight said, a shade of vexation passing over his face. 'Then all the things must have fallen out! And the box is no use without them.' He unfastened it as he spoke, and was just going to throw it into the bushes, when a sudden thought seemed to strike him, and he hung it carefully on a tree. 'Can you guess why I did that?' he said to Alice.

Alice shook her head.

'I hope some bees may make a nest in it – then I should get the honey.'

'But you've got a bee-hive – or something like one – fastened to the saddle,' said Alice.

'Yes, it's a very good bee-hive,' the Knight said in a

discontented tone, 'one of the best kind. But not a single bee has come near it yet. And the other thing is a mouse-trap. I suppose the mice keep the bees out – or the bees keep the mice out, I don't know which.'

'I was wondering what the mouse-trap was for,' said Alice. 'It isn't very likely there would be any mice on the horse's back.'

'Not very likely, perhaps,' said the Knight; 'but if they *do* come, I don't choose to have them running all about.'

'You see,' he went on after a pause, 'it's as well to be provided for *everything*. That's the reason the horse has all those anklets round his feet.'

'But what are they for?' Alice asked in a tone of great curiosity.

'To guard against the bites of sharks,' the Knight replied. 'It's an invention of my own. And now help me on. I'll go with you to the end of the wood – What's that dish for?'

'It's meant for plum-cake,' said Alice.

'We'd better take it with us,' the Knight said. 'It'll come in handy if we find any plum-cake. Help me to get it into this bag.'

This took a long time to manage, though Alice held the bag open very carefully, because the Knight was so *very* awkward in putting in the dish: the first two or three times that he tried he fell in himself instead. 'It's rather a tight fit, you see,' he said, as they got it in at last; 'there are so many candlesticks in the bag.' And he hung it to the saddle, which was already loaded with bunches of carrots, and fire-irons, and many other things.

'I hope you've got your hair well fastened on?' he continued, as they set off.

'Only in the usual way,' Alice said, smiling.

'That's hardly enough,' he said, anxiously. 'You see the wind is so *very* strong here. It's as strong as soup.'

'Have you invented a plan for keeping the hair from being blown off?' Alice enquired.

'Not yet,' said the Knight. 'But I've got a plan for keeping it from *falling* off.'

'I should like to hear it, very much.'

'First you take an upright stick,' said the Knight. 'Then you make your hair creep up it, like a fruit-tree. Now the reason hair falls off is because it hangs *down* – things never fall *upward*, you know. It's a plan of my own invention. You may try it if you like.'

It didn't sound a comfortable plan, Alice thought, and for a few minutes she walked on in silence, puzzling over the idea, and every now and then stopping to help the poor Knight, who certainly was *not* a good rider.

Whenever the horse stopped (which it did very often), he fell off in front; and whenever it went on again (which it generally did rather suddenly), he fell off behind. Otherwise he kept on pretty well, except that he had a habit of now and then falling off sideways; and as he generally did this on the side on which Alice was walking, she soon found that it was the best plan not to walk *quite* so close to the horse.

'I'm afraid you've not had much practice in riding,' she ventured to say, as she was helping him up from his fifth tumble.

The Knight looked very much surprised, and a little offended at the remark. 'What makes you say that?' he asked, as he scrambled back into the saddle, keeping hold of Alice's hair with one hand, to save himself from falling over on the other side.

'Because people don't fall off quite so often, when they've had much practice.'

'I've had plenty of practice,' the Knight said very gravely: 'plenty of practice!'

Alice could think of nothing better to say than 'Indeed?' but she said it as heartily as she could. They went on a little way in silence after this, the Knight with his eyes shut, muttering to himself, and Alice watching anxiously for the next tumble.

'The great art of riding,' the Knight suddenly began in a loud voice, waving his right arm as he spoke, 'is to keep –' Here the sentence ended as suddenly as it had begun, as the Knight fell heavily on the top of his head exactly in the path where Alice was walking. She was quite frightened this time, and said in an anxious tone, as she picked him up, 'I hope no bones are broken?'

'None to speak of,' the Knight said, as if he didn't mind breaking two or three of them. 'The great art of riding, as I was saying, is – to keep your balance properly. Like this, you know –'

He let go the bridle, and stretched out both his arms to show Alice what he meant, and this time he fell flat on his back, right under the horse's feet.

'Plenty of practice!' he went on repeating, all the time that Alice was getting him on his feet again. 'Plenty of practice!'

'It's too ridiculous!' cried Alice, losing all her patience this time. 'You ought to have a wooden horse on wheels, that you ought!'

'Does that kind go smoothly?' the Knight asked in a tone of great interest, clasping his arms round the horse's neck as he spoke, just in time to save himself from tumbling off again.

'Much more smoothly than a live horse,' Alice said, with a little scream of laughter, in spite of all she could do to prevent it.

'I'll get one,' the Knight said thoughtfully to himself. 'One or two – several.'

There was a short silence after this, and then the Knight went on again. 'I'm a great hand at inventing things. Now, I daresay you noticed, the last time you picked me up, that I was looking rather thoughtful?'

'You *were* a little grave,' said Alice.

'Well, just then I was inventing a new way of getting

over a gate – would you like to hear it?'

'Very much indeed,' Alice said politely.

'I'll tell you how I came to think of it,' said the Knight. 'You see, I said to myself, "The only difficulty is with the feet: the *head* is high enough already." Now, first I put my head on the top of the gate – then the head's high enough – then I stand on my head – then the feet are high enough, you see – then I'm over, you see.'

'Yes, I suppose you'd be over when that was done,' Alice said thoughtfully: 'but don't you think it would be rather hard?'

'I haven't tried it yet,' the Knight said, gravely: 'so I can't tell for certain – but I'm afraid it *would* be a little hard.'

He looked so vexed at the idea, that Alice changed the subject hastily. 'What a curious helmet you've got!' she said cheerfully. 'Is that your invention too?'

The Knight looked down proudly at his helmet, which hung from the saddle. 'Yes,' he said, 'but I've invented a better one than that – like a sugar-loaf. When I used to wear it, if I fell off the horse, it always touched the ground directly. So I had a *very* little way to fall, you see – But there *was* the danger of falling *into* it, to be sure. That happened to me once – and the worst of it was, before I could get out again, the other White Knight came and put it on. He thought it was his own helmet.

The Knight looked so solemn about it that Alice did not dare to laugh. 'I'm afraid you must have hurt him,' she said in a trembling voice, 'being on the top of his head.'

'I had to kick him, of course,' the Knight said, very seriously. 'And then he took the helmet off again – but it took hours and hours to get me out. I was as fast as – as lightning, you know.'

'But that's a different kind of fastness,' Alice objected.

The Knight shook his head. 'It was all kinds of fastness with me, I can assure you!' he said. He raised his hands in some excitemem as he said this, and instantly rolled out of the saddle, and fell headlong into a deep ditch.

Alice ran to the side of the ditch to look for him. She was rather startled by the fall, as for some time he had kept on very well, and she was afraid that he really *was* hurt this time. However, though she could see nothing but the soles of his feet, she was much relieved to hear that he was talking on in his usual tone. 'All kinds of fastness,' he repeated: 'but it was careless of him to put another man's helmet on – with the man in it, too.'

'How *can* you go on talking so quietly, head downwards?' Alice asked, as she dragged him out by the feet, and laid him in a heap on the bank.

The Knight looked surprised at the question. 'What does it matter where my body happens to be?' he said. 'My mind goes on working all the same. In fact, the more head downwards I am, the more I keep inventing new things.'

'Now the cleverest thing of the sort that I ever did,' he went on after a pause, 'was inventing a new pudding during the meat-course.'

'In time to have it cooked for the next course?' said Alice. 'Well, that *was* quick work, certainly!'

'Well, not the *next* course,' the Knight said in a slow thoughtful tone: 'no, certainly not the next *course*.'

'Then it would have to be the next day. I suppose you wouldn't have two pudding-courses in one dinner?'

'Well, not the *next* day,' the Knight repeated as before: 'not the next *day*. In fact,' he went on, holding his head down, and his voice getting lower and lower, 'I don't believe that pudding ever *was* cooked! In fact, I don't believe that pudding ever *will* be cooked! And yet it was a very clever pudding to invent.'

'What did you mean it to be made of?' Alice asked, hoping to cheer him up, for the poor Knight seemed quite low-spirited about it.

'It began with blotting-paper,' the Knight answered with a groan.

'That wouldn't be very nice, I'm afraid –'

'Not very nice *alone*,' he interrupted, quite eagerly: 'but you've no idea what a difference it makes mixing it with other things – such as gun-powder and sealing-wax. And here I must leave you.' They had just come to the end of the wood.

Alice could only look puzzled: she was thinking of the pudding.

'You are sad,' the Knight said in an anxious tone: 'let me sing you a song to comfort you.'

'Is it very long?' Alice asked, for she had heard a good deal of poetry that day.

'It's long,' said the Knight, 'but it's very, *very* beautiful. Everybody that hears me sing it – either it brings the *tears* into their eyes, or else –'

'Or else what?' said Alice, for the Knight had made a sudden pause.

'Or else it doesn't, you know. The name of the song is called "*Haddocks' Eyes*."'

'Oh, that's the name of the song, is it?' Alice said, trying to feel interested.

'No, you don't understand,' the Knight said, looking a little vexed. 'That's what the name is *called*. The name really *is* "*The Aged Aged Man*."'

'Then I ought to have said "That's what the *song* is called"?' Alice corrected herself.

'No, you oughtn't: that's quite another thing! The *song* is called "*Ways and Means*": but that's only what it's *called*, you know!'

'Well, what *is* the song, then?' said Alice, who was by this time completely bewildered.

'I was coming to that,' the Knight said. 'The song really *is* "*A-sitting On A Gate*": and the tune's my own invention.'

So saying, he stopped his horse and let the reins fall on its neck: then, slowly beating time with one hand, and with a faint smile lighting up his gentle foolish face, as if he enjoyed the music of his song, he began.

Of all the strange things that Alice saw in her journey Through The Looking-Glass, this was the one that she always remembered most clearly. Years afterwards she could bring the whole scene back again, as if it had been only yesterday – the mild blue eyes and kindly smile of the Knight – the setting sun gleaming through his hair, and shining on his armour in a blaze of light that quite dazzled her – the horse quietly moving about. with the reins hanging loose on his neck, cropping the grass at her feet – and the black shadows of the forest behind – all this she took in like a picture, as, with one hand shading her eyes, she leant against a tree, watching the strange pair, and listening, in a half dream, to the melancholy music of the song.

'But the tune *isn't* his own invention,' she said to herself: 'it's "*I give thee all, I can no more.*"' She stood and listened very attentively, but no tears came into her eyes.

> '*I'll tell thee everything I can;*
>   *There's little to relate.*
> *I saw an aged aged man,*
>   *A-sitting on a gate.*
> *"Who are you, aged man?" I said.*
>   *"And how is it you live?"*
> *And his answer trickled through my head*
>   *Like water through a sieve.*

He said "I look for butterflies
  That sleep among the wheat:
I make them into mutton-pies,
  And sell them in the street.
I sell them unto men," he said,
  "Who sail on stormy seas;
And that's the way I get my bread –
  A trifle, if you please."

But I was thinking of a plan
  To dye one's whiskers green,
And always use so large a fan
  That they could not be seen.
So, having no reply to give
  To what the old man said,

I cried, "Come, tell me how you live!"
    And thumped him on the head.

His accent, mild took up the tale:
    He said "I go my ways,
And when I find a mountain-rill,
    I set it in a blaze;
And thence they make a stuff they call
    Rowlands' Macassar Oil –
Yet twopence-halfpenny is all
    They give me for my toil."

But I was thinking of a way
    To feed oneself on batter,
And so go on from day to day
    Getting a little fatter.
I shook him well from side to side,
    Until his face was blue:
"Come, tell me how you live," I cried,
    "And what it is you do!"

He said "I hunt for haddocks' eyes
    Among the heather bright,
And work them into waistcoat-buttons
    In the silent night.
And these I do not sell for gold

Or coin of silvery shine,
But for a copper halfpenny,
   And that will purchase nine.

"I sometimes dig for buttered rolls,
   Or set limed twigs for crabs;
I sometimes search the grassy knolls
   For wheels of Hansom-cabs.
And that's the way" (he gave a wink)
   "By which I get my wealth —
And very gladly will I drink
   Your Honour's noble health."

I heard him then, for I had just
   Completed my design
To keep the Menai bridge from rust
   By boiling it in wine.
I thanked him much for telling me
   The way he got his wealth,
But chiefly for his wish that he
   Might drink my noble health.

And now, if e'er by chance I put
   My fingers into glue,
Or madly squeeze a right-hand foot
   Into a left-hand shoe

Or if I drop upon my toe
  A very heavy weight,
I weep, for it reminds me so,
Of that old man I used to know –

Whose look was mild, whose speech was slow,
Whose hair was whiter than the snow,
Whose face was very like a crow,
With eyes, like cinders, all aglow,
Who seemed distracted with his woe,
Who rocked his body to and fro,
And muttered mumblingly and low,
As if his mouth were full of dough,
Who snorted like a buffalo –
That summer evening, long ago,
  A-sitting on a gate.'

As the Knight sang the last words of the ballad, he gathered up the reins, and turned his horse's head along the road by which they had come. 'You've only a few yards to go,' he said, 'down the hill and over that little brook, and then you'll be a Queen – But you'll stay and see me off first?' he added as Alice turned with an eager look in the direction to which he pointed. 'I shan't be long. You'll wait and wave your handkerchief when I get to that turn in the road? I think it'll encourage me, you see.'

'Of course I'll wait,' said Alice: 'and thank you very much for coming so far – and for the song – I liked it very much.'

'I hope so,' the Knight said doubtfully: 'but you didn't cry so much as I thought you would.'

So they shook hands, and then the Knight rode slowly away into the forest. 'It won't take long to see him *off*, I expect,' Alice said to herself, as she stood watching him. 'There he goes! Right on his head as usual! However, he gets on again pretty easily – that comes of having so many things hung round the horse –' So she went on talking to herself, as she watched the horse walking leisurely along the road, and the Knight tumbling off, first on one side and then on the other. After the fourth or fifth tumble he reached the turn, and then she waved her handkerchief to him, and waited till he was out of sight.

'I hope it encouraged him,' she said, as she turned to run down the hill: 'and now for the last brook, and to he a Queen! How grand it sounds!' A very few steps brought her to the edge of the brook. 'The Eighth Square at last!' she cried as she bounded across,

*   *   *   *

*   *   *

*   *   *   *

and threw herself down to rest on a lawn as soft as moss, with little flower-beds dotted about it here and there. 'Oh, how glad I am to get here! And what is this on my head?' she exclaimed in a tone of dismay, as she put her hands up to something very heavy, that fitted tight all round her head.

'But how *can* it have got there without my knowing it?' she said to herself, as she lifted it off, and set it on her lap to make out what it could possibly be.

It was a golden crown.

9

Queen Alice

'WELL, this *is* grand!' said Alice. 'I never expected I should be a Queen so soon – and I'll tell you what it is, your Majesty,' she went on in a severe tone (she was always rather fond of scolding herself), 'it'll never do for you to be lolling about on the grass like that! Queens have to be dignified, you know.'

So she got up and walked about – rather stiffly just at first, as she was afraid that the crown might come off: but she comforted herself with the thought that there was nobody to see her, 'and if I really am a Queen,' she said as she sat down again, 'I shall be able to manage it quite well in time.'

Everything was happening so oddly that she didn't feel a bit surprised at finding the Red Queen and the White Queen sitting close to her, one on each side: she

would have liked very much to ask them how they came there, but she feared it would not be quite civil. However, there would be no harm, she thought, in asking if the game was over. 'Please would you tell me –' she began, looking timidly at the Red Queen.

'Speak when you're spoken to!' the Queen sharply interrupted her.

'But if everybody obeyed that rule,' said Alice, who was always ready for a little argument, 'and if you only spoke when you were spoken to, and the other persons always waited for *you* to begin, you see nobody would ever say anything, so that –'

'Ridiculous!' cried the Queen. 'Why, don't you see, child –' here she broke off with a frown, and, after thinking for a minute; suddenly changed the subject of the conversation. 'What do you mean by "If you really are a Queen"? What right have you to call yourself so? You can't be a Queen, you know, till you've passed the proper examination, and the sooner we begin it, the better.'

'I only said "if"!' poor Alice pleaded in a piteous tone.

The two Queens looked at each other, and the Red Queen remarked, with a little shudder, 'She says she only said "if" –'

'But she said a great deal more than that!' the White

Queen moaned, wringing her hands. 'Oh, ever so much more than that!'

'So you did, you know,' the Red Queen said to Alice. 'Always speak the truth – think before you speak – and write it down afterwards.'

'I'm sure I didn't mean –' Alice was beginning, but the Red Queen interrupted her impatiently.

'That's just what I complain of! You *should* have meant! What do you suppose is the use of a child without any meaning? Even a joke should have some meaning – and a child's more important than a joke, I hope. You couldn't deny that, even if you tried with both hands.'

'I don't deny things with my *hands*,' Alice objected.

'Nobody said you did,' said the Red Queen. 'I said you couldn't if you tried.'

'She's in that state of mind,' said the White Queen, 'that she wants to deny *something* – only she doesn't know what to deny!'

'A nasty, vicious temper,' the Red Queen remarked; and then there was an uncomfortable silence for a minute or two.

The Red Queen broke the silence by saying to the White Queen, 'I invite you to Alice's dinner-party this afternoon.'

The White Queen smiled feebly, and said 'And I invite *you*.'

'I didn't know I was to have a party at all,' said Alice; 'but if there is to be one, I think I ought to invite the guests.'

'We gave you the opportunity of doing it,' the Red Queen remarked: 'but I daresay you've not had many lessons in manners yet?'

'Manners are not taught in lessons,' said Alice. 'Lessons teach you to do sums, and things of that sort.'

'Can you do Addition?' the White Queen asked. 'What's one and one and one and one and one and one and one and one and one and one?'

'I don't know,' said Alice. 'I lost count.'

'She can't do Addition,' the Red Queen interrupted. 'Can you do Subtraction? Take nine from eight.'

'Nine from eight I can't, you know,' Alice replied very readily: 'but –'

'She can't do Subtraction,' said the White Queen. 'Can you do Division? Divide a loaf by a knife – what's the answer to that?'

'I suppose –' Alice was beginning, but the Red Queen answered for her. 'Bread-and-butter, another Subtraction sum. Take a bone from a dog: what remains?'

Alice considered. 'The bone wouldn't remain, of course, if I took it – and the dog wouldn't remain; it would come to bite me – and I'm sure *I* shouldn't remain!'

'Then you think nothing would remain?' said the Red Queen.

'I think that's the answer.'

'Wrong, as usual,' said the Red Queen: 'the dog's temper would remain.'

'But I don't see how –'

'Why, look here!' the Red Queen cried. 'The dog would lose its temper, wouldn't it!'

'Perhaps it would,' Alice replied cautiously.

'Then if the dog went away, its temper would remain!' the Queen exclaimed triumphantly.

Alice said, as gravely as she could, 'They might go different ways.' But she couldn't help thinking to herself, 'What dreadful nonsense we *are* talking!'

'She can't do sums a *bit!*' the Queens said together, with great emphasis.

'Can *you* do sums?' Alice said, turning suddenly on the White Queen, for she didn't like being found fault with so much.

The Queen gasped and shut her eyes. 'I can do Addition,' she said, 'if you give me time – but I can't do Subtraction, under *any* circumstances!'

'Of course you know your A B C?' said the Red Queen.

'To be sure I do,' said Alice.

'So do I,' the White Queen whispered: 'we'll often say it over together, dear. And I'll tell you a secret – I can read words of one letter! Isn't *that* grand! However, don't be discouraged. You'll come to it in time.'

Here the Red Queen began again. 'Can you answer useful questions?' she said. 'How is bread made?'

'I know *that!*' Alice cried eagerly. 'You take some flour –'

'Where do you pick the flower?' the White Queen asked. 'In a garden, or in the hedges?'

'Well, it isn't picked at all,' Alice explained: 'it's *ground* –'

'How many acres of ground?' said the White Queen. 'You mustn't leave out so many things.'

'Fan her head!' the Red Queen anxiously interrupted.

'She'll be feverish after so much thinking.' So they set to work and fanned her with bunches of leaves, till she had to beg them to leave off, it blew her hair about so.

'She's all right again now,' said the Red Queen. 'Do you know Languages? What's the French for fiddle-de-dee?'

'Fiddle-de-dee's not English,' Alice replied gravely.

'Who ever said it was?' said the Red Queen.

Alice thought she saw a way out of the difficulty this time. 'If you'll tell me what language "fiddle-de-dee" is, I'll tell you the French for it!' she exclaimed triumphantly.

But the Red Queen drew herself up rather stiffly, and said 'Queens never make bargains.'

'I wish Queens never asked questions', Alice thought to herself.

'Don't let us quarrel,' the White Queen said in an anxious tone. 'What is the cause of lightning?'

'The cause of lightning,' Alice said very decidedly, for she felt quite certain about this, 'is the thunder – no, no!' she hastily corrected herself. 'I meant the other way.'

'It's too late to correct it,' said the Red Queen: 'when you've once said a thing, that fixes it, and you must take the consequences.'

'Which reminds me –' the White Queen said, looking down and nervously clasping and unclasping her hands, 'we had *such* a thunderstorm last Tuesday – I mean one of the last set of Tuesdays, you know.'

Alice was puzzled. 'In *our* country,' she remarked, 'there's only one day at a time.'

The Red Queen said 'That's a poor thin way of doing things. Now *here*, we mostly have days and nights two or three at a time, and sometimes in the winter we take as many as five nights together – for warmth, you know.'

'Are five nights warmer than one night, then?' Alice ventured to ask.

'Five times as warm, of course.'

'But they should be five times as *cold*, by the same rule –'

'Just so!' cried the Red Queen. 'Five times as warm, *and* five timcs as cold – just as I'm five times as rich as you are, *and* five times as clever!'

Alice sighed and gave it up, 'It's exactly like a riddle with no answer!' she thought.

'Humpty Dumpty saw it too,' the White Queen went on in a low voice, more as if she were talking to herself. 'He came to the door with a corkscrew in his hand –'

'What did he want?' said the Red Queen.

'He said he *would* come in,' the White Queen went on, 'because he was looking for a hippopotamus. Now, as it happened, there wasn't such a thing in the house, that morning.'

'Is there generally?' Alice asked in an astonished tone.

'Well, only on Thursdays,' said the Queen.

'I know what he came for,' said Alice: 'he wanted to punish the fish, because –'

Here the White Queen began again. 'It was *such* a thunderstorm, you can't think!' ('She *never* could you know,' said the Red Queen.) 'And part of the roof came off, and ever so much thunder got in – and it went rolling round the room in great lumps – and knocking over the tables and things – till I was so frightened, I couldn't remember my own name!'

Alice thought to herself, 'I never should *try* to remember my name in the middle of an accident! Where would be the use of it?' but she did not say this aloud, for fear of hurting the poor Queen's feelings.

'Your Majesty must excuse her,' the Red Queen said to Alice, taking one of the White Queen's hands in her own, and gently stroking it: 'she means well, but she can't help saying foolish things, as a general rule.'

The White Queen looked timidly at Alice, who felt she *ought* to say something kind, but really couldn't think of anything at the moment.

'She never was really well brought up,' the Red Queen went on: 'but it's amazing how good-tempered she is! Pat her on the head, and see how pleased she'll be!'

But this was more than Alice had courage to do.

'A little kindness – and putting her hair in papers would do wonders with her –'

The White Queen gave a deep sigh, and laid her head on Alice's shoulder. 'I *am* so sleepy!' she moaned.

'She's tired, poor thing!' said the Red Queen. 'Smooth her hair – lend her your nightcap – and sing her a soothing lullaby.'

'I haven't got a nightcap with me,' said Alice, as she tried to obey the first direction: 'and I don't know any soothing lullabies.'

'I must do it myself, then,' said the Red Queen, and she began:

> '*Hush-a-by lady, in Alice's lap!*
> *Till the feast's ready, we've time for a nap:*
> *When the feast's over, we'll go to the ball –*
> *Red Queen, and White Queen, and Alice, and all!*'

'And now you know the words,' she added, as she put her head down on Alice's other shoulder, 'just sing it through to *me*. I'm getting sleepy, too.' In another moment both Queens were fast asleep, and snoring loud.

'What *am* I to do?' exclaimed Alice, looking about in great perplexity, as first one round head, and then the other, rolled down from her shoulder, and lay like a heavy lump in her lap. 'I don't think it *ever* happened before, that anyone had to take care of two Queens asleep at once! No, not in all the History of England – it couldn't, you know, because there never was more than one Queen at a time. Do wake up, you heavy things!' she went on in an impatient tone; but there was no answer but a gentle snoring.

The snoring got more distinct every minute, and sounded more like a tune: at last she could even make out words, and she listened so eagerly that, when the two great heads suddenly vanished from her lap, she hardly missed them.

She was standing before an arched doorway over which were the words QUEEN ALICE in large letters, and on each side of the arch there was a bell-handle; one was marked 'Visitors' Bell,' and the other 'Servants' Bell.'

'I'll wait till the song's over,' thought Alice, 'and then I'll ring – the – *which* bell must I ring?' she went on, very much puzzled by the names. 'I'm not a visitor, and I'm not a servant. There *ought* to be one marked "Queen" you know –'

Just then the door opened a little way, and a creature with a long beak put its head out for a moment and said 'No admittance till the week after next!' and shut the door again with a bang.

Alice knocked and rang in vain for a long time, but at last a very old Frog, who was sitting under a tree, got up and hobbled slowly towards her: he was dressed in bright yellow, and had enormous boots on.

'What is it, now?' the Frog said in a deep hoarse whisper.

Alice turned round, ready to find fault with anybody. 'Where's the servant whose business it is to answer the door?' she began angrily.

'Which door?' said the Frog.

Alice almost stamped with irritation at the slow drawl in which he spoke. '*This* door, of course!'

The Frog looked at the door with his large dull eyes
for a minute: then he went nearer and rubbed it with
his thumb, as if he were trying whether the paint would
come off; then he looked at Alice.

'To answer the door?' he said. 'What's it been asking of?' He was so hoarse that Alice could scarcely hear him.

'I don't know what you mean,' she said.

'I speaks English, doesn't I?' the Frog went on. 'Or are you deaf? What did it ask you?'

'Nothing!' Alice said impatiently. 'I've been knocking at it!'

'Shouldn't do that – shouldn't do that –' the Frog muttered. 'Wexes it, you know.' Then he went up and gave the door a kick with one of his great feet. 'You let *it* alone,' he panted out, as he hobbled back to his tree, 'and it'll let *you* alone, you know.'

At this moment the door was flung open, and a shrill voice was heard singing:

'To the Looking-Glass world it was Alice that said,
"I've a sceptre, in hand. I've a crown on my head;
Let the Looking-Glass creatures, whatever they be,
Come and dine with the Red Queen, the White
Queen, and me!"'

And hundreds of voices joined in the chorus:

'Then fill up the glasses as quick as you can,
And sprinkle the table with buttons and bran:

Put cats in the coffee, and mice in the tea –
And welcome Queen Alice with thirty-times-three!'

Then followed a confused noise of cheering, and Alice thought to herself, 'Thirty times three makes ninety. I wonder if any one's counting?' In a minute there was silence again, and the same shrill voice sang another verse:

'"O Looking-Glass creatures,"quoth Alice, "draw near!
'Tis an honour to see me, a favour to hear:
'Tis a privilege high to have dinner and tea
Along with the Red Queen, the White Queen, and me!"'

Then came the chorus again:

'Then fill up the glasses with treacle and ink,
Or anything else that is pleasant to drink;
Mix sand with the cider, and wool with the wine –
And welcome Queen Alice with ninety-times-nine!'

'Ninety times nine!' Alice repeated in despair. 'Oh, that'll never be done! I'd better go in at once –' and in she went, and there was a dead silence the moment she appeared.

Alice glanced nervously along the table, as she walked up the large hall, and noticed that there were about fifty guest, of all kinds: some were animals, some birds, and there were even a few flowers among them. 'I'm glad they've come without waiting to be asked,' she thought: 'I should never have known who were the right people to invite!'

There were three chairs at the head of the table; the Red and White Queens had already taken two of them, bur the middle one was empty. Alice sat down in it, rather uncomfortable at the silence, and longing for some one to speak.

At last the Red Queen began. 'You've missed the soup and fish,' she said. 'Put on the joint!' And the waiters set a leg of mutton before Alice, who looked at it rather anxiously, as she had never had to carve a joint before.

'You look a little shy; let me introduce you to that leg of mutton,' said the Red Queen. 'Alice – Mutton; Mutton – Alice.' The leg of mutton got up in the dish and made a little bow to Alice; and Alice returned the bow, not knowing whether to be frightened or amused.

'May I give you a slice?' she said, taking up the knife and fork, and looking from one Queen to the other.

'Certainly not,' the Red Queen said, very decidedly: 'it isn't etiquette to cut anyone you've been introduced to. Remove the joint!' And the waiters carried it off, and brought a large plum-pudding in its place.

'I won't be introduced to the pudding, please,' Alice said rather hastily, 'or we shall get no dinner at all. May I give you some?'

But the Red Queen looked sulky, and growled 'Pudding – Alice; Alice – Pudding. Remove the pudding!' and the waiters took it away so quickly that Alice couldn't return its bow.

However, she didn't see why the Red Queen should be the only one to give orders, so, as an experiment, she called out 'Waiter! Bring back the pudding!' and there it was again in a moment, like a conjuring-trick. It was so large that she couldn't help feeling a *little* shy with it, as she had been with the mutton; however, she conquered her shyness by a great effort and cut a slice and handed it to the Red Queen.

'What impertinence!' said the Pudding. 'I wonder how you'd like it, if I were to cut a slice out of *you*, you creature!'

It spoke in a thick, suety sort of voice, and Alice hadn't a word to say in reply: she could only sit and look at it and gasp.

'Make a remark,' said the Red Queen: 'it's ridiculous to leave all the conversation to the pudding!'

'Do you know, I've had such a quantity of poetry repeated to me today,' Alice began, a little frightened at finding that, the moment she opened her lips, there was dead silence, and all eyes were fixed upon her; 'and it's a very curious thing, I think – every poem was about fishes in some way. Do you know why they're so fond of fishes, all about here?'

She spoke to the Red Queen, whose answer was a little wide of the mark. 'As to fishes,' she said, very slowly and solemnly, putting her mouth close to Alice's ear, 'her White Majesty knows a lovely riddle – all in poetry – all about fishes. Shall she repeat it?'

'Her Red Majesty's very kind to mention it,' the White

Queen murmured into Alice's other ear, in a voice like the cooing of a pigeon. 'It would be *such* a treat! May I?'

'Please do,' Alice said very politely.

The White Queen laughed with delight, and stroked Alice's cheek. Then she began:

> *"First, the fish must be caught."*
> *That is easy: a baby, I think, could have caught it.*
> *"Next, the fish must be bought."*
> *That is easy: a penny, I think, would have bought it.*
>
> *"Now cook me the fish!"*
> *That is easy, and will not take more than a minute.*
> *"Let it lie in a dish!"*
> *That is easy, because it already is in it.*
>
> *"Bring it here! Let me sup!"*
> *It is easy to set such a dish on the table.*
> *"Take the dish-cover up!"*
> *Ah, that is so hard that I fear I'm unable!*
>
> *For it holds it like glue –*
> *Holds the lid to the dish, while it lies in the middle:*
> *Which is easiest to do,*
> *Un-dish-cover the fish, or dishcover the riddle?'*

'Take a minute to think about it, and then guess,' said the Red Queen. 'Meanwhile, we'll drink your health – Queen Alice's health!' she screamed at the top of her voice, and all the guests began drinking it directly, and very queerly they managed it: some of them put their glasses upon their heads like extinguishers, and drank all that trickled down their faces – others upset the decanters, and drank the wine as it ran off the edges of the table – and three of them (who looked like kangaroos) scrambled into the dish of roast mutton, and began eagerly lapping up the gravy, 'just like pigs in a trough!' thought Alice.

'You ought to return thanks in a neat speech,' the Red Queen said, frowning at Alice as she spoke.

'We must support you, you know,' the White Queen whispered, as Alice got up to do it, very obediently, but a little frightened.

'Thank you very much,' she whispered in reply, 'but I can do quite well without.'

'That wouldn't be at all the thing,' the Red Queen said very decidedly: so Alice tried to submit to it with a good grace.

('And they *did* push so!' she said afterwards, when she was telling her sister the history of the feast. 'You would have thought they wanted to squeeze me flat!')

In fact it was rather difficult for her to keep in her

place while she made her speech: the two Queens pushed her so, one on each side, that they nearly lifted her up into the air: 'I rise to return thanks –' Alice began: and she really *did* rise as she spoke, several inches; but she got hold of the edge of the table, and managed to pull herself down again.

'Take care of yourself!' screamed the White Queen, seizing Alice's hair with both her hands. 'Something's going to happen!'

And then (as Alice afterwards described it) all sorts of things happened in a moment. The candles all grew up to the ceiling, looking something like a bed of rushes with fireworks at the top. As to the bottles, they each took a pair of plates, which they hastily fitted on as wings, and so, with forks for legs, went fluttering about in all directions: 'and very like birds they look,' Alice thought to herself, as well as she could in the dreadful confusion that was beginning.

At this moment she heard a hoarse laugh at her side, and turned to see what was the matter with the White Queen; but, instead of the Queen, there was the leg of mutton sitting in the chair. 'Here I am!' cried a voice from the soup-tureen, and Alice turned again, just in time to see the Queen's broad good-natured face grinning at her for a moment over the edge of the tureen, before she disappeared into the soup.

There was not a moment to be lost. Already several of the guests were lying down in the dishes, and the soup ladle was walking up the table towards Alice's chair, and beckoning to her impatiently to get out of its way.

'I can't stand this any longer!' she cried as she jumped up and seized the table-cloth with both hands: one good pull, and plates, dishes, guests, and candles came crashing down together in a heap on the floor.

'And as for *you*,' she went on, turning fiercely upon the Red Queen, whom she considered as the cause of all the mischief – but the Queen was no longer at her side – she had suddenly dwindled down to the size of a little doll, and was now on the table, merrily running round and round after her own shawl, which was trailing behind her.

At any other time, Alice would have felt surprised at this, but she was far too much excited to be surprised at anything *now*. 'As for *you*,' she repeated, catching hold of the little creature in the very act of jumping over a bottle which had just lighted upon the table, 'I'll shake you into a kitten, that I will!'

10
Shaking

S HE took her off the table as she spoke, and shook her backwards and forwards with all her might.

The Red Queen made no resistance whatever; only her face grew very small, and her eyes got large and green: and still, as Alice went on shaking her, she kept on growing shorter – and fatter – and softer – and rounder and –

11

Waking

– and it really *was* a kitten, after all.

12

Which Dreamed It?

'YOUR Red Majesty shouldn't purr so loud,' Alice said, rubbing her eyes; and addressing the kitten, respectfully, yet with some severity. 'You woke me out of oh! such a nice dream! And you've been along with me, Kitty – all through the Looking-Glass world. Did you know it, dear?'

It is a very inconvenient habit of kittens (Alice had once made the remark) that, whatever you say to them, they *always* purr. 'If they would only purr for "yes," and mew for "no," or any rule of that sort,' she had said, 'so that one could keep up a conversation! But how *can* you talk with a person if they always say the same thing?'

On this occasion the kitten only purred: and it was impossible to guess whether it meant 'yes' or 'no.'

So Alice hunted among the chessmen on the table

till she had found the Red Queen: then she went down on her knees on the hearth-rug, and put the kitten and the Queen to look at each other. 'Now, Kitty!' she cried, clapping her hands triumphantly. 'Confess that was what you turned into!'

('But it wouldn't look at it,' she said, when she was explaining the thing afterwards to her sister: 'it turned away its head, and pretended not to see it: but it looked

345

a *little* ashamed of itself, so I think it *must* have been the Red Queen.')

'Sit up a little more stiffly, dear!' Alice cried with a merry laugh. 'And curtsey while you're thinking what to – what to purr. It saves time, remember!' And she caught it up and gave it one little kiss, 'just in honour of its having been a Red Queen.'

'Snowdrop, my pet!' she went on, looking over her shoulder at the White Kitten, which was still patiently undergoing its toilet, 'when *will* Dinah have finished with your White Majesty, I wonder? That must be the reason you were so untidy in my dream – Dinah! Do you know that you're scrubbing a White Queen? Really, it's most disrespectful of you!

'And what did *Dinah* turn to, I wonder?' she prattled on, as she settled comfortably down, with one elbow on the rug, and her chin in her hand, to watch the kittens. 'Tell me, Dinah, did you turn to Humpty Dumpty? I *think* you did – however, you'd better not mention it to your friends just yet, for I'm not sure.

'By the way, Kitty, if only you'd been really with me in my dream, there was one thing you *would* have enjoyed – I had such a quantity of poetry said to me, all about fishes! Tomorrow morning you shall have a real treat. All the time you're eating your breakfast, I'll repeat "The Walrus and the Carpenter" to you; and then you can make believe it's oysters, dear!

'Now, Kitty, let's consider who it was that dreamed it all. This is a serious question, my dear, and you should *not* go on licking your paw like that – as if Dinah hadn't washed you this morning! You see, Kitty, it *must* have been either me or the Red King. He was part of my dream, of course – but then I was part of his dream, too! *Was* it the Red King, Kitty? You were his wife, my dear, so you ought to know – Oh, Kitty, *do* help to settle it! I'm sure your paw can wait!' But the provoking kitten only began on the other paw, and pretended it hadn't heard the question.

Which do you think it was?

A boat beneath a sunny sky,
Lingering onward dreamily
In an evening of July –

Children three that nestle near,
Eager eye and willing ear,
Pleased a simple tale to hear –

Long has paled that sunny sky:
Echoes fade and memories die.
Autumn frosts have slain July.

Still she haunts me, phantomwise,
Alice moving under skies
Never seen by waking eyes.

Children yet, the tale to hear,
Eager eye and willing ear
Lovingly shall nestle near.

In a Wonderland they lie,
Dreaming as the days go by,
Dreaming as the summers die:

Ever drifting down the stream –
Lingering in the golden gleam –
Life, what is it but a dream?

THE END

The Backstory

Test your knowledge of Wonderland and have a go at making up nonsense verse!

Who's Who in *Alice's Adventures in Wonderland*?

Alice: A curious and polite little girl of seven who loves her pet cat Dinah.

The White Rabbit: A nervous animal in a constant rush, always frantic to please his superiors.

The Caterpillar: A haughty creature who asks puzzling questions. Alice chances upon him reclining on a mushroom smoking a hookah, a type of pipe for flavoured tobacco.

The Duchess: Alice meets the Duchess in the kitchen of her palace, nursing a baby. She is rude and violent towards her baby but later becomes rather too friendly to Alice.

The Cheshire Cat: We first encounter the Cheshire Cat in the Duchess's kitchen. He is known for his distinctive grin and ability to disappear and reappear whenever he likes.

The March Hare: Utterly nutty and full of nonsense, the March Hare spends his time constantly having tea with his friends the Hatter and the Dormouse.

The Hatter: As mad as the March Hare, the Hatter speaks only in riddles. In his world it is always tea-time and he is always attending his own crazy tea party.

The Dormouse: The Dormouse cannot stop falling asleep, no matter how hard he tries, although he is awake for long enough to tell a very strange story about treacle.

The Queen of Hearts: A foul-tempered, croquet-playing monarch, prone to shouting 'Off with their heads!'

The King of Hearts: A gentler ruler than the Queen, the King is no better at logical thinking.

The White King and the White Queen: two living chess pieces. The White Queen explains to Alice how she lives her life backwards.

VINTAGE CLASSICS

The Red King and the Red Queen: Also chess pieces, the Red King is asleep throughout the entire story. The Red Queen is very fast runner, although she never seems to get anywhere.

Tweedledum and Tweedledee: A pair of fat twins who recite 'The Walrus and the Carpenter' to Alice and have an absurd fight over a rattle.

Humpty Dumpty: an egg who sits on the top of a high, narrow wall and explains the poem 'Jabberwocky' to Alice.

The Lion and the Unicorn: these characters compete for the White King's crown. They think Alice is a monster.

The White Knight and the Red Knight: These are a pair of very clumsy knights who fight over Alice. When the White Knight wins he sings Alice a long and melancholy song.

How much attention did you pay to the weird and wonderful details of Alice's adventures? Take this quiz to find out how much of a Wonderland expert you are...

Alice's Adventures in Wonderland

1) Who does the White Rabbit mistake Alice for?

2) What kinds of creatures are the comical footmen Alice spots outside the Duchess's house?

3) Why has the Duchess been sentenced to death?

4) In the game of croquet what kinds of animals are used as the bats and balls?

5) According to the King, what rule has Alice broken that requires her to leave the courtroom?

Through the Looking-Glass

6) What are Alice's two kittens called?

7) Can you recite the first line from 'The Jabberwocky'?

8) What kinds of insects does the Gnat point out to Alice?

9) What type of cake does Alice attempt to slice up for the Lion and the Unicorn?

10) Where does the White Queen disappear to at the end of Alice's dinner party?

Answers to the *Wonderland* quiz – how did you do?

1. Mary Ann, his housemaid.
2. A frog and a fish.
3. Because she boxed the queen's ears.
4. The bats are flamingos and the balls are hedgehogs.
5. She has become more than a mile tall.
6. The white kitten is Snowdrop and the black one is called Kitty.
7. ''Twas brillig and the slithy toves'
8. A Rocking-horse-fly, a Snap-dragon-fly and a Bread-and-Butterfly.
9. Plum cake.
10. She dives into the soup-tureen.

Give yourself one point for each correct answer. If you got...

10 points or more: Fiddle-de-dee, you're an Alice whizz!

5 points or more: Your face has got SOME sense in it, but you *could* do some more swotting.

Less than 5 points: Off with your head! As the Duchess says to Alice 'You don't know much, and that's a fact'.

Who was Lewis Carroll?

Lewis Carroll's real name was Charles Lutwidge Dodgson and he was born in 1832, in Cheshire. As a young boy Lewis was excellent at reading and at school he showed himself to be a naturally bright pupil. His gift for numbers led him to study maths at the University of Oxford. He did very well there even though he admitted that he often didn't work hard enough. He suffered from a stammer but he was very good at mimicking people, telling stories and playing charades.

After his degree, Lewis Carroll had a career full of variety. He continued to live in his Oxford college, he taught and wrote books about maths, and he was ordained a church deacon. He also pursued his love of writing stories and photography. As well as the Alice books he wrote many poems, articles and short stories. Although he never married he adored children and spent a lot of time with his young friends, playing with them and taking photographs.

CLASSICS

VINTAGE

Was Alice a real person?

Lewis Carroll certainly knew a little girl called Alice. She was the daughter of a colleague at Oxford University named Henry Liddell. Lewis occasionally took Alice and her sisters out rowing and it was on one of these trips in the summer of 1862 that he invented a story about a character called Alice and her adventures underground. The real Alice begged him to write it down, and when he eventually did, *Alice's Adventures in Wonderland* was published in 1865. If you are very observant you might have spotted the fact that there is an acrostic poem (this means that the first letter of each line spells out a message) at the very end of *Through the Looking-Glass*. 'Alice Pleasance Liddell' is spelled out which suggests that these stories were inspired by her. But Lewis Carroll said that he often dedicated his work to the little girls that he knew.

Stuff and nonsense!

Alice gets pretty tired of listening to the people
and animals in Wonderland recite poetry to her.
And what strange poetry it is! Lewis Carroll and his
contemporary Edward Lear, as well as Dr Seuss and
Roald Dahl, are all well-known for writing rhythmic,
rhyming and funny poems, known as 'nonsense verse'.
Edward Lear wrote 'The Owl and the Pussycat' which
is a very famous poem – perhaps you know it? He also
wrote many limericks. These are poems which consist
of five lines with a strict rhyming pattern, and which
normally tell very silly stories. Here's one of Lear's:

> There was an Old Man with a beard,
> Who said, 'It is just as I feared!
> Two Owls and a Hen,
> Four Larks and a Wren,
> Have all built their nests in my beard!

And another:

> There was a Young Lady of Dorking,
> Who bought a large bonnet for walking;
> But its colour and size,
> So bedazzled her eyes,
> That she very soon went back to Dorking.

Have a go at making up your own limerick – you could be inspired by your home town, your friends and family, or people you see on the street. For instance, if you live in York, and you have a brother, your limerick could begin 'There was a young man from York, who would only ever eat pork'. Get the idea? Off you go!

Twinkle, twinkle, little bat
How I wonder what you're at!
Up above the world you fly
Like a tea-tray in the sky.

Remember the Mad Hatter's version of this famous nursery song? Why don't you get creative with nursery rhymes, and make up your own version of 'Baa Baa Black Sheep', 'Jack and Jill' or 'Three Blind Mice'. Keep the structure but change key words for something completely unexpected.

'Jabberwocky' is one of Lewis Carroll's most famous nonsense poems, and it's wonderful to recite aloud. It's a clever poem, because even though many of the words are made up, you can still understand the story it tells. What do you think the word 'brillig' means? What are the 'mome raths'? What does the 'Jub Jub bird' look like? Make up your own nonsense words and put them together to create a fantastical, atmospheric and exciting poem. Or, if you prefer drawing, why not create your own image of the fearsome Jabberwock!